THE BELLE *of* TWO ARBORS

THE BELLE *of* TWO ARBORS

Prose by Paul R. Dimond

With poetry by Martha Buhr Grimes

Publishing Services
Thomson-Shore, Inc.
7300 West Joy Road
Dexter, MI 48130

Published by Cedar Forge Press
Printed in the United State of America and Distributed by
Thomson-Shore, Inc.

19 18 17 16 15 1 2 3 4

ISBN – 978-1-943-29021-5
Library of Congress Control Number 2016917006

Publishers' Note

Many say the dead can't talk. We found out different. We hope you do, too.

Belle grew up and raised her younger brother in a big shingle cottage near Glen Arbor atop the little finger of Michigan's geographic mitten. At 21 she tried to fledge to college in Ann Arbor, but her brother, Pip, tagged along with his "Marmie." She wasn't our mother either, but she helped raise us as if she were, in our separate houses across a little park near the campus. We called her Marmie, too.

Born in 1899 and raised on Emily Dickinson's poetry, Belle died too young in 1953. She strayed from her two sheltering Arbors only a handful of times and permitted publication of only one poem during her life. No recluse, though, she gave as good as she got: with the help of her brother and their best friend, the Ojibwe David Ahgosa, she battled her demons and those her father, their family business, the projectors, the pedants, and the naysayers up north and in Ann Arbor threw at her. She also shared copies of some of her poems (and more of her letters) with each of her three great poet friends, Frost, Roethke, and Auden. She sang many more at family gatherings, her classes at the University, and the writers' camps she hosted at her Homestead overlooking Sleeping Bear Bay. When Belle died, we couldn't find any trace of the many hundreds of poems we knew she had composed.

In 1977, after Pip and the rest of our other parents died, Marmie had her Angel, David's blessed albino daughter, guide us to an old chest intended as Belle's trousseau. Our Marmie had locked more than a thousand of her poems, more letters, her journals, and a draft memoir safely away inside for this moment. As best we can tell, every word here speaks her truth, but we know she had a fertile imagination: how else could she say so much in such short poems? Now, Dear Reader, you will decide whether Belle's voice should join the others she helped sing to the world.

Ruth Belle Peebles
Paul Fitzpatrick O'Bannon
Empire Press
Empire, Michigan
December 1978

Belle's Seasons

THE BELLE *of* TWO ARBORS

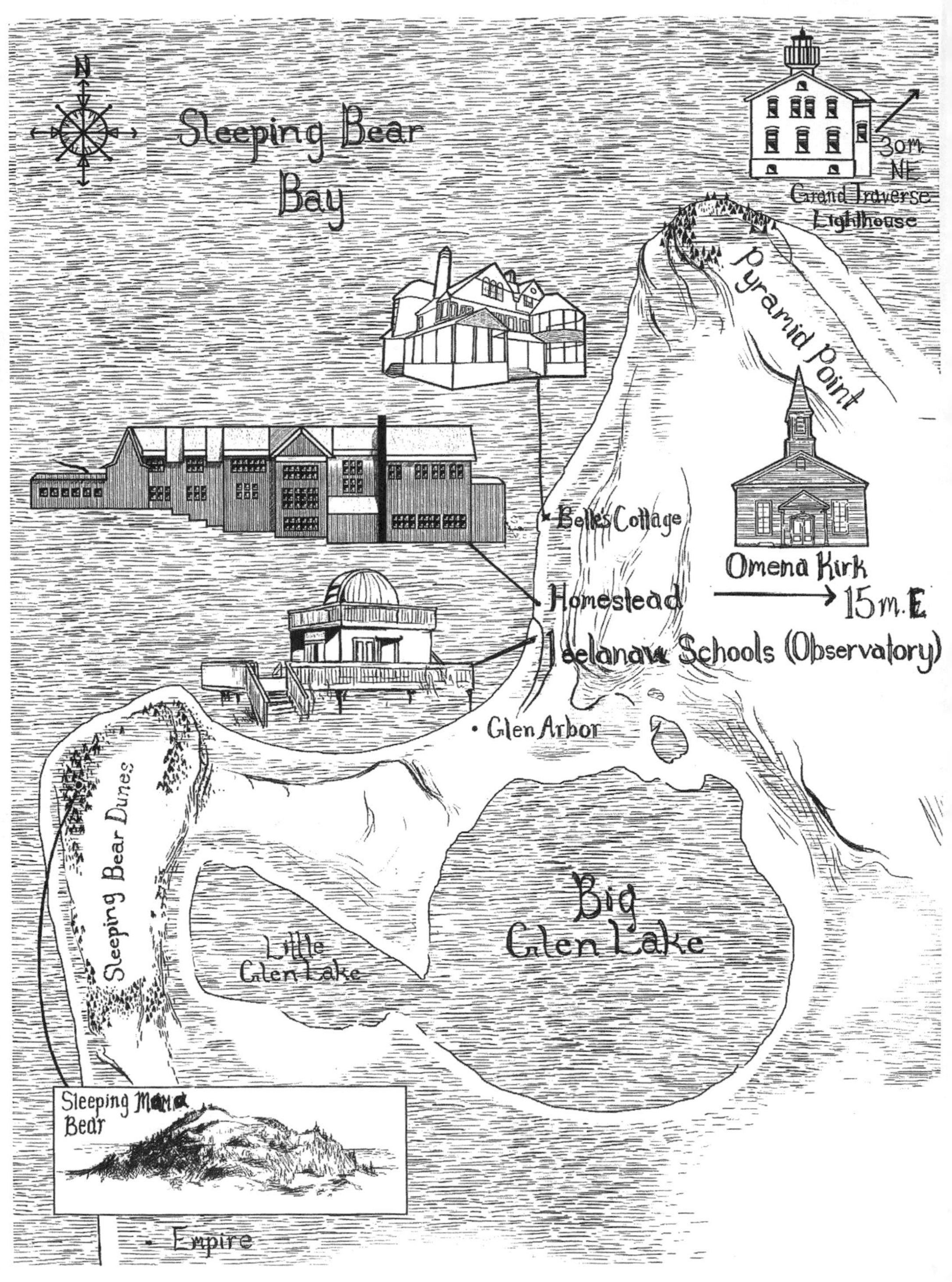
N
Sleeping Bear Bay
30m. NE
Grand Traverse Lighthouse
Pyramid Point
Belle's Cottage
Homestead
Omena Kirk
15m. E
Leelanau Schools (Observatory)
Glen Arbor
Sleeping Bear Dunes
Big Glen Lake
Little Glen Lake
Sleeping Mama Bear
Empire

WINTER 1913: GLEN ARBOR

The gentle rise and fall of the ice under our shanty didn't bother. The slosh of water from the fishing hole, washing my little brother's bobber over the boots he'd taken off, did. At the sight of the long pier in front of Bell Stove Works trembling, my frail Mama dropped her line and raised her gray-gloved hand to her ear to listen for any warning. There wasn't any, not even the whistle of the wind. As we waited for worse, the calm deceived. That certain slant of bright winter light now illuminated only a still sheet of ice on the bay and the solid buildings ashore. The black stove beside us stood sturdy and warm on the thick ice. Pip dropped his bobber back through the hole into the water, and Mama picked up her line. We waited for a mess of perch to bite.

ᔕ

After a four-day blizzard had cooped us all up and ruined my hope of a big party on New Year's Eve for my 14th birthday, January 3 had broken clear and mild. Papa left before dawn to join his men at the factory overlooking Sleeping Bear Bay. No dumb yes-man foreman, my father, Paul Peebles. He had the smarts, and ambition, to marry my Mama, Mary Bell, while she was still fertile despite her then 39 years. Papa soon took over running the stove works her father, Ian Bell, had founded in Glen Arbor.

Grampa also built our house as part of her dowry, along with a mile of lakeshore and dunes, woods, meadows, and steep hills. All in all, he'd bought more than a thousand acres on either side of the Crystal River from the first white settlers in these parts.

I rose in the dark house to prepare breakfast for Mama and my six-year-old brother. I mixed up the eggs, flour, baking powder, milk, sugar, and melted butter and poured the batter on the griddle-top, dusted the pancakes with powdered sugar, stacked them on the plates, and put the syrup from our big maples on the table. While Mama pecked at a single serving, my little brother ate three helpings and asked for more. I never could say no to him, even if his late, long birth nearly killed dear Mama, and she'd never been the same since. She'd lost an inch a year thereafter as her back stooped, her legs whittled to sticks, and she fell into a wheelchair. Pip wasn't to blame: What was my father thinking, getting Mama pregnant at 46, anyway? I knew: Papa wanted to sire a boy to take over the Bell Stove Works and continue its operation as Peebles and Son. Papa and Mama had the misfortune that they gave birth to me, a girl, first.

It's odd what we inherit from our parents and what we don't. Pip got his nickname because Papa named him Paul after himself and gave him a middle name, Ian, to seal the Peebles takeover of the Bell business. There was so much confusion, what with "Paul" and "Ian" ringing back and forth between my Papa and Grampa, that soon we all called our boy "Pip."

The little guy got his good looks from Mama. His hair was straight and dark as most of hers, his eyes the same pale gray-blue, his bright smile just as irresistible. Mama had a white forelock, about which Papa always started to tell a story to all who would listen. He said it made her a better looker than that beauty queen who'd become such a sensation in those new-fangled moving pictures. Miss Nesbit played the lover in the film—and in real life—of the rake Grampa and Mama hired from New York to design our home. "Thank heavens," Mama picked up telling the family yarn, "the hussy's husband had murdered the philandering architect at his Madison Square Roof Garden rather than our front porch"—or Papa would never have stopped regaling all within earshot of the racy tales of Stanford White. Sometimes Mama couldn't resist adding, her white streak, blue eyes, and bright smile flashing as if a young woman again, "Bell Cottage *is* the best shingle-style house in the country."

Mama was fiercely loyal to our home, as she was to my brother and me. Pip, bless him, was just as loyal to Mama and me, even if I couldn't help feeling a trifle envious he'd no doubt soon sport Mama's becoming white streak. With my dark red hank of unruly hair that Papa gave me, I didn't inherit Mama's striking looks. I also began to chafe at her undying devotion. Maybe as a teenager I wanted to try my new wings to see if I could fly outside by myself, but I shared Mama's fear of leaving the hearth that sheltered both of us for so long. Already taller than the older boys and gawkier than any of the prettier girls, I tried to hide my embarrassment at my early ripening as best I could at school. But I never got over the other kids whispering and pointing at me as if at a freak. At least at home I had a role, taking care of Mama and our boy. Papa talked once about hiring help, but Mama insisted we needed to invest every penny into the family stove works. My deft touch cooking, cleaning, mending, and minding also earned me Mama's thanks, even when our skin irritations at being cooped up for several days in a row sometimes made me wish I didn't have to tend her so.

Oh, there were times I also wished to shut my little brother out when he wasn't in sight, but I never could resist caring for him when he popped into view. With his cheeks white from the sugar and syrup dripping off his tongue between his missing two front teeth, he begged me to take him "to see the big boys pu' the s'oves 'ogehew." He couldn't yet enunciate his *T*'s and *R*'s. I could only nod.

After washing and drying his face, I helped Pip put on his warm leggings, button his winter coat, lace up his boots, and clamp on his red stocking cap. When Mama said she wanted to come along, I was surprised. She hadn't set foot outside Bell Cottage since our annual rite of delivering turkeys the day before Thanksgiving. At that time we'd first dropped by the homes of the men in Glen Arbor and Port Oneida who worked for Papa at the factory to say thank you. Next, we'd visited the poorer Ojibwe families left in their few remaining but better-kept frame houses in Ahgosatown. Mama said they'd prefer a job at Bell Stove Works, but Papa said it was too far from the east side of the peninsula. Too far to walk or to travel by horse and buggy, yes. "But not to catch a ride in those new Tin Lizzies?" I asked. "Not too far to set up camp next to Glen Haven and work at D. H. Day's lumber mill or big dock to the west of us," I pressed. Mama looked sad and shook her head. These men were good enough to convert and serve as deacons in the Omena kirk they founded and kept up; were they not good enough for Papa to hire?

Yet when Mama gave me her best smile, I never said no to her either. So I helped her put on her winter gear, gray gloves, and woolen cap. I steadied her as she hobbled out to her makeshift sleigh, a big sled with a seat and handrails. Pip and I strapped on our snow shoes and pushed Mama up the short lane to Sunset Shore Road. The frozen bay, pure white from two feet of fresh snow, extended west to Sleeping Bear Dunes. Far to the north, only a narrow strip of dark water rippled in the strait to the two Manitou Islands.

As we passed the mouth of the Crystal River, Pip wandered off to chase a rabbit. On his snowshoes his little legs raced across the deep drifts almost as fast. On his skates, he was even faster: Papa called his son "my river skater" because he picked up speed the longer he scooted along. On snow or ice, as on land, I lumbered, big and slow. In the Great Lake, I floated and swam for hours on end, not as quick as a brookie in the river, but as strong and, yes, graceful as a big sturgeon in the lake. Little Pip, so trim and wiry, was a sinker. Maybe his oddly sunken chest didn't hold enough air. As long as he could wade in the river to fish, dip his toes in the shallows to skip stones, or skate on a frozen surface, he danced with the best. Put him in water over his head, and he was lost.

I pushed Mama until Pip rejoined us at the crossroads of Glen Arbor. He pushed the sleigh the rest of the way on Lake Street to the stove works, only a couple hundred feet from the long pier on the bay. When the little boy popped his head through the backdoor, Papa blocked the way. When Pip tried to step around him, Papa stood his ground. Papa's brush-cut, dark red hair bristled, and his plain face, dark eyes, and flat nose couldn't hide his brute strength. He pushed Pip back. Seeing the crestfallen look of his heir to the family business, Papa turned to me. He directed me to go to the office, get the jigs and bait, and take Pip ice-fishing. Patting his boy on the shoulder, he added, "The stove's already lit in the shanty for you."

When Papa turned his back to shut me out, I stuck my foot in the door. When he glared at me, my eyes were now level with his. I stared back until he saw Mama bundled in the sleigh. When Papa gazed more sorrowfully at her, I asked, "Do you think it's safe for Mama out there?"

"Good God almighty, Martha, the ice's thick enough to hold a pallet full of our stoves." He had a business to run, and not enough time to play with his little boy this morning or to care for his invalid of a wife *any* day. Those were my jobs, and he'd given me what for the few times I neglected my duties. He turned and shut the door, but I managed to step back before it slammed on my foot. I had learned to stay out of Papa's way.

I tried to tell Mama we should go home and read poetry to Pip—whether Miss Dickinson or Miss Barrett or his favorite Rabbie Burns—as we'd done so often when Papa was busy, but she turned to the little boy. When he raced toward the office, she looked up from her sleigh and smiled. "Let's catch a mess of perch for lunch."

We pushed Mama's sled atop the snow to the fishing shanty a

hundred yards beyond the end of the pier, where the great lake steamers docked eight months a year. Pip and I took off our snowshoes and helped Mama off the sleigh. I opened the door. The big Bell Stove made the shanty so hot inside Mama said we could take off our coats and leggings. She kept her gray gloves on to fiddle with the hooks. When she saw our boots getting soggy from the top layer of the thick ice melting, she took off hers, propped her stocking feet on the asbestos board under the stove and told us to do the same.

I don't know whether I could have saved Mama if I'd helped her onto her sleigh as soon as our shanty came to rest after the first rise and fall of the ice, when the water sloshing through the fish-hole and the trembling of the big pier stopped.

The sound of the thunderous crack hit us as our ice shanty rose and fell the second time. The ice inside our shanty split in two, silver shards flew all around, and water erupted like a geyser from the fish-hole.

Mama toppled off her stool. Her gray woolen cap followed and floated, in slow motion, through the air until it came to rest on her shoulder. The white shock of hair splitting her dark head pointed through the open door to the dark water spreading between the two jagged sides of the ice splitting toward the pier. Mama pushed Pip out the door as the frame teetered and the studs creaked. The crack widened and then raced to shore as if the frozen bay had been struck by a giant cleaver.

Despite looking so frail sprawled on the ice, Mama pushed—hard—at my shin. I tried to pick her up, but she was too strong. "Save him," she said. The ice on either side of the widening chasm, inside the shanty and out, began to break up.

I stumbled out the door. I grabbed hold of Pip, turned, and looked back, but Mama only smiled through gritted teeth. As the big stove loomed behind her and began to sink, she didn't whine. She never had. She waved her gray-gloved hand, the look in her gray-blue eyes already distant, and said so softly I could barely hear, "Take care..."

I thought I heard her add, "...of our boy," but I wasn't sure and there wasn't time to ask.

The wood shanty formed a coffin: Mama and the big Bell Stove her father invented and her husband built sank, sputtering and sizzling, into the deep, dark bay.

The most damnable thought flashed through my head: *My wish came true, one less person for me to take care of.* As Pip began to sink, the frigid water hit me so hard it knocked that ugly notion out of my head before I could drown in guilt. The ice had already broken into chunks bobbing all around us. I had to swim Pip to shore.

I stretched out, rolled on my left side, and held my little brother with my right arm high on my right side. He didn't struggle or say a word. I kicked my legs and paddled with my free arm already feeling like a block of ice, but at least it served as a rudder. I swam, as best I could in this crabbed sidestroke, diagonally toward shore to get away from the deep channel for the big ships. Surprisingly, on this bright, cloudless day, the water was dark. Opaque with fine sand stirred from the bottom, the bay seemed too heavy to yield to my kick or stroke.

I couldn't tell how long I tried to swim, but eventually a strange sensation began to creep over me: my body became so numb it seemed to warm. Even my stone-cold left arm came alive, and I began to paddle more strongly. I guess I lost myself swimming in that water, now calm, no slosh, no sound except Pip's rapid breathing in my ear. No matter the cold or the distance to shore, fear didn't strike me down. Instead, a sense of exhilaration lifted me up.

I looked over my shoulder at Pip's face, his dark hair wet—already sprouting ice crystals—his lips blue and smile gone. Fear now clouded his pale blue eyes, usually so clear and deep. "Mawmie, don' leave me."

"I won't, ever." Even after he learned to enunciate his *R*'s and *T*'s, I would always be "Marmie" for him. I hated my first name, Martha, anyway. It always sounded so dour, maybe even unloved when my father said it. But I loved my Grampa and Mama, now both gone, and the family name they gave me as a middle name. I hugged Pip close. "Just hold on, and Marmie will take care of you." For the rest, even Papa, I vowed I wouldn't accept being called "Martha" ever again.

My left arm paddling so strong soon scraped the sandy bottom, and I felt the rush of excitement at swimming us to safety. Then the frigid water once again seemed to cool so it must have stunned me. The last thing I remembered, though, was a sense of relief. The great blue water had buoyed us up.

Sometime that evening Papa came to my bedroom on the third floor of the turret. I'd been dreading this moment since I fell into a deep sleep. Occasionally, I had heard one voice or another outside my door say "tremor," "upheaval," "quake," and "out between the islands"—once even a French word that sounded like "seiche"—but I was afraid Papa was angry with me for not saving Mama. Maybe I was just in shock from nearly freezing or too quickly thawing. When I heard Papa's knock, I bolted upright.

He sat down beside me. "I'm proud of you, Martha."

"Please, Papa," I blurted, "don't call me that anymore."

He was silent for a long while before he said, "You kept saying that when we dragged you and Pip ashore, all the way to the stove works and the sleigh ride home."

I couldn't remember, so I only nodded.

"What would you like to be called?"

"Bell."

"Your Grampa's name?"

"The name I also share with Mama."

I thought his short-cropped red hair bristled again, but he said, "How about we add the letter *E* on the end, so you can have a proper first name rather than just a last name?"

I was so surprised he didn't object, I just nodded. No point in arguing with him now about dropping the last name of Peebles I got from him.

He pulled a small package from his pocket and handed it to me. "Your mother and I had planned a proper birthday party for you over supper today, but…" There followed another long silence. "Your Mama was going to give this to you. She said it's for your eyes only." He handed me the gift, patted my hand, and turned to go.

"Wait. How's Pip?"

"You saved him, Marth…, I mean, Belle."

"What about Mama?"

"If we don't get buried by another blizzard, Pastor Weir will lead the memorial service Sunday at noon." He turned to go again.

"But what about Mama?"

"We couldn't risk trying to recover her body."

"But she wanted to be buried in the old cemetery behind the Omena kirk."

He sat down beside me again. I reached out but brushed against him. He must have been as embarrassed as I was by my new awkwardness, because he pushed himself away and said, "Not until all the ice melts…" He dropped his eyes. "I'm sorry, Belle." He shook his head. "Not until spring."

After he left, I set the package on my bedside table. I got up and locked the door on him, as he'd locked himself away from me. When I turned, I saw myself in the tall mirror above my bureau. I filled up most of the frame. Almost six feet tall, my shoulders stood square: Mama wouldn't ever let me slouch to hide my height, but my large frame hid most of my thickness. Underneath my wool gown, though, my two new big mounds, ugly as sin, rose. I wondered what Mama would advise now, given her prior order: "stand tall and throw your shoulders back, even if you aren't ever going to be a nimble, light-stepper on any dance floor."

I tried to throw my unruly hank of hair forward to see if that would offer any cover-up. No luck, the wild, dark, red, tangled mass just rode on top of my big chest. I closed my eyes but couldn't resist reaching up.

I dropped my hands quick, but my face, suddenly flush, still stared back at me from the mirror. A plain face, perhaps: eyes so dark navy they melded into my pupils, nose flat, lips neither a thin grimace nor a fat pucker. Skin not alabaster with the rouge cheeks of a stage star but, thank the Lord, not red freckled either. At least my teeth were straight like Mama's, not bad for smiling in good times, better for gritting in bad.

I looked deeper into the mirror and saw the reflection of the quarter moon peering through the clouds high in the sky. I turned and walked over to the window. A floor below, Pip hung out his open sash peering through the captain's telescope he got for Christmas. More than a wanderer on land or a tinkerer in the shop, he was a dreamer gazing deep into the heavens. He looked up. He tried to smile. Finally he lifted his hand. Not a wave, but a call for help. I nodded.

Pip knocked on my door, and I unlocked it. He dragged his telescope behind him and hopped on my bed, his orange-and-white furball of a cat, Mister Stripes, close behind. My brother couldn't resist the package on the table. He grabbed it but then looked to me for approval. Mama wouldn't mind if his eyes saw her gift; she never could resist him either. I nodded again, and he tore off the wrapping. He opened the small book, but, when he saw Mama's writing, he handed it to me as fast as he could. Seeing the green ink and fine scroll of her hand set me back some, too.

The title page read, *A Dome of Many-Coloured Glass* by Amy Lowell. Between the title and the author, Mama had written, *To my birthday girl: May you grow into the best of the new generation of poets. Your Mother, Mary Bell, December 31, 1912.*

A few pages into the slim volume, she'd inserted an envelope inscribed in her hand, "For your trousseau." I read the poem on that page, "A Winter Ride," to myself. Not appropriate for sharing with Pip *this* evening: too much joy kiting with the sun on a bright winter's day. So I flipped through the thin book until I happened on a section called "Verses for Children" and found "The Crescent

Moon." I read it aloud to Pip in hope that it might help him sleep. It started too breezily: "Slipping softly through the sky little horned, happy moon, can you hear me up so high?" After too many more stanzas flying too high, it careered to a point: "I shall fill my lap with roses gathered in the Milky Way, all to carry home to mother. Oh! What will she say!"

Bad enough Pip no longer could carry roses, or anything else, home to Mama. Thankfully Pip didn't seem to catch this cruel irony, but Miss Lowell's verse was so thick with sweet honey for me on this bitter day, I almost choked.

So why did Mama give me *A Dome of Many-Coloured Glass* anyway? I opened the envelope, unfolded her crisp stationery, and read her note:

My Dear Child,
The critics say Miss Lowell will be remembered as one of America's great poets. But after you read all her images, you'll know Miss Dickinson's and your songs sound much better. Don't ever listen to any teacher, or let any other damn fool, tell you different. Remember your voice always: poetry's meant to be heard not eyed, so say your lyric aloud!
Love, Mama

I couldn't help smiling at the memory of Mama scowling at Miss Patterson's comments in red ink splashed across one of my poems. Whether my teacher assigned an essay, a story, or a report, I always turned in a poem. Mama said, "What's that pinched-nosed, squinty, four-eyed idjit talking about? 'Put a capital letter at the beginning and a period at the end.' 'Incomplete sentence.' 'Too many dashes.' Hell, damn! You just forget all her scribbles and sing your song aloud to me just as you heard it when you composed it." When I started to speak, she cupped her hands to her ears as she so often did when she wanted to hear better and said, "Sing it proud, dear!" After I finished, she nodded triumphantly: "You keep right on singing, and I'll take care of Miss Patterson."

Through my smile at this memory, I saw that Mama wasn't here to take care of Miss Patterson—or me—any longer.

Pip tapped my shoulder. "Whewe's Mama's body?"

I didn't know how else to answer so I told him the truth: "Buried under the ice."

"How's she gonna get to heaven?"

There was a question without a good answer, but I replied, "We Scots are much practiced at getting lost at sea and finding our way Home."

"I'm nevew going in deep wawa again."

So I tried a different answer. I looked out the window. "Maybe her spirit rises separate from her body." I swallowed hard at that because Mama's passing tested my belief in the teachings of John Knox that Papa and our Kirk drilled into me.

After a long pause to follow my gaze, Pip nodded and tapped his big telescope. "I'll find hew." I didn't know he'd still be searching the stars forty years later, but I hugged him close. My boy would never lose his faith.

After I thought he'd fallen asleep, I turned and placed Mama's note back in the envelope, the envelope back in the book, the book in the drawer of the bedside table. When I began to turn off the oil lamp, I heard him say, "Mawmie, leave the light on fo' Mama." I turned and held onto our little boy, gritted my teeth, and cried and cried. Mister Stripes climbed between us and purred so I didn't have to listen to my own sorry thoughts. He lulled me to sleep. Bad enough remembering the scene unfolding; worse feeling guilty over my unbearable flash, thinking I'd only have to care for Pip now when I knew I'd miss my Mama forevermore.

Guilt and Pip's little cat couldn't stop me dreaming my Blue Salvation: That feeling of buoyancy while floating in the icy water, of growing warmth as I lost myself swimming, the thrill of fighting to save our boy and me, the burst of joy when my hand first felt the sandy bottom, the cold water stunning, the longer release of making it safely back to shore. This sense of relief enabled me to forget, at least for a while.

Buried beneath the thick down comforters, I got so hot that even sticking one leg out didn't cool me down. From some place too close by, I heard the sound of the ice cracking and saw Mama and the Bell Stove sinking in their shanty coffin. I woke with a start, thinking I'd never escape that horrible scene. I pushed the covers off both my legs to try to cool off, but not even Mister Stripes' purring could get me back to sleep.

I stood up, still flushed in my thick nightgown, and I opened the drawer and took out Mama's gift and note. I looked to make sure Pip was asleep, his orange-and-white fur-ball purring in his ear. Time to go to the secret place Mama shared only with me.

I unlocked my bedroom door, crossed the hall, and entered the attic. At the far end, under a huge quilt Mama had stitched together, stood the big wooden chest next to the floor grates. Inside, for my trousseau, she put books, family pictures, charms, silver, her wedding dress, her dolls, and her jewels in a big lockbox. I sat on the quilt atop the chest and looked north out the window. The moonlight danced across the ice floes thrown on shore and the dark water in the bay already freezing over.

I lost myself dreaming about the thrill of the water buoying me up and the relief of safely making shore. As if in a frenzy, a new song burst forth from my lips:

> Your lips are
> Blue Salvation—
> flowing over my
> hills and valleys

cooling the red heat
of my Passion—
soothing summer balm
after the wintry storm—

I replayed the poem in my mind. Not bad for a first try. At least it captured what I felt when the great lake embraced me, even if it missed the rest of what I experienced when that cruel crack took Mama down.

I removed the quilt, opened the chest, pressed the secret lever inside the lid, and took out the key. I gently pushed Mama's other gifts aside and pulled the locked box from the bottom. Inside were her jewels and a leather-bound book, my *Songbook* we called it, that she'd given me to write my poems and private thoughts.

I pulled it out and turned to the next open page. I listened harder as I wrote my new song down. I could hear I'd omitted that certain slant of light on this wintry day, the early warning from the initial seiche, the death knell sound of the crack when the ice split, and Mama's long, gray goodbye as she waved me toward shore. Something else missing nagged, but I was too tired coming down from my rush to figure out what. I inscribed my name and date at the bottom: *Belle, January 3, 1913.*

❧

The funeral in the old kirk in Omena wasn't as bad as I'd feared. More than a half century earlier, a band of 150 mostly Ojibwe converts built this white clapboard Presbyterian church with the tall steeple, high on the bluff looking south over the frozen Omena Bay on the west branch of Grand Traverse Bay. Today the sky was blue, and the noon light flooded the sanctuary. Even in the absence of a body, guests filled all the pews. I wouldn't call most mourners, though, as many felt obliged to pay their respects to a member of the Bell Stove clan, one of the few that offered a steady job and a decent wage to folks up north year-round. Then again, most didn't begrudge Mama her lineage because they remembered her father more kindly than they felt about mine. In fact, Mama, despite her barbs at home, minded her manners enough the few times she ventured out that she didn't make many enemies. Miss Patterson, on the aisle in the third-row pew on the other side, did give me the eye to let me know I'd have to mind her in school now. Most of the rest seemed a little sorry for my brother and me, even if they thought the end for such a long-suffering soul as Mama some kind of blessing. But what did those ignorant of how much she had shared with Pip and me know anyway?

When I turned to see if Miss Patterson had stopped staring, she looked right past me. From this distance her blue eyes didn't have to squint over the pince-nez she wore on her pert nose for reading the hymnal. Why, she'd even cut her long hair for the occasion. Rather than scrunched up in an ugly bun that always wanted to fall apart, her short bob, now more pepper than salt, framed a face I barely recognized, not unattractive at all, even becoming. I followed her gaze, turned, and realized her eyes had been fixed on Papa the whole time. Good Lord, what was she thinking? My Mama's dead body wasn't even going to be buried in the old cemetery outside the kirk this day.

Our little boy sat fidgeting with his telescope between Papa and me. Papa looked straight ahead the whole time. Occasionally, he touched his son, not to put his arm around him, but to tap him on the back to remind him to sit up straight, like a man. Pip did sit straighter, but he also edged closer to me. When he turned, looked back over his shoulder toward Miss Patterson, and gave his telescope a wave, I feared he might already have deserted to her camp. As I turned to scowl at her, I was relieved to see his older friend and mentor, David, the great-grandson of Chief Ahgosa, waving back at Pip from his seat in the back with the rest of his dwindling band, less than fifty now. Pip always had a knack for joining to play with the underdog, whereas I avoided all the boys and girls, always gawking at me so. I had retreated with Mama to the haven of our Bell Cottage, to care for each other and our boy and to share poetry. Without Mama, where could I escape now?

At least the hymns sped right along, more harmony than dirge. A few times they reached a crescendo when David's father let loose his deep bass: not even the patch covering the Deacon's right eye could block his *Alleluias* from lifting our memories of Mama and reverberating through the rafters all the way up the steeple. Like all his kin, David used the last name of Ahgosa rather than the Scots surname, Potts, awarded at his baptism in the Presbyterian Kirk. Like his forbears, David's voice still sang to other Gods our Kirk would never accept, but the native legends David shared about our Great Lake made more sense to me than the Bible stories from soil so far away.

Pastor Weir spared us singing Rabbie Burns' *Auld Lang Syne* or *Scots Wha Hae*, so the congregation didn't have to start wailing. He also spared us a sermon about a woman who set foot in this kirk only because her father and husband demanded that their offspring be raised in all the fire, brimstone, and guilt of John Knox. Instead he gave his strong voice to solo two poems of Miss Dickinson he knew my mother loved. With his sympathetic face, freckled over pale skin, red hair blond from graying, and upper left front tooth turning as if a snaggle, he abridged the first, but in a soft voice to make us all listen harder:

> There's a certain slant of light,
> On winter afternoons
> That oppresses like the weight
> Of cathedral tunes.
>
> . . .
>
> When it comes, the landscape listens,
> Shadows hold their breath;
> When it goes, 'tis like the distance
> On the look of death.

On this winter afternoon, the certain slant of light through the windows of the old kirk reminded me of Mama's distant look of death as she pushed me out of the fishing shanty to save Pip. Now, I hugged him all the closer: wherever Mama might be, I wanted her to know I'd make sure she hadn't died in vain for our boy.

Parson Weir boomed loud the second to close the service:

On this wondrous sea,
Sailing silently,
Ho! pilot, ho!
Knowest thou the shore
Where no breakers roar,
Where the storm is o'er?

In the silent west
Many sails at rest,
Their anchors fast;
Thither I pilot thee, —
Land, ho! Eternity!
Ashore at last!

Oh, how I wished I believed what I'd told Pip—that any God, John Knox's or any other, could raise Mama's ` from the deep to heaven for eternity. Unless she talked with me again, I would only see her buried in the Great Lake.

At least Mama would have been pleased that Parson Weir knew how to pause for a breath on a dash with Miss Dickinson and to sing out her exclamation points. Both sound better when sung right aloud than when read wrong silently on the page. Oh, how I hoped for Mama's sake my songs could also put Miss Patterson to shame.

The next evening Papa called me to his study on the first floor of the turret. He introduced me to Mr. Robb, "the company lawyer," who'd driven over from Suttons Bay. Mr. Robb's short stature, long white hair, and muttonchops contrasted with Papa's height and close-cropped, dark red hair. The lawyer explained he wanted "to share a problem that you can help us solve." Mama had executed a will that gave me her half of the shares in the Bell Stove Works my grandfather had left her, and she'd appointed Miss Schultz my guardian to protect my interests if any dispute should arise with Papa.

I remembered Mama taking me to Northport to visit Miss Schultz last year. Mama introduced her as "the only woman lawyer and the only lawyer for women in all of Leelanau County." So I turned to Papa and asked, "Do we have a dispute?"

"I hope not," he said. He leaned toward me earnestly. "We're busting at the seams in Glen Arbor, and I want to move to Empire."

"Move from *here*?" I demanded.

"Marth—" Papa started to shout at me but then paused to gain control of himself. "Sorry, I mean Belle," he said more softly. "The lumber company's vacating their buildings. It's my best chance to expand the factory."

"No, Papa, I *mean* from *here*, Bell Cottage, the home that Grampa built for us."

"Aw, no," he replied, "we're still going to live here." I made the mistake of letting down my guard. After a short pause, Papa continued, "I'll even buy you a car so you can bring our boy over to tinker with the stoves in Empire any time he wants." His throwing in a car couldn't salve the insult to me, now his 50 percent shareholder in the company he married into. "I'm also going to change the name to the Peebles Stove Works."

I don't doubt my hank of dark red hair lit up at that, but I took my time to compose my reply. "Papa, we do have a dispute now." When his face reddened into a beet, I turned to Mr. Robb and said as plainly as I dared, "Nobody's ever heard of a Peebles stove, but if Papa wants to change the name from Bell, then Empire does have a nice ring to it, leastways if Papa really means to grow the family stove business." With my best smile I added, "Sorry, I mean *Papa's* business."

Even Mr. Robb's beady eyes brightened, and he couldn't help his grin stretching to his muttonchops. "You ever thought about arguing before a jury, Miss Belle?"

I didn't doubt I'd still need to consult Miss Schultz down the line, but I only answered, "Doesn't appear we'll have to this time."

Mr. Robb nodded and said his goodbyes. After he left, Papa asked, "What would you think if someone came to live with us and helped you with Pip and the chores?"

I thought about blurting that Miss Patterson wasn't welcome in Mama's house. Instead I answered, "Thank you, but I can manage."

When he didn't argue, I excused myself and shut the door behind me.

I also shut my bedroom door and locked it every night thereafter on Papa. Pip was always welcome. Even on evenings when I was sick of having to mother him all day, I opened the door when he knocked. I'd promised Mama: Pip was now Marmie's boy.

SUMMER 1920: GLEN ARBOR

Papa wasn't a bad man, just distant, at least from me. He built the Empire Stove Works, and I tended Bell Cottage and our boy, Pip.

I thought there were two problems. First, Pip, a teenager at last, began to sprout into adolescence. Already six feet tall, and with an eye that wandered across the cheap postcard pictures of tawdry tarts as well as the heavens, he tinkered with telescopes, stoves, cars, skates, flies, fish, and every other object, real or imagined, that came within his reach. Of course Papa couldn't be bothered, so the burden fell on me: Can you guess the difficulty of me explaining the facts of life to such a boy?

The second problem was more difficult. At 20, with high school long gone and my majority in sight, it was past time for me to fledge. Even a big bird as lumbering, burdened, and tethered as me has to try to break loose sometime. On a late August morning, Papa took Pip to explore the stove works in Empire, and I drove my old Chevy Roadster over to Northport to explore my options with Miss Schultz. Money was no issue: Papa expanded the business so much since Mama died, my half of the profits swelled my trust to a size I never could spend, with the prospect of more to come. Miss Schultz, my trustee until I turned 30, added, "Your father's scrupulous in his accounting, and he takes no salary. I've invested all of your Trust fund in Liberty Bonds from the U.S. Treasury rather than bet on those risky bankers and their wilder Wall Street kin."

"Is Papa providing for Pip, too?" Miss Schultz dropped her brown eyes and shook her head. "You mean he's not taking care of our boy!"

Miss Schultz raised her eyes. Her long hair, more salt than pepper, piled on top of her head in waves to a high crown, made her round face look even pudgier and kinder, like the Gramma I always imagined but never knew. "Your father willed his half of the shares to Pip and made clear he wants to train *his* boy to take over."

I shook my head at that. While Papa always shooed me away from the stove works, I watched from the big hill above Empire and measured the raw materials as they arrived by boat and train, and then I counted the stoves as they left. I talked to the men over lunch at the picnic tables in the park. I snuck into Papa's study at home, reviewed the numbers in the double-entry journals, and saw how the revenues from the stove sales grew faster than the costs. Although there was a big expense in the materials and labor to build the increasing number of stoves discarded as "scrap" and a bigger lost opportunity in not making lighter stoves for cooking alone, it was hard to argue with the profits nearly doubling every year. Papa may have prevented me from learning about how flame works, the mechanics of building stoves, and how the men worked inside the plant, but he couldn't stop me from learning the rest of the business.

Although Pip loved experimenting with flame, he didn't give a hoot about the business. Instead, Papa complained, Pip pestered the men to borrow their tools to build his ever-larger telescopes, his latest a set of magnifying mirrors propped on a huge tripod so you looked down through the eyepiece rather than up the cylinder to see the night sky. That evening he had described the debate raging between Amy Lowell's brother Percival and another astronomer, George Hale, about "intelligent life on Mars." Lowell claimed he saw "vegetation, yes, crops, growing around the canals built by Martians to tap the water from the polar ice cap," while Hale saw only the expected "erosion of the surface of any dry, lifeless planet in space."

When I expressed my doubt about Mr. Lowell's sanity, Pip asked, "If there are eight planets orbiting around our sun, and billions of stars with, say, eight times as many planets, why would intelligent life be found only on earth?" That question would have stumped John Knox, too. Then he stunned me: "God wouldn't create such a universe fit for life in so many places and then waste the opportunity." Pip was doing more than daydreaming when he accompanied Papa and me to listen to Parson Weir preach the Presbyterian faith at the Omena kirk every Sunday.

After a long pause to consider how to respond, I asked, "How do you plan to prove that?" That's when Pip told me about some kind of "wireless telegraph" and explained the little "receivers" and "transmitters" he made out of crystal sets. He'd read everything he could in the papers and magazines about the inventors that were going to "broadcast on radio." He also tried to explain about "electromagnetism" and "radio waves." Although he got a little impatient with me, he allowed as to how he wanted to build "a dish with such big ears" and "an ear trumpet with such sharp focus" he could "listen for intelligent life and God's voice in space." It wasn't so strange, for a boy who already had as much trouble hearing as our Mama had, to want to build devices so he could listen better. But, good Lord, how big an aid to hearing was Pip planning? At least my brother had some mission in his life, where I had none, except to care for him.

"Miss Schultz," I finally replied, "my brother doesn't want to run the stove works." I couldn't resist a chuckle. "He's going to lose himself searching the heavens."

"He'll have to get out from under your Papa's thumb then, too." She paused. "What're you going to do with *your* life?"

I almost blurted back, "Run *our* family business," but I caught myself and answered, "I'm not sure."

"Still writing poetry?"

That question bothered even more. I'd gone to the attic and sat on the trousseau many times, in the bright white light of day and in the pale blue light of the moon, but I'd managed only a paltry sum of short verse since I wrote that last poem in my journal the day Mama died. Three lines at most: I never could string two together to make a song. Maybe it sharpened my internal editor, so I made each word count more. Each little snippet described one image or another of nature all around Bell Cottage: a flower, tree, beach, dune, river, bay, or Great Lake, ever-changing throughout each day with the light, the weather, and the seasons. I wrote each on a single scrap of paper. After re-reading, most blew into smithereens in my head. I tore those to bits. The few survivors I threw in the bottom of the chest. I saved my journal for my next real poem Mama would want to hear. "Trying, but not having much success," I admitted.

"Why don't you go to college?"

"Am I too old now?"

I guess a tear trickled from my eye because Miss Schultz pulled a handkerchief from the billowing folds of her white-frilled blouse and handed it to me. After I'd daubed up the damp enough to see her, she touched my hand and smiled. "You're plenty young enough. With Miss Patterson's help, I checked. There's a spot waiting for you at the University of Michigan."

"That's a long way, downstate. What about Papa and Pip?" Miss Schultz paused at that, and I stammered, "Th-th-they're m-m-my only f-f-family." More than another tear must have leaked out because she pointed to the handkerchief in my hand, and I daubed and daubed and daubed again.

Instead of asking me about how hard it might be for me to leave Pip and Papa, she tapped my hand and said, "It's time to say goodbye to your mother."

That knocked the wind out of me. I still had a hard time accepting that, without telling me, Papa got the crew from the Sleeping Bear Point Life-Saving Station to drag Mama's body out of the bay and buried her in the old cemetery next to the Omena kirk. Try as hard and often as I could to talk with her at her grave, Mama never answered. I still couldn't remember whether she'd ever said goodbye to me or just waved me toward shore and told me to take care of our boy. Oh, Mama, I know you cared, and I miss you so. But why didn't you ever say farewell to me? That's what I told Miss Schultz.

That prim lawyer lady with the kind face, warm smile, and gray, wavy hair rose, walked around the desk, and lifted me to my feet. She held me close in a powerful hug even though I towered over her. When I fell limp in her arms and bawled my big red head off on her shoulder, she whispered, "Belle, your Mama loved you. It's time for you to say goodbye."

The next morning I woke early and knocked on Pip's bedroom door. When he answered, I entered and sat down on the side of his bed. I told him I was going to visit Miss Schultz, stay with her overnight in Northport, and return in time to fix our Sunday supper. "Can you take care of Papa till then?"

"I don't want you to go."

"It's just for the day."

"You're planning to leave us, aren't you?"

"I've got to do something for myself first."

"Where are you going?"

"College, I think, but not till next fall. Don't tell Papa."

"I already figured that. I meant today." When I didn't reply, he continued, "Papa told me you visited Mama's lawyer yesterday. You need a better excuse now." When I told him I was going for a long swim to find myself, Pip said, "I'll tell Papa Miss Patterson's already back for the fall term, staying with her parents in Traverse City, and invited you to spend the night to help prepare for school."

My old nemesis had been a lot nicer to me ever since Mama passed.

She encouraged me to write poems again instead of the essays, papers, and reports I dutifully wrote for her as assigned. After graduating from high school, I typed the lesson sheets, ran the mimeograph machine, and, eventually, helped teach. She even gave me a set of Edna St. Vincent Millay's poems and pointed me to her anthem for women, "First Fig." Gave new meaning to burning the candle at both ends, even if it won't last the night: "But, ah my foes, and oh, my friends—It gives a lovely light!"

This past semester Miss Patterson and I had also read several of Shakespeare's plays aloud to our students: so much better to hear the sounds, beat, and phrasings than let only your eyes scan his verse. *The Tempest* was my favorite: I loved the aging conjurer, Prospero, playing out the Immortal Bard's last hurrah. After we finished school in June, Miss Patterson said it was time for me to take flight. I didn't know what to make of her advice. After all, I still didn't know her intentions with Papa.

I still wasn't any better at making friends my age. At six feet I towered over all the other young women and most of the men. What with mothering Pip, running Bell Cottage for Papa, teaching school, swimming alone for miles on end, and being the boss's daughter, there weren't many takers for my friendship. Didn't help that the only other time I ventured out—to play at D. H. Day's grandstand in Glen Haven in his annual tennis tourney—I surprised them all with my big forehand, except for David Ahgosa. A fish in water, I lumbered on land. Much fleeter afoot, he chased down all my winners in the finals until he wore me down and I gasped for air. First time a woman and an Indian swept the medals in any competition in Leelanau. Before I could move on, though, I needed to complete my unfinished business with Mama.

I ate a big breakfast and drove the roadster on the State Road through Glen Arbor. It was already dwindling so: after Papa moved the stove works, no more steamers stopped there, and the pier began to rot. I drove past the Indian Camp where 25 darkly burnished men and women braved the paler-faced neighbors to work in D. H. Day's burgeoning tourist empire to the west. I stopped in Glen Haven to consider the long journey ahead and marveled at its growth despite the decline in the lumbering trade, what with the rise in coal, kerosene, oil, and gasoline as fuels. Papa said that old Mr. Day was Sleeping Bear's King David: he always found a new way to expand his kingdom after the old one petered out. On my right stood the D. H. Day General Store, new gas pumps in front, to serve all the visitors who drove from Michigan, Indiana, Ohio, and Illinois to visit our little heaven on earth. The D. H. Day Sleeping Bear Inn across the street now had rooms only for his increasing number of guests, not his few remaining lumberjacks. The Day Tramway on the rails behind the store that used to carry so much wood now took all the guests for a ride to visit his tourist sites: the old D. H. Day Lumber Mill on Glen Lake, the new D. H. Day Shop and baseball field at the base of the dune climb, and the new Day farm he named after his Adirondacks home, Oswegatchi, with 200 Holsteins, 300 pigs, and 400 acres of cherry trees.

No dummy, that D. H. Day: while other lumber barons stripped the forest and scorched the land, he planted new trees and blessed his heirs and neighbors with 5,000 acres of what was already the best second-growth forest in the Midwest. The D. H. Day Pier at the north end of Glen Haven proved his perseverance: here, the biggest steamers still docked—with tourists and goods from Chicago and Milwaukee heading in and with passengers, the last of the lumber, and the beginning of D. H.'s farm products heading out. In western Leelanau, only Papa's single-minded focus on building our Empire Stoves offered more workers jobs than D. H. Day's new trade in tourism, farming, and retail.

David Ahgosa handed me a coin and said, "A penny for your thoughts?"

I looked at the pretty head of the Indian Princess coin. "What are *you* doing here?"

"Living with John Westman in the Indian camp and working for Mr. Day."

"But you were set to graduate next spring." His ruddy face blushed redder. He'd shot up over the last year, his dark eyes already level with mine, but he lowered his head; only his straight, long, thick, coal-black hair looked back at me. The brisk breeze rustling the beech, maple, birch, cottonwood, and aspen all around the village filled his awkward silence. I lifted my head and smelled the pure air of our great freshwater sea. The countless whitecaps breaking wave after wave on shore added a welcoming hum. "Hop in. I'm heading out to the Life-Saving Station."

He climbed aboard. I told him I was swimming to the South Manitou lighthouse, staying at the Coast Guard station overnight, and swimming back the next day.

He nodded but didn't say a word until I stopped at Sleeping Bear Point. He turned and said, "May the Great Spirit be with you." His dark eyes flashed, and he gripped my arm so tight I didn't know what to say. "Do you know the legend that the Manitous are the burial ground for the twin cubs that couldn't make it across the Great Lake to join their Mama Bear?" When I nodded, he pointed to South Manitou and continued, "Don't fear the tales of the old women who say only shipwreck, evil, and death lurk out there." He paused. "Manidoo is our Great Spirit. If you are worthy, she reflects what you most want. I'm going to be an alpha wolf for a new pack, brave enough to lope alone to scout danger and see opportunity and loyal enough to return and show my people the way. I rowed to South Manitou and received a blessing for my animal dream."

I touched his forehead. David, four years older than Pip, was only a tad shorter, just as handsome, but much stronger. Although quiet and reserved, he harbored a crush on me. He averted his eyes whenever I caught him staring, in school or out. "I'm more a fish in water," I replied. I couldn't help chuckling at the image I saw in my head: "A big, slow, ugly sturgeon, plowing along in my thick skin in the Great Lake."

David shook his head and placed the penny firmly in my hand. "You're as beautiful as this Princess. So is the sturgeon. You'll see: the Great Manidoo will watch over you and help you find your way."

David's firm touch and good wish wouldn't let the blowing sand's sting on my skin and the breaking waves' crash in my ears fill me with doubt. I trusted him with the key to my Chevy and said, "I'll meet you here tomorrow before the sun passes halfway across Lake Michigan. We can talk about your schooling then." I put the penny into the little pocket of my swimsuit.

"Wish me luck, too," he said. "I'm running up the west front of the dune in the morning without stopping. We call the great Sleeping Bear, 'Kchi Mokwa.' I will meet her at the top, and she will watch over both of us." When I searched his dark eyes, he dropped his head and his brave front. I couldn't resist burying his head on my shoulder. "Don't ever tell your brother," he whispered, "but I quit school when I learned my great uncle and some of his friends were shills, front men for buying thousands of acres of our lands here for white folks." I felt his whole body slump against me as he added, "Terrible personal insult piled on top of the Feds denial of thousands of land claims by other Ojibwe and Odawa here."

I shared how my father was the hired hand who'd married into my mother's family business but wouldn't ever consider letting me take over. I confided how I feared my Mama's last words were to take care of the male heir to the family throne, not to say goodbye to me.

David lifted his head and looked me in the eyes. "On your passage back from the Great Manidoo, you'll find your Mama is still on your side. Pip will be, too." I bussed him on the cheek and told him his rite of passage would also show him a better way.

I dived through the pounding waves into the cool water of Lake Michigan shortly after eight a.m., pointed toward the lighthouse, seven and a half miles away. I'd been swimming longer distances all summer, back and forth across Sleeping Bear Bay, from Pyramid Point to Glen Haven and back. Of course, the open water in the passage could get a lot rougher, and the dozens of shipwrecks between the shore and South Manitou testified to the even more unpredictable weather.

The wind quartered against me from the northwest, but the water stayed fairly calm in the passage—rolling swells, to be sure, but only a few whitecaps. I stroked a steady crawl but rested by floating on my back every hour. Lost in my element, I felt the soothing water flow over me. By keeping an eye on the lighthouse, I managed to swim a pretty straight line, but no Great Spirit greeted me as I approached South Manitou.

Two members of the Coast Guard crew raced to help me as I clambered ashore. There was no way to appear modest, what with my wet suit clinging to my big body, although I must say all my swimming that summer had cut much of the "baby fat" from around my thighs and middle. Of course, that only made my bosom stick out more. I'm not saying I pranced to meet the two sailors, but by the time we said our "Hellos" and "How dos," they were less anxious about my health and more interested in showing me off to their mates. Not often a person swims this strait, let alone a big mermaid.

Well-clothed in a dry uniform the men fought over to lend me, well-fed at the dinner mess, I slept in the quarters the captain vacated. Too tired to dream, no Manidoo graced me. I awoke alert and rested but none the wiser. I loaded up in the morning with pancakes fresh off the griddle but went light on the butter and syrup. The captain offered a ride home in the cutter, but I wanted to swim back, as I hadn't yet figured out how to say goodbye to Mama. He offered to follow in his powerboat, but I told him I didn't want any stinkpot ruining my good day swimming. I changed into my suit and ambled to the beach. I picked up a stone the size of a silver dollar and skipped it on the Great Lake. When it bounced seven times, I dived in to swim back to Sleeping Bear point, the sailors' cheers at my back.

My crossing started smooth enough: the water cool, a gentle breeze quartering with me from the northwest, what little current there was helping, the small waves riding with me. By keeping an eye on the high dune, I swam back straight toward the Point and fell into the rhythm and release of a long swim in clear blue water. Several hours and more miles later, the storm broke my reverie. A driving rain, a strong wind, and big waves from the west pushed me off course. It wasn't cold like the usual Nor'wester, but it was a powerful blow. Rather than fight by trying to swim southwest against this warp pushing me farther and farther east, I went with the flow and swam southeast. This allowed me to breathe more with the wash of the waves than fighting for air against the big chop. At worst I'd make landfall by the old pier at Glen Arbor.

In all the rain, wind, waves, and spray, I couldn't see any shore. I had to trust that the storm would keep pouring in from the west, the northwest, or even the north: that would help push me to shore somewhere along the shore of Sleeping Bear Bay. If the rain and wind shifted and blew from the southwest, the storm could push me off shore past Pyramid Point into Good Harbor Bay, and another several miles and hours swimming, probably late into the night. That would test my endurance and my will.

The longer I swam, the warmer the water and the wind felt. Not being able to see even the highest peaks on land proved unsettling, and my worry that the warm wind might now be coming from the south was disorienting. Instead of losing myself in my element to figure out how to say goodbye to Mama, I now felt lost. There was nothing to do but keep on swimming, and I disciplined myself to rest on my back every half hour or so. I don't know how many more hours I swam, but it was a long time. I began to flag—although not to get so delirious with fear I wouldn't make it—but the ache inside my chest and in my arms and legs grew. I'm not sure whether my limbs got lighter or heavier, but it took more concentration to stroke and kick.

I must have hit a different plateau in my mind because I don't remember the storm ending. Suddenly, I noticed the water below me was so blue and clear I could see the sandy bottom. I turned my head quickly to breathe to make sure I wasn't sinking and saw blue sky above. I turned my head back down and saw the sandy bottom again. Before I turned my head to breathe and look for shore, I saw one of our old sturgeon mates sliding gracefully along the sand. Longer than me and a third again as heavy, he looked like an armored marine dinosaur with tough scutes on his back. Big, yes, but a welcome sight: nowhere near ugly. He glided forward, led by what looked like a short crocodile snout, but his four barbel antennae hanging down gave him away. They scooted along to enable his toothless mouth to sweep up all he could eat from the sandy bottom. Captivated by the sight, I dived down and followed after.

Without warning the sturgeon veered to the left, and a small, white circle flashed ahead. It looked like a silver dollar, sparkling on a large black object between two ghostly goalposts. I swam closer and saw the remains of two tall studs sticking up and a crosspiece completing the frame, odd pieces of lumber, lying half-buried in the sand. There in the middle, holding the silver dollar, stood a dark, wide… what? A potbellied stove! I swam closer. With the light filtering through the water and the sand kicked up from the sturgeon, I couldn't see clearly, but I knew.

The scene came back to me. I saw Mama wave goodbye and heard her say, "Take care" to me. Not, "Take care of our boy." No, "Take care," she said to me, her voice full of love for me and of regret that she had to leave me, as well as our boy. I flashed back to Sunday evenings when Mama dried my freshly washed hair in her lap. She'd wrap a cotton ball around a matchstick, roll it in warm mineral oil and swirl the swab in my ear. She'd finish with a caress to the back of my neck. Oh, Mama, you did love me.

What a salvation: I knew I could say goodbye to Mama now.

My lungs searing for want of air, I looked down one last time at the silver dollar glinting against the black of the stove. The color wasn't silver. No, it was whiter, like the sand. But how could a sand dollar make it here? I reached down and picked it up: not the shell of a mollusk, but a stone circle rubbed flat and smooth by the ages.

I pushed off the sandy bottom, and when I surfaced, I was never so glad to see the last remnants of the old Glen Arbor pier, rotting in the surf a hundred yards ahead. My Papa, all his men from Empire, and Pip waved to me from shore. I treaded water and gulped down oxygen until I caught my breath enough to wave back. From the corner of my right eye, though, I saw the Glen Haven Coast Guard rescue squad racing toward me. David waved in the bow of that crisp, white surfboat. I waved back, flattened my body, and set out with my best crawl. After so many miles, and more hours, swimming over to South Manitou and back, I'd be damned if I'd let anyone, even David, rescue me with so little water left between the beach and me. When I reached the sandbar now spreading west from the old pier, I stood, turned, saluted to David and waved the rescue boat away. The Ojibwe youth dived in and swam after me.

I turned again, threw my shoulders back as Mama always advised and strode the few remaining yards toward shore. My father tried to run through the knee-high water to greet me but tripped and fell just before our paths crossed. His arms flew out. I leaned forward, braced my long legs, and broke his fall. He couldn't help hugging me. Pip, taller than Papa and me, barreled into us, and we three toppled together in the shallow water. Before we managed to regain our footing, David Ahgosa piled on, too.

I might have looked a bit bedraggled after so many hours battling the storm across the strait, but Papa, Pip, and David all looked silly, spray flying off their hair, faces, hands, and arms as they whooped at the sight of me. When we finally reached shore, I must say that Papa and Pip, clothes and shoes awash with water, looked worse than I did. Papa dropped his usual reserve and held me close again, but then he shouted, "Good God almighty, Belle, what in blue blazes did you think you were doing?"

In answer I stood tall right up to him, gave him a peck on his cheek and said, "Finding my Blue Salvation again." His men standing around didn't know how to react to my display of affection and independence, but when David began to clap, they joined right in. Out past the sandbar the Coast Guard sailors piped up with a cheer. To make my blushing worse, all the men ashore and on the boat hip-hip-hoorayed.

Thankfully, Papa could see I'd had enough and wrapped me in a big robe so I could dry off, drop my eyes, and allow my crimson color to fade. With Pip leading the way, Papa helped me through the crowd that seemed more intent on shaking my hand and clapping me on the back than letting me pass. Finally, we escaped into the safety of Papa's big Essex touring car. When David approached to join us, Pip shook his head at him. The Ojibwe boy dropped his eyes but handed me the keys to my roadster. I unclenched my fist and handed him the smooth white stone I'd found. As Papa drove off, David looked up and waved the age-worn stone that had guided me to Mama. I nodded to him with a big smile. The Great Spirit Manidoo had blessed my sturgeon dream and was helping me find my way. I hoped he had found a better way, too.

After supper I knocked on the door to Papa's study. He called me in and, when I entered, lifted his head and hand from the company books and directed me to one of the two big leather chairs in front of his big desk. "Papa," I said, "I'm going to college."

"This fall?" he asked as he raised his eyebrows but held his temper.

"No, next," I answered as soft as I could without him missing the answer.

"What do you plan to do about Pip?"

"Unless you're going to buy us all a house in Ann Arbor before then, he'll have to stay here with you," and, I don't know why, I added for emphasis, "at *Bell* Cottage."

Papa kept his frown from growing into a scowl and said as calmly as he could, "Belle, the business is growing so, you know I can't move down there."

"Yes, Papa, before my swim I met with Miss Schultz, and she told me how well you're doing with *our* Empire Stove Works. Thanks to you there's plenty of money in my trust fund to pay for my college and living in Ann Arbor."

Damned if Papa didn't set me back then. He told me I had a year to wean Pip. That was a low, cruel blow, even if I could never let Papa know how hard it would be for me to leave my boy. After a day with Papa's first display of affection for me I could remember, he was already scheming as to how my going would enable him to pull Pip under his wing to take over *his* business. He proceeded to rub my face in it: "It's time the lad learns from his father how to stand on his own two feet."

My red hair and usually plain cheeks must have flamed at that, but I only answered, "If you want Pip to spend time learning *your* business, you better hire his friend David Ahgosa at the stove works."

Papa nodded and said, "Good idea." Then he smiled and added, "You've done such a great job raising Pip, you've also freed me to focus on increasing *our* family business." I was dumbfounded. "You heard me. You own 50 percent." Then he floored me. "You were right: Empire has proven a hell of a lot better brand than Peebles." When I started to blush too much at his compliment, he held up his hand. "Now, look, you know I want to train Pip to run the company and I'm going to will my shares to him, but you'll always own half."

"Then why don't you start making stoves for cooking alone as well as heating?"

That staggered him but not for long. "Belle," he said tentatively, more as a question than a statement. He paused for a long time but then continued more certainly, "*We* want you to stick with your words for a while."

"*We...?*"

"Miss Patterson and I are fixing to get married next summer. She can help me raise Pip while you're away at college."

Miss Patterson? Since her gaze on Papa at the funeral, I should have figured. When I thought again about what Papa was saying, I wondered if he also meant he wanted me to return here after college to help with the business. "Papa, slow down so I can catch up." He nodded. "When did you ask Miss Patterson?"

"Yesterday, before I knew you'd taken off on your crazy swim across—"

"And she said yes?" I interjected.

"Well, she agreed we can get engaged for a proper courtship, after all our..." My ears perked up, but he didn't finish the thought. Instead he added, "I suppose she could find me as irascible and impossible as you do to live with, but I hope you'll help keep me on my best behavior so I don't miss my chance with her."

When he put it that way, how could I help but nod? After all, I was the one leaving Bell Cottage and Pip behind. "When I finish college, you mean I can come back here to live and help with the business?"

"This is half your house, and it will always be your home. But Miss Patterson reminded me you've got talent you've not explored much since your mother died." When I just sat there and didn't respond, he added, "She says if you apply yourself, you can sing as well as Miss Dickinson or that New England farmer, Frost."

Wouldn't Mama just laugh at the thought of Miss Patterson wanting me to go off to college and write poetry! I'm not so sure Mama would approve of Papa going courting to marry Miss Patterson, but maybe Mama knew something I didn't.

I needed to ask one more question: "Planning on more kids with Miss Patterson?" When he shook his head, I walked around his big desk and gave him a hug. There'd be time enough after college to see if I wanted to play a role in the family business. Bent on gazing at the heavens, my brother wasn't a threat to run the Empire Stove Company.

That evening I visited the chest in the attic, picked up the loose scraps of paper from the bottom and read several aloud:

fringed by pine forest
our snug shingled cottage home
nestled by the bay—

---

sweet maple syrup
pancakes puffing on the griddle—
heavenly breakfast

---

wooden chest of words
beneath Mama's hand-stitched quilt—
my attic retreat

---

beyond Bell Cottage
flows a meandering creek—
brookies hide—Pip seeks

There were a baker's dozen more. I scanned each, stacked them all together, tied them in a bundle and pulled out the lockbox. I closed the top of the chest and sat down on Mama's quilt. When spoken aloud, the words and phrases of my snippets did make sound, but I hadn't included any sounds in the verse. I stood, put David's penny and my packet back in the lockbox and took out my songbook. After I reviewed my goodbye poem from that night so many years ago, I was ready to sing a different song for Mama:

Mary Bell's Death

water below ice
spilling from our fishing hole—
sly silence—and then—

one long lonely Crack!
our fishing shanty's heaving sigh—
spinning silver shards—

brother 'neath my arm—
her gloved hand waving toward shore:
Mama's gray goodbye—

frozen arm flailing
reaching for life, pumping hard
through unforgiving gray shock—

now stroking steady
in peaceful rhythmic splendor:
Oh! Blue Salvation

I may have lost a bit of my thrill of the struggle and sense of climax at touching the sand, but at least I captured other changes in mood and, after so long gone missing, *sound*. This poem might give Miss Patterson more opportunity to wield her red pen, but I didn't care: the role of Mama's long goodbye in my life now played the central role in *my* song.

Mama, forgive me. I'm sorry I ever thought, even for an instant, that your dying spared me the burden of having to take care of you. Although such a guilty thought may have been a fact, it's not true. I miss you to this day and am grateful for every moment we shared, right to the last, when you said farewell.

I promise I'll get back to writing more poetry, for you and for me. You gave me an ear for sound-sense, and I'll never stop trying to sing for so long again. Mama, please give me your will to grit my teeth so I can carry on.

Fall 1920: Glen Arbor

Pip rebelled. He acted up in school and refused to look at Miss Patterson, even when responding to her questions. He didn't speak to David and never ran with him along the shore, even after Papa hired David on the condition the Ojibwe boy finish school. Pip stopped going to the stove works in Empire altogether and refused to join us at Pastor Weir's Sunday service in the Omena kirk.

At first I worried about my boy. Always a loner except for Mama and me and his underdog pal, David, he even stopped knocking on my door. Sure we'd eat breakfast together, and I'd drive him to and from school, where I helped Miss Patterson teach again. On my walks I'd catch glimpses of him fly-fishing for brookies in the Crystal River. Returning from my swims, I'd find him wandering the beach, searching for Petoskey stones, or running to Glen Arbor. When I opened the windows to let the cool night breeze into my bedroom, I could peek down and see him searching the heavens with one of his telescopes, but he never waved to me. Pip was at the age where strange humors coursed through his body and ruled his emotions. I knew enough to let my boy be.

The second Saturday in October, David Ahgosa flagged me down from Sleeping Bear Point on one of my swims across the bay. When I emerged from the water, he greeted me with a towel. As I dried off, he asked me to join him for a climb up the west face of the dunes to visit the Sleeping Bear. He stripped off his shirt and placed it under a large rock with the towel. I followed him along the beach and up the long, steep, slow climb to the top. There, we saw the shaggy green mound of the mysterious bear rising high above us. The muscles on his back rippling, David proceeded more rapidly up a shallow ridge to the west front of the large dome. He turned, and his darkly tan chest and taut tummy glistened. He pointed north, and I looked past the Sleeping Mama Bear still peering across the bounding blue water of the Great Lake to her two island cubs in the distance. As we looked above us, I saw long dune grass covered the big dome, along with the remains of an old beech grove, all held together by the roots of the trees and grass. The prevailing winds had already blown the few remaining leaves off, while the howling Northwesterlies had long since toppled most of the trunks and stunted the growth of the other beeches over time. Only cottonwood volunteers now offered any hope of a forest rebirth to hold this magnificent Mama Bear together.

David led me around to the east side. He tiptoed up the dome to avoid damaging any ground cover. He stopped near the top at a natural nest formed by several trunks. He pointed east to Glen Lake and the Day farm, with its picturesque barn with two cupolas, and north to the dirt road D. H. dug out of a hill into Glen Haven. He explained how Mr. Day, as the County Road Commissioner, was getting the state to pave his private road as a part of his dowry for his new supervisor. "Sven Surtr's fixing to haul mobs of tourists in dune buggies from Mr. Day's gas station to this sacred spot."

Papa had warned me to steer clear of D. H.'s new man, a swarthy Norse giant with ambition and forearms to match. Of course, Papa knew all about how to get ahead, marrying the owner's Old Maid daughter. At least Papa would be glad to hear that Mr. Surtr set his sights on King David's empire instead of ours.

When I began to chuckle at this thought, David gave me what for and told me we had to save this Mama Bear from such ravaging: "They'll lay gravel roads over the dunes to get here. Tens of thousands will climb this pinnacle and carve trails through the trees, underbrush, and dune grass. Our Mokwa will be lost in a blink of time."

The legend of this Mama Bear watching eternally over her two cubs lost swimming with her across the Great Lake just before they reached our shore would be forever defiled. Yet the huge mound on which we sat was already exposed to the prevailing northwest wind, and the harsher storms that blew across the Lake would erode her steep west bank. When I asked about this greater force of nature, David said, "That's no reason to kill her before her time." I took his hand and nodded. We ought to assure a reprieve for our Mama Bear at least until our children learned the power of her legend.

We tiptoed back down and huddled together in the warm sand. The lee of the big dome sheltered us from the Northwest wind. I shared everything about my passage to Manitou and back: how I found Mama and her farewell wish for me. David was oddly reserved about his race up the west front of the Mama Bear but assured me he'd found his way as an Ojibwe. The view east across the wide dunes, Glen Lake, Alligator Hill, Glen Arbor, and Sleeping Bear Bay to Bell Cottage soon mesmerized me. The hot afternoon sun above and warm sand at our backs made me sleepy as I basked in the sight, sound, and feel of the dunes' rolling mounds and sinuous valleys and of the shifting winds.

Suddenly, I woke with a shiver: the cold Northwest wind whistled above as the autumn sun fell early behind the Sleeping Bear. David's head lay cradled in my arms. I wondered at my holding a boy almost three years my junior so close. He opened his eyes, dark and clear, and I knew: I was holding him tight against our pasts, even though they'd always pry us apart long after he grew from boy to man. Too soon his hand brushed my cheek, and the wind blew the sand over the hollow we had made there.

∽

The next afternoon I drove to Glen Haven to meet with Mr. Day. In his office above his General Store, he shared stories with me about the old days when Papa boasted he could make Glen Arbor thrive with the Bell Stove works and big pier for shipping more than old D. H. could with all his lumbering, reforesting, and big dock for his Great Lakes steamers. "Times do change," he said.

Yes, Glen Arbor waned, its pier rotted, while Empire boomed instead when Papa moved the company there and adopted its name. Glen Haven took on a new face, too, what with all the visitors, whether from the big passenger boats or stream of cars, bent on touring Glen Lake, the Day farm and orchards, and the massive dunes. Before I could continue to my point, he said, "You're old enough to call me D. H."

"Mr. Day, thank you for teaching my family how to buy land, plant trees, and work with the Indians to make sure our little paradise will thrive for generations."

"Now, Belle, your papa told me you could butter and bargain with the best. So, why don't you just stop the buttering and get to the bargain."

"You know the legend of Sleeping Bear and how much that pinnacle atop the dunes means to David and his band of—"

"Hell's bells, girl," he interjected, "you know it's too long a climb for most folks to get there, and she'll only be able to attract more tourists to these parts if we can drive right up to her." He turned from his little desk and yelled out the window, "Sven, you better get up—" Before he could finish, the door to his office burst open. As I jumped out of my chair, my eyes stared right at an Adam's apple, big as a Macintosh, bobbing up and down. He stuck out his hand and swallowed mine in his big mitt. I couldn't keep my eyes from rising to the top of his dark head, more than a half-foot above mine, his teeth so big they looked like fangs. D. H. introduced this dark giant as his "future son-in-law."

I tried to make my points about the need to protect the Sleeping Mama Bear from hordes of tourists walking all over her fragile crown, ferried by dune-cars undercutting her trunk. Even sitting, Sven looked down at me; his huge frame made his chair look like a toddler's. Don't know if it was his bony cheeks or the big ridges over his eyes, but his expression seemed so hostile, even fierce, I soon ran out of words.

As I wound to a stop and stood to leave, old D. H. did his best to cover my embarrassing retreat. "Belle, we're still a ways from running any buggies over the dunes to your big Mama Bear. Costs a lot to build and maintain hard enough gravel pack on the dunes and to buy and outfit new vehicles to get to her."

Sven stood and said, "Good to meet you, Miss Belle." He turned to Mr. Day and added, "Vy don't ve ask Mr. Peebles if he vill invest so ve can get our Dunesmobiles varoomink sooner rather than later?"

"Let's think on that, Son," D. H. said, and I fled before I did any more damage.

The next Sunday, after cleaning up the mess from our midday dinner and putting the fixings in the icebox for our picnic supper on the beach, I set out for a swim across the bay to Glen Haven. A perfect Indian summer day warmed the air to seventy degrees, while the absence of frosts this fall left the bracing water not much colder than the hottest day in August. As I swam past the mouth of the Crystal River, I saw Pip reel in brookies returning to their spawning grounds. He stuffed only enough in his creel to grill on the campfire for our picnic. I missed the sight of Pip racing David on the beach, but I ached to hold the Ojibwe alone again.

The crimson of maples and yellow of the more plentiful birch had already faded, but the ochre of the few oaks ripened. Against the green backdrop of the new and old pines, the more muted leaf colors offered a pastel palette. An hour in, as I turned over to float on my back, the still water in the bay reflected this sight. Another hour, and the wind from the Northwest picked up and impeded my progress.

As I flipped over on my back, the *D. H. Day* Mackinaw Boat, a 19-footer with a single mast, mainsail and foresail, glided by with a confident skipper at the tiller and a lovely woman by his side. A gust of wind heeled the boat over toward me, and there sat David, riding high on the rail, pointing. We waved at each other and continued on our separate ways.

The Northern Michigan Transportation Company steamer *Manitou* sat moored at the big dock in Glen Haven. With berths for 2,200 passengers, this must have been her last run for the season. The life-saving crew at Sleeping Bear Point was already battening down the hatches for the winter; only the South Manitou Coast Guard Station would watch over the passage during the rougher weather ahead. In the bustling village, a gaggle of guests stood waiting at Sleeping Bear Inn to ride Mr. Day's tram for a fee to visit all his attractions on the way to the east front of what he claimed was "the largest moving sand dune in the world." Of course, "moving" meant that the prevailing winds off Lake Michigan blew the two-mile-wide dune only a couple of inches east each year toward Glen Lake—not so much as any eye could notice but enough so Mr. Day and his guides could brag.

On my swim back across the bay, I got to thinking more about saving our Sleeping Bear. When I had asked Papa if he'd heard whether Mr. Day was planning any new tourist ventures, he told me, "Old D. H. is still putting his money where his mouth is." First, as the newly appointed Chairman of the Michigan State Parks Commission, wouldn't you know Mr. Day gave 32 acres of prime lakeshore frontage and woods east of the Indian Camp and west of Glen Arbor for our first state park? Second, he was also carving through the trees on Alligator Hill between Little Glen and Sleeping Bear Bay to build a golf course and resort with hundreds of home sites for sale. Papa said King David wanted "to make our corner of the small tip of the little finger of Michigan's mitten the Adirondacks of the Midwest." Third, he started building a cannery. The King hoped his D. H. Day

Campground would attract thousands of campers to rent his boats, buy his gas and goods, and pay to see his many sights. He'd sell his fruit and tourist paradise by word of mouth, and hundreds would return to buy his lots and pay him to build their new cottages with his excess lumber.

I couldn't help smiling at the rivalry between Mr. Day and Papa either. Both of them started as hired hands and ended up owning the business. Each wanted to outshine the other: Papa by building our Empire Stove Works into a national player, D. H. by figuring out how to parley all his glorious land, verdant forests, and blue waters into an even bigger tourist empire. Then a chill hit me: Good Lord, Papa might agree to invest with D. H. in dune rides to make sure Sven didn't come courting after our Empire.

Not until I reached the mouth of the Crystal River did I realize I'd swum right past Pip's campfire for our picnic. I turned and saw the smoke rising from the hollow in the dune and the D. H. Day sloop moored on the beach below. By the time I clambered out of the water by the ship, I heard Mister Stripes screeching. I raced up the dune and found the skipper refereeing a wrestling match between Pip and David. As I approached, the older boy took my brother down. Seeing me, Pip squirmed, freed his left hand, and landed a sharp jab on David's nose. Rather than raise his aim, David pounded Pip's shoulders. Our orange-and-white striped fur-ball of a cat caterwauled in protest.

The skipper didn't appear worried, but I couldn't stand the sight. I launched my body at David. As we sprawled on the sand, I pinned him. I should have worried he'd belt me, but his closer contact sent a bigger jolt through me. Already beginning to flush, I pushed myself off before I caused any more embarrassment.

I scrambled up and faced Pip, but he refused to look at me. The skipper helped David up. As the two boys glowered at each other, this gentle man smiled. "You two must be great friends to go at it so hard without hurting anyone." I had to laugh at the truth of that, and the skipper turned and introduced himself. "I'm Skipper Beals, and this is my wife, Cora. Ma'am, which of these two belongs to you?" That set me back some, but it did offer a better excuse for my blush than David's touch: Did I already look such an old schoolmarm Skipper thought I was the mother of a teenage boy? When I nodded toward my brother, he asked, "Mind if I teach them the finer art of self-defense?"

That got all our attention, and he began to demonstrate the proper stance, posture, positioning of the hands and movements, first with Pip, then with David. Soon he had the boys taking turns trying to hit him, but he deflected their punches and countered with a light tap to their nose, chin, chest, or belly. This continued until the two boys tired so they couldn't hold their arms up any longer. Throughout this demonstration Skipper wasn't mean; he kept talking and explaining while Mrs. Beals beamed. I admired how he captivated the boys and made them forget their anger with each other by taking turns learning how to box with him. After a long while, he said, "Let's take a break to sort this all out." He turned to me and said, "Why don't you have a talk with your fisherman down by the river, while I talk with my navigator down by our sailing ship?"

Sure enough, it turned out Pip had been carrying a grudge since that day months ago when he'd tried to join David in the Ojibwe rite of passage, to run up the west front of the dunes. The two boys had added a bet: whoever won could invite D. H. Day's youngest daughter, Estelle, a real looker, to the annual Hob Gobble Nobble late fall party. Although Pip could skate a bit faster on the frozen ice, David ran slightly quicker on snowshoes over the deep snow, and the boys mostly tied when dashing across the beach, Pip was no match for his older pal over long distances, certainly not racing the thousand feet up the steep west dune-face. In fact, Pip admitted he'd never even tried it before, while David had trained for weeks to make sure he wouldn't fail.

To add insult to injury, with only a hundred feet to go, Pip cramped so badly he had to stop. After reaching the top, David returned and tried to console his taller but younger friend. Pip had to lean on David as a crutch on the slow trudge down the dune to the base at the shore of Lake Michigan and through the longer trek around the point.

When they'd passed my car at the Life-Saving Station, David had stopped to ask the crewman in the watchtower whether he'd caught sight of me yet. When the lifeguard shook his head and said a bad storm was brewing, David became concerned. When Pip asked David how he knew about my swim, David pulled out the keys to my roadster and tried to explain. Given Pip's defeat, injury, and humiliation, my boy took even greater offense at my sharing my secret with David. Pip *ordered* his friend to arrange with the Coast Guard to get the surfboat out to search for me. As Pip limped off to hitch a ride to warn Papa, he admitted he'd called to David: "Potts, if my Marmie makes it back safe, don't chase after her ever again."

Pip conceded that by the time I finally swam to safety at Glen Arbor later, he'd never been so happy to see me. But he *hated* the sight of David jumping from the surfboat and swimming after me and then me inviting his older pal to join us in Papa's car. Given the hurt my boy felt in so many ways that day, and the awful things he'd said to David, I could see how the two boys' friendship fell to a feud that lasted till now.

Pip was so embarrassed by the end of this story, I hugged him. Although taller than me, he would always be my little brother. I said I was sorry and tried to explain my chance meeting with David and how David had shared his Indian Head penny with me for luck. I lifted Pip's head, looked squarely into those endless blue-gray eyes, hoping they'd not see my different truth, and said, "David never made a play for me. He just wished me well." When Pip nodded, I told him how the sturgeon had shown me the way so I could say a proper goodbye to Mama. I sang the song I composed, and he said he'd keep looking for Mama in the heavens for both of us.

I asked whether David invited Estelle to the party. When Pip only dropped his eyes, I asked, "Will you take me?" He looked up. "I'll teach you, and you can drive us." When his blue eyes lit up, I added, "We can pick up David and Estelle, too." I didn't dare tell my brother of my other meeting with David but was glad to learn that David and I could share secrets no one else could know, not even Pip.

"I'm sorry I was mad at him," Pip said. "I like Estelle, okay, but not so much to let her split David and me." He lowered his head. "Marmie, I owe him an apology."

I picked up the creel and handed it to Pip. "You and David roast the brookies, while I go get the rest of the fixings. Invite the Beals to join us."

I was famished by the time I returned from our cottage with the picnic basket. The fish smoking in the corn husks in the hot coals set my mouth to water. I didn't let the two boys' jabbering stop me; I tucked away more than my share of roasted trout, potato salad with peas, sun tea, and the best cherry cobbler I ever baked.

The setting sun cast as rosy a glow across the bay as the campfire did across our faces. On close inspection, Skipper, although big, was a teddy bear of a man, ruddy skin under a full head of dark hair; Cora, more a lynx of a woman, small, sleek, deep brown eyes, and auburn hair cropped in a pert bob. This was their sixth visit from St. Louis, and they'd already fallen in love with our north coast.

As dusk fell, the fire flickered shadows across all our faces. David said he'd tell a story. His face, eyes and hair so dark his white teeth flashed, I thought for sure he was going to tell the legend of the Sleeping Bear and her twin Manitou Island cubs. Instead he began, "My great-grandfather told me the legend of the Great Lakes when I was a small boy. First the big ocean covered all our world and only fish swam. Then the long, hot sun dried up everything far beyond where we can see, and only insects crawled on the parched earth. Eventually, the big ice flowed from the north and gouged out the land, and nothing swam or walked here." He paused, and his eyes danced as the tongues of flame framed his dark face. He threw more pale driftwood on the fire, and its crackling increased our anticipation. "Finally, when the bitter cold retreated north, the warm sun melted the ice and gave us this Great Lake. We call this water our Nibi because it is the sacred spring of life—all manner of fish, fowl, wildlife, and man." As the wind echoed its *too-loo* through the pine, David swept his hand in a wide arc and continued, "The eagle spirit showed my grandfather how we must teach all our original people to share why we cherish this great water with others. Unless our every action helps conserve our Nibi for at least seven generations hence, the big sun will come back to steal the Great Lake, and only insects will crawl on the parched earth ever after." His eyes looked so fierce and sad, I knew, because he was determined to make amends for his Great Uncle's deceit.

Thankfully, Mrs. Beals clapped her hands and hugged the Ojibwe boy before I could. She explained she and her Skipper had been searching for a site for a camp to teach boys this lesson for two years: "You've blessed this shore as the perfect spot."

Pip added how this was also a good spot to search the night sky. He offered to build an observatory so the campers could learn to unlock the secrets of the universe.

David picked up with another story, "The Legend of the Lost Daughter." He began so softly, the lap of the waves and the whine of the ship's mast punctuated his words: "Eeinau was the favorite daughter of the Superior hunter to the north. He wanted her to marry the bravest of the young men of his tribe, but she flew on silken wing to the sylvan haunt in the shadow of the great dune that she had found far to the south. We call her Spirit Grove, Manitowak." Looking right at Cora Beals, David sang, "Beneath the shade of the big trees, where the perfume of the spring flowers wafted thee o'er waters blue, where the sun's last rays of day bathed thee in gold, where the night blesses thee with the green plumes of thine devoted lover, thou found this place. Ever after it is named after thee, the delight of life." He smiled. "Of course, we had no *L* in our language, so the first white man who recorded our tales added an *L* to her name because this place is a 'de**l**ight of **l**ife.' That's why we call it **L**ee**l**anau."

The crescent moon rose high, and the fireflies danced all around David's head. Oh, how I wished he was my age and this evening would never end. Mrs. Beals clapped again before I lost myself. As if on her command, a shooting star burst behind her pretty head. Pip and David nodded to me. The two boys knew we had to share our delight of life with Skipper Beals and his Missus. Only Papa stood in the way of the camp.

I knocked on the door to his study before I went to bed that night. Papa looked up from his account books as I told him about my supper by the campfire with Pip, David, and the Bealses.

He asked, "Have you decided where you want to live in Ann Arbor?"

"Miss Schultz arranged a room in a women's dorm across from the President's House." When Papa didn't respond, I continued, "She says the boarding houses for women off campus aren't right for me." When he still kept his lip buttoned, I explained, "Oh, Papa, I'll be so much older than all the other first-years—"

"Well, then," he interjected, "like to live in our own house down there?"

"You're not selling our stove business and moving the whole family?!"

He took off his reading glasses. "Don't plan to, but Pip and I will want to visit." With a smile he added, "Belle, I'm not going to let you become my lost daughter, ever."

"Do we have the money?"

"I was going to talk with you and Miss Schultz about investing some of your trust fund with me to expand our works to build your cooking stoves. If you and Miss Schultz agree, we can sell the land you find so enchanting to the Bealses for their camp instead."

"You never met them."

"Selling the land to the Bealses for a fair price will not only generate enough money to expand the plant in Empire and buy us a house in Ann Arbor, it will really get D. H.'s goat." I swear he almost twinkled as he crinkled his eyes. "King David asked me to *donate* that tract to his damn *D. H. Day* State Park."

"Can we keep this side of the river-mouth for our homestead?" He nodded. "And reserve the right to fish in the river and walk the beach in summer to Glen Arbor?"

"Good God almighty, Belle, do you want me to tell the Bealses that Pip wants to reserve the highest dune to build a barmy observatory and David wants to reserve your campfire site so I'll whittle some giant totem pole to tell Chief Ahgosa's legends, too?"

Time to take my chance: "I want you to talk some sense into Mr. Day so his new man won't start ferrying hordes of tourists in newfangled dune buggies to destroy the Sleeping Mama Bear." I explained my conversation with D. H. and Sven's suggestion that they seek an investment from Papa to finance the scheme.

"D. H. has got way too much capital tied up in developing his new Day Estates and canning business." When I didn't follow his drift, he explained: "Maybe David, you, and the new man all view the Sleeping Mama Bear as too much of an attraction." He chuckled. "You won't have anything to worry about once I tell old D. H. I wouldn't invest a plug nickel in driving folks to that shaggy old mound so far from the real thrill: running down the Dune Climb right next to the concession stand he already owns!"

"Is that all you think our Mama Bear's worth?"

"As long as that's what my fellow Scotsman believes most tourists think, he won't spend a penny to threaten her legend."

Papa was still smiling as I thanked him and excused myself. I guessed Sven would continue to argue that racing in a roadster, top-down, across the dunes would offer a bigger thrill. Given the failure of my plea on the merits, however, Papa's talking dollars and cents stood a better chance, at least for a while, of persuading old D. H.

I skedaddled up the two flights of stairs to the attic. My goodbye song to Mama had rekindled my sound sense, even if I couldn't spit out my new song all at once—it was too long. So I stood up, grabbed the lockbox, pulled out my songbook, sat back down on the chest, turned past dozens of poems since my goodbye poem for Mama, and began to write. It took several drafts, and more edits, but I think I got my first sonnet mostly right:

Delight of Life

We walk along the sandy shore among
piles of pale driftwood, carved smooth, bleached
 white
by decades of nature's slow and steady strum—
fuel perfect for a campfire any night

with you sitting close beside me to share
a rite of passage as old as Eden's vine;
joined by the slap of waves against the pier
a soft too-loo echoing through the pine

the whine of wind against a sailboat's mast;
amidst the burning crackle and shifting fire,
the silver crescent moon rising in the east
the flicker of fireflies sparking love's desire

fading like tiny stars to memory, dear—
as soon the imprint of our bodies here.

I could still feel David's touch to my cheek as we left the Sleeping Bear, or was it the wind of our delight of life tugging so at me? I couldn't ever tell, but I knew I'd compose poems with sounds as long as I lived. I pulled the Indian Head penny from the box, placed it gently on my new poem, added a few thoughts, and closed my journal.

ᔕ

I thought everything was okay with Pip. After the ice in the ponds and rivers froze early, two weeks before Thanksgiving, he laced on his skates and flew up and down the Crystal River, David in his wake. Soon, they joined to play hockey in the 50x150-foot ice rink D. H. Day had flooded in a big shed in Glen Haven. One day Pip asked me to drive him to a game. Even with his odd concave chest, he bulled through or skated circles around all the others, except for the Dark Ogre, Sven Surtr. Playing no favorites, the big brute checked him as if he were another grown man. Once, Sven caught Pip with his head down and checked him so hard into the boards that the walls shook. But Pip hopped up, and even Sven had to offer a grudging nod of respect.

On our drive back, Pip said he didn't want to run the stove business, although he did admit he liked playing with flame and wanted to tinker to help Papa build a stove for cooking only. When he mentioned David's joy at working with Papa at the Empire plant, I suggested he ask David to figure out how the men could make more stoves with less scrap.

Pip got to talking about tinkering with telescopes and radios. Nothing would stop him from searching for intelligent life in space and finding Mama and his God, too. I understood his joy: I shared my exhilaration when I first sang a song in frenzied creation and my deeper pleasure listening to the poem and adding a different slant of meaning. Then I even confessed my fear of moving away and living alone in Ann Arbor. But I encouraged Pip to pursue his dreams, and he encouraged me to compose my songs.

There was a problem, though, and it wasn't David Ahgosa going hot and heavy with Estelle Day after our double date. By Christmas break, Pip and I knew. My brother was still my boy, and I was still his Marmie. He didn't want to be left behind, and I didn't know if I could move to a new home in a distant arbor without him.

For my birthday on New Year's Eve, Papa gave me a book of Miss Dickinson's poems, *The Single Hound*. The lead poem described how Emily came to feel that her childhood friend who married her older brother was her second sister in the house next door, only "a hedge away." The stanza I liked best told how the poet now walked through life with her sister-in-law, "up and down the hills, I held her hand the tighter, which shortened all the miles." Miss Dickinson ended by plighting her loyal sisterhood to "Sue—forevermore!" She even signed her name at the end of the poem, *Emily*.

I went to the attic, composed one of my shortest poems, and inserted it into my songbook because I knew the problem:

Sibling Rivalry

In the deep Marmie
rests with fishes, on land
only my dear brother Pip—
My boy

Whether or not a selkie lost on land, I would never forsake my not-so-little brother.

Ironically, Miss Patterson told me the rumor out of New England literary circles: Miss Dickinson had offered her family homestead as the love nest for her older brother to tryst with a much younger mistress, the wife of Amherst College's new astronomer, only "a hedge away from" her sister-in-law's nose. Whatever I might say, even wish for a mate of my own, I also learned my fealty belonged first to my own flesh and blood, my brother, just as surely as David's did to his Ojibwe band.

Not long after, Papa left a picture postcard of the Sleeping Bear Dunes under my door with a note:

Despite that Nordic giant's handshake nearly breaking me, old D. H. got in his cups enough again he didn't argue when I

> *told him I wouldn't invest in any damn dune buggies. His big son-in-law tried to protest, but little King David shut him up: "Sven, we've got much bigger fish to fry." Leastways the Day Estates will occupy the Day clan for a decade before it ever turns a profit or, more likely I fear, bleeds them dry.*

I had to shake my head: the long cold winters and nights up north bred such heavy drinking among too many, including Mr. Day, Prohibition or no. Thank you Papa for influencing your old friend so, but I doubt Sven will ever stop seeking to bleed our Mama Bear dry. Eventually, I know David and I will have to make her legend more powerful to stop that Dark Ogre.

SUMMER 1921: ANN ARBOR

I swam back and forth the length of the big kettle lake, close to two miles from the diving tower and two big beaches at the northeast end to the water toboggan chute in front of the two grand hotels at the southwest. Hundreds of bathers crowded Groom's Beach and its neighbor with the long deck in front of the Stilsonburg stop of the Grand Trunk Railway, and more kept arriving on the train from Jackson. At the other end of the lake, hundreds of revelers crowded the big first-floor porches and hung off the second-floor balconies of the hotels. As the afternoon wore on, more folks from Dearborn and Ann Arbor emerged from the ping-pong train at the Whitmore depot and joined the parties ashore at the Clifton and Lakeside Inns. Many boarded the cute, little, two-deck steamer, the *Jenny D*, for a cruise to the beaches at the other end.

No other swimmer ventured out into the middle of the lake, but I swear the gnarled, old captain of the *Jenny D* sold tickets to gawk at the strange sight of a big mermaid swimming there. The lone lifeguard, sitting atop the big waterslide in the shallower water at Groom's Beach, closely followed my progress at first. A handsome, strapping specimen, he lost interest once he saw I could plow safely across the lake, lap after lap.

For the first day of summer, the temperature in the air soared to 90. After the chill of Lake Michigan, Whitmore Lake felt like a warm bath. I needed a break. I touched a corner of the floating platform of the diving tower, turned, swam out of the *Jenny D's* line of fire, and rolled onto my back. I closed my eyes to the late afternoon sun.

Without a splash the strongest arm I ever felt wrapped ever so gently around my big chest and began to propel me toward shore. I opened my eyes, but the sun sliding down made it hard for me to see. Although I hadn't been in any danger of drowning, I saw no harm in letting this merman save me.

His powerful sidestroke carried us past the diving tower and the waterslide. We coasted together to a stop on the sandy bottom in two feet of water. I opened my eyes and saw the lifeguard's face. What struck me was the smile, a broad grin with mischief at the corners. He shook his head, and the spray of water formed a rainbow until it hit my face.

"Serve towels with your showers?" I asked as I wiped my eyes.

He tipped his head back, laughing, and swallowed down the wrong pipe. When he raised his head and started coughing, I sat him up—the widest shoulders and biggest chest I'd ever seen. I pounded him on the back until he feigned begging for mercy.

I looked around. Thank heavens the hordes of sunbathers had deserted Groom's Beach and Stilsonburg because he kissed me on the lips. Although the water wasn't salt, he tasted of spice.

I managed to push him away, stood up, and said, "Thanks for thinking of saving me anyway, Life-boy." I splashed water on his face, dived into the lake, and headed for the waterslide. About halfway there I turned back to see where he was.

He stood and shouted, "Race you to the diving tower." I figured I had 10 yards left to the slide and another 25 to the finish line. I put on my fastest crawl, but a few yards from the goal, I felt the surge from his powerful stroke. No doubt I was better at marathons than sprints, but this was ridiculous. He left me in his wake. When I touched the floating deck, he reached down and easily pulled all six feet and 150 pounds of me up next to him. I was struck dumb at the speed of his swimming and the sight of his tan body: not an ounce of fat, huge feet and hands, short legs, and narrow waist rising in a *V* to his buff chest and broad shoulders. I feared I looked like a blob of blubber next to him, but his gaze suggested he didn't think I was that bad looking.

He stuck out his right hand awkwardly, dropped his eyes, and said, "Robert O'Bannon at your service."

Given the close contact we'd already shared, that introduction seemed an anticlimax. But I didn't know any better, so I answered, "Belle," and reached out my hand to shake. The mischief in his eyes should have offered a warning, but he shook my hand so hard I thought he was going to break it. When I began to return the favor, he just pulled me close, tilted my head down, and kissed me again, but ever so sweetly. My grip loosened at that, but I broke off before my longer legs quivered.

I dived into the water and swam toward the slide. He seemed to coast easily beside me, no matter how fast I tried to go. When we reached the slide, I looked up the many steps and four landings to the top. We emerged on a platform 40 feet in the air to quite a sight. The lowering sun shimmered on the surface of the lake. At the far end, the ping-pong train puffed south on tracks running through miles of farm fields, all the way down to the Huron River and the University of Michigan.

He tapped me on the shoulder and pointed southwest to a spire rising up in the sky from a thin brick church held up by narrow stained-glass windows. "That's St. Patrick's. My boys' choir sings evening Vespers tomorrow. I'll do a solo if you join us."

I guessed from his name, and that of his church, this would be another new experience for me. Mama and Papa never let me set foot in an Episcopal church, let alone one of the Pope's parishes, during all my Presbyterian days in Leelanau. I could see that St. Patrick's would dwarf my little kirk, but his Irish charm rang so pure, what was the harm?

I sat down atop the slide, and he maneuvered close behind. He pushed off, and we flew down. My shrieks climaxed at the bottom with a big splash and then a long sigh as he and the warm water cupped me. I couldn't tell whether his touch or the drop in the temperature as the sun fell caused my goosebumps. Maybe I was just nervous, never having spooned before. No matter, he sensed my need, swam me to shore, bundled me in towels, and, with roving hands, dried me off and warmed me up, thank you.

I offered him a ride, and we walked to my roadster. He turned his head while I turned my back, took off my wet suit, and put on slacks and a sweater. I shut my eyes while he did the same, although I did sneak a peek to see what the dark foliage below this merman's narrow waist might hold. I wondered how any woman could ever manage to take all that in.

Once in the car, he asked where I lived. When I told him off campus in a house on Cambridge, he asked, "A transfer student?"

"I'll be a freshman."

"I was worried you were older."

"Would that matter?"

"I'm a sophomore, and most college girls want to go out with upperclassmen."

"What do I do when I get to be a senior then?"

He grinned his most mischievous smile and said, "Continue with this older man."

"I'm 21, but I don't mind."

Judging from his look, he didn't either.

Paying more attention to him than driving, I let my roadster veer into a sandy buildup on the side of Lake Road just before St. Patrick's Church. We were stuck. He hopped out and pushed. I let the clutch out slow and came to a stop in front of the cemetery. He opened my door and took my hand, and we walked through the main gate a few steps, rose bushes in full bloom on either side, to two markers with the names Michael and Mary O'Bannon. "My grandparents. From Tipperary. Near the Rock of Cashel. I hope to visit the old sod after I graduate."

"Where does your family live now?"

"We'll stop by on the way back to town." He grabbed my hand to leave, but I saw a third marker with a single name, Thomas. "Tommy-boy, my kid brother," he mumbled. "Crushed by the thresher. An axle broke. My Da still can't forgive himself."

"I'm sorry. Do you have any other brothers or sisters?"

He shook his head. "My Ma never forgave him either." He held my hand as we walked to the car. He opened the passenger door for me and drove east on Northfield Church Road, jogged north, and then turned east again. He slowed and said, "What's your last name?"

"Don't really go by any."

"The Queen's not going to like it if I introduce you by your first name only."

"I hated my given name, Martha, so I borrowed the good Scots name of my Mother's family, Bell, and added the *E* on the end so there'd be fewer questions."

He turned into a short lane and drove up the hill to a tidy, two-story, white clapboard house with a trim, red barn in back. He walked me on the stone path to the front door. On either side, clusters of purple and blue iris and gladiola reached up for my chest. I did my best to run my fingers through my hank of red hair, but that didn't improve on the rumpled sweater and slacks I sported. Hardly go-to-meeting dress.

He opened the door and shouted, "Anybody home?" A short, attractive, brown-haired woman popped around a corner, squealed, "Robert," and crushed him in a hug. Down the stairs padded a tall, distinguished-looking man with a shock of hair as long his son's but white. He shook his son's hand, hard and long. My new friend introduced me to his parents. "This is Martha O'Bell, but she likes to go by Belle."

“Call me Grace,” his mother answered with a regal wave.

“Pleased to meet you,” I said, not daring to call the Queen Grace.

Mr. O’Bannon saved me from the awkward silence. He extended his hand. “Most people used to call me Thomas, but I go by O.B. now.”

“Howdy, Mr. O.B.,” I replied and tried to grip his hand as firmly as he held mine.

Although Mr. O’Bannon couldn’t hide the sadness in his dark eyes, he clapped his son on the back. “About time you brought home a healthy lass with a grip to match.”

After raiding the icebox for chicken salad and touring the barn with its new Ford tractor and old woolly sheep, we excused ourselves, and the last O’Bannon boy drove me back to town. “No red hair or blue eyes in your family,” I said.

“We call those types the late-comers.” He explained how that Norman stock represented one of the many invaders who crossed the Irish Sea, pillaged the land, and tried to conquer an unruly people. “We fooled them all: they’re all Irish now, and thanks to St. Patrick’s inspiration from our Rock of Cashel and Michael Collins’ fighting, we’re mostly a free country, too.” He asked hopefully, “Any of your kin Scots-Irish?”

I shook my head and chastised him for introducing me as “O’Bell” to his parents. After a pause I touched his arm and added, “As the daughter of independent Scots rabble, will you mind if I call you Rabbie?” I explained how my Mama reading Rabbie Burns and Emily Dickinson inspired me to write poems. “She called them all songs.”

He surprised me by belting out a Burns ballad. At the end of the first stanza, he sang, “Only thou I swear and vow shall ever be *my* Dearie!” with such a lovely lilt, I thought I might fly. When he hit even higher notes with a tremolo, claiming he’d die if I refused to be *his* Dearie, I couldn’t help the tears. “So please call me Rabbie,” he sang, “my Dearie Belle till the day I die.”

"You serious?" When he nodded with his biggest smile, I knew I was in trouble.

He pulled to the side of the road and said, "Cross your heart." I did, and he held my hand. I told him how it had taken me so long to fledge my nest by Sleeping Bear Bay. I told him about Mama's death, saving my little brother, my rite of passage swimming to South Manitou and back, and finally writing a poem to say goodbye to my Mama so many years later. I shared my long differences with my father and my growing appreciation for Papa.

He told me how the harvester had tipped, how he had lost his grip on "Tommy-boy," and how his little brother had lingered for weeks of pain and suffering after being mangled by the thresher. He shared how only the singing of Father Goldrick's boys' choir at the funeral in St. Patrick's saved him. "Say you'll join us at Vespers tomorrow evening to hear us sing."

"Aren't you too old for a boys' choir?"

"I direct the lads now. If I can raise the money, the founder of the Little Singers has invited us to bring our Wooden Crosses to sing at Notre-Dame in Paris."

Rather than ask what Notre-Dame was, I said, "Only if I can sit in the back of your church so no one notices I don't know when to bow and scrape."

"No problem, Dearie: Over time you'll learn."

I changed the subject before I challenged him on why he couldn't convert to Presbyterian instead. "With all your singing, do you write poetry, too?"

"Odd." He shook his head. "I don't have the sense of sound to write poems. I stick to short stories—and criticizing others' verse."

I squeezed his hand. "Dare I share my poems with you?"

"You must join the Whimsies." He explained how the student literary magazine worked. "Then we meet at Professor Roy Cowden's and read our stories and poems."

"Not sure I want to put my singing up for public review."

"I'll protect you from anyone who dares throw sticks or stones."

"Words can hurt me more," I squeaked as the lump grew in my throat.

"Cowden says Frost's joining us, too." Having just finished poring over *A Mountain Interval*, oh how I wanted to hear Robert Frost say his poems! When I nodded, Rabbie pulled the car out and soon turned right onto the much wider Pontiac Trail, eyes ahead but right hand firmly on my left knee. I must have rested my eyes because the next thing I heard was my door opening. I looked over his shoulder to neat, three-story brick buildings lining the street, their retail windows still lit up. As he helped me out, I looked back to the Diag—the open square at the center of campus—and the much bigger buildings of the University arrayed across the main quad, lit only by the rising moon.

Rabbie escorted me into the ice cream parlor. It had a crisp, black-and-white tile floor and a stamped tin ceiling, booths with black leather benches filled with people on our left and silver metal stools with round, black leather seats and more patrons on our right. He squeezed us into one side of the first booth that opened and ordered one strawberry sundae. When it arrived with two big scoops of ice cream side by side, dark red strawberry preserves dripping down, and a brighter red cherry on top of each mound, I almost laughed at the sight. Instead, I just tucked into my scoop. I don't know if I ate too fast or the sight of the sundae unnerved me, but a shiver soon raced down my throat; I swear a jolt hit my core so hard I got a cold-freeze that bounced all the way to the top of my head and back down to the tips of my toes. Rabbie leaned his big shoulder over and warmed me right up. When he picked up his cherry and placed it in my mouth, I returned the favor. He held my hand and licked my fingers, and that set off a different shiver.

We eventually finished, and I asked him for the keys. But Rabbie said he'd drive me home and walk to his night watchman job nearby. He pulled my roadster out and spun a nifty U-turn across the trolley tracks. As we approached the big rock at the corner of Washtenaw and Hill, he pointed to a big fraternity house under construction behind it.

"Two jobs, seven days a week?" I asked.

"No, Tuesdays and Thursdays I take the Interurban to Detroit to work out."

"For what?"

"A meet next week against Duke Kahanamoku and the boy wonder from Illinois."

"Who's Duke K-ka-han…?"

"Three golds in the 1920 and 1912 Olympics. Still holds all the world records."

I perked right up. "Can I watch?" When he didn't answer, I told him, "Jog right, around the little park and take the first left on Cambridge. It's the second house."

"The meet's at the Detroit Athletic Club, kind of like a fraternity, for men only."

"Good Lord, I don't want to join. I just want to watch you race."

"I'll see if Coach Mann can sneak you in."

Given my father's continued refusal to consider me taking over our family business, I shouldn't have been surprised at discovering another men-only club barring my entry, but it still hurt. As he stopped the car, my house loomed high on the hill. Georgian brick colonial, it stood two tall stories with double-hung windows, white muntins and trim, a big center entry, three dormers above on the steeply pitched roof, stately columned porches on either side. "Good lord, Belle," he said, "who's your landlady? It's bigger than my fraternity house!"

I felt like telling him, "All your boys-only clubs be damned, I own this," but I just hopped out of my car. I opened his door, helped him up, took the keys, and kissed him square on the mouth. Before he could engage me in any tongue wrestling, I pushed away. "I'll be there to hear you and your Little Singers tomorrow."

I sashayed up the walk into my Cambridge house without looking back. After bolting the door behind me, I raced up the stairs to the second floor and looked through the curtains in one of the front bedrooms. I saw Rabbie skipping across the little park, heading north to his night job at the building site behind the big rock.

I retired to my bedroom in back, opened my leather journal, thought for only a minute, let a few phrases sing, and jotted down the draft of my first poem to him.

Swimmer's Itch

Baptized in love I am
when your body porpoises
up to mine—

the warm swoosh of your waves
streams straight from my toes
to tingle my heart—

then you power on—
leaving me behind to flounder
in the cool splash of your wake.

I arrived at St. Patrick's late so I could sit unnoticed in a back pew. As I approached the church, I saw the bell tower rising up and up, the graceful spire above reaching higher and higher, its ability to support the big cross on top its own miracle—defying gravity. When I opened the door and stepped into the sanctuary, the evening sun flowed through the tall, narrow stained-glass windows in a rainbow of color and pointed to one available seat in the last row on the left. The heads of all the parishioners turned toward me. To my relief, I saw they looked above me, up to the choir singing *Alleluias* from the overhanging balcony.

I stepped quickly toward the back pew, but not fast enough. The pure voices suddenly stopped, and all eyes fell on my six-foot frame decked out in white, including a boxy, white linen hat that probably made me look a head taller. I tried to make myself small, bowed toward the altar, and turned to sit down. I tripped over the kneeler in the front of the pew and fell onto the bench with a whump. Thankfully, I missed the little white-haired lady next to me as she shied away with a fearful look.

After whispering my apology, I saw Grace O'Bannon gazing from the aisle seat in the front pew on the right. Beside her, Mr. O. B. smiled at me. I nodded, but when they turned to face the front, the Queen shook her head as she whispered in his ear. Father Goldrick raised his arms, and the angelic voices of the Little Singers in the balcony rose again. I didn't know any Latin, but the sound of the boys' choir lifted my spirits.

Father Goldrick recited two verses, no doubt psalms from the rhythm of his deep, booming voice. The boys' choir responded with a song that soared high as the rooftop cross. Father Goldrick answered with a chant that included a *Gloria* and a *Patri*. The Little Singers above answered and inspired the rest of the congregation to chant back.

Father Goldrick read a brief passage in Latin from the Bible in his sing-song way. Suddenly, all those around me fell to their knees, and the boys above and Father Goldrick began to chant back and forth at each other. Belatedly, I kneeled down, too. When the Little Singers above began another chant, the parishioners dragged me up to a standing position, and they responded in kind. The harmony of the deep baritone of Father Goldrick, the alto and soprano of the boys, and the high tenor of Rabbie then burst out with what sounded like *Magnificat*, followed by Latin phrases I couldn't understand. When this ended, the parishioners dropped me to my knees again and prayed for the Virgin Mary. Father Goldrick then joined the boys' choir in a sing-song, its rhythm unmistakably that of the doxology followed by *Our Father*, even if I couldn't make out a single word other than *Pater*. Father Goldrick said one more prayer and then signaled us all to rise. He looked to the balcony.

All I could see was the overhang. It didn't matter. A single tenor, so soft and high, cast his spell. As Rabbie sang *Ave Maria*, his voice picked up depth and volume until it reached a crescendo so pure I wanted to cry. When he finally lowered his voice after the last stanza in the final amen, I had to restrain myself from screaming for more.

After Father Goldrick said the Benediction, the little white-haired lady next to me clasped my hand and said in the kindest voice, "Peace be with you." Not knowing how to respond, I thanked her. With a nod behind me, she continued, "I hope to sit Vespers with you again: You inspire our choir."

I turned, and there Rabbie stood, wearing a white robe with a large wooden cross hanging over his big chest. He waved to me to join his glorious host of smaller charges in similar garb standing behind him. I managed to take one step before the Choir Master and his Little Singers of the Wooden Cross enveloped me. I couldn't foresee that Rabbie's damn Church, and his boys' choir and religious singing, would conspire to separate us for three decades, no matter how much we loved each other.

ဢ

The next week I was stunned by the Detroit architect's masterpiece. Not even the picture books Stanford White left at Bell Cottage to show off his firm's other commissions could match Albert Kahn's indoor pool at the D.A.C. Twenty-five-foot tall arched windows carved between ribbed beams rose gracefully into a vaulted ceiling in the six-story club. Four chandeliers, each with a six-foot ring of 24 bulbs, threw light on the water. The two lines at the bottom, dividing the three lanes, waved back. Five hundred men in tuxedos watched. A lucky few sat in folding chairs in the front row on either side of the length of the pool, behind brass railings. The rest stood behind on both sides, on both ends, and around the balcony above.

Duke Kahanamoku stood on the dark tile deck above the center lane. Handsome, a big smile, gleaming white teeth, easygoing, graceful—a picture of confidence even at age 31: he'd yet to lose a race. My Rabbie stood on his left, about the same height but much bigger in the chest and shoulders. He curled his toes over the edge. The new Chicago phenom paced on the right. Only 17, he glared at the Duke as if he were going to hunt the Hawaiian down rather than swim against the reigning champ.

All the other swimmers training at the D.A.C. and the Illinois Athletic Club who'd lost out in the preliminary races stood behind them in long, dark robes, many with dark swimming caps. I stood at the back of this crew, hunched down to hide my height, my red hair tucked under my swim cap, my dark slacks and sweater covered by my bulkier dark robe. Matt Mann signaled the swimmers to ready, and all three crouched.

Before I even sensed the shrill sound of the coach's whistle, Rabbie bolted into the lead, and the other two followed close behind. The water roiled as they raced down to the far end, turned, and swam back in a mad sprint. Rabbie touched first at the halfway point, and the D.A.C. crowd went nuts. Duke touched a close second, with the longer Chicago lad two yards behind. As they turned and raced down the pool, the chandeliers swayed, and the light flickered. At the far end, it looked like all three touched at the same time. The roar grew as they swam back toward the finish in a single wave. The Duke surged into the lead halfway home, but Rabbie hung on as he matched Duke's quickening pace, stroke for stroke. The Chicago youngster closed the gap, although his longer strokes seemed less hurried. The water surging behind his big, webbed feet propelled him even faster over the last few yards.

I forgot myself and craned over the heads in front. It looked as if Duke had won by a fingertip, but the crowd's roar suggested our local boy scored the upset instead. Matt Mann huddled with the two judges, from either side of the finish line, and the three men with stopwatches, one for each lane, from the end of the pool. A hush fell as the coach picked up a megaphone: "The winner, with a new world record, is…" Mann paused until the crowd begged. "Johnny Weissmuller!"

Duke congratulated Johnny, and so did Rabbie. The coach conferred with the swimmers. He asked the crowd, "Would you like to see who wins at fifty yards?" The men in tuxes screamed and stamped their feet so, I feared the balcony might collapse.

Mann escorted Duke to the start line in Lane Two and then placed Johnny on his left and Rabbie on his right. The crowd hushed when the coach gave the ready sign. He blew the whistle, and all three shot out over the pool, knifed through the water, and turned at the far end together. This time Johnny wasn't lagging. As they neared the finish line, the chandeliers did shake. Johnny appeared to touch out Rabbie and Rabbie to touch out Duke, or maybe it was the other way around. I couldn't tell. When I realized I was waving my cap in the air, I pulled it back on before my unruly red hair gave me away.

Coach Mann huddled with the two judges and the holders of the stopwatches. They shared a brief laugh, but we all screamed for the verdict. Finally, Matt picked up his megaphone and declared, "Dead heat, but a new American record for all three." The roar grew, and I swear, not only all the swimmers around me in their dark robes, but all of the black tuxedoed men stormed the coach, Rabbie, Duke, and Johnny.

As they swarmed, I made my exit and opened the door to the laundry. I took off my robe and cap, climbed into a huge roller-tub and buried myself among the clean towels. A half hour later, Rabbie and the coach escorted me down the back stairs and out the service entry to my waiting roadster.

Rabbie drove, I sat next to him, and Coach Mann leaned forward from the back seat. Mr. Mann was a gentle Scotsman. When I thanked him for arranging for me to watch the race, he said, "Rabbie tells me you're quite a swimmer."

"Not as fast, but I can paddle and kick for hours on end. It's my salvation."

"Woman of your ability and character can swim in the Olympics, too."

"But not train with you at the D.A.C."

"Hey, Coach," Rabbie interjected, "how about starting a swim team at Michigan this fall? You can train Belle on the side."

Mann frowned. "Remember, you guys failed to raise the money to complete the pool in the new Union, so I've got to head back East to support my family."

"Why won't the University pay for it?" I pressed Coach Mann.

"Although it's meant to serve all students, it's supposed to be a private club."

"Sorry," Rabbie said, "he means all the male students."

"Is there going to be a Union for women students, too?" I asked.

"The Women's League has started fundraising for a new building," Rabbie answered. Coach Mann added that all the Ivy League schools had new pools, but only Northwestern, Illinois, and Chicago fielded men's teams in the Western Conference.

The more I learned, the madder I got. My face must have turned as beet red as my hair. "Belle, I'm sorry about all this," Mann said, "but there's a lot of nonsense that goes around about women being too fragile to compete in sports."

"Well," I asked, "if there's no men's pool and no women's pool at Michigan, where does anyone swim when all the lakes freeze over?"

Mann couldn't help laughing now. "The men can swim at the new short-course pool at the YMCA on Fourth Street."

Rabbie didn't laugh. He said, "The women can take dips in the Plunge Tank, but it's only an oversize tub in Barbour." He explained that was the women's annex to the men's gym. "It does have a beautiful space for parties, though."

"Oh, do I go to tea there after I take a 'plunge' in that tiny tank?"

Rabbie and Mr. Mann fell silent. After we traveled through

Ypsilanti, I asked Coach Mann where he was spending the night. When he told me the Union but looked a bit sheepish, I asked, "Can you show me what needs to be done to finish the pool?"

"Well, at least we don't have to sneak you in."

"No," Rabbie picked up, "we just have to escort you through the back door."

The Union was a handsome building, brick with limestone trim, big windows, and a seven-story tower front and center. Entering through the "Ladies Entrance" on the north side, we walked on dark tile floors with oak wainscot and limestone on the walls, past the big Men's Grill and a tiny Lady's Dining Room. The two men hurried me through the Locker Room, for men only, into a cavernous space. The windows at our level were five feet high, but huge arched windows soared above. I asked how much it would cost to finish the pool. When Coach Mann answered $25,000, I did blink.

The next day I had my quarterly call with Miss Schultz. She said Empire profits had more than doubled again, as much from the savings in cutting the rate of scrap as from increasing sales. When I chuckled, Miss Schultz continued, "Your father made David Ahgosa the inspector, and his eagle eye embarrassed the men until they got it right the first time." I asked how Pip was doing. "Still tinkering at the shop, but he and David are hard at a new competition." When I said I hoped it wasn't boxing, she explained how D. H. Day's plan to sell homes around his course on Alligator Hill hadn't panned out, so he had begged the boys to "play golf there so [his] resort doesn't look empty."

Satisfied Mama Bear would be safe from Sven's dune buggies for another year, I said, "I've got a new sport, too. He's a faster swimmer, and we play tennis, too."

"You need me to head down there to chaperone?"

"Too late." I paused. "Miss Schultz, I take it the University's a good credit." When she confirmed my guess, I said, "Will you call

Fielding Yost and President Burton to see if they're interested in a loan of $25,000 to finish the Union swimming pool?"

"You gonna break up the ice on the frozen lake to swim in the meantime?"

"Not if you arrange to finance the damn pool now, Miss Schultz."

"Good Lord, Belle, they won't let you go swimming with men at the Union!"

"Matt Mann's agreed to coach my boyfriend and me there during off hours."

"One more thing," said Miss Schultz. "Miss Patterson's trying her best, but—"

"Good," I interjected. Whether called Bell after my Mama's father or Belle after me, the cottage was my family home, not hers.

Fall 1921: Ann Arbor

Most of the Whimsies cornered Frost by the window closest to the fireplace in Professor Cowden's living room. I retreated to the other end and observed. I was prepared to make a quick escape to the front porch of the craftsman bungalow if the poet made a move to make me say one of my poems. Fortunately, after regaling those crowded around him with reading several of his poems, making caustic asides about the "Imagists" and "Free-Versers," and giving accolades for Yost's football teams led by All-American Harry Kipke rolling over their opponents with more than "a point a minute," he asked a darkly attractive senior girl to recite for the group. She read two short verses. He offered a mild critique but warmly encouraged her to keep writing.

Frost followed her shapely legs, revealed by knickers fastened well above the knee and cinched tight around her narrow waist over comely hips, out onto the porch. Through the double-hung windows against which they leaned, I saw their animated conversation. His prematurely graying head bobbed in time with her pert brunette bob. Even when he shook his head at her, she only nodded in time to him.

As the evening wore on, I became concerned about the protocol.

Not about the pair's cooing, but about whether I could desert the poet to her and walk home alone. Rabbie had picked Frost up at the widow D'Ooge's house the poet rented for his family across the street on Washtenaw and had delivered him to my doorstep. Rabbie then left to join the swim team at the train depot for the ride to a meet in Chicago, and I walked Frost the several blocks west to the Cowden house. While I was trying to figure out what to do, a tap hit me on the shoulder. When I turned, she introduced herself. "Hi, Belle, I'm Stella Brunt." I didn't know what to say. "Frost says it's time for you to save him from my clutches." When I didn't respond, she added, "He scolded me so about using tired, old phrases in my poems, I can't take any more."

I waited for the poet to thank our host and say goodbye to the Whimsies. As he walked me through the front door, out onto the porch, and down the steps, I felt the many eyes on my back more than the chill of the late October night. I can't remember what Frost said as we walked, but by the time we passed under the full moon and got to my doorstep, I blurted out my first words, "Care for a nightcap?"

I wasn't much for drinking, particularly after getting sick on the rot-gut that passed for liquor during Prohibition at my first fraternity party. Rabbie had tried to warn me, but before I retched in public, he carried me up the hill to my house. I spent a long night on the floor of my bathroom, getting acquainted with the toilet bowl. Papa had laughed at this story, but he'd brought three bottles of his best Scotch from the old country the next time he visited and taught me to savor its taste.

I sat Frost down on the big sofa overlooking the little park below and lit the kindling in the big fireplace. When I returned from the kitchen with two glasses and a bottle of Laphroaig, his eyes of seafarer blue lit up, but he shook his head. With an impish grin, he said in a Scottish burr, "Ach, lassie, ye'd warm the cockles of my late mum's heart, but my favorite tipple is ginger ale." I returned with a bottle of Vernor's. He took a big swig and shook his head, but he dutifully took another swallow of our odd-tasting local pop. He told me how his mother, Isabelle Moodie Frost, revered her homeland and loved the name "Belle" we shared. When I asked about his father, he shook his head. So I told him about Papa. When he asked about my mother, I shook my head but did tell him how she'd inspired me with Emily Dickinson verse to compose "songs that sound to the ear rather than poems that please the eye." He toasted her good sense and asked me to recite one of mine.

Although I knew it by heart, I excused myself to get control of my nerves. When I returned, a copy of my poem in hand, I stood before him and sang my goodbye to Mama, "Mary Bell's Death." Frost closed his eyes and listened. When I finished, he asked me to say it one more time. This time his pale blue eyes fixed on me and, just like Pip's, seemed to see right through me into some deeper recess. After I sat down, he offered a toast: "I wish I'd written a song to say goodbye to my Belle, my mother."

His brown hair already graying at the temples, heavy lids sagging over the corners of his eyes, kindly smile, rumpled sweater, and old coat made him look fatherly, but the twinkle in his pale blue eyes and the purse of his lip made him seem younger. I pushed my poem into his hands so he'd have to read it.

Frost took a long time. "I feel like Higginson after he first read what Miss Dickinson sent him. It sounds a good song, but, good Lord, is it poetry?" He then went into a harangue about Amy Lowell's stream of words and phrases being as unsatisfying as "playing tennis without a net" and told me I'd have to learn to play by the rules, too.

I was stung by his invoking Miss Lowell to criticize my song, but I just gritted my teeth as Mama taught me. I told him the story of Mama's gift to me of *A Dome of Many-Colored Glass* and explained Mama's note telling me to keep on singing. "She told me, 'Don't ever listen to any teacher, or any other damn fool, tell you different.'" I paused. "Are you my teacher, or just another damn fool?"

"You must play tennis," he replied with a wry smile. "Knocked my first serve back over the net for a winner." He picked up my poem again and read it through. "After Emily died, Higginson helped edit the first two books of her poems with the Amherst astronomer's young wife, who'd become friends with Miss Dickinson's family." Now, I had to laugh: if the rumors Miss Patterson shared with me had any credence, the astronomer's wife was much more than friends with Emily's brother and much less with his wife. Frost ignored my chuckle and explained how they tried to straighten out her punctuation, grammar, line structure, and missing rhymes. Frost shook his head again. "Poetry is a cruel mistress. Composing without form is bad enough, but if you insist on doing it, then you've got to go out and defend it yourself." Now, I shook my head. He put on his Scots burr and said, "Ach, lassie, you can't count on anyone else editing your songs and selling the resulting poems to the publishers, the critics, and the public."

"You won't even be my Higginson?"

His ginger ale bottle now empty, he tried a sip scotch and made a face. "Every person's entitled to one vice, but mine's not liquor." I offered him another Vernor's, but he shook his head. "Your local brand tastes too much like ginger beer. A cup of tea, please?" I prepared my best Lipton for him. He took a sip, nodded, and continued, "Dickinson begged Higginson to be her preceptor, but while she was alive, he just told her to keep working because her drafts weren't ready yet."

"With what little time you'll share with me, what will you tell me?"

Frost paused a long time. He sipped and savored his tea. I couldn't tell whether he was measuring me or figuring out how to leave with the least embarrassment. Instead he asked, "Does your draft of 'Mary Bell's Death' leave anything out about that day your mama died and how you felt?" Was he a mind-reader who knew I'd written "Blue Salvation," too? I prepared for his scolding, but he was gentle: "Keep it for a while. Deepen it. Deepen it."

Sounded a lot like Higginson, but I put on my best smile and asked, "Do you want me to call you Preceptor now?"

"My Mama Belle called me Robbie. You can, too." He told me how after his father died, his mother returned to New England and raised her two children by working, teaching, scrimping, and pleading for support from her father-in-law, all the while reading books and poetry aloud to both her children and encouraging them to listen for their better inner voices and God's direction. "The Scots lilt to her speech made such a sweet sound, and she always encouraged me to make my verse sing, too." He dropped his head. "I wish she were still here, to see how far I've come." He paused. "Sometimes, I do hear voices, including hers." He chuckled. "But I haven't figured out how to talk back yet."

"Are you close with your sibling still?"

He flared at that.

"I didn't mean to pry."

He sighed, but his pale gray eyes hardened to a stony stare. "My sister inherited more of my father's craziness." He paused. "She chose to give in to the darkness, and I had to put her in Maine's State Hospital." His shoulders slumped. I didn't know what to say. After a long pause, he added, "I failed her, too."

As he lowered his eyes, I swear a tear began to roll out. I admit I touched his arm and put on my best front to try to keep up with Stella Brunt in nodding with him. Good Lord, what was I thinking? Frost was old enough to be my father, and married to boot.

The back door slammed, and I gave a start. Frost blinked and asked, "Who's this handsome young man?"

"This is my brother, Pip. Say hello to Mr. Frost."

The poet stood and greeted my brother but without extending his hand. The same tousled hair and pale blue eyes, they looked like father and son. Pip already had a streak of white running from his right temple to the back of his ear. "Pleased to meet you, Pip." Nodding to me, Frost added, "Are you also a poet, baying at this midnight moon?"

"I was at the Observatory, sir."

"A big telescope here, too?" Frost then recounted how much he enjoyed the view of the night sky from Professor Todd's Observatory at Amherst College.

"You can join me to observe on our new 37 ½-inch reflector!"

"What year are you at Michigan?"

"I'm a junior, but at Ann Arbor High. It's a block north of the campus, on State Street." He chuckled. "Michigan named our Observatory 'Detroit,' though."

"Have you read *Our Place among the Infinities*?" Frost pressed.

"Proctor's right."

"You don't buy the nonsense Amy Lowell's brother spouts about Mars, do you?"

"It'll be on view soon, and you can judge for yourself whether the canals are—"

"Boys," I interjected to end their spat, "it's past all our bedtimes."

"Pip," Frost countered with a warm grin, "I'd like to join you."

"Look forward to it, Mr. Frost," Pip replied in kind.

As my brother began to climb the stairs, Frost stood and said to me, "You must join us." I rose but again didn't know what to say. The poet added, "Miss Brunt told me she and Rabbie arranged for the Whimsies to hold their founding meeting at the Observatory because women aren't permitted in the front door of the Men's Union."

I knew all about that male bastion and couldn't help nodding. We proceeded to the foyer, where I opened the front door. As he shambled out onto the porch, he turned and asked, "Do you type?" When I nodded, he walked back to me. "Come to my house after lunch, and type up my poems for my next book." When I nodded again, he turned without saying goodbye and walked across the little park toward his house.

I walked up the stairway and, at the second floor landing, saw that Pip had already closed the door to his corner bedroom. I couldn't figure out what to make of Frost's gentle but insistent criticism of my poem nor of his encouragement, including working for him. I couldn't get to sleep, so I counted my blessings for Pip instead.

We'd learned how to manage pretty well together since he'd moved in. I ordered the groceries delivered from Alphonse on Forest or Mr. Strickland on Geddes, while he organized the dirty laundry to be picked up by White Swan every Tuesday and returned every Thursday, cleaned, folded, and pressed. I wasn't a bad chef from all my practice, but Pip soon surpassed me with his measuring and mixing of ingredients and experimenting with the cooking thermometer, making different dishes. Apart from a few burned brownies, runny fudges, and scalded stews, we enjoyed our good meals together, and we talked up a storm while we fixed dinner and washed and dried the pots and pans, dishes, and flatware afterward. I tended the garden the nurserymen helped plant, and Pip mowed the lawn. I handled the finances, while Pip took care of the maintenance and repairs. Every Sunday morning we made a game of putting the house in order before going to the First Presbyterian Church downtown for the 10:30 service. At 15, Pip was out to prove he was no longer a baby brother to be cared for or an uncaring, selfish adolescent to be sent back to Papa and Miss Patterson. He succeeded.

Pip was even civil at the dining or kitchen table when Rabbie joined us. Pip didn't appear jealous or hurt as he had been with David Ahgosa, but he didn't exactly embrace Rabbie as a possible brother either. The only time I ever heard Pip say anything negative about my boyfriend, it did give me pause, though: "Be careful," he warned, "he'll leave if he finds someone of his own kind to marry."

I felt like answering, "I'll enjoy him until I find a good Presbyterian to be my mate," but I feared I might not be the marrying kind.

Pip's presence did crimp Rabbie and me romping together as freely in the house as we had all summer. I wondered whether Pip closed his bedroom door to try to give Rabbie and me some space to play or to shut out our now-stifled spooning cries. So I asked Pip if he wanted to build a bedroom and bathroom in the attic above the big garage in back. Pip leaped at the chance, drew plans, and did most of the work. He supervised Mr. Hutzel's plumbing and heating work to learn all he could. Oh, I paid all the bills and offered to help, but he didn't want me in the way of his measuring, cutting, sawing, hammering, and plastering. By Thanksgiving, he'd be ready to move in. Not surprisingly, he completed his laboratory for tinkering there first. I wondered if I was fated to be the reclusive spinster poet, sleeping alone in my house while my brother carried on an affair with a married woman in his retreat. For the time being, thank heavens, I had Rabbie, and Pip wasn't yet a man.

Pip also worked with Washtenaw Gas Company to switch the boiler in the basement from coal to natural gas to heat our house and added a newfangled gas range in the kitchen. I swear he took both apart and put them back together, twice, to figure out how they worked so he could invent a better design.

We learned we didn't need any live-in help to disrupt our lives at Cambridge House. Mostly we could make do for ourselves and, only as needed, hire contractors, whether for building, heating and plumbing, planting, tending, catering, or cleaning.

I couldn't make do with Professor's Strait's Shakespeare class, though. The newly tenured Edmund "Ned" Strait, Exeter prep, Dartmouth undergrad, and Harvard Ph.D., rode roughshod over us. A short, chubby, caustic man, he read our short essays aloud in a mocking tone with a fake British accent and corrected our grammar, punctuation, and form even more than our Rhetoric instructor. He dressed the part, too: a tweed jacket, pressed twill pants to match, and contrasting Oxford shirt, colorful bow tie, and silk handkerchief folded neatly into his breast pocket, his long blond mane slicked back over his ears, not a hair out of place. His skin and eyes gave him away: pale skin blotched with freckles and red marks and beady, black eyes darting over his half-glasses so he could look down his nose at us. A Shakespeare scholar, he sneered at what he called our "crude Midwestern idiom." The year before, the English Department had split into two, the supposedly more academic literature and criticism folks of Strait's ilk in one group, and the rhetoric, composition, creative writing, and journalism folks in the other. Strait sought to show us he was the master of both.

After mocking several of our short essays, he saved his worst for last. Apparently one of the students had submitted a typed dialogue in rhymed couplets between two thieving braggarts—Nym and Pistol—making fun of the commoners' speech in a rural British pub. As Strait read this doggerel, he grew redder. "Who dares mock my class with this low stab at the Immortal Bard?" He tapped a ruler in his hand as he walked down each aisle, seeking a plea from the guilty party.

He stopped by my desk. "Miss Belle, I hear you fancy yourself a poet and too good to learn proper English diction." As he glared over his silly glasses and down his nose at me, I noticed a small mole with a single hair twitching at the corner of his mouth. "Do you know how to type, too?" I nodded. "I suppose you've also read Shakespeare before?" I nodded again. When he saw I was staring at the single hair in his mole now twitching more violently, he turned on his heel, strode to the front of the class and started reciting a scene from one of Shakespeare's plays I hadn't read. Strait's usual stentorian tone fit the mocking of two petty knaves so well I couldn't stifle my guffaw upon learning their names were also Nym and Pistol. The bell rang before he could take my laugh for an admission of guilt and wrap me on the knuckles.

A week later Frost hopped off the front porch of his Victorian and joined Pip and me for a walk on Washtenaw, past the eastern edge of the University and the longer trek up Observatory Street to the top of the highest point on campus. The shell of the new hospital loomed in front of us, but to the north and east the rising moon lit the Huron River Valley. From the corner Frost looked down to the Huron River and pointed east: "We must go botanizing in your

Nichols' Arboretum this spring." I could already see him striding in his shirtsleeves with a smile down the steep slopes there to the river.

When we turned west on Ann Street, Director Hussey waved from atop the 70 stairs to the Detroit Observatory, his residence and a classroom building, three domes rising above. Greeting us in front of the main entry, he pointed to the landmarks in the distance below: the seven-story clock tower of the county courthouse downtown and Hill Auditorium, the massive Angell Hall still under construction, the hulking new general library, and the Union on campus.

"Where's Burton getting the money for all the new buildings?" Frost asked.

"Not all of them are welcome," Hussey replied as he pointed to the huge hospital under construction across the street and to the smoke rising above the Observatory from the University power plant to the southwest. Turning to the new library in the heart of campus, he added, "When they tore down the old one, they destroyed the twin towers that displayed the University Clock and the five bells that struck the chimes on the quarter hour and the hour. We astronomers hate to see bell and clock towers destroyed."

"Poets, too," Frost said.

Hussey ushered us into the student tower, and we took turns peering through the eyepiece at the bottom of the six-and-a-half inch refracting telescope focused on the quarter moon. Huge craters jumped out at us. Inspecting the telescope, Frost said with apparent pride, "Alvan Clark, same maker as the *much* larger one built for Professor Todd at Amherst."

Hussey only smiled and walked us over to the larger dome housing the huge, 37 ½-inch reflecting telescope. "Except for the mirror, we built this in our shop here. It's one of the ten largest in the world." He explained how the single lens of the refracting telescopes in use since Galileo had reached its maximum possible size because of the huge weight of the glass. With a series of smaller lenses and mirrors magnifying the light, reflecting telescopes could see much deeper into the heavens. He also explained how they also incorporate spectrometers to explore the chemical properties of stars and the speed at which stars and galaxies move.

Hussey then hustled us back into the original building, up a staircase, and into the large dome that housed the 12 ⅝-inch refracting telescope. Seventeen feet long, the steel tube pointed through a sliding opening in the dome from atop a big stone platform. "The tube and lens weigh about a ton, and the pier, four times that. Good thing Tappan built a solid foundation 64 years ago, or Fitz's telescope would have sunk into the ground."

Frost eyed the huge cylinder. "Only half the size of the one Clark built for Amherst."

"Ours is a half-century older." He marched Frost up the 12-foot-wide ladder of steps to the viewing platform and sat the poet down at the eyepiece.

Frost looked and asked, "What am I seeing?"

"The too-much storied canals on Mars," Hussey replied.

Frost looked again and said, "Don't see any Martians staring back at us." He stepped down and helped me up. I saw lines that might look like canals, but there was no way to see whether they had ever held any water, let alone life.

Pip climbed up, looked, and walked back down with the director. Hussey walked us down the stairs into another room with lots of pictures, squiggly lines, measurements, and framed reports. He sat us around a conference table. The Director turned to Frost and, unable to conceal his contempt, said, "The lad tells me you wonder about the prospect of finding life on other planets."

"No, *I* wonder whether we poets can offer more insight into such questions than you astronomers," Frost replied. "When Todd showed me his observatory back in '17, that *renowned astronomer* said his mission had become finding intelligent life in space."

Hussey snorted. "Todd's gone as daft as Lowell."

Pip tried to intervene. "Aren't the sightings from the young astronomers at Mt. Wilson and at Lowell Observatory of galaxies receding almost as revolutionary?"

"Hubble and Slipher haven't proved anything yet, young man."

That set Frost off: "Pick a fight with someone your own age!"

"Mr. Frost," Pip interjected. "It's okay. The Director lets me observe through all the telescopes here." Seeing that Hussey was nodding too readily at this cover, my brother, bless him, added, "Of course, I've yet to convince him we should build radio antennas to listen in space, too."

"I've been hearing voices since I was a child," Frost picked up. Plucking his ears, he added, "Pip, I hope you prove I'm not as crazy as the Lowells." He then turned to Hussey and asked, "So, what do you make of the search for intelligent life in space?"

"Such questions are better left to the clergy, the philosophers, and *you poets*." Little did we know this narrow view would bedevil Pip's quest for the rest of his life.

I thanked the director for showing us around, and Pip shuffled off toward the student observatory, where he would spend the rest of the night searching the heavens. Without shaking the director's hand, Frost grabbed my arm and said, "We can still find our way out of a place that wants to put blinders on its astronomers." Hussey made some conciliatory remark, but Frost wouldn't hear of it and hurried me outside.

We looked west from the highest point in town all the way to the County Courthouse. The large luminary of the quarter moon in the sky lit the clock in the tall tower facing us, and the big hand glinted gold as it crossed the little hand to mark midnight. We zigzagged south down to the campus. As we walked past Hill Auditorium to the stores on North U, Frost apologized for getting into a debate with another "short-sighted scientist." He chuckled. "I will have to admit David Todd got so daft the College eased him into retiring to Florida my first year at Amherst." He paused. "Remember, his wife, Mabel, is the one who edited Emily Dickinson's first published books of poems."

He stopped in front of the ice cream parlor where Rabbie and I had shared a sundae and pointed to a sign in the window displaying a chocolate-coated ice cream: "Frost Bite—Ten Cents." Robbie hurried me around the corner to Wahr's Books and pointed at a sign in the window atop three of his books, *A Boy's Will*, *North of Boston*, and *Mountain Interval*. It read: "Frost Bark—Very Little Worse than his Bite."

Frost walked me across the street to the northwest corner of the Diag. He sat us down on a bench. "Sometimes, I feel like an itinerant piper, putting on an act here and lecturing there, all so I can get paid for my supper. Almost 50, and I don't have any way out, when all I really want to do is write poetry and walk in the fields and woods of a little farm. Not locked up in my family home like Miss Dickinson, mind you, but freed from this burden of having to be such a public character, barding all over."

Big clouds covered the moon and stars, and the sky turned an inky black. He finally sighed, and we meandered southeast on the Diag. As we passed the construction of the new Angell Hall, Frost said, "Hope Burton finishes this before all us creative fellows get burned up in that beat-up, old firetrap at West Hall where we've been relegated with the rhetoric crowd." When we neared the arch in the new Engineering building leading to South University, the clouds cleared, and the moon lit the clock in the tower of the adjacent building, the old Engineering Shops. As we passed through the arch and reached the corner, a bell chimed once behind us. The clouds returned, a cold wind blew, and the chill grew in the dark.

Frost grabbed my arm and fast-walked us until we reached the D'Ooge house. He pulled me up the stairs and sat me down on the porch swing. He paced, his hands clasped behind his back, his head tilted forward. After several minutes he whispered, "I'll be up all night composing. Can you come first thing in the morning to type?"

His sour mood gone, I caught his mania. I was also acquainted with the mystery of the dark, broken by the light of singing a new song. I nodded and skipped down the steps. When I looked back, he twirled around and disappeared behind the front door.

I stayed up all night composing a new poem until I got it right:

Star Struck

Night-eye aimed at space
where stars circle ebony—
one exploding bright.

Beneath a silver
moon, breaking through charcoal clouds,
shines the midnight hour.

In darkness, we wonder.
Chimes toll one—Alone,
I wander til dawn breaks.

I couldn't help wonder whether that was all between Frost and me, too.

The next morning I typed Frost's 80-line poem titled, "I Will Sing You One-O." As I clacked away on the Corona, he said the two long stanzas aloud until I finished. He grabbed the two pages, read the draft to himself, and recited it again. He took out a thick pencil, made several marks, put the poem down, picked it up, made a few more revisions, and pushed it back to me to type again. As I typed, he peered over my shoulder until he exclaimed, "No, make the first sentence of the second stanza read 'Then came one knock!'" He sang the next three lines, "A note unruffled/of earthly weather,/ though strange and muffled." He paused.

I asked, "Shouldn't the next line read, 'The tower said, 'One!'" When he nodded, I added, "Robbie, we barely got a glimpse of that Old Engineering clock last night."

"Nor saw any snow. That's why this grace note starts as if the poet's lying awake at night, imagining." When I couldn't help chuckling at another of his point-of-view subterfuges, he took offense: "But we *did* see planets, stars, constellations, cosmic motes, yawning lenses, and the clock tower. And we *did* talk and talk about creation and space." I had to smile at how Frost could jump from exploring nova in the heavens to narrow minds like Hussey, as the final line said, dragging us all down, man and nation alike.

I knew Pip would love Frost's poem: "Mind if I sing your One-O to my brother?"

"Only if it will keep him looking, no matter what any damn fool says."

"Your poem about your experiences observing with him will inspire."

Frost shook his head and paced back and forth on the other side of the table. He pursed his lips, started to speak, shook his head again, and paced back and forth some more. Finally, he stopped right in front of me. "You know, I've looked through plenty of telescopes, seen many a steeple, and heard many more chimes in my time."

"I didn't mean to say your different dream and unique sound had but one source."

Frost nodded. "You can share it with the lad, then."

"Do you think Pip will find anything with his star-gazing?"

Frost pursed his lips again, but his pale eyes now twinkled. "I hope he finds the voices of intelligent life and God in space, but I'm not sure that'll help us know any better where we really are here on earth. Maybe the looking, maybe that is all." I wanted to share my new poem with him, but I was too afraid he'd tear me apart again.

That evening Pip greeted me with his younger neighborhood pal, John Kraus, whose father taught at the Engineering school. Together they'd built a small antenna on top of the garage and a crystal receiver in Pip's new lab to listen to Ty Tyson broadcast Tiger games on WWJ from Detroit. They soon added a short-wave radio with big vacuum tubes to listen for voices from other radiomen all over the country. Pip and his little friend led me up the stairs to the third-floor guestroom on the west side of our house. Thomas Edison was John Kraus's idol, but he looked more like a little Ben Franklin as he scrambled onto the steep roof to complete stringing the odd set of dangling wires from the antennae atop the house to the receiver in the garage attic. Suddenly, a lightning bolt flashed through the darkening sky. As the thunder hit us, John lost his footing. Pip, bless him, caught his little friend's ankle before he slid off the roof, and I helped drag the boy through the window to safety.

With no sign of fear at his close escape from a hard fall, John followed Pip as we exited the house and climbed up to Pip's lab in the garage attic. John tuned the receiver until a clear voice from a New York announcer pervaded the room, interrupted every minute or so by the static from lightning strikes. Pip took over and waited several more minutes until a longer hiss marred the broadcast. It grew louder and louder until it began to fade and then disappear. "That's also the sound of electricity," Pip said and explained how the trolley threw off this charge as it rolled closer up Lincoln and turned east on Hill and then faded as it turned north on Washtenaw toward town.

"We take turns," Pip added. "John searches for static from trolleys, engines, and lightning, and I listen for—"

John, no more than 12, piped up, "Pip rigged another set of antennas on the attic roof to capture sound from outer space."

"Think he's going to hear any signals of intelligent life?" I asked.

"I don't know," John said, "but we're having a ball building all the new stuff."

Two weeks later I typed a longer poem for Robbie, "The Star-Splitter." It told the story of a neighbor in Littleton, New Hampshire, full of reckless talk of star-gazing and worse ways of trying to tend his farm at night by the light of a chimney lantern. He failed so at "hugger-mugger farming he burned his house down for the fire insurance and spent the proceeds on a telescope." Out of farm and house, he had to earn a living and found a job "as an under-ticket-agent on the Concord Railroad that gave him leisure for star-gazing." The narrator spent an entire night with his astronomer friend outside, observing, and the new telescope "split a star in two or three… and ought to do some good," at least "compared with splitting wood."

The last stanza began with a question, "We've looked and looked, but after all where are we?" The narrator of the poem offered in answer only another question: comparing this night of star-gazing with his neighbor's former nights farming by the light of a chimney lantern, "How different from the way it ever stood?"

That gave me the courage to pull out a copy of my "Star Struck" and hand it to him. Frost read the poem. "Is this a copy?" Afraid to ask what he thought of my poem, I only nodded. "Well," he continued in a gravelly voice full of irony, "It would be presumptuous for me to think your poem is about our evening star-gazing, walking, and talking together." I couldn't help chuckling with him as he folded my poem into his pocket. "Your song of being star-struck needs a lot more work, but I need to think on it before I say anything more." At least for now, *that was all.*

ꟹ

No matter how much Coach Mann urged me to speed up my stroke to match Rabbie's pace, I fell farther behind every lap swimming for the first 50, 100, and 200. And no matter how much Coach challenged his captain to swim quarter-mile after quarter-mile with me, my Rabbie began to slow after the first 50 and to struggle after the first 100. Four evenings a week, we met Matt Mann at the Union pool, and he wouldn't let up. Finally, Rabbie's times in the 50 and 100 began to improve by a second, and I picked up my pace to lower the time it took me to swim a mile by a minute. Try as we might, Rabbie never improved his time in the 200 or 400 enough to match the lower times Johnny Weissmuller kept throwing on the board in Chicago, and I never could speed up enough in the short races to threaten the women on our Olympic team. In the water Rabbie was born a sprinter; I, a marathoner.

At home, though, we matched up. After a late snack and light banter, we engaged in my bed. We had only one rule: Rabbie had to leave the house before six a.m. so he wouldn't be with me when my brother woke up. Rabbie told me we practiced "the rhythm method," but his version didn't make much sense. Instead, like clockwork, we spent four nights a week together in my bedroom after swimming at the Union pool. I loved the foreplay, the anticipation, the release, and the warm cuddling afterward.

Apart from my poetry class with Frost and his sessions with the Whimsies, I didn't see much point in college. The Shakespeare class offered only a stifling Strait-jacket; the sneering sarcasm of the toady Professor, masked in the voice of his villainous Shakespearean buffoon, stung me. I also hated the way he leered at me. I still liked reading books and stories, but I didn't have Rabbie's passion for literature and history either. Given all of that, I hoped that our rhythm method would lead to a child: What could the Queen do then but consent to our wedding?

I loved typing Robbie's poems after lunch during the week, even if some required more retyping, and more back and forth between the poet-singer and listener-scribe than "I Will Sing You One-O." Other times he'd call up to Mrs. Frost, read a line or two, and ask for her advice on spelling, grammar, or even tone. I also found Mrs. Frost a good companion, as she worried over the poet's growing schedule of appearances and tried to monitor the comings and goings of her grown children in and out of their unfamiliar house that she said was haunted by their wicked landlady, the widow D'Ooge. The Frosts' daughter Lesley enrolled at the University and joined a sorority but still felt as if an outsider. Their son, Carol, got antsy after Yost's football season ended. The third, Irma, missed their home and younger sister finishing high school in Bennington, Vermont, where their mother returned twice to see after the youngest child. I paid close attention to Mrs. Frost's worries over her family and Robbie; whatever the poet might say in his darker moods or dream in his mania creating a poem, she provided support to her troubled man and offspring to carry on, day after day.

I also enjoyed hearing Pip's excitement after school over his latest observation or wacky experiment before he headed off to play hockey on the naturally frozen ice of Weinberg Coliseum at the bottom of Hill Street or Drappatz Pond south of town. I snuck off once to the Majestic for a movie but preferred spending what time I had away from Rabbie, Robbie, and Pip, writing poems in my journal. When I couldn't sleep, I composed late at night. When I could sleep, I skipped class and wrote all morning.

Oh, two evenings a month I also attended Vespers at St. Patrick's, but mostly to listen to Rabbie sing. Although I learned to sit, stand, and kneel without any more threats to my seatmate, I never did learn the Latin Liturgy nor persuade the Queen I was anything other than a blasphemous Scots Presbyterian.

Another evening President Burton invited us to a dinner party at his house to honor Frost, but Rabbie and I sat next to Mrs. Frost to entertain her while Stella Brunt sat directly across the table next to Frost to fire his mood, which she surely did. To my chagrin Mrs. Frost asked Rabbie whether he could type. When he nodded, she invited him to join us at her house after lunch to help her with Frost's schedule and to type the poet's rising stack of letters and speeches while I typed his poems.

Frost made that evening a success with his performance after dinner. His self-deprecating remarks made it easier for the academics to swallow his flinty criticism of ivory towers, including "our Harvard of the West." The president even joined us undergrads in cheering the poet's conclusion: "The greatest test of a college student's character is found when he finds the work for which he will neglect his studies." Although I envied Stella when Frost winked at her at the end of this remark, he held me in his thrall when he closed by reciting several of his poems. The hoarse rumble of his hard-scrabble New Hampshire farmer voice punctuated the irony of his plainest words. His repeating of lines with different inflections made for different tunes of the same songs. I couldn't blame Robbie for finding Stella Brunt much more attractive than I.

When the toasts to Frost ended, President Burton said, "Our Fellow in Creative Arts once again shows why he's as popular on this campus as Fielding Yost."

"Let's put that to the test," Frost replied. "You schedule a reading for me at Hill Auditorium any Saturday afternoon there's a home game. Ferry Field will be sold out, and no one will be at Hill, not even me, because I'll be at the stadium, cheering for Yost's boys." Frost only proved the president's point.

The next day offered the low point of my first semester. Professor Strait asked me to come to his office after I showed up to his class for a change. He held the door open and followed much too close behind as he pushed me toward the chair in front of his desk. He leaned down and brushed my shoulder with his hand as he walked around and sat in the big chair on the other side. He picked up a straight-edge; touched it to his pale, skinny lips; and then began to hit it, hard, in his other hand. "Miss Belle, I didn't appreciate your ditty mocking me." I didn't say a word. He tapped the ruler on the table. "Skipping half my classes to play house with your young buck, Rabbie, and flirt with that old fool, Frost, will only serve to drag them down with you." When his stare over his half-glasses shifted down to my big chest, I held my head high and threw my shoulders back. His beady black eyes bugged out, and he tapped my hand with his ruler. The hair in the small mole at the corner of his mouth twitched until his thin lips finally parted, and he blurted, "Please, Belle, make every class and hand in every assignment or else."

He leered at me, but I didn't nod, blush, or take my eyes off him. He turned his head away and tapped the ruler, harder, on his desk. I got up. "Professor Strait, I wish I had composed that poem." I opened his office door and slammed it behind me. I vowed to make every one of his damn classes, hand in all his stupid assignments, and ace his final exam so he'd have no excuse to flunk me or to slander Rabbie or Robbie.

Rabbie and Frost stopped to pick me up for the final gathering of the Whimsies before Christmas break. An all-day snow blanketed the sidewalks, so we trekked on my street until the bright lights inside the Cowdens' house welcomed us. Punch beckoned at one end of the cozy living room, a crackling fire at the other. Frost made a beeline for Stella Brunt, her good looks already reflecting the glow from the fire.

Rabbie steered me to the punch, where Cowden offered a "tut-tut" at my beau for missing class because of a swim meet and handed me a glass, cranberry red, frothy on top, with bubbles throughout. I drained that quickly, and our host refilled my glass. Rabbie recounted to Cowden the repartee between Burton and Frost about Yost, while I downed that too. I remembered thinking the blizzard must have dried me out, as I drained another glass of punch. I fell into a big armchair whose soft cushions embraced me.

"Belle, you haven't read a poem yet," I heard in the distance. All the other Whimsies crowded around our poet-in-residence and host by the fireplace. Frost waved me forward with a folded sheet of paper. I thought for sure it was "Star Struck," but when I unfolded the note his stubby lettering read: *Sing your goodbye poem to your mama.*

My legs buckled, but Cowden held me up. So I threw my shoulders back and held my head high as my Mama instructed me. I tried to sing, but my voice quavered. By the time I finished squeaking "Mary Bell's Death," I was gasping for air. No one made a sound, and I didn't know where to hide. Finally, I heard Stella Brunt's muffled cry. I couldn't tell whether she was trying to stifle a laugh, but then saw her tears. She hugged me close and said, "I also watched my Mama die."

When I began to list, Frost took my elbow and said, "I wish you all a Merry Christmas." He walked me to the door, turned, and bowed. "And to all a good night." Rabbie O'Bannon grabbed my other arm, and I stumbled down the steps.

I don't remember much after that except the shock of cold when the deep snow jumped up and hit me in the face and the headache when Pip shook me the next morning in my bed. "Marmie," he asked, "you dead or alive?" He'd brought dry toast and tea. The Lipton's helped me wash down the toast and two aspirins. I fell asleep, but Pip woke me for lunch with chicken soup and crackers. "Going home over the break?" he asked. As Rabbie and I planned to practice at the Union pool afternoons and swim in my bed nights, I shook my head. "Can I borrow your car to drive home this afternoon?"

"If you mind the jog where the shortcut runs into the state highway."

He crossed his heart. "The Queen invite you to Christmas dinner?"

"I doubt she'll welcome me into her home any more than her pew at St. Patrick's."

"Why don't you take the train up for Christmas, and we'll drive back together?"

That would make my longest separation from Rabbie. "I'll call and let you know, okay?" When he nodded, I continued, "I've got something I want you and David to consider while you're there. If you two think there's a market, why don't you tinker with some burners and build a portable cooker for Mr. Day's campers?" Pip's grey-blue eyes now sparkled as if he'd already started to imagine a new design. "Remember to look both ways before you merge from the county road onto the Traverse highway."

Late that evening I got a call from Papa. "Pip's fine, but he crashed your car." He paused. "Praise the Lord, his concave chest must have helped him slide around the steering wheel on impact." I had to smile at the thought of this odd deformity saving our boy. I asked how the accident happened, and Papa said, "He got to daydreaming about some fool camp-stove and didn't see that the snow had drifted over onto the state highway." I held my hand over the mouthpiece so Papa couldn't hear me chuckling. "Belle, you there?" When I still couldn't answer, he almost yelled into my ear, "Damn it, girl, I'll buy you a new car and drive down with Pip to make sure it arrives without a scratch." Seemed I did better with Papa the less I said.

SPRING 1922: ANN ARBOR

The draw of Robert Frost and Amy Lowell promised to pack Hill Auditorium. Rabbie begged off to swim, but Stella Brunt invited me to join her at Martha Cook House for dinner before the show. She asked me to help enlist Frost to stay at Michigan another year. "President Burton's looking for donors to pay his salary. He's asking Horace Rackham, and we're going to see Governor Osborn. Will you talk with your father?" She explained how most thought Empire Stove Works financed the pool at the Union.

"Who told you that?" I asked. Papa had no idea Miss Schultz lent the money from my trust to finance the pool, and the transaction was supposed to be anonymous. Sure, Coach Mann and Rabbie figured I helped in some way, but they'd never tell.

"After noon, the Ladies Entrance doesn't lead to the pool for anyone but you."

"You don't think Coach Mann wants to train me for the '24 Olympics?" Stella must have seen my red hair flaring because she bit her tongue. I had to admit my times in the Olympic sprints didn't justify all the attention Mr. Mann gave me. Well, then, why was I spending twelve hours a week plowing mile after mile, lap after lap, all in my own good time? Sure, I enjoyed the camaraderie with Rabbie and Coach, but I loved the feel of the water flowing, buoying me up, that sense of welcome and peace—yes, the blue salvation in my soul I was able to find there after Mama said goodbye.

Yet I owed Frost, too. If he hadn't tethered me here, that beast Strait would have driven me back up north with Pip. Yet would it be right for me to pay my Robbie to stay another year? That seemed so much more, well, personal than lending money to build a pool, more personal than Rabbie and me. "Sorry, I'm not going home for the holiday."

"Join me to give thanks for the risen instead?"

That certainly would make it easier to avoid any scene with the Queen over an Easter goose at the O'Bannon farmhouse. When I learned Stella was also an older student—from having to leave her Ontario home to work for several years to save enough to go to college—I began to realize how far she'd come and wanted to go. She'd already set her sights on the former governor, regent, publisher, and now mining tycoon who had funded Frost's first year here. Maybe I should learn something from this woman. "If you're serving a Canada goose, I'll join you."

We walked across the Diag and up the broad steps to Hill Auditorium. Stella marched us down to the seats reserved by President Burton for his guests in the second row. Huge organ pipes rose behind the stage, and the parabolic dome spread over us. Another Albert Kahn masterpiece, the acoustics rivaled any in the world.

Frost walked on stage with Miss Lowell to introduce her. He played the modest, good-humored New England farmer as he shambled forward in a rumpled suit, hair tousled. Lowell played the star, decked out with jewels around her thick neck and fingers, a frilly white silk collar billowing from her capacious bosom, a red sash around her big middle, and a dark, tailored garment showing her broad hips with a larger bustle covering her bigger behind. Amy walked to an arm chair beside a big table, where her papers, a pitcher of water, a glass, and a big reading lamp awaited.

They both waved to the crowd and got a standing ovation. Miss Lowell pulled a pince-nez and a white handkerchief from the folds of her dress, sat down in the arm chair and nodded to Frost. As he began his introduction, she interrupted and bade him move the already lit lamp to another place. As he set the lamp down, she squinted through her glasses and directed Frost to set it in another place. As this charade continued, first titters, then laughs, and finally cheers arose when Miss Lowell nodded at the lamp's final resting place. They didn't need Charlie Chaplin to warm us up.

Frost continued his introduction by explaining to the audience the importance of the precise position of the reading lamp Miss Lowell carried with her: how else could she recite her poetic images unless she could see to read them? Unfortunately, he held the lamp-cord and pulled it too hard as he punctuated his remark. There was a flash, and all the lights on stage and throughout the packed house blew out. Over the sound of janitors scurrying, Frost and Lowell conversed back and forth in stage whispers that made light of what otherwise might have been a disaster. An unseen voice from the audience shouted, "Please smoke your cigar, Miss Lowell."

She was as notorious for her smoking habits as her "Boston Marriage" to Ada Dwyer Russell, and Frost encouraged her: "They'd like to see you do it."

Aping Mae West, Amy Lowell cooed, "Come on out behind the barn and join me."

In short order, the lights returned, a new bulb fit into the reading lamp, and all appeared well. Until either Frost tripped over the cord to resume his introduction or Lowell tripped over the folds in her dress settling her bulk down, and the water pitcher toppled and spilled. Frost set it upright in a flash. Miss Lowell retrieved several more handkerchiefs from the folds in her dress and made sure her papers were in order. Her composed and friendly reaction to what might have dismayed so many others won us.

Frost was just her set-up man. He completed a gracious introduction with this pointed compliment: "Although Miss Lowell may be the best poet at describing images with words, she puts all the rest of us to shame as a showman and businessman. No one has been more fought over, fought against, and fought about than Amy Lowell. Whether hailed or hooted, no one has a greater capacity to arouse her readers and audiences."

Amy Lowell didn't fail us either. Her short introductory sermon on the merits of free verse and saving the imagists and Ezra Pound from themselves might have sounded pompous on another occasion, but our appreciation of her stage presence compelled careful attention. Her voice didn't carry her poetry as well though, or maybe Mama was right: Amy's poetry made more sense seeing than hearing. After finishing one of her poems with a flourish, she waited for our response. She challenged us: "Damn it, clap or hiss. Don't just sit there." Thereafter, she welcomed our applause but also greeted any undertone of hisses with a riposte that drew a mix of laughter, clapping, and catcalls.

When she finished her performance and Frost thanked us in his puckish way for our attention, no one left the show disappointed. Perhaps they left like me: not persuaded that Miss Lowell's poetry was great, but certain she cut an imposing figure whose words could not be ignored, given her larger-than-life persona. I marveled at her ability to parade so in front of an audience. I could never stand in public and sing any of my songs, let alone mount the campaigns Frost and Lowell did for their poetry.

Stella and I took the trolley to Frost's home on Washtenaw, where he hosted Miss Lowell for several of the English faculty and a few Whimsies. Fewer Frost family members joined us than in the past. Carol Frost, tired of being at loose ends in Ann Arbor and under his father's thumb, had walked out of the house a month before and showed up a week later at the Frost farm in Vermont. Soon after, Lesley and Irma, still feeling like strangers at the University of Michigan, followed with the blessing of their parents.

Amy lit up a cigar as we entered the crowded living room. "Robert," Mrs. Frost said, "tell our guest how the widow D'Ooge may protest again." Frost explained how a fire started in the attic of the house after the last poetry reading, by their mutual friend Louis Untermeyer.

"This house must be a tinderbox, because his poems aren't the least bit hot…" Lowell eyed Stella and me. "…like mine."

"Don't listen to her," Frost said. "She's just mad because Louis said she carries not just a chip on her shoulder but an entire lumberyard."

Lowell didn't take this bait. "Frost, good to know two women can come together in Ann Arbor without starting a riot." With a big leer at me she added, "Why don't you introduce me to the redhead?" Without waiting for an answer, she pushed the Frosts and Stella Brunt aside and asked, "Do the men make fun of you for being so big and tall?" When I froze rather than answer, she patted me on the arm. "Want to go outside and share a cigar so we don't set the house afire?"

"Thank you, but I don't smoke."

"Have you read my 'Lady'?" I shook my head. "'Taxi'?" No. "'Venus Transiens'?" No. "'Madonna of the Evening Flowers'?" No. "'Clear, with Light Variable Winds'?" No. "'Nuit Blanche'?" No. "Anything of mine?"

"I never got past *A Dome of Many-Coloured Glass*."

"That can be remedied if you'd like a private reading." When I shook my head again, she shouted across the living room, "Frost, you sly fox." When he hurried back, she said, "You're keeping this divine creature from my best work and for yourself."

"No, I'm challenging Ms. Belle to incorporate the stirrings of her sound-sense into forms of poetry that may yet ring." Frost took Miss Lowell's arm and escorted her away.

"Saved," Stella whispered. I asked about the poems Miss Lowell mentioned. "They're *all* quite erotic, particularly when she describes two women's bodies engaging."

Professor Cowden pulled me aside. "Someone's spreading rumors among the faculty that you're ignoring your assignments." When I shook my head, he continued, "A memo circulating under the pseudonym Nym claims you're skipping Prof. Strait's class to swim with Mr. O'Bannon at the Union and play house with our poet in residence here." Cowden confided, "Nym is a minor character, a filcher and a coward, in several Shakespeare plays, who tattles to gain favor but in his final appearance gets hanged."

I had to laugh. Michigan's Nym was none other than Strait himself. Rather than tattle, I said, "I earned a B first semester. If Professor Strait continues to use a blind grading system, and I disguise my handwriting so he can't tell, I'll earn an A this spring."

Cowden smiled. "You know Strait and his academic high horses mock my courses, too." In a lower whisper he added, "We've got to mind our manners lest the literary crowd use their greater influence to try to put creative writing and poetry down."

"Is Frost in any trouble?"

"Both faculties, Rhetoric and Literature, resent the attention he generates."

"If Rabbie, Stella, and I organize the Whimsies to write a letter telling how much Frost has meant to the University, will that help?" The ever-proper Professor Cowden hugged me so I thought we might generate another round of rumors.

Miss Lowell's loud adieus made us turn to catch her grand exit. Frost said, "She's going to Detroit, where there's a hotel large enough to accommodate her retinue." The driver tied her excess luggage on top of the taxi, two younger women wedged in beside Miss Lowell in the backseat, and two older women squeezed in front with the cabbie.

Stella and I helped Elinor tidy up. As we opened the door to leave, Frost held me back. He pulled out a thick pamphlet. "Your mother was right about Miss Lowell, and you," he said as he handed me the upcoming *Whimsies* issue. "Don't know how star-struck you'll be, but the cover poem's for you. Thanks for helping with my work here."

When I got home and saw that my goodbye to Mama was the lead poem, I nearly choked. "Mary Belle's Death" was much too personal: damn it, Robbie, you had no right! Yet, when I finally calmed down enough to focus on the fine print on the cover and read Frost's verse, I admit I became more star-struck than angry.

Vol. II, No. 3 APRIL, 1922

WHIMSIES

MICHIGAN'S LITERARY MAGAZINE

"We make ourselves a place apart
Behind light words that tease and flout,
—But oh, the agitated heart
Till someone find us really out."
—Robert Frost.

The bloom fell off this rose a month later when I opened the letter Frost sent on his return to Vermont:

My Second Belle,
"Star Struck" is a piece with your death poem to your mother: Much well sung; less well written. Still, enough you shouldn't give up. Don't know if Michigan will pay me for an encore, or if I should concentrate on finishing my new book of poetry here. At least the family seems more settled now, but who ever knows for how long. Give my best to Rabbie and say hi to Pip.

He signed his kiss-off, *Frost*. I'll say! Strait may have bruised me with his ruler, but Robbie cut me with what he said and what he didn't.

Made me so mad, I gave my all to Rabbie and never said *boo* about Frost all summer. Yet if the great poet never returned, I would miss him and my work for him, his odd contraries, hard challenges, spare criticisms, and few encouragements included.

Winter and Spring 1923: Ann Arbor and Glen Arbor

The New Year broke cold, drear, and lonely. Frost had been scarce most of the first semester. Frustrated by Michigan's delay in signing him for another year, he'd committed to a cross-country tour of appearances all fall. When President Burton's offer came in mid-October, Robbie reported for only two days of politicking with the dean and the English faculty. Frost left for several readings in Boston, where he wrote me to complain about Miss Lowell's latest publicity stunt: she published an anonymous "rhymed screed" titled *A Critical Fable*, "lampooning" him. He headed off for 14 lectures in 14 days from New Orleans to Texas and then more readings back through Missouri and Illinois. No wonder he was sick with the flu when he finally got back to Ann Arbor in November. Mrs. Frost asked me to help nurse the patient in the smaller house they'd rented on Washtenaw, closer to campus. The more time he spent in bed, the ornerier he got. He even complained about having to go to a meeting of the Whimsies at Cowden's house. When he said he'd wasted so much time singing for his supper and suffering from the grippe he hadn't written a single poem for his new book, Mrs. Frost bundled him up, and they retreated to their Vermont farm.

Rabbie took off with Coach Mann in January for big tests against the Ivy Leaguers and the Athletic Club men out East. They asked me to tag along, but when Coach told me a 16-year-old phenom was training for the Women's Swimming Association in New York, I thought I had all the excuse I needed: "They don't have a race long enough for this marathoner." Mann countered that Gertrude Ederle's best distance started at three miles, but she was also a rare sprinter at a hundred yards. Rabbie threatened to bring Trudy back to Ann Arbor unless I challenged her there. Instead I gave Rabbie and his coach each a kiss on the cheek and sent them off.

Pip had driven up north again for the holidays. Papa called to let me know our Cadillac Phaeton arrived safe: Pip remembered to stop at the jog onto Empire state highway. Papa also bragged how David Ahgosa had already sold old D. H. Day 500 new camp stoves, but he complained Pip was tinkering with a newfangled gear for tilting and turning telescopes rather than the next Empire stove. "We're going to have to send that boy away to college to straighten him out."

Now facing 1923 all alone, I took to my bed, too. I managed to scribble one melancholy poem:

Dry Land

swimming on sand chafes
the pale skin of this lonely
selkie out of water

with sweet memories—
of the warm rush in my
blue deliverance

Thereafter I let the snow and the mail pile up. When you're down, it's easy to sleep, hours on end, day after day, week after week.

When I first heard the clang, I couldn't figure out what it was. When the brass-knocker on the front door refused to stop, I got up. I don't know if the Western Union boy thought I was a ghost, but he said, "Sorry, Ma'am," and handed me a telegram, his eyes riveted on me. I looked down, saw my robe flapping open to my goose bumps in the cold, and slammed the door.

Fearing bad news, I ripped open the yellow envelope: "Returning the 31st to earn my keep. Stop. Be at my house after noon to type poems for new book. Stop. Ready to discuss Star Struck. Stop. Your Preceptor. Stop."

The rest of the spring semester, oh, how Frost worked at a furious pace, and how we worked for him. Rabbie typed letters and drafts of poems in the morning while the poet slept; and I worked all afternoon, typing and talking back and forth with Robbie about revisions. He arranged his new book in three parts, with the title poem "New Hampshire" first, several long lyrics like "Star-Splitter" as Notes next, and many songs like "I will Sing You One-O" and shorter verses as Grace Notes. He worried that J.J. Lankes' woodcut illustrations for his new book weren't good enough. He reworked old poems and wrote new ones evenings and nights. When I asked him why he decided not to include "Design," the best short poem I'd typed the year before, he said, "Doesn't belong yet." Although the poem sounded a good grace note to me, maybe he thought its deeper slants might be read as too dark. No matter. Not even two more bouts with the flu and a long break in Vermont to tend the rest of his family stopped Frost from finishing.

Michigan's Fellow in Creative Arts made little time for the University. Even when he stopped by Cowden's home to visit his Whimsies writing group, he arrived late, left early, and refused to stop by my house for tea or ginger ale. When I brought Pip with me one afternoon to pry him away, Frost took a break but only long enough to say hello. He shooed Pip out with *The Illustrated Century Magazine* copy of "The Star-Splitter" with Lankes' woodcut. He never did make time to discuss my "Star Struck" poem again: the master was so driven by his work he made no time to advise his apprentice.

Finally I called Stella Brunt, who'd been scarce since her graduation. I asked her to join in hosting a dinner for the Frosts with Rabbie, Coach Mann, and his Missus. "I don't have a proper beau to bring to the party quite yet," she replied.

"But I need you to take his mind off his work and make time to play again."

"No," Stella said, "Amherst fired his nemesis Meiklejohn, and the new president's offered to hire Frost back."

"Is that why he's shutting us out down here?"

"Frost can't stand saying goodbye either, including to you."

That evening I tried to work through my frustrations in a poem:

Preceptor

The noted surgeon
aims his blade—cuts a fine line—
while his intern watches—

yearning for her chance—
yet taking notes for a future text:
Operating on Cadavers

To his assistant
the surgeon complains—Butchers!
Medical schools graduate butchers!

Even in old age
his skills save lives, while she only
preps for another cadaver.

I must have been feeling pretty sorry for myself because that night I didn't care if Frost left: My Preceptor would never, ever help me put my lyrics on the page; he only used me to help him prep his songs for broadcast around the world.

The next morning, though, I reread my poem. Even if I couldn't make the rhyme pattern work, I wasn't ready to give up. I called Stella. "Is Burton trying to keep him?"

"He's telling everyone that Frost's work on his new book demands his full attention for now, and its publication will bring great credit to Michigan."

"You mean the faculty doesn't want Frost back?"

"With the exception of Cowden and a few others, the rest resent Frost's growing reputation and vanishing teaching load."

I could sense Ned Strait's evil hand at work but asked, "Burton made an offer?"

"He can't get the Regents to commit to an endowment for a permanent position." When I asked about her governor friend, she replied, "I'm seeing him next week at his St. Mary's compound to ask."

Rabbie checked around, and, sure enough, Strait had poisoned the well by detailing Frost's isolation from students and faculty and by circulating more scurrilous accusations about Robbie, Rabbie, and me. Frost might be ready to quit, but I wasn't: Pip and I dragged our reluctant old friend up north.

On Friday afternoon we arrived at what even Papa now called *Belle* Cottage, whether out of pique at his Bell in-laws or a wish to bring Pip and me back home more often, I couldn't tell. Papa greeted us, but Pip raced off to meet David at the site where they planned an Ojibwe birch box and observatory for the Bealses' Leelanau camp. Papa insisted Frost and I stay to "nose and taste" his favorite Scotch, a 25-year-old Macallan. By a roaring fire on the back porch, Robbie graciously sniffed and sipped the Scotch with Papa, and they shared tall tales of their Scots heritage. When they started swapping ballads of our motherland's national bard, Rabbie Burns, I told Papa we had to show Frost our own little slice of heaven on earth before the sun set. Papa begged off, so Robbie and I bundled up against the late chill as March passed into April.

Drift ice sat stranded in the high dune grass, but no piles of snow marked the sandy beach. As we walked along the shore, Robbie kneeled down, took off his right glove, and dipped his fingers in the water. "Too cold for swimming."

I did the same but said, "Not for me."

"You an ice maiden?" he asked.

"Maybe more a hot-blooded mermaid," I answered.

"Ha," he said, "more a kelpie siren."

"No, in the deep, cold water here I'm more a danger to myself."

Before I realized how far we'd come, the weathered piers from the old dock in Glen Arbor rose in the bay before us. Frost asked, "Is that where your Mama said goodbye?" When I nodded, he bade me sit beside him on a silvery trunk of driftwood. "I'm heading back to Amherst." I didn't say anything, so he detailed the reasons. Closer to his family and their Vermont farm. Better pay, little teaching, and the prospect of a long tenure. Not far from his New York publisher. Closer to his rural New England roots. A small college that accepted his foibles, not a big university with all its demands and unseemly gossip. Burton couldn't even promise a position in the fall, and Frost had to provide for himself, Elinor, and the rest of his family. He'd be gone most of next year, shilling to sell his new book, anyway.

"Preceptor, you running away from this intern?" I said.

He shook his head, got up and walked back alone along the shore. Finally, he stopped, waved, and waited until I joined him. We walked back to the cottage.

I couldn't sleep that night. I wandered down to the kitchen in an old robe.

There Frost sat at the table gripping a stubby pencil, his eyes fixed on a short poem with several line-outs and insertions. Suddenly, he looked up at me, startled. He put his pencil down and paused before saying, "Rabbie's your man."

Taken aback, I managed only to say, "What?"

"I meant you love your Rabbie, not this old man."

"His different religion and stronger-willed mother make that fairy tale unlikely."

"But he's writing a love story for you."

What the hell was this, my Robbie as the know-it-all buddy standing in for my boyfriend to argue that Rabbie should serve as my husband, provider, and lover? Where was my Preceptor, who had yet to offer a single suggestion about my work in almost a year? I cinched my robe tight, grabbed his hand, and marched him up the stairs to the attic. I opened my chest and pulled out the lockbox. I bade him sit beside me and sang my "Blue Salvation." He asked to see the poem, and I opened my journal for him. He asked for a copy, and I obliged.

"Belle," he said, "this is what's missing from your goodbye poem to your mama. Put it in. Then rework the poem so you tell your truth but aslant, like Dickinson."

Now I was mad at him for acting as my Preceptor. I grabbed the songbook back. He tried to calm me, but I shooed him away and shut the attic door behind him. I sang all night, songs of lust for my lost Rabbie and hateful laments about the impossibility of my loving Robbie. None made it into my songbook, but several escaped shredding, including one wondering why David Ahgosa distanced himself from me with each passing year as he ripened from boy to man. Curious that a few chance encounters with that mystical Ojibwe stuck with me so: perhaps he was the most forbidden delight of life of all my boys. When dawn broke, I folded the papers together, tied them with a ribbon and placed them in the bottom of the trousseau Mama gave me.

What a joke! *Mama, I'm sorry if I'm not the marrying kind, but I'll be damned if I'll pay any man to serve as my husband against his religion or any man against his marriage. Oh, Mama, tell me how not to become a whore, because I fear I'll do anything to get Rabbie to marry me and Robbie to stay. Only David, I know, has no price.*

Another horrible thought hit me then: What was the difference between her dowry that bought Papa and me paying enough to pry my Rabbie from his Queen and Church or to keep Robbie at Michigan so I could be his secretary and…what? Oh, Mama, why do I try to drag you down to excuse my temptation? Right there I sang my new understanding, irony and all:

The Dowry and the Whore

A dowry might purchase
old daughter an avid suitor—
eager for the cash.

He may grow wealthy—
fat—and spend each evening
in his mistress's arms.

Should his wife complain—
she may end up on the corner—
for sale again!

No matter how much I yearned, I promised myself I'd never risk that fate.

The sun crossing the attic window woke me. I freshened up, put on my best face, and braved the stairs from my lofty turret to the big kitchen on the first floor. Papa, Pip, and Robbie sat around the big table, dipping hunks of bread in steaming potato, leek, and onion soup. I was so hungry I joined in all the dunking, slurping, and good cheer even if I didn't join their jabber.

Then I heard Papa say, "What do you think, Belle?"

"Sorry, Papa, about what?"

"Pip joining Mr. Frost at Amherst next fall?" When I didn't say anything, Papa continued, "Your poet friend says the College teaches boys how to become men and offers enough star-gazing to get that out of Pip's system, too."

My brother piled on. "There's also a new Donald Ross golf course, an artificial ice rink, and fly-fishing, and you can stay with the Frosts when you visit."

So this was what my brother's leaving me would feel like: a gunshot to my gut. Maybe my bribing Rabbie to overthrow his Queen wasn't such a bad idea after all, but I only said, "You willing to pay for it, Papa?"

"It'll be a good investment if Amherst teaches him how to stand on his own so he can run the business after I'm gone." He paused. "How about we split it?"

"Papa, why don't you use some of Mama's dowry to pay for Pip's college?"

Frost smiled at that, and Pip looked expectantly at his father. Finally, Papa nodded. "She's even tougher when it comes to my running our family business."

"I know better than to argue with her about poetry, too," Frost said. He proceeded to regale them with stories of how I "told" him "to rewrite" his "I Will Sing You One-O" and saw right through his "dialogue between the hugger-mugger farmer star-gazing and the poet pontificating in Star-Splitter." He turned to Papa and added, "Belle did compose the best of the student poems." Thank heavens Frost proceeded to tell Papa how I performed my song so well I'd fainted as if I were Sarah Bernhardt. "I think she might have enjoyed a few too many glasses of punch too."

Thus saved from having to sing "Mary Bell's Death" to Papa, I was reminded again why I was so mad at Frost for giving my song to the *Whimsies* for the spring issue. My poetry was too personal for publishing. I vowed *never* again.

Papa and Pip headed off for the stove works in Empire, Papa to get Pip's thinking on a new gas burner to heat water or steam for radiators. Frost declined their invitation in favor of a walk "botanizing" with me. I guessed he hadn't finished making up with me for stealing back to Amherst and, now, fixing to steal my brother away with him.

We climbed up the steep, wooded ridge. The warming sunlight through the leafless maples, beech, and birch left pools of melt and colorful sprigs of spring ephemerals. The white of Dutchman's Breeches hanging upside down as if from a clothesline. The purple, heart-shaped bloom of Wild Ginger. The unexpected yellow of the Dogtooth Violet. Frost pointed toward a patch of ground cover with a bright yellow petal and orange stamen and pistil.

"Green and Gold," I said.

"Thanks, I don't distinguish those hues so well."

"America's greatest poet is colorblind?" I had to laugh, but he dropped his head with a nod. "Maybe that explains the greater sense of sound in your songs."

"Perhaps, it also allows me to see sharper and deeper."

"X-ray vision?"

"Wouldn't my critics have a field-day with that notion?" He grabbed my arm, and we headed over the top of the hill. The last snow disappeared in slender rills running down the south slope. I pointed to a spring pool forming among the trees about thirty feet below and whispered, "Listen to the peepers."

"A lovely silver croak."

I chuckled. "Call it the irony of our Leelanau spring, ending too many months of hard winter with a surge of new life, but only here for a day, gone tomorrow."

"Michigan shares much with New Hampshire and Vermont." As if a foregone conclusion, he added, "Visit Amherst." He dawdled so over a bed of ferns beginning to lose its coat of ice, I walked away but almost tripped at an old fence, now only a tumble of stones, wood beams and rusted barb-wire. Thankfully, Frost's unexpected hand steadied me. Suddenly, a doe appeared on the other side, looking back at us. After eyeing us as if to make sure we wouldn't fall, she began to walk away. An onrushing snort of exhale brought her up short. A big buck, antlers long gone from last fall's rut, knobs yet to blossom into a rack, rose beside her. We two looked at the other two across the fence, and they looked back. Eventually, the doe ambled off one way, and the buck turned and raced the other.

"Robbie, I will see you when I visit Pip next fall," I replied.

We proceeded along the crest of the hill until we saw the mouth of the Crystal River below. We clambered down, and I led Robbie along the riverbank to the log bridge David Ahgosa built to cross to the sacred place where he told the story of the Lost Daughter. I pointed to the brookies running in the clear water rushing below. We climbed up the steep bank and walked through the birch to the clearing in the dunes. There sat David on a driftwood stump, pondering several sheets of birch bark. He waved, and I introduced this boy-man to my man-child: "David Ahgosa, my chief guide up north, meet Robert Frost, my Preceptor of poetry at the University down south."

David explained his plan for building a box out of the birch bark and how he used pen, ink, and smoldering coals to draw the figures. Frost smiled and explained how good poems also made good figures. David showed him how the visage of the eagle would fly in front, with a lone wolf, a big sturgeon, and a Mama Bear on the sides of the box. Frost chuckled. "With such imagery and construction, Belle's poems might yet also be built to last." They got to jabbering so with each other at my expense I excused myself.

"Where you going?" Frost asked.

"For a dip."

"It's much too cold."

"Not if I strip down to my scales." I walked through the birch and pine and down the dune to the shore. I dropped my clothes, ambled into the cold water up to my knees and dove into the bay. I felt the icy nettles as the cold water hit my skin, but within a few minutes, my regular kick and stroke warmed me. Soon the rush of water inspired me.

Fifty yards out, I heard a voice yelling on shore, "Belle, come back." I flipped over and saw Robbie. I waved Frost off but swam close along the shore, the water here not that much colder than the deeper water of the bay in summer. When I got to Glen Haven, I wondered how much longer Mr. Day could keep the big lake steamers docking at his pier now that Detroit was building cars most families could afford. I marveled at the huge Sleeping Bear Dunes rising on the left, the Lake beyond so Great it didn't end at the horizon, and South Manitou north across the strait beckoning again. Not today: too cold, even for me.

As I swam back, I wondered how we could conserve this unique place. Would a state or national park just invite more visitors to destroy it? Yet how could people who wanted to live here make a living if we restricted it to be conserved, undeveloped, forever? I didn't know, but at least this quandary gave me reason to meet alone with David Ahgosa again. Together, we might figure how to stop the Ogre Surtr from sucking all life out of the Sleeping Mama Bear with any damn dune buggy. Thank heavens Mr. Day had taken in a group of rich Chicago investors to pump money into Day Estates to make a longer go of building his "Adirondacks of the Midwest" on Alligator Hill instead.

My mind began to wander, and the rhythm of my stroke and kick faltered. My legs and arms felt heavier, almost leaden. I rolled on my back and closed my eyes.

"Belle!" I thought about responding, but I was content, floating in my element.

A strong hand grabbed one arm; two others, my legs. I opened my eyes and saw David and Robbie leaning from the small single-mast Mackinaw boat. I tried to wave them off, but they hauled me aboard. David touched my skin. I looked down and saw the bluish tinge. David directed Frost to man the tiller and wrapped me in blankets. Downy with satin trim, the covers didn't prevent me from shivering and shaking.

Frost yelled, "Warm her up before she freezes!" And, oh my, did my Ojibwe friend as we sailed back along the shore!

Until the thunder clapped, seemingly right above us, and David let loose of me. He yelled at Frost, "Head toward the shore!"

I poked my head out of the covers and saw a wall of small shells roiling the bay and moving toward us at a frightening clip, an eerily beautiful but frightening sight.

David took the helm. With the wind howling at our backs, he raced the Mackinaw boat directly at the beach. He yelled at Frost, "Pull out the centerboard." After Robbie hauled it out, David yelled to Frost and me, "When I say 'Prepare to come about,' duck. When the boat spins parallel to shore, jump toward the beach."

In less than ten seconds David issued his command. The boat spun about, and Robbie and I jumped out into no more than two feet of water. At the same instant David jumped up, shinnied to the top of the mast and leaned toward shore. With the forces from the wind, the boat spinning, and David's weight at the top, the mast slowly began to fall and the hull to tip over, David leaped into the shallow water. He huddled all three of us under cover of the hull as the tip of the mast stuck into the beach. The pounding of the hailstones on our makeshift roof sounded as if a powerful and long fireworks show was shooting off right on top of us.

From the deafening din, I saw tens of thousands of ice balls, many bigger than tea-cups, more the size of golf balls, many more the size of buttons and peas, falling like small bombs on the beach. The storm seemed to go on and on and on, but in no more than fifteen minutes, it stopped as suddenly as it started.

On returning home from this wild adventure, I excused myself and went right up to my bedroom in the third-floor turret. Recovering from another bout with the icy waters of Sleeping Bear Bay, I slept in my big bed past midnight. Starving, I tiptoed downstairs, warmed the leftover soup, and tore off chunks of bread. "Smells good," I heard Robbie say as he entered the kitchen.

We sat together at the kitchen table without saying a word and savored our late night meal, right down to the last crust and drop. Eventually, I got up, pulled the picture book of McKim, Mead, and White commissions off the shelf, turned to the section with their many Amherst College buildings, and showed him the loose pictures of houses designed by other architects in the town Stanford White particularly admired. Frost picked up the snapshot of one and showed me a handsome, many-gabled home set high on a knoll and shaded by big trees. "The President of Mass Aggie's home is my favorite." He paused, shook his head, and added wistfully, "I can't afford it, yet."

"You're welcome to stay in Ann Arbor." Now I'd said as much as I dared, but I'd have offered an endowment to pay the great poet to stay at Michigan.

He got up and puttered about, brewing us each a cup of Lipton's. After he set the tea on the table and took a big swallow, he said, "Belle, we've got to head back first thing in the morning so we can get on with my book." I shook my head. "I've written six grace notes already, and I need you to type them so we can make revisions." I shook my head again. "I've got more racing in my head."

I dropped my eyes. "But I told David we'd join him at the Omena kirk in the morning." Still standing, he patted my shoulder. By the time I looked up, he was gone.

I climbed the stairs to the attic, opened my notebook and sang:

Spring Break

We sidestep snow piles,
wander among leafless
beech and birch, hopeful

as colorful sprigs
dotting the forest floor,
eager now to bloom—

behind a fat spruce
doe eyes stare us down
and the buck nearby—

then she turns away,
toward the setting sun,
a lone eagle shrills,

a chill wind whistles
and shivers the barren trees:
can two ever be one?

Three days later, back at Cambridge House, I caught Rabbie O'Bannon carrying the draft of his novella. "Let me see it," I said.

"But I swore Frost to secrecy," he countered.

"Let me see it," I demanded. Rabbie handed me the typewritten draft, its hard cover bound by Smythe sewing on the left side, and I began to read.

"Good Lord, Belle, it's 95 pages." I kept reading, and he squirmed on the big couch in front of my fireplace. Despite all Rabbie's fidgeting, I completed Part 1 in a half hour, got up, and offered him a drink. He accepted a glass of Laphroaig, and I poured another for me. In Part 1 a teenage boy grows up, frolics, drinks, swims, dances, travels, and, yes, experiments with six girls. Mostly tender, self-deprecating, and funny, none of the stories crossed the line into graphic sex. Part 2 was another matter. Although it did offer a paean to the more mature and vital woman the young man then met, I was grateful Rabbie described her as a mysterious, slim, dark, hot-blooded Latin. Instead of a hank of unruly red hair, she wore tight crimson blouses, flaring red skirts, bright blush on her cheeks, carmine lipstick, and ruby barrettes to show off her flowing black hair. That she emigrated from the Caribbean, confessed her sins in the Catholic Church, and hated deep water helped, too. Thank God, no one could mistake this character for me. Because the scene Rabbie wrote at the end was so hot, I took his hand, and we flew to our nest. I forgot his Queen.

Next morning, Mrs. Frost opened the door to Robbie's rental, the home of the long-time chair of the English Department who'd died two years before. She led me into Frost's den. A pile of draft poems greeted me by the Corona. Ten lyrical "Grace Notes," the first rued the short life of the spring ephemeral flower ("Nature's first green is gold… But only so an hour") and the other brief breaths of first life ("So Eden sank to grief. So dawn goes down to day. Nothing gold can stay.")

The fifth, titled "Two Look at Two," cast a different spell. As night begins to fall in late autumn, two lovers decide to turn back from their walk to the hilltop: "'This is all,' they sighed. 'Good night to woods.' But not so; there was more." First, a doe looked at them around a spruce tree across "a tumbled wall with barbed-wire binding," until the doe "sighed and passed unscared along the wall. '*This* then is all.'" But no, "a snort bid them wait" and an "antlered buck of lusty nostril" now stood looking at them around the spruce until he moved on. "Two had seen two, whichever side you spoke from./'This *must* be all.' It was all. Still they stood…" Another, much different dreamscape spun by the master poet: I knew better than to think it reflected our walk together atop the ridge.

The tenth poem, "The Onset," began with a dark view of winter letting "death descend" as if "life had never begun." The second stanza answered the long winter's storm with the new life of spring: "It cannot check the peeper's silver croak." The snow would "all go downhill/In water of a slender April Rill." He concluded with something like the sight as we drove into Omena and saw the old kirk: "Nothing will be left white but here a birch,/and there a clump of houses with a church." Yet Robbie once again wove the scenes and phrasings together with such grace and punch as to conjure a much different dreamscape and to sound a different tune each time read aloud.

I couldn't help wondering whether Frost was saying that nothing so gold as the spring flower or the unlooked-for moment can ever last but, like each season and dawn into day, must also pass. Or was he saying that such moments are complete, maybe even eternal, because they are so ephemeral?

Frost touched my shoulder and asked, "What do you think?" Rather than tell him, I showed him a copy of my "Spring Break." He read it twice, slowly. He said, "Sing it," and I did. "Work on making it read on the page as well as it sounds said aloud." He folded my poem and put it in his shirt pocket. Before I could say anything more, he asked, "What say you of Vincent Millay winning the Pulitzer?"

I tried to read his expression to see whether he felt aggrieved that she, much younger and a woman no less, had beaten him to the prize he coveted. His pale blue eyes and full pursed lips did not give him away. "You'll win next year with your new poems."

"Like Vincent, I won't leave anything to chance." He confided in his best stage whisper, "A year of campaigning, a few choice words from well-placed friends, and *New Hampshire* will win the prize for me, too."

For the last meeting of the Whimsies, Frost agreed to referee our work for the year. Rabbie had written a long letter to President Burton, blunting the criticism that Frost had made himself scarce in his second year at Michigan, except to the two students who served as scribes for his new book. Privately, Roy Cowden also shut up the more hurtful campaign of whispers spread by an anonymous faculty member within the two English departments about Frost, Rabbie, and me. Ned Strait covered his tracks so well, only Cowden and I suspected who "Nym" was.

I invited Stella to join us at Cowden's home for our final goodbye to our great poet friend. The evening droned on, as Frost announced one prize after another, none for Rabbie or me. As we clapped for the winners, Stella whispered, "Don't give up hope."

Just then Frost announced, "For the best fiction work, Rabbie O'Bannon and his *Keystone*. How he found the time to write a short novel with all the work I loaded on him all year, and winning the Western Conference Swimming Championship for our school and two medals in the intercollegiate meet, I can't fathom." Rabbie gripped Frost's hand so hard, I worried he'd break it. Instead all the

Whimsies cheered. Rabbie finally let go, and Frost said, "Let me tell you this young man's imagined a great character, a woman that every one of you should wish to get to know as your mate for life or best friend."

All eyes turned to me, and I reddened. Frost, in his most down-home way, said, "Oh, no. Rabbie's *Keystone* is a little Spanish spark-plug, not a big, red-headed mermaid." That brought the house down but didn't help my blush. The emcee continued, "And now the *Whimsies* annual award for the best literary work, Belle's…" He paused while he pulled a paper from his coat pocket and unfolded it.

Please, Lord, tell me I didn't share "Dry Land," "The Dowry and the Whore," or "Preceptor" with Frost.

The one he chose, "Spring Break," wasn't much better, but Frost did say all 15 lines rather than make me sing. He added, "Belle shares Emily Dickinson's great sense of sound and irony, and her greater lack of grammar and punctuation." I managed to mumble my thanks without fainting.

As Stella and I walked home, she said, "I meant don't give up on getting Frost back here. Burton's pressing to commit the funds from the Lit School budget, and I'm putting the arm on Chase."

Not even "Governor" any longer.

"Belle," she continued, "I know you can't pay to keep Frost here: Chase decided to leave his wife, and I'm not paying him so I can be his secretary either." When I had chuckle at that, she added, "Listen to me. Just don't get so uppity you tell Frost you don't want him back. After a full year away with only those boys at Amherst, he'll beg us Whimsies to reel him back with Burton's bait of a lifetime appointment at Michigan."

Fall 1923: Amherst and Ann Arbor

Matt Mann doubled Rabbie's training sessions to get him ready for the Olympic trials next spring. That meant my time swimming at the Union was limited to weekends when Rabbie snuck me in. Oh, Coach offered to train me, but my times were too slow. Instead I agreed to host Ms. Ederle later in the fall and help her train with him. At least, that would give me a reason to skip the boring literary criticism classes in the mornings and swim with Trudy until the men reclaimed their pool at noon.

With no typing for Robbie, no poetry seminars, and no Pip, I was at loose ends. Even the prospect of working on the literary magazine faded when a stuffier crowd of domineering men took over, changed the name from *Whimsies* back to *The Inlander*, and moved the office to the Union's male bastion. Although Rabbie and I trysted in our nest all night now, my days grew longer as the time the sun shined each day grew shorter.

In early October Frost wrote:

I've tried to make sure Pip's made a home with the College boys, but I fear they're more Eastern high-hats than solid Great

Lakes folk or good rural New England stock. I had better luck introducing him to the Emeritus Astronomer David Todd, who escaped his insane asylum for a last hurrah at the College. I also took Pip to the Evergreens to meet Emily Dickinson's niece. She calls herself Madame Bianchi after a minor Russian prince who married her for her money and left her with nothing but his title. Pip disarmed her by sharing how her aunt's poems inspired you to compose. Nevertheless, Pip misses you terribly: Mrs. Frost insists you stay with us for a visit. Stanford White designed Todd's Observatory here, and I'll also show you the big house on Sunset that I admire as much as he did. I enclose a town map I've marked with all the sights so you won't get lost.
Robbie

Pip's few letters hid any anxiety about being away from home. They sounded more a young man exploring new places, people, and challenges. He also indicated that the astronomer Todd encouraged his search for voices in space. Pip included a detailed drawing of the odd box in the shape of a horn on a circular track he'd designed for the big hill above our stove works: *Marconi says there's static interference on transatlantic calls, and it's not coming from any electric trolleys nearby. If it's from space, I'm going to track it down from Empire Bluff with this big ear.*

He also wrote about his two closest friends, his freshman roommate, Charles Cole, and a sophomore, Charles Drew, he met working out at the gym:

The two Charles are as different as can be. Cole is great fun and a brilliant lad. He organized our class of '27 to steal Sabrina when no one in the class of '24 expected. With only a couple of our other strong boys, we managed to hide the 300-pound statue off campus, in a little barn in back of the Astronomer's House below Todd's Observatory. Drew is quiet but sprints down the

> *field every game for a touchdown. He challenges me in the gym to score more goals on the ice this winter and in the lab to invent a radio telescope to search in space. First time I found friends—besides you and David—I'd follow if asked.*

Two weeks later Mrs. Frost sent an invitation:

> *Belle, you must stay with us. Your brother's a delight to host, but he reminds us how much we also miss Ann Arbor. Turn left on Dana, and halfway down on your left you won't miss our house. Elinor*

I screwed up my courage and drove to Amherst through Canada with an overnight stop near Syracuse. The second day a flat tire near Stockbridge held me up for two hours. I drove through the dusk along Northampton Road and turned up Dana. The fading light only made the mix of red brick and yellow clapboard houses and fall colors more impressive. When I arrived at the Frosts' rental, I had to smile: red brick, with two double-hung windows on each side of the big front door, five more on the second floor, and three dormers on the roof: a 3/5-scale model of my Cambridge House.

Mrs. Frost greeted me at the door and waved off my apology for being too late for dinner. Pip and Robbie both hugged me—Pip because he did miss his Marmie and Frost because he hated shaking hands. While I snacked on leftovers at the kitchen table, Frost invited Pip and me to attend one of his "small readings" that evening. Pip begged off, as he was meeting Professor Todd at the Observatory to finalize their plan to develop a new "speed camera" to photograph the light from stars behind the sun during the next eclipse.

"Whatever for?" Frost asked.

Pip said they were to going to see if they could confirm the initial proof by the British astronomer Eddington from the 1919 solar eclipse of one of Einstein's theories: "Newton's construct of gravity is wrong.

Rather than the Sun 'pulling,' space warps around such heavy objects: that's how the light from distant stars bends around the Sun." Frost, still as perplexed as me, nodded at Pip's enthusiasm. My boy apologized for leaving before he could "cloud the cosmos more." He invited us to join him tomorrow morning for golf at the Orchards "to explore another mystery together, albeit here on earth." Frost accepted before I could warn him how well my brother played.

When Pip left, Mrs. Frost suggested I stay with her to rest up after the long journey. Robbie wouldn't hear of it. He walked me along Dana, away from the campus, until we turned right, toward the town center. Frost pointed down a cross-street, even farther from the College, to a big white clapboard house with many gables, set back high on a knoll. "Not quite as big as your house in Ann Arbor," he said with a shrug.

"More elegant than my shingle cottage up north."

"No view of the Great Lake, dunes, and islands, though," he replied.

"High enough to see west across the valley, all the way to the Berkshires."

"The street *is* called Sunset," Frost said, "just as I marked on the map, but it's called Goodell House, after the old President of the Mass Aggie College who built it." He touched my arm. "When I get rich like you, the town-folk will call it Frost House."

"Do you begrudge my inheritance?"

"I struggled for years working my farm to support my brood and earned every penny I ever got selling my poetry and singing for my supper at more damn readings."

"No one ever offered a hand-up?"

"Not like yours," he grumped.

"Then I'll buy a copy of your new book so you can buy your *Sunset* House."

"You will not!"

We walked to Main Street in silence. At the corner we faced the picture-book New England town, the long commons aglow with streetlights, three-story brick commercial buildings at one end, churches, stores, mansions, and fraternity houses lining each side, and the College rising on the hill at the far end. At the very top of the campus, an illuminated clock tower shone above all.

"Tell me true," I said, "did you use the one here or the one in Ann Arbor for 'I Will Sing You One-O'?"

"Oh, Johnson Chapel has only one big bell, but the tall church steeple directly across the quad houses a real carillon."

"That's no answer."

"Poetic license, my Belle," he replied with a squeeze to my arm. We walked down the far side of the commons, past the DU and Beta houses. When we turned left at the edge of the campus, a huge harvest moon rose in the night sky. "Many's the time I walked alone, beyond the lights of this, and many other towns, to bear my dark soul to that one luminary clock so high above this earth." When I said I was also acquainted with that night light from gazing out my attic window up north, he sat us down on a bench by the Chi Phi house. "You're right," he said. "My father's father gave me an annual stipend, a free home, and a farm to raise my family so I could write poetry." Frost paused. "I never did make a dime tilling his rocky Derry patch. When he died, I sold the Frost homestead and moved the family to England to make my name as a flinty farmer poet from New England. Even when I rage at the critics calling me a regional bard, I've played that role pretty well ever since, eh?"

"Robbie, you're going to be rich as well as famous."

"Then you'll be my guest at what will be *my* Sunset House sooner than later."

We walked into the fraternity and up the central stairs. In a corner suite 12 boys crowded around us on two leather couches and six table chairs. Frost and I faced them in two comfortable armchairs. The fireplace at our back threw off so much heat, Frost took off his jacket. The boys' eyes lit up more when I stripped off my V-neck sweater.

Frost started by reading Dickinson's "Certain Slant of Light" that Pastor Weir had recited at Mama's funeral. He then pulled from his pocket a typed poem heavily marked with his thick pencil at the end. I heard my "Mary Bell's Death," but he tacked on my lines from "Blue Salvation." My blush gave me away. He then read one of his grace notes I'd typed, "To Earthward." Frost repeated lines to make different tunes of each song. "Okay, men," he asked, "what do these three poems share in common?"

One boy said, "Death." Another suggested, "Light." A third said, "No, dark." A fourth said, "Sweet and sour." A bear of a man in back drowned the others out, "Irony."

Frost turned to me. "What do you say, Miss Belle?"

"Convey your meaning at a slant. That's what Miss Dickinson says in the first poem. That's also what you do in the third as your poet ages, from appreciating the purely sweet to the 'after-mark, the bitter bark and burning clove.'"

"Just as you do with sounds and rhythms in the second poem," he replied, "moving from 'sly silence' to 'lonely crack,' from the 'gray goodbye' of death to—"

"Professor Frost," I interjected, "I don't like the way you tacked my separate song about the sense of calm after a climactic storm onto my lyric about my Mama's death."

"—Blue Salvation," he continued as if he hadn't heard me.

"Thank you, but I will hold your suggestion awhile, and deepen it, deepen it."

"Gentlemen," he said, "you now see why in Amherst it's a mistake to argue with a woman poet who speaks her mind with her own slant."

When Frost finished his ramblings over a half hour later, good humor and fellowship filled the room. I almost felt like one of the boys when Robbie waved the hulking figure behind the couch up and introduced the young man as the "Alpha, the President of Chi Phi and captain of the hockey team." Robbie stuck his finger, hard, in the boy's big chest and told him how Michigan recruited my brother to play on the Varsity there but Frost brought Pip here: "Make sure you put the rush on him."

"Has your brother made friends with any upperclassmen yet?" When I told him about Charles Drew, he said, "Drew's in Omega Psi Phi," and then whispered, "A fraternal order for the only two Negro students here and the few coloreds at Mass Aggie."

"Don't be surprised if Pip chooses to join Mr. Drew."

The Alpha reddened at that.

On our walk back, Frost stopped at the corner of Boltwood and Main, pointed right to Emily Dickinson's Homestead and her older brother, Austin's, home, The Evergreens. "Tomorrow, I'll introduce you to Emily's niece, Martha. The self-styled Madame Bianchi holds the originals of the many poems Emily shared with her mother."

"Where are the rest of the originals?"

He paused and put a stubby forefinger to his lips as if pondering. He explained how most thought Mabel Todd still hid a big trove Emily's sister had given her to edit, even after the Dickinson heirs winning "a lawsuit over a piece of land" shut her up.

"Is Mrs. Todd in Amherst now to help take care of her husband?" Frost nodded. "You mean *all* of Emily Dickinson's original writings may be right here?" When his blue eyes lit up, I blurted, "Will you introduce me to her, too?"

Frost replied in a low voice, "Pip should introduce you to the Todds." He put his arm around me and whispered, "Maybe we can find out what the College needs to do to negotiate a ceasefire between the two warring sides to get hold of all the originals." The prospect of seeing Emily Dickinson's creations excited me, so I nodded.

ಌ

The next morning Frost played a different game than golf, one mulligan after another—on the tee, from the fairway, even putting. On the fifth hole, his pitch landed near the pin, but his ball rolled into a gully. "Who ever heard of building greens as upside-down saucers?" he complained. Pip explained that our fellow Scot Donald Ross was the architect. The final four holes, Frost put his last ball in his pocket and botanized through the trees. Meanwhile, Pip striped his tee shots down the center and flew his fairway shots onto the greens, missing another three-foot putt on the ninth for a one-over-par 37. I traipsed after my ball in the rough, hit from tall grass to sand bunker, skulled chips across the green, but sank a ten-foot putt on the last hole for one over 50.

On the drive back through the Notch in the Holyoke Range, Frost said "golf spoiled a good walk, but I'll show you a thing or two about real sport on the tennis court." Pip had a physics lab and said he would meet us at four for a lecture by Niels Bohr. Without offering any reason, Frost dropped me with Pip at North Hall next to Johnson Chapel and said he'd meet me at the court. Pip walked me down to the edge of the College's hill and pointed south. Midway down to the playing fields, a half-dozen courts nestled on a plateau. Although dubbed "clay," the red topping appeared much softer and more porous than the hard mud of the few "clay" courts at Michigan.

Long after Pip left, I heard "One-O" ring from the big clock tower in Johnson Chapel, quickly followed by the harmony of the bells ringing in the church steeple across the quad. I wondered what was keeping Frost but swept the court, careful not to mar the chalk lines. Eventually he showed up, dressed in white pants, pressed with a sharp crease, white sweater and shirt, and new tennis shoes so white they looked like spats. "Sorry, I had to pick up my new Davis bat and wait for the boys to string it with catgut." He handed me a rickety old Tad with loose strings. He looked askance at my old sneakers, brown slacks, and tan blouse. He twirled his new racquet. "Rough or smooth?" When I answered "Rough," he replied "Smooth" without rubbing his finger over the decorative braid at the bottom of the face. "I'll serve," he said, looked up at the sun, and pranced out to the baseline on the south side to avoid the afternoon glare when serving.

"I don't get to choose side?"

"Belle, you don't have my old rheumy eyes."

"We're not going to switch after the odd games?"

He shook his head. I walked to the other baseline.

Frost stuffed two balls in his left pocket, tossed one up with his left hand, and smashed it with the new racquet in his right. The ball sailed so high over the net, it just missed hitting me. "Strings must be too tight." He hit his second with topspin and drove the ball into the bottom of the net. "Just practicing," he said. I retrieved the ball at the fence behind me for him. He wailed another first serve into the deuce court that landed a few inches behind the service line. "Check the mark," he said. I circled the round splotch on the dusty red surface. He looped his second serve in, and I smacked the ball cross-court with my big forehand, perhaps a bit too high. I thought I saw a puff of chalk as the ball landed near the far corner, but he called "Fifteen-love" as he got set to serve to the ad side. When his first serve landed in this time, I blasted a backhand right down the sideline, but I couldn't tell whether it landed on the baseline or not. Frost marched up to the net to pick up the third ball and returned to serve to the deuce court. "Thirty-love," he said. He managed to claim the first game when I returned his next two good serves down the middle and short, and he hit two devilishly angled drop-shots winners for which my lumbering was no match.

I proceeded to hit every ball within my reach hard, but well inside the baseline and the sidelines. Frost became so frustrated with the big pace on my ball he started trying to hit harder for winners. After I won the next few games, he changed tactics again and started dinking the ball, hitting drop-shots shots followed by lobs to move me up and back and looping angled shots to run me from side-to-side. As I was no lynx, this served him better. We had long points, some with the ball going back and forth ten to twenty times, and he won two of the next three games.

As he started to serve the next game, he said, "Four all."

"Robbie, I think it's three-five."

"No, you lost track." And it was hard to keep score when we didn't change sides or call total games before we started each new game. I shook my head, gritted my teeth, and dug deep into all my reserves. I won his serve and mine by lumbering as fast as I could to hit his devilish angles, slices, and lobs back with more pace and power.

"Another set?" I squeaked while trying to catch my breath.

"Sorry, I've got to get the boys at the shop to restring my racquet. It's too tight." The sweat poured down his face, and he mopped his brow. I handed him a ladle filled with water from the bucket by the net. He slurped half and poured the rest over his head. I did the same as, truth be told, even close to fifty Frost was in great shape and his deft touch forcing me to lumber around the entire court wore me out.

Without shaking hands, he tapped my arm, and marched me up the hill. He looked at his watch and said, "Just as well we quit before I got my revenge in the second set after tuckering you out. Mrs. Bianchi expects you in half an hour, and you need to clean up."

Frost also looked like he'd been in a fight with a chalk monster and lost, white socks, shorts, and shirt all streaked with red clay. "Robbie, I think we need to get you cleaned up, too."

"I'm not going." When I shook my head, he said in a stage whisper, "I fear she believes my act as a New England farmer sage here will upstage Emily Dickinson's legacy as the Belle of Amherst."

Frost's ambitions, and Miss Dickinson's fame, went far beyond that. "Remember when you complained Amy Lowell wrote her verse as if playing tennis without a net?"

"You didn't warn me you played like the second coming of Helen Wills."

I wanted to experience Miss Dickinson's creations so much I didn't protest.

ഗ

Atmospheric Hudson River landscapes greeted me from the walls of the parlor in the Evergreens. After I told Madame Bianchi how much my father's gift of her book of Emily Dickinson poems meant to me, she told me the history of her home and how her mother hosted salons for many dignitaries, artists, and celebrities "passing through our little village." Closing in on 60, she wore a dark suit over her solid frame. Her dark hair, pulled back in a wave, revealed penetrating eyes and a severe demeanor. Yet she smiled warmly as she autographed a copy of *The Single Hound*, put her arm around my waist, and said, "Belle, your brother told me so much about you, please call me Mattie." She explained how her publication had been inspired by her mother's close collaboration—her "spiritual converse"—with her "sister-in-kind and in-law." Mattie asked me to recite one of my poems, and I sang "Mary Bell's Death." She recited one of her poems, so erotic it made me blush. Pointing to the marble sculpture of the nude *Cupid and Psyche*, she said, "Can you match that?" I sang my "Blue Salvation," and she clapped. I asked if I might see the originals of her aunt's poems.

Mattie walked me across the hall to the library. The pale walls set off the dark fireplace mantel, big globe, and bookcases topped by vases, paintings, busts, and knick-knacks from the Dickinson heritage. There were no copies of any of the books of poems and letters edited by Mabel Todd. Instead neat rows of papers rested atop the ornately carved black table in the center of the room and in all the cases around the walls. A handsome young man, at least 20 years her junior, rose to greet me. "Belle, this is Alfred Leete Hampson. While I make tea, please show her Aunt Emily's originals."

I lifted one of the poems from the table. I felt the paper and examined Miss Dickinson's odd scratchings. One by one I picked up dozens of poems on scraps of paper, wrappers from French chocolates, exotic envelopes, and inserts in letters from Mattie's Aunt Emily to her mother. Each time my spirits soared, until I compared one handwritten poem after another to the published versions in *The*

Single Hound. At the sight of all the revisions, removing capital letters, dashes, and exclamation marks—even changes in line form—my heart sank. Why couldn't anyone let Emily speak for herself?

Mattie returned with the tea, and Mr. Hampson whispered in her ear. She nodded and said to me, "Alfred's just as dedicated to retrieving my Aunt's legacy for her rightful heirs as I am. He's helping me organize a new and *complete* collection of Emily's poems." She paused. "We're also organizing *my* Aunt's letters, including for the first time the hundreds of letters she shared only with my mother." Mattie added, "I'm writing an introduction to explain how the love of a married man Aunt Emily renounced as a young woman led to her long seclusion across the hedge."

She waited for me to respond, but I didn't.

"You know," she finally said, "that other woman's visiting Amherst now to care for her daft husband." When I nodded, Mattie put her arm around me again and whispered, "I wonder whether you and your brother might prevail on her to return all of Aunt Emily's writings she stole from Aunt Vinnie so we can bring the entire collection together under one roof?"

Good Lord, what had Frost gotten me into now? I managed to blurt, "What if the College provides the one roof?"

"I'll never agree to *give* my collection to Amherst. That homewrecker's refusal to return Emily's creations forced me to sell the Dickinson Homestead."

I offered my condolences and retreated by saying my goodbye as best I could.

Alfred walked me to the front door and whispered, "Miss Belle, you need to understand that Madame Bianchi is committed to explaining how her mother was Emily Dickinson's best friend, confidante, reader, and sounding board, except at the very end of her father's life, when Mrs. Todd drove a sword through the Dickinson family."

"I understand the double hurt she feels about her father's mistress being editor of her aunt's poems, but I don't see what that has to do with College."

"Amherst did not reward the Dickinson family properly for their decades of loyal service." He paused, walked me onto the front stoop, and closed the door behind us. "The College also refused to fire David Todd to end the scandal and instead promoted him to full professor." He pointed across the street and down the Dickinson Grove to the disputed house and land at the far corner. "After Mattie's father died and the Dickinson family finally put an end to the Todds' fraud, Amherst made Professor Todd Secretary of the Faculty and built a big house and the best observatory of any college in America for him." He paused and pointed farther south to the College rising on the hill. "After that bugger went insane, President Meiklejohn even made him *emeritus,* and a Trustee purchased a posh house for the Todds in Coconut Grove. Amherst's refusal to bid on the Homestead when Madame Bianchi had to sell was the final straw."

I thanked him for showing me Miss Dickinson's originals. As I looked east to the large brick house where Emily composed all her poems and, with her sister, Lavinia, provided a haven for their brother's affair with Mabel Todd, I had to admit Frost might be onto something: "Mr. Hampson, Professor Frost says there's a new president at Amherst. He might wish to make appropriate amends to Madame Bianchi and the Dickinson family legacy."

He squeezed my hand, nodded, and waved goodbye.

The next day I visited Mabel Todd at the Observatory House. In her mid-60s, she looked a pixie, with lovely white hair and lively dark eyes on a pretty face only age had weathered. Even though a stroke hobbled her right hand and leg, she stood straight to greet me, but only five feet tall. She wore a well-tailored suit with lovely white flowers painted on the lapels. She led me into the parlor, much larger than the one at The Evergreens. I sat down on one end of a sofa, and Mrs. Todd sat on the other. She began, "Your brother's such a tonic for The Astronomer."

"Pip enjoys your husband's tales of chasing solar eclipses, and he loves tinkering with new devices to help capture moving pictures of the next one."

Mrs. Todd handed me a book she had written, *Total Eclipses of the Sun*. I opened it and found that Mabel had dedicated it to Amy Lowell's brother, Percival, "Intimate Friend of Celestial Spaces." Mrs. Todd did get around. She pulled out two snapshots, the first a photo of a rustic cabin nestled among the trees by a rocky shore. "After our success writing textbooks and travelogues and lecturing all over the country, David and I built this retreat for our families." When I expressed my admiration for the scene and told her about my family home on the shore of Sleeping Bear Bay in Michigan, she asked, "Did you have troubles with the loggers cutting down your forests, too?" When I nodded, she told me how they'd decided to buy all of Hog Island to preserve the trees. I shared how Papa joined with a wise lumberman to plant second-growth forests in Leelanau.

Mrs. Todd handed me the second picture, an exotic home, nestled among tall pines, with a broad veranda and three arches opening onto a palm-tree garden. She also picked up a second book, *Corona and Coronet*, showed me the picture of a huge sailboat, and read the subtitle of the book: "Being a Narrative of the Amherst Eclipse Expedition to Japan in Mr. James's Schooner Yacht *Coronet*, to Observe the Sun's Total Obscuration 9th August, 1896." She explained how she spent a good part of the year after Austin died sailing the Pacific and back with her husband's former student. Mrs. Todd pulled a newspaper clipping from the chest and handed it to me. It had a photograph of her sitting in a wicker chair on the veranda of her home in Coconut Grove. She called it "Matsuba." The caption under the picture read:

> *Mrs. Mabel Loomis Todd, whose life reads like a page from "Who's Who," is now in Florida "resting" and writing three books, preparing her private museum, and entertaining. She is the dean of American woman lecturers, having been on the*

platform for a quarter of a century. Her writings range from the only authoritative book on the total eclipses of the sun to sonnets and travel stories.

"You see," she proclaimed, "I had another full life after Sue and Lavinia Dickinson closed Emily to me." She added with a note of pride, "And, after our daughter learned she and her husband couldn't have children, Millicent followed the love she found with us on all our expeditions abroad. She just earned the first dual doctorate—in geography and geology—Harvard ever awarded."

"My Mama reciting Emily Dickinson's poems from your collections inspired me to compose."

"Without my work, and enlisting Mr. Higginson, no one would have had that chance." She added, "But I suppose you've met with Sue Dickinson's daughter, too."

"She showed me the originals in her possession."

"*A Single Hound* makes as many changes as Mr. Higginson and I ever did."

I didn't nod but instead added, "She's planning a new edition of letters revealing that her Aunt Emily became a recluse at an early age when she renounced a love with a much older man because he was married."

Mabel Todd shot to her feet. "That's the mad wish of Sue Dickinson and her daughter, seeking more revenge on me for the love Austin and I shared."

"You should publish the rest of Emily's work so she can speak for herself, then." Mabel Todd blanched, lifted her fist to her mouth, and bit at it. I added, "Madame Bianchi's preparing what she's calling 'The Complete Poems of Emily Dickinson.'"

"Follow me," she said as she rose and placed her good arm in mine. I helped her walk out the back door. I paused to look up and saw the dome of the observatory Stanford White's firm designed for David Todd high on the hill. We walked to a large shed at the back of the yard. She opened the door, and the sunlight flooded through all the motes onto a dusty trunk. I helped her to the chest, smaller than Mama's trousseau for me but made of fancy camphorwood. She took out a key, and, as she opened the latch and lifted the lid, there was a soft tinkling of bells. No one inside Observatory House could have heard this feeble alarm. Inside rested many big, brown envelopes containing dozens of packets of poems, folders full of letters and various loose papers, stacks of carefully typed copies, and two locked metal boxes.

Mrs. Todd yanked a canvas off a large object next to the chest. There sat a large bronze statue of a nude goddess on a big rock. "How did Sabrina ever get in here," she exclaimed. When she sat down on a crate, I draped the sheet over the statue and told her about my brother's letter disclosing his freshman class prank.

While she began to leaf through the envelopes, folders, and packets, I looked to a nearby crate that served as a bookcase. It held copies of several books, including the three collections of Dickinson poems and the book of correspondence Mrs. Todd had edited. "All published by Roberts Brothers in Boston?" I asked.

Mrs. Todd nodded. "Only the last collection failed to win an audience, because the Dickinson heirs stopped me from my campaigning to promote Emily's poetry. I put all the poems Lavinia gave me and all the letters I collected in this chest." She handed me one of the packets and said, "I call these fascicles because Emily copied her poems on separate pages and then fastened them together into a booklet with twine. That's the closest she came to a final writing and publication of her creations in a book."

She raised a single sheet of paper from one of the other folders and showed me the poem Emily sent to her, "A Route of Evanescence." Mrs. Todd explained how she played the piano and sang at the Dickinson Homestead and left a painting of an all-white woodland flower as a gift for Emily. She handed me a thank-you note from Miss Dickinson. The elongated scrawl was difficult to decipher, so Mrs.

Todd recited: "That without suspecting it you should send me the preferred flower of life seems almost supernatural. I cannot make an Indian pipe but please accept a hummingbird."

I now understood the poem as a puzzle, about a small bird beating its wings to stand still in the air, an exotic white plant, and mail from Tunis. I looked at Mabel Todd, still so tiny but lovely, and nodded. Pretty as a hummingbird. A musician, singer, painter, writer, correspondent, and world-traveling pixie sprite, she would have been quite the prize for Emily's older brother. "Tell me what Emily Dickinson was like."

"I never saw her." Mrs. Todd dropped her eyes. "She was always in her room or in the shadows on the stairs." Fearful as I already was of leaving my safe Arbors, was that going to be my fate, too? I must have grown pale, because Mabel asked if I was all right.

A new thought struck me: Emily might have put up with her brother's affair playing out in the Dickinson Homestead despite her long friendship with Austin's wife, "Sister Sue," but Emily refused to meet his illicit lover or become her friend. "Did Emily write you any other letters?"

The color rose on Mrs. Todd's cheeks as her eyes darted to one of the locked tins. "None worthy of publication," she said and gathered herself. "After reading most of Emily's poems and letters, I know she lived a spirited life, enjoyed the Brontë sisters, Shakespeare plays, the Bible, music, painting, and imagining adventures the world over. She felt more deeply, flashed brighter, and flew higher and farther than any bird in America, all while secluded in her Amherst cage." Mrs. Todd paused. "Mrs. Bianchi's letters won't support her mother's vengeful gossip. Emily Dickinson lived as a non-conformist, yes, but not as a forlorn recluse who forswore the love of a married man."

"How many of her poems have you already edited and published?"

She eyed her trove. "Less than half of these."

I leaned toward the chest and asked, "May I?" When Mrs. Todd nodded, I read dozens of the poems. My excitement grew at holding

Emily Dickinson's compositions in my hand and seeing how extraordinary they were. My heart raced as I flew with all the exclamation points, paused with the dashes, rose with the capitalized words, and pondered with all the poems aslant. I couldn't resist singing several aloud.

"Different than my edits," Mabel admitted. "Better read aloud. The pause of the dashes invites you to fill the void and feel the beat, while the exclamations do carry you right along to—OH MY!" She laughed but then shook her head. "I barely convinced Thomas to work with the versions I'd already edited to appear more regular in print."

"So far, I also write my odd songs mostly for myself and a few friends, maybe because my preceptor Frost also says they need more work. But if I die tomorrow, I hope any editors will publish my poems as I sang them."

Mabel pointed to the chest full of poems and smiled. "I know, but as you can see, Mrs. Bianchi will commit fraud if she claims her next collection of poems is *complete*."

"What if you were to publish the rest of yours?"

Her age showing, Mrs. Todd sighed. "I won't publish again until I'm sure we can avoid more embarrassment from Sue Dickinson's daughter."

Following Frost's instructions, I offered, "What if both sides agree to donate the original poems and letters you each possess to Amherst College?"

Mrs. Todd deflected the question. "Sue's daughter is only interested in getting the royalties on new editions of Emily's poems and speaking fees."

I looked inside the camphorwood chest again. "What's in the other tin?"

"Austin's letters, my diaries, and…" She paused and dropped her eyes.

I still couldn't fathom why her affair or the lawsuit over a strip of land, both buried for more than a generation with Austin, stopped Mabel from publishing the rest of Emily Dickinson's poems and letters. So I asked instead, "Well, then, can anyone else speak for you to challenge Madame Bianchi's claims about *her Aunt Emily*?"

"I've been in touch with Amy Lowell to see if she'll write a biography to tell the truth." I must have been unable to refrain from shaking my head because Mrs. Todd said, "You don't think that's a good idea?"

I phrased my response carefully and offered it with a bit of humor: "Like Frost, Miss Lowell's mostly about securing her own place in history, don't you think?"

"Yes, they're both pretty good campaigners, as was I before my stroke."

"How about *your* daughter?" While Mrs. Todd pondered that, I added, "Maybe it's also time to find a better place to keep these treasures safe." When she had to nod at that, I said, "I'm sure the College has the best facilities to preserve such important papers."

Mrs. Todd looked to the two metal boxes in the chest again and shook her head. She pulled one of the books out of a nearby crate. She opened it to the title page, *Poems of Emily Dickinson*, "edited by two of her friends." She took out a pen, scribbled a message, and handed the book to me. The cover included the embossed Indian pipe Mabel Todd had drawn for Emily Dickinson. I opened the book to the title page and read the note. *To Belle: Publish while you can for after you die only others can edit for you or destroy your poems as they please. Mabel Loomis Todd. Amherst, 1923*

"Recite one of your songs for me," she said. I said "Preceptor." "One more please." I sang "The Dowry and the Whore." She clapped. "A last one." I chanted my lament, "Dry Land." She closed the lid on the chest and locked the latch. "Belle, don't worry. Even if Sue Dickinson's daughter outlives me, I'll ask my daughter to deliver my originals to the College at an appropriate time."

As she closed the barn door behind us, I replied, "I'll ask my brother to get his mates to take Sabrina somewhere else so the search for the statue won't lead here."

I helped Mrs. Todd walk back to the Observatory House where she had built a new life with "The Astronomer" after moving on from editing Emily's poems. On my walk across town to Frost's rental, I reviewed my meetings with Mrs. Todd and Madame Bianchi. I didn't see how Amherst College could ever resolve the blood feud between two such headstrong and divided women and acquire the poet's originals from both sides.

At dinner that evening, Frost and my brother talked up a storm. Pip described how the rapid-fire camera he and David Todd built could operate from a plane flying above the clouds to capture the best images ever of the corona from a solar eclipse. He also explained how Mars might be too far from the sun to support life.

"Damn it," Frost said, "if Earth's the only planet that's the right distance from our sun, how are you going to find another orbiting any of the more distant stars?"

Pip explained how Bohr's lecture on atoms and Todd's pictures of the Sun's corona made him think all stars must burn continuously from huge explosions but that the voice of intelligent life carried by a radio signal would make a different sound.

"What hearing aid are you fixing to listen for voices, then?" Frost demanded.

Mrs. Frost interjected, "Enough. My head's spinning."

Robbie hushed her and asked Pip, "How much of what you're telling me results from your hearing inner voices as I do?"

Pip answered, "⅓ such imagination, ⅓ observation, and ⅓ cussedness." Pip nodded with a smile to the great poet: "Maybe roughly the same as your creations."

Frost turned to me. "What do you think?"

"You and Pip are both crazy enough to see miracles in the smallest drop of water or a single atom and in the biggest Great Lake or greater universe."

"Oh, pshaw," Frost retorted, "you're just trying to avoid a good argument." He looked to Mrs. Frost. "Is it okay if we leave it that Pip should look for signs of intelligent life in space, and I'll keep looking for signs of intelligent life here on Earth?"

"Yes," Mrs. Frost replied, "but don't you think Pip's odds may be better?"

Frost had to chuckle at that, but Pip said to Mrs. Frost, "Given that we scientists can't ever seem to agree on what we see, Mr. Frost's vision as a poet is likely keener."

Robbie nodded in triumph. "Belle, what did you learn from your meetings with the Dickinson-Bianchi and Todd camps?"

I first recited the wrongs Madame Bianchi felt the College had inflicted on the Dickinson family and the longer list of unearned favors she felt Amherst had bestowed on Mabel and David Todd. "Oh, I knew it," Frost exclaimed. "I'll advise President Olds to award Madame Bianchi an honorary degree to make amends for the insults and to offer a substantial sum for all the originals to make up for not buying the Dickinson Homestead." He rubbed his hands together.

Mrs. Frost looked at her husband. "Set a good precedent for honoring you, too."

Robbie couldn't help nodding at that. Before I could even begin to explain the greater difficulties with Mabel Todd's originals, he turned on me: "If you ever get a poem right, that's why you'll have to publish and campaign to sell and defend it yourself."

I managed only to say with as much sweetness as I could, "Any time you think my songs are near ready, Preceptor, will you let me know?"

"Why does every aspiring poet seek my help editing and publishing?"

"I'll search for my true voice to sing to please myself, then, thank you." I got up.

"Damn it, Belle," Frost shouted after me, "think of this game of poetry as an adventure, like diving off on one of your long swims in your cold Lake Michigan."

"Even in that deep water, you know I can't make it on my own."

As I retreated to my guestroom, Frost added, "Don't forget we're all invited for lunch with Bohr at the president's house tomorrow at noon."

Mrs. Frost followed shortly after. I sat on the bed, and she sat in the chair by the dresser. "Mr. Frost wouldn't say those things unless he believes you've got potential as a poet." When I didn't respond to this damning with faint praise, she lit into me: "Oh my, you poor young dear, don't you understand? You'll also have to grow a tough skin to get through all the readings and criticism." I wondered if Frost had enlisted his wife to gang up on me, but she must have seen me shaking my head because she added, "To get anywhere, you'll also need to find a partner to manage your schedule, listen to the slights, heal the hurts, and take care of your home and family."

She sighed and shook her head. "Some days I wish he'd never shared his poems with anyone but me. It's a trial losing him to his campaigning and all the other demands on him." When I didn't respond, she got up. At the door she stopped. "Maybe you are right to protect your privacy, but your arguments with Robert wear on me."

I couldn't help but nod at that. "I'm sorry, Mrs. Frost." I'd also worn out my welcome. "I very much appreciate your looking after Pip and hosting me, but I best be getting back to Michigan in the morning."

She stepped forward, gave me a hug and said, "Please call me Elinor." When I thanked her, she added, "Don't worry, Pip's going to shine here, too."

At first light I woke and headed back to Ann Arbor. As much as I was inspired by seeing, holding, and reading the original Dickinson poems, I wanted out of the blood feud between Mattie and Mabel over Emily's archives, and I surely didn't want to cause any more friction in the Frost family.

Good Lord, tell me I'm not as smitten by this older married man as Mabel Todd was by Austin Dickinson. For sure, I don't have her stomach for all the clandestine outings and other excess baggage. I'm more the ugly duckling, bound to be a homebody spinster, than the hummingbird, flitting to and fro from such an affair and then escaping by sailing around the world.

When I returned to Ann Arbor, a worse sight greeted me. Professor Strait stood at the head of my class in literary criticism. He leered at me as I sat down in the back. I tried to make my big self as small as possible. He explained how our instructor had been badly injured in a car wreck. Egad! Nym would be our substitute for the rest of the semester. He proceeded to wave a copy of *Henry V* in the air as if it were a prop. His bow tie bounced, and he strutted around as he read another scene involving Nym and Pistol. When the class mercifully ended, he said, "Miss Belle, see me in my office."

To avoid protesting at the ritual repeat of his earlier performance as he sat me down, rubbed against me, picked up his ruler, and started tapping, I clamped my teeth shut. I kept my eyes on him, even when he peered over his silly half-glasses to leer at me. I set my hands firmly on the shallow desk between us to fend him off. "Now, that the old bard's gone home to his little boys' college and Mr. O'Bannon's practicing with the men, how about we make a fresh start?" He reached out and tapped his ruler on my right hand, first softly, then more urgently. I folded my hands on my lap. He set the ruler on the table and opened a notebook. "I see you've already missed six classes and handed in two papers late." He lifted his eyes and said, "Miss Belle, one more absence or late assignment, and I'll flunk you, is that understood?"

"No." I stood up. "I have to drop this class now—" He rapped the ruler on the desk. "—now that I have to help train Gertrude Ederle for the Olympics in the Union pool. It's only available to us women in the morning, when this class is scheduled."

As I turned to leave, he tapped his ruler on my rear. I stood stock still at the shock. "If you stop foisting your Up North doggerel on Mr. O'Bannon and playing house with him, he might even qualify to teach here, albeit only in the Rhetoric Department."

I turned back, stood tall, and threw my shoulders back. "I suppose you think he should stop his creative writing with Professor Cowden, too." Rather than answer, his beady eyes bugged out, looking me all over. "Nym, I hope Rabbie won't ever have to listen to you mock Shakespeare's verse with your petty villains and pompous bull."

As I left, he sputtered, "Cowden better stick to his Diction and Usage, too."

Thankfully, Trudy Ederle proved a charm. Already harder of hearing than Pip, she shared his determined wonder of discovery. A big, New York City gal, she still enjoyed our smaller town, the short trolley rides to the Union for our early morning workouts and to the Majestic for shows, our drives out Lake Road to St. Patrick's and back to town for sundaes. Even at 17, she was a hit at the frat parties and danced the night away at Barbour Gym balls. I usually begged off and let Rabbie escort her. When Trudy left for Thanksgiving, I was glad I missed her more than he did.

One thing was certain when she returned in early December. Although fast in the sprints, Trudy and Rabbie would have to train even harder for the next five months and swim their best to qualify for the Olympics. Coach Mann wisely pitted them against the big bull of a freshman, Paul Samson, to improve their times.

I'd sent the Frosts a thank-you note for hosting me, but I didn't expect to hear back. Pip's first letter described how he'd managed a midnight heist of Sabrina: *We unveiled her on top of the Octagon at the entrance to the College to give the Class of '24 what for: Case closed!* Subsequent letters described his observing through the big refracting telescope, tinkering with his designs for "huge hearing aids" to capture radio waves, and, since November, skating with the hockey team and studying how the pipes under the outdoor arena froze the ice. He also shared that he'd *met a terrific townie from Amherst High, even if she's too fast for me*. Pip's last letter asked,

> *What spell did you cast over the captain of the hockey team? The Alpha's rushing me so hard, he says I'm to take his place on the ice and at his fraternity house. I'd prefer to join Drew, but I guess I'm not welcome there any more than he is at Chi Phi. I don't understand why Indians and Negroes are viewed as so different from us, when Charles showed me how we all bleed the same color.*

Late in the afternoon on November 20, a package arrived at the doorstep of my Cambridge House. From the stubby-penciled lettering, I knew it was from Robbie. I ripped off the paper and found a copy of New Hampshire, with all the handsome woodcuts illustrating the title poem, notes, and grace notes. An envelope stuck out from the fourth page. I opened the book and saw Frost's dedication, "To Vermont and Michigan." He'd scrawled below in his stubby hand, *Belle, You and Burton are the reason for Michigan: This New Hampshire's dedicated to you. Your erstwhile Preceptor.*

I opened the envelope and pulled out the note:

> *My second Belle,*
> *I find I got a good deal more Ann Arboreal than I suppose I should have at my age. Don't be surprised if I show up at Michigan next fall.*
>
> *Pip and Bohr got me thinking. Apparently individual atomic particles fly into a screen such, you can't tell when and where any one will land, but the pattern the whole mass makes, you can predict. Just like us, the individual flies where and when it will, but the great mass still moves, whether forward or back, at our predictably slow snail's pace. Such uncommon sense*

might persuade me to drop my quarrel with the scientists and English Profs whose diktats ruin most colleges.

Please be our houseguest here the third week in December when you drive to take Pip back home for the long holiday. I promise not to be so ornery. We've also got more work with President Olds on the Dickinson-Todd feud. He's prepared to offer Sue Dickinson's daughter a degree and a tidy sum to buy Emily's poems and letters. We now need your advice on Mrs. Todd's collection.

Robbie

I called Stella, and she told me Dean Bursley had found the money for President Burton to offer Frost a lifetime appointment. As "Permanent Fellow in the Creative Arts," he'd be responsible for only one seminar. My Rabbie further complicated matters. After I visited Papa up north and he returned to the Queen's grip, he'd been distant. He didn't spend nights with me because he needed to study for some "big" exam, but I didn't want to miss my chance with him. So I wrote Pip and told him to take the train home.

Yet I still owed Frost a letter, and I didn't want to discourage him from accepting Michigan's offer. Amherst's prestige and money could still talk. After all, the College's own Calvin Coolidge was now President of the United States. I wrote Robbie:

This particle's stuck in Ann Arbor and will miss visiting you and Mrs. Frost. Pip will have to take the train home. I also don't want to get in the middle between Madame Bianchi and Mabel Todd. For what it may be worth to you, though, Mabel loves the College, but she's hidden things in two locked boxes in her trove that prevent her from parting with her cache. As determined as Madame Bianchi is to capture Emily's legacy solely for the Dickinson heirs, she'll never give up her originals as long as Mrs. Todd or her daughter pose any threat. Looks like an impasse, but you and President Olds will know better than I ever will.

Rumors swirl here that our President Burton's going to woo you back to our fairer arbor, for life. I can't promise any botanizing, but your Frost Bites still sell well, and your new book's dedication to Michigan assures not only greater sales, acclaim, and fortune here, but also a long line of college lasses (and lads) who will want to serve your every beck and call. Don't let my presence here give you and yours an excuse to stay there.

Despite Rabbie's continued distance over the next two weeks, I was feeling pretty proud of myself until I got Frost's reply:

Miss Belle,
I had the pleasure of taking Pip and his new girl to dinner last night. Rachel Goldberg is as short as he is tall, as ripe as he is lanky, and as pert and demonstrative as he is reserved and dreamy. I advise you to drive out here and take him if you want him to come there for Christmas.

Pip has won Mrs. Frost, and she insists that you stay with us as long as you wish to rest up for your long drive back with Pip. You need have no worries about your reception here, and I promise not to argue with you over keeping your songs to yourself.

I shared your letter with President Olds, and he's decided to talk with Mrs. Todd to see for himself. When you come to rescue Pip, we can meet with old Olds to explore what else can be done. That way we won't have to upset Elinor with any more talk about archives and the College.
Frost

I was so mad: How dare Frost share with President Olds my personal letter bowing out of any battle over Emily Dickinson's archives.

Driven by ambition to be the best poet of all, was Frost setting up another chip for bargaining with the College? Worst of all, truth be told, I didn't see how my University stood a chance of winning Frost back from Amherst.

Fortunately, with a rush of emotion, I thought I knew where to turn: Rabbie's distance made me miss him all the more, and I vowed to ask the last of the O'Bannon clan to marry me. The Queen be damned, my true love was going to make the Olympic team and have a brilliant career as a professor and writer. With Pip no longer needing me as his Marmie, I wanted to bear and mother Rabbie's children, support our family in my two Arbors, and compose new poems for my babies and me.

That evening, however, I felt a different song welling up:

Chanteuse Lament

Lovely little nightingale
in the willow above the pond
pining for her two true loves:

a graceful gliding basso swan—
plumage like white silk against the night—
sentinel to his aging mate

and that plucky meadowlark—
weaving among clover and Queen Anne's Lace—
twilling his seductive song.

She warbles of thwarted Love
until she can no longer sing—
then, she takes to Wing.

The next morning the postman dropped off a brief letter from Pip. He wrote he was having a great time with Rachel but he'd take the train to Ann Arbor; we could drive up north for Christmas with Papa and his Miss. Pip closed by noting *the poor daft Professor Todd had to be taken back to his asylum after he made an advance on a tenth grade girl at Amherst High*. I wondered if Ned Strait would ever be forced to accept such a fate. Probably not: He was too discreet, pressing himself on his coed students only behind closed doors and spreading his ugly rumors through a pseudonym.

Later that afternoon I sat on the couch in the living room of my Cambridge House, watching the flames dancing in the fireplace. Rabbie and Trudy wouldn't arrive from swimming for an hour, so I pondered how the feud Mabel Todd and Madame Bianchi had over the Dickinson legacy would ever work out. Rabbie's familiar knock on the back door interrupted. As he entered, I blurted, "Where's Trudy?"

"I skipped practice this afternoon." He looked flush and huffed, as if he'd run all the way from campus in the thick snow. He ripped his boots off and bade me sit next to him. He held my hand gently and said, "I'm going, Belle."

"You've worked hard and earned your trip to the Olympics in Paris, and you're taking your Little Singers of the Wooden Cross to perform at Notre Dame!"

Rabbie laughed and shook his head, his shock of black hair and dark eyes dancing in the firelight, and he told me how he'd won a Rhodes Scholarship to study at Oxford. Struck dumb, I heard him add, "No matter what happens with the Olympics, we can marry this spring, honeymoon in Ireland and Scotland for a month, and live in Oxford for the next three years!"

The pain in my stomach spread to my chest, so I could only parry: "What's the Queen say?"

"Belle, I want you to help me raise our children Catholic."

"What if I want to raise our children Presbyterian?" Why couldn't I just say yes after all my resolve to ask him to marry me?

Rabbie got up, pulled a bottle of Jameson's Irish whiskey from his overcoat, and poured us each a glass. "To us, Belle: We can make this work."

Trudy popped in the front door, rushed up to him, and exclaimed, "First Phi Beta Kappa, now a Rhodes, next an American record in the 50 and the Olympics!" Why hadn't I said that to my Rabbie? She yelled at me in her too-loud voice, "Aren't you excited for him!?"

I took a closer look at our house guest. Almost as tall as me, her shoulders hunched to hide her bigger body. Yet her enthusiasm lit her plain face up as a gawky teenager growing into maturing young woman of real substance. If she cut her hair in a pert bob, her infectious good cheer could turn any head, including my Rabbie's.

He offered Trudy an Irish whiskey, but she poured herself a glass of water and raised her glass. "A toast to Michigan's conquering hero!'" After a brief celebration, Rabbie excused himself with a peck to my cheek and a punch to her shoulder. Trudy slid close on the couch. "After the Olympics I'm going to need more support."

"Are you Catholic?"

"I can't hear you. Speak up."

So I yelled the question at her.

When she nodded, I wondered whether she wanted me to release my Rabbie to her, but Trudy pressed on: "Will you help me show the world that a woman can swim better than any man after I win in Paris?" I swear she almost jumped in my lap: "Lend me the money so I can train to become the first woman to swim the English Channel." I sat there, stunned. "There'll be a ticker-tape parade down Broadway, movie and book deals, a tour with Johnny Weissmuller… and I'll pay you back. I promise."

I heard myself answer, "Let's show 'em, Trudy." When she hugged me, I added, "The Women's Swimming Association won't refuse my donation for you."

"Belle," she whispered, "do you ever get the feeling that the sea is a like a friend you've known all your life?" When I didn't respond, she continued, "When I swim, I never feel alone in the water. I talk to it."

"When I swim," I replied, "the water's my blue salvation, a mother that buoys me up and never lets me down and a lover that holds me close and never says goodbye."

Alone in my bed that night, approaching my 24th birthday, I pondered the fork in the road ahead and sang a song for my journal:

True North

I am guided
by an inner Pole Star
to Leelanau—

and though I stretch
like a compass arm
to know the world beyond—

I cannot break
its grip—on me—
or on my Heart!

I was too much a homebody to chase Rabbie across the Atlantic, no matter how much I wanted him to marry me. Whether separated by place, religion, heritage, age, my phobias, or another woman, I couldn't join him any more than David or Robbie could ever join me.

Winter 1926: Glen Arbor and Ann Arbor

We sat low in the sand. Our backs rested against a driftwood stump. Only our heads peered over the shallow bowl and between the beech, birch, and pines to the bay, frozen all the way to North and South Manitou. As the winter sun began to set early in the afternoon, the bay's blue-white ice faded to pale pink and then the gray of dusk. The campfire warmed us against the northwest wind howling through the passage, and the Leelanau eagle on the front of the birch box in the tree watched over David Ahgosa and me. Pip's grinding, filing, and hammering inside the new observatory dome serenaded us.

David wanted to leave Papa's stove works in Empire and start his own business in his native home. He'd moonlighted at D. H. Day's orchards and cannery in Glen Haven and wanted to grow cherry trees and run a fruit business with his dwindling tribe on their land near Omena. "Have you saved enough to survive until you can start selling?" I asked. He shook his head. "Do you have any partners to invest in making jellies, cobblers, and pies?" He shook his head. "What about the Days?"

"I'm quit with them: Sven tried to bully me into helping him convert old Fords into dune buggies." With pride he added, "I got up every time he knocked me down."

Seeing his swollen black eyes and bruised chin, I wanted to scream but asked only, "What happened to Day Estates since D. H. brought in the Chicago money?"

"No more lots sold." His grin revealed a tooth chipped from his bout with the big brute. Marketed as "America's Premier Resort Community, Estates Ideally Restricted to Caucasians and Gentiles only," Alligator Hill wasn't ever going to be any exclusive Harbor Springs. As if reading my mind, he vowed, "I will make a thriving home for my kin. The treaties of '36 and '55 stole our traditional lands and sent us to our new home: Ahgosatown is where our Ojibwe Band will rise again."

"Should I call you Chief?" I blurted.

"No, only the Ogemaw for our extended Ahgosa clan." He raised his dark eyes. "In the fall of '28, when Spring Blossom turns 18, we're getting married."

My mind raced in so many directions, but I willed myself not to protest. After several false starts, beginning to say more than I should, and a few more stumbles, thinking through what I could say, I made my offer to this willful Ojibwe. If David agreed to work for five more years at the stove works, I'd lend him the money now to purchase more land and to plant and cultivate more fruit orchards for his band. If David agreed to work at the stove works for another five years after that, I'd lend more money to finance a warehouse and plant to make jellies, juice, and pies. Both loans would include a schedule of payments to pay down the principal over 20 years, a mortgage on the land, buildings and equipment to secure the loans. Finally, I offered to include in the loans the cost of paying for the services of my classmate at the Business School to advise him on his family business.

"Who?" David asked. I told him about my learning at UM with

Kurt Knutsen and how I hoped he'd become my business partner up north. "What about Rabbie?"

"He's still recovering in a sanitarium in Switzerland."

"You paying for that, too?"

I lowered my eyes as I shook my head. Eventually, I peeked up. His dark eyes still searched mine. "Maybe our religious differences split us, as the divisions between us latecomers and your original people split Estelle and you."

His gaze did not waver. "I can't give you a mortgage on the land."

I remembered his pain at his forbears' bad land dealings. "Going to buy back the land your forbears sold to white men and then some?" He nodded. "Okay, if you fall six months behind on your payments, then I get to appoint a new CEO, and we'll split all profits. Whatever the results, you'll own your land and business free and clear at the end of 25 years."

"I'll make sure I never give you cause to replace me."

Although we now had a deal, I felt empty, as if our business arrangement stood as a barrier to our, what, friendship or more? He looked up to the magical bird on the front side of his birch box in the tree above. With the northwest wind whistling through the pine and the light from the campfire flickering on his dark face, he asked, "Do you see the watcher?" I looked up and admired the strong visage, sharp eyes, high cheeks, square shoulders, and proud chest of the eagle. "I imagined you when I made her, keen sight, healing powers, truth teller."

"No unruly red hair, though."

With a nod he smiled, but I felt the sting of his touch as his gentle fingers graced my cheek. "If you're willing, we can work together to preserve this place as I make amends and help my band rebuild." He extended his hand again, but I brushed it aside and embraced him. Night fell quickly, and David held me close as we huddled together by the campfire in the shelter of the hollow in the dune and the longer vision of his eagle on the birch box, watching over us. I touched his puffy eyes and felt his tears.

"Come see," Pip yelled from the door to his observatory. We gathered ourselves, walked up, and saw a shutter cleverly mounted on a track that moved a window around the dome in synch with the telescope. It kept the cold out in winter and the flies out in summer. David and I took turns looking through the 14-inch reflector at the surface of what appeared to be only a small part of a huge planet. The lens focused on a big scar that grew before our eyes. When I stepped back, Pip nodded triumphantly and said, "We're watching a comet crash into Jupiter."

I shook my head, whether in wonder or disbelief. "What would that do to earth?"

He snapped his fingers: "One good-size meteorite blasted a 100-mile-wide crater in Mexico and wiped out the dinosaurs for thousands of miles around."

David shook his head but, with a nod to me, said to Pip, "We need you to help us conserve our special Leelanau place." When Pip looked puzzled, David explained how old King David's empire was already beginning to falter, not just the lumbering but also the golf course, lots on Alligator Hill, and soon his farm. "His son-in-law doesn't share D.H.'s regard for nature. He's bent on growing tourism by racing cars across the dune to overrun our Sleeping Mama Bear."

David then turned to me. "We also have much work to clean up the stove works." Although I knew, I hadn't admitted it. He laughed at my guilty look.

But Pip answered, "Cutting back on all the scrap at the factory was a good start."

David and Pip proceeded to make a list of how they'd shift all our boilers, forges, and generators from dirty coal, wood, or oil to cleaner, more efficient, and less expensive natural gas.

It hit me then: "America's Flame," I blurted. I had to work with Kurt to figure out how to make this our trademark to sell future products from our Empire enterprise.

"Let's also enlist the Bealses and their campers in conservation," Pip said.

"Help me with your tinkering so my dwindling band can once again prosper."

"Help me build an ear trumpet on Empire Bluff to listen for voices in space."

I couldn't help but support both my boys' dreams. Even if David were to marry his betrothed in too few years, I'd never be able to wean myself from him either.

ɞ

When I returned to Ann Arbor in mid-January, Frost's letter greeted me:

> *Miss Belle,*
> *I return at the end of the month. Sickness and scatter in my family continues, but not much I can do about it and I'm too old to go back to farming. All the years of my versifying, teaching, and campaigning have taken a heavy toll on us. Join me for lunch at One-O every afternoon. I need your help for my next book.*

His request caught me off guard. Our great President Burton had died too young in February of 1925, after he fell ill nominating President Coolidge for re-election at the Republican Convention and never fully recovered. I had dragged myself back from my long leave up north that May to bear witness at the memorial service. Frost, Michigan's soon-to-be Permanent Fellow in Creative Arts, gave the eulogy for Burton to a packed house at Hill Auditorium. Many of the academic pedants looked down on Frost and thought his folksy talk on learning and teaching was a lot more about the poet's than Burton's views. But I thought that was the highest compliment Robbie could pay any person, dead or alive, as the two, born in the same year, were remarkably kindred spirits on the subject. How else explain the warm but brief visit of Frost to Ann Arbor in the spring of 1924 for two readings that led to Burton sealing Frost's permanent return to Michigan that fall? Yet Frost begged off starting his fellowship here in order to stay at Amherst for the 1924–25 school year anyway.

Twelve months late, Frost had finally shown up in Ann Arbor in the fall of '25. Although he basked in the accolades from the locals for the Pulitzer Prize book he'd dedicated to Michigan, Elinor made him rent a house on the far side of the Huron River so he could concentrate on composing. He did join a meeting of the new student literary magazine, *The Inlander*, but stood largely aloof from campus life, even after Elinor returned to Vermont to care for poor Marjorie, sick again. Murmurs, no doubt spread by the academic pedants of Strait's ilk, suggested that the new President Little wouldn't put up with Frost's ways.

I read on. *I'm feeling mighty guilty about my duty to our late president to teach one poetry seminar to earn my year's keep. What with all my other obligations, I hope you'll sign up and help get the Three Graces to join us.* He meant his three favorite coeds after Stella graduated and I transferred to the new Business School rather than face Strait again on my return to Ann Arbor. Frost continued: *I tired of having to read bad poems of juvenile boys for a living and hope to see my favorite girls again. I must also admit I miss hearing your up-north tunes, even if not yet in good form.* This unexpected bittersweet bark from my erstwhile preceptor almost made me puff up.

Not for long, though, as the bard hit me with his two closing lines: *Besides, Cowden tells me your participation in my seminar will finally give you enough credits to graduate with a B.A. in creative writing. Whatever else, that should make it worth your while!* For someone who dropped out of Dartmouth and Harvard, Frost wasn't one to talk. Bad enough that Madame Bianchi's new books, *Complete Poems of Emily Dickinson* and *Life and Letters*, were incomplete and over-edited and foisted Mattie's family gossip about what caused her aunt to become a recluse. Worse that he should add an exclamation point to mock Emily Dickinson and me. Why, the old curmudgeon had no idea why I'd dropped English for Business.

He signed off *Robbie*, but I knew he just wanted to make sure I'd start by preparing at least one decent meal a day, lunch, fix his pot of afternoon tea, do his typing and scheduling, and listen to his bark until there was nothing to do but fix dinner, too. Then he'd shoo me out so he could write all night. Yet all my classes at the Business School did end by noon, and I no longer had the will to swim all afternoon.

Frost included his final review of Amy Lowell, dead at 51. His postscript read:

> *Without Miss Lowell's early reviews of my two books from England, I might still be waiting to launch my career on this side of the pond. How did I repay her? I gave her the respect of my criticism and never stooped to publish an anonymous screed mocking her, as she did me. Do you think the attached fails to grant her poetry its full due? I hope not, but whoever knows?*

As I pondered this question while reading his review, a knock on the front door startled me. I looked through the peephole and saw the big chest pushing through the opening of the big raccoon overcoat, rumpled double-breasted suit, and wrinkled white shirt, no tie. I opened the door and said, "Happy New Year, Teddy." My odd freshman hulk of a friend shambled in, threw his fur coat on the couch, and slumped down.

"Got one of your single-malt Scotches?" Theodore Roethke rasped from his insolent slouch. He already reeked of bootleg hooch from the silver flask he stuffed in one of his many pockets, along with books, journals, paper, a green pen, and snacks.

"How about you take a dip in the pool to sober up and get rid of your stench?"

He gave me whatever he thought must have been his most appealing leer and said, "Only if you strip and join me in the hothouse, Big Mama."

I had to laugh. At six-foot-two, with large upper body, mass of unkempt light brown hair, outlandish garb, and expensive Johnston & Murphy shoes to match, he looked the caricature of a Chicago gangster. Yet he was just a lonely boy, angry that his father died too young to allow him to take over a large set of floral greenhouses, one bigger than three football fields, with a total of more than a quarter million square feet under glass. The first in his family to go to college, Roethke tried to fit into our big university by distinguishing himself as above it all, but he pledged Chi Phi to find a safe place in which to hide and, at odd hours, study to play and win the game of college.

He landed in my backyard in response to my ad to help complete my new pool and take care of the grounds. With no partner to save me swimming lengths across Whitmore Lake anymore and less interest in sneaking in for an hour at the men's pools at the Union or the YMCA, I'd taken the plunge at Cambridge House instead. Unfortunately, the contractor went out of business before finishing the decking and garden around the two narrow lanes, 75 feet long, between the house and the garage with Pip's vacant quarters above.

Roethke looked such a big bear of a boy the first time he came to the door and introduced himself, I couldn't resist hiring him and calling him "Teddy." He got me back two weeks later. He strode onto the tennis court with shorts that revealed two legs so spindly I couldn't see how they could carry his big body, but he hit tennis balls across the net harder and with fewer errors than I did. Of course, the one time I managed to split sets all fall, he broke his racquet on the net-post and walked off. When he learned my brother still called me "Marmie," he dubbed me "Big Mama."

Teddy was worth the aggravation. He finished the decking and built a big glass house to cover it. He added flowers inside, in beds by the house and in big pots around the deck. The winter sun beating through the south-facing glass heated the water in the pool to 65 degrees on a sunny day. Cranking the windows open in summer to the cool drafts under the big elms would hold the water under 75. Lying in a chaise on the deck or swimming in the pool with the fragrant flowers all around felt like escaping to my Garden of Eden. So far, I hadn't gone swimming with Teddy.

Despite appearing as if he caroused day and night, Roethke made time to study every afternoon from three to six, when no one else could suspect him. He also wrote, fiercely, about how the war between his father and uncle over running their greenhouse killed both and the business; tenderly, about flowers, trees, wildlife, and the smallest spark of life in nature; descriptively, with an eye for the telling detail, personal example, and insightful metaphor, even about the contributions of the Junior Red Cross in his hometown. Although his tough-guy bluster didn't admit it, he also was a real Presbyterian, a graduate of Alma's summer Bible study program.

"Teddy," I replied, "I'm not a reliable lifeguard for drunken sailors."

"Drive me to Lefty's instead?" He'd roped me into chauffeuring him to this speakeasy on the Detroit River once before, but not even the Canadian Club the bootleggers raced in speedboats from the Hiram Walker distillery to avoid the T-Men could make up for the smoke, hubbub, gangsters, broads, and bouncers. I shook my head.

All of a sudden he looked as helpless and forlorn as the big, lost boy he was. I couldn't help sitting down next to him and stroking the back of his head. "Teddy, what's the matter?"

There followed the strangest story I ever heard. He said he'd gone back to Saginaw for the long Christmas holiday to work in the pickle plant to earn enough money to keep up his act here for the second semester. He worked the 12-hour night shift with six other misfits, one an old Negro, "Big Whack." The two became friends sharing their flasks of Old Crow on breaks in the darkest corners and coldest hours of the night. On the job they took turns walking around the narrow deck atop the big vats and stirring the pickles with big oars while leaning over the safety railing. When Teddy showed up for work one evening, Big Whack had gone missing. Ted finally convinced the police to conduct a search, but no one knew where the old man had run off to.

"This morning I told the cops Big Whack wouldn't have volunteered to leave a paycheck behind. That's when the boss agreed to drain the vats. This afternoon they found his body." A sob interrupted his story. I hugged the big lug, and he managed to say in a hoarse whisper, "The sight of his body—his skin, his nose, ears, and mouth—already pickled was too much."

I couldn't help holding him close now, cradling his head on my shoulder. Damned if he didn't try to bury his face in my bosom below. "Teddy?" No answer, he nuzzled my too responsive breasts. I pushed him away and said, "Theodore Roethke, you made that story up, didn't you?" He lifted his head and shook it, no shame on his face, but the hint of a smile gave him away. "When did this happen?"

"Last summer," he admitted. "Pickle factory closed for the season come fall." A sheepish show of teeth divided the plain bottom of his face from the more attractive top.

"Do you know how to type?"

"Can't even hunt and peck."

"If you can help me with Robert Frost's scheduling, I'll get you into his creative writing seminar." You'd have thought I'd promised to spoon with him. He rose, picked me up, set me down on the floor, and began dancing. I got to enjoying his Foxtrot so much I almost forgot myself. Eventually, I managed to ask, "How old are you?"

He stopped, held me at arm's length and admitted, "Eighteen… almost, and I haven't ever written a poem."

I stared in disbelief and shook my head. Half again his age, I didn't know how to let the poor boy down. I took his hand and led him to our glass house. "Teddy," I said, "keep your drawers on yourself and your hands off me in the pool." Surprisingly, he didn't violate either command after we jumped in. Nor did he fake a drowning to get me grappling either. Then again, it would have been hard for a six-foot-two-inch body with that big a chest to fool even as gullible a soul as me in water only five feet deep. This was another boy I was meant to mother, not marry.

After we got dried off, he said as he left, "The Rhetoric and English classes here seek to deaden all interest in writing, so I'm game to try something different with Frost and you." Oh, how I knew what Ted felt!

ꝏ

I woke early the next morning in a cold sweat from my recurring nightmare: *The insistent rap on the window below, the beady eyes peering over his half-glasses down his nose at me. I rose and raised the lower window sash to shoo Nym away, but he held out a bottle of Talisker as if the key to my den. Why I opened the front door, I don't know—maybe it was the fever that was the first sign of my long grippe—but he entered my study, shut the door and window behind him, took down two glasses, and poured us each a double shot. I tried to retreat to the big chair behind the desk, but he steered me to the chair in the corner facing him. He said he came to apologize and persuade me not to transfer to the new Business School. He said he knew I'd missed Rabbie heading off to the Olympics and then Oxford, but I was the most gifted of all the English majors. "If you'll let me tutor you as my doctoral student, I'll help you become the first woman on the Literature faculty." He poured another double and toasted me. All I could focus on was the single hair twitching in its mole at the corner of his mouth as he leaned his face toward me. Only when I felt his lips pressing against mine, that single hard blade scratching away, did I awake again, screaming at Strait to leave.*

After the better part of a year retreating up north to try to recover from repeated bouts with flu and to repress this bad dream did I begin to stop being afraid to fall asleep. I told only Miss Schultz about Nym's attack and my nightmares. She did her best to console me, and I confided I stopped his assault by cracking a bottle of Talisker over his head. "That dirty little man's not worth your wasting good Scotch or any more of your time." I conceded that I was ready to go back to Ann Arbor in the fall of 1925, but only as a transfer to the Business School. She nodded but said, "Just don't let Nym stop you from composing poems while you're learning how to help run your family Empire."

That afternoon Kurt Knutsen, all five foot, eight inches and 145 pounds dripping wet, sat in a deck chair by the pool. A second-generation Dane, he'd grown up in the tough textile district of New York City and learned to survive despite his boyish blond good looks by keeping his mouth shut, avoiding fights, and melding his smaller body into the larger crowd. He enrolled at Michigan to learn business so he could return to New York as a financial whiz and earn enough to shut the bullies up. In Ann Arbor he grew a short-trimmed mustache, slicked down his hair, put on horn-rimmed glasses, and wore trim, navy blue pinstripe suits with a regimental tie.

After watching him strut his stuff the first few weeks at the Business School, I made different plans for him. I wanted him to partner with me to run our Empire enterprise and take it to new heights. First, I had to find a way to make it worth his while to stick around until I could persuade Papa that Kurt was our man.

Fortunately, we soon became the odd but inseparable study pair: the big, plain bird with red hair, afraid to say a word in class, and the dapper little blond dynamo, chirping away to encourage the rest of us. Tappan Hall, named in honor of Michigan's first president, was a stately, old, red brick building. It sat back from South U between Alumni Hall and the President's House. Kurt made it my new nest so I could fledge from Ned Strait and his ilk. My partner developed the best head for numbers, risk and reward, and management and organization, while I learned to apply my odd flair with observation and words to marketing and advertising. I loved studying the cases compared to the stuffy rhetoric, criticism, and literature classes. Kurt peppering me with ideas, questions, and suggestions made it easy for me to forgo the few credits I needed to earn my B.A., if not to forget Rabbie O'Bannon and my need to bury Nym.

While I lounged in slacks and a sweater by the pool, Kurt wore the business attire that I never could get him to take off. Nevertheless, I wasn't going to let him fly away as I had Rabbie. "Coach Mann's bringing Trudy Ederle over to explore how we can help her swim the English Channel and capitalize on her fame." I explained how Trudy had failed in her first attempt last summer. She'd fired the trainer who, unaccountably, pulled her out with only a mile to go; then she fired her manager after she found out he'd planned to steal much of the money she'd have earned. Having won a gold and two bronze medals at the 1924 Olympics, and set dozens of U.S. and world records, the girl was already a sensation. Her failed attempt at the English Channel last summer only raised the stakes for her second try. "Will you make Trudy your first client?"

"I can't believe you're conspiring to get me to move back to New York City."

"I've already got your next assignments, all up north."

"Taking me in as your partner?"

"To help Trudy, I'll pay you a salary and donate my insights." I then explained my plan: he'd find the support so Ederle would have everything she needed to swim the Channel, but we needed to protect our 19-year-old from burning herself out touring the world thereafter. "We need to make her a national icon instead."

"You don't think she's got the glamour for showbiz?"

I explained her youthful enthusiasms, difficulty hearing, and fear of answering questions in public and how we could help her instead become the symbol for our Empire, "America's Flame, the woman every man and woman admires."

"Good, then let's tout Trudy Ederle as The Spirit of America for her crossing."

"In addition to helping run our family business, will you help my brother and our best friend build a golf course and a cherry business up north?" Before he could answer, the loud knock on the front door signaled Trudy's arrival.

The following Monday Teddy and I showed up at Frost's gull-winged, white clapboard Greek Revival on Pontiac Trail at the stroke of One-O in the afternoon. Frost greeted me with his puckish grin. "Who's this bear?" he asked as he gazed at Roethke's unusual costume, bulk, and face and avoided shaking the big brute's hand.

"I'm Theodore Roethke, Mr. Frost, Class of '29. I hope my helping you helps me decide whether I should consider writing as a career."

"Can you type?" Frost asked. Teddy slowly shook his head, and his raccoon coat, several sizes too big, swayed with him. "Can you cook?" Teddy's head and body didn't stop swaying. Frost turned to me and complained, "Haven't you gotten Rabbie back yet?" When I shook my head, Frost said, "Belle, we don't need a Frosh."

"I'll do the typing, poem-work, and cooking," I answered, "and he'll help organize your schedule and travel." When Frost gave me one of his doubtful frowns, I added, "He's so handy he built me a glasshouse over the swimming pool in my backyard, and he can fix your furnace so there won't be any more fires."

Even Frost had to smile at my reference to his run-in with his first landlord in Ann Arbor, the widow D'Ooge. "If you'll let me paddle in your pool, I'll let this big Teddy Bear tag along, so long as he doesn't make a mess here."

"If he's out of here by two, will you admit him to your seminar?"

"I suppose he's never written a single poem."

Teddy's swaying continued, but his brash tough-guy mask fell with his face. "Don't worry," I said, "the Three Graces and I signed up with him."

Frost reluctantly edged his hand out, but Teddy grabbed it and wouldn't let go until the aging poet said, "Uncle." They'd get along fine.

After light lunch and conversation, Frost complained to Roethke about the large stack of requests on the table. Eventually, Teddy arranged three piles: a big stack for *No, thank you* replies through the summer, a stack of *Maybes* for next fall, and only one *Yes*, another honorary degree. "You'd think Michigan would have offered this Pulitzer poet a doctoral degree after my eulogy for Burton and accepting this lifetime position."

"The Master of Arts wasn't enough?" I said.

"Dartmouth's offering to put a doctorate on top of their M.A." Frost made a sour face. "Can you believe that the new Little President's wife asked me to work with her poetry group?" He put on his best puckish grin and added, "Why, that would *Rob* all the Creative Arts from this Permanent Fellow!"

"Couldn't be worse than the English classes here," Teddy said. "By the end of the first semester, Professor Strait had beaten all love for writing out of me."

"You'll enjoy my seminar then, Mr. Roethke," Frost said. "I promise I won't do any teaching if you start writing again."

Only then did I explain how Strait and his crowd of pedants were the reason I transferred to the Business School. The great poet nodded but said, "Some days a third person will join us here, for odd jobs, conversation, or botanizing. He grew up poor, also quit school, supported himself living in the Canadian wilderness, and has written several promising poems. He wants to hone his rough-hewn, northern voice with me."

"Is he a freshman, too?" Teddy asked.

"No reason to subject him to getting Strait-jacketed by the rhetoric and criticism crowds here." He paused. "Be good to Van Dore, okay? I don't want any mistaken college airs ruining his rural tune."

Teddy said his goodbye, and Robbie put me to work typing new poems. The first one, he said, "will be my contribution to President Burton's memory." Mistaking my headshake as wondering why he hadn't also talked about helping hone my up-north voice, he explained, "Long before the Little President raises the money to build a bell tower to honor Big Burton, my 'luminary clock' will be published."

So I finished "Acquainted with the Night."

He asked, "You going to contribute to the bricks-and-mortar memorial?"

"I don't see the relevance, since you know your one luminary clock at an unearthly height against the sky isn't any bell tower, but the moon." When he nodded sheepishly, I hit back: "I already persuaded other donors to match my gift so Mrs. Burton can live with his memory without having to beg." That brought Frost up short. So I asked, "Compared to 'One-O's' commentary ending with musings on naysayers like Hussey dragging us all down, why so much more personal in your poem about battling the Black Dog here?"

"The new book's going to be about the contraries, the small fights we each can make to spark a little life amidst the inevitable dark. You know, whatever happens, my poem says it right: Our short time on this earth is 'neither right nor wrong.'"

His tone hinted at something more but I couldn't tell if he was worried about dying young like President Burton and Amy Lowell or something else. So I asked, "How are Mrs. Frost and Marjorie doing?"

"I'm still working to provide for them, even if it kills me, all right?"

He began to pick up his handwritten drafts as if to dismiss me, but I held fast to the longest one, "The Lovely Shall Be Choosers."

As I read it aloud, Frost calmed down. When I finished, he said, "At long last my ode to my Mama Belle. What do you think?"

I thought it as inadequate as his answer to my question about the recovery of his wife and daughter. "You need to hold it awhile…" I began.

His puckish smile appeared, and he finished, "…and deepen it, deepen it."

"Robbie, I'm serious. You need to get beyond all the contraries and say your goodbye to your mother."

"Still working on yours?" When I nodded, he sat down across the kitchen table and clasped his big hands together. His thick fingers intertwined to form a roof, and he pressed his big thumbs together as if to enter through the door into the church. "The strike to Marjorie's heart and lungs isn't going to kill her, but I don't know if she'll ever…" He unclasped his fingers and thumbs so the tips touched and formed the interior ribbing inside the cathedral. "Elinor will never be the same." I didn't know what to say, so I placed my hands over his. "It's not just Marjorie's illness, Irma's mind never being quite right, Lesley's wanderlust, and Carol's always beating himself up." He paused. "I've worn Elinor out, too." I remembered my conversation with Mrs. Frost but bit my tongue. As if reading my thoughts, he said, "Not the constant campaigning, teaching, and politicking to promote my poems. No, I'm still such a bad man I got her pregnant."

"How could you? She's 50!" My hands flew to my mouth. "Fifty-two, and her recovery from miscarriage has been hard, very hard."

"Hell Damn, Frost, I thought my papa was an animal when he got my mama pregnant at 46, and Pip's birth proved so hard, she became an invalid."

He picked up another of his drafts and handed "Acceptance" to me. It described how a bird understands the change to darkness as the sun sets and swoops to its remembered tree. He nodded, placed his big hands over mine, and said the final line, "Let what will be, be."

Thank heavens, I escaped without having to make dinner for that contrary man.

When I returned to Cambridge House, Trudy had a pile of noodles and a tomato basil pesto sauce ready. I put garlic and butter on slices of Italian bread and baked them. She drank whole milk, and I downed what passed for Chianti during Prohibition. As we ate, I explained why I wanted her to become the icon for our Empire enterprises after she crossed the Channel.

"Can I wait to decide about becoming America's Flame until after my swim?" she asked. Near deaf, she was nowhere near dumb: she wanted to make sure Kurt and I were devoted to her goal first. I nodded.

"What percentage will Kurt take of any endorsements and support I earn before and after the swim?" I assured her I was paying Kurt's complete salary, and she owed him nothing more. Of course, I added, I hoped Kurt would return as my partner up north, but he was also free to choose a different course.

"Can I endorse other products, or does your family business want exclusive rights to my image?" I had to laugh at that, but I assured her she was free to take on other clients so long as they didn't compete with stoves or furnaces. "I don't have the body to go half-naked in any B movies with Johnny Weissmuller." I knew better but held my tongue because a brighter future beckoned. "I'm better seen than heard," she added in her usual loud voice but with a new note of resignation. "I don't want to do anything that risks making me look deaf and dumb."

"Trudy, you won't ever have to go on tour." Then it hit me: "What if we make your hearing loss part of the challenge you're meeting to swim the Channel?"

"Will that put me in a position to help deaf kids learn too?" When I nodded, she added, "Coach Mann helped find a new trainer who's crossed the Channel in both directions." We took our tea and sipped it on the big couch in the living room in front of the fire. "What kind is this?" she asked.

"Lipton's, the best Scotland has to offer."

"Wonder if Kurt can figure out how we can make that America's brand, too?"

I nodded with a smile.

"Belle, what do you hear from Rabbie?"

That brought me up short. I could still feel Rabbie tingling me so I ached. She told me how disappointed Rabbie had been at not being able to shake his cough so he could swim a leg in the finals of the Olympic relay race. Trudy paused, and now I hoped she was going to let me off the hook. Instead she asked, "You paying for his care in the sanitarium?"

I shook my head but now couldn't help blurting, "Did you meet his new girl?"

"Mirja's a Caribbean original. Wears red skirts and blouses that show off her slender body, with curves in all the right places, topped by a striking face and long, silky black hair. She's a sparkplug, so much energy, so curious, so friendly." Good Lord, she was the Keystone in Rabbie's novel, and with the last name Fitzpatrick, no doubt Catholic as well as Irish. "I never saw them after Paris, but Johnny told me she had a flat in Oxford and a house in London and had chased Rabbie until he got so sick he couldn't escape."

"Rabbie sent me one postcard that fall, hinting he had another girl in his frieze, but the letter he sent me before he went off to Switzerland…" Trudy cupped her ears to make sure she wouldn't miss the most important part of this story. "He wrote he had consumption and had to go to a sanitarium in the Alps." I had to calm a catch in my throat. "Trudy, I was frantic. I wired and offered to nurse him and pay for everything, no strings attached. He wired back that he'd already agreed to let Mirja care for him."

That night I pulled out my songbook and reread the poem I wrote when Rabbie told me he'd found another to care for him:

True Love

although she cradles
the fragile egg of love
gently in her ivory hands
careful not to crack its gossamer shell

that first line
thin as filament

slivers its way around
into an opalescent web—

too soon
their porcelain passion
shatters into slender shards

I drafted my first new lyric since I discovered I'd lost him. I guess it included some of Frost's "Acceptance," too: "Let what will be, be."

The Turtle

She lives inside her painted shell
That's hard against her back—

Her cozy home that grows with her
Protects her from attack—

It keeps her heart sequestered, too,
When erstwhile lovers call—

After she lays her barren eggs,
On—Alone—she plods.

I wondered when and where I'd ever again make my stand for what Frost called the "contraries," the small stands against the overpowering tides of life till death.

Two days later I got my first chance. Five minutes late to Frost's once-a-week seminar on the third floor of Angell Hall, I ran into Professor Strait at the door. When he said he was fixing to "monitor" the class, I blocked his entry, folded my arms under my big chest, stared down at him, and dared him to do anything more than leer at me. When he tried to step around me, I pushed him back, hard: "Over my dead body."

Even Frost must have heard the commotion because he burst out of the door. I said, "You know Professor Strait, but he also goes by Nym." That embarrassed the rotund fop so much, he retreated down the hall. When I explained what Strait had intended, Frost returned to class and rambled about the divisions on English faculties between the "rhetoric and diction mob, the literature and criticism police, and us creative fellows." He soon closed the class: "What do you say we wind down these sessions? Write at least one decent poem, one you treasure enough that you want me to give it back to you rather than tear it up. When it's ready, call me to make an appointment. We'll meet at my house so we can read and discuss it together, one-on-one, okay?" I couldn't blame Frost if he'd also had more than his fill of Michigan's Nym and its two, deeply divided English Departments.

Spring 1926: Glen Arbor and Ann Arbor

Pip, home from Amherst for spring break, rode in the backseat of our Lincoln with Robbie. Kurt sat in front with me. Frost peppered Pip with questions, and we learned that my boy had been the leading scorer on the hockey team and was elected captain for his senior year. He said he refused to run for Alpha of Chi Phi because his fraternity brothers wouldn't let Charles Drew share his room this term. "Besides," he added, "I want to study for a Rhodes. Oxford's New College with its Savilian Chair has been a hothouse for astronomy since 1619." I wanted to know what this meant for his relationship with Rachel, but I knew to ask my brother later when we were alone.

Frost had no such qualms. He tapped me on the shoulder and yelled, "Is Rabbie going back to Oxford in the fall?" Keeping my eyes fixed on the road ahead, I nodded. "Will he finish next spring, then?" I shook my head. "Good," Frost screamed. "When Pip moves to England, you can get back together with Rabbie and see if you can sell your poems over there as I did before." He paused. "I'll set you up with the editor for my London publishing house." When I didn't respond, he continued, "She visited me stateside, and she's a real fireplug with sense and sass." Then he hit me with a gut shot: "Mirja Fitzpatrick doubled sales of all my books across the pond." I couldn't breathe, and I slowed the car. "She can also make you an All-American poet despite all the Brits who are wild about ex-pats like Pound and Eliot."

I pulled the car to a stop on the side of the road and got out. Kurt and Pip held me up until I could breathe again. I asked Kurt to drive and slid into the front seat. I turned to Frost and said, "Rabbie's already taken by your red-hot Latin lover, publishing flash." Frost threw up his hands in apology, as if he didn't know, but I continued, "I'm not going to England, ever. Not for Rabbie. Not for Mirja. Not to publish what you always say are my too rough-cut, unfinished poems." Frost looked to Pip and to Kurt. Finally, Robbie murmured an apology, but we rode the final two hours to Belle Cottage in silence.

Papa greeted us at the front door as if he couldn't have gotten along another minute without us. Despite his show of good cheer, new worry lines cut deep furrows in his face. His shoulders slumped as if his burdens had grown too heavy. His breath already smelled of alcohol, and he couldn't wait to sit us by the fire to share another spot of Macallan. At least that gave Frost an excuse to regale Papa with stories of Pip's accomplishments at Amherst and plan to compete for a Rhodes to study "the cosmos" at Oxford. Papa didn't share Frost's enthusiasm for this any more than I did.

I took over before the old poet had a chance to stick his barb into me again. "Pip, can you and Robbie show Kurt around before the sun gives out?" At first Papa protested, but I told him, "We need to talk," and headed toward his study.

"What's wrong?" I asked Papa. He settled in his big chair, and I sat across from his huge desk in one of the two well-worn leather chairs.

"She left me."

Miss Patterson was still schoolmarm for her young charges and caregiver for her aging parents. She didn't have enough left over to be a live-in partner for any full-time mate, let alone one with Papa's appetite. "Did you give her a share of our business?"

"Miss Schultz made sure my half will all go to Pip."

That was a relief, because I knew it was going to be hard enough to convince Papa to put up any of his share to hire Kurt and groom him to take over, but first I had to ask, "Did you provide for Miss Patterson?"

"The trust I set up for her will pay handsomely, but…" He paused. "I can't keep up with the business growing. Pip doesn't want to help run it. Even David Ahgosa's bridling under my big thumb. Besides," he looked up with his first smile, "I'm making a lot more money dabbling in the market."

"Papa, are you borrowing to buy stocks?"

"Eighty percent margin, 400 percent profit in less than a year."

I guessed how much he must have at risk. "Did you pledge your share of the business?" He nodded but hung his head, and I saw how much his bald spot had grown on top. "Neither of us may borrow against our share without the other's consent." He looked up. "You agree to work with Miss Schultz to sell your stocks now, or you'll forfeit your share of our Empire to me."

"Hell, what's it matter anymore, anyway?"

"Papa, you know you don't want me to replace you as Chairman and CEO." Hard as that was for me to say, it was the truth for him, and he nodded. I also shared how Kurt was going to work with Trudy Ederle to make her the symbol of the Spirit of America and retain her as the icon for our America's Flame to sell our gas stoves and furnaces. When the hint of a smile lifted one corner of his mouth, I told him about my plan for Kurt helping with our family Empire.

"Belle," Papa replied, "we'll have to see about your Mr. Knutsen: Unless you're giving him your shares as a dowry, he'll have to earn any percentage from me."

"My recollection is the father of the bride pays the dowry." Before he choked on that, I said, "Despite my overtures, Kurt has shown no interest in bedding me."

"He's a fool, then." Papa added, "So am I. I'm sorry I ever prevented you from marrying your Catholic songbird."

"Papa, I couldn't bring myself to convert."

"John Knox may send me to Hell, but I don't know why I believed Scots Presbyterians had to marry each other." He poured us each another shot. "Tell our boy I won't disown him if he marries Rachel." Even if Papa couldn't see me as CEO of our Empire, I didn't take offense. Hard truth was, I no longer could see it either. Kurt was our man.

After dinner I retired early, too numb to risk more conversation or go to the attic and compose any new lyric. Yet I had so many thoughts swirling in my head, I couldn't sleep. I needed to fight against the spiral down from anxiety to a dark hole, but I was so tired. Soon though, I heard Kurt's gentle knock on my door and welcomed him. He expressed his regret over Frost's remarks in the car, but I told him I'd survive. He saw right through me. He sat on the bed beside me and held my hand. I laid my head on his shoulder, and he patted it gently with his other hand. Could I see Kurt as my mate for life? Not one I could love as madly as Rabbie, get as mad at as Robbie, or share as much magic with as David, but oh how I wished he would hold me now or, given our difference in size, let me cradle him.

Instead, he said, "I had a good talk with your father and brother. After I help Trudy, count on me coming back to build America's Flame."

I wanted to put my finger in his mouth and my tongue in his ear, but I only lifted my head from his shoulder. "Thanks. We need you."

"On the walk across the ridge this afternoon, I also agreed to help Pip and David develop their new links." He explained how we could finance the club through initiation fees, annual dues, and fees for lodging, food, and play for members and guests. He proposed coordinating with the Bealses to share the cost of building a lodge for golfers in three seasons, hunters and leaf-peepers in fall, skiers and snowshoers in winter, fly-fishers and mushroom foragers in spring, and families of the campers in summer.

"Would it help our business if the Bealses expand their camp beyond Christian Scientists and also include girls and start a college prep school the other nine months of the year?" Kurt embraced this idea but also suggested we hire Bobby Jones to design the course. Jones, the winner of several U.S. Amateurs and a U.S. Open, was a national hero because he refused to turn pro. Yet we couldn't make the same mistake as D. H. Day had with the Chicago investors at Alligator Hill. "Pip won't go for a club that's for Gentiles only and excludes persons of color, like his Negro friend from Amherst or David Ahgosa."

"If we exclude any of our customers at our club, it will hurt Empire sales, too."

"No lots for sale either, ever," I snapped.

Taken aback, Kurt stood up and extended his hand to shake, but I pulled him, a head shorter, toward me until I buried his head in my ample breasts. He pushed me away, his face flush from embarrassment. He shuffled toward the door, opened it, and turned. Never much for a poker face, I must have looked crestfallen because he stepped back and kissed me, once, on the cheek.

"As long as I work with you," he added, "I need two weeks off over Easter, two more over the fourth of July, and two more over Thanksgiving, to go home to Fire Island, okay?"

Before I could scream, Pip pounded on my door, bounded past Kurt, and jumped on my bed. "David really took to your new man." Kurt retreated and closed the door. Pip asked, "Will he make a good mate for you?" I must have looked down because my brother said, "Not sure about Rachel and me anymore either."

"Papa said he won't stand in your way if you decide to marry."

I didn't know how to read him, a boy of many moods, as he shook his head. The white streak in the hair above his ear already made him look as distinguished as any leading man on stage or screen. I never could read his gray-blue eyes, but his bony face looked fragile. He explained that Rachel planned to throw him over at the end of this school year to "latch onto an underclassman she can better train to mind and marry her." He paused. "Maybe that's for the best. If we don't break off now, I won't be able to keep resisting."

Just the thought brought back the anticipation of the rise, explosions, and long plateau Rabbie always gave me. Maybe I should have held my sex hostage to his marrying me. No, then I'd have no sense of the joy of love, or was it just the joy of sex?

Pip must have seen the blush rising on my face because he said, "Marmie, I didn't mean to drag Rabbie in as Frost did."

"It's okay." I even managed to laugh. "I can't stay mad at the old bard for long."

Pip eyes searched into places I didn't want him to go. "Do you still love him?"

"Rabbie or Robbie?" I said.

While I pondered that, he said, "Whatever happens with Rachel, promise you'll visit if I win a Rhodes."

I knew I couldn't let my fear of leaving my two Arbors stand in Pip's way, but I couldn't help asking, "Why go to Oxford to study?" When he didn't answer, I pressed, "You want to follow in Rabbie's footsteps?"

"No, Charles Drew convinced me." Pip reached out his hand. "Marmie, when his grades weren't good enough for a Rhodes, he decided to teach at a Negro college to earn money for medical school so he can show how blood knows no skin color. He told me not to pass up a Rhodes and my search in the stars. I swore I wouldn't let him down."

"Okay, I will come see you in England," I said as brightly as I could manage, "but I need you to come home in the summer and over Christmas to help with Papa, Empire, and our new Homestead Golf and Outing Club."

"This will always be my home, but…" He paused, and I feared he was going to say he was fledging from me. Instead, he said, "Cambridge House, too. And Michigan may offer a better place to pursue my research than up north when I finish at Oxford."

No matter his odd moods, he would be my boy to the end. At least I could hope.

After Pip left I heard Papa's knock for the first time since Mama died. I opened the door for him, and he stood uncertainly at the threshold. I sat him in the big chair by the window. What more was there for us to talk about at this hour of the night?

"Belle, I always loved your Mama, but she stopped loving me back after you were born." He looked down for the longest time until he mumbled, "That's why Miss Patterson and I were… friends… so many years before we got married."

"What about P-P-Pip?"

"A mistake: Your mother decided she'd had enough of Miss Patterson ministering to my needs, and…" He paused again. "I never should have given in. Pip's birth nearly killed her, and she never… I'm sorry, Belle."

My head spun. How could I have misunderstood all these years?

"Please say something," he said. When I didn't respond, he added, "Can you forgive me?"

I nodded but then blurted, "What are you going to do without Miss Patterson?"

A wry smile crossed his face. "Every three months we're going to take two weeks off together."

Damn, I thought, as his words brought to mind the recent conversation with Kurt. Kurt wanted his different kind of love away from Belle Cottage and Empire, too. Good Lord, Mr. Knutsen could take over the family business without having to marry the boss's daughter, and then he could sell to the highest bidder so he could return to New York a rich homosexual.

Soon after Papa left, I heard the stage whisper saying my name. "Robbie, come in before you wake the whole house." Frost entered with a sheaf of papers, his stubby handwriting, marks, and erasures beckoning. He must have stayed up late, writing. "Run into another doe and buck?"

"More of your ephemerals," he replied, "but the long wait in the line outside your door to get an audience didn't kill any off yet." He handed me one of his new poems, "Spring Pools."

"A different take than 'Nothing Gold Can Stay'?" I asked.

He nodded with a puckish grin. "This one's a warning, to the trees that have it in their pent-up buds to darken nature and be summer woods…'"

"Then," I interjected, "shouldn't the next line start with, say, 'Think again'?"

Frost thought about it, struck out the first four words, scribbled a new four and sang his new tune with "Let them think twice." "What do you think now?" he asked.

"Not nearly as contrary as the one three years ago."

Still standing, Frost nodded with a smile that turned into a yawn. "Belle, have you ever written a poem about how you feel about life in Leelanau?"

I got up, cinched my robe tight, walked him to the attic, got out my journal, copied "Delight of Life" on a sheet of paper, and handed it to him. As he added my copy to his sheaf of poems, I announced, "It's in the form of a sonnet." Frost nodded, yawned again, and said, "I'll read it in the morning before we drive back to Ann Arbor so you can type all my drafts."

"But we just got here," I blurted. Then I thought better and assured him, "I'll use the typewriter stowed in the den downstairs and be done before we'd even get to Clare."

I woke to a soft but insistent knock on the door. I looked out the window and saw dawn was breaking. I rose, opened the door, and David Ahgosa whispered, "Come with me." I nodded, closed the door on him, and got dressed quickly.

David walked me fast down the stairs, out of the house, up the steep hill, and across the ridge. Just after the tumbled-down wall where Frost and I happened on the buck and doe three years before, we pulled soundless to a stop; our breath fogged in the early morning chill. The shallow spring pool beneath the tall trees yet to leaf out reflected the sun rising to the east, the blue sky and puffy clouds above, and a dozen spring flowers blooming white, blue, and gold. I had also enjoyed my spring ephemeral blossoming in the water with Rabbie and was sorry it had dried up since. Even if such a season never passed my way again, I would remember its tingle. I wondered whether Frost's dark had always prevented him from opening fully to such light, no matter how bittersweet the memory might seem at times afterward. Maybe that explained his tendency to hold back in many poems, in contrast to Miss Dickinson's different slants of meaning that so often bared her soul.

I felt David's hand pressing mine. I looked up and saw he pointed to a clearing in the trees beyond. There, camouflaged by the dabs of snow mottling the tall brown grass, lay a newborn fawn, quiet, calm, and scentless. I wondered whether I would ever have the opportunity to give birth to such a delight of life, let alone suckle, nurture, and raise her. The early sun lit the morning dew all around the fawn. Each droplet looked a tiny blue ocean. Strange how the rising spring sun in morning casts a clear blue light all over our north coast, while the setting fall sun at the end of day casts a warmer, rosy glow.

David squeezed my hand and walked us without a sound past the fawn to the edge of the opening. There I saw the 200-foot drop to the Crystal River below, the view opening across the bay to the Sleeping Bear Dunes and Lake Michigan, where the sun would set. David turned and pointed from right to left across the valley floor below, back up a gentle slope toward the rising sun, down the gentle meadow toward the bay again, and back up to another clearing atop the ridge with another 360-degree vista. Yes, this was the layout for our golf course. David knew this place better than anyone, but I said, "I'll find a golf architect to help you design with nature."

"Why do we need anyone else?"

I began to explain how the economic success of our new club would depend on its, well, what exactly? I doubted myself in the presence of this splendor and David's magic, but I explained how Kurt and I hoped to use Trudy's Spirit of America to brand our Empire stoves and furnaces as America's Flame.

"As long as your big-name designer lets me point the way," he said, "we'll be fine here."

I looked out over the bay, across the straits to South Manitou and back. "David, I want you to be my manager, trainer, and spotter this summer. When Trudy sets off from France, I'm setting off from Sleeping Bear Point." He pulled me close and held me tight against the cold morning wind whistling through the trees.

Within a few seconds, I felt my heart beating in time with his. Our breath merged in a silvery fog of satin that cupped us. Was I contrary enough to fight to make this moment last? "If I dye my hair and tan my skin, may I be your Autumn Moon?"

The rising sun soon cleared the fog our breath had blown to form a sheltering tent. David let go, but my cheek still felt the tug of his breath. That night I sang:

Northern Light

morning light shines on dew,
breaking through the fog
of our silver breath
with blue clarity

sunset casts a rosy glow
over the hills and valleys
coloring the sand and sea
in shimmering hues

the pulsing green curtain
of Northern Lights dances
across an ebony sky
in luminous ecstasy

praise for this gift of northern light,
cycling from generation to generation—
blessed sparks of life.

The next afternoon I drove to Glen Haven. The dark giant greeted me at the tall green gas pump in front of the store. "Vill her up, Missy Belle?" His huge shadow blocked the sunlight streaming over the dunes. Before I could answer, D. H. Day, a big cigar in his mouth, hopped down the front steps of his store and told his son-in-law to check the oil. Mr. Day pumped the gas into my Phaeton, the rag top down.

"Sales pick up yet at your Day Estates?" I asked. He chomped on his cigar and shook his head. The droop in his big moustache and shoulders suggested he'd aged into his 70s. "Good Lord, the way David Ahgosa is selling your stoves and building his Ojibwe orchards," I added, "you'd think the Chicago mob would have taken off their damn deed restrictions so folks of color with enough green in their pockets might buy."

He turned his head, took another chomp, and spit on the ground. "Should have followed your papa's advice and invested instead in—"

Sven slammed the hood shut and interjected, "Scenic rides with thrills and—"

Little old D. H. raised his hand, and the dark giant shut up. "I might have done a damn sight better if I'd invested more in Glen Haven, my farm, and the Dune Climb concession." A shadow loomed over us. The dark giant was quick for a big man.

"Missy Belle, your oil is vull up, but it's seventy-vive cents for the gas."

I handed Mr. Day the change and put on my best smile. "Why don't we get together in June to compare notes about how to conserve our little corner of paradise? Bring Sven, too." I couldn't tell whether the ogre bared his big teeth in a scowl or a grin, but he'd soon ascend to King David's throne.

ᔕ

The next Monday, after lunch around Frost's big kitchen table, the poet grumped at Teddy, "Have you written a poem for me yet?"

"I submitted an essay on the war between my father and my uncle over—"

"I know, killed them both." Frost shuffled through his papers, picked up two pages filled with Roethke's green ink, and returned the draft.

Teddy looked at the paper. Frost left no comments. "Well, what do you think?"

"Tragic story, but when I suspended classes, all I asked for was *one poem*."

Teddy pulled his fat wallet from a pocket inside his double-breasted suit coat. He made a show of emptying the contents from a number of folds, flaps, and crevices in the billfold onto the table. The pile grew. He pawed through the mound and eyed one piece of paper after another. I thought Frost might throw a fit, but the practiced poet who fumbled on stage to win his audience smiled and began to laugh. Finally, Teddy raised his meaty fist up and displayed a tiny prize as his triumph. He unfolded it and handed the scrap, no bigger than three inches by three inches, to Frost.

"Not bad." Frost handed me "To Darkness" and asked what I thought. I read it and liked the different slant of meaning on how to see in the face of being blind.

I searched on the table in Frost's pile of papers and found one of the poems I'd typed for him at Belle Cottage. I read aloud the first stanza of "What Fifty Said." With an ironic edge, it conveyed a bitter slant, telling how the pedantry of old, know-it-all English professors beat the stuffing out of aspiring college students.

Teddy clapped his big hands together. "You take a class from Strait, too?"

"No," Frost replied, "but I suffered his type at Dartmouth and Harvard: Made me quit school!"

Whereupon, I continued with the second verse, about how such students once aging into succeeding generations of old teachers should instead "go to school to youth to learn the future."

As Teddy rose and bowed to Frost, I couldn't help thinking what a good rebuke Frost's poem offered all the Nyms on English faculties who couldn't stand creative writers. Yet the old bard rummaged through his pile and found a longer poem, written in his stubby pencil, titled, "The Bear," and read it aloud. It described the "uncaged progress of the bear" wandering cross-country in the fall as he pulled a tree down "as if it were a lover and its chokeberries lips to kiss goodbye."

Frost paused. "Theodore, you may think you're just as free to roam, but you act more like the poor caged bear fighting an inward rage."

The poem then described how man's pacing back and forth is confined at either end by the telescope and the microscope, where, like a bear, he "can sit back and sway his head… between two metaphysical extremes." Frost paused to study Teddy as the big boy swayed back and forth on his chair, eyes shut and nose up, listening hard. As Frost continued to say his new poem, he scowled at Teddy's swaying "back and forth… from cheek to cheek." Frost concluded, "A baggy figure, equally pathetic when sedentary and when peripatetic."

Teddy grimaced so his face grew red, and soon his big snout did, too, as he continued to sway on his butt back and forth as if a big, mad caged bear. I laughed to try to break the tension, but Teddy just leaned forward, still swaying from cheek to cheek in his chair. Suddenly, the big young man reached his huge mitts across the table, shook Frost by the collar, and roared. Robbie looked to me for help, but I didn't know what to do. Frost turned, studied Teddy more closely, and began to laugh. Teddy let go and chuckled, too, although his smile was again limited to a self-conscious show of teeth.

No matter: The odd pair joined to put on a show as much as the evening Frost and Amy Lowell jousted at Hill Auditorium.

Frost stood and patted Roethke on the back. "Keep on raging, including against that dark legacy your father and uncle left."

As I walked Teddy to the den where he could sort through letters and requests and work on Frost's schedule, he whispered, "Big Mama Bear, don't let any of the other fellas know I'm composing, okay?" When I didn't answer, he added, "I've got a certain image to keep up so I can take cover in my fraternity." I could only nod.

I finished typing, revising, editing, and retyping Frost's new pile of poems. I got up to leave before he could ask me to cook a late supper and keep him company in his lonely house that evening. Instead he asked, "Do you like that bear of a boy?"

I couldn't resist nodding, and neither could Frost.

I don't know whether Teddy overheard us, but he emerged from the den in a rush and said in his most manic voice, "Big Mama, let's treat our poet friend to a dinner in the glasshouse and garden I built!"

To my surprise, Frost chimed in, "I accept, but I need to get cleaned up first." So I left Teddy to chauffeur Frost so I could get home to fix dinner.

A half hour later, Teddy pulled to a stop in the driveway in front of the garage and raced Frost through the cold rain into our glasshouse. I watched from the kitchen window as I finished preparing the chicken salad, slicing the French bread and setting the kitchen table. Teddy explained how he built the glasshouse, showed how the pulleys could open different parts of the glass roof, slalomed around the flower pots on the deck patio, and bragged about the many different blooms he planted and nurtured. Both needed towels to wipe off the many splatters that fell on them from Teddy's exhibition opening and closing the glass roof panels in the rain.

Over dinner Teddy entertained us with stories of his hijinks, on campus in class and at the tennis court, off campus at fraternity parties and acting the tough guy at the speakeasy downriver, even working and playing when younger in the much bigger glasshouses in his Saginaw home. Throughout, Teddy showed off by downing shots of scotch, while Robbie and I sipped Lipton's from our teacups.

Over dessert of Sander's ice cream and hot fudge, Frost shared that Elinor would be returning in two weeks with Marjorie and Irma. "Carol's staying behind with his wife and baby at the farm in Vermont," he continued, "while Lesley mans her bookstore in Pittsfield." He fiddled with his teacup for quite a while before adding, "You know, I've gotten used to our routine, writing all hours, sleeping till noon, working the rest of the day and evening with Teddy and you, walking the Huron riverbank with Van Dore and the Arboretum with…"

Roethke interrupted our guest by clinking his glass of scotch against Frost's teacup and saying, "It's been great for me, too."

"But I don't see how it'll work with three more people in our house day and night," Frost said, "and my family will still be divided, some here and some there."

I felt sorry for Frost, two of his children grown, two more not yet fully fledged, but all still dependent on Elinor for succor and Frost for money. I reflected on how I couldn't bear my brother being gone at Amherst, let alone Oxford. Although Papa was a bit more than five hours away, I'd always be there for him. If Mama had survived, I'd never have left our cottage up north unless she moved in with me here. "You know Elinor and the two girls are coming to rescue you from our arboreal clutches," I said, "and return you to your New England home with everyone there."

"We could winter here and summer there," he said.

"What?"

He sipped his tea. "A house in Ann Arbor and a farm in Vermont."

"You think your wife will want to travel back and forth so?" I asked.

"Till death do us part."

"What if Elinor needs to stay there to tend to your children?"

"Another reason you and Ted need to help every day after lunch here." Frost looked to Roethke and added, "You can also help persuade Elinor, Irma, and Marjorie to make a life here, and we can save Vermont for summer, early fall, and two-month breaks in winter and spring."

Teddy tilted his shot glass up, drained it, and looked through the bottom at us. Through this thick glass lens, his eyes grew bigger. He started swaying back and forth on his butt, playing the manic bear once again. When I couldn't help giggling and even Frost began to chuckle, Teddy leaped up and said, "Let's go for dip in the pool instead!"

He kicked off his shoes and took off his shirt, slacks and socks. In his boxer shorts and undershirt, he looked even more the bear with his big barrel chest. He raced out the back door and cannonballed into the pool.

As I cleared the table and Teddy splashed outside and yelled for us to join him, Robbie bent over, took off his shoes and socks, and rolled up his pant legs. Frost walked out and joined Teddy in the glasshouse. As I finished stacking the dishes in the sink, Teddy yelled, "Big Mama, get a swimsuit and I'll race you a length, for the gold medal!"

I only took off my shoes and stockings and walked out into the glasshouse. I flopped down beside Frost and we dangled our feet in the water. It was cold, because it had been cool and overcast all day, with intermittent showers, so the sun's warm rays never could get through the cloud cover to heat the pool from the night chill. Teddy swam over and dared me to race again. When I shook my head, he whipped his big arms across the pool surface. A mountain of water drenched Robbie and me. "Serve towels with your showers you big lug," I screamed back at my manic Teddy Bear.

That only egged the bear of a boy on. Teddy leaped forward and grabbed at my arm to pull me in. Frost leaned across with both arms to defend me from Roethke's onslaught. Somehow, their arms got entangled. When Teddy stepped back, he pulled Robbie into the pool by mistake. Frost landed with a big splash.

When Robbie regained his footing and stood up with Teddy's help, our guest only shook his head and the water sprayed off his sopping hair. He looked stunned, and soon he began to shiver. I could see the bumps rising from the pale skin on his hands like on a plucked goose. Good Lord, the last thing we needed was for our guest, too often stricken by grippe or worse, to catch a bad cold or the flu.

Teddy pushed and I pulled until we got Frost out of the pool and onto the deck. I raced back into the house, got several big towels and a robe from the linen closet, and threw them out the back door to Roethke. Teddy tried his best to dry Robbie off. Roethke kept apologizing, and Frost saying he was all right, but Robbie's teeth began to chatter. I hurried Frost and Roethke into the downstairs bathroom. I told them to take turns warming up in the hot shower, while I went upstairs to grab dry clothes for them.

Eventually, the odd duo appeared in the living room in Pip's dry clothes, much too long for Robbie and much too tight for Roethke. We tried to exchange pleasantries, but soon Frost asked Teddy for a lift back to his house on the other side of the river. They said their goodbyes to me with forced good cheer.

I retreated to my bedroom, put on a dry warm robe, and pulled out my songbook. I hopped into my big bed and tried to compose, but no lyric came. I jotted down words now and again to try to describe the images, sounds, and conversations of the day, but I crossed most out. Finally, I opened my mouth, and a new song poured out. I ended it with a long dash so the last sound faded into a sigh.

At Risk

Inside my glass house
I glide back and forth
in the Blue Salvation of my pool,
cool water flowing gently

along my length
like a mother's soft caress.

Outside, the nosy world
peers in, eager
to cast aspersions,
foul as day-old chum,
hoping to hook
my embryonic will.

It would not be wise
to hurl stones—
Instead, I Swim—

When I woke, the sun had already reached its highest point in the sky. Coach Mann and Kurt Knutsen were due to arrive in ten minutes to discuss how we could best help Trudy. I dressed, raced downstairs, and brewed a pot of tea.

They soon arrived and shared their plans for Trudy's crossing. "I offered the *New York Times* an exclusive," Kurt began, "but the editors refused to pay for the rights to cover a public event. So I signed up the *New York Daily News-Chicago Tribune* syndicate." When I looked skeptical, he added, "Don't worry, the *Times* will be all over the story, too." Kurt proceeded to list the other sponsors he'd already lined up: the *Saturday Evening Post*; Macy, Hudson's, and the Sears catalogue among the retailers; the drinks Coca-Cola and Lipton; Ford and Northern Pacific among the transportation brands; Wilson and Christ-Craft for sports; our Empire and Upton Machine Washing among the stove, furnace, and appliance makers. "They'll pay all expenses just for the right to bargain for Trudy's name, and the entire country will root for our Spirit of America to plant the Star-Spangled Banner in Dover when she crosses the Channel." Kurt assured that Trudy reserved the right to review the merits of each company and its products before endorsing any if she "wins the race, but the field's getting crowded. Already, four other women plan to beat our girl across."

"If Trudy wins," I asked Matt Mann, "what are the chances Michigan will hire her to coach a women's intercollegiate swim team here?"

"Trudy'll be so famous, why's she going to want to coach?"

"If Trudy agrees and I finance a pool at the new Women's Athletic Building, how about I pay to move your swimming camp to Sleeping Bear Bay with her?"

"My daughter will disown me if I move from the place she loves as her own."

"I can't fight you on that, at least if you start a camp for girls there, too."

Ever before the proper Scots gentleman, Coach Mann startled me with a hug. I should have known: "Let's break out the Laphroaig for the new women's pool," he said.

That afternoon I drove to Frost's house to type his drafts. Teddy must have been embarrassed by our mishaps the night before because he was nowhere in sight, but Robbie appeared not to mind. He just had me go over his schedule and reply in the negative to request for talks that didn't fit or weren't worth the trouble. He said only one thing about his dunking: "Our bear of a boy does have a manic streak: you need to watch out lest you get bowled over next time."

While we sat at his kitchen table, I gave Robbie a copy of "At Risk." He read the poem once and then again before he nodded and stuffed it into his pocket. I asked, "Aren't you at least going to say 'Hold it awhile, and deepen it, deepen it'?"

"That was Star Struck." At least Frost remembered. "I reread it the other day." He explained that the editor of *The Dearborn Independent* had asked for his help to get contributions "from the best local poets." I began to freeze. "I sent him your Star Struck and one of Van Dore's more rugged wilderness sonnets."

I sputtered and eventually managed to squeak, "No!"

"It'll offer a new start for you, better than *Whimsies*."

"Preceptor," I screamed, "you had no right."

"You gave it to me and asked for my help, remember?"

"Not ready yet," I said as evenly as I could. "And give me back my glasshouse poem."

"You owe me that one for class."

"You already have my 'Delight of Life,'" I answered.

"You wrote that long ago."

I shook my head and tidied up his papers on the table. Frost appeared to mark-up "At Risk." He folded the draft in two and gave it back to me.

I opened the paper and read his thick scribble. He hadn't made a single correction. Instead, there was a note at the bottom of the page: *Belle, after a couple of years more writing, you can publish a book of poems in England and then go on a tour when you get back to promote your songs here. You should include your glasshouse poem, but the lead should be "Delight of Life" and the title of your book,* Up North. *Robbie*

I excused myself as politely as I could and drove back to my Cambridge House. Frost never would understand why I couldn't bring myself to publish my poems: they were too personal to publish, in his lifetime or any of the others' that I refused to embarrass including mine.

Two days later, Frost looked terrible. He had caught a fever, sore throat, and cough. His nose and eyes were red and runny; his face, ashen; his breathing, labored. The doctors at University Hospital said it was only a bad cold, not even the flu, but Frost looked a sorry mess, wheezing and snuffling in bed. Teddy and I had only a week to try to get him in shape before Mrs. Frost, Irma, and Marjorie arrived.

The next morning, I relieved Teddy from his night shift tending our sick poet. I made breakfast and lunch, carried it on a tray into Robbie's bedroom, stayed to make dinner, and then let Teddy sup with Frost and tuck him into bed.

He wasn't a terrible patient although I did get tired of his saying the oatmeal in the morning was as "freezing" as his feet and the tea at lunch as "boiling" as his head. I was tempted to spike his morning coffee with whiskey and his later tea with Scotch, but I found the secret on the third day. I added honey to his tea, laid a cold compress on his forehead, and gently rubbed the aches and pains out of his back, shoulders, legs, and feet. When he rolled over, I tucked his hands under the covers, leaned over, placed my long fingers on either side of his head, and massaged his temples.

When I arrived the next morning to prepare breakfast, Teddy complained that Frost had given him a hard time last night by demanding a "Templer." Roethke slumped in his chair and rested his elbows and head on the kitchen table. He looked up with bleary eyes and added, "I won't make it through another night with the Old Bard unless you show me how." I stood behind his chair and told him to lean back. I bent over and massaged his temples so he'd be ready for Frost that evening. When Teddy's eyes began to bug out, I told him to close them. When he began to hum, I punched him. When Teddy only offered me his best toothy leer, I knew Frost had recovered from his bad cold.

I shooed Teddy out, set the table, and added a sheaf of Frost's handwritten poems, a typewriter, and plain paper. I woke Frost and told him to show up for breakfast, clean-shaven and fully clothed, in 15 minutes. When he began to protest, I shushed him and returned to the kitchen to make griddle cakes and bacon. I brewed a fresh pot of Lipton's. While he ate heartily, I began typing one of his drafts. I stopped every once in a while to ask a question or offer a suggestion, and Frost responded as if there'd never been any break in our routine preparing his new book. After lunch I made him take a nap, but by three o'clock, he was back at the kitchen table, peering over my shoulder, reciting and dictating changes as I typed.

I cooked a light supper for him and prepared to leave. Frost bade me sit at the kitchen table and said, "Tell me more about your Ahgosa friend." So I did. He ate heartily but listened carefully for 15 minutes without asking any questions. He took out a paper and a stubby pencil from a pocket inside his rumpled coat and made a few notes. I described the morning up north when David and I had witnessed something like Frost's spring pool, as well as a fawn, the layout for our new golf course, and the shared embrace of the silver tent of fog formed by our breath.

"Have you written about that?" he asked.

"Only the setting, but I still miss the tug of his breath on my cheek to this day."

Frost raised a hand to his face, wrote another note, and stuffed it into his coat pocket. "A powerful image, one we've all shared on a chill morning strolling in the woods, alone or with a friend," was all he said.

I cleared the table and said goodbye. Robbie rose and expressed his thanks for my helping him recover from his latest bout with another cold. He pursed his lips as if to say something more but didn't. He stood awkwardly. He hated shaking hands and a hug might be too intimate. Instead, he lightly tapped my shoulder in farewell. I left, but the mark burned all the way home.

That night I couldn't sleep. I tried to think about composing a song celebrating the moment I felt the pull of a man. Instead, I couldn't stop wondering why, in the end, I was doomed never to share my love with a good mate for life. I sang a lament:

Siren

Like the mermaid siren
painted on a Grecian urn
I wait for love.

Tempted would-be lovers
pass my way but
reject my warm embrace—

unlike the queen bee's suitors
whose consummation leads
to their mortal fate.

From afar
I feel their lusty gaze
and bid them near.

Like the mermaid siren
captured on the vase
I wait… and wait.

The next day I arrived at Frost's house in time to prepare lunch, and Teddy joined shortly after noon to eat with us and help Frost for the next couple of hours with his pile of requests for readings, speeches, and teaching. Elinor, with the two younger Frost daughters in tow, arrived early in the afternoon, before Teddy left. That gave me a chance to introduce him so the mountain of a boy could buffer me from any disputes. After a seemly half hour of talk, I excused myself and tried to drag Teddy out with me, but Marjorie had already taken a shine to this odd bear.

I got a call from Elinor that evening, transmitting Frost's request that I show up the next morning to type. I did but left my questions and suggestions in writing and made myself scarce from the Frost house for a week. Late one afternoon Teddy stopped by and told me Irma had met a man she liked, Marjorie was a peach, Elinor took a shine to Wade Van Dore, and Robbie and his missus seemed to be settling happily into Ann Arbor.

That would be the first time in six semesters of trying, I thought, but I didn't say anything to Teddy.

The second Monday in May, the mailman delivered a note to Cambridge House in Frost's stubby, smudged handwriting. *Dear*

Miss Belle, Mrs. Frost and I request the pleasure of your company on Friday evening at eight o'clock to celebrate with the rest of our poetry seminar and the Inlanders and Outlanders. RSVP. Robert.

Not wanting to ruin the good luck of everything going so well in the Frost household without me, I called Teddy and told him to extend my regrets. Instead, he dropped by Wednesday evening with a bottle of Talisker and a determined look. He handed me another note from Frost: *Belle, your regrets are not accepted. I need you here so we can show those stuffed-shirt Inlanders a thing or two about poetry. Cowden's agreed to stop by with Roethke to wrestle you here if you try to stay away. Robbie.*

I looked up from the note. "Teddy, are you taking advantage of Marjorie?"

He only replied, "She's a sweet kid."

"She may be four years older than you, but she's still weak from—"

"I grant you she's a looker, but Irma's the one who's latched onto a beau." Teddy told me about the son of a Kansas farmer and Irma's plan to marry him.

"You double-dating?"

"Irma's too… well, oh, I don't know. And Marj—"

"*Marj?*" I interjected. Why, my shambling bear with all his tough-guy Chicago gangster masks and worse antics had made himself a part of the Frost family! Remembering my walks with Robbie, I said, "I suppose you and *Marj* also go botanizing in the Arb."

"No, only shorter walks to the river until she gets her strength back."

"Well, you're not typing Frost's poems all day," I said. "What do you do?"

"Play Backgammon, Parcheesi, Checkers, Hearts, and Whist," he said.

"With Frost and Elinor, too?"

"We also share tall tales, sad ballads, and rollicking poems: Burns, Kipling, Carroll, Wilde, Barrie, Poe, Twain, Dickinson, Wylie, even Lowell."

"Amy?" I queried. "I suppose Mrs. Frost has also fallen for you." When he beamed, I couldn't help thinking *This might yet prove the spring to keep Robert Frost a Permanent Fellow in Creative Arts at Michigan: Third time's the charm.* "You and Professor Cowden don't have to kidnap me on Friday. I'll drive myself, thank you."

I drove across the river on the Broadway Bridge and turned up Pontiac Trail. I parked opposite the white clapboard structure, a two-story central main core with a four-column front porch on the first floor, a classic second-story and full-windowed gable above, flanked on either side by matching one-story wings with corner columns, double-hung windows, six lights top and six bottom, with striking, carved wood panels below. I entered the hall of the packed house. The crowd spread from the parlor and study in front to the bigger living room and kitchen in back. Frost, dressed in a rumpled tweed coat, white shirt with collar open, and baggy brown pants over his weathered leather shoes, broke off a conversation with Cowden and the Three Graces. To greet me, he also ignored the pleas of several of the *Inlander* boys for his attention. He called Irma over and introduced me to her fiancé, John Cone. Marjorie and Teddy soon joined us. Finally, Frost waved to his missus. Judging by the hug Elinor gave me, the Frost household might well be one big, happy family in their new home on the north side of Ann Arbor.

As Cowden tried to pull Frost away to meet with another gaggle of his admirers, Robbie asked about Stella Brunt. "She and Chase Osborn are circling, trying to figure out how they can spend more time together, respectably or not," I replied. Cowden shook his head at me as he escorted Frost to join the gang waiting in the living room to share time with the great poet.

The punch beckoned in the parlor, but I let it flow elsewhere. Not that I was going to win another prize, but I didn't want to make a fool of myself fainting again. Irma and her betrothed excused themselves and left for a walk to the river. Mrs. Frost excused herself to oversee the kitchen. Finally, Teddy and his Marj couldn't take me any longer either and drifted away. The hubbub grew, and I retreated out the back door and sat on the back porch. Occasionally, one or another of Frost's flinty comments or wry remarks drew a roar from his throng of admirers inside.

Roy Cowden sat down beside me and offered a glass of punch. I didn't refuse. He said he'd missed my participation in the student literary groups, and he asked how I was enjoying business school. Before I could answer, he said, "Sorry, I was just trying to make small talk before we get down to business." I downed my glass of punch, and he gave me his. "I haven't touched it, and you may need it." I swallowed that, too. "Amherst's new president came to town and made one hell of an offer to Frost." I only nodded my head. "No teaching, no more than 10 weeks on campus total, same pay, promise of more, full professor, tenure for life."

"Michigan going to match the terms?" I asked.

"If Burton were still alive, yes, but with his death, our faculty won't stand for *no* teaching load for Frost," he said. "Many are mad he's getting paid at all after he canceled the classes for his writing seminar. Nym's spreading ugly rumors again, about that, Roethke, Van Dore, and you." Teddy wasn't going to prove the lucky charm for keeping Frost permanently at Michigan now, third try or no. "I've talked to the department chair, though. Will you serve as Frost's teaching assistant for a six-week seminar once a year, as well as his secretary?" I froze. "The University will pay you."

Did they think I needed their money? I was incensed. "And if I earn a Ph.D. for studying and writing poetry, publish in the best journals, sing my songs on campuses all across the country, and win a Pulitzer, will you consider me for professor, too?"

"Belle, you know I will, but I can't tell you how long it will take the rest of my colleagues to consider another poet, let alone a woman, for tenure on the faculty."

"Professor Cowden, as much as I want Frost to stay and as much as I respect you, I hope you'll understand why I won't prostitute myself for the University and all its Nyms and Straits to keep Frost."

I got up and walked toward my car.

Teddy grabbed me before I reached the street. "Big Mama, you can't leave."

I shook my head, but he placed a small glass of amber liquid in my hand. I nosed the smoky peat and savored the Scotch. He handed me another glass, and I knocked it back, too. Damn: "You brought the Talisker you just gave me?" When he nodded, I couldn't help laughing, took his arm, and walked back into the cauldron I'd just left.

Frost was already performing, giving out awards for the best short story here and the best long fiction there. Contrary as he was, he seemed oddly out of sorts as he honored one of the Three Graces and offered only condolences to the *Inlander* boys. "Next," he said, "I'll read you the best short poem from the University of Michigan in 1926, and I do mean short." He recited Teddy's "To Darkness." Frost gave the four lines a wry caste, as if blindness were just another condition that humans had to accept, no different than his "Acceptance," where the bird knows that when light fades at end of day, it's time to nest.

Teddy shambled up to Frost. Theodore Roethke stood tall and waited until the crowd quieted. He sang his song in a baleful voice with such sad eyes, we all felt as if we'd become blind. He said it again. He enabled us to feel the sixth sense nurtured by such darkness to see by a different light.

The silence continued for several seconds after Teddy finished, until Frost clapped his hands, and we all joined. "Mr. Roethke's already a complete poet," Frost said. "He knows his verse is meant to be heard rather than eyed, and he won't let any other speaker, no matter how much more experienced, substitute for his voice."

Frost's next words hit me like a fist in the gut, and I couldn't breathe: "Miss Belle, would you care to recite *the* best poem from Michigan?" Oh, Lord, there was nothing I could do but walk up beside him. But my mind went blank, and I couldn't remember the first line of my glasshouse poem. I whispered my confession in Frost's ear, and he said back in his stage whisper so all could hear, "Not 'At Risk.'"

He turned to the audience, bowed to me, stood up, and with a grand gesture pulled a folded page from the inside pocket of his coat. With another stage whisper, he confided, "This is an older poem so we can forgive its author, even one so young, not remembering her perfect sonnet." He cleared his throat, and with a voice clear as crystal, no hint of any New England flint or Frost wry, he sang my "Delight of Life." A tear fell from that old curmudgeon's right eye when he finished the last line, holding the last word with his hum for several moments, and then letting it fade with the sand and the remembrance of leaving love and up north behind.

There was another long silence until Frost picked up the bottle of Talisker from the table. He made a show of filling a glass and handing it to me. He picked up his ginger ale, raised it high, and said, "A Toast to the Belle of Two Arbors, Glen and Ann."

I'd miss this man, but Hell could freeze over before I'd admit it. I held back my tears, threw my shoulders back as Mama always instructed, clinked my glass to his, and gulped down the shot. When Frost offered to pour another, the crowd cheered, but I threw my glass over my shoulder. Thank heavens Teddy was still there to catch it in his big mitt, because my glass flew directly at a set of double-hung windows, six lights above and six below, at least one of which wouldn't have survived the crash.

When the party broke up, I looked for Mrs. Frost to say my thanks for hosting, but she'd already retired upstairs. She must have known this was her husband's valedictory before leaving Michigan. As I turned to go, Teddy gave me a bear hug and whispered, "Frost wants to see you." As I disentangled myself from the many folds in his thick fur coat, he added, "Don't let him get away from here."

Before I could respond, Robbie grabbed my arm and led me

through the hall, out onto the front porch, and across Pontiac Trail. We scrambled across the Ann Arbor Railroad tracks and down an embankment. We crossed Plymouth Road and turned up Broadway. When the rise steepened, he slowed to walk up the long hill. He finally turned right and led me to a bluff called Cedar Bend, high above a big ox-bow in the Huron River. Across the valley, dwarfed by the new General Hospital in the foreground, hid the Detroit Observatory where we had first explored the mystery of Mars and men.

"Despite all my grump and grouch, and Nym's snoot and slander," Frost began, "I do like this place." With a wry glare, he added, "Despite the Huffy Astronomer and that huge new hospital obscuring our view of the stars."

He took off his tweed coat, laid it on the ground and bade me sit beside him, hands on our knees, leaning forward, looking, for what?

"Must be your bestowing prizes on me." I faked a swoon and leaned closer.

Frost didn't bite. Instead he pushed me away as he barked, "Belle, marriage, decent or not, is the one institution of the ages that causes the least possible pain between the sexes." He shook his head. "The least possible is all I say."

How could I respond to that? "Buy your Vermont farm or retreat yet?" I asked.

"Eyeing a stone house near Bennington and a Gully Farm near Bucks Cobble."

"The house in Amherst you covet, too?"

"What with all the medical bills, not sure we can afford anything."

"Pshaw," I said. "Pulitzer prize-winner, America's favorite poet, and another best-seller on the way, what's Holt paying you, anyway?"

"Royalty of 15 percent on new books, plus 100 dollars a month."

"Ask for another five percent after the first 5000 in sales on *all* your books, triple the monthly salary, and make sure Holt agrees to publish your collected works, too. What with your readings and teaching, you'll be rich." I paused. "Enough so you can afford what you want for your family and Amherst College will make a loan to buy the house on Sunset in town, too."

Frost opened his eyes wide, pursed his lips, and whistled. In his best Scottish burr he said, "Ach, lassie, care to negotiate for me?"

"No, but you can buy your rental here for a good price. Based on your increased earnings, I'll put up the mortgage for you." Now I'd done all I could to keep Frost.

"I do love our house here with the hen and chicken architecture, a large middle with two little wings." His smile blossomed into a chuckle. "Cozy inside and solid, tough walnut throughout." He shut his eyes as he paused, and the smile left his face. Finally, he opened up. "Belle, the family's been happy here this spring. Irma's found a man who can stand her contraries, your Teddy's giving Marjorie good cause to recover, and even Elinor enjoys our home here, but..." He paused and peered across the river valley to the University Hospital rising so high on the other side. "Amherst made me an offer I can't refuse."

I swallowed hard before I said, "Your only obligation as a Permanent Fellow and full Professor of Creative Arts here will be one six-week seminar a year, and I'll serve as your teaching assistant and do your typing. The University will pay you 25 percent more than Amherst." That did go beyond what Professor Cowden suggested, but if I was going to take one for the Michigan team, why not splurge? "Trudy's affliction must be catching, Robbie. I can't hear you."

In the softest voice, no stage whisper or puckish grin, eyes downcast, he answered, "I watched my father die from womanizing, boozing, and marathon swimming, and I..." He stopped and looked at me. "Belle, I've watched too many of my poet friends diminish as they fall harder for one younger woman after another."

"From my experience," I told him the truth, "you may be at risk as a teetotaler from a sniff of good Scotch once in a long while, but never as a good husband from womanizing." I tapped his hand as I stood up.

He rose and touched my elbow. "I'm sorry, Belle," he said. "The Little President may think he means well, but he can't protect me from Nym and the other academic snobs on the English faculty." He paused. "Maybe only Burton could make me forget I'm a yank from New England who wants most to live on a farm with family and challenge young people to write, write, write at colleges nearer by."

The following Wednesday Teddy stopped by my house after class with the inevitable request: "Frost needs your help typing poems." After lunch in our glasshouse Eden, we drove together across the river. Frost greeted me with three drafts. I started typing the long one first, several pages, but his inserts, scribbles, and whole stanzas lined out made his already stubby hand hard to decipher, let alone understand the gist. Several times I had to stop and ask what word or phrase he meant by his hen-scratching and where an insert belonged.

When I finished, he asked, "What do you think?"

The poem took the form of a lengthy dialogue between a man, Fred, and his unnamed wife. Framed by the metaphor of a brook that somehow ran west from its source and away from the Atlantic Ocean, the conversation proceeded apace until the man's musing that life also began in the backwater and went against the customary flow. Wasn't my favorite, but I said, "Contrary enough, I suppose, for this book."

"It needs work, I grant you, but 'West-Running Brook' is going to be the title poem, even if I can't ever seem to capture everything I mean to convey about…"

While he continued his pondering, I typed the draft of the short poem, titled "A Winter Eden," with only two marks on the five stanzas. I told him I loved the description of the winter garden, bunnies coming out to "sun and romp" atop a "plane of snow one level higher than the earth below…so near paradise all pairing ends." Yes, "Here loveless birds now flock as winter friends."

After Frost recited the rest of the poem, he looked at me expectantly, and I answered, "Thanks, Robbie. I enjoyed sporting with you as winter friends in our brief time together."

"We've had our moments in autumn and spring, too…" Frost paused and pursed his full lips. I never could tell whether this pose signaled whistle or words. He continued with his whistling New England words, "…as we can never see the future."

"And 'Let what will be, be.'" Before Frost could reply, I continued, "I like hearing a poem about winter that's brighter than your mostly darker musings in this collection. I need to sing one about the winter delights of Leelanau."

"Glad to be of service, my younger Belle." Frost beamed.

I should have known he was setting me up for a sucker-punch. "A Minor Bird," only eight lines, described a poet wishing that a nattering bird "would fly away." He goes to the door to shoo the beaked bother "When it seemed as if I could bear no more." Frost concluded, "...there must be something wrong/In wanting to silence any song."

I handed him the typed page, got up, and left. I hated my Robbie describing all his student acolytes, including me, as "The Minor Bird."

He trotted after, waving a pamphlet, but I kept going, all the way to my car. "For God's sake, Belle, I took care to call 'The Minor Bird' a 'him' as if Van Dore or Roethke." Damn: I *was* the Minor Bird that so irritated Frost. I managed to start the car before he put his paw on my shoulder. "I gave the first draft to the Three Graces so they could use it as the cover poem for their last go-round with the student magazine."

I felt like screaming but instead tried to focus on pushing the clutch in and shifting into first so I could escape without further embarrassment. As the gears whined and the car jerked forward, I saw Frost in the rearview mirror, waving the pamphlet.

He yelled, "It's the issue where the Three Graces and all their boyfriends take potshots at Nym in their short stories!"

I was so stunned I let my car grind to a stop and stall. I leafed through the literary magazine and read the choice lines he'd underlined about the different "Nym Sanders" characters. I came to one where the woman narrator described her difficulty learning how to drive a stick shift under the thumb of the know-it-all, unwanted older suitor. I couldn't help chuckling. Soon, we were laughing together.

When I finally started the car and began to pull away, Frost yelled after me: "If you keep at it, you can do anything." Too bad I knew what he meant: I hadn't done anything yet. Sad to admit, but I didn't share his indomitable will to publish and campaign. No, the mere thought of publishing or reading a poem publicly made my stomach flip and closed my bellows until I gasped for air. Frost was one of a kind.

After the announcement that Amy Lowell won the Pulitzer posthumously, he sent a picture postcard of the big woman performing in her full regalia with a note:

> *No more guilt about my final review of the late Miss Lowell's work: helped her win the prize. My negotiations with Holt and Amherst go better than I ever hoped, thank you. I will do my best to compose and sing until I bury all the Nyms and other academic pedants. You should keep writing, too. RF*

I thought back to our first late-night walk around Ann Arbor so many years before: Frost barks did often sound as good as his Frost bites tasted, no matter how bittersweet:

Oh, how I will miss this contrary bard not barking at me going forward!

Summer and Fall 1926: Glen Arbor

On August 7, as the hands on the luminary clock in the clear night sky passed One-O, I waded into the water in front of Sleeping Bear Life-Saving Station. David Ahgosa had coated me with a mix of olive oil, lanolin, and Vaseline. He had opened his collar and lifted a white pendant over his head. It was the polished white stone I'd given him after my first rite of passage to South Manitou and back finding Mama's farewell. I warmed the stone in my hand, draped the pendant back over his neck, and pressed it against his heart. "Hold this until I really need it."

For good luck I wore my All-American red- and white-striped swim suit and tucked my hank of red hair inside a blue cap. Trudy and I pulled on our goggles and shouted "Cheerio!" at the same time: she set off from Cape Griz-Nez, France, for the white cliffs of Dover, while I began my swim to the Manitou Islands and back.

Thanks to Kurt Knutsen, Trudy's following boat included her father, sister, and trainer, as well as reporters from the *New York Daily News* and the *Chicago Tribune* who paid handsomely to write the "official" story. Reporters from other U.S. and European papers boarded a second tug, several determined to scuttle Trudy's swim to preserve their paid scoops with other challengers.

I dived in, and David followed in the prototype for the Chris-Craft Cadet that Papa and I had bought with the Bealses to launch the new summer girls' camp, Leelanau School, and soon-to-follow Homestead Golf and Outing Club. The water felt only brisk, and the winds held steady at only a few knots from the northwest. I swam the seven miles to South Manitou in good shape. I treaded water near the southern tip, ate cereal and fruit, sipped the Lipton's David passed over the side in a bottle without touching me.

Aided by the following breeze, the six-mile swim over to the southwestern point of North Manitou passed in a dream as the water and air warmed. At this pace I'd beat the time of the fastest man swimming the English Channel by three hours. Where the Atlantic Ocean rushes into and out of the funnel between Dover and Calais to the North Sea, the shifting tides, prowling sharks, and stinging jellyfish presented greater challenges, to be sure, but the fresh water of these straits wouldn't buoy my body up as well as the Channel's salt water. I headed back southeast toward the mouth of the Crystal River. My six kicks and two strokes per cycle, 28 strokes per minute, continued to power me forward for the first three hours.

Soon a strange squall gathered ahead and raced straight at me. No way could I beat into the teeth of this storm. So I pointed southwest toward Sleeping Bear Point. I lowered my kick to four beats for every two strokes. When the downpour hit, the Manitou passage roiled, and the wind battered my left side. I learned to roll more into the big swells and breathe only out of the right side of my mouth.

Suddenly, the rain pelted me, a wall of water rose, and the rogue wave rolled me over. I swallowed so much of Lake Michigan, I thought I'd drown. David rumbled the Cadet up as I struggled to cough, but he touched me only with his steady voice and refused my reaching hand. After I finally cleared my lungs and recovered my resolve, I continued my swim across the storm toward Sleeping

Bear Point. Nearing exhaustion and losing hope, I hit ten hours into my crossing before the so'easter passed. Only another three hours in calmer weather, and I'd land back at the Life-Saving Station where we began. I caught my second wind.

An hour later I heard the throaty rumble of the engine as David pulled the Cadet beside me again. He pointed ahead. I saw another storm, this one racing over Sleeping Bear Dunes right at us. I turned southwest. When the wind and rain blasted me, it broke my rhythm. I began to flounder as my hands and feet became blocks of ice. David pulled the boat up and yelled above the storm's roar, "Autumn Moon, you must come out." When I didn't respond, he held the white stone out for me and shouted, "Now!"

"What for?" I heard some voice I didn't recognize in me say. I bobbed on the rough sea until I regained my bearings. Although the chop belted my right side, I swam on. I kept my arms rising and falling, my feet kicking, and I inhaled enough air to stay afloat. I swam on and on and on and on.

I made landfall at 6:31 p.m., several hundred yards to the west of the mouth of the Crystal River. My exhilaration overcame my exhaustion. I lumbered on rubbery legs toward the beach and saw that David had made no secret of my crossing this time either. The Bealses and their 200 campers joined in cheering as they raced from their lookout under his birch-bark box. Pip and Papa reached me first and draped me with soft towels. This time Pip also embraced his best friend, David Ahgosa.

My brother had been so moody and distant all summer I knew he must be missing Rachel. Now, his gray-blue eyes sparkled. Pointing to a tall antenna rising from the dome of his observatory, he shouted, "Marmie, you made it, only three hours after Trudy. She swam the Channel two hours faster than any man ever has!"

The *New York Times* remarked, "The record of Miss Ederle's nineteen years shows her to be courageous, modest, sportsmanlike, unaffected, and poised. She has beauty of face and figure and abounding health despite a childhood illness that impaired her hearing. She embodies the best of our country. She is the Spirit of America."

That didn't tell half the story. All the way across, the second tug tried to ram Trudy to disqualify her, while Kurt's boat maneuvered to defend her space. Heavy winds and big tides blew her so far off course, her circuitous route nearly doubled the distance of her crossing. After 12 hours swimming, when the sea roiled so she couldn't make any progress, Trudy had refused the pleas of her trainer to give up and climb aboard. The *New York Daily News* reported Trudy saying, "I knew I would either swim it or drown."

In the murk of the storm at dusk on the Dover coast, thousands of well-wishers lit bonfires, sent up flares, and shined search lights to guide Trudy. The pictures showed her strong, steady strokes until she finally reached England. In her red cap, two-piece suit, and still-intact yellow goggles, she walked ashore, shoulders back and head high, to the cheers of the crowd. Only five men had swum the channel before. One of them was Trudy's trainer, who'd finally made it on his 17th attempt in 1911, but it had taken him 23 hours. The *Daily News* quoted him: "No man or woman ever made such a swim. It is past human understanding." When she doffed her cap, her short bob with a curl complemented her smile and figure. An All-American icon was born.

Some in Trudy's now-growing entourage wanted her to tour Europe and visit her ancestors' home in Germany, but Kurt persuaded her to seize the moment and return to New York. A ticker-tape parade down Broadway gave two million fans the opportunity to fete Trudy in person, while tens of millions more gobbled up the news reports of this extraordinary woman. President Coolidge dubbed her "the best American girl." Offers poured in from all over.

Kurt called me from New York: "Trudy's falling for the rush of new friends, hangers-on, and hucksters who want her to earn quick bucks, including a charlatan from Paris who claims he'll make her a million by showing off her two-piece suit swimming in exhibitions throughout the U.S. over the next year."

"Tell her I want her to come to Belle Cottage to celebrate *my* rite of passage across the Manitou Straits." Kurt laughed at the suggestion. "Throw in the prospect of David Ahgosa sharing his legends in sign language so she can learn how to communicate with the young girls and boys, hearing and deaf alike, she's going to inspire." Kurt was all ears on the phone now. "Finalize all bids from major companies for long-term contracts to market with her brand." When Kurt didn't respond, I added, "Hell Damn. Tell her Matt Mann's going to join us, to ask her to run his girl's camp in Canada and coach the new women's swim team at the University of Michigan."

We met over Labor Day weekend. It took two days for Trudy to wind down from all her other offers, including from Hal Roach for a slapstick movie that could set her up for his move to MGM; Adolph Zukor for a comedy, *Swim Girl, Swim*, produced by his Paramount Studio; Flo Ziegfeld for a role diving into a glass swim tank to spice up his *Follies*; and a proposal from Broadway songwriter and wannabe promoter Billy Rose to headline a travelling *Aquacade*.

I found we communicated better when only one other person joined Trudy and me. Pip broke the ice. His own hearing impairment getting worse, he could sit and chat with her, each shouting at the other in Pip's newfangled ear trumpets—really just an oversized telephone receiver—to magnify the sound. Trudy heard Pip when he said he hadn't figured out how to make hearing aids small enough they wouldn't get in the way of speaking parts in the new talking movies or answering questions at press conferences.

By a campfire on the dune under the protective eye of the eagle on the birch box, David shared his legends of Sleeping Bear, Leelanau, and the Great Lakes. He showed her how signing worked. He taught her how to answer in a softer voice. Soon Trudy also began to see how she could understand by reading David's lips.

Matt Mann shared with Trudy how little he made coaching the Michigan men swimmers and running his summer camp. I assured Trudy the Women's Athletic Building would open with a new pool for the Michigan women's varsity in a year or two. Not much compared to her offers for performing, but a steady supplement to the larger amounts she could earn as the new Spirit of America from endorsements.

Trudy asked Kurt and me what we thought of "a few exhibitions" before going into coaching. Kurt explained how none of the corporate sponsors "will go forward if you choose to become a clown in a movie comedy or a sexpot in stage folly, a vaudeville Aquacade, or a cross-country series of local swimming exhibitions."

"You mean you don't want me as America's Flame for Empire if I try a few performances before I help Coach Mann open the girls' swim camp next summer?"

We sat on the back deck overlooking Sleeping Bear Bay. The afternoon sun shimmered on the water, and the big Dunes reached for the horizon. The wind and waves quieted as if to hear the answer. "That's up to Belle," Kurt said, "as I'm starting as General Manager of her family business in two weeks."

Trudy turned to me and demanded, "Whose side are you on?"

I asked Kurt to give us time alone. I patted the spot beside me on the bench and spoke so she could see my lips. "I'm so proud of you." She nodded. I pointed to the Manitou Islands across the deep blue water of the straits. "You inspired me to make my crossing." I kissed her cheek. "I will support whatever you want."

"I was shaking the whole ride down Broadway," she croaked.

"Fooled me," I said, as I wiped away her tears, "and millions of others too."

"I want to be America's Flame." She squared her shoulders. "Tell Kurt I'll also review every other endorsement proposal, even after he starts working for your Empire."

At dinner Papa said Mr. Day and his son-in-law agreed to put off the scheme for dune rides to our Sleeping Mama Bear for a while longer: "That's the condition I set for loaning them money so they could expand their orchards and cannery." Our celebration after dinner with a sniff of Macallan may have seemed small compared to the millions who cheered Gertrude Ederle's crossing, but, together, we set out on another journey.

That evening I went to the attic and composed another lyric in my journal. Feeling the pull of my home I dreaded ever losing, I sang of spring awakening:

Up North

My yearning for Leelanau is like a disease—
the sun through my window bids me awake:
a chorus of robins sings from the trees

to return to Her bosom, where She offers ease
from the thorns and the thistly losses that ache—
my yearning for Leelanau is like a disease—

The shoreline's now free from its ice-sculpted frieze,
and frothy white waves roll, tumble, and shake.
Five or six finches peek out through the leaves—

I dream of the pond near our bubbling creek,
the nest of a wood duck and her handsome drake—
my yearning for Leelanau is like a disease—

a riot of flowers—the hum of the bees,
the honeyed fragrance of spring in their wake,
a redheaded woodpecker taps on a tree:

Soon Brown-Eyed Susans will sway in the breeze.
The squawk of the seagulls, the bluest of seas—
My yearning for Leelanau is like a disease:
A chorus of robins sings from the trees.

Depending on how I sang my song, sometimes its rolling refrains sounded a bittersweet lament ending with a long dash, but other times I chanted them as my personal anthem and closed with an exclamation point. I resolved to let my deeds conserving this sacred place speak in all time ahead. Whatever else, I memorized my Up North song so it could inspire—or console—me to my last go down.

ꕤ

Six weeks later Frost wrote:

> *I regret to report Pip is in the infirmary, not consumption or grippe for he has no cough, only sore throat and fever. Although Rachel appears peaked, she ministers at his bedside. Your boy needs you. Mrs. Frost joins me in insisting you stay at our new Sunset House the College so obligingly financed. As the children all muddle along elsewhere for the time being, you shall have the run of the guestrooms.*
>
> *No lectures, I promise, but I may seek your help with my next book and your other good advice. Speaking of which, Holt will also up my contract. Supper's on me at the College's new Lord Jefferey Inn.*

I called the physician all the students dubbed "Mister Brown." The College had assured us the good doctor knew his limits, most important when to refer any boy for treatment to the hospital in Northampton or, God forbid, Mass General in Boston. Brown told me Pip had contracted "a bad case of the kissing disease, probably from his young Townie girlfriend." He advised my brother to stay in the infirmary until his fever subsided, three weeks at most. When I asked if I should come to help Pip, he replied, "Not unless you want to stop his Miss from seeing him." My respect for Dr. Brown rose.

I called the infirmary the next morning at 10 a.m. and heard Pip shushing someone in the background. "Could that be Rachel?" I asked.

"No, it's the damn frosh in the next bed acting up because Rachel's flying paper airplanes to cheer me up."

"You two back together for good?"

"Marmie," he whispered, "I can't talk about that now, but I'll be okay, okay?"

"Pip, let Mr. Frost know it won't be necessary to open his new house to me for a visit now because you're going to be okay, okay?"

Two weeks later Pip's letter arrived in the mail. His fever subsided so quickly, Mister Brown released him early. *He says my only risk is too much spleen, so my contact sports will be limited to hitting golf balls and playing with Rachel.* The captain of the hockey team would miss his last season. As I read on, I could see that this stab at good humor presaged more trouble for my boy. Although he expressed no regret over her infecting him, Pip noted, *She still surprises me.* After Rachel broke up with him last spring, refused to respond to his letters all summer, and declined his invites to parties at Chi Phi the first two weekends in September, Pip said he was almost resigned to her leaving him for good. *Yet the next Saturday she showed up at my room and told me she wanted only me. I couldn't resist when I should have. She says she wants to quit Mass Aggie, get married, and start a family in Oxford or Michigan. What do you think?*

I thought Pip could do a lot worse than Rachel. After almost three years together, including a three-month separation and then sticking together after Pip got sick, maybe they'd make a good pair. Still, I had a nagging doubt and wrote Pip back:

> *I don't know why Rachel left you last spring. Maybe to find another boy to carry her through after you leave. Maybe because her parents told her to marry only a good Jewish boy. Maybe in the hope you'd miss her so much you'd propose to her. But I don't have any experience marrying, so you'll have to judge*

yourself. Remember Papa's not going to disown you, whatever you decide.

I do know you shouldn't make any decision based on money or giving up your dream to study the cosmos and find the voices of God and man in space. If Oxford's your next step on that quest and you choose to marry, I will support you as I always have and always will.

Love, Marmie

Ten days later Pip replied: *I love Rachel. Even when she's tired, sick, and cranky, I want to be with her.* I wrote back: *Why don't you delay making a final decision until you bring Rachel home for the long holiday break? You both can decide then whether she can stand a Presbyterian Christmas, you can put up with Hanukkah, or you're going to make your own family celebrations, religious or no.*

ఌ

Frost wrote me in his stubby handwriting at the beginning of November:

My Second Belle,

Michigan signed me up for a poetry class for two weeks in the spring term. Sign up Mr. Roethke and any Graces you can find, and you'll be my teaching assistant. I'll do my best to quell the stampede from the Inlander boys by limiting the seminar to 15. I'll be staying down the street from you at Dean Bursley's so I can drop off my drafts of poems for my new book for you to type. But I don't want to catch cold by our big Teddy Bear dragging me into your glasshouse pool again. In the meantime, send me your suggestions for our seminar. Robbie

Pip's recovering nicely, and Rachel's beginning to glow again.

I prepared a list of 15 poems, 10 a good blend of happy-sad drinking songs, for Frost. I added a sizzler from Louise Bogan, one of Amy Lowell's short but sassy *haikus*, one of Millay's cheekiest invitations to love, and Emily Dickinson's hottest poem, "Wild Nights." To test whether Frost would even read my suggestions, I included a five-line *tanka* from Jun Fajita, a photo-journalist gaining fame in some modern poetry circles with this other ancient Japanese form. I set a schedule for the class: five poems each day, all 15 by the end of the first week. The second week each student would say a poem he or she had written. I posted the list of poems and class schedule to Frost.

☙

Pip and Rachel arrived at Belle Cottage shortly after noon in early December. I smiled at the contrast between the two. She bounded up the front porch, bundled in a bright red parka, matching snow pants, big fur-lined mittens, boots that looked like mukluks, and a red stocking cap with matching ear flaps and tassel that Pip had bought her. My boy trailed behind in his usual mishmash of old shoes, baggy pants, weathered pea coat, and bare head showing off the white streak on one side and long, dark hair flopping over his forehead and his back collar.

I wondered what the proper attire might be in Oxford next fall and reckoned tweedier than that of my brother. He looked different, too, taller than I remembered, his long legs and arms longer, his long fingers longer. Still gangly but stronger, his chest remained oddly hollowed. I couldn't tell whether Rachel was dressed as one of Santa's chubby helpers or the blushing bride-in-waiting, ready to build an igloo. The way she hung on Pip's arm and every word, she acted as if she'd never let go.

In the hall I helped Rachel take off the first layer and then one more before she stepped out in black pants and a dark cable-knit sweater whose bulk couldn't hide her substantial endowment. Her eyes and hair matched her garb, and her ruby lips, rosy cheeks, and pert nose made her appear more luscious, even ripe.

Papa and I had decked the living and dining rooms with fir garlands and boughs of holly but avoided any other sign of religious decoration for the holiday season. After lunch Pip drove to the stove works in Empire to join Papa, Kurt, and David. They wanted to tinker with a new air intake and exhaust system for our gas furnaces.

Rachel joined me in the kitchen to help clean up. After the last pan had been wiped dry and put into the cupboard, she poured us each a cup of tea, and we sat at the kitchen table. "Last week my mother screamed and ran Pip out of our house when he asked permission to marry me." I couldn't blame my brother for deciding to ask Rachel before he returned home for the holidays, but then she began to cry. "I'm pregnant." I sat right up at that. "My mother wants me to put the baby up for adoption with a Jewish family." I swallowed hard. "I want to marry Pip and raise our child."

I had a number of questions but asked only one. "Have you told him yet?"

"After he proposed to me."

I had to give Rachel credit: she didn't use her pregnancy as a club to get Pip to marry her. "Let me talk to him. Whatever you two finally decide, I'll support."

That night Pip came to my room. He showed me his latest design for his huge horned trumpet. It was beginning to shape up. I even understood when he showed me how its odd, four-sided flare would capture radio waves scooped up from deep in space. He talked about how much he looked forward to studying with the leading astronomers in England, marrying Rachel, and raising their new baby together there.

"How're you going to deal with Rachel's mother?"

"We want to get married here, now, so she won't be able to say no."

Given Rachel's age, I didn't know if she could without her parents' consent. "We'll have to talk with Miss Schultz first to see if Rachel can." I paused. "Whatever her advice, do you think you should then talk to Mrs. Goldberg, too?" He nodded through his grimace. "One more question: Are you sure the baby's yours?"

"The baby *will* be mine." Always a willful boy, he'd brook no doubts.

Next morning Pip, Rachel, and I met with Miss Schultz. Although Massachusetts courts might not respect Michigan's judgment, Rachel did not need her parents' consent to marry if Pip and Rachel intended to make their permanent residence here. When we got home, Papa said, "Mrs. Goldberg called several times, and she's on the line again." We trudged into his study, and he handed me the phone. "She says she'll only speak to Belle." Pip grabbed the phone, tried several times to talk but then shook his head when Mrs. Goldberg wouldn't stop screaming through the phone, "No, only your Marmie!"

I picked up, and Mrs. Goldberg began, "Belle, even if Rachel pulled the pregnancy card on you, too, Mr. Goldberg and I don't want her marrying your brother."

"Pip and Rachel plan to wed in a civil ceremony before our circuit judge here."

"You don't even know if your brother's the father." When I didn't respond, she continued, "This isn't personal to Pip. We can't accept our daughter marrying *goyim*."

Not personal? I saw red, remembering how Rabbie's mother had said much the same thing to me. "You can't stop her."

"She needs our consent."

"Not under Michigan law."

I heard Mrs. Goldberg arguing with Mr. Goldberg but couldn't make out what they said. Mrs. Goldberg came back on the line. "Tell Rachel that Mr. Goldberg and I will disown her if she marries your brother."

"That's not my province." I handed the phone to Rachel, but Pip took it and told Mrs. Goldberg he would be a good husband to her daughter and a good father to her grandchild. I could hear her shouting to speak to her daughter. Pip handed the phone to Rachel. She listened for a long time but told her mother she was going to marry Pip tomorrow. As Rachel began to hang up, I took the phone. "Mrs. Goldberg, when the baby's born, I hope you and Mr. Goldberg will join in holding your grandchild."

I didn't relay what she replied: "Never. You've already stolen our daughter."

After a private wedding at Belle Cottage with David Ahgosa as Best Man and me as Maid of Honor, we held a baby shower and gave presents to celebrate Rachel's marriage with Pip. Papa also welcomed the prospect of his first grandchild: He might yet find a male Peebles to run the family business.

The newlyweds headed back to Amherst to find an apartment off campus. My boy had finally fledged his Marmie's nest. I could only hope Pip and Rachel would eventually return from Oxford to Michigan so I could be a part of their new family, maybe even help them raise their offspring.

ᔓ

David must have sensed how troubled I was because he stopped by Belle Cottage the next afternoon. He invited me to don snowshoes for a trek to figure out how we could lay out plans for the rest of our soon-to-be golf and outing club. The bright sun low in the cold sky offered little warmth. Its crystal light appeared almost blue as it reflected off the fresh powder. David loped on top of the deep snow up the steep ridge without making a sound. I followed slowly, pounding in his tracks and huffing for air.

I joined David at the crest. He quieted my panting by showing me how to breathe more deeply, as I did when swimming. I heard the chatter of the few birds in the pines. I listened as the breeze whistled through the beech and birch. I heard the light thwack as a pine cone bounced, even the rapid pit-pats as a jackrabbit raced across the snow.

David moved north across the crest. I imitated his quiet gliding gait. He pointed to the meadow that fell east down the ridge until it rose up the treed hill on the other side. “Skis,” he said. He retraced his steps and pointed to a wide opening in the pine forest that ran down the hill, all the way to the docks on the Crystal River, where the raised boathouses protected our Chris-Craft and Mackinaw in winter. “Toboggan run.” David glided across the crest and pointed to the meanders farther south in the river, frozen solid. “Skates, sticks, and pucks.” He nodded toward the Bealses’ camp in between, pointed to the layout for their new school and the path through the trees, all the way back up the steep slope to where we now stood. “Snowshoes.”

David turned and pointed down through the trees on the steep slope to the base of the ridge. “The Homestead.” When I looked puzzled, he said, “Our four-season lodge, four stories tall, made of cedar. It will look west over the bay to the Sleeping Mama Bear, her two cubs, and the sunset.”

I could see Pip inventing a mechanical rope tow to carry people, toboggans, and skis up the hill on the snow, but it would be a steep climb for golfers to trek up with golf bags and clubs. “What about a clubhouse for golf up here?” I asked.

“Right where we’re standing, low-slung, all-wood, blending into the trees, with views of the course east,” he answered, “and of the bay, island, dunes, and sunsets west.”

I took off my snowshoes, David did the same, and we sat and huddled close together to survey our Homestead. As one of the shortest days of the year began to draw to a close, the setting sun fell to dusk in the cloud cover and cast a blue light across the frozen bay. He held me close, and our breathing soon came together as if one.

That night I composed another sonnet, this one for David Ahgosa:

Crystal Moment

We follow deer tracks into the silent wood,
The crunch of our boots the only sound.
Around us shaggy boughs of pine bend low,
An offshore breeze swirls wisps of snow.

Our campfire rings a sculpted mound of white
Blazing bright with each shaft of morning light
Filtered through birches and ancient oaks—
Like memories that burn and fade in smoke

A crimson cardinal weaves among the trees,
A snowflake lands upon your ruddy cheek,
You kiss me once, your lips do not linger—
No fire for us this cold December.

By sharing this crystal moment with the snow,
We consummate the love we might have known.

Spring 1927: Ann Arbor and Amherst

Not having heard from Frost by the end of February, I distributed my tentative class schedule and the poems selected for the first week of his spring seminar. On the Sunday before the first class, Frost called and asked, "Are we ready?" Before I could answer, he said, "I'll drop by after dinner to make sure."

Frost arrived at 7:30 and handed me a big sheaf of his poems to type. We sat on the couch in front of the fire, he with his ginger ale and me with a cup of Lipton's. He talked amiably about how much he missed his "Arboreal friends, Michigan Wolverines and the Sleeping Bear." I shared the news from around town and up north. Finally, he asked, "What should we do for the seminar?" I showed him the list of poems for the first week, handed him copies of each, and shared the schedule for students to read their own the second week. He looked these over as if he'd never seen them, jotted a few notes and asked, "Was 'Wild Nights' published in a Bianchi or a Todd-Higginson collection?"

"I suspect Mrs. Todd took particular pleasure in picking it, but..." I had to chuckle. "She and Higginson rounded the rougher edges."

"But this version's still so graphic."

"Even a virgin recluse has passion, Robbie."

Frost then read aloud, "Wild Nights—Wild Nights! … Futile—the Winds—To a Heart in port— … Rowing in Eden—Ah, the Sea! Might I but moor—Tonight—In thee!"

His full lips pursed so I thought he might explode. Before he had the chance, I said, "Just another blend of your happy-sad drinking song."

"More like a siren in ecstasy after stealing her mariner's heart."

"Maybe more a passionate wish than an exultation over any deed done." When his full lips fell to a frown, I added, "As in Miss Lowell's *haiku*, 'Afterwards I think: Poppies bloom when it thunders. Is this not enough?'"

His pales eyes brightened, and he did whistle. "I know. Her 'Hokku,' as she called it, also makes me wonder." He finished his pop and got up. "I'm game to give your approach a go, even the *tanka* you included in your post to test me." With a wink and his puckish smile, he added, "Don't worry if the discussion of these poems, or the student readings of their own, flag."

I didn't know how to respond, but it didn't matter. He recounted the story of one of his first teaching jobs, to would-be teachers at a normal college. The first assignment he gave his class was Mark Twain's short story, "The Celebrated Jumping Frog of Calaveras County," wherein the owner of an "edercated" frog named "Dan'l Webster" bet forty dollars that his frog could jump farther than any other. A stranger took up the bet and managed to stuff quail shot down Dan'l's throat "that filled him pretty near up to his chin." Sure enough when the starter "touched up" the two frogs from behind, the stranger's frog "hopped off" while "Dan'l couldn't budge."

Frost continued, "When I asked the class what this story taught them about teaching, I didn't get any answers."

He looked to me to see if I wanted to offer a reply. Remembering his unwillingness to grade his students' poems, I said, "Don't cram too much stuff down your students' throats, or they won't be able to learn."

"Drat," he said, "You ruined my punch line. *There are two kinds of teachers: those who try to fill their students with so much quail shot they can't budge, and those who give them a little kick in the rear and the students fly much farther on their own.*" With that, Frost touched my hand. "I'll be here Tuesday for lunch to get back to work on the book."

The seminar rolled along better than either Frost or I had any reason to hope, nary a sign of Strait seeking to monitor our odd gatherings. Sure the old bard got to telling stories about poetry, learning, and life, but each student jumped at the chance to say what they thought about one poem the first week and to recite their own the second. Frost made few critical comments on any student work, only once remarking of a too-pretty poem by his favorite Grace, "My Dear, there is a difference between fetching and far-fetching." He wrote on every draft, "Keep writing, RF."

The class met at my house the last Friday. In ten minutes the first four students recited their poems. I'd saved Roethke for last. He didn't disappoint. He offered a parody of Frost's own "What Fifty Said," suggesting that students come in knowing they know nothing but after teaching for 30 years think they know everything. We all held our breath, waiting to see if Frost would take umbrage and put Teddy down. Instead Robbie sang from memory "The Bear" and laughed with Teddy as the boy in his outsize fur coat swayed back and forth from one cheek to the other, eyes shut and snout uplifted.

Teddy returned the favor by rising and singing Frost's "What Fifty Said." The big bear of a boy swayed back and forth on the balls of his feet and towered over the rest of us sitting around my living room. As he sang the last line, "I go to school to youth to learn the future," he searched the many pockets in his outsize fur coat until, at last, he pulled out his flask and offered it to toast Frost.

The 53-year old poet, looking younger than the day I met him, made a show of standing up to the bigger boy, unscrewed the cap, whiffed the fumes, and fell back. Frost made as if to knock back a big slug, but he sputtered and coughed until Teddy slapped him on the back. Robbie turned to me. "Share a sniff of Talisker with all our friends while I savor my ginger ale."

Rather than remind him that Teddy and I had finished that bottle after the last of our working sessions on his new book—retyping for the fifth time his lengthy but still unsatisfying title dialogue, "West-Running Brook"—I walked to the bar and poured 17 shots of Laphroaig. I advised sipping, but our big Teddy Bear never minded me. Only two of our mates needed any assistance breathing after they followed suit and choked while gulping the Scotch down. Soon Teddy rounded the crowd up and left.

"How do you think my new collection will be received?" Frost asked.

"If you ever finish the title poem, your book won't lack for buyers."

"And the reviews?"

"If you want another Pulitzer, get cracking with Holt on your complete poems."

Frost rubbed his full lips with his stubby forefinger and thumb, and his large brow furrowed. "Will you stay at Sunset House for Pip's graduation, or do I have to sign up to teach another seminar here in the fall?"

"You didn't stay at my Cambridge House, so I don't think it's fair for me to impose on you and Mrs. Frost that way."

"What would that fat fop Nym say about that?"

"Too much," I conceded.

☙

The third Saturday in April, Pip called. Rachel had fallen ill a few days earlier, mild headache, heartburn, and somewhat elevated blood pressure. He'd taken her to the Mass Aggie's infirmary right away, but the doctor there treated her on an outpatient basis for three days before admitting her for bed rest and further observation. Anemia set in, and Pip transferred his wife with unborn child to the hospital in Northampton. "Marmie, Rachel looks terrible, but she won't let the doctors take the baby."

"Do you want me to see if the specialists at University Hospital here have any suggestions for the doctors there?" After Pip said he welcomed that, I asked, "Have you told Rachel's parents?"

"She won't let me."

"Don't you think they should know?"

"You're right. I'll call Mrs. Goldberg now." He paused. "Will you follow up with her, too?" I couldn't say no.

First, I talked with the University doctors specializing in women, babies, pregnancy, and birth. They warned of the grave risks to mother and child associated with such symptoms and promised to talk with the doctors in Northampton. Unless Rachel's condition improved in the next 24 hours, an emergency cesarean section was the best hope to save mother, if not child.

Then I called Mrs. Goldberg, and she said, "Your brother already called."

"Rachel's very, very sick."

There was a long pause. I heard Mrs. Goldberg arguing with her husband. "Tell your boy that Mr. Goldberg and I will visit Rachel this afternoon."

I drove my Phaeton 17 hours, straight through the night, stopping only for gas. I arrived at the hospital in Northampton at noon on April 19. I walked into a white room with two single beds, white linens, separated by a white curtain. On one side lay Rachel, Pip holding her hands on her big belly. I barely recognized her, her face so puffy and pale, her usually full lips drawn so tight they looked like wisps of ash. Underneath Pip's hand, I saw her fingers so bloated and white they looked like fat stubs of chalk. She moaned. Pip looked up, his pale gray blue eyes full of hurt.

On the other side of the curtain lay an older woman, all alone, one leg in a white cast propped up in the air by a trapeze and the other missing below the knee swathed in white dressings. Her thin, white hair, wet and matted against her forehead, the rest of her face contorted in pain; her skin was so papery it looked like blue-white ice. Her hands reached to touch the part of her leg that wasn't there. She screamed.

I approached a nurse in the white hallway. She wore a white uniform with white shoes, a white hat pinning her salt-and-pepper hair back. I asked to speak to Rachel's doctor, but she said he was still in surgery, operating on the last of the victims run over by the drunken old woman in a terrible car crash. The nurse returned to the room with me. The nurse had more success administering some kind of pain-killing shot to quiet her patient than we did quieting ours. When Pip excused himself to go to the men's room and the nurse left, I put a cold compress on Rachel's forehead. I leaned over and gently massaged her temples. I could feel the beat of her racing heart. She stopped moaning and opened her eyes. I had never seen such a depth of hurt. I continued rubbing her temples and whispered, "Rachel, it's Marmie."

A spark of life appeared in her eyes. She opened her mouth. But then her thin, pale lips drew shut, and only another moan emerged. I massaged her temples, and she struggled to take several deep breaths. She looked over my shoulder, grabbed my hands, and held on with surprising strength. "Don't let them kill my baby," she said.

A man in a pressed white coat, white bristles on his unshaven face, towered over us. "I'm Dr. Sawyer," he said. We walked out to the hallway.

"Did you talk with the specialists from Michigan this morning?"

"And the doctors from Boston Lying In." I waited for him to continue. "The only option left is to deliver the baby immediately and hope for the best." He looked so tired.

"How long you been in the operating room?"

"Fourteen hours."

"Any other surgeons available for Rachel now?"

"Not here." He shook his head. "No one better qualified until you get all the way to Boston, and I'm not sure Mrs. Peebles will survive the ride."

"Do Rachel and Pip know?" He nodded. "What are the chances?"

"Although she says the baby's likely short of term, better than even odds for the child, less than that for the mother; I'm sorry."

"And if you don't operate?"

"Convulsions, seizure, and death for the mother within a day, which will also kill the unborn child." I shook my head. "The specialists from Michigan and Boston agreed we'd wait until this afternoon in hope of some improvement, but…"

He turned his head and looked through the door at Rachel. I saw her body stiffen and her lips twitch. It looked like the seizure of a little boy in school I had seen when I was seven; he had never returned. "Did you talk with Mrs. Goldberg?"

"She said it's in God's hands."

Pip returned, and we walked into the room. He held Rachel's hands and rubbed gently across her belly. "The doctor's going to operate to save you and the baby."

She looked over his shoulder to me: "Help Pip care for our baby."

I left to call Mrs. Goldberg at her home to invite her to share the vigil. When I returned, Rachel, ashen and anxious, lay on the gurney under a white sheet. Pip leaned down and kissed her. "When you wake up, I'll lay our Ruth or Rob in your arms."

"No matter what, don't give up our baby," she answered. Pip held her hand, all the way out the door and down the hall. Soon he returned, and we sat together, waiting. The old woman on the other side of the curtain made no sound. Pip sat stony-faced, buried in the inner universe to which he often escaped. I felt helpless.

Within the hour the baby, surprisingly plump, dark-eyed, dark fuzz for hair, rosy cheeks, and red lips, slept peacefully in the nursery. Baby Ruth was a miracle because Rachel died on the operating table before the baby was born. Somehow, the mother still managed to will her child to life. When the baby began to caterwaul, a matronly nurse held the pink-faced little screamer up to Pip with a bottle.

My boy didn't flag. He cradled his child in one arm and tickled her lips with the nipple. He smiled and cooed as the baby eagerly suckled, gurgled, dribbled, and appeared to smile back. When the baby sated herself, Pip asked the nurse if he could say goodbye to Rachel. At first she shook her head, but then she said she'd ask. Within a minute she stuck her head in the door to the nursery and waved us forward. Pip carried his baby, and I followed as the nurse led us down the hall and around two corners to the recovery room. There Rachel's body lay, still on a gurney. Her arms and hands were as pale as the thin white sheet on which they were folded. Eyes closed, face serene, she felt no pain. Pip laid the baby on her arms. "Marmie and I will take good care of our Ruthie."

The nurse gave my brother several more minutes to say goodbye. As the baby slept in Rachel's arms, Pip's angular face contorted. Desolate and distant, he couldn't say a word or even cry. I vowed to help him raise the baby as a gift from God, sorry I'd ever wished for this opportunity, determined not to let my guilt stand in the way of loving Ruthie as if she were mine. I tapped Pip on the shoulder, and he picked his baby up. Ruthie was as vulnerable, loving, and small as Mama's baby the day I had lifted him up. I raised my boy Pip ever after. I would mother Ruthie as no one else could.

We walked down the hall and returned Ruthie to her cubby. In the rush of emotions, we'd not introduced ourselves to the nurse there. Mrs. Peck smiled and gave us both a pat. "All hours we'll be here to feed your baby whenever she wakes up. We'll clean her bottom and feed her until you're ready to take her home." I didn't even know where Pip and Rachel lived or whether there was room for me. I had no idea what arrangements needed to be made. Mrs. Peck added, "If you need more time to sort things out, don't worry. Baby Ruth's a gift for all of us, too."

When she left, I said to my brother, "Ruth is such a lovely name."

Pip's bony face contorted: "We'd planned it as a peace offering to Rachel's mother." He shook his head. "Won't do much good now."

"Pip, do you think Rachel would prefer to be buried with her kin here?" His gaunt face now looked stony, as if he couldn't express any emotion, but he nodded.

We left the nursery and walked down the hall, right into Robert Frost. He reached up and grabbed Pip by the shoulders. "I'm so sorry about your Rachel." Pip dropped his head, and the old man held him for the longest time. "You, the baby, and Belle are staying at my house, right through to graduation."

"What about the rest of your family?" I blurted.

"Mrs. Frost's already at our Stone Cottage in Vermont with Marjorie, but we'll all come back if you ever need help." He must have seen my surprise because he continued, "Elinor insists you three make our Sunset House yours for the rest of the semester." I never was so glad to see that contrary man in my life. He added he'd take Pip, stop at his apartment off Belchertown, pick up his clothes and the things for the baby, and drop them at our home away from home. He gave my boy a friendly push down the hall. He whispered so Pip couldn't hear, "You've got business to settle with Rachel's parents in the waiting room."

I knocked on the door and entered. Mrs. Goldberg rose, a gray-haired vision of her daughter, 40 years older. Her simple black dress was neatly pressed but washed so many times it had faded, black shoes polished but worn thin.

"Mrs. Goldberg, I'm sorry about your daughter." She did not blink or nod. "Rachel was so brave, even after she knew." I paused. "She saved her baby."

Mr. Goldberg sat impassively in his chair, a black suit old but pressed, black shoes polished but with holes worn through the soles. He looked much older, stiff, almost as a statue, his face pale and stone-like. I looked to him, but his watery eyes fixed on his wife. As

Mrs. Goldberg continued to stare at me, I couldn't figure out whether she was fixing to attack Pip for killing her daughter or figuring how to challenge Pip for custody of the baby.

Eventually, Mrs. Goldberg said, "It's not Pip's fault."

I didn't know what to say, but I noticed Mr. Goldberg's hands shook and his fingers trembled. *Parkinson's*, I thought. What was it Frost said I had here, "business to settle"? Mrs. Goldberg was too poor to pay for the care Mr. Goldberg would need. I asked, "How...," but clamped my mouth shut before I said "...much." Good Lord, what was I thinking? Mrs. Goldberg had just lost her daughter.

Mrs. Goldberg continued, "Rachel chose your brother as the father." She paused. "Please make sure he's as good a father as any *goyim* can be for a child of David." Mrs. Goldberg said this with resignation, as if she'd prefer to smite me with a sword.

"I hope you'll let me make arrangements so you can join as grandparents."

Mrs. Goldberg squared her shoulders. "We don't want anything more to do with you, your family, or the newborn." I recoiled at her attack. The short woman stepped forward and demanded, "All we want is our baby back." I shook my head dumbly. "We will bury her beside her older brother, Rob, she so adored." She dropped her eyes. "He died in the trenches in the War."

"May my brother say his last goodbye to Rachel at the burial, too?"

Mrs. Goldberg turned to her husband. His head now shook as hard as his hands and fingers, but he willed himself to nod. Mrs. Goldberg said, "Our daughter's name will appear on the gravestone as Rachel Goldberg only."

She still viewed the wedding as null and the baby illegitimate, sacrileges both. "I'm sorry for the loss of your daughter," I said, "as I am for the death of my brother's wife." I looked at Mrs. Goldberg. "Rachel decided to name the baby Ruth after you, and you will always be welcome to hold her as your grandchild whenever you wish."

Mrs. Goldberg took that in slowly, turned, walked back to her husband, sat in the chair next to him, held his hands in hers, and bowed her head. "We only need to know where to call to let you know the time of the burial tomorrow."

"We'll be staying in Amherst, at the Frosts' house on Sunset."

I couldn't sleep that night. I scribbled several opening lines, but no song followed. My mind roiled with the images and sounds of a dying wife and willful mother, a newborn baby sleeping in lifeless arms, my boy losing his mate while she gave him a daughter, a mother disowning her daughter in life but reclaiming her remains in death. I couldn't figure out what to think or say. Finally, I sang a different lyric:

Babel

I hear a baby's lusty cry
for mother's milk—
while, atop the Tower,
shaman, ministers, imams, rabbis, and priests
all claim the true god—
Little Ruthie does not care!

Johnson Chapel filled the next morning at nine a.m. The College had no denominational affiliation, but religion and moral philosophy confronted all Amherst students. For Pip, a Presbyterian in a New England town without a kirk, Chapel provided time for prayer and reflection with the God he thought he would surely find in his heavenly search for the voices of His creation.

This was not the first time that the chaplain, the Right Reverend Donovan, and President Olds presided at a gathering to mourn a death in the Amherst family. Twice in Pip's four years, the new College Church hosted a memorial service for a faculty member. This was the first time for a young person, the wife—and mother of the child—of a fellow Amherst student, but Frost felt more comfortable in Johnson Chapel, where he'd spoken so many times before.

Students and staff packed the main floor and balcony. The chaplain offered a brief eulogy to Rachel, while the president offered consolation for the loss of Pip's wife and hope in Ruthie's birth.

This was the first time Robert Frost offered a benediction at the College. He introduced his poem by telling how my brother as a teenager took him to an observatory and took on "a crotchety, old academic who couldn't see beyond his peers." Frost thanked "Pip for inspiring this old poet to open my eyes to search the galaxies above as the flowers below, to seek signs of life in distant planets as the nearest bud, to see creation in the death of shooting stars as the pine cone gives birth in a forest fire."

"Now," the poet continued, looking down at my brother, "you must carry on." In a steady voice, firm and strong as New England flint, a ramrod-straight Frost said his "Stopping by Woods on a Snowy Evening." Most critics read this poem as a story of a lonely rider stopping his horse on his last trip home and thinking of all the things he must do before he dies. None who heard Frost say it to my brother that morning heard that tone. No, Frost concluded in his most matter-of-fact voice, "The woods are lovely, dark, and deep, but I have promises to keep, and miles to go before I sleep… And miles to go before I sleep." A daughter to love and nurture, a quest to find the voice of God and man in space, who could know what else: a life full of promise and promises yet to keep.

Frost offered my brother, and the rest of us there, no alternative to keeping on. Pip and I needed the bucking up as we emerged from Johnson Chapel onto the quad: the bright sun that greeted us quickly fell behind a gloomy, gray overcast.

A handsome young man stepped up, embraced Pip, and introduced himself, "Miss Belle, I'm Charley Cole." He turned to my brother. "I talked to Charles Drew last night. He's sorry he couldn't make it up from D.C., but he wanted me to tell you not to give up your child or your dreams of studying on a Rhodes at Oxford." My brother nodded as the long road ahead seemed to brighten, if only a bit.

I drove Pip to the hospital in Northampton. We fed baby Ruth in the nursery and then headed cross-country through the drizzle and mist to the Jewish Cemetery of Amherst, a good 10 miles northeast of the town. We parked off the road and walked respectfully behind a short line following the body, covered with a plain white shroud, carried by six bearers. Seven times the rabbi, holding a polished shovel, halted on the way to the gravesite not far from the entrance. Mr. Goldberg followed slowly, Mrs. Goldberg helping him on one side, a tall young woman on the other. Two older couples came next, then eight young women. A short young man trailed behind with us.

When we reached Rachel's grave, next to her brother's, the rabbi said only a few words, and only one stood out for me: when he nodded to Mrs. Goldberg and the baby in Pip's arms and called them both "Ruth." The cantor sang what sounded like a psalm in Hebrew. The bearers lowered the shrouded body. The rabbi took the shovel, pointed down, and pushed three loads of dirt into the grave. He placed the shovel in the ground, and Mr. Goldberg, with the aid of Mrs. Goldberg and their tall companion, pushed three more piles of dirt atop his daughter's body. Mrs. Goldberg pushed three more piles of dirt in the grave and stuck the shovel in the ground. The young woman, willowier than Rachel, followed. Her long hair covered the left side of her face. Pip nodded and whispered, "Sister Rebekah." The mourners and pallbearers each took a turn. Mrs. Goldberg shook her head at the young man beside us but nodded to Pip and me, and we helped push the earth to fill the grave.

A burial chant led by the rabbi followed, with responses from all the mourners. Pip and I could only hang our heads, as we did not know the words. I looked down to the short young man next to us and saw he was crying. I wondered how he'd managed to alienate Mrs. Goldberg even more than Pip.

The rabbi and Mrs. Goldberg helped Mr. Goldberg lead the mourners out, followed by Rachel's older sister. We passed in rows of two between the two parents and offered our condolences, but Mrs.

Goldberg turned and led her husband away before the lone young man, Pip, or I could say anything.

Pip talked to Rebekah. After she introduced him to the short young man, I pulled the rabbi aside and introduced myself. He expressed his condolences and asked about the baby. I explained how Ruth was healthy, how she would be staying with Pip at Frost's house, and how I'd help mother her. He offered to help, but I explained I needed his help for something else. I asked how far along Mr. Goldberg was with his Parkinson's.

"He'll need a wheelchair within a few months, then much greater care."

I wrote a check to the rabbi and gave him my address. "Give me your estimate every quarter, and I'll advance the funds for what he needs."

The rabbi expressed his thanks.

"You must never let Mrs. Goldberg know the source, or she'll reject it."

A week later Pip drove northeast of Amherst once again. I held baby Ruth. When she cried I soothed her, by singing poems, whether mine or those of Frost, Burns, Dickinson, or even Amy Lowell. When we arrived at the Jewish Cemetery, we saw Rebekah and her short friend arranging pebbles atop the new gravestone. Ruth started crying when we came within sight of the carvings: "Rachel Goldberg 1909–1927" and, below, the trunk of a tree. Oh, a life cut off much too young.

Rebekah walked over and asked Pip whether she could hold the baby. When she cradled Ruth, the baby quieted, and the long hair fell away from the side of the woman's beautiful face. A large, purple birthmark covered the area between her left cheek and ear. The young man, his dark eyes filmy, came up, gently touched Rebekah's arm and hummed. Baby Ruth, not yet able to focus, looked for the sound and began to gurgle and coo. No lovelier duet ever graced a grave, and I forgot the birthmark as I watched this scene so full of love. Maybe this young man was lucky to have Rachel's sister to console him, but Pip was more blessed to have Ruthie.

Rebekah handed the baby to me, took Pip's hand and led him to the gravestone. She handed him a large pebble, and Pip placed it atop the others. As he looked into the distance, his whole body slumped. Rebekah held my brother and comforted him.

I couldn't hear what they said, but the young man introduced himself, Bernard Brodsky. A second-year student at MIT, he had gotten to know Rachel over the summer when he worked at the physics lab at Amherst to help pay for his tuition. Pip returned, took the baby from my arms, and kneeled by her mother's grave. Brodsky, tears now flowing down his cheeks, hummed again. Pip held the baby, still cooing and gurgling, said the Lord's Prayer, sang the doxology and said his final goodbye.

All the while the older sister held the young man up, her left arm wrapped around his waist. Pip returned, holding the baby, Rebekah touched his arm and young Brodsky, still humming, gently placed the tip of his little finger on Ruth's tiny hand. When the baby tried to grasp his finger, he pulled back and walked out of the cemetery.

ཡ

The week of graduation, Elinor returned with Frost to Sunset House. Pip's class chose the poet as their only honorary member, the Class Choregus, for sharing his "happy-sad blend of drinking songs." Mrs. Frost loved Ruth, and Pip and I welcomed her help. She even accepted the stream of classmates who continued to drop by, ostensibly to help with the cleaning, washing, and meals, but mostly to share their affection and support for Pip and his baby. Elinor offered them tea, juice, ginger ale, and cookies.

Marjorie drove down for graduation weekend. She looked pale and thin, despite her delight in Ruth and show of good spirits. I pulled her aside, and she admitted she'd suffered from the grippe and stayed in bed most of the winter, exhausted and anxious about her illness. She asked after Teddy, and I told her the bear of a boy was as incorrigible as ever.

"That's mostly an act," she replied.

"You were good for him."

"He was good for me." A little color rose in Marjorie's cheeks, and she left to join her father and Pip with Ruthie.

Mrs. Frost approached and said, "We're thinking about a trip with Marj this fall for a change of scenery." I offered to host the Frosts in Ann Arbor and up north. "She's not well enough to see Mr. Roethke yet." With a sigh she added, "I just don't know what to do anymore. I worry so about Marj and the rest of the children."

Mrs. Frost and I watched as Marjorie held the baby and Pip and Robbie finished loading the car for the long drive back to Michigan. Elinor touched my arm and said, "Ruthie is such a blessing for Pip."

"For me, too," I replied.

Marjorie and Ruthie got to cooing at one another and then laughing.

"Maybe for Marj, too," Elinor said.

"Oh, how I hope so," I replied as I grasped Mrs. Frost's hand.

Pip took his little girl and hummed a sweet lullaby. Frost joined in with a Burns ballad, and soon the three of them were dancing cheek to cheek. Marjorie joined them in their rollicking, and soon Elinor and I followed step.

On my drive home to Belle Cottage with Pip and our baby girl, a new song rolled into my head, a happy-sad blend of Pip losing a dear mate but gaining a daughter, of my never finding a mate but now mothering a second child, of my fearing to fight against the contraries of life but learning to sail with my Ruthie, as the shifting tides of time marched on. By the time I got to my attic nest, I came to my senses: no baby deserved the burden of being sung to sleep with such expectations placed on her. Instead, I composed:

Marmie's Lullaby

Daisies droop their weary heads
White tails curl in forest beds
Sparrows sleep in downy nests
Time for baby's eyes to rest.

Sunset paints the clouds with copper
Sailors turn their prows to port
Honeybees on the wing to hives
Gossamer wings as soft as sighs.

Pine scent fragrances cooling air
Squirrels are seeking hidden lairs
Farmers put their plows away.
Until the morning dawns the day,

Close your eyes, my tired babe—
Stars are winking through the trees,
A silvery moon sails high above:
Happy dreams, my dearest love.

I vowed to teach our girl how to swim so she'd also come to love the embrace of Sleeping Bear Bay.

A gift and note from Stella Brunt also inspired me when we got home. Her note read: *The cover of the enclosed may show the way to honoring our dear President Burton. Might even remind Frost to return to Michigan.* I tore the plain wrapping off the two heavy, thick rectangular objects and found two copies of the *Michiganensian*, the yearbook put out by the class of '27. There, in the center of the handsome, black leather cover, stood a slender red brick beacon, rising gracefully in narrowing stages through golden clouds and blue sky to a glorious carillon. Judging from the colonnade connecting the tower to four-story buildings on either side, it had to be more than 200 feet high. Underneath this ethereal *bas relief*, the caption read, *Burton Campanile*. Good Lord, the One-O from such an immense carillon at such a height might just ring all the way to Amherst.

I mailed the second copy to Frost with a note:

> *Thanks to you and Mrs. Frost for taking Ruthie, Pip, and me in when we were most in need. I don't know how we could ever express how much this meant to us. As a token of our gratitude, I hope the cover on the attached gift reminds you that Michigan will always welcome you. It may take quite a while before Burton's proposed bell tower ever rings One-O to call you back. In the interim please remember that Pip, Ruthie, and I will be at the front door of Cambridge House and Belle Cottage to welcome you, Elinor and Marj into our two sheltering Arbors any time.*

Summer and Fall 1927: Glen Arbor, Oxford and Ann Arbor

Ruthie gave Papa a second chance at fathering, our first summer home. When she grasped his little finger with her tiny hand, he cooed. When she cried, he fed her, held her close, and entertained her with his funny faces and dozens of birds, rabbits, and fish he whittled out of driftwood. When she smiled, his worn face lit up, and the years dropped away. When she needed changing, Papa would fight Pip and me for the opportunity to clean up the mess, dust her bottom, and give her the reward of more bottle. Baby Ruth thereby gave Kurt space and time to run the business in Empire, David to manage the stove works, and Pip to tinker with the design of our gas furnace, build his horned antenna on Empire Bluff, and help David and Skipper build the Homestead lodge.

Charles Lindbergh might have trumped The Spirit of America's Channel crossing with his nonstop solo flight across the Atlantic in his *Spirit of St. Louis*, but he didn't diminish our "America's Flame." Rather than crow that her ticker-tape parade down Broadway was bigger or argue that her feat was more demanding, Trudy joined in cheering a second American hero for his spirit of adventure and courage. Their crossings thereby joined in the public's mind to double the size of their respective achievements, popularity, and fame. The flame of America's best girl only burned brighter.

ᔓ

On the last day of July, I drove through Glen Arbor to Glen Haven to see D. H. Day. He looked all of his 75 years, drooping moustache and thinning hair all white, nose longer and redder. Yet his body was as wiry as ever, and he still sported a big cigar. He greeted me and asked whether I'd join him in buying back Alligator Hill from the Chicago investors who'd bought him out. "You and I could still make Day Forest Estates the Adirondacks of the Midwest."

Rather than talk about my family's commitment to the Homestead, I replied, "I see you're putting your sales proceeds to better use here." He'd remodeled, repainted, and refurbished his yellow clapboard Sleeping Bear Inn and expanded his red cannery building. In front of his general store, he'd put in new red pumps that filled the gas tanks of several cars as we talked. But steamships for the masses were fading, and big-city moguls hadn't bought any lots for summer cottages on his second-growth forests.

"Belle, you're right," the old codger replied. "I'm arranging to sell the rest of my dune land to the state when I die for a fair price—more than your Miss Schultz offered on your behalf, thank you—and the feds have agreed to transfer their holdings so we can preserve Sleeping Bear in a state park as one of America's great tourist attractions."

"Going to reserve only the concession for your shop at the dune climb?"

"Despite your Papa's good loan and better advice to expand our fruit business, I repaid him. I'd like you to test the pros and cons of our scenic dune rides."

The Dark Ogre drove right up in a new Ford, ragtop down. D. H. opened the passenger door, sat me in front, and hopped in back. We drove along his new state highway, freshly paved, to the Coast Guard

Station. Sven pulled the car hard left, and we raced up the gentle rise on a gravelly path through the aspen, birch, and beech. When we emerged on the dune, Sven floored the accelerator.

Mr. Day leaned forward, patted my shoulder, and yelled in my ear, "Don't know if a scenic ride offers enough of a thrill to attract riders—"

"Look at the fox over there," Sven interjected, pointing to the right, but he steered the car hard left, off the trail, and roared the Ford down a steep slope. I nearly flew out of the convertible. My heart beat in my throat so hard I managed only a sigh when Surtr slowed at the base of the hill, turned, and cruised to a stop at the top of the next dune. The view west across white-capped Lake Michigan, spreading blue all the way to the horizon, took my breath away. Sven turned and sped south, toward the big hump of the Sleeping Bear rising in the distance.

When we arrived at the east front of Mama Bear, Sven pulled to a stop. Glen Lake, the Day Farm, and the still-vacant resort, links, and landing strip cut through the forest on Alligator Hill all beckoned. Mr. Day lit one of his big cigars and puffed away with pride.

The Ogre didn't try to drive over the big hump. Instead, he yelled, "Look at the big buck up there."

When I peered up into the brush and fallen trees leading to the pinnacle, he jerked the wheel to the left and raced the Ford down another steep dip. I flew in the air again. When we landed, my bones and teeth rattled this time. Just as unsettling, when Sven slowed at the bottom to turn, the car stuck in a drift of soft sand. The giant and I got out and pushed as D. H. steered, his mouth clamped shut on his cigar. When we managed to get the Ford back on firmer ground, I climbed in front, but Mr. Day waved his cigar for Sven to sit in back. Old D. H. cruised back to Glen Haven. He pulled the Ford to a stop by his general store, gave Sven a shake of his head, and escorted me to my car.

"What do you think, Belle?"

As the Ogre stood on the front porch of the store and glowered down, I said, "More than enough thrill." I put on my best smile, waved at Sven, and whispered, "But Mr. Day, you might want to wait until you can modify your dune car so it has shoulder harnesses to hold the passengers in and bigger tires so they don't have to get out and push." D. H. chomped on his cigar. "Can you steer clear of the Mama Bear, too?"

He took a pull on his cigar, thought awhile, and exhaled. "Damn it, girl, the whole dune's named after her."

"Won't be much left after your son-in-law leaves her drowning in his wake," I replied, loud enough so Surtr could hear.

"David Ahgosa tattooed Sven pretty good with his bare knuckles about that, too." D. H. chomped down on his cigar again. "Okay, if I ever decide to run a fleet of dune buggies, I'll tell Sven and my boys to steer well clear of Mama Bear, okay?"

I knew that would last only as long as D. H. lived, but I nodded and asked, "What do you think of our plans to build a golf and outing club and Homestead Inn?"

"Hope you sell plenty of stoves to cover your losses if those Chicago boys get Day Estates Resort and lot sales humming before you open."

"They don't have our secret weapon."

"I did hear Pip's been setting course records all over our north country."

Although my brother had honed his game so he could compete with the best in Michigan, I said, "No, we've signed up the British golf course doctor, Alister MacKenzie."

Old D. H. shook his head but smiled. "Belle, I wish I had enough money and time to work with you to conserve more of this place." He took a big puff of his cigar. "You're a damn sight prettier and a lot smarter than that stubborn old Scotsman you've got for a father." The toll of time furrowed his brow. "He and I've done pretty well, though, but you've got a lot more time ahead than we do."

I couldn't help lifting that dear man up. "Thanks for challenging

Papa. Together, you planted the trees that regenerated our forests and our lives."

"Leastways, we avoided the infernos that burned up whole towns from all the slash left by the cut-and-run lumbering crowd on the Lake Huron side."

"Pip, David, and I will build on what you and Papa taught us," I said.

"You best keep an eagle-eye on Sven or engage him in your cause after I'm gone."

A week later I visited the big, horned ear trumpet on the highest point above the bluff south of our stove works in Empire. Fifteen feet long, the aperture flared from a shallow two-foot by two-foot square at the listening post to the 10-foot-high, 10-foot-wide scoop at the end. The entire contraption sat on a circular platform to spin the horned trumpet around its horizontal axis. A metal ring encircled the big horn midway out and could rotate the scoop on its vertical axis. Pip put the big hearing aid through its paces and explained how a crude pen recorded sounds, even when he didn't have someone listening for "cosmic static." When I asked what he'd heard, he replied, "At first, mostly the lightning." Pip looked over Lake Michigan for another storm. "When we paid more attention, though, we captured a steady *hiss*."

"Where's it from?"

"Haven't figured that out, yet." Pip paused and looked up. "Originates so close to the sun, it could be our big solar furnace fusing and firing. Maybe much farther away."

The next week Pip drove me to David Ahgosa's orchard. Already, 10,000 cherry trees stood in neatly planted rows on the sides of the rolling hills, with a good mix of larger pear and apple trees at the top. David, Pip, and I climbed the tallest hill and looked east, to the choppy blue waters of Grand Traverse Bay and the greensward of Old Mission Peninsula, from which David's forebears fled 75 years before. To the west we looked across Lake Leelanau and Good Harbor Bay to the rougher waters in the Manitou passage. Small pears and apples already flooded the trees all around us.

"How long before your first harvest?" I asked David.

"This fall." He pointed to the large sheds on the shore east of his village. "Your brother helped us design the gas burners for the big boiler pots to make jellies and jams."

"Pip, you helping David get away from our Empire enterprise?"

"Don't worry, I'm good for at least ten years," David replied. "I'll need your second five-year loan to build what we need for pies, crumbles, juices, and—"

"What's with the vines on that steep, rocky hill to the north?" I interjected.

"Pip's also helping figure out how to ferment grapes into wine."

"I suppose you used the broken pallets at the stove works to make the stakes?"

"Just making sure there's no waste." Both my boys made me so proud.

I left and headed up to Northport to confer with Miss Schultz. She assured me the planning to include a world-class swimming pool in the Women's Athletic Building was going forward and that my loan to finance it was secure. "You should hear the Director of Women's Physical Education talk, though: 'The social position of women does not permit any physical exploitation or unladylike competition.'"

"Tell him to tell that to Trudy's face."

"*She* did. *Doctor* Margaret Bell says, 'Participation in varsity athletics can disrupt the functioning of the female reproductive system.'"

"Hell Damn. What's the Little President say?"

"He's holding his powder, hoping the issue will go away so he doesn't have to bring yet another dispute to the Regents."

"Can we help finance a new women's and children's hospital?" I asked. Miss Schultz replied, "Maybe, that'll also give us standing to tell the Regents to let Trudy coach her team to a national championship." The little lady, hair now gray, stouter body covered in a frilly blouse and tailored coat, still fought for me.

Two weeks later, I asked Dr. Alister MacKenzie, "What do you think of David's layout for the Homestead course?"

"I'd like to hire the lad." Already close to 60, the dapper gentleman with a trim mustache wore matching tweed knickers, vest, coat, and cap, his tie tucked into his shirt. "The big drop-off from the tees on the holes down to the river will be spectacular, but we'll need to make sure the closing holes aren't so steep as to ruin the good walk on the way back up."

He patted David on the back. With Pip they led the way down the ridge toward the Crystal River. The American golf course architect Perry Maxwell and I followed. We paused to look up to the low-slung, rough-hewn cedar-sided clubhouse under construction atop the ridge, with glorious views in all directions. "How many courses can you stand for us to design in Michigan?"

"No more than three," I answered.

"Want to keep your Homestead exclusive," he said, more statement than question.

"Exclusive in terms of the attraction, but not the color of the members: our one bar is the ability to pay, in green."

Maxwell chuckled but did admit he and his mentor were heading down to Frankfort tomorrow to explore developing a new course for an exclusive development that wanted to sell lots to rich white folks.

"What are they going to call it?"

"Crystal Downs."

"If you do go forward there, we'll offer a good rate for their members to play, dine, and drink here." Might as well let everyone see we had the best course in the Midwest.

Below us Dr. MacKenzie and the boys chattered together, pointed, and walked back and forth through the pine, maple, beech, birch, and aspen. When they reached the Crystal River, they followed the bank to see the new construction at the Bealses' school.

I left to join Skipper and my Papa at the Homestead Inn, nestled against the steep hill. Vertical cedar siding climbed five stories to the peak of the center gable. Matching sets of double-hung windows divided into four long lights would reflect the sunset over Sleeping Bear Bay in all its crimson glory.

"Papa," I said, "it's too steep a hike to the golf course. How are the guests at the inn ever going to make it up to the clubhouse?"

"No worries, lassie, Pip's designed a funicular."

Skipper interjected, "David and Kurt will build it at the shop over the winter and have it running by the time the first nine opens next summer."

"What's a funicular?" I asked.

"A hill-hiking railway," Papa proudly proclaimed.

"Two cars connected by a cable," Skipper added, "with a passing lane midway."

"Great for carrying skiers up in winter, too," Papa said.

I nodded but added, "Too bad we didn't outbid the Chicago investors for Mr. Day's Alligator Hill."

"You're not going for that crazy notion that you can buy cheap now," Skipper said, "and then sell dear to the Uncle Sam for a national park, are you?"

"I'm relying on the dearer notion that we can buy for a fair price now," I answered, "and conserve the rest of our Delight of Life here forever."

Skipper blanched. "You don't want me to trade my campsite south of the Sleeping Bear Dune Climb to the Chicago boys so I can develop a golf and ski resort with D. H. on Alligator Hill instead?"

"No!" I yelled. "We'd prefer to make you a partner in our golf and ski resort here, thank you."

"Enough with the dickering, you two," Papa said, "Let's go sniff the Macallan." Much as I admired Papa, old D. H., and the Skipper, I knew I had a lot more work ahead with David Ahgosa and Pip to conserve our corner of Leelanau Peninsula. Sven Surtr represented only the first wave of a new generation of less considerate projectors.

On the back porch of Belle Cottage, Pip cradled his baby and conferred with Dr. MacKenzie, Maxwell, and David. Papa poured the Scotch, the sniffing and tasting began, and the conversation flowed.

"How many trees have to go?" I asked.

"Not many," the good doctor assured. He also explained how we'd do a controlled burn every few years and let rabbits keep the woods clear and grass short. "Don't want any golfer searching for a wayward shot to spoil the brisk pace of play."

Papa asked, "You a fellow Scot rather than one of those Yorkshire plodders?"

"Call me MacKenzie with a capital *K*," the doctor exclaimed. "My parents were both Scots. Once I put down my saws, sutures, and military camouflage after the Boer War, I adopted the spirit of our old St. Andrews' sod, too." He raised his glass in a toast.

"My kin lived in Peebles," Papa replied with pride in his family name.

"Why don't you join Pip and the baby this fall, and I'll show you around?"

Kurt and David piped up to let Papa know they'd take care of our Empire enterprise and oversee completion of our inn and clubhouse. Pip smiled and said only if I also joined to help him with the baby. I hadn't crossed the Atlantic for Rabbie or Trudy, but maybe Papa, Pip, and our new girl could hold me up; might convince my boy to let me continue to mother Ruthie when he returned home after finishing Oxford, too.

That night I sat on Mama's chest in the attic and opened the window to the moonlit bay below. The west wind whistled through the trees, and the waves of whitecaps broke gently in a warm hum. I let David Ahgosa show me the way, and I sang:

Eden on Earth

I see the gentle pine-scented hills
rise above the dappled waves
that lap the shores of Leelanau;

I walk the quiet wooded paths
listening to the chorus of songbirds
as they twitter in the trees;

I smell the pungent smoke of campfires
by our majestic lake
and search the August sky for shooting stars;

This surely must be paradise on earth.
Adam and Eve lost theirs;
Let this not be our fate.

Ojibwe guide, show me the way:
What magic medicine will protect
these sacred dunes and this great lake?

I vowed to return from the trip across the pond with all my family to find out.

ග

The *H.M.S. Majestic*, the flagship of the White Star Line, landed in Southampton at noon on September 15. Pip and Papa had never been happier to see landfall. Even at 55,000 tons, the largest passenger ship in the world rolled with the sea. They'd been sick for five days. Good thing I didn't tell them the full story. White Star named her after a sister ship of the *Titanic*, sunk by the Germans in 1916. Germany transferred the older but larger *S.S. Bismarck* as compensation in 1920. The cruise line rebuilt and renamed her in 1922 when a dangerous crack appeared mid-ship.

Although baby Ruth and I sang, played, ate, and slept with apparent ease throughout the voyage, I wasn't in much better shape. The farther we traveled from my two sheltering Arbors, the more I doubted my ability to cope. With Pip and Papa laid up in their berths, I held onto baby Ruth for everything I was worth.

Pip and Papa scrambled down the gangplank as fast as their wobbly sea legs permitted. I carried Ruth, her eyes wide open to take in all the sights of a busy port. At least she hadn't inherited my phobias. I was so engrossed in promising her I'd never hold her back when she was ready to fledge, I didn't see the face that greeted me when we reached the wharf. A flash of satiny crimson rising up and kissing Pip on the cheek opened my mouth just enough to greet Rabbie's open lips as if he'd never left. Only Ruthie's squeal saved me from burying my tongue deep in his. I straightened myself as best I could, and Rabbie introduced me: "Belle, meet Mirja Fitzpatrick."

I held onto Ruth tightly as I surveyed the lithe sprite in front of me, as vibrant as the character that Frost first shared with me from Rabbie's novella. Beside her vitality, I felt the big, slow, fearful creature I was on my darkest days. Her long, silky black hair was plaited in a braid down to her shapely rear. Her green eyes flashed from a tan face with rouged cheeks and lips. A silver necklace with jade bangles jangled between comely breasts pointing out from her red satin blouse. "Belle, you're as glorious as Frost says…" She relieved me of Ruth. "…and I want to read your every poem."

Ruth's little fist pulled on Mirja's necklace, glistening in the midday sun. My little babe wouldn't let go, even while Mirja settled Papa, Ruthie, and me in her spacious, three-bedroom apartment in Oxford. On Broad Street above Blackwell's Books, a stone's throw from Rabbie and Pip at New College, it was convenient for her trysts. Yet Mirja returned to London during the week for her day job as an editor at the William Heinemann publishing house. Rabbie and Pip ate meals with the other boys at New College but often joined us to help Papa and me with the baby and to explore Oxford.

What a beautiful old city: winding cobblestone streets; stone walls; dozens of Gothic colleges with chapels, museums, and theaters; and my two favorites, the domed Radcliffe Camera and adjacent Bodleian Library in the center—all bordered by two lovely rivers, the Thames and Cherwell. The pall of sooty air hanging over Oxford left the great buildings black, but I escaped to the storied reading rooms, where I buried myself.

On my second visit to the Lower Camera, I must have looked lost as I pored over Shelley's first folio. A gangly undergrad, pasty long face, hair sticking up in all directions, slouched down beside me. Wearing a rumpled tweed coat, brown tie askew, he asked if I'd mind if he joined me. I didn't, and he introduced himself, "Wystan Auden, The House."

When I introduced myself, as I always did, simply as "Belle," he squinted at me and asked, "Are you Scots Presbyterian?"

I wasn't sure what to say, and I only managed to nod.

He said, "Somerville, then?"

That stumped me, so I shook my head.

He explained it was the second women's college. The first, Lady Margaret Hall, named after the mother of King Henry VII was reserved for what he called "us good Anglicans." The second, named after a great Scottish mathematician, who managed the feat despite being a woman, took all comers, "including you Presbyterian heretics."

His good humor loosened the knot holding me back, and I said, "No, I write poems, but I'm here helping take care of my brother's baby while he's studying cosmology at New College on a Rhodes."

Auden clapped his hands over mine and explained how he'd shifted from biology and medicine to English and poetry last year. "Let me hear one of your verses."

All eyes in the Lower Camera turned on us. Before we got shushed, he walked me out. I invited him to Mirja's apartment down the street, as I didn't want to stick Papa alone with Ruth for too long. I sang my "Up North" anthem on the way.

"I like the sound," he said, "but where's up north?"

I explained how Robert Frost had taken me under his wing and suggested I collect a number of my poems about the Leelanau Peninsula in northern Michigan and call it *Up North.*

Much to my surprise, he squeezed my hand. "Hmmm, I also like Frost's folksy tunes."

When I squeezed his right back, Wystan blushed and withdrew his. "What's 'The House?'" I asked to cover any embarrassment.

Auden explained how King Henry VIII took over Christ Church College and made it the cathedral home for the Church of England's Archbishop of Oxford.

Outside the apartment I heard Irish ditties from the piano and knew Mirja was back. When I led Wystan in, the dark beauty rollicking across the ivories played a wilder Latin number, and Papa danced with our little baby. Ruth saw me and raised her hands. I took her from Papa, cradled her close, and invited Wystan to join us. The lanky lad romped and stomped with us as Mirja raced down the keys all the way to the lowest notes before heading back up to the highest with a flourish.

When I introduced Wystan to her, she asked, "Are you the poet friend Isherwood brags will be the next Shelley?" While Wystan nodded sheepishly, I explained how he found me reading Shelley. Mirja handed me an envelope and said, "Chris told me I should sign Wystan up for Heinemann before the Faber brothers grab him." She explained to Wystan how Heinemann was preparing the European publication of Frost's next book. She added, "Frost tells me Heinemann should launch this All-American Belle so she can return home to a hero's welcome, as he did so many years before."

"Capital idea," Wystan said, "her *Up North* will sing."

"Belle shared her poems with you," Mirja exclaimed.

"Odd form, but her villanelle does roll right along, *My Sweet,*" he answered.

I fled with Ruth into the nursery. I sat down in the comfy rocker, fed her a bottle, and sang "Marmie's Lullaby" until she fell asleep. I opened Frost's note:

> *Dear Belle,*
> *We hoped to travel with Marj this fall to England, but she's fallen ill again. Don't fret about me waiting for Burton's Bell Tower to ring me back. Michigan's asked me to do another course in creative creation, even shorter this time, three hours in one week in December and another three in March. If you cross the pond again by then, I trust you'll assist. Invite your big Teddy Bear.*
>
> *"West-Running Brook," poem and book, finally threatens birth, thanks to your excising "The Lovely Shall Be Choosers." Time for you to let go, too: Mirja can midwife your creation so Heinemann can give birth to your "Up North" poetry over there.*
>
> *Don't let her stealing Rabbie away stand in the way either; she didn't even know he had deserted you. Blame that fool papish boy for thinking he couldn't raise his children under our darker Scots cloud.*
>
> *I trust Pip and you are also enjoying playing with your new charge Ruthie as much I do playing with my grandchildren. It's not too early to teach the cute tikes that learning like life is a game, too, at times hard and vexing, even ordinary yes, but also rewarding with wonder and discovery. And don't worry about any supposed mistakes in her education: who can ever know what's best when there is so much in our kin beyond our ken?*
> *My missus sends her best. Frost*

By the time Ruthie awoke and we returned, our course for the next two weeks had already been set. Mirja had persuaded Wystan he should drive Papa and me on a tour: to meet Dr. MacKenzie at his home course, Alwoodley, north of Leeds; to show us the Pennine

Moors Wystan roamed as a boy near the North Yorkshire mining village of Rookhope; to explore Papa's home-place in Peebles in the Scottish Borders; and to find my mama's kin in Helensburgh on the Firth of Clyde. Having finally settled down in Oxford long enough to feel the fist in my chest beginning to relax, I said to Papa, "That's a bit much for the baby, don't you think?"

"Mirja's agreed to help Pip take care of Ruthie while we're gone," he replied.

From Mirja's smile I guessed that wasn't all she'd take care of. "We can't ask Wystan to chauffeur us for so long," I replied.

"My sweetie, Chris, is away for two weeks, playing with another boyfriend," Auden replied, "and traveling with you will beat my moping alone here."

"Honestly, Wystan, we've only just met."

Auden looked at me as if I was crazy, but Mirja interjected, "That divine *Mister* Isherwood is such a naughty boy!"

Egad! For the second time, I'd mistaken an offer of friendship for an advance. Did I already look such an Old Maid that I attracted men who preferred their sex to mine? I looked at Mirja radiating and knew that would never be her problem. She added, "While you're gone, Ruthie and I will go with Pip to study with the great astronomer Eddington in Cambridge."

My brother popped through the door. He'd grown into such a tall, angular, oddly handsome man, I shouldn't have been surprised that Mirja fell for him. His pale blue eyes fixed on her. I blurted, "Cambridge for two weeks with Mirja and Ruthie?"

His face glowed.

I looped my arm around through Auden's, nodded to Papa, and asked, "When do we leave?" I didn't dare hope what all this might mean for Rabbie and me.

Two weeks later one of the other boys visiting Rabbie's room in New College taunted Wystan: "You're a poofter." The 20 boys crowding around Mirja and me turned and watched. The brat had red hair, a red mustache, and a red face. His tweed coat, flannel pants, and regimental tie were just as insolent. "You shame all Oxonians," he told Auden.

Pip and Wystan each rested one arm on the old stone mantel above the roaring fire in the paneled room, its wood a rich ochre patina from centuries of waxing and rubbing. Between them stood one empty Laphroaig bottle and a half-empty Macallan bottle.

I'd grown to admire Auden on our trip, ever-friendly and informative in sharing his old haunts and legends in the Yorkshires, ever-curious in learning about the golf gods from Dr. MacKenzie at Alwoodley and St. Andrews, ever-attentive to Papa's need for refreshment and even greater urge for relief along the way. Kindred spirits, I shared with Wystan my poems about the legends of Leelanau, my "Mary Bell's Death," and my yearnings for renewal with the dunes and Great Lake, and he shared his stories about the lore of his Pennines. He explained how the lead mines scarred his favorite landscapes, while soot from burning coal cast as black a pall over Charles Rennie Mackintosh's School of Art in Glasgow as the buildings in Oxford. I talked about how we faced the same conundrum of nature versus development in Leelanau County and how I hoped that natural gas and our Empire stoves and furnaces might offer hope for a cleaner future. He talked about his home: rivers carving sharp gorges and caves in the limestone landscape, while rain and runoff eventually rounded the tors and crags into lovely green hills and valleys. We visited dear Mama's seaside hometown in Helensburgh on the banks of the Firth of Clyde. There we also toured Mackintosh's acclaimed commission for a strikingly modern private home and the less impressive Larchfield School where Wystan interviewed for a teaching post.

Earlier this day, Wystan had taken me to the Ashmolean Museum to see one of the earliest Renaissance paintings concerning the age-old issue of man versus nature. Piero di Cosimo's *Forest Fire*, circa 1500, looked like a sorcerer's colorful version of an ancient wall carving.

Two and a half feet high, it spread almost seven feet across the wall. The big coral bulls, tawny lions, fearsome boars, other beasts with human faces, and all variety of birds fled from the roaring inferno in the forest. Was it ignited by lightning, men rubbing sticks together, or an act of God or the devil? A few small, dim men appear to concentrate on bringing water from the nearby lake to put out the fire. Although the figures looked almost flat, the landscape with green meadows, blue lakes and sky, and the forbidding forest on fire gave great depth and vitality to the scene. Surprisingly, Wystan had held my hand tight in the hush as Cosimo's wild art washed over us.

The red-headed lout broke my reverie: "You can't even keep up with a damn *Rhodie huckleberry*." Auden listed as he turned to face this assault, while my brother held more firmly onto the mantel. I had no idea what inspired their drinking contest.

Rabbie O'Bannon, already loyal to Wystan, took three steps and decked the double-insulter with one punch. Mirja raced over, helped the florid boy up, and shook her head at Rabbie. Wystan stumbled over, held the boy's left hand, and said to Rabbie, "Mr. O'Bannon, meet Mr. Isherwood." Rabbie apologized, but Auden turned to his lover, "tut-tutted," and said, "Teach you: time wounds all heels."

Mirja invited the combatants back to our apartment "to heal all wounds instead." On our walk along Broad Street, we learned that Isherwood had instigated the drinking contest to initiate my brother into another of Oxford's odd rituals. Auden's longer-standing taste for Scotch did not match Pip's greater capacity. I told Mirja she should sign Wystan up for her publishing house instead of badgering me. "He'll soon rival Frost in America and Yeats here." Mirja took another look, but Auden didn't look very promising: Pip and Rabbie held the listing poet up, while his lover pushed from behind.

As we opened the door, Papa greeted us with a rollicking reel, and Ruthie shrieked for joy. The rest of the room filled with smiles, except for me: bad enough, I'd fallen for a good man who didn't want my kind; worse, Rabbie showed no interest in me.

ᔓ

The next morning I got up early with Papa, and he asked whether Pip and I could manage if he headed back home. He missed his work with Kurt and David at his Empire, overseeing the new Homestead and, well, his trysts with Miss Patterson. Before I could reply, Mirja, wearing a teal satin robe, her long silky hair brushed to a shine, said, "When Mr. Peebles sets sail, I'll move back from London and help with Ruthie here." Since it was Mirja's apartment, how could I object?

After Papa set sail, we settled into a regular domestic pattern: Mirja or I handled any feeding or changing at night. Pip, excused from sleeping in his quarters at New College, woke early to feed and change the baby, prepare breakfast, and play with Ruthie. By 10 a.m. Pip headed off to the library, the observatory, or the pitch; Mirja headed to her study to read and edit manuscripts; and I played with Ruth and prepared lunch. We three ate together at one p.m. Mirja or I cared for the baby the rest of the afternoon and prepared dinner. On my afternoons off, I usually joined Auden in the Bodleian, Christ Church, the Ashmolean, long walks, or punting the Thames—always sharing poetry, whether ours or others. As often as not, Rabbie or Wystan would join us for dinner, and in the evening Pip and I took turns caring for Ruth and putting her to bed. Surprisingly, when Pip stayed home for the evening, Mirja usually joined him, Rabbie showed me the town, and Auden repaired to his privacy. When I stayed home, Rabbie joined Ruthie and me while Mirja played with Pip and Wystan. I didn't mind my old boyfriend's attention.

Three weeks after Papa left, Pip invited his "most kindred spirit in all academia" to stay for the weekend. My brother had latched onto the odd clergyman while visiting Eddington in Cambridge. A mathematician and engineer by training from Belgium, Georges Lemaitre appeared in his long black frock and stiff white collar as a stout novice priest. His horn-rimmed circular glasses suggested he might be as much insightful scientist as Catholic seer. Abbé Lemaitre had studied Einstein's equations and the universe under Eddington but disagreed with both. In an accent tinged with his Flemish, Georges explained, "Their steady state theory of the universe doesn't make sense."

"What's your proof, Father?" Mirja asked.

"Hubble's observations confirm what Slipher's suggested," Abbé Lemaitre began. "All the galaxies continue to recede from one another." He cupped his hands and fingers together into a small ball and then opened them wide as his arms flew up and apart. "Over time the universe keeps inflating from an explosion in the primordial atom."

"Georges," Mirja replied, "sounds like you better watch out or you could prove as much a heretic to the Catholic Church as Galileo before you know it."

"The high priests in academia are more skeptical of my theory." A sad, older look fell over his face as he explained: "Einstein says my math is correct but my physics is abominable, while Eddington says my theory, 'although elegant, is repugnant.'"

"When you join us in Empire will you help us understand the source of the odd hiss recorded by Pip's big, horned ear trumpet?" Mirja asked. Good Lord, was she already planning to move back with Pip and become his wife and Ruthie's mother?

I offered to stay home with the baby while the others escorted Abbé Lemaitre to his speech at New College and on to dinner afterward. After they left, Rabbie knocked on the door and offered to help with Ruth. Even as we put my baby down for the evening in her crib and I sang her to sleep, Rabbie touched my hand, my arm, my shoulder. When he laid me down on the couch in the parlor, I tried to shake my head. I didn't know whether he was jealous of Mirja's passion for Pip or testing whether I might yet offer more, but, oh, how I ached for him—and, oh, how his touch thrilled. The baby slept through all our thrashings and couplings, whether on the couch or floor or in the bath.

Thank heavens my cries concluded before the good cleric returned with Mirja and Pip. Sitting together, primly playing cribbage, Rabbie and I looked like old friends passing the time while the baby slept. I was sure Mirja could smell the change in the room, and her grip on Pip's hand only tightened. Yet when she fixed her green eyes on Rabbie, I saw her firm hold on him.

For two weeks I continued the charade of playing with my Rabbie while Ruthie slept, but I couldn't take the unspoken any longer. "You still intend to marry Mirja to bear your babies and raise them Catholic?" I asked him.

"I'm letting God decide." I slapped his face. With a hurt expression, he explained how he'd tried to beget a child with Mirja for almost two years but failed.

"Unless you make up your mind to marry me, no more religious trials, thank you." Oh, how I wanted to join him but not as a dam to his sire in some misbegotten test of God's will. My time away from my safe Arbors over, I decided to sail home.

The next morning I asked Pip if I could take Ruth back with me. He protested, but I couldn't tell whether he'd miss our baby or the excuse she provided to tryst with Mirja. Finally, I persuaded him I could take better care of our baby at home than he could manage in Oxford. Pip promised to rejoin us for a long break over the holidays.

When Mirja found out, she asked if I would share my poems so Heinemann could get first crack at publishing *Up North.* Instead I replied, "Do you believe marriage should be shared only by couples of the same faith?"

"Only if they're planning to have children," she said.

Oh, Pip, I'm sorry for you, too.

On the passage home, I read the poems I'd composed on 27 scraps of paper. Some made me cry; a few made me laugh. Only one did I copy in my songbook:

Worlds Beyond

The mystery of the stars
the wonder of afar
if only we could travel
from earth to outer space
we could see ourselves
with another face
perhaps discover distant life
worlds not mired in war and strife.

Oh! The mystery of the stars—
If only we could stretch that far…

As much as I wanted to, I couldn't throw one other poem overboard:

My Golden Laddie

A golden laddie one fine day
Stole my smitten heart away—
Twas in a field of new mown hay.

I pine for him from morn to night,
His bonnie smile his dark eyes bright—
Our afternoon of pure delight.

His lips were warm, his body firm,
This maiden had no will to spurn—
I was butter in his churn.

A golden laddie one fine day
Stole my smitten heart away—
How I yearn for his return!

When I arrived at the depot in Ann Arbor, I posted a letter to Professor Robert Frost at Amherst College I'd written on the train ride from New York:

Ted Roethke stayed at my Cambridge House while I visited Oxford, but I just arrived back, in time to help host your poetry seminar. Our Teddy Bear and two of the Three Graces will join us, as will Stella Brunt.

Ruthie's too young for the class, but you'll find she's grown into a happy child and loves hearing songs, mine and yours. Pip's staying in Oxford, but I'm not sure how long he'll last. His tutor sees no point in searching for voices in space, and the rest of the physicists and astronomers there mock his big horned trumpet recording a hiss.

You were right about Mirja. She's hard to resist, but I managed to keep my verse from her press. She proved a big help playing with Ruth and more than adopted Pip, but I hope she doesn't desert him as Rabbie deserted me because we darker Scots don't share their Catholic light.

Give my best to Mrs. Frost and Marj.

Roethke picked the baby and me up in my vintage Phaeton, ragtop down. I held Ruth tight as Teddy raced the roadster around Washtenaw. I didn't ask him to put the top up because the baby squealed with delight at the cold breeze.

Teddy dropped us off next to the glasshouse in back. I opened the door into our Garden of Eden, much warmer and more luscious inside than out. Ruthie scrabbled in my arms. She crawled to the side of the pool. I stripped down, jumped, and beckoned my kin to join me. She paused for no more than a second and then fell toward me. Her little body submerged only for a second, and then she bobbed up and floated into my welcoming arms. Ruthie knew how to crawl faster in our pool than on the ground.

I clutched my little mermaid to my bosom as Teddy carried our luggage from the car.

After I put Ruth down for a nap and sang her to sleep with "Marmie's Lullaby" and "Up North," Teddy and I talked in the kitchen as we prepared supper. He recited the poem he'd written for Frost's seminar, "Silence." I asked if I could read it. He handed me a piece of paper splashed with his green ink. I took my time to decipher the writing, opened my old Corona, typed it out, and handed him the clean, black-type copy.

Sitting slumped in his chair, the vest of his gangster suit unbuttoned, his quiet voice couldn't mask his inner storm as he asked, "Belle, what do you think?" His brow pulsed, his eyes bulged, the sinews on his thick neck stuck out, and his body shook. He began to weep. I pulled his head to me and rubbed his temples. "It's all right," I said and quoted his verse, "What shakes your skull to disrepair shall ever touch my inner ear."

Teddy gently pushed me away and looked up. No leer. No ribald joke. No pretext. "You saw right through me all along, didn't you?"

"Many of us share your darkness. We're so afraid to speak of it to others, it's a relief for you to say our despair shall never touch another ear."

"Do you think the Old Bard will like it?"

I couldn't help chuckling. "If he can stand the pain of hearing you say what he so often feels but holds back, he'll hug you close, too." Teddy reached up, pulled me down, and buried his head in my breasts. This time I pushed him away, but ever so gently.

Baby Ruth caterwauled from the nursery upstairs. Teddy asked if he could bring her down. I handed him a bottle. "Good luck changing her diaper, too."

When the baby quieted, I tiptoed up the stairs to the landing and heard Teddy singing poems. One I recognized as mine, several from Frost, two children's verses from Bogan, one from Millay, all thankfully innocent. The rest I assumed were his.

Over supper Roethke wanted to learn all about our trip. Rather than disclose the diverse triangles among Pip, Mirja, Rabbie, Ruthie, and me, I told him about Wystan Auden. Teddy asked for more. "He's got the sensitivity of Bogan or Millay and the fire of that Irish bard Yeats," I said, "but he'd benefit from more of Frost's common touch."

"Do you mind if I head off to the library to read Auden?"

"He hasn't really published much yet." Teddy looked so crestfallen, I added,

"If you hadn't been in such a hurry to put another rush on me, you could have read my copy of his first 18 poems." I retrieved the limited edition and handed it to him. He read several of the poems, and his whole body slumped when he saw how good they were. "Teddy, there're more than enough ears in this world to hear your voice, too."

The next week, when Roethke shared his "Silence" with Frost over lunch at my house, Robbie did like it, although he again warned our big bear to fight against falling to darkness or mania. Teddy paid little heed. Maybe he thought the depths of despair and the heights of mania brought out his best writing. A dangerous risk, yes, but Roethke was more of a gambler than Frost: he shared more of Dickinson's wild nights than Frost's more lyric allusions, ironies, and contraries.

Then again, I might have read too much into the young poet ignoring the old bard's warning: Teddy's attention fell on my houseguest, Stella Brunt. Her dark hair, still cut in a pert bob, and her liaison with the governor only made her shine more. Frost also couldn't resist his first flirtation at Michigan either. Our conversations around the kitchen table and the glasshouse pool danced so, even baby Ruth took delight. Only once did she cry: Teddy made the mistake of telling Frost he and Yeats might at long last have to step aside for a younger generation, and he proceeded to recite one of Auden's first poems. Frost took such loud offense, I had to sing a lyric from his new book. The sound soothed hurt feelings, and Ruthie stopped her wailing. When I sang our anthem, "The Bear," Teddy began rolling back and forth, Ruthie started clapping her hands in time with the tune, and Frost joined with us.

That evening I managed to enlist Dean Bursley to take Frost and Roethke over to Professor Cowden's home to meet with the latest crew of Inlanders so I could finally talk with Stella alone. As we sat on my big couch, I asked how she managed with Governor Osborn. "His wife keeps us from marrying, but I'll become his assistant, manager, and muse." I shook my head. "Well, Roethke and Frost keep coming back to you."

"Not the same as with your governor," I replied. "None are devoted to me."

"How do you manage caring for baby Ruth and your interests here and up north?"

Feeling sorry for myself, I said, "Trudy Ederle and David Ahgosa are the only two friends I have left." I omitted Kurt because I still feared he was using our Empire as a way-station to set himself up for a move back to New York and his mate there.

"You've got so many more friends than that," Stella said.

Yes, I had to admit: all my family, including baby Ruth now, Miss Schultz, even Rabbie, Wystan, Matt Mann, Roy Cowden, the Bealses, Dr. MacKenzie, my Teddy Bear, and Robbie, not to mention others who'd already passed: Mama, President Burton, and, just this fall, dear old D. H. Day. "Would you trade them all so you could live with one man under cover of being his secretary and adopted kin?" Stella asked. I thought hard about Rabbie and David, even considered my three odd poet friends, but shook my head.

On Friday afternoon I invited Trudy Ederle to join our final seminar. After the last of the participants read, Frost closed with Teddy's "Silence" and my "At Risk." As if on cue, Stella, Trudy, the big bear, and the rest stripped down to their swimsuits. Frost took Ruthie and sat in a chair far from Roethke's big splash and more dangerous grasp, but my baby begged to get in the pool. I dived in and held out my arms. She jumped in and crawled after me to the other side. I handed her to Trudy and shouted, "Your first recruit for the 1944 Michigan and Olympic Swim Teams."

"How much," Trudy yelled, "did you have to pay to override Dr. Bell's veto?"

Nothing, I signed, *more than make sure University Hospital could focus on reducing the loss of life to mothers and babies during pregnancy and childbirth.*

I don't know what the Little President thought of my performance on behalf of Michigan, but I learned I'm blessed: I'm not alone after all.

Summer and Fall 1928: Glen Arbor and Ann Arbor

I reread Rabbie O'Bannon's letter as I sat alone atop the ridge overlooking the bay and dunes. I needed the sight of my delight of life unfolding below to lift my spirits.

For Oxford's extended winter break, I had hosted Mirja at Cambridge House because the Queen wouldn't for Rabbie's first visit home in four years. Despite my misgivings, our guest proved such a help with Ruth and so much fun, I found it hard not to like her. Mirja also spared me any lovemaking in my home, at least until after Ruth and I left on Christmas Eve to join Papa and Pip for our holiday up north. Yet, I guessed she'd also find an excuse to join us at Belle Cottage and make merry with my brother.

Sure enough, while Rabbie interviewed for a teaching job at the UM English Department the first week in January, Mirja headed north. She regaled Papa with stories of how her late Irish rogue of a father built his empire, starting with running rum in the Caribbean, then acquiring the docks in Cork and Kinsale in his home country, followed by Liverpool and Manchester in England. When Papa asked why he hadn't conquered Glasgow, too, Mirja said, "He sold the lot for a merchant fleet." When Papa asked about her mother, she danced the Tango with him. Papa begged off a Flamenco encore, but the beat of her castanets inspired Ruthie to cluck so, Mirja took our baby as her partner.

When we returned to Ann Arbor, Rabbie hadn't won a teaching job, but the faculty did waive any course requirements and invited him to write a dissertation for a Ph.D. Mirja asked me to help her look for a house near campus. When I introduced her to Olivia Hall's son, she fell in love with the historic Italianate on the corner of Hill and Washtenaw, just across the little park from my Cambridge House. She didn't care that Mr. Hall didn't want to sell. She knew there was a price.

So, I feared, did I. All winter and spring, Pip had called once a week from Oxford to inquire after our baby Ruthie and to listen to her cry "Pip-Pip-Pip" on the phone. He wrote me only one letter, a long one, including an explanation why he found such delight in Ruthie's "pipping." With Mirja he had visited the Royal Observatory and met the Royal Astronomer, who had invented the "six pips" that signaled Greenwich Mean Time to the world. Pip wrote, *Sir Dyson enjoyed meeting a namesake for his time signal, but Mirja and I learned to make better use of it. Either of us may request a visit by phoning and singing a short pip; a reply of a longer pip signals "the coast is clear," while silence warns "stay away for now."*

Good Lord, I didn't want Pip rigging up any private walkie-talkie with chimes between Cambridge and Hill to communicate in his secret code with Mirja if she married Rabbie. I did call the architect of our house to figure out how to connect Pip's garage attic to the nearest corner of the house with Ruthie's nursery, though. Samuel Stanton proposed a second floor brick bridge, with a pitched roof, double-hung windows and dormers, over the west end of the glass-house. It captured his original Georgian architecture, offered Pip a separate entrance through the garage, private quarters, and easy access to Ruthie's room. The builder, Mr. Koch, completed the new addition in time for Pip's return.

After Rabbie's first letter, dated January 31, expressed his *deep regret* that his *prayers to beget a child with me hadn't been answered*, I prepared for Rabbie marrying Mirja and moving across the little park. He must have resigned himself to accept that Mirja's desire to raise a family with him did not mean her love for him was exclusive.

The second, dated March 1, noted he'd accepted Michigan's offer to join the faculty as an instructor with the prospect of joining the tenure track as an Assistant Professor as soon as he completed his Ph.D. He had closed: *Will you consider seeing me again if I leave Mirja behind?* My heart skipped a beat at that.

His third, dated April 20, asked: *If we were to marry, would you permit our children to be raised Catholic? Even if you don't convert, the Queen can't object then.*

I replied as I had to his first two letters: a postcard with another scene from Whitmore Lake with only one word written on the back, *Belle*, but this time I added a heart under my name.

His fourth letter, dated May 10, was sweet: *Belle, Oxford awarded me a blue for coaching our swim team to a win over Cambridge. I look forward to racing to catch you again. As ever, Your Rabbie.* Knowing how much he had missed swimming because of his long battle with TB, I added one line to my last Whitmore Lake postcard reply: *If you're hankering to swim and spoon with me again, you're more likely to catch me in the bluer waters of Sleeping Bear Bay or my glasshouse pool. Your Dearie Belle.*

Now, as I reread his last letter, dated June 1, only the sights of my Leelanau home kept me from feeling like a woman scorned, lost to love forever:

> *Dear Belle,*
> *I'm sorry, but Mirja just told me she's bearing our baby. We must wed, and Father Goldrick has agreed to forgive our sin and offer the sacrament of marriage in old St. Patrick's on June 15.*

In time I hope you will forgive Mirja, our child, and me.
I will love you forever.
Rabbie

Teach me to get my hopes up. I'd fled to Belle Cottage up north: Pip could represent our family at the nuptials in St. Patrick's. I don't know whether I hoped my brother would ravish Mirja on her wedding night to spite Rabbie or Mirja would leave my brother alone so he could find another love. When I asked Pip, my boy made clear his relationship with Mirja was not my affair. So true!

ᔕ

A week later I headed over to Glen Haven in my Phaeton, top down, the crisp spring wind blowing through my hair. I passed the Day general store, inn, and cannery and turned west before the Day pier onto the road along the shore. I drove past the Life-Saving Station but didn't see any sign of dune buggies. I returned to Glen Haven and bought a Nehi pop. I savored the orange nectar and asked about the Day family's plans for the tourist season: no word of any dune buggies. I bought a postcard of the Dune Climb, Day concession stand, and Day Farm, plus two quarts of milk.

I proceeded back on the shortest state highway in Michigan to the junction with the main road, from Glen Arbor to Sleeping Bear Dunes. As I slowed at this crossroad, a big Ford pickup careened around the corner. When I swerved, the two bottles broke and spilled milk all over my lap and the postcard. I tried to mop up the mess. A huge shadow blocked the sun, and I heard, "Vatch vere you're going next time, Missy Belle." I saw red. I pushed opened the door and shoved the Ogre in the chest so hard he fell over backwards. Now, I towered over him. "Next time, you watch where you're going, or you're going to get somebody killed."

Sven scrambled up. I feared the dark giant might deck me. Instead he spat out, "Not iv my new buggy is the only von racing to the

Sleeping Bear." He dusted himself, turned on his heel, hopped into his truck, and continued into Glen Haven. I saw the oversize, balloon tires that could propel his customers across the dunes to Mama Bear.

I fumed all the way back to Belle Cottage. After I changed clothes, I hiked atop the ridge again to my spot overlooking the bay. I sat and thought about losing Rabbie and confronting Sven Surtr. A soothing voice said, "A penny for your thoughts?" The Ojibwe boy was now a man, full-grown. He walked on this earth so quietly you never could hear him, his voice so soft you listened all the harder.

"Another one?" I said.

David handed me a second Indian head cent in mint condition. I didn't have to tell him about Rabbie because he'd already talked to Pip. He sat beside me. As the west wind blew, I told him about my latest scrape with the Ogre. Once he made sure Sven hadn't punched me, we watched the whitecaps rising on the bay as the breeze stiffened. The late afternoon sun sparkling off the water soon beckoned. He grasped my hand, and we walked through the forest so quietly we scared up not a single rabbit, squirrel, toad, butterfly, or bird. Down the steep ridge toward the harbor at the mouth of the Crystal River, he headed us to the Chris-Craft. He hopped in beside me and started the engine. When he reached deep water, he pushed the throttle down and held me close. The powerboat planed, and we flew across Sleeping Bear Bay toward Glen Haven. His handsome bronze face scanned far ahead as he captained us.

He didn't pull into Glen Haven to fight Sven. He didn't pause to wave as a few tourists walked down the gangplank of one of the last of the dwindling number of big passenger ships. He flashed by the Coast Guard Life-Saving Station at Sleeping Bear Point and then headed south on Lake Michigan. A third of the way to Empire, he slowed, pulled close to shore and secured the boat. From the storage compartment behind us, he removed a picnic basket; then he stepped up to the prow and jumped onto the beach.

He held out his hand, and I joined him at the base of the steep dune. He carried the basket in one hand and held my hand in the other. He stopped several times on the climb up to let me rest. When we reached the top, a sandy sea greeted us, with rippling waves rising and falling over the hills and valleys, as big swells. We skirted the big hillock of the sleeping Mama Bear, the west side already threatened by a tiny blowout. On the south side a deep sand path, almost a trench, rose to the top. I thought of the song written by a Beulah man my mama used to sing to me, "Sleeping Bear Pinnacle, towering high, undisturbed by the world's din and blare." Bygone history, I rued. "Do you miss old D. H., as much as I do?" I asked. David looked up to the pinnacle and nodded. "The State Park won't stop Sven Surtr now either," I added.

"Nor would the Department of Interior if our Sleeping Bear were a National Park." He explained how "the Great White Fathers in Washington" allowed the slaughter of wolves and feeding of bears in Yellowstone and dammed the wildest corner of Yosemite. "They treat our National Parks no better than the original people they herd into *reservations* out west, and they refuse to recognize us at all here despite the treaties they got the first Ahgosa Ogema to sign." He pointed to the view east, across the expanse of dunes down to the glassy blue of Little Glen Lake, the rustic red roof of D. H. Day's picturesque barn and white clapboard farmhouse below and the forest green of Alligator Hill. Beyond, our softer green Homestead golf course snaked its way down from the heights of the darker green forest to Sleeping Bear Bay. "Belle, we can do better here."

I sang my "Up North" song. It had become our anthem to save Mama Bear, his band's sacred Nibi and our delight of life for at least seven generations hence. That's when David shared the story of how "land stolen from other Ojibwe and Odawa bands in an 1817 treaty" helped fund the original Michigania school in Detroit and the new university when it opened in Ann Arbor in 1837. All I could do was squeeze his hand.

He led me down a gentle dune, south to a cottonwood grove, and spread a red blanket in the hollow. He opened the picnic basket, took out several glass jars and fed me the sweetest cherry, pear, and apple preserves I'd ever tasted. The wind's gentle flutter of the leaves serenaded us as the dapples of light brushed our cheeks. We took turns slaking our thirst with water from a blue pottery jug. It was so cold and fresh, I found I had to drink more slowly lest a chill spike my throat, but it tasted so pure, I couldn't stop. The water splashed over my face and down the front of my blouse.

David took out a chamois and dabbed it against my cheeks and chin. So soft it absorbed every drop with a touch, he rubbed it gently over my lips and down my neck. He unbuttoned my top two buttons and—yes, please don't stop—rubbed it over my breasts. He whispered so softly, "This is my last summer."

"Is this rite of passage for you or for me?" I said as I unbuttoned his shirt and rubbed the polished white stone circle pendant resting against his chest. I placed my left hand on the back of his neck and pulled his head down.

The gentle, tender, slow, long, deep, and complete love we shared that summer, I will never forget. The memory, without more, had to last both our lives. Our vow to protect Up North had to last much longer.

ꟹ

Kurt and Dr. MacKenzie arranged an exhibition match for September 15 to publicize the completion of the first nine holes and beginning of the back nine of our Homestead Golf and Outing Club. With the help of Grantland Rice, they pitted Walter Hagen—recent winner of the British Open and leading pro, with nine other majors—against Bobby Jones—the recent winner of the U.S. Amateur, plus six more majors. Pip teamed with Jones and David Ahgosa with Hagen in a best-ball match. The red of the maples, the first tinge of russet of the few old oaks, and the yellow of the aspen and birch contrasted nicely with the greens of the pine forest and our course. Lake Michigan and Sleeping

Bear Bay shone as the sun warmed the air and the wind blew white clouds and rippled whitecaps across the brilliant blues above and below.

Kurt invited Trudy Ederle to join us to trumpet our America's Flame as well. Kurt knew the rest of the press couldn't bear the thought of Grantland Rice capturing another exclusive. Sports and business writers from New York, Detroit, Chicago, Cleveland, and Atlanta showed up to find out what was so special about our Empire in our distant northwest corner of the Lower Peninsula to attract such sports icons.

In the morning Trudy stood up for our Empire stoves and furnaces. Kurt explained their safety, reliability, efficiency, and lower cost, but America's Flame stole the show with a demonstration of how Pip's latest burners compared with other sources of heat. Trudy passed a white plate over wood, coal, and oil fires and displayed the resulting lines of soot collected on the surface. In contrast, passing a white plate over the gas flame left only shining white, no residue at all. Pip showed how the wood, coal, and oil all burn with yellow to red colors because of the waste carbon that didn't ignite, while natural gas burned completely in a pure blue flame. David took the press on a tour of our plants: the reporters had never seen an industrial facility so clean that no finger could find grime anywhere, and there was no waste or scrap either. When the Ojibwe chairman shared the Nibi ethic that guided all our operations and Kurt explained its importance to producing better products at lower cost built to last, Papa beamed.

The golf exhibition attracted even more attention. Dr. MacKenzie explained his layout to the press as they walked each hole, from the big drops from tee to green on the first holes down to the Crystal River, to the middle holes snaking through the forest valley, to the ninth, climbing to the top of the meadow overlooking Sleeping Bear Bay. Hagen, shooting three under on his own ball and aided by a 35-foot birdie putt from David, finished the first nine two up over Jones and my brother. We broke for lunch at the clubhouse. Nestled in the woods atop the ridge looking west over Sleeping Bear Bay to Sleeping

Bear Dunes, it provided a perfect setting for the golf doctor to share his design for the second nine. MacKenzie pointed out how the holes down the meadow offered stunning views over the water and difficult greens, while the three finishing holes snaking back up to the summit of the ridge would challenge any golfer and make the libations at the nineteenth all the more welcome. Based on our Homestead course, Jones announced Dr. MacKenzie would help him build another in Augusta, Georgia, to host an invitational for the best golfers in the world. Irrepressible, Hagen piped up that he hoped the design there would be as accommodating to his game as our course here.

Dr. MacKenzie and our Homestead made Hagen eat his words the second time around the front nine. The wind picked up, and he shot three over. Only David's spectacular approach stiff to the flag on the eighth for a birdie to halve kept Jones from singlehandedly closing out the match on this next-to-last hole, what with his eagle and three other birdies on the second nine. All even going into the last hole, Pip stood much taller at the tee. Although his backswing ended only parallel to the ground, his longer club, wielded by his sinewy arms and blacksmith hands flowed through a much bigger arc. His ball sailed high over the trees that the others could only skirt, driving uphill. Although Pip's ball nestled in the long grass, he took out his spoon and scythed through the rough. His second shot flew high over the trees, cut the second dogleg, landed at the front edge of the elevated green, and climbed toward the flag. The others, taking the safer route with three shots to the green, could only watch as Pip willed his longer putt into the cup to claim the match for the all-amateur team with an eagle.

The powerful Hagen lifted my boy off his feet and then congratulated David and Bobby Jones. He walked to the architect MacKenzie and bowed. As reported by Grantland Rice, Hagen said, "Damn it, Doctor, don't make Jones' new track any tougher, or I'll never win there." Alister only nodded and then winked at Bobby Jones.

We rode the funicular down to the Homestead Inn and sniffed and tasted Papa's best Macallan while we watched the sun set. The clouds cooperated so we could see the red orb sink into the horizon and light a pink sea of crimson islands. At dinner we fed the celebrities, journalists, and other guests with fruit from David's orchards and game from our forests. The choir from the Leelanau School accompanied the best pies from the Ahgosas' Grand Traverse Company, all topped by ice cream hand-turned by Skipper Beals' pupils. I picked Ruth up to go. All the faces glowed except David's and mine. His new bride by his side, we could only nod goodbye to each other.

Kurt, bless him this once, rose to escort Ruth and me home. Grantland Rice met us at the door. Perhaps, he said it best, "Your Empire is a paradise on earth. Now, that we're going to tell the rest of the world, preserve it if you can."

"I'm not alone," I replied. "On your way back, visit the community David's building at Ahgosatown. You'll get your exclusive on this peninsula we now call Leelanau. He's going to show us all the way to conserve this sacred place, forever."

Grantland Rice got his story, and the word of America's Flame, the Homestead Golf and Outing Club, and the fruits and pies of David's band spread.

I returned to Belle Cottage, put my baby down and sang a new lullaby to her:

Letter from Upstream

A silver flash
Glinting in the sun—
Finally! A trout
About to make a run.

I raise my pole
Plant my waders wide
Arc my cast
Toward the other side.

I play my line
Hoping for a bite
And hook a hubcap:
What a sorry sight!

Then, I spot a log
Lumbering down the stream
But no—it's a tire:
I'm having a bad dream.

Close your eyes, my darlin',
Beseech the Nibi hear:
Protect these crystal waters
That flow so cold and clear.

Three weeks later, Fielding Yost and Coach Mann dedicated the Gertrude Ederle Pool for the Women's Athletic Building, atop the knoll at the east end of Palmer Field. Pip and I rehearsed Trudy. When she took the podium, she didn't miss a beat. She promised to follow in Matt Mann's wake: to serve as a steward for this new pool in order to help women experience the rewards of improving through training, being part of a team, and competing against others with grace, win or lose. Trudy promised to do for girls and young women in this pool what Matt Mann had done for a generation of boys and young men at the Union pool: to help children grow into adults, to build character and fitness, and, yes, to train swimmers to represent the University and our country.

The cheers echoed from the high ceiling to the tall arches overlooking the women's tennis courts. When the assembled press asked questions Trudy couldn't hear or see, Pip signed to her. She answered in a voice as clear as the big yellow block "M" on the front of her navy blue letter sweater. By God, Michigan women would finally be able to swim and compete for a varsity letter in the Gertrude Ederle Pool.

Stella Brunt joined the reception I hosted for Trudy, her new recruits, and the first teen members of our Ann Arbor Women's Swimming Club. Stella pulled me aside and whispered, "Chase has agreed to match any amount you donate to endow the salary to hire a woman as a tenured English professor if we call it the Frost Chair."

That set me back some: I preferred loaning money to build the pool in the Union or the Lying-in at the Hospital rather than making gifts for faculty salaries. I also wondered what Frost would think of my endowing a chair in his name designated for a woman: was Robbie cantankerous enough to want one of his Graces, or female Whimsies or Outlanders, to break up Strait's pedant, all-boys' English Department?

I topped up two glasses with Laphroaig, offered one to Stella, and clinked my glass against hers. Mirja, ripe with child and face flush, joined us and said, "I'll put up my share, too." So much for any secrets between Stella and me, but I wasn't going to turn down Mirja's money.

"How about a different pact," Trudy broke in, "the three of us march through the front door of the Union and sit down in the men's-only Faculty Club there?" We looked to her. She was our spirit, our flame, our inspiration. Stella and I could talk a good game, but we had only one leader who'd put her whole life on the line to prove she could compete with any person, regardless of sex. Trudy turned, picked up two more glasses, and poured Laphroaig into each. We sealed our lips together by sniffing and tasting the Scotch. I don't think I'd ever seen her drink a drop of alcohol before, but Trudy Ederle tossed the whole shot down in one gulp.

ନ

A week later the mail arrived at lunch while I fed Ruth. I saw a big package wrapped in brown paper marked with Frost's stubby black letters. I stuffed my baby full of the best homemade apple and pear puree fresh from David's harvest and put her in her crib with a bottle of water for a nap. I proceeded to the sanctuary of my pool.

When I opened the door, Teddy surprised me. His big body floated languidly in the warm water, only his head and hands sticking out with a fistful of papers. "Hey, Big Mama, jump in." I'd seen him only three times in the past several months, when he pinched off dead flowers, cleaned the debris, and made sure I hadn't "neglected" *his* "Garden of Eden." He said he'd been too busy working as a teaching assistant for Rabbie's first-year writing course: "Do you know how long it takes to comment on 90 two-page essays each week?" How he managed to read a sheaf of student writings while floating in the pool, I couldn't imagine either.

I looked down at my sport coat, sweater, and skirt and answered, "Sorry, Teddy, not dressed for the occasion."

"Strip," he said, but his usual tough-guy pose couldn't hide his shaking. Beneath the water, I saw the whale of a bear was covered only by his hair, and he trembled. I sat down beside the pool and waved the package. "I'll open this Frosty gift rather than risk you heating me up." I ripped the paper off and found two copies of *West-Running Brook*, each with an envelope stuck inside. I first opened the copy with the envelope near the beginning and found the lead poem, "Spring Pools," where he wrote, *To Belle, Without you, this brook would never have run at all let alone west. Frost*

I opened the envelope. His letter was short but bittersweet:

Belle,

Thanks for challenging me to write "Spring Pools," "West-Running Brook," and all my other contraries in this collection better. My Collected Poems with Holt will surely secure another Pulitzer if this book fails, as you predict. Who knows, if I live long enough, my life's work may yet earn a Nobel. In the meantime, the larger share of the royalties and increase in monthly pay won't hurt. RF

I opened the second copy to the envelope marked "Mr. Roethke" stuck almost in the back. "Frost sent you an autographed copy of his new book and a thank-you note."

Roethke placed his papers on the deck. He climbed out, and I bundled him in a warm robe, but this didn't hide his reek of liquor. "Do you want me to read Frost's letter?" When he nodded, we sat down on a chaise. "Mr. Roethke, Don't let the universe cramp your style: you are meant to write, not practice law. Don't let the dark cage you: roam free. Don't let the academics trap you: write, write, and write, as you will."

I handed the letter to Roethke. As Teddy read it to himself, tears welled in his sad eyes. I rose, picked up his papers beside the pool and saw from the green ink he was also working on a poem. I sat my butt down on the chaise across from him, lifted my snout, shut my eyes, and swayed back and forth. A smile crept across his face. "You need practice to qualify as my Big Mama Bear, but you may now read my new verse."

I read Teddy's rough draft of a poem in progress he titled, "Reply to Censure." It seemed his answer to the "pedantry" of too many English professors, those "inveterate defamers of the good who mock the deepest thought and condemn the fortitude whereby true work is wrought." To the academic "cravens" who Frost and Roethke hated so because they "reviled just men," Teddy answered, "The bold wear toughened skin…" He'd crossed several attempts at the final three lines out with his green pen.

"What happened?" I asked.

"Took another literature class from Strait to show him I deserved better than the *C* he gave me first year," he roared, "but the little creep told me this morning I was failing." He paused. "I've only composed three measly short verses and begun this fourth. I'm not a poet, and I'm not sure I can earn a living as a writer or an academic. So I'm quitting English and going to law school next fall, as my Mom always wanted."

Rather than talk about how Rabbie thought Ted's short stories and narrative analyses were the best of any peer or how he saw different slants of meaning as only a great poet can, I said, "Why don't you let me type your essays and the poem with one of your draft endings so Strait can at least read them instead?"

I quickly waved an envelope with the letter Auden had sent me. He grabbed it and read Wystan's account of meeting a new Rhodes Scholar, Robert Penn Warren, "a red-haired, freckled lad who shows promise despite his odd accent, Southern." Wystan enclosed a copy of a Warren poem as it was going to appear in the *New Republic*.

Teddy read "Self-Possessed Friend" and lit up. He grasped my hand in his big mitt and, as if willing me in his mania, said, "You must publish, too."

"While you, my big, brave Teddy Bear, skedaddle off to law school?"

Before he could answer, Pip opened the window of his sitting room in the addition above the glasshouse and yelled down, "Mirja's wet."

Water broken. Premature labor, I thought. "Carry her to my car in the garage," I yelled back as I rose to help my brother. As we raced out the door, I asked Teddy, "Call ahead to the hospital, get Rabbie there, and take care of Ruthie."

Mirja fainted in Pip's arms as I drove up Washtenaw and raced past the observatory to the Emergency Room. A team of doctors and nurses from the new Lying-in took over, but not before Mirja quickened enough to whisper, "Tell Rabbie the boy's name is Paul." I couldn't bear another funeral from childbirth.

Fortunately, the cesarean saved Mirja, so she could tell Rabbie first. The newborn, only five pounds, had to incubate more under a lamp. In a few weeks he could caterwaul.

Mirja and Rabbie insisted Pip and I serve as Paul's godparents. Whatever Pip's trysting with Mirja, I vowed not to succumb to Rabbie's pull. Instead, I sang a lullaby for Ruthie and the new baby, Paul:

Born Friends

in the quiet woods
two fawns bend across a stream
to nuzzle noses

Spring and Fall 1929: Ann Arbor and Glen Arbor

I held a graduation party for Roethke. Elected to Phi Beta Kappa, he graduated with honors—*magna*, not *summa*, due to the grades from Nym. Not bad for the hulking lad who dressed and acted like a Chicago gangster to hide his harder study and better writing from his peers. His roommate Crouse and several of their Chi Phi brothers made the short walk down Washtenaw to join us, along with a handful of good-looking coeds who saw through his act. Only Rabbie appeared from the English faculty, although Frost did send me a signed copy of *New Hampshire* with a note to give to our big Teddy Bear.

We convened in the glasshouse around my pool. The spring blooms exploded with color, and the unseasonably hot, humid day made them sparkle with dew. Teddy arrived late. He'd exchanged his double-breasted suit for a tweed jacket and slacks. Soon he stripped down to his shorts, jumped in the air, grabbed his knees, and cannonballed into the water. When Ruthie dived after, he hugged our toddler. His fraternity brothers soon followed, while the handful of girls magically appeared with swimsuits.

Thankfully Trudy finally showed, or Teddy might have kept the pool party going for hours. He challenged her to a race, but she said she'd already packed for the long drive to run Matt Mann's swim camp for girls. He pleaded so, she eventually unpacked the two-piece suit from her Packard and returned in her full glory. Roethke handed Ruthie to me and joined Trudy on the deck at the far end of the pool.

"Can you handle a hundred laps?" America's greatest swimmer asked.

Teddy dived and in mid-air yelled, "One!" Before his big body crashed with a belly flop, Trudy landed far past him. She swam almost three laps to Teddy's one, but he touched her out and raised his hand as if he'd won. Trudy held it high. Ever the showman, he lifted her above his head and sang "The Victors." He no longer appeared bulbous or hairy like a bear. Although not trim, he was big and strong, not fat. Even his big nose fit his face better: not cute to be sure, but not unhandsome either.

Teddy followed with a short speech thanking Ruthie and me for allowing him to share *his* Garden of Eden: "It kept me sane, long enough to graduate despite the best efforts of Nym and most of the English Department to drive me crazy." He exempted Rabbie: "You showed me that teaching can engage students in writing." He concluded by thanking his mother and sister: "When Dad died," he paused to clear his throat, "you stayed home and supported me so I could make it through."

Before anyone could cry or cheer, Teddy invited everyone to leave: "I've got a stash of Hiram Walker's Canadian Club and Lefty Clark's best music waiting for us back at Chi Phi." With that, he grabbed his clothes. He paused by the back door, kissed Ruthie on the cheek with his big lips, and asked me, "Care for a rematch tomorrow?"

"You know I can lap you."

"Not on the tennis court." He hugged me so hard, I thought he'd crush Ruthie. Instead she squealed with delight, and I felt warm all over, despite his drenching me.

Of course, Teddy left his book from Frost to give him an excuse to return so we could talk. A week later he appeared at the kitchen door wearing cream slacks and a tennis sweater, looking as dominant as Bill Tilden.

"Did you throw away your fur coat?"

"In storage for next winter," he answered, giving me the eye.

I couldn't divine what he intended, so Ruthie and I fed him lunch. While I cleaned up, he played blocks on the floor with her. Before I knew it, they'd built a tower, 15 floors in all, at least five feet high. He helped Ruthie stand on the kitchen table and balance the last block, a red one, on the tippy-top. Before I could applaud their construction, Teddy sat down on the floor with Ruthie. Together, they toppled the tower and shrieked with joy as the blocks tumbled around them. He got down on his hands and knees and made a game of picking up each block with Ruthie as he sang a rhyming ditty about needing to clean up lest "*You* become Dirty Dinky." Ruthie joined in singing the refrain as they took turns placing each block in a neat row in the box under the sideboard.

Teddy pointed to the glasshouse, and Ruthie and her playmate dashed out to the pool. I guess it didn't matter to them that neither had a suit, but I refused to join in the buff. I opened the kitchen window to monitor their swim and savored a cup of Lipton tea. A half hour later, Teddy returned, thankfully wearing a terry cloth robe. He handed a tired Ruthie, swaddled in soft towels, to me. I took my little girl and began to carry her to her room upstairs, but she demanded that her big friend follow.

As I put a nightgown on Ruthie, Teddy asked, "No diapers?"

Before I could respond, she replied, "Mawmie says I'm a big gewl now!"

With that Teddy tucked her gently into her bed. "Want a story, Kiddo?" There followed a nonsense poem about a "monstrous whale with no tail." When the "big lubber tried to spout, the best he could do was jiggle his big blubber." As he repeated the four-line song, Ruthie laughed when he jiggled his own middle and then hers every time he said, “Blubber.” The fourth time he sang in a softer voice, lengthened the words, and spoke of the “monotonous whale.” The fifth time through, he closed her eyes, and she fell asleep during the sixth before he whispered his last “Blubber.”

We returned to the kitchen, I poured us each a cup of tea, and we sat at the table. Wrapped in his robe, he told me his plan: he would take one class at the Law School in the fall while serving as Rabbie’s teaching assistant again. “But what I really want is to apprentice with you…” He pulled out a well-worn copy of Elinor Wylie’s poems. “… and cut my teeth on you women poets with a better ear and sense of lyric.”

I got up, went to the study, and returned to give him my well-worn copies of Dickinson’s published songs. “What would Ned Strait say about this?”

“To hell with that little snoot! I want to become a great poet or a poor fool.”

“Why not start with a poem to say goodbye to your dad?”

He froze before me.

I stretched my hand across the table and placed it in one of his big mitts.

He gripped my hand but dropped his eyes. “Maybe I’ll learn this fall I can make a better living as a lawyer than trying to relive my youth and make sense of my father.”

“Let’s go botanizing instead.” I opened Frost’s *New Hampshire* and said three short poems, “Fragmentary Blue,” “Blue Butterfly Day,” and “A Dust of Snow.”

He reached over, claimed his gift, and read the longer “Two Look at Two” back to me. I had to laugh at his intensity reciting the poem. “It’s not funny,” he said.

No, it wasn’t, and neither was he. Even when at his most manic entertaining, Teddy’s eyes spoke the dark depths of depression. “Frost said he’s hired Van Dore to tend the Vermont farms, and he’s going to help Wade put together his first book,” I replied. “If you want to help the Ahgosas with their orchards up north, we can start this summer with me typing any nature poems you may compose instead."

He lowered his eyes again and shook his head. "I've got to help Sis with Mom in Saginaw." He walked to our glasshouse and returned fully dressed. "But I promise I'll hide away and write in my notebook about my memories of the greenhouses, the fields, the woods, and my reflections on growing up but still seeing as a child."

"This fall," I replied, "we can meet every Friday afternoon for lunch and then work for a couple of hours on your poems while Ruthie naps." He picked up his gift from Frost and the books of the women poets, stood awkwardly, and turned to go. "If you can, plan on joining us at Belle Cottage for Thanksgiving, too." When he stopped at the door, I rose and kissed him gently on the cheek. "I'll show you the buck and doe, and we'll savor the harvest from David's orchards."

He shambled out the kitchen door, through our glasshouse, and into his separate world. I wondered whether any of us can ever see into the interior space of another when it's so murky and we don't dare look inside our own.

ꙮ

The next morning, as I packed Ruthie's clothes with mine, I saw a big pickup parked outside our garage. Pip and a young man with close-cropped hair loaded radio equipment and batteries in the truck. I finished packing and, with Ruthie toddling after, carried two bags out. Pip and the young man relieved me of the luggage. "Marmie, you remember John." I looked hard and, yes, finally recognized him as the younger radio tinkerer from years before. "He graduated from Michigan this spring, moved with his family into new house with a barn in the country off Arlington." John Kraus leaned down, introduced himself to Ruthie, and showed her the wires, plates, and mesh.

"What radio gizmo you two planning to build now?" I asked.

"I'm just getting back at it," John said, "after one too many crashes trying to learn how to fly glider planes."

"He's going for a Ph.D. in physics here," Pip said, "and I'm inviting him up north to help me figure out the source of the buzz my horned trumpet's capturing."

"We've got plenty of room," I said to John, "and Pip could use the inspiration."

Cut off by Mirja since little Paul's birth, my brother had moped around for six months. He rebelled at his astronomy advisers here suggesting he get back to observing the stars rather than playing with radios and cosmic rays. He found solace only when plotting a new golf course with Dr. MacKenzie for the University, across the street from "The Big House that Yost Built" for the football team. Pip tossed his golf bag in the trunk so he could lose himself in the good doctor's spirit on all 18 holes at our Homestead.

I stopped by Strickland's to pick up three Cokes and a bag of chips for our long ride. I also grabbed too many Sanders goodies but held onto the big pile in my arms. I rounded the aisle to pay at the register in front, and Ned Strait barged into me. Everything crashed to the floor. As Nym leaned down to help clean up the mess, he whispered, "Kept your Teddy Bear from a *summa*, and your Rabbie will never get tenure here either."

Mr. Strickland replaced the broken Cokes, bagged my mound of snacks, and accepted my apologies and pay. As I left, I saw Strait speaking amiably with the owner and nodding toward me as if he'd come to my aid rather than landed another low blow. I got to my Phaeton, handed the goods to Pip, and saw Nym get into his car empty-handed, no groceries. Why that fat creep had stalked me to deliver his latest insult!

The news wasn't much better at Belle Cottage. After Papa, Kurt, David, and Miss Schultz greeted us with supper and Pip put Ruthie down for the night, we met around the dining room table. Kurt explained the challenge. The only good news: through March, sales of kitchen stoves and portable camp stoves boomed, and orders for our furnaces grew apace. The bad news: except for the campers, sales had stalled since. A big inventory of unsold kitchen stoves already clogged our warehouse in Empire.

"Papa," I asked, "what do you think?"

My father, wringing his hands and tapping his feet nervously next to me, looked pale. "I feel it in these old bones. It's going to get worse: real bad for a long time."

"Miss Schultz," I asked, "we set to weather a long storm?"

"No exposure to stocks." I wanted to tell Papa to thank us for saving him and our enterprise from his reckless gamble, but he looked so beaten-down there was no point. "You could shut Empire tomorrow," Miss Schultz added, "and live off the interest on your U.S. Bonds."

"What if we don't shut down?" I snapped.

"Depends," Kurt answered, "on whether we can cut costs to match the sinking revenues."

Papa, his hands shaking, rose for a shot of Macallan.

"David," I asked, "how go the sales of your fruit, pies, and jams?"

"Slow and getting worse," he confirmed. The Ogema would need relief on his loan, but he was too stubborn to ask. "The Days' sales fell even more."

"What do you recommend?" I asked Kurt.

"Shut down the main line for stoves and slow the production of furnaces. If we lay off half our workers tomorrow, we might break even, at least for the summer."

David said, "Let's divide the crew in half and give each six weeks off instead."

When Kurt questioned David's ability to manage the work flow, David explained how he could form smaller, more flexible teams, each able to handle all three lines. "That'll allow us to make whatever mix and volume of products we need."

"Willing to put your head on the line," Kurt demanded.

David didn't flinch, and Pip said he'd join with his best friend to design a new gas stove made out of stainless steel.

Kurt nodded, and Papa poured a spot of Macallan for each of us. "Thank God," he said, his hands still shaking, "you young folks are in charge." After we finished sniffing and tasting his aged single-malt, Papa added, "Kurt, I'll sell you the third of my shares for half the price you offered when you first came on board and transfer the rest to Pip."

"Sorry, Papa," I said, "we need your help to weather this storm first." I was much more worried Kurt would walk out now, when we needed him most, and it was time to put him to the test. "Kurt," I said, "I'll sell you a third of my shares for the price we agreed, since Papa's just named you CEO."

"Fair enough," Kurt replied. He raised his glass, and we all took a big gulp. Maybe he was more interested in being our partner than jumping ship for New York City.

As our war council broke up, I pulled David aside. "How's the club doing?"

"Reservations are up to play the course and stay at the inn."

"Trade you the interest on your loan for produce, fish, and game to feed our guests?" At least we owned the Homestead Club and our half-interest in the inn free and clear, while the Bealses' school and camps generated a regular stream of parents paying to drop off, pick up, and visit their kids year-round. Thank heavens Dr. MacKenzie stocked our course with rabbits, to mow the grass and clean up the forest floor at no cost!

An hour after I fell asleep in my third-floor sanctuary, I felt someone trying to climb into bed. When I sat up, the full moon cast a silver glow on her dark head. I sat in the rocking chair with Ruthie beside the window. Sleeping Bear Bay, the dunes, and the islands shimmered in the light, as they had for thousands of years. I shared the stories of Sleeping Bear, the Manitou, and the Lost Daughter. I sang a new lullaby:

The Legend of Ruth

Twin fawns are sleeping in the wood,
Fox kits are in their den,
A gentle breeze rocks the maple,
Where roosts a mother wren.

Trillium nod their snow-white heads,
Morels sprout near mossy logs,
Ducklings swim upon the pond
Serenaded by bull frogs.

Of the many blessings
Spring has brought this way
The best is little Ruthie,
Our delight of life each day.

Ruthie gave me hope we could grow our empire here while conserving our Leelanau for generations to come, but, Lord, how long would it take to ride out the coming storm?

ℴ

Five months later, on the Wednesday before Thanksgiving, I dropped Teddy at the main office of the Ojibwe cannery on the shore side of the state road in Ahgosatown, a mile north of the Omena Kirk. Behind the retail shop and sheds, neat rows of houses cascaded down the gentle slope to the boat docks in the cove, sheltered from the rough water of Grand Traverse Bay. David Ahgosa's wife, Spring Blossom, carried baby Davey close to her, in a colorful sling. Only his dark hair, forehead, brows, eyes, and nose peered over the top, but I could see he was going to be as handsome as his parents. She offered fresh pears and apple juice as refreshment. Spring Blossom would show Teddy the harvest in the sheds until David returned to walk him through the orchards.

I begged off, as I had to drive to meet Miss Schultz at the Grand Traverse Lighthouse.

I got into the car and looked back. Teddy opened the door to the first shed and pawed through bushels of cherries, apples, pears, and grapes. He towered over his hosts, mother and child, as if a huge bear, until he bent down so they could converse together on the same plane. Teddy stuck his little finger in a soft pear and offered it to Davey, who raised his head from the sling and eagerly sucked the sweet juice. Although Teddy still wore his oversize raccoon coat, he dropped his tough-guy pose for the more sensitive man-child he was when his inner demons let him be.

I drove along the shore road, through the Ahgosa clan's burgeoning orchards, and couldn't help wondering why Miss Schultz set our meeting at the lighthouse at the tip of the peninsula. I drove up the final dirt road and saw her there, atop the sturdy, weathered brick keeper's house, waving from the catwalk outside the big tower. From the second floor, I climbed up the steep ladder, shimmied through the narrow hatch, and clambered onto the landing in the tower with the big light. She welcomed my smile with a frown and a warning: "It is going to get worse, a lot worse."

I was more hopeful: during the first three weeks in November, the stock market had risen and regained half its losses from the October crash.

Her hair, now all white from her 70 years, shook back and forth. As if reading my hopes, she barked, "Dead cat bounce." She continued, "The Fed's not lowering interest rates fast enough, Congress is cutting spending, and Hoover's fine with a tariff on foreign trade." Her white head and the white frills on her blouse shaking, Miss Schultz added, "We're heading for a Great Depression."

When I asked if she had any good news, she said, "Our U.S. bonds are worth more. Now, what's your latest scheme?"

"First, tell me what you learned from the new president at Michigan."

"You and your friends should make a pledge to fund the Frost Chair only if your donations are contingent on the University hiring a woman to fill it." She explained how five years ago an alumna donated $35,000 to the History Department for a woman professor, but the faculty, all male, didn't even look for a qualified candidate.

Trudy was right: we'd have to do more than put up our money to change the culture at Michigan. The old *Inlander* article said what most in academia still felt: including women on the faculty was another "*Very* Dangerous Experiment." More than that, Ned Strait and his ilk thought it was heresy. "Think we can enlist Ruthven's support for hiring women as faculty through a new kirk, then?" I explained how the crash had soured our congregation's appetite to pay for a new church but UM's president wanted to go forward, on the very site where Frost had rented his second house.

"The Frost Kirk today, the Frost Chair tomorrow," she exclaimed.

"Tell Ruthven we'll advance a loan for the new church if Michigan raises the funds for the student center and assembly there."

Miss Schultz nodded. A savvy adviser and better friend—willing to tell me what I didn't want to hear and willing to stand with me when I didn't listen—I couldn't imagine. How would I have ever gotten along without her?

She walked me out to the catwalk and pointed north to the Beaver and Fox Islands, west to the twin Manitous, and finally south to the big breakers crashing on shore below us all along Cathead Bay. She told me how, more than a half-century before, the keeper and his wife had saved her life. At 15 years old, she'd run away from her Northport home, walked eight miles to Cathead Bay and along the beach to the point below the Lighthouse. A late fall storm blew across the Great Lake, and the surge pulled her into the roiling inland sea. The keeper saw her, threw a lifeline, and pulled her ashore. In the sheltering home under the flashing light, the keeper's wife had helped the adolescent girl see her way to an independent future.

"I'm repaying my saviors by buying up the land around here, all the way to the south end of the bay, and I'm fixing to leave enough money to preserve it in a land trust so it can serve as a beacon for future generations." When I protested she had many more years to go, she interjected, "Belle, my memory's already beginning to walk on. Can I count on you to help here after I'm lost again?"

I leaned down and whispered, "How could I refuse?"

"I want you, Pip, Spring Blossom, and David to serve as the trustees." Miss Schultz added, "Has David told you the Feds refuse to recognize his band under the old Indian treaties and now conspire with the state and private landowners to deny their rights to fish, hunt, and gather on all our land and waters?" When I didn't respond, she said, "My land trust will protect these historic treaty rights of the Indians." When I asked if Papa, Pip, and I could also preserve these rights on our land, she pulled my head down and whispered, "You tell David, as the Ogema for his Ojibwe clan, he can protect these rights for members of other bands on his land, too."

The wind whipped through my unruly red hair, and I felt a shiver, a fright at the thought of losing Miss Schultz too soon. I must have teetered, because Miss Schultz held me up once more, as she so often had.

ෆ

I drove up the long lane by the Crystal River to my home. All the leaves were down, but the late afternoon sun lent a rosy cast to the grassy dunes leading to the blue expanse of Sleeping Bear Bay beyond. As I passed the Homestead Inn, there stood Teddy, practicing his big serve on the tennis court. I jumped out, picked up a racquet leaning against the net post, and stepped to the baseline on the other side.

"Ready?" said Teddy.

Before I could answer, he whistled a big serve into the far corner of the service box. I took too big a step to the right and, although managing to rake the ball crosscourt deep, skidded and fell hard on my keister. He rifled a forehand down the far sideline. I watched helplessly, but the ball landed just in back of the baseline.

When I called "Out," Teddy smashed his racquet on the ground and screamed, "You cannot be serious!" He raced up to the net. "It wasn't even close to being wide."

I suppose I should have just given him the point. Instead I said, "Teddy, you hit it long." When he looked at me as if I'd insulted him, I did: "If you'd paid any attention to me falling, you could have just bunted the ball back rather than try to show off."

Teddy stalked off the court and headed up the steep hill. Soon, his pace slowed as he began to snake back and forth through the trees. I ran to the far side of the inn and rode the funicular to the top. I walked past hunters telling tales about the big bucks that got away and laughing at the fool below climbing the "cliff." I poured two steins of draft from the keg behind the bar and greeted Teddy as he climbed onto the deck. His face flush and sweaty, he chugged his beer. He headed down the gentler slope to MacKenzie's greensward in the valley. I had to run to catch up. I handed him my stein. His unruly hair matted flat with sweat, he said, "I'm sorry. Forgive me?"

After a big breakfast the next morning with Papa and Ruth at the kitchen table, I drove Teddy to visit our stove works in Empire. David showed how a third as many workers organized in small teams produced twice as many portable camp stoves, a new line of lanterns, half as many furnaces, and Pip's new line of stoves. One third of our prior workforce had retired or moved down south over the summer. The remainder worked half-time for half pay in teams, each able to make all our products, no time lost switching lines or twiddling thumbs while waiting to unclog bottlenecks on a long line.

I pointed Teddy out the door to visit the other boys at the radio scoop on Empire Bluff so I could talk with Kurt. We met in the warehouse, where we still had a two-month supply of cast-iron stoves. Kurt said we'd never make another, and Trudy did look right at home in the display ads, cooking on America's Flame in stainless steel. The best advertising—good word of mouth—was also spreading fast. He suggested an exclusive deal to build for Sears, but I didn't want to risk losing our brand to theirs. "Why not also approach the Upton Brothers down in Benton Harbor?" I asked.

"I'll see if they're both willing to sell for us but use our brand instead of theirs." He paused. "I need to talk with you about David and Pip."

"They're not fighting again," I said.

"No. They've worked miracles together, reorganizing the plant and inventing the new stove. They've given everyone here hope, but…" He paused again.

"But what," I demanded in a voice that disclosed too much about my affection for my grown brother I still loved as a son and the Ojibwe boy I still loved as a man.

Kurt explained how David was running a big business in Ahgosatown, serving as the headman for his band, acting as the manager for the Homestead, and helping Skipper Beals. "And if Pip heads back to Ann Arbor, David will watch over your papa, too. If we're going to keep David, you need to run the Homestead." He paused. "Belle, I need you to help me navigate in this big storm." I told him I couldn't separate myself from Ruth and Pip. "His hearing's gotten a lot worse: Pip won't ever get a job teaching."

"If you ever leave us for the Big City," I asked, "can Pip run our Empire?"

"He's more valuable as an inventor, and David will make a better CEO," he replied. Hell Damn! Kurt didn't think I could run our Empire either.

I walked to the top of the bluff and saw Pip and David clambering around, under and over the big horned contraption. Teddy leaned out the door to the little station house and relayed instructions to John Kraus inside. Pip guided me into the shed and showed me how John had recalibrated the pen graph to capture the radio soundings. When his radio pal shook his head, Pip added, "We need to build a more powerful receiver."

I looked outside at the big trumpet, two huge gears to turn and to elevate the telescope to scan the heavens, and said, "How can you build a bigger radioscope?"

"Pip and I came up with a different approach," John answered.

The two stepped outside, set off in opposite directions, walked a long way out, and spread their arms wide. When they returned, Pip said, "We put a big parabola at my end," and John added, "We mount a bunch of antennae on a wall that we can tilt at the other end." In unison, they said, "We put a reflective surface in between and..."

I cut them off: "How much?"

"Two or three football fields' worth," John said.

I shook my head, confused.

"Sorry, Marmie," Pip said, "several hundred thousand dollars."

He knew we couldn't afford that, even before the crash, but I asked, "What do you call your new contraption, anyway?"

"Big Ear," Pip answered, cupping his hand to one of his. I should have known.

"What's the new antenna spinning on top of the station doing here?" I asked.

"It's a transmitter to send our signals into space," Pip answered.

"Any life forms from other planets reply yet?" Teddy asked with great interest.

"Given the distance, we'll be lucky if Ruthie's great-grandchildren hear back." Pip paused. "We did capture echoes from a crazy stunt pilot rolling in a thundercloud."

I put one arm around my boy and the other around John. "Don't give up, ever."

As Teddy and I walked back to the car, I thought about Mirja and little Paul arriving early for Thanksgiving. It would be the first time they'd seen Pip alone since we moved up north at the beginning of summer, and I didn't know what to expect. Everywhere I turned there was another challenge, another problem, another responsibility, whether here or in Ann Arbor.

Teddy broke my reverie. "How much of this territory is yours?"

I pointed south along the bluffs overlooking Lake Michigan. All our plantings provided the green of the pines, the brown of the tall grass, the gray of the maples, and a scattering of white birch, leaves long fallen.

"Dwarf trees?" he asked.

I looked again. With more than a decade of growth, the oldest already stood much taller than my big friend. "When Papa acquired these tracts, they'd been clear-cut. We planted a new forest that's already flourishing, thank you."

We drove around the south and east sides of Glen Lake. I pulled to a stop at the top of Miller Hill and showed Teddy the panoramic view. "From where the Crystal River meanders from its source at Fisher Lake below, past Glen Arbor, to its mouth by the Homestead Inn, we own the better part." Teddy and I hopped back into the car. I took the shortcut to the state highway heading east and turned north on the first dirt road. By the meadow I parked, walked Teddy halfway up the finishing holes of the Homestead course, and pointed north, all the way to Pyramid Point where our land now ended.

He waved goodbye: "Big Mama, I'm heading off to botanize." Teddy could make me laugh. One hundred yards out, he stopped and turned his big snout up, sniffing the bracing northern air. "Belle, my senses are gathering material for a new poem."

☙

My day didn't end after dinner. I had so many separate meetings Papa let me use his study so I could hold court behind closed doors. Rather than sit at his big desk, I turned the two big leather chairs so they faced each other. Spring Blossom came first, followed by Mirja, David, and Roethke. Spring volunteered to help David run the Homestead, but I told her I wanted her to help me instead and to take over as soon as she was ready. I offered her an apartment for her family in the inn, next to the big kitchen. She added, "My brother can manage our businesses so David can focus on Empire."

Mirja came next. I'd missed seeing her and baby Paul, and I said so. She replied in a soft voice, "I can't go on without Pip." I asked whether she thought that was fair. "That's between Rabbie and me."

"Mirja," I replied in an even voice, "I mean for Pip." I might have added for Rabbie and me, except I'd learned I could live with regret but not guilt. Mirja didn't blink. Although Pip might always be my boy, he'd become a father and a man, more independent than most. Despite sharing Ruth and parts of two homes with me, he'd decided he wanted only whatever Mirja might offer. "Whatever you choose to do or not with Pip, can you keep your affair from Ruth and little Paul and from our guests at the resort?" She nodded. "Then you best stay in the guest room that adjoins Pip on the second floor, and little Paul can share Ruth's room in the attic next to me." She didn't argue, not even when I told her Pip would have to move up north.

Instead, she asked about Pip's research. "Mirja, please keep him dreaming until the University or some other source with enough money decides to fund his Big Ear." She nodded with a big smile and tapped my hand as she left.

I was rubbing the spot when David entered steaming, "I can't accept your favors, not the job for Spring Blossom, not the apartment for our family at the Inn, not the work for my mother-in-law." He sputtered, "They're my responsibility, not yours."

I bade him sit in the other chair and told him I needed them to help *me* run the resort. "I haven't done a good enough job?" he protested.

"We need you more now running the plant in Empire."

"You want my band to quit our family's business for yours, too!"

"I've invested too much in your Grand Traverse enterprises for that."

When he proposed that his cousin take over, I shook my head. He conceded Spring Blossom's brother would do a better job, but David didn't know what to say to his cousin, who was older and more attuned to Ojibwe ways.

"He can help us here, then. We'll pay him for fish and game for the Homestead, and we'll respect your rights to hunt, fish, and gather on all our land." I greeted David's big smile with another bolt: "I'm also exercising my option to take a share of the profits of your Grand Traverse business in lieu of interest and principal." Before his grateful whoosh ended, I told him about my conversation with Miss Schultz and all her plans for a land trust. I asked if he and Spring Blossom would join Pip and me to serve as trustees to preserve her legacy. When he nodded too readily, I said, "You going to respect the rights of all the other bands on your land, too?"

After a long pause, he nodded but said, "Except for gathering any fruit from trees or crops we plant until after we harvest."

"What are we going to do about the Dark Ogre invading our Mama Bear?"

Before David could answer, Roethke barged through the door. David shook his head but got up and squeezed by before Teddy threw his fur coat on the chair and sat down. There the big man sat with his new rustic look, a lumberjack in red and black plaid shirt and big work boots. He handed me two sheets of paper, green ink flowing across three long stanzas with blotches and inserts. Titled "The Coming of the Cold," the draft began, "The late peach yields a subtle musk..." and ended, "Winds gather in the north and blow... and soon winds bring a fine and bitter snow."

I looked out the window, and sure enough, the north wind pelted snowflakes against our window. His descriptions of smell and sight abounded, but I couldn't hear any sound. I handed the two sheets back to him and said, "Sing it to me."

Without looking at his poem, his voice rose and fell in a steady rhythm so I could hear his tone even when he sang of silence, "The loose vine droops with hoar at dawn."

"So much better read aloud," I said and handed him my new song:

After the Harvest

Frothy waves hasten back and forth
along Lake Michigan's sandy shore,
keeping time with the thump of the wind—

Sweet scent from a cider press
mingles with the pungent tang
of smoke that coils from chimney tops—

Aspens, birches, maples, oaks
layer the forest floor with color:
crimson sepia, orange, and ocher—

Underfoot leaves crackle and crunch,
squirrels hurry to hollowed logs
to store their cache of seeds and acorns—

Hopeful children, buttoned up tight,
Pull wool hats low over ruddy ears
Haul out sleigh bells, skates, and sleds—

While hot chocolate simmers on the stove,
Winter sneaks in with downy flakes
that dance wildly in the frosty wind.

After Teddy finished my poem, he winced and muttered, "Not always." He reached into a pocket inside his fur coat, pulled out a book, and handed it to me. *Further Poems of Emily Dickinson*, Madame Bianchi's latest contribution, with Alfred Leete Hampson. I had to laugh at the subtitle: *Withheld from publication by her sister, Lavinia*.

"What's so funny?" he asked.

I told him just enough of my history with Madame Bianchi that he understood when I concluded, "Just another excuse to add to her campaign for the Dickinson legacy after saying she'd published Emily's *Complete Poems* five years before." I skipped the new book's long introduction, scanned several poems, and shook my head. I told him how I came to see that Mabel Todd, Thomas Higginson, and now Madame Bianchi took liberties "editing" Miss Dickinson's songs. Seeing his sad eyes, I couldn't resist singing "Wild Nights!" in Emily's original lyric as a refrain.

Teddy rose and said, "I'll be up all night working my poem until it also sings." He kissed me smack on the lips. "Big Mama, I'll wake by noon if you want a rematch."

After Teddy left, I had time to ponder whether we were ever going to be able hear all Emily's poems sing for themselves as she'd composed them.

Pip entered and slid into the chair beside me. "What are you going to do about your studies?" I asked.

"I'll tinker, skate, fish, and play more golf here while you help me raise Ruth."

I felt like hugging my boy but asked, "Can you help in Empire and Ahgosatown too?" He nodded. "Spring and I need help with the club and the inn, too."

He said he'd also take Skipper Beals' new apprentice under his wing. "Major Huey's got his heart set on Mrs. Beal's sister, the school, camps and Homestead."

"I talked with Mirja, and let her know she's welcome to visit here any time."

He smiled, brushed the streak of white hair above his ear and turned his pale, blue-gray eyes on me. Despite looking gaunter every year, he was a handsome man, not the least because he didn't let his handicaps or my doubts limit him. "We'll be fine."

"Pip, could you ever fall for Trudy instead?"

"Nah, she's family, like a sister." I didn't know what to say. "I've been playing with the old crystal radio sets John and I used to build." He explained how he was going to build a hearing aid "so small it'll fit inside her ear." All I could do was nod to my boy.

Papa came last. From behind the desk he pulled out his big wooden office chair and held it for me. When I sat down, he rolled me back to the desk. He walked around the desk and sat down in one of easy chairs. "Our boy going to be all right?" he asked. I nodded. "You and Ruthie, too?"

"We're all going to spend more time here than in Ann Arbor." When a frown crossed his face, I added, "Papa, it's going to be okay. Our Empire's going to make it through, too."

"I don't have much time left," he said. I listened harder. "I need some time alone."

"Good Lord, Papa, you seeing Miss Patterson here again?"

"Damn it, Belle, there's no privacy when there's so many of you underfoot."

I don't know why I hadn't caught the catch in Miss Patterson's voice when I last talked to her. "No," I said, "I won't trade you Ruthie's and my rooms for your office."

"May I pay for a room at the inn so I can visit with my former wife there?"

"Only the garret overlooking the tennis courts, where no one can see her knickers."

"Belle, open the big drawer on your right."

I pulled it out, and a large sculpture whittled out of a big stump looked up at me. In the center behind a big desk sat a woman with a proud visage. Immediately behind, an old man stood proud. On one side stood a short man with a moustache, flanked by a tall, dark man with flowing hair. On the other side, a taller man holding a baby leaned in, with a big young woman in a swimsuit and a short, stout old lady in a fluffed-out blouse.

"Oh, Papa," I cried. He rose, handed me the keys, and placed his hands on my shoulders. "Can you whittle Spring Blossom and

Davey?" I asked. When he nodded, I added, "Mirja and little Paul, too?" He nodded again.

"Madame Chairman," he added, "I turned the Ogre down, and the Days can't get a loan to start running their damn dune buggies." While the Depression had dashed many dreams, it had saved Mama Bear for a while longer. He pulled out a *National Geographic* magazine and turned to the pictures of huge totem poles carved by the original people in the Northwest. "I showed these to David, and he said *totem* derives from the Ojibwe word *odoodem* and means the kinship group. We're fixing to carve one for our two clans under his birch bark box."

I rose and kissed my father on the top of his bald head. I used to think he was so much bigger, distant and fearsome.

That night I snuck into the attic and imagined the worst we could face:

Depression

Factories all have closed their doors,
proud men are begging in the street—
their family must have food to eat.

Rain clouds are rumbling in the west
a silver ring encircles the moon
icy winds swirl about the dunes,

lightning flashes, thunder booms—
I turn from the lake and run in fright,
no stars appear on this dark night.

Rain pelts the shore, a flash of light
while I seek safety in a hollow,
trying to stem the fears that flow.

Oh, maybe I did shed a tear over not having a mate to share the journey, but I was lucky to have a good family, friends and partners. I added the final stanza:

> No, I'll not succumb to sorrow,
> for I know that dawn will follow—
> and the sun will shine tomorrow.

Spring 1931: Ann Arbor and Glen Arbor

Little Paul dragged his big sprinkling can around the pool to help his mother water her bougainvilleas, bromeliads, anthurium, hibiscus, orchids, begonias, and oleanders. With Teddy off to graduate school at Harvard for the year, Mirja made the garden inside our glasshouse a riot of Caribbean colors. Yes, Mirja made sure Roethke's carnations, roses, and irises flourished, but they now provided only variety for her more exotic tropical blooms. Dressed in a crimson swimsuit that showed off her dark tan, silky black hair, and long legs, Mirja danced from plant to plant.

Try as we might, Mirja and I couldn't coax the little boy into the pool. Not even Ruth, with all the wiles of his best friend and big sister, could entice him to dip his face. Paul became his mother's helper poolside as I swam laps with my little girl.

We'd managed up north. Kurt and David eked out a profit for our Empire, selling more camp stoves, cutting our costs, and, thanks to Trudy's appeal as America's Flame, increasing our share of shrinking stove sales. In places with gas pipelines, Kurt worked with the utilities to offer furnaces for factories and office blocks that still ran with low-cost, long-term heating contracts. He even talked a few gas companies into hooking up whole neighborhoods and offering similar terms to heat homes and apartments.

Pip invented a valve to shut off the gas if it didn't burn. He also convinced the pipelines and utilities to add an odor to the colorless, scentless natural gas so leaks could be detected and repaired before any explosion. We all learned from Trudy's biography: openly meeting problems pays off better than trying to cover them up.

Pip took over David's responsibilities repairing and building facilities at the camp and school, mentoring young Major Huey, and helping Spring Blossom make sure our inn also served the shrinking needs of our Homestead Golf and Outing Club. Pip helped her brother solve any mechanical problems in Ahgosatown to deliver produce and products to meet the declining market demand. All the while Pip continued to search with his horned trumpet on Empire Bluff for the sound of intelligent life in space. His golfing prowess also attracted many hundreds to our MacKenzie course. His reputation as the new face of our Empire grew. It didn't hurt that the press covered Pip's hearing handicap and linked him to Trudy's All-American Flame.

No, we didn't thrive as the Depression deepened. Total output and demand in the country had fallen by more than a quarter since the 1929 crash. The Day Estates on Alligator Hill and the main steamship line serving Glen Haven folded. The dock, railroad, and cannery there soon fell into disuse. D. H. Day's heirs struggled to make a go of his inn and general store in Glen Haven and farm and orchards overlooking Glen Lake.

Nevertheless, sharing our natural paradise on Leelanau beat the lot of tens of millions of other Americans, without work and losing hope in more desperate cities and dust bowls. No point in counting our blessings, though: we all had too much work to do.

Except Papa. Oh, he puttered around the stove works in Empire, encouraged Kurt, David, and their men, and held court in the clubhouse bar or by the stone fireplace at our inn. Mostly, though, he enjoyed his trysts in his garret with Miss Patterson, his more frequent sniffs of Macallan at home, and his frolics with Ruthie. The grandchild and grandfather loved spending hours on end together, and they always included little Davey when Spring Blossom was busy running the Homestead.

ೞ

Roy Cowden invited me to lead a spring term poetry seminar and start graduate school. The University's great Broadway playwright, Avery Hopwood, left his estate to Michigan to establish annual student awards for creative writing. Cowden asked, "If you win the poetry prize and get an advanced degree, why shouldn't you be the first woman professor in the new English Department?"

Ned Strait and his ilk, I knew. Nym was already calling in his markers to wrest control of the world's largest student writing prizes from Cowden.

But Spring Blossom didn't need me getting in her way during the less busy winter and spring seasons at the Homestead, and Kurt said he'd call with David every week while I was in Ann Arbor to discuss the rest of our business. Pip wanted to join me to see whether the University would support his radio astronomy, even if he couldn't teach, and Ruthie jumped at the chance to see more of Mirja and little Paul.

For my poetry seminar, I supplemented the list of poems I'd used with Frost and established a schedule for student presentations. Trying to compose any new poems as a participant in the graduate writing seminar run by Cowden proved harder. I even tried to write floating on my back in the pool, as Teddy had, but nothing worked.

Cowden knocked at the back door of the glasshouse. Mirja, watering the pots closest to the door, beckoned. Wearing a tweed coat, pressed slacks, and paisley tie, he held a book in his right hand and waved it as he navigated her thick jungle. "Belle," he said as he continued the short walk to the poolside, "Frost thinks he's going to win the Pulitzer, and he asked me to—" He stopped in mid-sentence as his left foot hit Paul's watering can. Cowden hopped on his right foot to avoid kicking the toddler, but his foot became entangled in the handle Paul still gripped. Cowden dived over Paul's head toward the pool, but the bucket now dangled from the professor's foot. The little boy, refusing to let go, trailed behind in a swan dive. Cowden threw the book across the pool, but an envelope fluttered out. The first director of the Hopwood Program landed with a belly-flop. Paul landed more gracefully but sank with his watering can.

While Cowden scrambled to his feet, I dived after the little boy. His eyes, not dark jade like Mirja's but more a light green, stared wide open. No sign of fear, he held his breath. He was just a sinker. Paul extended his hand, and I sat him on the side of the pool. Ruthie swam to us envelope in hand, climbed out, and hugged her best friend.

Cowden, except for his sopping hair, looked ready to stand in front of any class. I straightened the knot on his tie before he got lost sputtering apologies. I offered the good professor towels and directed him to the bathroom, where he could change into a robe.

I couldn't resist picking up the book that had landed, facedown, pages splayed open. On the title page, by *Collected Poems of Robert Frost*, I found a one-word salutation in his stubby handwriting: *Frost.* Ruthie handed me the wet envelope, and I plucked his note from inside. The stubby letters in lead pencil hadn't bled as ink might:

Belle, The only major difference I see between my original West-Running Brook and my Collected Poems is I ignored your advice and included "The Lovely Shall Be Choosers" this time: I got the inside word a second Pulitzer is coming my way.

This should relieve me from any obligation to write another "Goodbye to Mama"—at least for as long as you don't finish yours!

Cowden says he's induced you to return to teach, study, and write poetry this spring. He's induced me to return for another of my creative visits in the fall. I trust you will help me avoid cramming shot down our students' throats. As ever, Frost

Although I hear Mrs. Todd and her daughter are coming out of hiding with an expanded version of Dickinson letters, our new president plans to award Madame Bianchi the first honorary degree Amherst has ever granted a woman. Perhaps, this will ease the sting of the Todds' shot across her bow.

That evening I picked up his *Collected Poems* and read "The Lovely Shall Be Choosers" aloud; it sounded better that way. Its cadence, the voice of the unseen oracles, their offering to the poet's mother of seven joys that sour, and the courage she displayed to persevere without saying a word to the very end, all sang more to me.

I pulled out my songbook and reread my two previous attempts to say goodbye to my mother: "Blue Salvation" and "Mary Bell's Death." I don't know whether it was Frost's letter twitting me with exclamation point and dash, but I sang again:

Goodbye to Mama

water below ice
spilling from our fishing hole—
sly silence—and then—

one long lonely Crack!
our fishing shanty's heaving sigh—
spinning silver shards—

brother 'neath my arm—
her gloved hand waving toward shore:
Mama's gray goodbye—

frozen arm flailing
reaching for life, pumping hard
through unforgiving gray shock—

now stroking steady
in peaceful rhythmic splendor:
lake lips caressing

the hills and valleys
of my cold suffering soul—
O! Blue Salvation…

I wrote the poem in my songbook but typed copies for Frost and for Cowden's class—and five for submission, anonymously, to the Hopwood competition. I wrote Frost:

I know you don't really think the poem to your Mama Belle made all the difference, but I do hear its sound better now. Your note mocking my style inspired me to sing my "Goodbye to Mama" at last. If it meets your challenge, I hope you'll share any better goodbye to your mother you may hereafter compose.
As ever, Your Younger Belle

P.S. I don't hold out much hope for your president getting "Aunt Emily's" papers out of Madame Bianchi's clutches. I fear the honorary degree will instead put off the time Mrs. Todd's daughter stops hoarding the rest of the Dickinson originals.

I posted the note to Frost's office at Amherst. All spring I waited but never heard back.

ᔓ

With six weeks left before the end of the semester, Cowden asked me to join him in his office at Angell Hall. He handed me his copy of "Goodbye to Mama" and said, "I need you to submit another poem for the Hopwood."

"This one's not good enough?"

"I retained three judges for each prize, and..." His voice trailed off.

"Does it count for your seminar at least?"

He took the poem, wrote on the bottom, and handed it back: *This is the best poem from any student. Makes me wonder why I never sang goodbye to my mother after she died. R. W. Cowden 4/20/31.*

"You sure you're not just getting even for the dunking in my glasshouse?"

He chuckled. "You need to submit at least one more poem for the competition." When I didn't say anything, he added, "It's important if you're going to break into the male bastion here by proving a woman's fit for our faculty."

"Tomorrow still the deadline?"

He nodded. "Five copies, typed. Use a pseudonym so no judge will guess it's you."

When I got home, I called Mirja, and she agreed to invite Ruth and Pip over for dinner. I sat down with my journal by the pool. I jotted several notes about spring and love, starting with the first buds and blooming as the flowers open. I looked around the exotic garden, lush and ripe, a springtime that lasted throughout the year. I jotted several more notes, now a bit more ironic, of the folly of endless love and eternal youth.

When I looked up, dusk had already given way to night. Ruth's bedroom window was open. Pip must have tucked her in so she could call down to me if she woke. Whether he retired to his private quarters alone or with Mirja, he never announced, but his lights were off. I looked up, and a meteor flashed across the sky. I sang a new song:

Shooting Star

Prone upon my blanket
High upon this hill
I search the August night
Hoping that I will

Spot a shooting star
Blaze across the sky.
Above, celestial twinkling,
And then I see one fly

Like silver on black velvet
It arcs from east to west.
If you were not looking,
You would miss its shiny crest.

Shooting stars give lessons
of how to live our lives
for if we are not looking
what matters will pass us by.

I submitted five copies under the name Caroline Herschel for the Hopwood competition. I made two extra copies of both my new poems; I sent one set to Auden at the Larchfield Academy on the Firth of Clyde and the other to Teddy's home in Saginaw.

ಌ

On Monday evening, June 1, Mirja, Rabbie, Pip, Trudy, and I hosted a dinner for Frost at Cambridge House. Robbie walked with his old friends Bursley and Cowden and joined our two other guests, Stella and Chase Osborn. Frost greeted Stella as if she were his long-lost star, but the governor said, "Stellanova Osborn, my new star." Dark hair in a pert bob, full lips highlighted with blush, and full figure trim as ever, she did look fetching.

When Frost began to congratulate his first benefactor at the University on his new bride, Stella shook her head. "Chase could only adopt me."

"As his daughter?" When Chase nodded, Frost turned to Pip. "Good to know your interest in the heavens has spread to the governor, too." Frost ignored Cowden's "tut-tut" and asked, "Figured out if the voices you're hearing in space come from sunspots, novas as luminous as Stella, galaxies colliding, or more intelligent life?"

While Pip admitted his inability to determine their "heavenly source," I sat our guests at the table. I put Frost at one end, with Stella on one side and Mirja on the other. I sat at the other end and entertained the governor and Bursley. Pip and Trudy signed next to each other on one side of the table, while Cowden and Rabbie belabored each other with the latest carping and gossip in the English Department on the other.

Frost's cheeks grew rosier as his tongue wagged between the two stars, and his now whitening crown of hair only made his blue eyes sparkle more. I don't know how he found time to tuck into the crown roast the butcher, Mr. Clague, provided, but there wasn't any left on his plate when our caterer, Mrs. Strieter, cleared. The lighter dessert of my homemade cherry sherbet did slow his conversation with Stella and Mirja long enough that each had time to daub the red melting from the corners of his smile.

I also managed to catch Bursley's encouragements to me. "Cowden says your poetry seminar is a hit with the undergrads. Your graduate work is superb. Keep it up, and the tenure track will open to you." After the last dollop of cherry ice, he leaned toward me and whispered, "We're negotiating to make Frost's stint next fall a regular visit every year." He didn't ask me to donate or to serve as Frost's teaching assistant. "Don't worry, Belle, with the surprise Cowden's giving him tomorrow, the funds I've got, and the pledges from Mirja, Chase, and Rackham, money won't be a problem."

Osborn nodded with a smile. "Stella tells me your family's bought a swatch of coast and forest on the northwest corner of Leelanau Peninsula."

"Several thousand acres," I said, "but not the Sleeping Bear Dunes."

Chase winked at Bursley. "Couple years back, I gave my preserve on St. Mary's River to the University, to be run as a part of its Biological Station at Burt Lake."

"We're still buying rather than giving away land for now," I replied.

He chuckled at that. "At least old D. H. Day—before he died, bless his soul—and I made sure the State Parks got the main part of the Dune."

I perked right up at that. "Think you could help us work with the state to prevent any dune buggies there?"

"Can't risk old King David rising from his grave to smite me," he said, "but if you're ever of a mind to turn Sleeping Bear into a national park, I did just work with the Secretary of the Interior to persuade Congress to authorize funds so the Park Service can take on Isle Royale."

"Not sure I trust Sleeping Bear with the National Parks any more than the State."

"At least the Feds won't be so beholden to the Day heirs, and you could throw in your land for a fair price to boot."

My face felt like it flamed to the color of my hair. "We're not planning on running our Empire at a loss any time soon."

"Miss Belle," he said with a smile, "I see why Stella admires your style."

"Governor Osborn," I replied, "maybe there is another wrong you could help Dean Bursley right though." Both men were all ears now. "The precursor of the University was founded in 1817 in Detroit as a part of another federal land grab, including from the Ojibwe and Odawa bands that the settlers had already driven out. The eventual sale of these lands helped fund the University when the newly admitted state authorized its location in Ann Arbor in 1837." I paused. "Do you think you could get your man in Washington to join you in asking the Regents to award five scholarships for qualified Indians so they can afford to enjoy the blessings of the University they helped found?"

Both nodded at that. Even if they were 114 years late at making proper amends, David Ahgosa would have nodded too.

Along with the sniffing and tasting of Papa's best Laphroaig, Frost held court in the living room. He pressed Rabbie on his approach to Freshman Composition with three, two-page essays and personal conferences with each student every week. Cowden confirmed that, despite early grumblings, demand for the course had spread, so Rabbie was hiring and training more new instructors for next year.

Frost said, "Too bad Rabbie wasn't teaching the Frosh when Mr. Roethke started."

Suddenly, Cowden and Bursley were all ears.

Frost chuckled. "If Belle and I hadn't rescued him from Ned's Straitjacket, Teddy wouldn't have starred at Harvard this year and won a position at Lafayette College." Apparently Teddy now shared more with Frost than with me. "You boys should hire him here. By fighting all his demons," he added as if challenging his two faculty hosts to disagree, "he will also make himself quite a poet."

Rabbie knew how to humor the old bard and asked how he'd managed to sing in top form without break or decline.

"Writing each poem," Frost began, "is a performance, in belief and will, as much as talent and inspiration." He paused, nodded to me, and added, "Sometimes persistence, too." He pulled a folded sheet of paper from his pocket.

I shook my head at him: no broadcasting my "Goodbye to Mama," thank you.

He put my song back. "You can't worry a poem into shape, even if it takes years to ripen. But when it does, you've got to engage it like a big game, as Yost's teams did."

Mirja pressed, "But how do you stay at your peak for so many… decades?"

"You never know the outcome of any poem you start until you've written the last word, no matter how long it takes." Frost patted the pocket that held my poem.

As the party broke up and all the other guests departed, Frost lingered. "Will you take me to your new kirk on the site of my second home here?" he said.

We walked across the little park with Mirja and Rabbie and then up the hill to their house. As Robbie and I continued past the big rock, Frost stopped in front of Chi Phi and said, "I missed our Teddy Bear tonight. Did you forget to ask him?"

"I sent two of my poems and an invite."

We continued down the hill to the new First Presbyterian Church. The Neo-Gothic architecture, tall sides clad in limestone, and steep-gabled roofs in slate, offered a welcoming arch with a large rose window over two massive wooden doors. "Good Lord," he said, "this looks more like the King's Cathedral at Christ Church."

As we entered the narthex, he stopped, picked up the gong, and struck the bell from the tower of the old church downtown, once. The sound reverberated through the main sanctuary, from the tall walls to the soaring ceiling. "Remember One-O?" Before I could reply, he marched down the center aisle to the front pew on the right. We sat in the hush for several minutes. He rose as suddenly as he'd sat. He led me out the door on the south side and cut through the alley to Hill Street, turned south down a side street, and stopped in front of Bursley's home. "Belle, help with my seminar in the fall."

"Unless I'm needed up north," I replied. Frost shook his head. His pale blue eyes pleaded, so I added, "It's a struggle, for our Empire, the Homestead Club and the inn, and the Ahgosa enterprises. A lot of families depend on us to keeping going."

Robbie slumped, and his big head dropped. "Oh, I know. Oh, how I know. I'm going to teach at least one long seminar outside

Amherst each semester and double my speaking engagements until this Depression ends." When he pursed his lips, I asked after his family. He told me his son gave up the Vermont farm and moved his family to Santa Barbara for better prospects, but consumption now gripped his son's wife. Lesley was divorcing her husband while going through a hard pregnancy on Long Island, and Irma was "still fighting with her husband, her demons, and me."

"I'm sorry," I said. When he didn't continue, I asked, "Marj?"

"She was doing so well, flourishing in her second year of nursing school in Baltimore until..." His shoulders sagged. "Not pleurisy this time... tuberculosis." He looked up. "We've got her in a sanitarium in Boulder. If Elinor's heart doesn't act up again, we'll go to her this summer, and if Marj is well enough, we'll..." He paused.

"I hope you'll find a healthy new grandchild and mother, a new Marj, and—"

Frost interjected by raising a stubby finger. "Just promise you'll help me here this fall it at all possible." I couldn't help nodding and giving my dear friend a pat on his hand.

❧

The next afternoon 200 nervous contestants sat in the biggest lecture room in Angell Hall. The presence of Pip, Mirja, and Trudy, I attributed to a show of support if I lost. Only Rabbie had a reason for being there: his students all wrote, wrote, wrote for the undergraduate Hopwood prizes. Teddy showed up as the doors closed. At least it was too warm for his raccoon coat. Yet decked out in his new professorial garb—tweed jacket with leather elbow patches, dark plaid shirt, and blue tie loose at the collar—he looked more as if he expected to win the first major Hopwood prize in poetry.

Professor Cowden presided and gave a brief introduction as to why the late Avery Hopwood and his mother Jules gave the money for these prizes: to encourage each generation of Michigan students, undergraduate and graduate, to practice the art and enjoy the wonder of writing. For Cowden, as for the Hopwoods, English at a great university meant creating literature—essay, screenplay, drama, short story, novel, and poetry—as much as reading the great old works, critiquing new ones, or struggling through rhetoric exercises. Roy was singing to the choir, and we cheered his music.

Except for a lone cough from the back. I turned and saw Ned Strait peering over his half-glasses and down his nose. Nym was monitoring the Hopwood proceedings in hope of finding fault to fuel his takeover from Professor Cowden.

The rest of us clapped for each winner as Roy made the announcements and presented the checks. I joined more heartily when one of Rabbie's students won, and even more so when a student in my seminar won the undergraduate prize in poetry, but I was more impressed by the Major Award for an essay going to Dorothy Donne. Also an older student, I'd enjoyed the lyrical quality of her prose when Cowden asked me to read an early draft. I'd written Roy, *Mrs. Donne would have made a great Whimsy: tell her we'll all be worse off if she doesn't start composing poems, too.*

Only the major prize in poetry remained, and Cowden introduced Frost. "We're honored one of the Hopwood jurors joined us. This is fitting, as Robert Frost wrote many of his great poems here while he inspired several previous classes of Michigan students. As you know, his *Collected Poems* won the Pulitzer this year. On behalf of the National Institute of Arts and Letters, I also have the privilege of honoring our Creative Fellow with the inaugural Russell Loines Award for Poetry for his extraordinary lifetime achievement." Cowden held up a framed sheepskin and a check.

Frost rose. He shambled up to the podium and, in his usual "aw, shucks" manner, bowed to Cowden and took the check. "Grateful as I am for the welcome award…" He paused, waved the check, and confided in his thundering stage whisper, "One thousand dollars!" He stuffed the check in his coat pocket and continued, "But you're not here to listen to me talk or read poems… although I do promise to return for two weeks in the fall to share my wit and… doggerel…" He paused for our easy laughter to subside. "Well, your prior president, Mr. Little, did send me packing when he compared me unfavorably to Edgar Guest and his doggerel." Our now less-easy laughter did not deter him. "No, I'm here to recognize a new talent, a big one, from this university, even more than to award the major Hopwood Poetry prize to a student enrolled at Michigan." Cowden, standing behind Frost, looked perplexed, but he knew better than to interrupt.

Frost reached into his rumpled coat and pulled out two pieces of paper, each folded into thirds. He made a show of unfolding and reading each to himself. I wondered whether he'd picked someone else for the prize but had decided he ought to read one of my poems as a favor to me. *Anything but "Goodbye to Mama,"* I prayed.

"Before I recognize the talent, will the person who used the pseudonym Caroline Herschel please step forward to accept the first Major Award for Poetry?"

What was this, some joke?

"Now, don't be shy," Frost continued. "Shooting Star is a good poem, the best of a commendable lot of 24 other qualified submissions that I and the two other judges reviewed." Then I looked back at Teddy and understood. Grinning from ear to ear, he swayed from one cheek to the other in his chair. His bulbous nose nodded with glee. I'd lucked out with my poem, but Frost was really here to tout his bear of a boy as the big, new talent. Better to stand up, accept my prize, and retire from the stage so the two showmen could put on their final act for the crowd.

I walked up and stuck out my hand, but Frost shook his head. I pointed to the last check on the table behind him.

"Belle," he blurted, "who's Caroline Herschel?"

"The first astronomer to sight a repeating comet, in 1786."

Frost picked up the Hopwood check, eyed it, pulled the Loines check from his coat pocket, and compared the two. He grimaced, shook his head and whispered in a loud aside, "A thousand smackers for decades of singing poetry for my supper and 1½ times that to a student for writing one unpublished poem!"

The audience clapped, my friends and the undergrads in my poetry seminar louder than the rest—except Roethke, who whistled, snorted, and stomped his feet. No wonder: he knew he'd be next.

Cowden stepped forward and, in a stage whisper reminiscent of the performance Frost and Amy Lowell put on 10 years before at Hill Auditorium, said to Frost, "You know we do require anonymity in every submission for a Hopwood."

When Frost put on a dumbfounded look, laughter erupted throughout the hall.

Frost shrugged his shoulders, smiled, held up his hand, and waited for the inevitable silence. "Sorry, Professor Cowden," he said. "I misunderstood when I called to tell you a contestant inadvertently shared a poem with me, not knowing I was a judge." As if that were sufficient answer, he continued, "Belle sent me the final version of two prior drafts of a poem that'd been itching at her for nigh on 20 years. You know," he whispered as if bringing the audience in on a secret, "we first met and worked together on an old student literary magazine here called *Whimsies* a decade ago."

Cowden, Stella, and Rabbie cheered at that, while the rest of the audience once again laughed but even more warmly. I looked out into the crowd and saw Teddy still rolled from cheek to cheek in his chair in anticipation, while Nym scowled in the back.

Without further ado, Frost recited "Blue Salvation" and "Mary Bell's Death" from memory. His phrasing and intonation weren't what I intended, but his interpretation captivated the Hopwood crowd. Even Teddy stopped swaying. Frost pulled a paper from his pocket and said, "Belle challenged me to write a better goodbye to my mother than 'The Lovely Shall Be Choosers,' although," he added in his stage whisper, "it was good enough to help me win a second Pulitzer and now a Loines." He recited his poem. "Of course, I returned the favor and challenged Belle to write a better goodbye than my first try or her first two. This spring she did." He proceeded to say my "Goodbye to Mama" in a soft voice with such passion I cried. When he finished, there was no sound other than the stifling of other sighs in the audience. Frost concluded, "Trust me, Belle, you won this game with your last word."

Teddy rose and started to clap. Others began to join, except Ned Strait, who sneaked out the back door. The clapping spread and sped up. I took the applause, and I walked back to my chair, stunned that Frost had intended to honor me all along rather than our big Teddy Bear. Frost also knew enough not to say another word.

Cowden closed even more briefly than he began. "This day we've done Avery Hopwood's wish—to encourage creative writing at this university—proud: we've set a bar that will challenge us, not just for years but for generations to come."

Most of the Hopwood participants, students, teachers, Frost the juror and performer, Cowden the director, and guests Pip, Trudy, Teddy, Stella, and Governor Osborn joined the party Mirja and Rabbie hosted. Pip couldn't stop congratulating me and telling Frost how right he was for recognizing my talent. Bursley stopped by and rescued the great poet. Cowden brought a glass of punch, and I handed him my check endorsed to the University for the Hopwood Program. "A down payment on the Annual Hopwood Lecture to go along with the student awards," I said. Cowden loved the idea, and I added, "Make sure you invite a great woman writer to speak."

Before he could respond, Frost returned and said to Cowden, "You didn't tell me Untermeyer was one of the other judges."

"Louis even offered to share Belle's poetry with his editor at Harcourt Brace."

"All right," said Frost, "I'll send her poems to Holt, too."

Cowden turned to me. "Publishing will help get you tenure here."

Surprisingly, Frost didn't join in badgering me. Instead he said, "Roy, if you hire both Mr. Roethke and Miss Belle to inspire young writers here, then your Hopwood Program might just make Michigan America's hothouse for writing."

"Dean Bursley and I need your help to make sure Ned Strait and his academic pedants and literary critics don't try to take it over and squash it," Cowden replied.

"Only the infusion of younger blood will overcome these infernal infections among hidebound faculty. I fled this place because of your Nym, but his ilk pervades every English Department, Amherst included. Let us celebrate the good progress we made today with a drop of Mirja's punch and my promise to return in the fall."

After I downed a few too many more glasses from the bowl, Roethke started playing the piano and I submitted to stumbling through a jig with Rabbie, a reel with Robbie, and a rumba with Mirja and Stella. When Mirja took over her keyboard, Teddy swept me off my feet with his nifty Foxtrot. After the third number, he guided me through the crowd and leaned against the corner of the carved wood mantel above the brick fireplace. "Tennis tomorrow morning," he demanded.

Hardly an invitation to romance, but I nodded.

"When I saw Frost in New York," Teddy added, "he told me about your mistake sending him your 'Goodbye to Mama,' and we concocted the scheme to honor you today anyway." The big bear hugged me. "You flummoxed him with Caroline Herschel." He lifted me up as he never had before. I protested that he was setting me up so he could desert me for the East again. He got down on bended knee and held my left hand in his two big paws. "Not until I've properly *courted* you all summer." I couldn't help laughing. "I'll be back here, teaching and writing with you year-round, as soon as I finish my Master's thesis. I'll show Nym and the rest of the toadies my poetry sings too." I almost forgot Ned Strait would do his best to blackball Teddy as much as me.

ഗ

Then June 2, 1931, proved so memorable I couldn't forget it for the rest of my life.

Mirja pulled me away from Teddy's hold in the parlor and walked me up to the phone in her sewing room on the second floor. "Kurt needs to talk to you," is all she said.

I put the receiver to my ear and listened.

"I'm sorry, but your father's dead."

"How?" I heard myself ask.

"In Miss Patterson's arms, in the garret at the inn."

I didn't know how I could tell Pip and Ruth or whether I'd ever be able to say goodbye to Papa. I sat in the chair and tried to compose myself. "We'll set out at dawn tomorrow," I told Kurt. "Can you make arrangements with Pastor Weir for a memorial service?" I rang off, and Mirja helped me up. "Tell Pip to meet me out back?"

She nodded and turned to go. At the door she stopped and said, "I'll have to tell the guests, too. We can't go on partying. Not now."

"Rabbie can tell them after Pip and I leave for Cambridge House, okay?" I retreated down the back stairs, into the kitchen, and out the back door. I looked up to the myriad of stars. I didn't know about heaven, but I would have given anything to hear my father's voice calling down, whether into my little ears here or even Pip's bigger ear on Empire Bluff.

Pip joined me, and I told him, not the details of where and how, but that Papa had died. My boy fell into me.

"We've got to tell Ruthie," I said.

"I don't know how."

I didn't either.

ᔕ

Three days later the white walls and ceiling of our old Omena Kirk held us. In the front pew on the right, I sat on the end next to the center aisle, Pip beside me, holding Ruth's left hand, then Mirja, little Paul in her lap, holding tight to Ruth's right hand. There was room for four more, but the rest of the congregation packed all the other pews, with dozens more standing all around. If Papa had died in 1913, I doubt anyone other than our immediate family would have shown up to pay their respects. In the years since, though, Papa had even replaced D. H. Day as the acknowledged leader of our northwest corner of Leelanau County. Maybe the Depression made Papa a better man, too, as he came to rely more on an immigrant from Norway and an Ojibwe down the road to carry his dream forward. No one begrudged him his liaison with Miss Patterson.

I turned to look for her. In the pew behind us sat Kurt, Miss Schultz, Trudy, Teddy, and Rabbie. Skipper and Cora Beals and Pip's mentees, Major Huey from the camp and John Kraus from the radio observatory, sat behind them. An unexpected guest, Alister MacKenzie, walked up the aisle, handed me a telegram, and sat beside Skipper. I scanned the rest of the pews, and there, farther back, sat Miss Patterson. David Ahgosa and his growing band stood proud in back and along the sides of the kirk. Towering in their midst, Sven Surtr bowed his head, too.

While Pastor Weir's wife played the prelude on the piano, I rose, gathered Miss Patterson, David, Spring Blossom, and little Davey, and walked them back to our pew. I didn't hear any gasps from the congregation. David and his wife hugged Pip as they slid by, and little Davey kissed Ruth. I was sorry I hadn't thought to make sure more of David's band could sit, but I could do something about another of my oversights. I vowed to talk to Skipper Beals so Ruthie and other qualified girls as well as boys, Ojibwe included, could learn at the Leelanau School.

Without Emily Dickinson's poems to hold him up, Pastor Weir's eulogy for Papa lacked the power and punch of his memorial for Mama. Maybe the lower key served us all better, as Papa died peacefully after a much longer life. So I listened to Pastor Weir describe Paul Peebles' accomplishments and legacy, his support for regenerating the forests and restoring the natural bounty of Leelanau, and his helping assure the dignity of work, and the pay for food, shelter, recreation, and education, for hundreds of families.

My mind began to wander. I opened the thin, yellow paper. The telegram read:

> 04 JUNE 1931
> DEAR BELLE. STOP. SO SORRY ABOUT YOUR PAPA PASSING. STOP. WILL SEND BY POST MY SIX ODES HIS LOVE OF BURNS INSPIRED. STOP. YOUR GOODBYE TO MAMA SINGS. STOP. MAY IT CONSOLE YOU IN THIS TIME OF LOSS TOO. STOP. WYSTAN.
> LARCHFIELD ACADEMY, HELENSBURGH, SCOTLAND

Auden's welcome condolence made Frost's note all the crustier:

> *It's hard enough to write a goodbye to one parent. It took you three tries to sing your "Goodbye to Mama," and you still find my goodbye to my mama wanting. Dont go mad composing a farewell to your papa. He was a good man and died without suffering. Let him rest in peace so you can get on with the living: please help his beloved Ruthie carry on without him.*

❧

Then I heard our girl whispering to Pip, little Paul to Mirja, and Davey to his father. *Oh, dear Robbie*, I thought, *you've already buried two of your children and fear you'll lose more before your time on earth ends: Hard as it may be, easier to let a mother or father go.* And I shuddered at the thought of ever having to bury Ruthie.

Pastor Weir closed his eulogy with the 23rd Psalm: "Yea, though I walk through the valley of the shadow of death… I will dwell in the house of the Lord forever." The voice didn't sound like Papa. I remembered Mama's gray glove waving and her voice wishing me well as the ice broke. I knew why Frost's note bothered me so. How I could I ever sing goodbye to Papa when he'd never had the chance to say farewell to me?

As the memorial service drew to a close, Pastor Weir invited the congregation to join us in one hour for a reception at the Homestead. Rabbie and Spring Blossom took Ruthie, Davey, and little Paul back to Belle Cottage, while Pip, Kurt, David, Miss Patterson, Miss Schultz, Teddy, Dr. MacKenzie, Mirja, and I buried Papa beside Mama. Eight good men, chosen by lot, six from Empire and two from the Homestead, bore the casket for the committal of his body.

Dr. MacKenzie pulled me aside. "Your father and I talked about walking the new course in Augusta with Bobby Jones, but it's taken too long. I'm so sorry."

"Think Mr. Jones might invite Pip to play in the first invitational there instead?"

"Ach, lassie, the Lord willing, I'll also offer him a few tips for those links." He pulled out a slim book titled *The Spirit of St. Andrews*. Dr. MacKenzie inscribed his name below it. "Just in case I don't make it, share my secrets with the lad."

Teddy held me and offered to hold me up, while Miss Schultz knew enough to tend to Miss Patterson so I didn't have to. I grasped Pip's left hand, and David gripped his right. As the pallbearers lowered Papa into the big hole, Kurt, bless him, let out a cry. My heart broke, and I couldn't help weeping.

Parson Weir recited the burial prayer, but I wouldn't leave. I picked up a shovel from one of the men, pointed it down, and pushed dirt from the mound beside the grave over Papa's remains. I listened as the clods and stones struck the casket, and my heart pounded with the drumbeat. I handed the shovel to Pip, and he did the same, as did David, Kurt, Teddy, and the rest, until the mound beside Papa's grave covered his coffin.

Pip and I picked up several loose stones and placed them on top of Papa's marker. Kurt added another stone and said, "April 20, 1865–June 2, 1931. A long life to be sure, but the dash says so much more: he lived a full life, and his greatest joy was you two. He left knowing you both would carry on, for his Ruthie and for the rest of us."

Miss Patterson pulled a Petoskey stone from the ruffles in her blouse and placed it on his marker. She whispered to me, "You know I loved him so."

Good Lord, didn't she remember I had to hide the old lovebirds in the garret of the inn? I only replied, "Stay with us for as long as you wish." Thank heavens, Miss Schultz had already made sure Papa's trust provided handsomely for her.

David lifted the flat, round stone that had guided me to Mama's watery grave. He draped the pendant atop the marker. "This charm will watch over your Papa as he walks on toward the sun until his spirit flies to his resting place. Then I will embed it in the totem pole we carved under the birch box, where the two watchers will protect your father's clan as mine."

I looked south over Omena Bay, caught a whiff of Macallan in the brisk breeze, and felt Papa's presence. An eagle circled overhead. I heard Papa say, "Farewell," felt a touch to my cheek, and he was gone. The big bird headed west toward Sleeping Bear Bay, and David picked up his stone circle from the marker.

"Did you hear him?" I mouthed to Pip.

My boy shook his head but whispered, "Did you smell the Scotch on his breath?"

I vowed to help my brother build his Big Ear. Oh, Papa, I don't know what voices our boy will find, but he deserves the opportunity to hear.

That night, while Ruth and little Paul slept in the bedroom on the other side of the attic door, I sang my elegy for my father:

Papa's Goodbye

A gentle breeze among the birches sings,
And graying clouds float silently above—
Your wooden casket cold to touch, on wings
Death, blasé Thief of my paternal Love—

And yet your whiskey breath wafts in the breeze,
Your lips—I swear!—caress my tear-stained cheek—
So I turn, slowly, and vainly reach
For your Arm so late I have sought to seek—

And o'er our heads a golden Eagle soars,
Illumined by a single shaft of Sun—
A Sign that You will haunt these Blessed Shores—
That your earthly journey is far from done:

O Woe, its lonely lament fills the Sky,
My Hopes muffled in a mournful Sigh—

I hoped my bow to Emily Dickinson's wilder emoting in this old sonnet form worked. When I wrote my lyric down in the journal, I put a period at the end first and then tried an exclamation mark, but both shut my voice off. I thought for a long while and substituted a dash. It worked, not as a pause, but to extend my sigh.

I wasn't sure I'd ever share my poem with Frost. Instead, I locked it in the trousseau Mama meant for me and said my farewell: *Papa, I will miss you forevermore, but I am grateful you became my father and most supportive friend, right to the end. Thank you for saying goodbye to Pip and me. We will carry on.*

Spring 1934: Glen Arbor and Ann Arbor

Abbé Georges Lemaitre, David Ahgosa, John Kraus, and my brother huddled inside the shed over the instruments and charts recording the hiss, static, and other sounds. Pip pointed to the faint line at the bottom, straight as an arrow. Suddenly, a new line shot up. A second later a thunderclap rumbled so, even Pip nodded and said, "Lightning."

Lemaitre stopped here on his way to Princeton after an historic meeting at Caltech in Pasadena. There he shared his theory of the beginning of the universe with Hubble and Einstein: how a small, dense mass exploded, and over time millions of galaxies formed and continue to race apart. John's imitation of the stout priest raising his hands from a single point at his waist up and out to form a space-time cone as the universe expanded over time made me laugh.

"Belle, forgive their lack of manners," the priest said with a bow.

I asked what Einstein thought.

"He said my *theory* is the most beautiful explanation of creation." He frowned. "But your boys point out a fatal flaw."

"The minor detail," interjected Pip, "that Hubble's most recent calculation of the age of the universe suggests the good father's primordial atom exploded billions of years *after* the geologists say the earth was born."

Lemaitre rubbed his round spectacles on his cassock. "What more can I do?"

Out of the corner of my eye, I saw another pen blipping slowly across the paper. Pip pushed us out the door and pointed west. "See the big ore boat?" A lightning bolt flicked down several seconds before its clap of thunder rocked us. We couldn't even see the Great Lake, let alone a freighter, through the storm. Pip pointed up to his latest odd contraption spinning atop the shed and led us back inside. He explained how it transmitted short-wave beams over the lake but included a receiver that detected the beams bouncing back off a passing ship or plane.

John nodded to Lemaitre and said, "The steady line recorded by Pip's horned scoop may be the remaining flicker from the big explosion you say started the universe."

Lemaitre sighed. "Okay, okay, I promise I will speak to Einstein again in Princeton, as well as the radio astronomers at Bell Labs, and Eddington when I get back."

That afternoon before dinner, I convened a war council for our enterprises in the kitchen. Kurt concluded, "Unless we find an independent source to finance installment sales of all our stoves, we'll be selling through Sears in its name and lose our brand."

"I'd rather put up all the stocks we bought last year as collateral," I retorted.

"No, Marmie," Pip answered, "you bought those at the all-time lows, and it's time to let America's Flame cook on her own. We can mortgage our plant, equipment, inventory, and brand to get whatever financing we need."

I knew my boy was a seer in the heavens, a tinkerer on earth, and an inventor without peer, but when had he become a financial wizard, too? When Kurt grinned broadly and said he'd go to Wall

Street to secure a line of credit that would see our Empire through this Depression, I could only open the last bottle of Macallan to toast Papa's memory and the future of our family firm.

As our meeting broke up, David joined me in Papa's study and warned me that Ben Peshaba planned to petition the Bureau of Indian Affairs for recognition of the Grand Traverse Band of Odawa and Peshawbestown and wanted the Aghosas to join on behalf of their Ojibwe band. When I noted that the Secretary of the Interior had asked and the University of Michigan had granted five Scholarships for Indians, he shook his head: "You know I don't trust the BIA to keep its word. Why should I run the risk of diluting our Grand Traverse enterprises in Ahgosatown?"

I turned in Papa's chair and looked out over Sleeping Bear Bay to the Dunes and Lake Michigan beyond. The wild spring storm had finally broken, and the surface of the big bay looked a sheet of glass. The sun fell below the cloud cover and reddened as it crossed the horizon. The crimson rays reflected off the water and the underside of the cloud bank, all the way back over Belle Cottage, and formed a scarlet tunnel for my entire field of vision.

I saw my immediate problem more clearly now: Kurt's face had lit up so when he talked about going to Wall Street, we risked losing our CEO. More and more, he turned over day-to-day operations to David and focused on strategy, the larger financial issues, and closing big deals: joint ventures with the natural gas utilities, a contract with the CCC for camp stoves, and financings with J.P. Morgan. Kurt had gotten so good at navigating through the Depression, he could become a king-maker, helping dozens of companies survive and thrive. Each time he came back from his retreats to Fire Island and New York City, he was energized. What kind of life did our isolated corner of Leelanau offer him, compared to the Big City? "David, whatever you decide, you will also have a big stake in our Empire."

After dinner I asked Kurt to join me in the study. He sat in front of Papa's desk in one of the two red leather chairs, their surfaces grown soft with age, and I sat in the other. I looked at this man: small, yes, but handsome; not a hair out of place on his head; his moustache trim; his dark suit, white shirt, and navy tie pressed; his gold-rimmed glasses circling clear eyes that absorbed everything within his sight. No sense wasting time with small talk. I reached out my hand and touched his. "Will you be my partner?"

"Business, marriage, or both?" Good Lord, how to answer that I thought, until he continued, "I just can't be your mate."

"Let's stick to business, then: You staying with Pip and me at Empire, or shifting to Morgan?"

His trim moustache wrinkled ever so slightly and his eyes blinked once, but he didn't remove his hand. "Belle, I don't know."

Sending Kurt off to New York to get financing was like offering this cool Dane catnip. "Kurt, you've carried us so far, we've been through so much and…"

He raised a forefinger to my lips, and a tear trickled down his cheek.

After Kurt left, I drafted notes to Frost, Auden and Roethke:

Dear Robbie,

Please offer Marj and her husband the opportunity to come to Ann Arbor for the birth of their baby at our new Lying-in at University Hospital. It's the least Pip and I can do for all you did for us with Ruthie in Amherst.

So glad to hear Van Dore still tends your farm and composes poems. I'm embarrassed to admit my voice has fallen silent again.

Ironic you report that after Mabel Todd's death, your President King continues his exclusive courting of Madame Bianchi. Given her recent retort—Emily Dickinson, Face-to-Face: Unpublished Letters, Notes, and Reminiscences—don't be surprised when Mabel's daughter answers with her own poisoned pen.

As ever, Belle

Oh, how I hoped Robbie and Mrs. Frost would take up my offer. Marj had such a history of illness, I worried the hardship of childbirth and risk of infection would strike her down in a hard Western town like Billings, where she'd moved with her husband. I was also sorry working to save my family Empire had prevented me from serving Frost on his last visit to teach as I'd promised. Worse, I wasn't there to protect him from Ned Strait and his Nym slanders; Frost was so offended, he'd never return to Michigan.

Oh, how I also feared for Wystan, a gentle man with such a creative flair and unique gift of expression. I found his *Six Odes* about his time teaching school in Helensburgh moving. Maybe it was just the memory of our trip together to Mama's home place along the Firth of Clyde, but I heard the echo of Rabbie Burns in his voice. The current draft of his verse play with Isherwood was more troubling: whatever their flirtations with any collectivist state, Nazi Germany was no place for such a curious fellow and his male mate.

Dear Wystan,

I fear for you and Isherwood living under the thumb of Hitler. If your homeland no longer suits, please consider my home in Ann Arbor your refuge. It offers the prospect of teaching at Michigan, freelancing as you wish, and writing as you will. If this isn't your cuppa, I can help you settle in New York through my CEO here and his investment banking partner there. You can then judge for yourself whether FDR's experiments offer a better way out of Depression than the monarchs, fascists, and communists. I'm sorry I don't enclose any poems in response to your extraordinary Odes, but I haven't composed any worth sharing. Faithfully yours, Belle

Next I wrote Ted Roethke:

Jealous as I am of Miss Kunkle, I hope she will provide a good marriage and a new family for you. Lord knows you need such a blessing, but you must also complete your Master's at Michigan. Rabbie says it's the only way to rise in academia as high as your poetry will surely take you with the public. I promise to thrash you on the tennis court this summer and ask one favor in return: will you ask your new mentor Humphries to introduce me to Louise Bogan? Seeing as I've lost my voice helping the family enterprise up north and Cowden sees no other prospect for a women on the English faculty, I convinced Stella and Mirja we should import accomplished women poets to give readings. We've already enlisted Millay for a visit this spring, and we'd like to ask Ms. Bogan.

I walked up to the attic, opened Mama's trousseau, pulled out MacKenzie's little book, and walked down to Pip's room. "The good doctor wanted me to share this with you." Pip opened *The Spirit of St. Andrews* and began to read.

A week later I drove Pip, Ruthie, and John south to Ann Arbor, where Pip loaded his clubs, knickers, and suitcases into my big, new Lincoln touring car. Pip had earned his way with his good play last summer, and my boy wasn't going to pass up Mr. Jones' request to play in his first Augusta National Invitational. Kurt made sure Grantland Rice knew that America's Flame accompanied my boy, along with their older chaperone and longtime friend of the Peebles family, Mirja Fitzpatrick-O'Bannon.

I shared responsibility with Rabbie for taking care of Ruthie and Paul back in Ann Arbor. The first week the kids stayed nights through breakfast with Rabbie at Hill House. He drove Paul to St. Thomas school, and I walked Ruthie to Eberbach Elementary. Ruthie and I ate lunch together at home, and I picked up both kids after school and drove them to my house. Rabbie joined us for dinner and then took the kids to Hill House for the night.

On Sunday afternoon we took Ruthie and Paul to the heartwarming new family movie at the Michigan Theater, *Anne of Green Gables.* The rural setting of Prince Edward Island reminded me of up north. After dinner at the League and ice cream sundaes at Drakes, little Paul and Ruthie begged so to spend nights at my house, we changed our pattern of care. Rabbie joined us for dinner most evenings and picked up Paul in the morning to drive him to school. Rabbie also spelled me when I needed to confer by phone with Kurt and David or Spring Blossom.

Mirja called on Wednesday evening to report that Pip couldn't wait to tee off in the morning with Jones and Hagen: "He's sick of practicing his lousy putting."

I asked how she was doing.

"I'll never stop loving your boy."

My hope of throwing Pip and Trudy together because Mirja had to play the role of chaperone had no chance. Who was I to offer Pip advice anyway when no lover had graced my bed for so many years now? Ruthie was more than enough blessing for a woman my age. Yet at 34 I couldn't stop my body yearning for the tingle of lying down with a man again.

While Rabbie read stories and put Ruthie and Paul in their separate twin beds in her room upstairs, I swam laps in the pool to lose myself as best I could. In the odd light thrown off by the three incandescent fixtures above, the new exotic plants glowed red, pink, orange, purple, even blue, while the carnations extended their familiar red and white well-wishes. The water, warmed by the sun during the bright spring day, poured over my shoulders and down my back and surged around my breasts and down my torso with each stroke. After an hour swimming, blue salvation was at hand. I rolled on my back in a state between euphoria and sleep.

I must have dreamed. First, his irresistible pull wafted over me. Then I felt the water part as he knifed silently into the pool. His strong arm wrapped gently around my neck and pulled me to shore.

I opened my eyes, but the light from the chandelier blinded me. I admit it may have taken awhile to wake myself against his riptide tingling me to the core. I struggled free and stood up.

Thank heavens, I had on my swimsuit, so my breasts didn't bob on the surface as headlamps. I jumped out, put on a thick robe, cinched the belt, and turned to face him.

Rabbie stood in the pool. His shoulders and chest looked as powerful as ever, but his face had lost its Irish charm and confident smile. "I'm sorry," is all he said. He climbed out, and I couldn't help staring at his naked body while he walked to the linen cabinet. He pulled out another robe, cinched it tight, and walked away.

"Rabbie, we need to talk," I heard myself say. He opened the kitchen door, and I whispered, "Please."

He slowed, and I followed after. He walked into the bathroom, closed the door, and returned fully clothed. I led him into my paneled study. I bade him sit in the comfortable, green leather chair in front of the big, carved desk, opened the bar beneath the bookshelves, and poured us each a small glass of Laphroaig. Making sure my fingers never grazed his, I handed him a glass and sat in the green leather swivel chair behind the desk. I savored my Scotch and watched as he sipped his with much less pleasure.

"Sorry you never acquired a taste for Scotch and my Kirk," I said too lightly.

"Sorry you never acquired a taste for Irish whiskey and my Church." He tossed his Scotch down. He got up, picked two other glasses from the bar, filled both to the brim with Jameson Malt, and set one before me. In one swallow he downed the other.

"No, I won't risk all in a drinking contest with you." I sipped my Laphroaig and pushed the glass of Jameson across the desk.

He sat down and sipped it now. "What I resent most is not Mirja's love for your brother or his affair with my wife. It's your providing cover for them, your acting to make sure Paul and Ruth suspect nothing, and your being Mirja's best friend and protector here." His face reddened.

"Would you prefer I let them run around and embarrass you and the children? That I keep Ruthie and Paul apart? That I stop providing cover for Mirja and Paul passing as white?"

As I spoke, the color drained from Rabbie's face, and he stood up. "No," he spat out, "I lied. I resent even more your not loving me again."

I felt my blush but willed myself to shake my head. I replied softly but with a wry note, "The Queen would still object."

He couldn't help nodding as his broad shoulders slumped. He knew his mother's iron will on matters of religion, marriage, family, and me. "Being Irish, I guess I inherited the abiding sense of tragedy that sustains me through what can at best only be temporary spells of joy. I still regret ours ended too soon." He shook his head. "I'll pick up Paul tomorrow morning after breakfast."

As he turned to leave, I said, "I promised the children we'd go over to John Kraus' after school to listen to the reports from Augusta."

"I'll drop Paul off then."

"Dinner back here at 6:45?"

After a long pause, he nodded. I didn't know whether I was grateful or sorry Rabbie kept on walking out the front door and down the well-worn path to Hill House.

I returned to bury myself swimming laps in the pool. Why did Rabbie's damn pull linger so after all these years?

∽

Ruthie, Paul, and I listened every afternoon to the radio broadcasts John Kraus picked up. When a gust of wind on the first day knocked Pip's short iron into Rae's Creek on the devilish par three to go three-over after three, it was all I could do to keep from crying like Ruthie. When Pip settled down to shoot par the rest of the front side, even little Paul cheered. It didn't hurt that his playing partners, the host Jones and the favorite Hagen, also finished over par.

Our spirits flagged after Pip buried his approach in the bunker on the 10th and took three to get down for another bogey. Already four-over, disaster lurked on every hole ahead. A string of pars on the next six holes kept Pip at four-over. At the par-five 17th, Pip pushed his drive into the fairway bunker, and his ball rolled under the big lip. He managed to blast out sideways but still had 260 yards to the flag. He smashed his spoon with a slight draw. The ball landed short, curled around the green, and stopped six inches from the hole. Pip scrambled to a par on the last to close with a 76, five worse than the old pro Hagen but tied with his host, Bobby Jones.

The next day Pip managed to shoot a very good one-under-par, despite missing three putts inside four feet, while Jones disappointed his fans again with a 74 and Hagen limped in with a 76. At three-over Pip acquitted himself as the low amateur in the field and tied with Hagen, five off the pace set by Horton Smith, the great pro from Chicago.

For the third round, Hagen played with Pip again. With a strong wind gusting to over 30 miles an hour, the old pro carved out a masterful two-under-par, to close within three shots of Smith. Pip salvaged pars from all over the course: tall grass, bunkers, woods, and water included. Yet he also missed four putts under five feet for bogeys. He also called a penalty stroke on himself on the final hole when the wind kicked up and moved his ball ever so slightly on the green while he addressed his putt. Unfazed, he willed his 25-footer into the cup for a 76.

Of all people, Walter Hagen tipped Grantland Rice off to the story of Pip's valiant play and his better sportsmanship. The great sport columnist wrote:

> *Some bottom-fishing carp complain Mr. Jones invited Pip Peebles to play as a pay-off to the memory of Alister MacKenzie. Here are the facts. I know because I witnessed them. The Peebles family arranged a four-ball match in the fall of 1928 so Bobby Jones could play their new course, the Homestead in northern*

Michigan, overlooking Sleeping Bear Dunes and Bay. Jones teamed with Peebles, the young Empire industrialist who had the wit to hire MacKenzie; and Walter Hagen teamed with David Ahgosa, Peebles' childhood friend and Ojibwe neighbor. Pip's eagle on the last hole sealed the win for the Jones team and demonstrated Dr. MacKenzie's knack for designing a championship links, with risk and reward on every hole.

Given the untimely death of the great architect Jones chose to help design Augusta National, it's only fitting Pip once again teed-off with the best amateur and best pro in the world to open Bobby Jones' first Invitational here. That Pip now stands only a shot back of his host for low amateur after three rounds, and better than most of the pros, only confirms the merit of his game. Pip is also a true sportsman. When the wind blew his ball on the 18th green here today, he didn't flinch. He called a one-shot penalty and calmly sank his long putt for a par. When his hearing failed as he grew from boy to man and his wife died in childbirth, leaving him to raise a baby girl alone, he didn't give up then either. He graduated from Amherst College, won a Rhodes scholarship, and has become one of the nation's leading inventors and a great father.

There is more to the story. Pip and his family also helped America's greatest swimmer, Gertrude Ederle, become America's Flame ever since she swam the Channel, despite her also going deaf. Trudy has walked every one of the 54 holes here with Pip. Only her coaching the U.S. women for the 1936 Olympics will delay the wedding bells for this All-American couple. Pip Peebles' good play and better sportsmanship at Augusta National has shut up all the carp who complained he didn't deserve an invitation to play here.

When I read the column to Ruthie and little Paul Sunday morning, they cheered. But I cried, for I knew the rest of the story. Thankfully,

Grantland Rice, Pip's daughter, and Mirja's son did not. I could only hope Walter Winchell wouldn't find out about Pip's love affair with his married chaperone either.

The final round, Pip confirmed his mettle, once again paired with Bobby Jones. Bobby shot two-under on the front nine, while Pip skied to 41, including four more misses on side-hill, five-footers. While Jones finished with nine straight pars, Pip stormed back with four birdies and an eagle at the par-five 17th. At the last hole, he sank a fast, five-foot, left-to-right side-hiller for 30 on the backside. Pip thereby tied his opening-day playing partners, Bobby Jones and Walter Hagen, at plus-six.

When Horton Smith birdied the 17th to win at four-under-par, Grantland Rice had another story. The great sportswriter recounted the masterful play of the pros and amateurs over MacKenzie's masterpiece. Bobby Jones had welcomed 58 pros and 14 amateurs to the first Augusta National Invitational. Despite the host's modesty in naming his event, Rice said it should ever after be called The Masters.

When Pip got home, he returned Dr. MacKenzie's little book. "Hide it so I won't ever be tempted to spoil a good walk again." He held up his long hands and spread his bony fingers into a huge, gnarly fan. "My heart nearly gave out every time I putted."

So much talent and imagination, so strong and independent, yet also so hobbled. "I know right where to put *The Spirit of St. Andrews* to keep you safe, but only if you promise to teach Ruthie and Paul to play golf so they can enjoy the good walks with you, playing our Homestead course." My boy gave me a grateful hug.

∽

The last day of March, a letter from Frost arrived at Cambridge House:

> *Dear Belle, Marj gave birth to a girl on March 16 in Billings. I was too sick to go, but Elinor was there to help. She raced back*

to care for my old grippe and reports mother and daughter are doing fine. I appreciated your good offer, but I remember my mother Belle's advice: the first Oliver Wendell Holmes said the safest place for a mother to bear a baby is alone in a manger, where the nurses and doctors can't spread the dread fever. Given our family history of sickness, though, I best only say our girl Marj and baby Marjorie Robin have made it safely through the darkest part of the woods. Give Pip my cheers on not letting the golf spoil a good walk and a better story in Augusta. Hope Ruthies healthy and thriving. Frost

Oh, how I hoped Marj and her baby would thrive, but I could hear Frost's darker fears under his lighter tone. Good Lord, the man deserved a break, and so did Marj.

Pip and I packed up the evening of April 22 to head north. Pip needed to tinker a new camp stove to fulfill our contract with the CCC, and Kurt wanted my help on how best to market our stoves on our own. The next morning Pip had one last meeting to persuade the Astronomy Department to let four students intern up north for credit, studying the readings of his horned trumpet on Empire Bluff.

As I walked out the door to pick up Ruthie at school, I met the Western Union man. He handed me the fragile yellow envelope. I dreaded opening it.

BELLE. STOP. MARJ HAS AWFUL FEVER AND INFECTION. STOP. MRS. FROST AND I TRAVELED BY TRAIN TO BILLINGS. STOP. NOTHING TO DO BUT PRAY FOR MARJ NOW. STOP. FROST.

Frost sent a brief telegram from Rochester on April 29. Marj had survived the flight on the small plane and was beginning a new serum at the Mayo Clinic. A week later I received a letter from Frost describing the injections and transfusions, and Marj's high temperature and delirium. *I try to talk with Marj to encourage her by reaching my hand to hers and saying, "You—and—Me." Curse all the medicos in Billings for forgetting the sanitary precautions they'd been taught in school.*

I cried with Frost's May 15 note:

> *Belle, Marj died today. She battled for all she was worth without complaint, even when her fever ran over 110. We tried to move heaven and earth to save her, but we moved nothing. I don't know how Elinor will bear up, as this is the cruelest burden, but I must stay strong for her, even with the horrible truth you know: I took Marj to Mayo too late. Frost*

Before I could begin to think about how to reply, Pip walked in and handed me a letter from Abbé Lemaitre. I gave him Frost's note and read the good priest's letter.

> *My dear friend and fellow dreamer,*
>
> *I regret no one else at Princeton, Bell Labs, or Cambridge will finance radio astronomy to help your search. In contrast, there is great interest in the echoes you and John Kraus get from bouncing your radio waves off moving objects. No doubt this is a piece with the interest in applying Einstein's theories to building a bomb as the rumblings of another great schism in Europe stir.*
>
> *As a lone priest whose theories are only as good as the evidence, I do wish you every success in observing and recording the echo from the original big explosion I am convinced created the universe. Your horned trumpet is a marvelous invention, and your proposed Big Ear holds even greater promise. Do not let any of the naysayers stop you. I look forward to hearing about your discoveries.*
>
> *I remain your faithful servant, Georges*

"I'm so sorry about Marj," Pip said in his level, quiet voice. "Would it do any good if I shared our experience with her husband? Ruthie's such a blessing."

My brother had just learned that Bell Labs, Princeton, and Cambridge, like the University of Michigan, offered no hope for supporting his research into the cosmos, but I asked, "Have you talked with Mirja about getting a divorce and you two marrying yet?"

He read my lips. "That wouldn't be right for little Paul or Ruthie."

I had to laugh: For such a lonely boy and man, Pip always thought of others first. "Well, then, did you discuss Grantland Rice's wedding bells for you and Trudy?"

"Sorry, Marmie, she's leaving. The president of the U.S. Olympic Committee threatened not to field a women's team in Berlin unless Trudy can develop new stars."

"Let's invite her up north for a goodbye party to thank her and wish her well."

"Do you think it'll also be our goodbye party for Kurt?" Pip asked.

"If so, do you want to take over running the company?"

He shook his head. "Do you?"

That set me back, but I needed more time to think. "What about David?"

"He's the best person to run the operations, but you should lead our Empire."

"I'll talk to Kurt, and then we can think about it more together, okay?" When he nodded, I added, "Frost and his son-in-law will both appreciate your letter."

That weekend little Paul and Davey raced across the beach. At six and five, they replayed the dune dashes of Pip and David Ahgosa more than two decades before, but this time a small girl, Ruthie, now age seven, scampered with them. Kurt, decked out in a navy blue captain's jacket and white hat, huddled close to me in the stern of our Mackinaw boat. I trimmed the sails with my left hand and looped my right arm around him to set the tiller. The boat heeled over from the brisk wind out of the southwest and pushed us together. With the last rays of the sun firing a rainbow in the spray from our bow-wave, I said, "You can't leave all this."

Kurt peered through the circles of his horn-rimmed glasses at the three kids racing together along the beach to the cookout on the campfire beneath David's birch box and Papa's totem pole. He took off his glasses, wiped the spray off, stuffed them in the front pocket of his navy blue sport coat, and looked at me. A gust of wind blew his white skipper's hat off. As it flew past me, he lunged to grab it but missed. Still holding the tiller with my one hand, I reached up with the other and caught his hat as we fell together.

As we sailed toward the reflection of the setting sun off the windows of the Homestead Inn, I clapped his hat back on his head and set him upright. "If I were to become your partner at Belle Cottage and father our children," he said, "could you stand my friend staying in the garret you reserved for Miss Patterson and your Papa?"

I lifted my hand off the tiller now. The bow of our boat spun to port, and Kurt fell into me again. This time he deftly pushed the tiller so we headed again across the wind toward the mouth of the Crystal River. "That would be hard," I replied.

"Because you couldn't stomach my infidelity or I'd embarrass you at the inn?"

I placed my hand on his on the tiller. "No, Kurt, I just can't live that way." He didn't let go of my hand. "If you want to become a full partner in the business here with Pip and me instead, I'd welcome putting you and your mate in the garret any time."

That ever-dapper man took his handkerchief out of his pocket, wiped his eyes and buried his head on my beating heart. I rested my head on his and wondered why I couldn't cry any more about losing another good man who wasn't meant for me.

The next morning I enclosed Pip's sealed letter for Willard Fraser inside the larger envelope I mailed to Frost. All those who accused my Robbie of being so driven to defend his reputation and to campaign for his poetry as to forget—or worse not to care for—his family and friends missed the measure of this man. Yes, the poet too often bristled with sharp hackles, but the man fought his darker side to help his family and friends in the worst of times, as he'd helped Pip, Ruthie, and me. Even when railing against the sickness, scatteration, and death visited on his family, and suffering the loss of his youngest child, I knew he and Mrs. Frost would make room to care for Marj's baby. And I told him so in my letter, thanking him again for all he'd done over the years and wishing him well in nurturing Robin. I explained I enclosed a letter from Pip for Willard Fraser, sharing his experience as a widower raising a child. I closed:

I also enclose a poem I composed walking our dunes. Yes, I shed tears for your Marjorie and for you, but I also remembered your benediction at Rachel's memorial service in Johnson Chapel. You reminded Pip he had to go on. A poet is who you are: you have promises to keep and miles to go before you sleep. Please give Robin a hug and hold her close: May she comfort and bless you, too.

Blue

(for Marjorie)

she stands alone
on this weathered dune,
the great lake below
twin to the azure sky—

on the jagged horizon
she can barely see
two tiny islands bob and
weave in the churning waves—

a cobalt wind hurls
slate clouds from the west
to blot out the sun and
buffet the sandy shore

with blue tears.

After lunch the next day, I donned my old two-piece swim suit, greased up, and struck out across the bay. With the water still so cold, I hugged the shore. As I passed Glen Arbor, only the stubby pilings of the big pier remained. The old Bell factory loomed above the beach, still boarded up. If this Depression ever ended, maybe we'd yet find a tenant to bring this shore back to life, too. I swam on and found my rhythm. My internal fire warmed me up, and the water now seemed only cool as it buoyed my spirits.

"Belle!" I heard a man's voice scream. "Marmie!" I heard a little boy's voice plead. I raised my head and saw Davey and Davey's big cousin bobbing in the water, their fishing skiff capsized. Three motorboats roared ahead. I swam as fast as I could, but Sven Surtr reached the two in the water first, while the two other boats raced away. When he raised a big paddle, I screamed. The Dark Ogre yelled back, "I've got them."

I closed the gap quickly but was surprised to see Sven fishing boy and man out of the bay. When he raised his big paddle over me, though, I dived deep. When I surfaced, the giant still loomed over me, his boat's wake sloshing over my head. "Damn it, Sven, why don't you jump in here if you want a fair fight!?"

He'd put his big paddle aside and only lowered his hand. Behind him, I saw Davey wrapping a towel around his cousin's head to staunch the blood. "Vill you shut up so ve can get Meester Ahgosa back to your Homestead vor repairs? The boy is vine."

I grabbed Sven's hand, and he pulled me in. As I gave Davey a hug, Sven gunned the engine, and I fell into the gunnel. Davey explained that six men had boarded their skiff, thrown them overboard, ripped their nets, and sunk their fishing boat. The two motorboats had raced away when the "dark giant" came to the rescue.

I scrabbled to the back, where Sven manned the tiller. Through the roar of his engine, I asked whether his men were responsible for the attack. "Ve don't like the Indians stealing our vish off Glen Haven, but ve aren't vigilantes." In the midst of the Depression, he didn't have to be: the local sheriff and the state conservation officers tried to stop the Indians. When we entered the harbor at the mouth of the Crystal River, I invited Sven to join us for a fresh fish dinner at the inn.

The giant shook his head with a grin and said, "Join us tomorrow vor a ride up the dunes in my souped-up Vord?"

That night I escaped to the attic. I hoped to see the moonlight on the bay, showing the way, but only an inky black roiled. I thought of Teddy still raging but out East, lost to Michigan and me. Trudy also lost, to New York to train better swimmers for the Berlin Olympics. Kurt going: high odds he'd move back to New York to join his partner and a big bank. Frost distant, anchored in New England with his family ties and troubles. Me tethered to my Empire and my clan up north. Papa, old D. H. Day, Mama, even Dr. MacKenzie, long gone.

Miss Schultz, of all the cruel fates, lost her sharp mind to dementia. On my last visit she sat by her window, a book in her hand, her mind not knowing why she couldn't understand. I held her hand and said the poem I wrote for her:

> She sits beside a mullioned window
> An opened book in her hand.
> Her cobwebbed eyes
> Meander across the page
> Among snakes of gray
> For an occasional word
> That might emerge:

Something gay—amethyst, for example,
or vermillion.

Maybe a glint rose in her eye as I recited "For Miss Schultz," or was it a tear? I didn't know then, and maybe I was just feeling sorry for myself at losing too many of my friends and not being able to defeat Strait.

Yet I could still count my blessings. Thank heavens for my boy, Pip, and our girl, Ruthie, the Ahgosas, Mirja, and little Paul, and, dare I say it, Rabbie. We might appear an odd crew in many eyes, but we did damn well given all our intertwining histories, possible frictions, and worse. What to make of Sven, I still couldn't rightly tell. Whatever else, the Dark Ogre wasn't a deceitful devil like Nym.

Fall 1934: Ann Arbor and Glen Arbor

The *Michigan Daily* roiled with articles and editorials the third week of the football season. Two years before, Coach Kipke had ended Fielding Yost's practice of barring Negroes from playing for the Varsity by starting Michigan's All-American track phenom Willis Ward at end. Winning two national championships in 1932 and 1933 proved that adding such color only helped the Maize and Blue. With the loss of many star players to graduation, the 1934 season opened with shutout losses to Michigan State and Chicago. Georgia Tech Yellow threatened to boycott the third game unless Ward stayed off the field at Michigan Stadium. The student paper asked whether Athletic Director Yost "knew or should have known of this outrageous threat when he scheduled the Yellow Jackets."

The morning of the game, Mirja led me into my study and locked the door. "Did you hear about the protest at the football rally last night?" She explained how an ugly row arose between students for and against benching Ward.

"Let those damned Yellow Jackets forfeit the game before we tell our first colored player this century he can't play." It was the least I could say for my playing an ugly race card with Rabbie about Mirja and Paul.

"I fear for Mr. Ward's life if he plays," Mirja replied. She told me how Rabbie's best student had stopped by Hill House late last night after he'd returned from visiting the Georgia Tech players to ask them to show better sportsmanship. "They treated Arthur Miller like a damn Yankee, roughed him up and told him they'd 'kill that nigger boy if he takes the field.'" Mirja blinked away the tears and told me how she'd been called a "Pickaninny" and pushed around by white workers as a child. "I had nightmares so bad, my father sent me to school in a Dublin convent. I've passed for white ever since."

"I guess Willis Ward doesn't have that option."

We heard Pip's knock, and Mirja unlocked the door. "I talked to Mr. Ward's roommate during the team breakfast at Barton Hills. The team captain, Gerald Ford, told Coach Kipke, 'I quit,' when he learned Michigan and Georgia Tech agreed to bench Willis and their best end."

I didn't know whether to be grateful or outraged.

"Ward told Gerry instead, 'Captain, you damn well better play and beat those Southern boys, or it'll be another 40 years before Michigan lets another black man play football.'"

"Where is Willis?" Mirja asked. When Pip said he'd dropped Ward off at the house his Negro fraternity rented, she said, "Take me there." I knew my brother shared the pain of discrimination Michigan visited on their different physical traits.

Michigan beat Georgia Tech 9–7 that afternoon, but Mirja told me she feared Willis Ward had lost. "He'll never be the same. We learned Yost let him know over the summer that the game would have to go on without him, but Willis hoped against hope Michigan would stand up to the Yellow Jackets and Jim Crow in the end. When only Gerry Ford stood up for him before the game, Ward was crushed."

Good Lord, why must caste—race, sex, religion, physical

differences—divide and diminish all of us so? The University should be ashamed, I thought. I felt guilty, too.

ᔕ

Two weeks later Edna St. Vincent Millay wore a crimson gown, trimmed in gold braid. Draped from her alabaster shoulders, the plush velvet swayed behind her as she floated to the front of the Hill Auditorium. She needed no introduction. Her book of sonnets, *Fatal Interview,* had sold 40,000 copies in the depths of the Depression. Her appearances across the country sold out to tens of thousands more to see and hear her.

Her amber red hair, pulled back from her forehead, fell easily to the nape of her neck as she turned to face the 4,300 crammed into the great concert hall. Professor Cowden, Stella, Mirja, and I sat in the second row center as guests of President Ruthven and waited with anticipation. Miss Millay surveyed the crowd. She wore no jewelry, rouge or lipstick, but her red dress and hair, fair shoulders and cheeks, and gray-green eyes made her look as if a colorful sprite or forbidden siren, as you please. She pushed the microphone aside and said in a clear bell of a voice, surprisingly deep for one so small, almost a throaty contralto, "I hate these amplifiers, so be quiet if you want to hear."

She held us in her thrall as she said her poems—some cheeky, others suggestive, others of betrayal and death, many with biting irony or resigned humor. She swayed as she spoke. Sometimes she spread her feet wide, and other times she wrapped her long gown around her arm, always wrapping us around her expressive fingers with her velvet voice and feline touch.

"My friends, men and women, call me Vincent," she said and sang her love sonnets: some, so torrid I blushed from the tingle; others, so pained I shared her anger; the last, a lamentation so full of mourning I almost choked trying not to weep.

She paused after the clapping, crying, and coughing died off, looked down, and then raised her face and her voice. In a white heat, this redhead in a crimson dress rose up and roared her final poem, the anthem for women that Miss Patterson shared with me so many years ago when I didn't appreciate the meaning of burning the candle at both ends so it won't last the night: "But, ah, my foes, and, oh, my friends—/ It gives a lovely light!" The audience exploded as we women rose as one, clapping, shouting, whistling, and cat-calling. She bowed only once and then ambled away as gracefully as she'd arrived 90 minutes before. Despite our calls for more, our last sight was her fine hair and velvet gown flowing behind her like a red tide and disappearing ashore stage right.

The party Mirja hosted for Miss Millay at Hill House went on much longer. The spiked Caribbean punch, Mirja's piano, the RCA Victor records, and the dancing flowed onto the east porch. As Vincent drank, danced, and dazzled, her crimson gown and hair turned scarlet, her pale freckled face flushed, and her grey-green eyes flashed emerald. As the night wore on, she smoked, drank, and chatted up Mirja. I entertained her husband, Eugen Boissevain, with small talk and introductions to our other guests. He split his attention between worried looks to Vincent and too many refills of punch.

When he began to list, I sat him in the chair with arms at the head of the dining table. I walked to the parlor and found Vincent and Mirja molded together in a slow tango. When Vincent saw me, she said, "Cutting in, my Belle?"

"Should I drive Mr. Boissevain home and put him to bed?"

Millay returned to the dining room with me. "Oh, Uge, what are we going to do with you now?" He reached out, and she folded herself as if a cat on his lap. She motioned to me, and we lifted him by the arms. Although he insisted on wearing his bulky raccoon coat, we managed to stuff him upright in the front seat of my convertible, top down. Vincent leaned down to him and said, "I'll be along later."

I drove around the block several times, hoping the cold rush would sober him. I pulled into the garage. I managed to drag him out of the car, but the stairs presented a challenge. He put his hands on the banister and pulled, and I put mine on his rear and pushed. At the top I guided him forward. When I let go, he fell like a sack in Pip's big bed. He mumbled and rolled over. Within seconds he began to snore in his stupor.

I walked through my brother's sitting room to the main house and slumped on my bed. I fell into a deep but troubled sleep. I dreamed of Vincent. At one point, I thought I heard a rustling sound under my door but was too tired to get up.

When I woke, the sun already beat in my window. I found a folded slip of paper under my door. *For Belle,* it said. *I patched these lines together as thanks for your taking care of Uge last night.* It began, *Into my scarlet vessel of great song/Let us pour all our passion.* It ended even more explicitly, *And many loved, but Sappho loved & sang. Vinnie*

Wine From These Grapes hit the bookstores on November 1, and Millay's fans quickly purchased the entire 35,000 first printing in two weeks. She sent me an autographed copy with a brief note: *Sorry we had to leave before you rose, but please join us at Steepletop, where Uge challenges you to a tennis match. I hope to return to Michigan soon, but, in the meantime, share one or two of your songs. Vincent*

Not a chance I'd risk, but a poem kept rumbling through my head about the many "Senses of a Woman." I tore up several drafts and finally gave up, but did I need Sappho to inspire me to love and sing again? One thing for sure: for my sake and Ruthie's, many more years would have to pass before I'd ever allow myself to taste such forbidden fruit.

Teddy's letter reporting his progress arrived shortly thereafter with a set of mixed messages. He wrote first about his meeting Louise Bogan at Humphries' house:

> *I was so overcome by hero worship, I acted like a country oaf at his first party. Eventually, I blathered, "No woman can sing*

as you, Miss Bogan." She retorted, "Young man, fawning all over me won't do." She's almost as tall as you, but willowy and more mature. But damn her and her Irish digs: she delighted in calling herself a "lowly Mick" and me a "big Kraut." The worst you ever called me was Teddy Bear. I didn't muster the courage to ask her about a reading at Michigan, but I'll pursue her to ground and then enlist her for you. You'll see she's quite the dame, even if a Mick! I enclose her review of Millay's new collection.

The rest of Teddy's letter offered less hope:

I'm wearing out my welcome at Lafayette. Mary's parents know I'm a brute, unfit to marry any good woman, let alone their daughter. They also know my time here's closing. I'll return home to Mom and Sis this summer again, this time with no prospects. If you'll talk to Cowden and Strauss about hiring me to teach at Michigan in the fall, I promise I'll finish my Master's this summer.

I read Louise Bogan's glowing review of Edna Millay's new book. The conclusion: "She has crossed the line and passed into regions of cold and larger air." Maybe, Michigan could offer a perfect home to rekindle Miss Bogan composing poems, rather than settling for writing more reviews.

A few days later I wrote Teddy and encouraged him to enlist Louise to speak at Michigan. I also shared what I'd learned from Cowden and Rabbie:

Both said you need to apply early. Get recommendations from your friends at Harvard and Lafayette and from your new supporters like Humphries and, if she's yours, Miss Bogan. I'll talk to Frost, too, although his stock has fallen here since he halted his annual visits. Although Strait and his toady allies can't understand how, you did earn your Phi Beta Kappa and Magna here and accolades for your teaching out east. If you complete your work for an M.A., how can the Nyms stop you from getting a job at Michigan this fall? After all, Strauss did choose Roy Cowden over Ned Strait as the permanent director of the Hopwood Program.

✧

With Thanksgiving at hand, I needed to get back up north. Against my better judgment, I invited Rabbie to join Mirja and Paul for the holiday, but he begged off so he could finish his doctoral thesis before he headed to Oxford for the winter term. His tenure in the English Department assured despite Strait's threats, he wanted to spread his wings to see if it would inspire a novel. But what did I know? Maybe Rabbie needed to say his goodbye to a lover in Ann Arbor before he crossed the pond.

I drove Mirja and Paul in my touring car. Top up, we made it before Kurt left for New York. A blizzard socked us all into Belle Cottage for a week. It gave me time to wear Kurt down and cut a deal so he'd run our Empire through June 30, 1937. I hoped David would grow enough by then, he'd take over so I need continue only as Chairman. I feared my limits enough not to want to test them as CEO.

With financing for installment sales and channels for distribution of our stoves secure, protecting our brand presented the new challenge. In order to coach the women swimmers at the 1936 Olympics, Trudy had to forgo all endorsements. Trudy and I issued a joint letter explaining how Empire Enterprises supported her commitment to help our amateur athletes perform their best in Berlin. Pip also made a personal gift to the Women's Swimming Association so its training programs would include girls who had difficulties hearing or seeing. Grantland Rice ran another column that concluded, "Our nation thanks Trudy for sacrificing her professional interests when the Olympic Spirit called her back to coach the women's swim team for the Berlin Games." We'd done our best to brand our America's Flame in the hearts of all our customers.

On the eighth day, the snow stopped, the clouds cleared, and the strong west wind blew the snow off the frozen Crystal River. After giving belated thanks to a full house with a turkey and all the trimmings at noon in the Homestead Inn, Kurt and I rode up the funicular and skied down the hills and through the dales of our course. Ruthie, little Paul, David, Spring Blossom, and Davey skated, while Pip pushed Mirja in a sled, up the Crystal River toward its source. After an hour Kurt and I took a break at the clubhouse. Sipping hot chocolate, we sat on the east porch and looked for the skating party below. Little Paul and Davey, leading the pack, already looked like river skaters as their long strides propelled them toward the mouth. Ruthie hustled after, followed by Pip, pushing Mirja on the sled, ready to help his acolytes ahead if any fell. The bright sun lighting all our faces and the other blessings of this day gave reason for thanks.

I looked for David and Spring Blossom but couldn't find them. Suddenly, David raced around a bend in the river and caught up with Pip. The two men called ahead, and the children stopped. Pip helped Mirja up, while David turned the sled and sped back up the river. Kurt and I rode the funicular down to the base and ran to the frozen river. Mirja and the children already walked toward us, skates in hand. I asked Kurt and Mirja to take the children to the inn and for Kurt to drive our biggest car back.

David and Pip raced down the river, pushing Spring Blossom on the sled. When she reached me, the Ojibwe woman was flushed and breathing hard, no fever, but doubled over in a pain.

"We've tried so hard I won't lose this baby."

Lord, how many times did we have to go through this? Kurt arrived in his Cadillac sedan. Pip laid Spring Blossom gently in the backseat, while David slid in the other side, took off his coat, held her head and shoulders in his lap, and covered her up.

I leaned in. "Do you want to say goodbye to Davey?"

She shook her head. "I don't want him blaming the baby if I don't make it."

Spring Blossom wasn't thinking clearly, not only about Davey but about her baby. No unborn child could survive with more than four months left to a full term. Pip said he'd help Mirja with Davey. I hopped into the front seat and urged Kurt to hurry. The Glen Arbor snow crews had plowed the roads to the stop sign for the county road and state highway to Traverse City, where Pip had crashed so many years before. This time the police car from Empire met us at the corner and escorted us with lights flashing.

After stabilizing Spring Blossom, the Munson Hospital doctors called the Lying-in at University Hospital to determine whether they'd have to perform an emergency abortion to save the mother. When the answer came back negative, I arranged for a private plane to fly us to Ann Arbor the next morning.

Thanks be, we learned Spring Blossom would survive and the baby had a fighting chance to be born. But the pregnancy with so many months to go would be very hard. Bed rest close to emergency care offered the best hope. I called Kurt and asked him to forgo his visits to New York so David and Davey could stay in Ann Arbor with me to lend support to Spring Blossom. He agreed on the condition that Pip stay to help him run the plant in Empire. "Kurt, forget the garret. You and your partner can stay in Papa's room for as long and often as you wish."

"I've got my apartment in Empire."

I thought about that but knew it wouldn't work for Kurt and his mate, not with the ugly banter and worse rumors the ex-lumberjacks working for us would spread from tavern to town. "It'll be hard enough in the shelter of Belle Cottage."

ও

Two weeks later I received a letter from Frost:

Elinor brooded so on the loss of our Marj and the return of dear Robin to her father this fall, she suffered a heart attack. She says she recovered to take care of me, but I'm taking her on the train to Key West for the winter to recuperate.

I don't know how you got the gumption to tell me to keep writing, but Willard found Pip's letter and your "Blue" more sympathetic. I also find holding, hugging and playing with dear Robin a joy, thank you.

I've been toying with writing longer verse to explore more contraries. Do you think the Fascists in Europe any worse than the Utopians here who want to socialize the risk inherent in our human condition? In all events, your poems are now good enough to share with others through the only means civilization knows if you won't go out and bard as a minstrel in public: publishing in print.

Frost

Speaking of Blue, what the hell's Kipke done with
Yost's point-a-minute teams? 21 points and 1 win in
8 games? For shame.

I wrote back to his forwarding address in Key West:

I am very sorry for Mrs. Frost's heart attack. Please take good care of her. Lord knows, she's the only one who ever could talk sense into you, but I enclose my poor poem, "Defying Gravity." I shared it with young Auden to warn him from sounding like the siren song of the left. Please don't you sound like Father

Coughlin and that coward Ned Strait, spouting their right-wing claptrap.

In this hard time, I do ask one favor. Will you write a recommendation to the Chair, Cowden, and Bursley so Ted Roethke can teach here next fall? For better or worse, Michigan is his home every bit as much as Amherst is yours; and the University might just take him in this time.

Rereading this letter, I see my tone is intemperate. I therefore enclose another poem, my "Papa's Goodbye," in apology. You will see we followed your good advice and let go of each other. Ruthie, like Robin, has proven a blessing.

As ever, Belle

No sense burdening Frost with the real shame of Michigan: Athletic Director Yost, Coach Kipke, our football team, and the rest of our University community. We were all losers for our prejudice as much Ned Strait for his.

Fall 1935: Ann Arbor and Glen Arbor

Teddy burst through the back door of our glasshouse, carrying a bottle of champagne. He threw his big raccoon coat down on the chaise next to mine.

"Big Mama," he blustered, "I got me a job starting next week, at the Cow College."

The sweat beaded on his forehead, and his big cheeks and bulbous nose flushed. He was already drunk. As I'd been up north all summer, I hadn't seen him, but Cowden called to let me know Teddy hadn't finished his Master's and, except for Frost's early response to my request, didn't get any of his other recommendations to Michigan until mid-September—much too late. But at Rabbie's urging, Chairman Strauss contacted his counterpart in East Lansing to see if there might be an opening for our tortured young poet.

I didn't like the way Teddy stood above me and leered down. I guess I should have been grateful I'd worn a swimsuit for my hour of laps in the pool, but it was still wet and clung to my every curve. "How'd you pull that off?" I blurted.

"Deluged State with telegrams from my Harvard backers and my friends at Lafayette," he bragged, puffing his big chest out.

"None from Michigan?" I asked to try to cool him down.

"Maybe Rabbie," he answered and shambled into the kitchen, waving the bottle of champagne. Before he returned, I raced to the linen chest, put on a robe, and cinched it tight. I stood awkwardly as he set the glasses down on the table between the two chaises, shook the bottle, popped the cork and sprayed the champagne, first in my face and then his. He grabbed me and began to lick the drops running down my cheeks and chin.

"Easy, Teddy Bear," I said and tried to push him away. When I couldn't, I stepped back but tripped on the chaise behind me.

Teddy eased me down, on top of his fur coat, then filled the two champagne glasses, handed me one, and offered a toast: "To a great year back home, Mama Bear." He clinked my glass and sat cross-ways on the other chaise, his feet on the ground, facing me as I reclined on his coat. He took off his rumpled tweed jacket, reached in the inside pocket, pulled out a piece of paper, and tossed it to me.

"It's my antidote for your wonderings about Vincent's lesbian love," he said.

He chugged his champagne, filled his glass up, leaned over, and poured more into my glass until it overflowed. The liquid blurred his green ink, but I tried to decipher his hen-scratching with its many insertions and deletions: *She… taught me Turn, and Counter-turn… she the sickle, I the poor rake… but what prodigious mowing we did make.*

"What's this all about, Teddy?" He only grinned wildly, and I read on.

Well, of course I knew, and he knew I knew. He fell on me and pressed his lips against mine.

"Teddy, not this way," I screamed. The bear of a boy slid to the deck in a heap, put his head in his big paws, and cried. "What happened?" I asked.

"Louise called me her Pomeranian stud, and…" He paused to gather himself. "She says if I work hard I might become a *minor* lyric poet, but I'm going to show her. I wanted to show you, too, but you deserted me this summer." I helped him up, wrapped him in his raccoon coat, and held his hand.

Eventually, he stopped weeping. "I should have finished my Master's and put my application and recommendations in early here." I rubbed his temples until his shaking stopped. "I used writing that history for Pa Crouse on his utopian new town in Hartland as an excuse, but I did need to help Mom at home again and earn some money so Sis can enroll here."

What a strange man-child, never able to free himself from his family and his wild mood swings. Maybe our glasshouse here was just a substitute for the one he grew up in, but much as I loved him, I was no surrogate for the father he lost or the older women he still needed.

I laid him down on his chaise and left to make tea. When I returned, he sat up. I handed him his cup and faced him from the other chaise. "Teddy, you need help." When he shook his head, I added, "Counseling, at our kirk or the University Hospital."

He pushed himself up, put on his tweed jacket, and picked up his raccoon coat. He held out his hand, and we walked to the Presbyterian Church in silence. He entered the sanctuary, marched to the front pew, sat down, and bowed his head. After a few minutes, he stood up and marched me back up Washtenaw. He stopped in front of the Chi Phi house, pulled a couple of typed pages from his inside coat pocket, and handed them to me. I saw it was a review by Miss Bogan praising eight of his poems. "Belle, I'm going to be the next of the great mad poets." He sauntered toward his jalopy.

"Teddy," I called after, "I'll be here this whole school year if you need anything." His legs wide apart, his whole body swaying, he never looked back, but I guessed he'd hidden his depression from Louise Bogan and wouldn't ever call her for help.

On my way home, I stopped by Hill House. I needed to unwind

with Mirja before heading home to greet Pip and Ruth, who were driving down from Belle Cottage. Pip wanted Ruthie to go to the Eberbach school. Mirja and I had an hour before Rabbie picked up little Paul from St. Thomas and our two kids could renew their friendship.

Mirja and I sat on captain's chairs under the shade of the big oak at the south end of her garden walk. We sipped iced tea. A vibrant tan and touch of rose in her high cheeks had finally replaced the sad sallow of her long recovery from her miscarriage last spring. Pip had rushed down to help Mirja for the first week to comfort her, but he headed back up north to help run our enterprises when Rabbie cut short his Oxford stay. For another four weeks, I helped take care of little Paul and Davey at Cambridge House, while David helped will Spring Blossom to term and Rabbie nursed Mirja. I toasted Mirja on her return to good health and her better looks.

"Paul and I missed Ruthie and you terribly all summer," she said. She leaned toward me and whispered, "It was Pip's baby I lost." She choked away the catch in her voice. "I tried so hard for so long with Rabbie to deliver a baby sister for Paul, but now I can't ever bear..." She paused. "Oh, Belle, I'm sorry."

She knew I always wanted to bear a baby, but I only replied, "I'm blessed Pip shares Ruthie with me and you let Paul grow up playing with us, too."

"It was hard for me this summer, watching Spring Blossom nurse her baby, until she let me hold her and I learned Angel was a blessing for all of us." Mirja paused. "That tiny gift of life made me see I wanted to get better, too."

Although most would have viewed Spring's baby, born pale all over, as a human freak, her translucent skin and lips, light blue eyes, and white, fuzzy hair, forming a halo, did make her look an angel. Thank heavens the Ojibwe culture always respected albinos, in nature and at home, as extraordinary beings to be protected and revered. Angel would have to wear a hat, long clothes, and dark glasses outside to protect her skin and eyes from sunburn, and I knew her father, mother, and brother would raise her so she could share her special blessing the rest of her life, as she had as a newborn with Mirja.

"Teddy stopped by and broke down this afternoon," I said. I paused to sip my iced tea to get what I wanted to say straight, but my hands shook so, I spilled some down my chin, and it dribbled down my throat and chest onto my blouse.

Mirja handed me a napkin. As I cleaned myself up, she said, "When Rabbie got back, he did everything he could to get Teddy a job here this fall, but…"

"I know our boy was his own worst enemy again, and Strait and his faction here can't forgive him his crazy…"

"Nym's corps can't stand the popularity of Rabbie's writing class either."

"Will you let Rabbie know Ted may be heading for a big fall?" At least forewarned, Rabbie could help if our Teddy Bear of a man-child called him.

Later that afternoon Mirja dropped Paul off to play with Ruthie. The two children raced up to her room. Pip set off to catch up with John Kraus and left me with his other acolyte, young Mr. Huey, in town to catch the train to Amherst. The Major had been a big help up north all summer.

"What do you plan to do after you graduate next spring?"

"I'm marrying Helen, and we're going to work at the camp, school, inn, and if you and Pip are willing, the club."

"We welcome both your help." Then it hit me. "Did you ever meet Robert Frost?"

"I had him for class my first semester freshman year. I liked the way he left us to write and think on our own, but…" He paused. "But I was studying so hard to prove that this Midwest hick could earn all A's, I burned out after the first couple of months. Feeling lonely and sorry for myself, I took a walk into town and saw him walking fast toward me. Hoping he'd solve all my problems with a fatherly talk about two roads diverging in a yellow wood, I said, 'Good evening,

Mr. Frost!' Instead he recoiled with a louder 'Harrumph!' and passed me by."

"He is a bit of a curmudgeon at times."

"I recovered," young Huey said. "In fact, he's still my favorite teacher." He paused. "But his talk at the final chapel service *argued* that FDR's New Deal falls into the dark hole of the Utopians with their calls for raising society and social contracts above the individual and personal freedom."

"What do you make of that?"

"Mr. Frost does better when he sticks to poetry," Huey replied.

I liked this young man so much I had to laugh, but he looked abashed. "I did once twit Frost," I said. "Told him he was only the second best poet from Amherst."

"I took a course on Miss Dickinson's poetry last fall from Professor Whicher."

"Which of her songs did you like best?" I asked.

"Wild Nights," he answered with a straight a face.

"Maybe I better warn Miss Mautz about her major."

"Too late, Miss Belle," the Major said with a broad grin.

"We need more of your kind up north, Mr. Huey." Oh, how I'd wished there'd been just one like him when I was young enough. Then I remembered: three had graced me. Just my hard luck, I wasn't the right kind for marrying Rabbie, David, or Kurt.

ഗ

Over the Thanksgiving holiday, David, Spring Blossom, Davey, and Angel hosted us for a feast with their burgeoning band of nearly 200 Ojibwe and, now, Odawa in Ahgosatown. The whitecaps scudding across the Grand Traverse Bay offered the only relief from the cold, gray day outside. Inside, the bowls of fresh grapes, apples, and pears lent their festive colors to each table. The cherry and black currant jams in saucers added more flair, while the big orange pumpkins carved in wild faces blessed our sumptuous dinner of venison, wild turkey, mashed squash, and rhubarb.

After we all helped clean up, Pip, Ruthie, and the Ahgosa family piled into my Lincoln touring car, and we headed north on Bay Shore Road, through Northport, all the way to Grand Traverse Lighthouse and the tip of Leelanau peninsula, where we'd scattered Miss Schultz's ashes. We left Ruthie and Davey skipping stones on the rocky point. The west wind and the waves breaking on shore serenaded our climb up four flights to the big light at the top of the house. As we scanned the panoramic view, the setting sun peeked through the gray clouds. It lit Angel's white curly hair atop her head, poking out from the papoose cloth slung around Spring Blossom's neck and shoulder. Angel showed us the way: she pointed to the west-facing white crescent shore to the south and the green second-growth pine forest spreading back to the east. Unlike the cold and stormy day that greeted Miss Schultz so many years ago, the red rays of the setting sun warmed our faces, and the gentle lap of the whitecaps breaking on shore hummed a welcoming tune in our ears. Oh, how much we all owed this great lady: that common debt would hold us together as we worked to make this sacred place her living legacy.

As the chill of dusk set in, we drove back through Northport and down to the home of the Ahgosa clan. After we dropped them off, we cut across the dirt roads until we reached the Manitou Trail and headed through Leland. As there was too little light for Pip to read lips, Ruthie begged me to tell her stories about Miss Schultz. I obliged and concluded by sharing how she helped Papa, Pip, and me purchase so much land on our side of the Peninsula. As we parked beside Belle Cottage, the clouds parted, and moonbeams danced across Sleeping Bear Bay and lit the big dunes beyond. All of age eight, Ruthie hopped out and asked, "Can we call the land we're helping Miss Schultz preserve the Leelanau Park?"

Pip looked across the Crystal River to the birch bark box and totem pole in the trees our Ojibwe friend said was the enchanted place that became a new home for the lost princess. "Let's suggest the name to David and Spring," I answered.

Ruth smiled and pointed up, where high clouds passed across the three-quarter moon. A silver glow rimmed the smiling face in the middle. "Sure looks like Miss Schultz approves," I added.

"No," said Ruthie, "Angel blesses the name Leelanau for Miss Schultz's park."

I looked up again. As the clouds passed, the moon glowed white with a gilt rim against the clear night sky, and I also saw Angel Ahgosa's face.

The next morning we stopped at the Empire plant. Papa's factory had doubled in size, but David made sure it ran clean, bright, and efficiently. He showed me the hub where the men built burners for all our gas appliances and the flexible spokes where they worked in teams to assemble the diverse finished products. The same number of men now worked full-time to produce five times the goods produced in Papa's best year.

David and I walked into the tinkering lab at the back of the plant and found Pip playing a game of Battleship with Ruthie on a shop table. A plywood screen separated their ten-by-ten grids so they couldn't see where the other had plotted their battleship, destroyer, cruiser, and submarine. Ruthie screamed whenever she hit one of Pip's ships and grimaced whenever she missed or Pip hit one of hers. With a call of "E-10," Ruthie nailed Pip's last ship, the submarine, and squealed with delight.

On the next shop table, Pip had split the surface with an upright black screen. On one side a small radio transmitter turned slowly, and on the other a car moved back and forth on a model railroad track. "What's that?" I asked. Pip lobbed a little shell from a makeshift catapult over the screen, while Ruthie tried to vary the speed of her car to avoid being hit. I nodded: another battleship game.

Pip picked up an oddly-shaped car. "John and I invented this stealthy one so it bounces the radio waves off at odd angles, and you can't figure out how to hit it."

Pip and his acolytes did have fun playing games, whether for the joy of the search or the rush of beating each other to the punch. I heard a clanking and looked over to a metal barrel revolving on its side over by the wall. "Do you test whether your cars and ships can withstand a direct hit by tumbling them in there?" I signed to Pip.

Pip stepped over, pushed a switch on the wall to *Off*, and opened the door. I reached in and pulled out one thick flannel shirt after another, big buttons on all thirteen. I felt one of the shirts, hot and dry, and smiled. Before I could congratulate him on this prototype or ask him how long before we could produce and sell his new clothes dryer, he pulled Ruthie to the adjacent gas stove. "Would you like to light a burner?"

"Ruthie's not to play with matches," I said.

"Don't listen to Marmie this once. Just turn the knob." She turned it clockwise. Small sparks flew and lit the gas burner, and a circular ring of blue fire formed. Pip said, "That's an automatic igniter." He pulled Ruthie to the next stove along the wall. She turned one of the burners, and another ring of blue flame appeared without any sparks. I looked more closely at the other three burners and saw a small flame, a pilot light.

"Can we go and listen to the horned trumpet?" Ruthie asked.

"Let's show the Major and Helen how to run it," I replied. Pip looked doubtful. "The Leelanau students will want to hear noises from space there as much as they want to see the stars through your telescope at the school." Ruthie looked expectantly at her father. He tensed his jaw, and I saw how gaunt his face had become. Pip grasped Ruthie's hand, and they raced up Empire Bluff to his old research station.

The next morning Pip knocked on the door to the study and entered with the Ogre from Glen Haven.

"Sven's got a proposal for us."

The dark giant folded himself into the old leather chair. I couldn't believe my ears as he humbled himself, explaining how the Day clan had fallen so far in the Depression they'd have to close up shop, "unless you and Pip loan us the money to buy a small fleet of dune buggies." When Pip nodded, I couldn't believe my eyes. "Ve vill steer vay clear of Mama Bear." Sven paused. "Ve vant to verk vith you, Pip, the Bealses, and the Ahgosas so this place can thrive."

"Why should we trust you?"

Pip answered, "We'll have a mortgage on his property and concessions, with a right to foreclose if his cars do any damage to the dunes." When I asked what David said, my brother replied, "Sven's also agreed to respect the bands' fishing, hunting, and gathering rights on his lands and harbor. David will deck Sven for *any* breach this time."

I chuckled, until Sven bared his fangs. "What else?" I pressed.

"Miss Belle, ve vill help spread the legend of Sleeping Bear and this Sacred Nibi so it lasts vor at least seven generations hence."

Was this really the Dark Ogre talking?

D. H. Day, Papa, and Mama had to adapt to tough times before; maybe I could, too. So I gritted my teeth and said, "Mr. Surtr, if your deeds don't match your words, I will fill the gas tank of every one of your damn dune cars full of sand, and I will fill you full of buckshot."

The giant only grinned now.

ᔕ

Two weeks later at Cambridge House I received a letter from Frost:

Dear Belle,

Sorry to hear Michigan didn't hire young Roethke. Maybe just as well, though, for Bursley tells me Cowden barely beat back a putsch from Strait to lead the Hopwood Program. Not sure the Cow College north of you is any better. Seeing as Michigan now ignores my recommendations, perhaps I can help him get a better position out east or west.

I enclose a draft of a poem I'm including in my next collection. I'm calling the book A Further Range because I'm ranging from New Hampshire, Vermont, Massachusetts, and Michigan to the West and, despite your warnings, from the contraries of plain country folk to the city bigshots that seek to rule us. Although my slant of meaning differs from your "Defying Gravity," I'd still like your opinion on whether I've gone too far. Of course, the more controversy the poem generates, the more sales, but I can't bear so much controversy the Book-of-the-Month Club changes its mind about distributing my further rangings.

Frost

Your "Papa's Goodbye" nettles: Makes me sleep less at night, trying to find just one adequate goodbye. When it finally surfaces, I will share it with you.

I read "To a Thinker in Office." Not nearly as direct as the suggestions in his previous letters to me and his chapel talk at Amherst College, that FDR was leaning far too left: "The last step taken found your heft decidedly upon the left" while "One more would throw you on the right" and "Another still—you see your plight." Frost proceeded to twit the man in office for thinking this was "thinking," when "it's only rocking, or weaving like a stabled horse."

I didn't see any cause in these musings for the Book-of-the-Month Club to withdraw its support for Frost's new book. I read the poem again, out loud this time, and once more to myself. His tongue was stuck so firmly in his cheek, the poem didn't offer much depth or sound-sense in its slants. Yet the more I thought about Frost's lack of sympathy for FDR doing his best to help us all fight the Depression, the more angry I got.

Dear Frost, I wrote with my tongue in cheek:

If you take the final two words "in Office" out of the title, "To a Thinker" might carry you with fewer hackles to the lighter chuckle of your bard at the end. No cause for worry, though:

the poem won't offend any of your publishers, even if it does offend me. Here's my poem with a different metaphor and slant of meaning:

Depression II

What would happen to the hive
If the flowers ceased to grow?
Who would feed the fecund queen?
Where would all the workers go?

Eden's on its slide to grief
Although the bees are able—
No pollen for them to store,
And no honey for our table

The phone rang, and Ruthie knocked on my door. "Uncle Teddy's crying." I got up and put the receiver to my ear. Expletives arose between the sobs.

"Teddy, where are you?" When he told me Mercywood, the private mental sanitarium west of town, I asked, "How'd you get there?"

"Pa Crouse and Sis brought me, after I went overboard seeing if I could get to a higher state, working, writing, running, drinking, and popping pills for weeks on end." When I asked whether his "higher state" helped, he replied, "Closed in on Nijinsky's trance, but got lost in the woods talking to a tree." He paused. "Six hours floating in the hydrotherapy tub here today, and I'm writing again." When I asked if he could get to sleep, he replied, "Doc Klingman's got some magic pills that'll put me away for the night. You'll see, Big Mama, I'm going to be okay."

I called Rabbie, explained Teddy's call and asked whether he'd heard anything from Michigan State. Rabbie hadn't but said he'd make a few inquiries.

Shortly before breakfast, Rabbie called back. Teddy had walked out on a class, tramped for hours without shoes or jacket in the cold, barged into the Dean's office, and rambled incoherently. Teddy submitted to "treatment" at Sparrow Hospital and "rehabbed" with a colleague until he started talking crazy again. He fled to Saginaw, where his sister and his patron committed him to Mercywood. When I asked what else, Rabbie confided, "Nym sent another screed to a buddy at State he calls Pistol. They spread all the dirt Strait could find or invent to get Roethke blackballed there, too."

"Does Teddy know?"

"The Chair there only told Ted he wasn't well enough to teach next semester and gave him what they politely dubbed an 'unpaid leave of absence.'"

"Bastards threw him out in the Depression," I muttered. "Any hope here?"

"I'd take him back to teach as many of my writing sections as he can handle. But Michigan won't offer Ted a tenure-track position, and Strait would only spread more poison here." He paused. "If Ted will only give Cowden and Professor Ray any excuse, just one paper, they will make sure the Department grants him a Master's Degree, and the Chair will give him the thumbs-up at schools out East, where his friends from Harvard and Lafayette can help get him a job."

"Get our bad Teddy Bear out of their hair," I said.

"Some might call it helping a Michigan Man."

I'd let Cowden and Bursley down, too, quitting teaching and my thesis too many times for my family, business, and up north. Strait had all the dirt he needed so this Michigan Woman wouldn't be wanted as a faculty colleague either, but Teddy needed a job and another chance. "I'll make sure he earns his degree this spring, even if I have to decipher his green-ink splotches and type the damn paper for him."

Dr. Klingman showed me into the hydrotherapy room with several metal pools of various shapes and sizes. The biggest accommodated

Teddy's length and bulk, and he floated easily, thankfully with a swimsuit covering his private parts, as well as a green pen in one hand and a newfangled spiral notebook in the other. The adjacent table included several more pens and books of poetry, by Auden, Millay, Wylie, Bogan, Frost, and Blake.

He greeted me with a smile. "My good doctor, meet the bane of my claim to fame in tennis, swimming, and poetry, the incomparable Miss Belle, better known to her family as Marmie." He placed his green pen and notebook on the table. Without rising, he extended his arm as if a reigning monarch. I curtsied, kissed his hand, pulled a wooden chair over, and sat next to his big tub. He reached across to the other side of the pool, flipped the switch on the wall, and smiled as the pool bubbled, burbled, and splashed all around him. I stood up, walked to the wall, flipped the switch off, returned, and said to Dr. Klingman, "Will you excuse us? Mr. Roethke and I need to talk."

Teddy smiled at that. With all the other spas burbling around their patients, we could now speak frankly without any eavesdroppers. "Wanna read my latest poem?" he asked as he handed me a slip atop his notebook on the table. I struggled to decipher the green ink splotches. The short poem began, "This elemental force was wrested from the sun;" proceeded to describe a river source trying to leap out but locked in his bones; flowed to wisdom flooding the mind until a seed bursts into fruit; and ended, "Around a central grain/ New Meaning grows immense."

I didn't cotton to his "Genesis" much, so I asked, "How do you like this spa?"

"They call it a sanitarium, but it's really an asylum." I swear he rolled like a big bear in that tub, but not one drop of water sloshed out. "If you listen close, you learn the inmates are quite sane, but the nuns are crazy." So I asked when he wanted to get out of this loony bin. "I float for seven hours at a time, so I've got another five to go." He could make me laugh. Until he cried, "You know Michigan won't take me back."

"Can you go home to Saginaw for the winter?"

"Pa Crouse owes me enough to pay for several months here." I doubted that and asked if he could stay with Miss Bogan instead. "Can't risk letting her know what's happened." So I asked about Miss Kunkle. "We're still corresponding, but Lafayette won't take me back either." Before I could decide whether I could risk taking him in, he exclaimed, "Belle, say you won't marry me."

"You big lug," I said, "is that your backhanded way of proposing?"

His manic eyes bugged out as he nodded but said, "Belle, I'm even crazier than you, and I shouldn't burden you and Ruthie with my…" He pointed to his notebook.

I picked it up. On the first page he'd *printed* in a clear and careful hand, "Open House," three stanzas, six brief lines in each of the first two, four in the last. It began, "My secrets cry aloud. I have no need for tongue. My heart keeps open house." My pulse began to race. I sang the rest of his poem aloud. He closed with his enduring anger, "The deed will speak the truth in language strict and pure. I stop the lying mouth: "

Only blank space followed the colon at the end of the fourth line of the third stanza, but the sound-sense and intensity of the rest of his poem made me feel, well, yes, *elated* that *nothing* followed the colon. "Teddy, why don't you just put a period at the end?"

"I need two more lines for symmetry and sound!"

"No, your 'Open House' shows you'll be right."

"You mean shows I can write."

I must have blushed at his pun because he grasped my hand with his big paw. "Theodore Roethke," I said, "you are a good man and will be a better poet."

"No. Remember, I'm going to become a great poet or a poor fool trying?"

I gripped his hand for all I was worth. "And we're going to write one paper so you earn your Master's this spring, to put Michigan and State behind you."

"But I can't let go of Mom and Sis." Even more softly, he started to cry.

In bed that evening I felt the energy of Teddy's "Open House." I pored through my songbook until I found my glasshouse poem, "At Risk." I copied it on a scrap of paper but substituted a colon for the dash at the end to mimic Roethke's unfinished draft:

It would not be wise
to hurl stones—
Instead I swim:

I could barely wait for morning to share my lament with Teddy in his tub so I could show him how to erase the top of the colon to make a period. No point letting symmetry ruin an otherwise good poem when the last stanza already sings *because* it's *shorter* than those that come before.

My poem might also remind him that he could go on, no matter what any damn fool at his alma mater or the Cow College said. I kept from Teddy—and everyone else—one other thought about "At Risk." No matter how long it took, I vowed to rise from my glasshouse and hurl one stone that would shatter Ned Strait so he'd have to stop spewing his rancid chum, inside or outside Michigan. Hell Damn, why couldn't I live with Teddy at Cambridge House and care for him in our glasshouse pool whenever he fell down?

Fall 1936: Ann Arbor and Glen Arbor

Dear Belle, I didn't want you to think my leftward travels mocking the little monarchs and shorter fascists of the right on the mainland meant I'd given up "On This Island." As you will see from the first poem I enclose, every time I return to these shores, I see my home in a new and, yes, fonder light.

I picked up the first of the two poems Auden sent and read it. The lilt and beat of the opening, "Look, stranger, on this island now the leaping light for your delight discovers," carried through to the end, describing how the clouds above reflected the ships below, "That pass the harbor mirror and all the summer through the water saunter."

His letter continued, *I also enclose a review I wrote for the British edition of Frost's* Collected Poems. *I do like his verse, but maybe you can send it along with a note to limit the bruise my praise will cause him.* I pulled the typescript out and set it aside on my desk in the library at Cambridge House. His letter concluded:

I'll spare you reading the two-act play I wrote with Chris. When you read the second poem, imagine two British madcaps, one a Lord Stagmantle, the other his Lady Isabel Welwyn, jumping on each other's shoulders, trying to get a better view of the tragedy—one twin killing his brother in an attempt to scale a mythical F6 mountain mammary to prove he's more worthy of the favor of their mother, Mrs. Ransom. Of course this satire's over the top, but don't you think we Brits deserve to have our aristocratic pretense and hero-worship pricked, too—at least as much as the petty dukes and little men with mustaches who seek to rule the continent?

When I read the first two stanzas of the second poem, I didn't get the joke: "Stop all the clocks, cut off the telephone" flowed right through to "Let the traffic policemen wear black cotton gloves." I heard the searing anger of a survivor at the death of a loved one. The next three stanzas made the satire plain: Auden's madcap pair described a Dr. Williams opening a vein to pronounce death and demanded that the Sergeant arrest the man who winked, while Lamp exhorted Gunn to put pedal to the metal of his "motor-hearse" and drive the dead man to his "grave at ninety miles an hour."

I looked to Trudy and Ruthie swimming slowly in the pool. After Brundage had fired her as coach from the Berlin Games because her only real star, Eleanor Holm, had two drinks, the U.S. Women's swimming team won but two bronze medals. This contributed to the smashing victory of Hitler's all-Aryan team over the USA. Thank heavens, Jesse Owens swept the dashes, broad jump, and relay, or the media might have made Trudy the symbol of America's much-reported decline during the Depression. A wicked storm had tossed Trudy down the stairs on her return voyage and broken her back. We brought her back to Ann Arbor for surgery and to recuperate at my house.

I read Auden's review. Wystan called Frost a "nature poet" and praised his "colloquial voice" of a small New England farmer who shared "good village gossip" with "little fuss." For Auden, Frost's restraint came because, "though reason is an uncertain guide, it is the light by which man must live."

Dear Wystan,
So good to hear you sing of your Island home: it's the best poem you've shared. Inspires me to see afresh and sing with such a clear voice.

Your daft duo's satiric death call left me wondering whether you might also take another fresh look: What if you drop the last three stanzas and see if the first two allow you to compose a different ending, to make a commanding eulogy by a mourner on the death of a loved one?

I will share your review with Frost and add a note. Read a few more of his poems aloud, and you'll hear he's as much a conjurer in his different tones as Shakespeare's more dramatic voice of Prospero in The Tempest.

I couldn't stand watching the newsreels of that little Fuhrer closing the Olympics with his self-proclaimed Aryans sending the rest of us packing. I'm embarrassed the head of the U.S. Olympic Committee played into the Nazi's hand by proclaiming this the "finest Olympiad in modern history." At least one of the most cantankerous blue bloods on your Island sounds the warning: Hitler spells trouble. I hope FDR will listen to Churchill because there are too many here who praise the Third Reich as a model for rebuilding our broken economy. Belle

Trudy took a break, toweled off, and sat down on the chaise next to mine. She picked up Frost's new book, *A Further Range,* and read his scribbled inscription aloud: "To Belle, Hopefully not too contrary for you nor too right for the Pulitzer Committee. Robert Frost, from your Sunset House, Amherst, June 10, 1936." She asked, "What's he mean, 'not too contrary nor too right'?"

"Take a gander at 'To a Thinker,' near the end of the book."

She scanned the poem. "FDR, leaning left and right, always fretting and fearful, does deserve twitting."

"Why do you say that?"

"The Nazis took down their most offensive signs for the Games, but behind the scenes, Hitler's goons rounded up the Romani and the Jews. More will follow," she added, "but the President just lets that little creep with a mustache strut."

"What did Avery Brundage say when he suspended Eleanor and fired you?"

"'I'm fed up with all you women at the Olympics, an embarrassment without shame in public and ineffective in the pool as on the track,'" Trudy yelled. "But I think Eleanor rebuffed his other propositions first."

Another Strait man in power, I thought.

Ruthie swam over to the side of the pool, hopped out, and gave her coach a hug. Our girl plucked Frost's best-selling book from Trudy's hand. "Any songs for me?"

"Try 'Neither Out Far Nor In Deep.'" It was one of many with a lighter air, swifter beat, and punchier sense of sound, floating from mountaintops to seashores, than the darker verse of *West-Running Brook*. Far from being too contrary, *A Further Range* offered a *delightful* read. Frost would deploy his allies to rebut the elitist critics and convince a majority of the Pulitzer Committee he deserved the prize for learning how to compose anew.

Ruthie read the poem to herself and bounced her feet with the beat. She handed the book to Trudy, who read the poem with her head bobbing in the same rhythm. "Can we drive up north?" Trudy asked. "If I'm ever going to swim in open water again, I need to look out farther—or is it further?—and go in much deeper in Sleeping Bear Bay."

"Oh, let's," Ruthie said. "Let's bring Paul and Mirja, too."

Although we'd only been back in Ann Arbor two weeks, I also

wanted to return, to see if the bay, beach, dune, and forest of Sleeping Bear Bay would inspire me to sing as lightly and insightfully about my home place as Frost and Auden did about theirs.

That evening I reread Ted Roethke's note. Not so full of bluster, he thanked me for helping him finish his Master's, pay for Mercywood, publish three more poems, and secure a position at Penn State through the good offices of Rabbie O'Bannon and Roy Cowden. *State College is in the middle of nowhere, and teaching Argumentation to engineers, scientists, and farm boys poses ironies for me. But this is a fresh start, and I'm going to make the most of it.* He added he'd already settled in: He made a mess of his room in the University Club; befriended the library's *Kitty (last name Stokes)*; and *successfully whipped enough of the boys at tennis to make me coach.* He concluded his letter with a request: *Will you let me know what you think of the enclosed draft? May be too corny, but it's my first attempt to think back to my father.* In a postscript he added, *I'll return home next summer to help Mom and Sis again, and I hope to share a cup of tea in our glasshouse if you can escape your up north for a day.*

I read his short poem with wonder: the language so simple and the memory so evocative of "Days of another summer. Oh that was long ago!" The little boy hurried to keep up with his father: "Matching his stride with half steps." The boy watched his father dip his hand in the shallow of a river with such sharp detail, the punch line struck evev harder: "But when he stood up, that face was lost in a maze of water." In "Premonition" the adult Roethke looked back on that scene as a little boy who already knew his father would, too soon, be lost forever.

Dear Ted,
I don't know if I ever thanked you properly for making this glasshouse my haven. Your poem made me appreciate how much you put into building it: not just your considerable engineering, construction, and horticultural skills, but also your memories of

the much bigger greenhouses of your childhood. You put heart and soul into this pool house, as you do in your "Premonition." Thank you for both.

Your draft is not "too corny to publish." It just sings in a different key. Rather than experiment with your mania, why not keep looking back deeper with your contemporary eyes to explore your time growing up? That's how I read your "Premonition." I hope to toast your new start in our glasshouse soon. Belle

The next morning, as I mixed Ruthie's favorite cereal of Kellogg's cornflakes with whole milk and blueberries, she opened Frost's book and began to sing: "I found a dimpled spider, fat and white…" My ears perked up, and I remembered typing a version of that poem in my first year with Frost. Ruthie finished the song of the spider trapping a moth in its web. What brought the "kindred spider" and "then steered the white moth thither in the night?" Frost shared his bafflement: "What but design of darkness to appall—if design govern in a thing so small?" Surely, Frost's old song fit the further rangings of his new book, another of his many stays against confusion even if dark.

I wrote Frost a brief note thanking him for his gift and letting him know Ruthie and I couldn't stop saying his poems. I enclosed Auden's review. *I told Wystan what he calls your folksy ways really sing with the voice of a conjurer every bit as powerful as Shakespeare's Prospero. Don't get too mad at Auden: you were his first idol as a poet. Forgive this wayward upstart, for he will in time learn your more cunning ways.*

ᔓ

On an unseasonably warm September day, the air grew crisp and clear once we drove past Cadillac. The Civilian Conservation Corps planting millions of trees made our north country smell greener, too. This welcome transition reminded me of the others ahead in Leelanau and the ones behind in Ann Arbor: David stepping up to run our burgeoning Empire as Kurt began to step back in preparation for his move to join Morgan Stanley; Major Huey and his bride stepping forward to run the Homestead Inn and Club as Spring Blossom moved back to Ahgosatown to raise her Angel and Davey and help her brother grow their Grand Traverse businesses; Pip and I spending the school year in Ann Arbor with Ruthie, with Pip investing more time in his new research lab and me wanting to spend more time at Belle Cottage; and our dear Trudy facing an uncertain future, without any immediate prospects. Rabbie and Paul appeared content: Paul delighted that his parents and Pip, Ruthie, and Marmie were close by, while Rabbie reveled in writing much-acclaimed short stories and inspiring more and more students to write, write, write. But who can ever know what goes on inside another family, particularly one bound up in a love triangle? Mirja sat beside me, oddly subdued.

While the Depression abated somewhat with a third straight year of modest economic growth in the U.S., unemployment still deprived 17 percent of Americans of the dignity of work and the wages to feed, shelter, and support a family. Across the globe the seeds of division and dictatorship, right and left, grew in this economic despair, the old monarchies crumbled, and the winds of war gathered. While FDR tried to quiet the sympathizers of the brown shirts and reds by isolating the U.S. from such outside influence, I didn't see how we could stand apart. I authorized Kurt to make arrangements with the new Morgan Stanley investment house to finance the sale of America's Flame products to the rest of the free world. Neither Pip nor I could stand the America Firster apologists (like Michigan's own Father Coughlin and Ned Strait) for the Third Reich.

"Mirja," I said, "I thought the Irish couldn't stand the Brits."

"We hate the threat of the Nazis more."

"Any alternative to war?"

"Not unless one of Hitler's generals or lovers kills him."

I turned my head so I could see her. Gorgeous, smart, and willful as she was, Mirja would make the perfect assassin. "Would you volunteer?"

"If I had the shot."

I had to chuckle but then asked, "What about your family?"

When she noted that Paul was too young, Rabbie too old, and Pip's research too valuable, I said my thanks, too. With support from the War Department, and Mirja and me, Pip had bought a big farm across the Huron River and built quite a research facility. Not yet the scale of Bell Labs, Loomis' Tuxedo Park, or MIT's teeming complex, but Pip's insights inspired a hothouse of talent, tests, and tinkering.

"I couldn't live without Pip and Ruthie either," I said. When Mirja nodded, I asked, "Something else troubling you?"

"Willis Ward." He'd refused to try out for his best events in the Olympic trials because he feared Brundage would bench him again, as Yost had before. "He's working for Henry Ford on 'labor relations,' but Pip and I offered to help him through law school." Mirja was still navigating the color line. I offered my support.

That afternoon Trudy and I swam from the mouth of the Crystal River to Glen Haven. I stroked slowly and took a break to float every ten minutes so Trudy could keep up. Trudy labored, and I found no blue salvation swimming in the Great Lake. I was just grateful when we made it to the old pier.

As arranged with Sven Surtr, Trudy and I cleaned up, showered, and changed into dry clothes at the D. H. Day Inn. He offered to take us for a spin in one of his new dune cars. "You need to see how badly the old Mama Bear's eroded," he insisted.

"From the Great Lake wind and storms pounding her west side?" I said.

Sven nodded and asked, "Vhat if ve try to restore Mama Bear?" Back to the same dilemma: do you conserve by letting nature take its toll or by trying to restore such a treasure to the way you found her? David arrived in his car from Empire to retrieve Trudy and me. "For now," Sven said, "maybe ve help keep her legend alive."

David punched the big man's chest, hard. "Don't you dare damage any other part of the great dunes with your thrill rides either."

When the dark giant pushed his chest hard against David's chin, I stepped between them. They glared at each other but didn't push me out of the way. Maybe they'd had enough of punching each other out.

That evening, after Mirja and Pip put Ruthie and Paul to bed in their room next to mine and retired to Pip's bedroom below for the night, Trudy and I finally got to talk alone. We pulled the two leather chairs in Papa's study up close. I offered her a sniff of Papa's favorite Scotch, but she refused.

"I got into enough trouble for Eleanor drinking."

"You weren't her chaperone," I said, trying to be supportive.

"Didn't matter." She turned her head, and I saw her pretty bob as she hid her eyes.

"My name's mud; no one wants me, and I don't know if I'll ever recover to coach again."

I knew—oh, how I knew. Like her other sponsors, we couldn't risk bringing her back either. "You okay financially?"

"If I mope around home the rest of my life…"

That smarted, so I turned my head away. To go from the world's most recognized athletic figure and an American icon to the drunken sailor dismissed as the coach of the women's Olympic swim team that got swamped—and a cripple to boot—was more than a comedown: it was a knockdown, maybe for the count. "What are you going to do?"

"Billy Rose asked me to put up money for an Aquacade, and he'll get Johnny and Eleanor to serve as the headliners. All I'll have to do is wear my two-piece and float."

Oh, dear Lord, that was the road to ruin for Trudy. Feeling guilty, I lowered my head but asked, "Did Billy Rose propose to you, too?"

"Being deaf and all, I'm hardly marriage material." Oh my goodness, how could I let Trudy throw away her life savings with such a hustler? Yet who was I to say anything, when I wasn't willing to bring her back as America's Flame? "Billy's waiting for Eleanor to get a divorce so he can marry her."

That gave me a better idea. "How about a long swim next summer, from Toronto, across Lake Ontario and the Erie Canal, and down the Hudson River to Manhattan?"

"Can I ride a barrel the whole way, including down Niagara Falls?"

"No, a Helen Wills, Babe Didrikson, or Helene Madison will cheer at each stop."

"Another parade down Broadway when I make it to Manhattan?" she asked.

"Trudy, Mayor LaGuardia will meet you with Mrs. Roosevelt and the Dean of Barnard." When she looked puzzled, I explained, "You'll coach there. If all Seven Sisters field teams, we'll challenge Avery Brundage to add *more* Olympic events for women."

"We'll be lucky if he doesn't eliminate all women's sports instead."

"Not with Grantland Rice making your summer-long comeback story even bigger than your Channel crossing!" I explained how we'd get Kurt to enlist Kellogg cereals and Schwinn bikes to put up a challenge to match the donations by fans all along the route to the Women's Swimming Association: "Corn Flakes for the cheering crowds at every stop and relays of girls riding red Aerocycles and ringing their push-button bells."

Trudy shook her head. "Belle, you know I can't swim like that anymore."

I pinched her midriff and said, "You do have a long way to get back in shape."

Trudy giggled until I stopped tickling her. "Okay, let's do it." I saw the determined look on her face and knew America's Flame could make it all the way back.

The next day, Mirja and I hiked up the hill in back of Belle Cottage with Paul and Ruth and headed north across the top of the ridge with a picnic lunch. The Homestead Course, full of golfers, ran through the early fall reds and yellows of our lush forest. We looked back out to Sleeping Bearing Bay, where our old Chris-Craft Cadet bobbed as Pip spotted for Trudy swimming, albeit slowly, on her own again.

We kept walking north, through the woods along the ridge, until we reached the clearing leading down the meadow to the old Thoreson Farm below. We set our picnic lunch on a red-and-blue plaid flannel blanket. After we finished eating, I shared the plot to heal Trudy.

Ruthie said, "Marmie, can we swim with her, all the way to the parade?"

Before I could answer, little Paul asked, "Who's playing a violin out there?"

We all heard the high-pitched sound until it was replaced by a big huff, then a second and a third. Leaves rustled and branches cracked. A big buck, at least eight points on its antlers, muscles bulging from its huge shoulders, eyes glaring and nostrils flaring, raced across the clearing to the woods on the other side. There several doe scattered, and the big buck, his huge haunches bulging, powered after them.

Little Paul jumped up and said, "That was so great!"

Ruthie, short and compact, hugged her best friend, a half a head taller. I wondered how soon we'd have to put them in separate rooms. The pair raced into the woods.

Mirja pulled at my arm. "Not sure we ought to let them watch," but it was too late. Ruth and Paul returned, eyes wide, and breathing as hard as the buck moments before.

"Why did the buck beat on the little doe's back?" Paul asked his mother.

I was so glad Ruthie hadn't asked me—until she blurted, "That's how they get a fawn, silly boy."

Mirja and I needed to talk before we let them share a bedroom tonight.

We walked down to Port Oneida. We stopped at the old port, only a few weathered dock pilings left, and shared cool lemonade from our Thermos. Ruthie pointed to Pip's Cadet and Trudy swimming slowly toward Pyramid Point.

After we passed a few neat farms, we reached the tidy green-painted cabins of the sister camp the Bealses ran for girls. We headed through the woods up the steep slope, and emerged atop the dune, 250 feet above the shore below. Pip waved up to us from his Cadet. Ruthie and Paul raced down in bounding leaps. Mirja and I followed at a safer jog. Ruthie crawled out to Trudy a hundred yards in the bay, while Pip cruised in and picked up Paul paddling gamely five yards offshore.

Mirja and I waded to the boat with our picnic basket, and Pip helped haul us all aboard. I rubbed Trudy's back and shoulders, while the two kids took turns sitting on Pip's lap, steering, as we cruised beside the sandy shore to Belle Cottage. The prevailing northwestern wind picked up, and the rising whitecaps slapped our starboard side. Pip slowed the Cadet. When the wind died down, Ruthie and Paul raced the boat the last several hundred yards to the mouth of the Crystal River. Pip docked the Cadet in its berth inside the little harbor teeming with Mackinaw Boats for the Leelanau School.

David Ahgosa drove up with Davey, Spring Blossom, and Angel. Davey, as tall as Paul but darker, raced to greet us, his little sister, covered from head to foot, in tow. The children set off across the bridge and along the beach. They stopped to skip stones. Mirja and I dashed after, Spring Blossom following more cautiously with Trudy. I raced past the children, pounded through the surf, and dived. The bracing fresh water hit me with a cold but loving tap, and I squealed with joy. Mirja and I took turns hoisting the young ones on our shoulders and launching them, making sure we'd catch Angel as she dived in. Even Trudy joined in slapping the water and laughing with us.

Angel rode in atop Davey's shoulders as he ran ashore, while Paul carried Ruthie on his back. Trudy, Mirja, Spring Blossom, and I followed, hand-in-hand, in a row four-abreast. I lingered on the beach and watched as the rest climbed the dune to the ring of trees and then disappeared in the bowl of the firepit by the birch box and totem. Only the waves lapping on shore and the breeze ruffling my hair made a sound. No woman had ever been blessed with such a loving family in a place of such glorious beauty.

A poem flew into my head as I experienced my freshwater coast—and myself—anew in midlife. I sang it as I walked into our sacred grove:

Fresh Blessings

I breathe in deeply Leelanau's pure air,
aqua waves sing a gentle song to me.
Her blue embrace, a mother's welcoming—
I am home, at last, from a distant sea.

The dunes beyond climb gently to the trees,
aspens and pines where finches build their nests,
quiet shade beneath shelters herds of deer—
for the weary traveler, a place to rest.

From shore I see the verdant Manitous,
a sandy crescent curves around our coast.
When ribbons of scarlet furl across the sky,
We'll meet at the fire ring with trout to roast.

I offer the Nibi this grateful prayer
for sacred land generations can share.

That night in the attic, I wrote my new poem in my songbook and made three copies. The first two I included with short notes to Auden and Roethke. I spent a longer time writing to Frost. I knew he must still burn at Auden's review. Rather than risk opening the scab, I decided to engage him more lightly—and deeply—in his new book:

Dear Frost,
It's been so long since we talked, I don't know what to call you anymore. Your last name offers the most possibilities: a cantankerous curmudgeon, addressed in cold anger; a whimsical,

even friendly mentor, said with affection; and shorthand for America's poet laureate, written with respect. I suppose I could put Mr. in front of Frost, but that wouldn't offer much of a limit. Robert alone sounds too formal. Rob doesn't sound like you. Robbie, particularly if sandwiched between My and Dear, might be read as too suggestive.

I'm so glad you finally found a proper home for your "Design." Ruthie can't stop singing to its beat and rhyme, and I can't help marveling at its vivid images and ironic twists. How many ways do you intend for us listeners to hear the single word "appall"? So many different slants of meaning, it ranges further.

Your poem "Neither Out Far Nor In Deep" inspired me to take another look at my shore up north. I enclose "Fresh Blessings" for your review. The first Frost, I know, will find it unworthy; the second Frost, I also know, will take delight and encourage my singing; and the third Frost, I dare hope may hear my voice and say this lyric's worthy of publishing even if I must hold it back. As ever, Belle

ಌ

The fall in Ann Arbor should have been one of my happiest, what with Ruthie and little Paul both here, Trudy joining Ruthie, Pip, and me at Cambridge House to rehab, even Rabbie joining Matt Mann to help train Trudy for her new quest. Yet I was strangely lonely. When Ruthie wasn't swimming with Trudy, she played golf with Pip and Paul until dusk on Michigan's MacKenzie course. Sure, I continued to sing poems with her at bedtime, but she spent more time at Hill House with Rabbie and Paul, reading and writing short stories. After we returned from Thanksgiving up north, the city flooded an oval in Burns Park, and Pip coached Paul and all the neighborhood boys playing hockey there. Ruthie, short and stocky, laced up her new skates and bowled the faster boys over whenever they came near.

I should have joined in the swimming and golf at least, but I felt fat and logy. I couldn't stand myself: why impose on others?

Kurt dutifully called once a week, but it was already clear David Ahgosa was ready to take over as CEO. Kurt had also lined up all our dealers to host Kellogg corn-flake breakfasts to launch Trudy every morning next summer, bike relays to cheer her along during the day, and barbecue dinners on our Empire camp stoves every evening. And Grantland Rice had agreed to cover Trudy's story of recovery and redemption, from beginning to end. Spring Blossom called twice to assure me the Hueys managed the Homestead better than we ever did. She and her brother also kept the Grand Traverse fruit enterprises singing. She said her Davey was growing fast and already looked the river skater David and Pip had been as boys. Spring's only off-key note concerned Angel: daylight bothered her eyes more, but sunglasses helped so far.

Not needed at home or my empire up north, I retreated to the chaise by the pool and the bed in my room above. I was too tired to compose. The first week in December, notes from my three poet friends greeted me at Cambridge House. Auden wrote:

> *Thank you for your generous words for "On This Island." Your lyrical "Fresh Blessings" inspires me to visit your peninsula. Although a pacifist at heart, I've come to share your view on Germany. If you can assist with shelter and other succor, Chris and I may yet escape the madness here for your fairer shore.*
>
> *Our composer friend, Benjamin Britten, seconds your proposal for "Stop All the Clocks." While I struggle with a new ending, he's beginning a score for a singer we both like with such a sad voice. With her help, we hope your "Funeral Blues" will wet many more eyes than the madcap satire inspired uneasy laughter.*

Ted's letter wasn't as encouraging. *Belle,* he wrote,

I think my one talent in poetry may be writing big about the small. Not sure I can take a painful journey back to my childhood. In fact, I doubt I'll ever want to include "Premonition" in any collection. Already 28, and your big brute Theodore hasn't written enough poems for a book, but I will return next summer to help Sis with Mom in Saginaw. No toasts earned, but I'll bring the Scotch to your glasshouse if you'll commiserate with me.

Enough with my complaining: Kitty Stokes my fire, the students take to my excursions, there's tennis to play and coach, drinks all around, a few decent colleagues. Maybe, I'm just meant to teach, live, and write about the small things in this backwater. What troubles me most, though, is the lightness of your lyric about the delight of your home up north: how does such good cheer fit with the pain of your death poems for your Mama?
Roethke

Oh, my big Teddy Bear, you see right through me, don't you? My happiness and light in "Fresh Blessings" masked the greater darkness and isolation that was now my lot in life.

Belle, Frost wrote:
You've got Frost I, II, and III right, but you forgot the final Frost: I say you need to read your poems to an audience. My friend, Harvard Professor, and Director of Bread Loaf, asked me to invite you to do so next summer at our Writer's Conference in Vermont. Time your west-inclining brook runs east.

Note I say nothing more about you publishing, lest you run from my advice or, like poor Van Dore, depend on it too much. Despite my buying him a farmhouse and trying to help him publish, he's retreated to the Canadian wilderness, this time with a wife and young child.

We're heading west to San Antonio for the holidays and a family reunion, including with our young treasure, Robin. Please give my best to Pip and a hug to Ruthie. I imagine she's one of the reasons you're singing more lightly now. RF

I take nothing for granted, but the Pulitzer Committee should share your view of my further rangings: Devoto will slay my critics in public, while Untermeyer persuades the members in private. I hope Auden will in due time listen to you, too.

Could I manage to combine a victory lap with Mirja, Pip, Ruthie, and Paul, cheering Trudy next summer, with a stay in Vermont for a reading of my poetry with Frost at the Bread Loaf Writers' Conference? I breathed deeply and tried to sing one of my songs, but my bellows didn't work. Ever so slowly, I regained my breath, but the pounding in my head and the flashing in my eyes continued through the night.

Pip, Mirja, and Trudy dragged me out of bed before lunch the next day and took me to the dedication of the Burton Memorial Bell Tower. When the old main library and its bell tower had been torn down and replaced by a new structure designed by Alfred Kahn to house 20 times as many books, President Burton proposed a campanile twice as tall to house a carillon to remember the boys we lost in the World War and to mark the hours of life on campus. When he died in office in 1925, we lost much more than our Permanent Frost Fellow in Creative Arts. Fortunately, Burton's successor's tenure had ended without inflicting too much more damage. Although I supported Eliel Saarinen's more ethereal beacon for the ages at the center of a cloister at the north end of Ingalls Mall, the Regents decided to adopt the similarly evocative but sturdier design Kahn proposed to stand alone next to his stocky Hill Auditorium masterpiece, the Big House for the Arts. Michigan's first athletic director Charles Baird donated the funds to cast 55 bells weighing 43 tons in England and finally shamed all the rest of us who loved President Burton into anteing up to build his memorial tower. In less than six years Burton had built the University of Michigan into the Harvard of the West for generations of students and faculty to follow. Along with hundreds of others—alums, faculty, and town folk—I donated to build the tower in his honor. Right on the main campus in the center of Ann Arbor, the Burton Tower and Baird Carillon brought academics, athletics, the arts, and town and gown together.

The cold, blustery December day reminded me that Burton had been as flinty, willful, insightful, and, yes, when he chose, as warm as Frost. When the 55 bells concluded their dedication serenade with the 24,000-pound bell striking One-O, I hugged Pip and saluted Frost in absentia.

As the crowd of donors and students broke up after the dedication, I asked Pip to squire Trudy and Mirja back to our place: I had to see and feel the big bell that struck one o'clock. I walked up eight flights, where the carillonneur greeted me in a small room in the center of the huge bell chamber. He sat at his keyboard, thin wooden handles for his hands and fat pedals for his feet. I explained why I wanted to touch the big bell. He escorted me around the 55 bells to what he called the "Bourdon" in the southwest corner. He explained the word came from the French word "groan," for the deeply resonant sound of its low pitch. "Stand back. I'll go inside, strike it once, and leave you to hear and feel it for yourself."

I squeezed into the southwest corner, where the adjoining pillars formed a wall so I couldn't see the plaza so far below. The big bell rang the deepest, loudest bass chord I ever heard. Ever so slowly it tailed off to a barely audible groan. Ears still ringing, I walked through the cold, whistling wind and touched the bottom of the big bell. I felt its rumble, still alive in my hand. My arms reached only an eighth of the way around, but the reverberation tingled my core, until the big bell faded to a stolid block of cast bronze.

I stepped back and made the mistake of looking over my shoulder, south through the opening that stretched from the floor where I stood to more than 20 feet above. I looked up to the top of the bell chamber, and my head began to spin. I looked down to my feet and over the precipice, only a few inches in front of my toes, down, down, down to the ground far below. I closed my eyes, breathing as deeply as I could, and all the energy drained out of me as the wave of panic passed. I opened my eyes and felt the vibration, the echo of the One-O from a few moments—and 15 years—ago.

Oh, Frost, where had the time gone? What had I done? What did I have to look forward to? Not any reading at Bread Loaf, my dear Robbie. I managed to crabwalk to safety and breathed in the fresh air as deeply as I could. I looked across the campus, past Angell Hall, where Frost performed for the first Hopwood Awards; past the Union, where I helped build the pool for Matt Mann and where Rabbie and I swam; past Tappan Hall, where Kurt and I plotted to build Empire together; past the arch on the far corner of the Diag, where I first heard One-O chime; all the way down Washtenaw to Hill House, where Mirja held me up when Papa died, and Cambridge House, where I helped raise Pip, Ruthie, and little Paul, and where Ted Roethke built me a glasshouse. Oh, how I wanted to lose myself forever in that hothouse of flowers and cool water, swimming.

I shut my eyes, braced myself against the side of a 20-foot tall column, and leaned over the edge to get a closer view. When I opened my eyes, a blizzard of snow hid all the scenes and the memories. I looked down again but couldn't see the ground. I looked out and, in the swirling snow, saw a young Ojibwe brave flying toward me, beckoning. I stepped forward to greet him, but when I looked again, David had vanished. I wanted to fly after him in the swirling snow that would carry me to him.

"Marmie!" I heard a high voice, as clear as the smallest carillon bell, calling. I felt two little hands grab my thighs. I heard her singing "Marmie's Lullaby" and knew she'd never let go.

"Angel," I said, "what are you doing here?"

"We need your help," David Ahgosa said as he lifted his daughter up with one arm and swept me off my feet with the other. "Sorry we're late, but our appointment with the eye doctors at University Hospital took longer than we expected."

"How did you know I was in trouble?"

"Our Watchers: Eagle, your papa, and our Ogichidaakwe, Angel the spirit leader."

Thank heavens, they helped me see: I had much more work to do with the Ahgosas up north but also with Trudy, Pip, Ruthie, Mirja, and Paul here.

That night I composed a poem:

Winter Bell

From this aerie
she has watched her fledglings
fly into the blue—

now the wind blasts
sandy sweeps across the dunes
waves dash for shore—

through white swirls
she spies a silver flash—
and flapping sturdy wings

she dives headlong
into the blustery storm—
an eddy of eagle and snow—

battered and buffeted
she struggles to free herself
from the maelstrom—

then, in the distance
the echo of a chiming bell—
she breaks the chain

of winter's hold—
and soars to her nest,
where she will wait

for spring

Fall 1937: Ann Arbor and Glen Arbor

Ted Roethke floated in the pool in our glasshouse. I sat in the chaise and recited in a sing-song voice Auden's four odd drafts of long ditties in dozens of quatrains formed by couplets. "Sue" told the story of an errant society babe through the words of fashion magazines and the view of the sleeping pills that Sue used to kill herself. In "James Honeyman," a driven mad scientist invented a deadly new gas, the British war ministry ignored him, he shared it with a foreign agent, and when war broke out, the foreign power dropped a bomb, killing James, his wife, and his little boy with his own invention. In "Victor," a poor boy, raised by his strict father to live by guilt, became a workaday clerk who couldn't resist marrying runaround Anna; after baiting by his father's ghost, Victor chased after his new wife and killed her with a knife.

I sang the first three ballads in as satiric a tone as I could muster, but Ted repeated his favorite lines with a more gleeful roar. I laughed along with Ted's refrain at Auden's deliciously vicious harpooning the first three "very British types"—the fashion snob, the nutty scientist, and the sexually repressed religious prig.

Teddy exclaimed, "God, that man Auden's a ceaseless bellows of ingenious verse. He may yet challenge Yeats."

I read the last ballad with increasing unease. "Miss Gee" rang closer to home: it told the story of a prim woman of deep faith who repressed her sexuality so much she dreamed of her vicar chasing after her, denied the pain growing inside her so long she came too late to surgery, and died on the cutting board, her body only another cadaver for the Oxford medical students.

I asked Teddy, "Do you think I'm Miss Edith Gee?"

"You don't have a squint in your left eye, lips thin and small, narrow sloping shoulders, and no bust at all," he said, but he didn't look at me.

I told him about my panic attacks and depression last fall, culminating in my dream in the Baird carillon at the Burton Tower and Angel and David saving me.

Teddy pulled himself out of the pool in a rush of water and said, "No, Belle, Miss Gee's a metaphor for people, men or women, who deny their creative desires and end up getting sick."

"How do you figure that?"

He quoted the quatrain, "Childless women get it—cancer—And *men* when they retire." He sat on the adjacent chaise and faced me. "Belle," he said, "your creative fires find lots of outlets."

"Childless like Miss Gee," I replied.

"You wouldn't know it from looking at Ruthie and you." When I didn't respond, he added, "Not to mention Paul and Angel."

"I tried, very, very hard, when I was younger to have a baby, but no dice." When Ted's big face looked back at me impassively, I asked, "What do you make of my fear of leaving my two homes and my refusal to publish my songs?"

He lifted his big hands, rubbed his face, and then reached out to me. "We're all crazy and find different ways to cope, to escape, to fight, and to forget."

Thinking back on his antics, his costumes and dodges, and his troubles not too long ago, I had to smile. I patted his hand. "Thanks for reminding me."

"I'll go with you if you ever decide to read your poetry, to New York with Bogan, Bread Loaf with Frost, England with Auden, even State College, PA, with me."

"I couldn't even go with Ruthie, Paul, and Mirja to cheer Trudy this summer."

He wrapped his big mitts around both my hands. "Damn it, Belle, Trudy would never have started her amazing comeback without you."

"She is America's Flame again," I exclaimed but then bit my lip because I knew I had missed the cheering crowds at every one of Trudy's stops along the way, the relays between stops growing to thousands of kids on bikes, the ticker-tape parade, but most of all just swimming beside Trudy. I withdrew my hands and reclined.

"Good Lord, the way Grantland Rice covered the story from start to finish, you didn't need to be there."

I looked over, and we both knew that wasn't true.

"Okay, how about this? Rabbie's talking with Cowden about starting a summer writer's conference. What do you say we help him organize it at the Homestead? We'll get Frost, Bogan, maybe even Auden, and one night you and I will read our poems for the campers?"

"You want Mirja and me to finance it for you?"

He nodded, but his sad eyes said more.

"Will it help you get a teaching job back here?"

When he said he'd been talking about it with his only ally in the Academic Old Guard here, I nodded. Yet I knew Michigan wouldn't hire Teddy until I silenced Ned Strait and his ilk once and for all.

❧

A month later at Belle Cottage, I received a note from Roethke: *Forget the writers' conference there for a while: I'm too busy at Penn State, drafting new poems for my first book. You may read the enclosed as this Big Bear's play off Auden's satiric ditties, but it's serious. As you're familiar with Pip and Trudy losing their hearing and your little Angel's battle for sight, which one of the senses do you want most to last?*

His poem, "Prayer," was perfectly typed. Ted might be busy writing poems, but he was also busy with Kitty Stokes if she'd do his typing. She'd better figure out how only tougher love offered any prospect of marriage, or Teddy would continue to heed the call to return to his childhood home in Saginaw instead.

I sang the 11 short couplets. I heard the rhymes and alliteration but couldn't catch the sound-sense. Roethke prayed for sight if he could choose one sense: "Take Tongue and Ear—all else I have—Let light attend me to the grave." I wrote him back:

Dear Ted,
You know I'll choose sound. In fact your claim to only sight as the last sense you'd want to lose isn't borne out by your poem. First, my sources tell me you've become a great cook. Ergo, your "Tongue" cannot be "generations dead." Second, your "Sight" must also be off. Unless you used a warped looking glass, how can you call your Byronic mien a "comely head?" Third, although you concede your "Eye" is an "instrument of lechery... more furtive than the hand," you still claim your "Eye's rape is gentle" compared to "the Hand" because it's "never more violent than a metaphor." Then you give yourself away by saying "Lip, Breast, and Thigh cannot possess so singular a blessedness."

Oh, no, I've felt your roving eye and watched as you've "blessed" so many other women. You see, I know your sense of sight also includes your sense of TOUCH. That's why I know I don't have to worry about you and yours limiting yourselves to sight as "only the abettor of the holiest Platonic love."
As ever, Belle

P.S. Thanks for relieving me of any more panic at thought of a public reading up north, but you and Miss Stokes are welcome to stay at Belle Cottage this summer.

I'd missed Ruthie and Pip terribly all fall but reveled in helping David with the operations in Empire, Skipper Beals and Major Huey at the Homestead and Leelanau School, and Spring Blossom with Angel, Davey, her brother, and their band's enterprises in Ahgosatown. The hopes for any sustained economic recovery had faded with another drop into recession. David ran split shifts with time off to share the more limited work and to reduce costs faster than the falling demand. Spring also worked out trades and barters for fresh produce, game, and fish at the Homestead, and she canned and stored more jams and jellies to be sold if robust growth ever ended this grinding Depression.

Her sharing Angel and Davey with me every day at Belle Cottage or the Homestead proved the greatest blessing and tided me over until Pip and Ruthie joined us for a long Thanksgiving holiday. The snow came early, and the three children joined Spring, David, Pip, and me for a picnic lunch bundled by the campfire. The firelight danced on Angel's white features and the birch box swaying above her in the trees. The curly silver hair flowing from her red wool hat into a halo capped her otherworldly look. When Ruthie and Davey started dancing around the fire, she joined and held out her hands, and soon we four adults linked arms with the three children and circled the fire, dashing faster and faster until David broke off and cracked the whip.

Pip, Spring, Davey, Ruthie, and I piled together into the snow bank around the rim of our sacred pit, but Angel grabbed the totem pole and held on tight. She started swaying; sang in her high, clear voice; and beckoned her father. David Ahgosa lifted her up. Angel took off her mittens and placed her hands over Papa's stone. She rubbed it, faster and faster, until it, well, groaned in a deep, low note.

Angel waved to me. I stepped forward, once again on trembling legs, right to the edge of our totem pole. The wind blew, and snow swirled from the trees so thickly I couldn't see. I felt the little Angel's glow as David placed her in my arms. She took the mittens off my shaking hands. She directed my bare fingers to Papa's stone. I felt the reverberation, until it waned as the Bourdon had a year before. "Thank you for watching over me," I said to Papa and our Angel. I reached up higher, to the proud eagle on top. I turned to David and said, "The Eagle's watching over you too." He smiled, for he was buying more land for pennies in the Depression to reclaim his band's heritage.

That evening after I put Ruthie to bed and she fell asleep, I opened my trousseau in the attic, took out my journal, and composed a poem. A Bourdon rang with such a low pitch, the narrator couldn't hear it but still felt its rumble reverberating through time. I thought of that night so many years ago, when Frost and I heard the older chime ring. I felt his presence, so long gone and distant, close at hand. Maybe, the sense of touch rounds out the sense of hearing as much as second sight guides our feelings.

Ruthie kept me company at Belle Cottage for the holidays, but she begged so to share Christmas with Paul, Mirja, and Rabbie, Pip and I drove down to Ann Arbor with her early. At Cambridge House a letter in Frost's stubby hand greeted me:

Belle,

Its been a rough fall. The doctors had to rip a vicious cancer from Elinor's womanhood. She bears the outrage so stoically I can't stand it. After all the years of her tending me and all my complaining, I wish she'd scream, but, no, she suffers me in silence as she has so many times before. Maybe I need to get sick so she can chide me again for acting as a spoiled child. I don't know, maybe life's too full of grief to bear, but, somehow, we do carry on.

Lesley is here with her children, helping her mother. She typed the enclosed poem. Although the critics will no doubt argue over its many possible meanings as much as 'Stopping by Woods on a Snowy Evening,' let your old friend know if, at long last, I met your challenge to sing an adequate goodbye to my Mama Belle. Whatever else, I hope you'll like the metaphor of "The Silken Tent" however interpreted. Frost

His poem sang in the delight of his metaphor: A single sentence danced on the page and flowed through all 14 lines of his perfect sonnet. I could feel the brush of wind on my cheek from my mama's gentle farewell wave so long ago. Thirty years later the bond she forged was indeed a silken tie I still welcomed. Yet Frost's woman was no fiction without weight. No, her silken touch was supported by a "central cedar pole that is its pinnacle to heavenward and signifies the sureness of the soul." If read as his mother, like mine she never complained no matter what and stayed strong as long as she could to nurture her child. The same could also be said of his wife Elinor to her husband.

Then, it hit me, as I felt anew the after-mark of David Aghosa's tug on my cheek in the silvery satin fog our breath formed as a tent over us so many seasons before: Frost's metaphor may also describe the memory – or hope – of such a lover's pull.

My Dear Robbie,
I'm sorry about your Missus and pray for her recovery. I doubt you getting sick will help her rally: you must stay strong, for her and for your family.

Your Silken Tent sings beyond my challenge. Eons from now, the elegist will still say it as a memorial for a mother (or for a similarly selfless nurturing wife), but your critics will longer debate its many possible meanings. They miss the magic of your best poems: tied by the senses to daily experience on this earth, your voice soars by the pull of metaphor into a dream that sounds a different tune each time heard. Indeed, I hear another in your perfect sonnet, a proposal to engage a lover that <u>no</u> woman could ever resist. In this regard your new poem tops the

rush of "Blue Salvation" I included in my "Goodbye to Mama" at your urging.
Auden changed the final stanzas to one of his Marx Brothers satires and created a searing "Funeral Blues" for a lost mate. Without changing a single word, your new poem offers more divergent readings. Oh my Scots minstrel bard, please take care with your magic powers as they tripped me up once again.

In thanks, I attach a song to let you know that our dear Burton's Bell Tower at long last rings at Michigan.
As ever, Your other Belle

For Frost

Up the tower stairs I slowly climb,
Careful to stare straight ahead—
Past the stony walls I go,
Ascending higher, vertigo at bay,
Until I reach the chamber.

Searching, I stand among them—
Fifty-five majestic bells of bronze—
Where is the one among the many
that rang those many years ago
when we walked this way at midnight?
Were we falling with the snow?

The carillonneur knows its place,
Secures me in a southwest corner,
Strikes this special bell for me
Whose timbre is so deep and low
You must listen closely for its groan.
I touch its base, feel its solid rumble:

Oh, yes! The Bourdon! One-O!

Summer and Fall 1938: Ann Arbor, Glen Arbor, and New England

Auden shambled down the steps of the New York Central platform with a battered valise that had carried him from England to Japan, through China, and halfway back. His transcontinental ride across North America included this stop in Ann Arbor on his way for a final fortnight in New York City before returning to England. Hair tousled, shirt wrinkled, tie askew, suit rumpled, hands in pockets, his pale face and smile still looked as fresh as when we first met, a decade before. Mirja, in a white satin blouse and flower-print skirt, and I, in a navy silk top and tan bottom, stood back. Wystan stepped forward, grasped one hand each from Ruthie and Paul, and said, "Show me your home."

We all piled into my new V12 Lincoln Zephyr, beige top down, green body shining. Auden sandwiched between Mirja and me in the front seat, while Ruthie and Paul piled in back and hung on his shoulder. Wystan gave each a colorful Chinese doll. Pointing toward Hill Auditorium, Mirja said, "That's where you'll wow a full house next year, even more than Millay or Frost." As the carillon from the bell tower punctuated her proclamation, I turned and drove past

Drake's, jogged onto State Street, and slowed to show off the 500-foot length of Angel Hall with its classic columned central entry.

Paul piped up, "That's where my pop teaches," and Ruthie chimed in, "Marmie says you're going to teach and write here, too."

Auden laughed with his two charges that hadn't seen him since the year they were born but already took to him as if their godfather.

"Children, please," I said, "Wystan's only agreed to visit for the day."

I circled the Law Quad, its stone buildings and towers rivaling any of the colleges in Oxford. "Um," Wystan said, "I already feel right at home, but, good Lord, how big is this university?" He pulled a green pack of Lucky Strikes from his shirt pocket, plucked a cigarette, and lit it with a snap of his Zippo. As I drove past the arch on the corner of the Diag, I told Wystan my story with Frost of hearing the chime ring "One!"

"That's my place," Paul yelled as we passed the rock at the corner of Washtenaw and Hill. One block farther, and Ruthie screamed, "That's mine!"

I pulled up the driveway and parked next to the glasshouse. Pip emerged with an iced tea for Wystan and grabbed his small bag out of the backseat. Mirja, Ruthie, and Paul escorted our guest into our exotic garden and showed him every blooming flower. I finally managed to get him to safety on a chaise before any of the pitchers, water wheels, or Venus flytraps attacked.

Wystan told us about his trip to China with Isherwood and their upcoming book. "We're going to call it *Journey to War*." Looking to Ruthie and Paul, he added, "Thank heavens this one will end before you're old enough to fight."

"You volunteering?" Pip asked.

Our guest knew enough to answer directly back so my brother could read his lips. "Won't bear arms, but if England wants me, I could stand for the Medical Corps."

"Whatever our lot," Pip said, "we'll each find a way to help." He told Auden about the long struggle of his best friend at Amherst College to make a difference as a Negro. Charles Drew was working on a new kind of blood bank to save the lives of those wounded in the war. "He says blood knows no skin color."

"Nothing I write will make that kind of difference."

"You might get inspired by seeing Pip's *top secret* war lab," Mirja said. Ruthie and Paul pulled at Wystan's hand. I packed sandwiches and a Thermos in the picnic basket. Mirja warned Pip, "Make sure you're back in time to freshen up for the 5:30 party at my house to show Wystan off." As Auden rose he handed me several pages.

The Cowdens, Bursleys, and Stevenses—my good friends Angelyn and Albert from the kirk—arrived at Hill House at the appointed hour, along with their neighbor from the west end of Cambridge Street, a respected Milton scholar, Warren Ray. No Wystan, Pip, Ruthie, or Paul. Soon a dozen other members of the faculty arrived, including, our resident Shakespeare man, Ned Strait.

An hour late Ruthie stormed through the back door, yelling, "Pip shot a 68!"

Paul, following close behind, said, "I broke 90 from the big boys' tees."

Auden, his skin sunburned, followed. "I lost only one ball in MacKenzie's Lake Ness monster, but the creek past the final hole swamped me." He looked at the puddle forming under his feet. "But I did need to hit my ball out of the ditch to salvage a 99."

Pip walked in last and accepted the blame for being late. It didn't matter. Wystan had already won over all his curious suitors, except Strait, who looked down his nose at Auden as he did every creative writer. Mirja pressed drinks on Wystan and Pip. In his winning accent and wry wit, Wystan shared his insights on the war already breaking out across the Pacific and building across the Atlantic.

"Who's Auden trying to fool with his silly, pacifist plays?" Nym muttered. "That stuttering dandy's no Shakespeare!"

Warren Ray, looking every bit as much a Harvard Ph.D. and

Renaissance literary man, showed his Crimson peer the door. Ray hadn't forgotten his Midwest manners, from growing up in small-town Illinois and graduating from its state university. He returned to engage our guest in a discussion comparing Milton's epic poetry and Shakespeare's dramas with Wystan's verse plays. Ever modest, Auden thanked Ray but deflected any hint of praise: "I copy madly from both and have great fun creating my own voices."

At 8:30, Auden and I walked back to my house. We convened in my study. His hands fumbling in the chair in front of my desk, he began, "Our long travels left us in a hole. Don't suppose you might help Chris and me?"

Ruthie knocked on the door with Pip. After Wystan gave Ruthie a good-night hug, I walked out and mouthed to Pip, "Pack Wystan a set of clothes in your traveling bag." He nodded. "Put $500 into his coat pocket, too." Ruthie nodded. She'd learned how to read lips, too.

I returned and poured us each a Laphroaig. We sniffed and savored as we had so many years before. "Where are you going to call home now?"

He lit another cigarette and explained how all his travels led him to America, "a land of lonelies and yet still-young hope, where I can write alone, perform in public, and live anonymously, but first Chris and I are heading for a last fling in New York."

I told him about Kurt Knutsen, his move to New York, with a cottage on Fire Island, and gave him the phone numbers.

"I'll give him a ring," Wystan said, "but we older men need younger inspiration."

"Avoid soliciting any boys you may end up teaching."

Wystan took a deep drag on his Lucky Strike.

"Wystan, it can get you fired over here."

"Hmm." With a rising inflection to his accent, he said, "The masters don't beat the boys in school and then console them in bed on this side of the pond?" When I shook my head, he mocked, "But it's okay for the faculty stiffs to shag the girls?"

"Good Lord, it's bad enough there's not a woman professor in the whole of the English Department here," I sputtered, "without you joking about a teacher sexually abusing his charges, as the one who walked out on your party this evening tried on me."

Wystan took a last puff on his dwindling cigarette. I pushed an ashtray across, and he snuffed the butt out with one hand and dumped the ash from his other. What kind of host was I not to notice he'd been using his hand as an ashtray? "Belle, that made me lose my faith for a long time, too, but I'm coming back to the original Anglican view. No matter how weak, we're all God's creatures." Wystan could make me smile. "Perhaps a small bit here for starters, maybe a reading or a seminar for aspiring poets so we can see whether Michigan makes any sense for me?" Before I could add how judging the Hopwood prizes might also help, a wince crossed Wystan's badly sunburned face. I left to get "Marmie's cure." I pulled soft gauze from the first-aid kit in the kitchen and dipped it in a mix of lukewarm tea and milk. I placed the wet pack gently on his face, ears, neck, arms, and the tops of his hands. Whether it was the cooling with evaporation or the tannin absorbing the burn, he perked up. "Thanks, *Deah*!"

With a twinkle he added, "You can assure the God-fearing folk here I'm *just* an old, married man." He explained how he'd wed Thomas Mann's daughter, Erika, so she could escape once the Third Reich shut down the cabaret she started with her lesbian friends in Berlin. He lit another cigarette with his Zippo, took a long drag, and exhaled. "Until death do us part, good friends, yes, but God forbid, no sex."

I couldn't help laughing. I rose and added a drop of Scotch to my glass. To which he replied, "If I promise to visit up north, may I have a sniff, too?" I began to pour into his glass and said, "Say when." I kept pouring. "Say when!" I stopped just before the Scotch slopped over the top of his glass. He picked it up and poured half into mine. "Shall we say next summer, over Independence Day, to celebrate my becoming an American?" I clinked his glass.

When he asked if I had any new songs to share, I pushed his drafts across the table and dropped my head. "Couldn't even find my ear to hear your sonnets from China."

"Hmm." I looked up, and his hazel eyes rested easily on me. He doodled with his pen and pushed his poems back across the desk. "They're for you." I looked down and read his postscript: *I hope these will inspire you to compose. When they do, let me know your thoughts on my newly titled* Sonnets from China. *As ever, Wystan*

ও

The first week in August, Mirja, Pip, and Paul visited Belle Cottage. Although Ruth protested, Mirja and I moved Paul into Papa's old room on the second floor of the turret. To get even, Ruth invited Davey to a "kids' sleepover" after dinner. When Spring Blossom and I consented on the condition that Angel also spend the night, Angel in Ruth's room and Davey in Paul's new guest quarters, Ruth objected. Eventually, she charged into my room and demanded to party with her bigger boy friends. I looked to the pale, white-haired Angel to see if she'd take offense. Instead, she waved Ruthie away, hopped up on my bed, and snuggled close. "What that?"

I'd been reviewing my round of letters with Frost since Elinor died in order to figure out how to respond to his most recent plea. "We have a dear friend, who lent Pip and me his home when Ruthie was first born, who's lost his wife and can't figure out how to go on." I paused to look at Ruthie, now fuming in the doorway but listening for my answer. "I'm trying to write a poem to help cheer him up."

Ruthie stepped forward. "I'm sorry Mr. Frost's still—"

Angel interrupted, "Marmie sing?"

I looked down at her, more closely, and saw her eyes, no goggles, so pale the faint blue took on a pink hue. As I sang my bittersweet, almost mischievous "Silent Tree" in the cadence of a nursery rhyme, Ruth peered over my shoulder:

Silent Tree

My upper lip is finely starched;
You will not see me cry
Although my wife's deceased
And so bereft am I.

Why then won't you talk to me
And Listen when I speak?
I've lost my dearest love
And from you—Not a Creak!

Silent as stone, as she was
When I grumbled. Ignore me now?
Bloody hell and Damnation!
I've a mind to cut you down!

Ah, your branches sway like lilies
In this whisper of a breeze.
And You offer me an apple—
Red as blood, it serves to ease

the mighty suffering of my soul.
Your gentle leaf upon my cheek
Like a heavenly soft caress,
And the sweet juice that you release

Mingles with my salty flow.
All my Joys and sorrows mated—
Reminder of eternal truth:

Laughter and tears are fated.

Angel clapped, and Ruthie began to riffle through Frost's letters and poems.

"Sorry," I said, "they're not for you to read."

"But I'm a big girl now."

"Too big for sleepovers with boys, yes, but not big enough for Mr. Frost's throes."

Before Ruth could pout, Angel pulled four pieces of paper from my pile and said, "Marmie sing more?" She couldn't possibly read yet, but she could see that a poem looked different than a letter. She'd pulled out Frost's "The Silken Tent" and my two poems from the Burton Bell Tower, all three written before Elinor died, and the draft of his poem "Carpe Diem," written after her death. I sang "Carpe Diem" first. Both children snuggled close as they heard in Frost's voice the irony of misunderstanding the present because you learn to appreciate it only after the moment's past, the more so in this instance, after the death of a beloved. I followed with his "Silken Tent," and the children reached across me to hold each other's hand. I finished with my bell tower poems. Ruthie shrieked with delight, and Angel glowed at the memory. My daughter gave me a goodnight kiss, picked her little friend up, and carried her back into her room.

I put Frost's letters in order and reread them. In the first he took out his sorrow with bitter regret over his wife giving him the silent treatment through her death and over his daughter Lesley blaming him for all their family's woes. *The thought of living alone nearly finished me off,* he wrote. In the second Frost revealed anew the lover's quarrel he had with Amherst. After the College held a service for Mrs. Frost at Johnson Chapel, including *19 honorary pallbearers,* he couldn't bear to sleep alone in their Sunset House and resigned. He suggested he'd spend the summer in his Vermont summer home, *although I'll probably bother Carol, Lillian, and Prescott at their farm more, where dear Robin's visiting. I hope Lesley, and even Irma eventually, will also forgive their father.*

A June 2 letter he wrote on the day he packed up his belongings at Sunset House signaled greater trouble. His stubby handwriting and train of thought jerked across the page so unsteadily, I knew he'd dropped his usual ginger ale for too much Scotch. He described the urn holding Elinor's ashes: *I wish I'd died with her.* He boasted *Amherst paid me 50 percent more than I did for the house. Although the College won't be building any library to honor me now, this score will tide me over until I'm able to sing for my supper again.* The letter ended, *None of my children will have me. Do you think I'll ever find another mate who will take me in?*

His fourth letter, from July, opened by blaming himself for *dragging Elinor through so much, but she's gotten her revenge and struck me down so low I can't sleep and have taken to drink, swearing, and telling every friend I ever had off.* Frost closed by telling how the wife of one of Mrs. Frost's pallbearers, the head of the Bread Loaf Writers' program, invited him to stay with her and their two children at a friend's. *I tried to beg off but was too down after my great joy Robin left to return home out west. When Kay offered to help sort my correspondence, type my replies, and set my schedule, I couldn't stand being alone a moment longer.*

I read the last letter, dated August 1, twice:

> *What a mess. When I fell into my dark trances moaning and Kay brought me back with a slap, I acted the bad man I am. I then did the only honorable thing and asked her to marry me, but she told me no, she'd never leave her family. Yet she did offer to become my assistant after Bread Loaf.*
>
> *I'm so torn up I beg you come to the writers' conference to make sure I don't do anything worse. Ted Roethke will join us as an instructor. You can appear as his guest, but you'll have your own room at the inn. I know this plea runs against your inbred homing inclination for your two Arbors, but I don't know where else to turn.*
>
> *Frost*

I tried to scatter Elinor's ashes as she wanted, but Hyla Brook is so grown over, it doesn't run, not west or east. Her ashes therefore still remind me what a fool I am.

Dear Robbie, I wrote:
I enclose a new poem for you. Make of my "Silent Tree" as you will, but you will have to decide whether you prefer the bitter-bark aftertaste of Kay's forbidden fruit to biding your time for a woman who's free to share more with you. Remember, whatever else, you can still find and pay an assistant to type and help manage your schedule, household bills and such.

This once I will fledge my arboreal nests, although I doubt I will be able to make you an honest man. Beware though: with my stronger will, I will team with Teddy to challenge your weaker flesh against any partner you choose on the court.

Don't worry about a library bearing your name: your poems will be hard enough to get rid of anyway. Before your last go down, I hope you sing more love ballads than laments, even if your best will be heard by us awestruck ear-readers as sounding both types of tunes if not more. Trust your other Belle: to write, write, write more poems for many, many more years is your lot. And Robin and the rest of your brood of grandchildren will continue to provide fertile ground for your wonder and doting.

Ted Roethke called me the next afternoon. "I'm carrying you to the doubles championship of the literary world, preliminary round at Steepletop on August 16 and the finals at Bread Loaf on the 18th."

"Frost put you up to this."

"He also arranged an interview for me in Bennington on the 17th."

"Don't bother having your Miss Kitty Stokes drive you to Steepletop, then."

"You still won't leave your—what does Frost call them—arboreal nests?"

"I'll pick you up in State College: It's on the way."

At nine in the morning on August 18, Teddy and I appeared on Bread Loaf's red clay courts, decked out in our all-whites, shorts for him, skirt for me. Only Frost's blue canvas Ked's marred his team's all-white. At age 64, his all-white hair only burnishing the twinkle in his blue eyes, the old poet pursed his lips into a cocky smile. "Miss Belle and Mr. Roethke, allow me to introduce you to Mr. Stegner, the Western States' singles and doubles champion only a few years back."

Tall, craggily handsome, with wavy brown hair, he reached across the net and shook my hand. "You look like the God I always imagined," I said.

"Pleased to meet you, Ma'am, but call me Wally."

Roethke turned to Frost. "Rough or smooth?" When Frost said "rough," Teddy spun his racquet, picked it up, showed Frost the face with no decorative braid at the bottom, and turned the end toward his old mentor. "Sorry, it's W." Before Frost, already reddening, could sputter his protest, Teddy added, "But I'll let you choose."

"Serve," Frost said without hesitation and tossed three new balls to Stegner.

"We'll take that side," said Roethke as he led me around the net and Frost glared.

As we crossed, I said to Stegner, "You and I will have to make sure the score is announced after every point and game, or these two will be at each other's throats."

The ball and the match went back and forth, with Frost holding his end up surprisingly well. He stood in the middle of his side of the court and chopped back everything within his reach. Stegner covered every one of our lobs over the poet's head and poached whenever we tried to hit a winner up the middle. After losing the first set, I worried my bear of a boy would begin to act up. Instead we both picked up our play and won the second because Stegner overruled Frost's blind call of "wide" when I aced him with a slider that nicked the line on set point. I suggested we four declare victory and retire for iced tea. Stegner agreed, but Frost protested, "I'm as fit as you youngsters, and I give no quarter."

Ted and I pulled away in the third set despite Wally covering more and more of the court for his tiring partner. Frost started arguing line calls and croaked, "Didn't you hear the ball tick the net?" when Teddy hit a serve Robbie couldn't reach. With Roethke set to serve at five-two for the match, Stegner whispered, "The other instructors treat Robert as a deity and tell me we're to bow to him."

Instead Roethke served so hard into the corners, Frost failed to make a single return, but Stegner kept hitting winners until I crossed and knocked off one of his rockets. The ball ruffled Frost's white pants as it passed between his legs.

"She shoots, she scores," Teddy exclaimed as he lumbered up to the net. All the while Frost sat on the ground, swearing, and looked for a bruise on his shin. Teddy climbed over the net to shake hands. In a pique Frost swung his racquet. Roethke stepped back, and the force of the swing sent the older poet sprawling. I sidestepped over the net and helped Frost sit up. His pale blue eyes soon glazed over, and he moaned. Stegner raced to pick up a water bucket and towel. I splashed a ladle over Frost's head. Robbie jerked, but his eyes did focus. Stegner and Roethke helped walk him to a bench outside the courts.

I shooed the two younger men away, sat next to Frost, and held the ladle so he could sip some water. Up close, he still looked a catch for most women, particularly those of us flirting with 40. Still breathing hard, Frost swallowed a sip of water down the wrong pipe and coughed. The ladle tipped and doused him again, this time down the open collar of his shirt. I dabbed his mouth, chin, neck, and chest with the towel. I helped him up and dusted the red clay off his still-firm butt.

He returned the favor. "Confound it, Belle, you're still a far sight better than most any player, man or woman," but his frown did shade into a smile.

"I'll take you for a drive so you can cool off and clean up before lunch, then."

"I've got a lecture at four, you know." On our drive, top-down in my flashy green Zephyr, Frost confided that Mrs. Morrison reminded him of his mother. "I've known Kay as long as you, too. I met her when her Reeling and Writhing Club invited me to teach a poetry class at Bryn Mawr." When I asked what he thought of engaging with such forbidden fruit, he pursed his lips: "Don't know if I have the will to choose, anymore."

Robbie wowed us with his performance in the Little Theater that afternoon: the easy humor, the voice so alive with crags and trills, the reading of poems from memory, and his long-rehearsed trick of appearing to craft a poem on the spot. He called his "new lament" an example of "the pang that makes poetry." Suddenly he lifted his outsize head, his face and eyes brightened, and he compared the figure a poem makes with that of love: "Both begin in delight, but no one can really hold that the ecstasy should stand still in one place. Both incline to the impulse, yes, but then they run the course of lucky events and end in…" He paused and, for the only time, appeared to glance at Kay Morrison, before continuing, "…at least a momentary stay against confusion."

He paused again, and I swear, he winked at me before he began to say the poem I typed for him so many years before, "To Earthward." When he got to the part about craving "the stain of tears, the aftermark of almost too much love, the sweet of bitter bark and burning clove," a lot of snuffling could be heard in the crowd. He closed, "I long…

to feel the earth rough to all my length." Oh, old bard, please no, not to your grave yet!

Kay Morrison, a slim woman of amber hair and good posture, never gave any hint that Frost's "Figure a Poem Makes" might be inspired by hers. The eyes of several men strayed from the stage to Bread Loaf's Queen Bee. Bernard DeVoto, co-director of Bread Loaf with

Ted Morrison, shifted his eyes, made all the beadier by thick, circular glasses, from Frost to Kay, but she maintained her poised pose.

After the performance the Morrisons escorted Bread Loaf's star to the inn for drinks and small talk so their paying customers could get their money's worth. The wannabe writers hung on every word of Frost and the other faculty. Charles Foster introduced himself to me as the Amherst student the Morrisons invited to Bread Loaf on a scholarship to honor Mrs. Frost. I explained how I was also a Frost acolyte, albeit from a much earlier era, when the poet was at Michigan. "Frost's mind still seethes and rolls as he invents a poem on the spot," he exulted. I had to laugh at the conjurer's ability to make his listeners believe such calling out was an act of creation rather than of memory.

Kay eventually freed Frost from his throng of admirers and ushered him into the night. As I began to leave for my room, I heard Teddy tell Wally, "If you thought Frost took his losing hard, you should have seen Vincent Millay's husband rip off his white ducks when Belle beat him at Steepletop." When I didn't stop, Teddy lumbered after. "Join Wally and me for drinks?"

I shook my head.

"DeVoto always hosts a private after-party at his cottage for the other luminaries and staff."

"I liked you more as a rebel Chicago gangster than as a social-climbing academic."

"I'm still an outcast at most colleges," he replied, his eyes sadder than ever.

Time to lay aside my objections to the pecking order at Bread Loaf and help my Teddy Bear overcome Ned Strait's blackball: "Let's go out and strut our stuff." Our nifty Foxtrot stole the show at Benny Devoto's, but our host had eyes only for Kay Morrison. During one break Stegner told us Benny had gotten him a job at Harvard. I looked over at the stocky man, but his nostrils flared like a buck during rut as he saw Frost approach Kay. DeVoto trotted over to separate them, as Wally assured Teddy, "If your poetry's half as good as your tennis, Benny will help you land a better teaching position, too."

Thereafter, Frost and I joined for tennis in the mornings, always singles, never a partner or a game. Robbie reminisced about "his many arboreal friends" and rued that "Little's coming and Strait's slanders made it impossible to stay." Of Amherst he said, "A men's college in a small town is too confining for a new widower, unless he's inclined to stink up the boys' pew." Most afternoons Frost disappeared, and Teddy squired me to Bread Loaf events and around its village of Ripton.

Frost offered a short seminar at one p.m. on August 26. After sharing only a few of his "further rangings," he excused himself and retrieved me from Roethke. Frost took my elbow, and we walked across the road and up a long trail into the Green Mountains. We emerged into a glade, in front of a big beech scarred by an iron spike. We sat down on a rock ledge and leaned against the thick trunk. Robbie pulled out a flask and took several gulps. "Gave Kay a copy of 'Silken Tent' right here before this witness tree but titled it, 'In Praise of Your Poise.'" He paused, but his pursed his lips suggested more.

I grabbed the flask and took a big gulp. "Good Lord, what's a witness tree?"

"When the colonists surveyed new land, they blazed a tree at the corner of every section. Pry off the bark, and there's a perfect negative of the marks they left."

I nodded, for I knew that feeling, oh so well. I made as if to peer under the bark. "You're safe: no picture here." I asked more seriously, "How're you coping now?"

"After Archie MacLeish's thin gruel this evening, I'm escaping early tomorrow to stay with Irma and her family in Concord Corners." I knew that was doomed and shook my head. "But I'm going crazy here!" He finished the first flask and pulled on a second.

"Be a Creative Fellow at Michigan this fall and stay at Cambridge House," I said.

"Type my poems, arrange my schedule, feed me, and keep me company?"

"Robbie, I'm but sorry I can't. I have to help run our family businesses up north, but I can find you eager and qualified young people to help you in Ann Arbor again."

He shook his head, and I'd never seen those pale blue eyes look so down. After a long silence, he lifted his big head, looked into the woods beyond the clearing, flared his nostrils, and snorted.

I had to laugh and asked, "Another Buck?"

"Not 'Two Look at Two' this time," he said as the deep lines in his face formed a frown. "I fear it's up to Kay Morrison whether it's 'One or Two' for her."

"Your Benny buddy also hovers over Kay whenever she begins to preen for you."

Frost's face contorted with rage. He swore. His whole body shook. He moaned. I lifted his head, but his pale eyes looked so blank I couldn't tell if he was still here. I slapped him lightly on the cheek. He stopped shaking, made no sound but looked to me for help. I couldn't resist holding him tight until he croaked, "I need to come up for air."

When I relaxed my hold, he planted such an urgent pucker on my lips I began to tingle all over. Oh, how I much I had always yearned for my Robbie!

He paused to take a bigger pull from the second flask, and I did, too. He fell as if swooning on me, as I had so many years before when he left Michigan for Amherst. I didn't know why, but I ever so gently pushed him away.

"Will you stay here till the first frost?" my Robbie beseeched, and I couldn't help smiling at his phrasing. "During the spring term I could also spend time at your house in Ann Arbor and your cottage up north."

"What about your new Missus Miss?" I asked.

"The rest of the year you can visit me, some here and in Cambridge, maybe Dartmouth… " He didn't finish, and I couldn't blame him: he knew how I was tethered to my two safe Arbors in Michigan, and I knew how deep his roots ran in New England.

Yet he grasped my hands in his and pleaded: "Belle, I need someone to make me an honest man so I won't fall…" He paused again.

I loved this dear bard and good man. I dropped his hands, pulled him close again, kissed him full on his lips and lingered for what seemed an eternity, but I finally stood up while I still could. I pulled him up for the walk back.

After a long trudge he broke our silence. "How the hell does Pip put up with sharing Mirja?"

"As tough a question is how Rabbie puts up with sharing her."

"He must be limp," Frost said.

I still felt Rabbie's pull when he had almost overwhelmed me not so many years before. "That's just wishful thinking on my part as much as yours, I fear."

"After all these years wanting to love Rabbie, how do *you* keep shutting him out?"

"A threesome's not my cup of tea," I answered.

"So you think Kay's playing me for the fool I am?" When I didn't answer, he wailed, "But I'm too far gone to settle for Plato's game with her."

He stormed down the hill. Eventually, he turned and yelled, "If you don't dally, I'll have time to freshen for MacLeish." I joined him. "Archie's a toady tool for the New Deal," he added. When I offered that MacLeish had also earned a Pulitzer, Frost retorted, "He used to be a good man, but his political campaigning's made him a bad poet."

A slim man with tiny glasses perched on his nose greeted us on the porch of Frost's cabin. "Miss Belle," Robbie said, "meet my longtime friend and ally, Louis Untermeyer."

Untermeyer offered a smile and his hand. After Frost walked into the bedroom, Louis asked, "Are you married?"

"Mr. Untermeyer," I replied, "you thinking of proposing, too?"

"Oh! How long have you known Robert, Miss Belle?"

"Since he first taught at Michigan, and I was one of his students."

"You're one of his Whimsies," Untermeyer said, and his smile grew.

"Maybe not his first favorite," I replied, "but his longest and most prized."

"You're the one who befuddled Robert for the poetry prize at the inaugural Hopwood awards. I am *so* glad to meet you."

"Not because I never sent you my poems to submit to your publisher?"

He laughed at that but added, "For now, delighted to know that you're the one Robert bats the tennis ball with in the mornings." He paused. "I drove over from my farm on the other side of Lake Champlain because he said he needed me. It appears Benny has spread much unseemly gossip about our troubled friend, but I'm relieved to see you're also the woman Robert disappears with afternoons to...botanize."

I shook my head at that, but only replied, "For the first time in more than a decade, I ventured forth from the shelter of my two Arbors, on the other side of Lakes Erie and Huron. I also drove here only because Robbie said he couldn't go on without me."

Frost emerged from the bedroom, said not a word, and left his friend behind as he escorted me out the front door. He fast walked me to the Little Theater. I led Frost to the next-to-last row, where only two Bread Loaf students sat. I caught Teddy's eye, and he settled immediately behind us in the back row.

As MacLeish began his reading, Frost said, "Surprised Archie took time out from his campaign to become the nation's head librarian." I shushed him, as the two students shook their heads at him, got up, and found the only two vacant seats several rows ahead. Frost leaned over, picked up their mimeograph programs, and began to fold them. The crinkling disturbed others nearby. Three times Frost pursed his full lips, but I gripped his knee to quiet him.

Frost turned and nodded to Teddy. I hoped Robbie was sobering up, but he tapped his ears and said in his stage whisper, "Archie's damn poems all have the *same tune*."

As I nodded for Teddy to sit next to Frost, MacLeish announced, "You, Andrew Marvell," perhaps his most loved song, 36 lines rolling and folding into one lilting sentence. I turned to join the others fixed on the Pulitzer poet upfront. The commotion beside me turned all heads back. Somehow Frost had lit the programs on fire. I stamped the burning papers out and apologized to Mr. MacLeish. Teddy clamped his big paw on Frost until MacLeish finished reciting his masterpiece to a standing ovation.

I suggested we put Frost to bed, but Robbie hurried after MacLeish, the Morrisons, and the other luminaries to DeVoto's cottage. Roethke and I followed. When Frost walked into the kitchen, his young Amherst acolyte, Charles Foster, had the good sense to hang on his mentor's sleeve. As Frost prepared a large Scotch on the rocks, Roethke added reinforcement, but Ted Morrison approached and said, "Robert, please be good for what's left of the evening."

Frost glared at his Bread Loaf host. "After this bottom's up, I'll be fine." He chugged his drink, refilled his glass, swore three times, stalked into the main room, and hunkered down on a big couch in the center, as if to hold court.

DeVoto flitted about, from Kay to Ted Morrison, from MacLeish to Stegner, from Roethke to Frost, trying to keep the conversations up and the tensions down. I made my way to MacLeish to invite him to sit and talk with his old friend. Unfortunately, DeVoto reached MacLeish before me and asked him to recite his new verse play for radio, *Air Raid*. What a mistake! Frost saw this as more of MacLeish's drivel campaigning for position with FDR, and he hurled offensive remarks as MacLeish recited.

Kay Morrison looked to DeVoto, and he brayed, "For God's sake, Robert, let him speak!"

When MacLeish finally finished, I pushed the Morrisons and

DeVoto aside, introduced myself to the honored guest, and walked him to Frost. Foster sat on one side of Robbie; Teddy, on the other. I sat MacLeish on the arm of the sofa so he and Frost could chat. I leaned down, took Robbie's empty glass, and said, "Be civil until I get back." I kissed him lightly on the cheek and whispered, "Care to make Kay jealous?"

Frost nodded, turned to MacLeish, and started in on an English critic who had pigeon-holed Frost as merely a "regional" poet.

I returned with two Scotches on the rocks to hear MacLeish say, "Jesus H. Christ, Robert, I'll go to England and spank him for you. You're the foundation, and we all know it."

"I'm an old man who needs such flattery," Frost replied.

I handed each a drink, and they toasted.

"God damn everything to hell so long as we're friends, Archie."

MacLeish, his arm resting on the sofa in back of Foster, reached over and tapped Frost affectionately on the shoulder. "We are, Robert. We are."

I motioned to Teddy and whispered, "Can you hitch a ride back to State College?"

He nodded, but with eyes sadder than ever. "You sure you're not needed here?"

I looked to Robbie and Archie, talking earnestly but affectionately. I turned back to Teddy and saw behind him DeVoto still fuming to Kay and pointing at Frost. I wanted no more of this scene. "Time for me to get back to our glasshouse," I answered.

"Thanks for helping me," Teddy said, "even if I still can't join you there."

"You got the job at Bennington?"

"Not yet, but you and I did win the doubles championship of the literary world."

I kissed his big mug.

He gave my big butt a love tap. "Don't give up on me, Big Mama."

He paused. "One of these days I'll also be a better poet than the Grand Old Bard."

I approached MacLeish and extended my hand. "It's been a pleasure meeting you." He rose and shook it with the same grace with which he spoke. I leaned down, kissed Robbie on the cheek again, and said in a stage whisper, "Time to get you to bed."

Frost rose, offered his arm, and escorted me out.

DeVoto ran after, yelling, "You're a good poet, but, Robert, you're a bad man!"

I pushed Frost forward, and he swore the rest of the way. His pale eyes looked so tired I sat him on his bed and tucked him in. He reached for me, but I only brushed his cheek with my palm. As I leaned down and whispered my goodbye, I felt the damp from his tears and began to choke up. Oh how I feared this would be our last farewell.

I willed myself to stand up, turn and walked out onto the front porch. There, Untermeyer greeted me and said, "I'm sorry I misunderstood." When I couldn't yet gather myself to respond, he continued, "I've never seen Robert this lost. Miss Belle," he added, "I lost two wives through my womanizing and a son to suicide. Each time Robert helped buck me up. Thank you for helping him in this crisis, and I do hope this will help him get back to his life work of writing poetry again, too."

He extended his hands in thanks and when I grasped both, he said, "I'll report fully next spring, when I come to Michigan to serve as the next Frost Creative Fellow."

I managed a smile at our small world. "I hope Mrs. Morrison proves a better and longer-lasting helpmate for Robbie."

I retreated to the inn, where Wally Stegner intercepted me. "Sorry about the ruckus between Benny and Robert." He paused. "Please forgive Benny, too, as he's also in the throes of a personal crisis."

"You this much of a saint to everyone who passes your way?" I asked.

"Only with folks who earn their spurs."

I must have blushed at that, but his missus was a very lucky woman.

I wondered whether Frost and Mrs. Morrison were so fortunate, but I had to admit she exhibited extraordinary poise, and Robbie surely needed such a woman to tend him if not also to make him mind. This was about much more than typing drafts and helping organize his schedule.

I couldn't get to sleep. I composed a poem that might help Robbie remember how much he meant to me, and so many others, despite all his recent profanities, drunkenness, and mania:

Museum of Bad Words

She kept a glass jar
in the cupboard
growing fat with quarters
relinquished every time
he said a hell or damn.

For the really bad words—
the ones that start with "f"
or take the Lord's name in vain—
she fined him a dollar.

I don't know what she did
with the money when he died—
a donation to the Smithsonian, perhaps?

Even so,
I would pay decades of quarters
to have the Old Bard back.

I composed a note and left it in an envelope with the poem for Frost at the front desk.

Dear Robbie,

Remember your telling me so long ago, "Marriage, decent or not, is the one institution that causes the least possible pain between the sexes?" I came to the same conclusion as another Old Maid, Emily Dickinson: engaging another's spouse isn't for us, but we both put up with a brother's love for another man's wife. Perhaps the best proof of your view of marriage is that it can survive even when threatened by such affairs of the heart. Whatever you decide, I hope you read the enclosed poem as a sign that your Scots kith and kin, Rabbie Burns, Belle Moodie, and I, are all proud of our All-American Makar, Robert Frost, poet and man.

As ever, Your younger Belle

P.S. Pip hates sharing Mirja, but he continues because he loves only her and that's all she offers. Over time he's also come to love her son, Paul, as if his child. He's a devoted father to our Ruthie and never flaunts his affair. I'll keep a room open for you at Cambridge House and my cottage if you ever want to travel from your New England haunts and return to Michigan, whether for a visit or a longer stay.

I left Bread Loaf before dawn and followed the sun and the Erie Canal on Route 5 across New York State. I stopped twice at places where Ruth, Pip, and Mirja had joined Trudy on her legendary swim from Toronto to Manhattan. At Buffalo I crossed the Peace Bridge over the Niagara River and barreled through Canada on Route 3. I gunned my green Zephyr across the Ambassador Bridge into Detroit at dusk and picked up U.S. 12. When I turned onto Washtenaw, the load I'd been carrying the entire time away lifted. I rolled up the driveway, parked by the glasshouse, and hopped out.

I saw Pip and Mirja jumping up from a single chaise and covering themselves with towels as best they could. They always tried their best to be discreet, even around me, but they had no idea I'd return this evening. As I walked by the pool, I waved. "You don't know how good it feels to be home!" I skipped up the back steps and asked, "Where's Ruthie?" Pip and Mirja now looked guilty and pointed to the second floor.

I raced up the stairs, shouted, "I'm back," and burst into her bedroom. She sat up and pulled the covers to hide her chest, but I saw her breasts had begun to bud. Beside her, Paul peeked out from under the covers, his dark shirt buttoned, short-cropped dark hair and clear eyes looking clean-cut as ever.

He said, "Hi, Marmie" in an innocent voice.

I only said, in as a level a tone as I could, "We'll sort this out downstairs."

I retreated to the kitchen, where Pip stood, tucking his shirt into his khaki pants, while Mirja sat at the table and buttoned her crimson satin blouse. I tried to control my voice but said louder than I should, "Fine sitters you two make for our babies!" Pip and Mirja both apologized. I tried to cool down. How much damage could a budding 12-year-old girl and an 11-year-old cub inflict on each other, anyway?

Ruth held Paul's hand as the pair walked into the kitchen. Although a head shorter, Ruth possessed a dark beauty, coal-black eyes, long raven hair rolling down to broad shoulders, and a surprisingly large carriage that would only become more imposing as she blossomed. Too soon, she'd grow into her mother Rachel's image, a vixen irresistible to all the boys. Paul, lankier and as darkly handsome, also stood straight; his pale green eyes, still fearless, gazed steadily at me, ready for whatever might come next. After Mirja grasped Paul's hand, I took Ruthie's and led her to my study.

I sat in my chair behind the desk, and she sat in one of the two leather chairs in front. "We were only exploring," she opened.

I looked at the mail on my desk and saw the envelope from Auden. "How long?"

"Less than a year." Good Lord, I hadn't even gotten to that question yet, but I thanked our good fortune we'd made them sleep in separate rooms up north so their clandestine "exploring" didn't go on all night. Yet there was so much opportunity in the forests of Leelanau and here botanizing in the Arboretum.

"Have you, well, um, had any signs of your womanly, ah, flush?"

"A period?"

When I nodded, she dropped her eyes.

"You know the buck and the doe we saw up north?"

She nodded.

"In humans it's a longer and more beautiful rite of passage to becoming a woman." I continued, "It's not dirty. We just need to take care." I opened a desk drawer and pulled out a Kotex.

"Oh, Marmie, I already know all about that."

I walked around the desk and sat next to her. "You also know how men and women make babies?" She blushed but nodded. Where did kids learn this stuff so young these days? "Then you also know you're too old to go exploring with Paul anymore."

Holding back her tears, she said, "Are you going to stop us seeing each other?"

I shook my head. "But you're going to have to do your reading, writing, and playing outside each other's bedrooms; keep your clothes on when you're together; and no more kissy-face, huggy-bear."

Ruth nodded.

I rose and lifted her up.

"He's my best friend, and I've always loved him so."

I felt more than heard her sigh, whether of relief, resignation, regret, or resistance, I wasn't sure. Whatever else, I knew I'd stay in Cambridge House with Pip and Ruth this school year. Helping my family was more important than conserving up north, trying to write poetry, or keeping up with my poet friends.

Rather than separate Ruthie and Paul, we pitched in to keep them too busy to explore each other. Rabbie picked up the short-story writing sessions. Pip took them to tinker in his lab, stargaze through his telescopes, and play golf at Dr. MacKenzie's University course. Mirja chaperoned them to dance lessons. I played tennis with them, and we read Frost, Dickinson, and Burns and wrote poems together. Mirja and I took Ruth and Paul to visit the Burton Memorial Tower to learn to play the bells. Thank heavens, the carillonneur had arranged for permanent screens to fill the space between the pillars since my last visit. When the two kids held hands to try to wrap their arms around the Bourdon, I wondered if our program to keep them only friends was doomed.

We also spent time steering them into separate activities. I swam with Ruth, and Rabbie encouraged her to compete. Pip sneaked Paul into junior hockey practices. Mirja took Paul to the local printing companies so he could learn how to produce books, and she taught Ruthie how to draw.

Maybe Ruthie doing so well inspired me, for I wrote Rachel's mother:

Dear Mrs. Goldberg,
Ruth will soon be as comely as her mother. She thrives in school and loves reading and writing. She calls me Marmie, and she swims like a porpoise, already much faster than I ever did. Pip's never married again, but he's a very good father to your grandchild.

Ruth knows that her mother died giving birth. I know she'd appreciate a letter from you. I'd also be glad to arrange a visit any time you wish. Please give my regards to Rebekah. She was so thoughtful to Pip, the baby, and me in Amherst. We are still grateful.
Sincerely, Belle

Later that fall, the harsh ringing on my bedside table woke me. I picked up the phone and offered a sleepy, "Hello."

"You okay, Belle?" asked Kurt.

I knew something must be the matter but said, "Just caught me napping… You?" I heard Kurt stifle a laugh. Or was it a sob?

"My partner left me, for the younger boys that appeal to Auden and Isherwood."

"Good Lord, how young?"

"Of age, but not yet men." There was a long pause. "Belle, I need your help on another matter. I'm switching to Lazard Freres. We're creating a relief fund to help as many Jews escape as possible. Will you shift your business and investments with me?"

"Of course, and I'll talk to David and Spring about the Grand Traverse enterprises, too." I paused. "If it'll make a difference, let the Uptons know we're with you."

"See you over Thanksgiving."

Maybe Kurt would always be my business partner.

The talk of the rising fascist evil reminded me I owed Wystan a letter. I began by telling him how much Ruth and Paul enjoyed his visit. *You inspired both to wield their pens.* I paused before deciding how to phrase my invitation to visit next summer. *We look forward to seeing you over the Fourth of July. If you bring a companion, we've got a garret in our Homestead Inn that's provided privacy to two generations already.*

I enclosed my new poem and wrote, *My "Museum of Bad Words" may not be much, but it's a start on my singing again, for the first time in a while.* I paused and thought about his draft sonnets. All began with two quatrains and concluded with two tercets; they flowed, bounced, burrowed deep, flew high, told his history of man and God, but always brought me back to what could no longer be escaped on this earth. The last closed, "And maps can really point to places where life is evil now. Nanking. Dachau." I concluded my letter:

> *The sweep of your sonnets carried me right along to the same conclusion you reached: Germany and its Nazis are evil, and*

only war will stop their aggression against ideas that must not die. I take heart your voice and insights will make as much of a difference as Pip's war lab or Drew's blood banks. Your Sonnets from China ring. I look forward to hearing the rest. Be well and safe, Dear Friend.

I reread my note to Wystan to make sure I hadn't said anything hurtful. I slipped it into an envelope and mailed it in care of his mother to his family home in England.

Later that morning two letters arrived. The first read:

Miss Belle, I live with Rebekah and the young man from MIT you met here, now a Physics professor at the College. I'm glad to hear Ruth thrives, but my daughter and son-in-law don't need any reminders they bear no children. Leave well enough be for the sake of us all, including the child. Mrs. Ruth Goldberg

Maybe our girl's namesake was right: I vowed to continue to help Pip raise Ruth without prying into what we left behind in Amherst.

Dear Belle, Frost wrote:
Kay set me up in an apartment across the river in Boston. The Morrisons will rent the farmhouse next summer below the witness tree, and I'll stay in the guest cabin down the hill. I'm paying Kay for serving as my secretary and business manager. If all goes well, I will buy the farm, plus a home close to her in Cambridge, even if I pour more of my heart into my poetry than into her cup.

I enclose a draft of a new poem. I shared it with Wally Stegner, who kept me company on the tennis court after you fled. Our Teddy Bear's reading also did us proud at Bread Loaf. He's working on a collection of good poems that will help him get a good position, maybe not back to your glasshouse Eden but forth to my greener Vermont pastures.

My best to Pip and a hug for Ruthie too. I made up with Lesley, but I fear Irma's losing more ground and Carol's in a state again. Robin, Prescott and the rest of the grand-children do give me joy (and the hope that all these Frosts will all thrive as only Lesley has among my children.)

Your poem reminded me I owe you an apology for putting up with my bad self. However your several musings about The Silken Tent also remind me that you should just enjoy the words, phrasing, metaphor, and different possible tunes all aslant without more. Isn't that enough to offer a stay against confusion? One of these years I do hope to return up north to see how the forests grow your Papa, Pip and you planted so long ago. In the meantime I thank you for helping me when I was lost and couldn't go on alone: I think I'm finding my bearings and will continue to write, write, write – and teach – for as many years as I have left. I promise I will also be in better tennis form so Wally and I can beat you and Ted the next time we meet, even if with your home-court advantage at your Homestead Inn.

Robbie's new poem "I Could Give All to Time" suggested he'd made his fate with Mrs. Morrison: "Why declare the things forbidden that while the Customs slept I have crossed to safety with? For I am there and what I would not part with I have kept." But I knew this slant was just one of many, as with "The Silken Tent" and most of his other great poems. Rather than speculate on any particular meaning, maybe it was better to just enjoy his poems and experience the full pang of each reading anew, as if a child full of wonder without more.

Stegner was right, though: in Frost's seventh decade, our mutual friend's phrasing and sounds still sent us ear-readers headfirst into a boundless wondering. As for Teddy, I couldn't imagine how he'd escape his demons despite his good act at Bread Loaf, but only death would ever end his drive to become a great poet. Yet I was sorry to admit my two poet friends would now go on without me. Oh, Teddy might stop by our glasshouse when visiting his mother in Saginaw and Frost might send me another note, but neither would ever make Michigan his home again, let alone with me. The time to let Frost know I'd serve as his host, helpmate, and so much more had passed and Ned Strait would never let Michigan forget Roethke's madness. Much as I'd miss my dear Robbie and bigger Teddy Bear, time for this reclusive Old Maid to burrow deeper into my arboreal nests to help Ruthie grow to find her way.

FALL 1941: ANN ARBOR AND GLEN ARBOR

"Go, Ruthie," we all screamed, with Rabbie, Pip, Wystan, and Paul making up in decibels what Mirja and I shrieked in more piercing notes. The chandeliers bounced light off the high arched windows in the Union pool, as they had before, when Rabbie and I swam there. After lagging the field the first three laps, she powered to catch the last boy ahead of her. When the two touched the wall, we couldn't tell who won. When they climbed out of the pool, the boy stood a head taller than our girl. Girl? Ruth might only stretch to 5'2", but she'd filled out, with her big shoulders and bust tapering to a narrow waist erupting into full hips and lean, powerful legs, with feet so big they looked webbed.

Matt Mann declared, "Phil Enns touched out..." The cheers of the boy's family drowned out the next few words until we heard, "...but Miss Peebles' time is only 1/10 of a second off the American women's record for the hundred!"

We lifted Ruth high. Paul, only 13 but already as tall as me, reached up, but maybe he was only cheering her, too. He bore his mother's dark good looks, except his eyes shone with a lighter green hue.

When we set Ruth down, I couldn't help noticing she was more than flushed by her swim. High cheekbones, full lips, and ripe figure made her the spitting image of her mother, Rachel. Her dark eyes sought only Paul.

Standing next to them, Auden still looked pale and boyish. He clapped Ruthie and Paul on the back. "I'll escort you two to the pool party in my new car." When our whimsical chauffeur pulled up next to the glasshouse in his sea-green 1939 Pontiac Coupe a half hour late, I asked how he'd managed to buy such a rocket. "Another of my benefactresses," he said with a wink.

I thought about retorting, but I was glad to see him enjoying our company. His dear Mum had died in August, and the love of his life, a blonde-haired, blue-eyed Jewish boy with whom he'd vowed to live in wedlock forever had jilted him for younger and more virile men in New York. Wystan had called to see if he could escape to Michigan to heal up. He'd been such a hit in his lecture at Rackham Auditorium last winter and judging the Hopwood poetry submissions in the spring, Roy Cowden agreed to ask the Chair of the English Department to make an offer. When Ned Strait got wind of this, he organized the academic snobs, literary critics, and rhetoric pedants to oppose the appointment of any more Frost Creative Fellows. He also whispered in the Chair's ear that Auden was a homosexual who would prey on students. Rabbie, Albert Stevens, and Warren Ray joined Cowden in vouching for Wystan as one of the English language's finest poets, albeit not yet much tried as a college teacher.

The Chair invited me in and said he was prepared to hire Auden on two conditions: For as long as Auden stayed at Michigan, I agreed to waive the provision of my gift requiring women to hold the position half the time, and I agreed to work with Rabbie, Mirja, and Prof. Stevens and his wife, Angelyn, to keep the poet from engaging any of his young charges in "untoward activity."

As to the first, I reminded him the English faculty was already 200 strong "with nary a woman in sight," to which he replied he couldn't even get Millay, Bogan, or Moore to sign on as a Frost Fellow, and I was too busy with my Empire up north and raising Ruthie to teach here.

"Just saving you from fending off another of Strait's attacks, that I bought a faculty position," I replied, but I agreed to both conditions. No point arguing about Strait's "untoward" plays for coeds.

Auden agreed to Michigan's offer so long as he taught only one small class each semester on great works of his choosing, literature, librettos, and, yes, poetry, but only from Dante, Shakespeare, Goethe, and Eliot. Although Wystan also agreed to tutor Hopwood poetry candidates, he refused any public readings. He wanted to focus on composing what he dubbed a "Christmas Oratorio dedicated to my Dear Mum."

We arranged for Wystan to rent a house away from all the lures on campus, coincidentally on the very site where Robert Frost had lived on Pontiac. Henry Ford had fallen for the Greek revival and moved that house to Greenfield Village. In its stead a smaller two-story, split-level, stained-wood home now stood. Auden agreed that an older student and committed heterosexual could live there to cook and keep house. Angelyn Stevens, my friend from the kirk and ardent fan of Auden's poetry, agreed to take his one class each semester and attend any informal sessions Wystan held—"at-homes" he called them. The only incident at Auden's house involved a woman student who drank too much of the Scotch Wystan set out on his sideboard as a good host. When the Dean of Women complained, Mrs. Stevens assured there'd been no "untoward activity," and Auden agreed not to offer any liquor. From then on, the students brought their own.

When Ruthie skipped down the steps of the kitchen to our glass-house in a stunning new red swimsuit, Wystan asked, "Ruthie, *deah*, do you invest as much time in writing as swimming?"

"Yes, but I like your poems and Mr. Frost's better."

"Not also your Uncle Teddy's?" he asked, as if taken aback.

"We-e-e-l-l-l, he does make up the best nursery rhymes."

Wystan chuckled at her imitating his speech. "Ted's a great sports fan, too. He took me to watch three beastly, brutal, but oh so beautiful boxing matches at Penn State."

"Several of Marmie's poems are knockouts, too." Ruthie continued, "Like Miss Dickinson's best, they don't hold back, like so many of Frost's, and they sound better than yours. Uncle Wystan, why don't you write reviews of Marmie's poems?"

"Hmm... well... publishers of reviews want their readers to be able to buy the poems so they can see for themselves." When she turned on me, Auden said, "Ruthie, *deah*, maybe one day she will let *you* organize and publish her poems." Not finished, Wystan floored me: "Until then, every afternoon ask your Marmie if you can hear the new verse she's composed while you've been away, working at school."

ᔓ

Wystan invited me to his wife's lecture at the welcoming, honey wood-walled theater in the women's League a few weeks later. Cast in the large shadows of her novelist father, Thomas, Erika Mann presented an impassioned argument against Hitler and "The Other Germany." We all understood it despite her thickly German accent, close-cropped hair, tie, shirt, and slacks. At the reception in the League afterward, Wystan shepherded his erstwhile wife respectfully among the guests but left as soon as it wouldn't appear rude.

All fall the specter of world war washed over us, with news from the fronts in Russia, Britain, North Africa, China, and the Pacific Rim. Pip spent long days at his war labs across the Huron River, encouraging a hundred scientists. He tested and refined his radio-wave-echo devices: he called them radar. He also developed and tested various means to avoid detection, including chaff, clutter, and oddly shaped model planes, ships, and tanks. He said whoever won this cat-and-mouse game would win the war.

The Brits had already proven the value of radar with their chain of finders circling the United Kingdom and a comprehensive air defense system that enabled the RAF to respond to wave after wave of Luftwaffe air strikes. Pip worried we weren't deploying radar quickly enough nor building a similar system of air defense to protect us from sneak attack. Others at Pip's lab worked on various sound-wave devices to detect and track ships and submarines at sea and to guide torpedoes; John Kraus worked on new ways for ships to escape detection and to avoid triggering mines. Even isolationist industrialists in the Midwest converted their plants to build war material.

As the weather grew colder, Wystan stopped by more to sit by the pool and soak up the warmth in the glasshouse. He'd shamed me into writing every morning, but I spent too much time trying to compose epic poems. He gently suggested I might do better with my stubbier Dickinson roots than his longer flights of fancy. He also told me about a promising young graduate student in his class from "Paradise Valley, some 'black bottom' section of Detroit, he says." Wystan added, "I think you'd call Robert Hayden a 'Negro' here. Only glasses as thick as Coke bottle bottoms enable him to see at all, but he's got a way with words and a passion for history and composing." When I asked Wystan whether he was tutoring young Hayden for the Hopwood poetry prize, a wry smile broke out. "I'm trying to help him understand that poetry needs to be about exploring the unknown and writing as you would say at a slant, not political diatribes."

"Ha! Forgetting your anti-establishment and left-leaning polemical plays when you were you were younger, I suppose?"

"No, I learned from hard experience that poetry makes nothing happen." With a smile, he added, "Then again, Robert may already be farther along in extracting the dross from his search into slavery and emancipation and composing historical allegories than Isherwood and I were with our political satires." He lifted his head. "I'm going deeper into history—and religion—with my next epic, too."

His Christmas Oratorio purported to tell the Incarnation story, but it was a much, much longer allegory describing Auden's loss of faith and long path back to Christ. His working title, *For the Time Being*, suggested this struggle would continue. The musicale grew and grew with each new part (Advent, Annunciation, Temptation, Summons, with more to follow)—each new chorus, soliloquy, narrator, and character already much too long for any conceivable score.

The next time he stopped by the pool, I said, "Good Lord, Wystan, I'm worn out: How much more is there?"

"Umm… It's a long way across the desert."

"You still mooning over the loss of your mate?"

"Only all night and every day," he answered.

"Why don't you invite him to join you when you visit your, ah, wife in L.A.?"

"Not sure her anti-Semitism won't drive him farther away."

Other rumors swirled on campus: Auden solicited a boy in his class; his housemate, Charles Miller, was his live-in lover; the drinks at his "at-homes" led to all-night sexual bacchanals. Nym charged "the fairy's even harboring a bitter, four-eyed colored man who's not satisfied with abolition of slavery and has the gall to challenge Anglo-American institutions and traditions."

Angelyn and Miller, joined by Rabbie, assured the Chairman that all the sexual innuendos were false and that Robert Hayden was an upstanding citizen and promising poet, but that didn't shut Strait up. So I invited Wystan to bring a friend to the Homestead garret for Thanksgiving.

"Thanks, but Charlie and I will instead serve up more of our Platonic pap with the turkey so the forked tongues here can wag more." He paused. "Belle, I hate to say this, but I still love young Kallman, no matter how much he strays."

ꕥ

The following Friday, after dinner at Belle Cottage, I met with Kurt, Pip, David, and Spring Blossom in Papa's study. David had picked up where Kurt left off in pursuit of defense orders for our camp equipment, stoves, and furnaces. With Spring Blossom and her brother, David made similar preparations for all their Grand Traverse enterprises.

I asked David for his thoughts on the Homestead. "Sorry, but you'll soon have to run that, too." Pip and Kurt both nodded. "Belle," my Ojibwe partner added, "I'm leaving to help run supply logistics from the Munitions Building in D.C. once the war begins."

"Davey's going to the Leelanau School," Spring added in a soft voice, "and Angel and I will stay with you here until the war ends."

What was this, a conspiracy to make me CEO? I gulped down my panic of never having run anything in my life and asked David, "Will you set up meetings for us with your key people?"

When he said only one of our foremen was too old to fight, I wondered how I'd ever manage.

After our board meeting broke up, I asked Pip to stay. Maybe I was envious he'd get to live in Ann Arbor, keep Ruthie and Mirja, and tinker at his war lab while I lived alone here. Before I could protest, Pip said, "I know you're making a big sacrifice to run Empire." I nodded. "And living alone up here is going to be hard, too." I nodded again. "Ruthie, you and I can visit back and forth regularly, a lot more than David can with his family." I had to nod again. "He needs you to help Spring with Angel and Davey and with the Grand Traverse enterprises until he returns, okay?"

"How's this all end?"

"We'll win this war, and you'll write poetry. I'll invent devices so I can hear you sing, and Ruthie and Paul will marry and share their children with us as we grow old."

That night I sat on the old trunk in the attic and reviewed the songs in my notebooks and on my paper scraps for the first time in years. Oh, how those short poems sang to me again, as Emily Dickinson's had so many years before, when I was only a girl. Outside my window I heard a high-pitched "Hoooo… Hoo… Hooooo." I looked out but couldn't see anything in the dark. "Hooo… Hoo… Hooooo," the owl sang again. It sounded more like a mysterious breath than a whistle or hoot. "Hoooooo." I looked again and now saw his round face, hooked nose, two tufts, and big eyes. The owl's hoot rang in my ears, and I knew who belonged up north, come what may:

Who wonders an owl
in the beech outside my window—
Who will save this land—

halt the desecration
of our dunes before Mama
Bear is blown away—

block pollution from
our crystal river and lakes
If not you, then Who?

The next day after lunch Pip, Ruthie, Angel, and I bundled up and drove over to Glen Haven. Sven Surtr filled up his modified black Ford from the big red gas pump in front of the Day general store. Pip hopped in back with the girls, and I sat next to Sven to see for myself whether his thrill rides damaged the dunes. Top down to the cold northwest wind, he said, "Better buckle up, Missy Belle, iv you don't vant to vly out."

"We can do without your fox dip and big buck bull by Mama Bear, thank you." The Dark Ogre gunned the engine and raced along M-209 to the life-saving station, where he turned onto a gravel road and then roared through the cottonwoods up the dunes. While I held on for dear life, Ruthie screamed, "Faster! Faster!"

On top of the dunes, the balloon tires rolled easily over the sand, no track in sight, behind or ahead. Sven pointed toward the eroding Mama Bear in the distance. As we approached, Sven slowed. Her west front had blown out more from the prevailing wind and big storms blowing across the Great Lake, but her east front showed no ruts or any other signs of man.

When I had to nod, Sven's grin showed only big teeth. "Where'd your fangs go?"

Surtr replied by spinning the steering wheel and flooring the accelerator. We raced so fast down a big embankment, I had to clamp my mouth shut not to lose my lunch. When we got back to Glen Haven, I swear Angel's eyes glowed through her sun-goggles. Sven helped me out of the car, shook Pip's hand, and said, "I hope to repay my debt to you by the end of next summer."

Ruthie piped up, "Can we come back for a ride tomorrow?"

My legs still shaking, I said, "Mr. Surtr, we will watch you like hawks."

⁂

Ten days later Ruthie, Wystan, Mirja, Rabbie and I parked in front of the Stevenses' home, only a block away from the Coliseum. With Albert and Angelyn, we walked to watch Paul and the rest of the Ann Arbor Junior Wolverines Pip coached play against Detroit's Junior Red Wings. Only 13, Paul was as tall as most of the older players, but he didn't look nearly as big. He had yet to fill out, but he danced around the ice faster than any. He carried a magic stick with a nose for the puck, poke-checking the hard, black rubber disk off Red Wing sticks, carrying it around the defense, and setting up his wingers or dekeing the goalie for a score. But the Detroit junior team, the best in the Midwest last year and undefeated in six games this season, sent waves of Red Wings at Pip's Maize and Blue and outshot and outhit our boys. As center-man, Paul became the target for many of the checks, but he kept his head up and avoided any big collision. With 30 seconds left in the game, the Red Wings led 4–3 and launched another wave at the Wolverines' net. At the far corner of the crease, the Red Wing center reached to tip the clinching goal in, but Paul lifted his stick, stole the puck, stick-handled around one

Red Wing attacker, and powered down the side boards right in front of us.

At the blue line, Paul crossed to the center and made as if to split the defensemen. When the two pinched together to crush him, Paul pushed the puck through their skates, danced to the right, picked up the puck, and raced, head looking only ahead, toward the goal. Yet his big Red Wing counterpart, skating back as fast as he could, never broke stride as he closed from the left and took dead aim at Paul.

Rabbie, Angelyn, and Wystan rose in one voice: "Look out!"

Mirja and Ruth shrieked, "Shoot!"

The Junior Wolverine shot just before the vicious check sent him flying. The puck flew into the upper right-hand corner of the goal. The red light came on before the horn blew, but the sound of Paul crashing into boards rose above the roar of the crowd. A hush fell over the arena as our boy lay crumpled on the ice, no movement, no cry, dead still.

Pip jumped over the boards and shuffled across the ice. Rabbie ran along the front row of the stands toward the far end of the arena, jumped onto the ice, fell, got up, and kneeled beside his son. All the other players stood silent in a circle.

The black-taped blade of Paul's stick inched along the ice. His left glove unfolded and re-gripped the knob. The black boot and silver blade of his right skate moved. Finally, his head lifted to look around. Rabbie and Pip helped Paul to a sitting position. Our Maize and Blue boy rose with his magic stick, his left hand still clutching the knob. The other players sorted into two lines and took off their right gloves; Paul led his older mates in shaking the hands of every Junior Red Wing.

The next day started off well enough. Ruth, Pip, and I joined Mirja at St. Thomas for early Mass to say a prayer of thanks for Paul's health and to hear Rabbie lead the boys' choir. Wystan, wearing bedroom slippers, flapped up the aisle and squeezed into our pew as the procession ended. The Latin Liturgy, the incense, the pomp, and the mystery of the Catholic Eucharist offered plenty of opportunity to say thanks. I looked over to Wystan, his eyes closed, head uplifted, singing his loudest with every chant. When Rabbie offered his full-throated tenor solo this morning, Wystan listened until the last tremolo and whispered to me, “Quite a set of pipes.” When Paul’s solo closed the Mass, Wystan listened raptly: the boy’s greater range, from alto through tenor to the first hints of bass, transported the English poet to a higher plane.

Mirja invited Wystan to join us at Hill House. “Sorry,” he replied, “I’ve got to help Angelyn teach Sunday school at the kirk and then rush back home so I can host another of my benefactresses for dinner.” Just like Wystan to view church as an extension of home. He wore his bedroom slippers in both.

For our early Sunday dinner, Mirja served a Caribbean jerked beef, spicy rice, and mango salad. After we cleaned up, Mirja played the piano while Rabbie, Ruth, and I replayed yesterday’s game and our boy’s narrow escape from serious injury. Paul, although very sore around his right shoulder and neck, appeared more ruffled by Ruthie saying, “I was worried you’d forgotten hockey’s a contact sport.”

Sporting a bruise on his cheek, and proud of his four points, including the first and last goals, Paul looked at her, offended.

“Well,” she said in four syllables, imitating Wystan’s speech, “you did manage to skate away from all the Red Wings until your last shot.” She folded her arms under her breasts, smiled, flashed her dark lashes at him, and added in Wystan’s manner, “Uhmmm.”

Paul now laughed and leaned closer so Ruth could massage his sore neck.

The phone rang. Rabbie answered, hung up, and said, “The Japanese attacked Pearl Harbor.”

I signed the words to Pip. Rabbie turned the radio on. John Daly interrupted CBS Radio with a bulletin. V.J. Kaltenborn followed with the day’s events, but we knew what the attack meant: the U.S. would join the war against the Axis.

Pip excused himself to go to his lab across the river. Paul and Ruthie begged to join him, but he shook his head. "May we listen to the radio in your suite?" she asked.

Pip nodded; he had kept one large antenna and big receiver to capture signals from the biggest commercial stations all across the country. Paul and Ruthie stood up and raced out the back door.

As I got up to leave to head home a half hour later, Mirja pulled me aside. "We need to talk tonight, alone, without the kids, Rabbie and Pip."

I joined Ruth and Paul in Pip's sitting room above the glasshouse. They fiddled with the dials on Pip's big radio to catch the latest. Shortly after six I left them to prepare supper. I thought about asking them to help, but I had to admit the news kept coming: the announcement that President Roosevelt would speak to a Joint Session of Congress tomorrow, Winston Churchill's stirring words, the leaks about how the Japanese continued to negotiate for peace during the attack, the reports of damage to our ships and planes. Besides, I needed some time alone to think about the logistics of my move up north and who to hire to cook for Pip and Ruthie here.

At quarter to seven, I climbed the stairs and walked down the hall to the entry to Pip's quarters. Door still open, what I saw made me stop: Ruth had taken off her blouse and pulled Paul's head to her bare breasts.

"Ruthie," I said softly, "I need you to help set the table."

She lifted her hands off his head.

Paul had let his hair grow long for the winter. There, in back of his right ear, I saw a pale spot for the first time. As Ruth sat up and pushed his head away, the spot seemed to gleam against his mass of dark hair. Paul tried to turn to look at me, but I held his head firmly and examined what was surely the beginning of a telltale white streak.

"Sorry," he said, and I let go. Paul rose, fully clothed, and said, "I'm sorry, Marmie."

Ruth calmly buttoned her blouse. "I'm not."

"Mirja and Rabbie are joining us for supper. Ruthie, we'll sort the rest out later."

While we ate, we listened to the news on WJR. After we cleaned up, Paul and Rabbie made ready to head home, but Mirja asked to stay and talk with me. After I saw Ruthie to her room, Mirja and I sat in the two chairs in front of my desk in the study. I told her about how I had seen the white spot growing in Paul's hair.

She nodded but said, "He doesn't show any sign of hearing loss."

"Yet!" I paused to control my temper. "How long have you suspected?"

"Since I got pregnant with Pip and miscarried, I've been watching."

I took a deep breath. "When did you see the first white hairs?"

"Last night when I checked his head for injuries," she answered.

I'd worried about Paul being Pip's son, too. "How do we tell Ruthie and Paul?"

"We can't," Mirja said. "It'll kill Rabbie."

"He's going to see for himself soon enough."

"Not if Paul doesn't lose his hearing," she replied.

I remembered the doctors saying that hearing difficulties accompanied the white streak no more than a quarter of the time. "Okay, but Ruthie's too…" I paused. What did I mean to say: headstrong, determined, sexy, needy, what? I knew her mother Rachel had trapped Pip, and if Ruth wanted Paul, he'd have to be a saint not to fall.

"I know," Mirja said with a nod before I finished. "We can't risk any incest."

I thought about my doubts, whether another man had gotten Ruth's mother pregnant, but I wasn't about to discuss this with Mirja nor explore it with Ruth. That was up to Pip. For now, the only safe course was to separate Ruth from Paul. "We'll enroll her in the Leelanau School," I answered, "and she can live with me at Belle cottage."

"Pip won't mind the separation?"

"Not if you don't cut him off," I said, even if I knew he'd miss his girl terribly.

That evening I waited for Ruth to knock on my door. When she did, I invited her onto my bed. I saw the red around her eyes.

"Marmie," she began, "Paul's too good for me." I had to shake my head at that, but she continued, "He won't ever take off his clothes or unzip his pants." The tears began to flow. "Is something the matter with me?"

I pulled her close. "No. No. No."

"I hate the girls at school making fun of my shape, and the boys leering at me."

I hugged Ruthie, lifted her head, and wiped the tears under her eyes. "We can put a stop to that." She listened as I explained how I had to run our Empire up north. "Davey's going to the Leelanau School, and Angel and her mom are going to spend a lot of time at our cottage. Do you want to join us?"

"What about Dad?"

"We can visit here, and he can take long weekends to join us up north, too."

"Won't he get lonely?"

I didn't say anything.

Ruth nodded. She knew about Pip and Mirja. "What about my swimming?" was all she asked.

"Let's build a glasshouse and pool at the Homestead." I paused.

"I'll ask Dad if it's okay." Oh, how I loved our girl.

ᔓ

Wystan stopped by after lunch later in the week with his swim trunks. The bright sun beat down on the glasshouse, and we lazed in the warm water. "Sometimes I wish I were square," he said as we climbed out and toweled off. When I asked if that was a compliment, he said, "Yes, but, hmmm, well, also a lament, I suppose." He pulled two folded pages from the inside pocket of his jacket on the chaise.

"CK's agreed to join me in California on holiday." He unfolded the two pages and handed them to me. "I'm going to offer to enroll him in school and to live with me."

His scribbles hard to decipher, it took me several minutes before I got the drift, and another 10 before I could piece together the details. In the form of a letter, it was a "Christmas Poem" for Chester Kallman.

"You don't think this is too, well, graphic?"

"Isn't that the point, *Deah*?"

When I couldn't help chuckling, he added, "Angelyn's found a cozier brick house on the other side of Burns Park, and I want to have you and Ruthie over for dinner when we get back for second semester."

"Sorry, Wystan, but I've got to move up north to run the family business."

"Hmmm..." The corners of his mouth began to turn up. "Is Ruthie going with you?"

I nodded.

"Pip, too?"

I shook my head.

"Will he mind terribly if I bring CK and his younger beaus to your Garden of Eden on bright days and share the pool?"

"That's not a good idea if you want to continue teaching here."

"I can't take being celibate any longer."

I shared the feeling but didn't want to admit it. "I've got a different Christmas present for you." I went into my study and added five $100 bills to the envelope with copies of my poems. I wrote "To Wystan" on the front. I walked back and found Wystan at the kitchen table, revising his poem. I stuffed my envelope inside the pocket of his coat and said, "Several of my new poems for you."

He looked up as he scribbled furiously on his rewrite. After a few minutes, he picked up his drafts and stuffed them inside his coat pocket with my envelope. "Unless Mr. Kallman has other ideas,"

Wystan said with a grin, "I look forward to hearing your voice." He paused. "Um, what if your poems will do better than mine in seducing him?"

I had to laugh, but I couldn't resist asking, "Do you think your sexual preference goes against your Christian faith?"

"Ever since the first apple, don't you think we've all been tempted?" When I had to nod, he added, "Not even in Ann Arbor can I do better than St. Augustine's prayer, 'Make me chaste, dear Lord, but not yet.'"

As he rose to say goodbye, I knew how that dear man attracted so many of us older women as his patrons along his different way. I kissed him, and his lips were soft and sweet. "As far as I'm concerned, Wystan Hugh Auden, you are wasted on men."

ꕥ

Two days later I reread Frost's letter with concern. Over the past two years, he'd shared brief notes describing his moves to live near Kay in Cambridge and Ripton and about the Morrisons traveling with him on winter trips to Florida. The anguished letter he had written after his son, Carol, committed suicide last fall was full of regret; Robbie said he'd always taken the wrong way with his boy and failed him. Only Wally Stegner, whose father had also shot himself in the head with a gun the year before, could console Frost enough so Kay could get him to bury his troubles in his work. Frost's new letter used his Harvard College address to encourage a private reply:

> *Belle, it's been a cruel fall. I finally buried the urns with Carol's and Elinor's ashes in the Old Bennington Congregational cemetery. Damn Holt's going light on my new book, and who will read poetry in the middle of a World War, anyway? More and more Kay treats me as a doddering old fool: no, No, NO! She caught me rereading one of your poems in bed last week. She burned it right in front of my face. So I fired her, and now she*

refuses to come back. I don't know how much longer I can go on alone.
As ever, Robbie

P.S. I'm sorry I didn't comment before on your good poems, but I enclose two of mine for you, one more than 20 years old, one new, both to go in the opening "One or Two" section of A Witness Tree.

The old poem proceeded "along a darkened corridor of woe" to a "crypt [with] stony pavement in a slime of mold," where the narrator says, "I will throw me down…and spread out in the figure of a cross." Yet in this prayer's march to death, whether by suicide or not, it ended with a plea: for someone to tell him if religion's "not to be my fate, before too late." Thankfully, his second poem proved Frost was no more ready for his last go down now than 20 years before. He returned to the Garden where the birds add "an oversound" to Eve's "daylong voice." Frost's sonnet concluded, "Never again would the birds' song be the same and to do that to birds was why she came."

My Dear Robbie,
Frost Barks again? Listen to your Belle: Don't blame Mrs. Morrison for wanting to keep you all to herself. To help you, I enclose a poem I wrote long ago, "Crystal Moment." It's about the pull I felt knowing David Ahgosa could not take me as his mate, but it should help you convince her she shouldn't fear you straying with me. At the same time, offer Mrs. Morrison a sweeter Frost-Bite confection: if you dedicate your new book to Kay for her part in it, your Silken Tent will sing to her, too.

If you also burn your puling old prayer, then you and your lady-friend manager will also celebrate your first joint effort as a best-seller and Pulitzer prize-winner. Your "overtone" continues as eternal as that of your Eve bird: Never again will poets' song be the same, and to do that is why you came.

Another challenge may also help. Auden's teaching here and composing another of his verse plays, this one about Christ. Given the dialogues you've crafted so well before, I ask again why not dabble in drama? Not sure anyone will ever rival Shakespeare, but you'll drive your critics mad displaying your mastery of yet another form. As ever, Belle

P.S. I include a new poem. I suggest you burn it and this letter, at least if you want Kay to continue as your minder-in-chief for the duration.

Choices

Is your love
like a golden gift
waiting at my rainbow's end
to mend my tattered clothes
and cobble my worn down sole?

Yet here I sit
under azure skies
beside a field of daffodils.

With gold I could
wear diamonds
and wrap myself in sable
travel to your noble estate
sip champagne from a crystal glass!

Yet here I sit
beneath a maple tree, listening
to the hum of honeybees.

Not sure I ever had any such choices, not with Rabbie, David, or Kurt, not with Robbie, Teddy, or Wystan, but the prospect of listening to the hum of my Leelanau home with Ruthie did raise my spirits.

The next morning before Ruthie and I headed up north, Pip pulled me into the first-floor study. He was terribly sorry to see us go. I said I'd miss him too but was glad he agreed we should keep Ruth separate from Paul.

His blue-gray eyes lit into me with surprise, as if I were one of the alien voices he hoped to find in space. "No, it's all the other boys trying to take advantage of Ruthie and the girls' taunting her in school," he exclaimed. "Half-brother or not, Paul's the only one who treats her with respect and is a true friend." He paused and placed his big, bony hands on my shoulders. "I appreciate the sacrifice you're making, running the business and helping Ruthie get through this rough patch." His long face looked gaunter than ever. A film formed over his eyes. He pulled me close. "Marmie, you and Ruthie better get going, or I'll quit the lab and come with you."

I didn't want to let go of my boy either. To hell with this damn war.

The next weekend Pip drove up north. I told him how Davey Ahgosa and Major and Helen Huey had already helped Ruthie make friends with the students and staff at the school and how our girl gave me the support I needed to work with the older men and younger women to help our Empire retool to serve the war effort. "Ruthie's already building the new glasshouse pool with the Hueys and Davey."

Ruth also gave her father the joy he needed so he could return renewed to his long days and nights inventing at his hush-hush War Lab. She consoled the Ahgosas when David couldn't get leave from the Munitions Building in D.C. to join us. She led us in joining hands and singing songs at the old Omena kirk. Maybe Ruthie was just putting on a happy face to buck the rest of us up. If so, she fooled me.

I began to count my blessings, until Sven Surtr showed up at our front door. He towered over me in a red-and-black plaid Elmer Fudd hat with ear flaps and matching hunting jacket. "I hear Missy Belle needs help at the plant." When I nodded, he continued, "I'll verk vor you but only till dune cars *varoom* in summer."

Pip appeared over my left shoulder. "Thanks, Sven. Your in-laws are welcome, too." The big Viking took off his cap, bared his fangs in what others might see as a smile, and shook Pip's hand. When he extended his arm to me, I took his hand but couldn't help scowling at my brother as the pain rose from the giant's grip. Was I really supposed to let this wild man work for me? When Pip nodded, I nodded at Surtr, and he released me.

Pip had also brought two postcards for me. Auden's, a picture of the Pacific surf lapping at the feet of bathers on the sandy shore, included a note:

> *Dear Belle, thank you. Before I wear out my welcome at Michigan with CK or get drafted, may we share your delight of life up north? Remember: every day, compose a lyric and share your voice with Ruthie. Cheers, Wystan.*

Frost's postcard of two skinny pine trees in South Miami offered a cheekier tone:

> *Belle, your old poem did placate Kay, and your new poem reminded me I need to keep on keeping on and I can do this only with her help, lest I get lost being alone again. The Frost Bite worked, and she agreed to accompany me this winter to our balmier Pencil Pines. Damn your challenges, though: A biblical Broadway play? But why shouldn't this aging bard one-up young Auden with operas about two of the best characters in the Old Testament, Job and Jonah! RF*

I couldn't help chuckling and wrote an ironic lament laced with not-so-sweet humor:

Who's the Luckiest Bitch

She was an old yellow lab going to seed,
mother to twelve litters, in heat for thirteen.
Never once had she just said no—
She watched her puppies come—and go.

She was a coifed French standard
mated with an aging King Charles breed.
When she learned the demands he made,
Her ardor for him began to fade.

She was a romantic Irish setter
living on an island in the North Sea.
Her dream mate barked on the distant shore.
Handsome, yes, but he couldn't swim that far.

I re-read my poem and laughed at the irony: despite becoming an Old Maid, I was luckier than all three. Even so, better not share my poem with Frost…Or Auden…Or Roethke. I tucked it into my most recent packet of poems in Mama's chest in the attic.

Spring 1943: Glen Arbor and Ann Arbor

Nym sat behind his desk and tapped his ruler on his palm. He looked more florid; red splotches now spread all over his fat face. He sneered over his half-glasses and down his bulbous red nose. "I proved your three Creative Fellows frauds: The first, a lecherous old proselytizer of doggerel who's reduced to scolding us academics who see through his mask... The second, a maniac upstart who fell to drink, debauch, and despair because he couldn't cut it in my classes... The third, a queer coward whose juvenile satires and turgid poems fail on this side of the pond."

Strait's whispering innuendos about Auden in the fall of 1941 had only set the stage for his campaign the next spring to drive the English expat out. Nym broadcast stories of Chester Kallman diddling his college mates during Wystan's notorious "at-homes." In triumph Ned pounded his ruler on the desk.

I reached across, grabbed his straightedge, and smacked his hand. He cowered in his chair. I felt like bending him over and paddling his big butt. I'd come to his office to see if I could persuade him to hold his tongue so Louise Bogan could serve as the next writer-in-residence.

As I rose to leave, he sneered, "Your money no longer carries any weight here."

He stood and hit his open palm with his fist. "Miss Bogan won't sully Angell Hall as the next Frost Fellow, either." As I opened the door, he yelled, "I gave you your chance, but you thought you were too good for me and you failed here all on your own. Even in wartime, there's no room for women on this faculty."

I turned back, pushed Strait down on his desk, and spanked his butt. When he cried out, I hit him again. When he moaned, I raised my hand to hit him harder, until I realized he had said "more."

My eyes flew open, but the floaters firing in my retina blinded me. My palms were clammy, my heart raced, and my nightgown was drenched in sweat. For only the second time since I retreated up north after thrashing Strait in his office in Angell Hall last fall had this nightmare struck me down. Thankfully, my bit for the War didn't leave me much time to fall into such a dark pit.

I breathed deeply to get a grip and stumbled from my bed into my attic sanctuary. I pulled my songbook from Mama's trunk and focused on my most recent:

Blue Spruce

Her arms encased in puffy white
as if she might attend a prom,
but she is rooted upon the hill—
can only sway to nature's song.

When the wind begins to blow,
her fluff as soft as eider down
will swirl on winter's icy breath
and waltz across a sweep of lawn.

I will watch from my cozy perch
beside this window laced with frost,
remembering dances long ago,
our bodies gliding across the floor.

The cold, late March night had combined with the lake-effect snow to dust the spruce outside my attic window with a fresh layer of fluffy white. Resonating with the echoes from my poem, this scene led me to reflect on my times dancing with Rabbie, David, and, yes, even my Teddy Bear Roethke so long ago. While I hoped my lyric danced as nimbly, I knew my "cozy perch" here continued more as a lonely portal: already 43, the prospects for a new love were unlikely; for any kind of marriage, a much longer shot; for bearing a child, nil.

Then it finally hit me: Yes, Nym might claim to be Strait, but he was a pervert. His exultation dominating me in his office paled in comparison to his cries for more when I hit him. Rather than forget that dark scene, I'd remember it for the time when exposing him would silence him, once and for all, even if it also did me in.

ᔕ

Belle Cottage did ring with life again: the younger voices of Ruthie, Davey, and Angel and the nurturing tones of Spring Blossom, often joined by Major and Helen Huey, and even Pip and David Ahgosa when they escaped their war duties to join us. The Empire plant hummed along, with more than 700 workers—75 percent women, the rest, like Sven, too old to go to war—producing more camp gear and gas stoves for the military effort abroad and gas dryers and furnaces for the new barracks, VA hospitals, ports, ships, and factories at home. Thanks to Major and Helen Huey stepping up on the unexpected death too young of Skipper Beals, the Leelanau Schools and Camps also survived. Helen, teaching Latin and composition, became Ruthie's favorite teacher. The Grand Traverse Ojibwe Enterprises boomed to meet the rising demand from the war and the expanding economy at home.

On the eastern front, the Soviets turned the Axis back at Stalingrad. In North Africa the Allies routed the Germans. In the Pacific the U.S. forces halted the Japanese advance and waged a sweeping counteroffensive. When, where, and how Allied forces would invade Western

Europe to join the Soviets in squeezing Hitler was all the talk. Pip, with his counterparts at MIT, Stanford and Bell Labs, invented smaller and smaller radar and evasive devices for more—and more lethal—ships, planes, and even tanks and artillery to find, foil, and fight the enemy. David helped supply our massive deployments. Kurt and Lazard helped finance the War, and once again I tipped my cap to dear Miss Schultz's bet on the U.S. winning by buying more War Bonds.

Even with our successes, though, we acknowledged our failures: Five years before, Auden had foreseen the evil of Dachau, and although Kurt's efforts to evacuate Jews from Europe helped save thousands, how many millions more fell in Hitler's concentration camps?

At home we had our own stench. Pip's mentor Charles Drew protested the prohibition of Negroes from giving blood for his plasma bank. The Armed Forces relented but only to the extent of segregating blood from blacks and whites. His proof that blood knew no skin color having failed to trump the Jim Crow brass, Drew returned to teach at Howard and practice at Freedman's Hospital. War is hell, but so is racial caste. Pip vowed to make it right for his friend, somehow, sometime.

Maybe Auden's protégé, Robert Hayden, had been right: his "Black Spear" poems that won the Major Hopwood prize in 1942 used historical characters and different narrative voices, perspectives, and dialects to reveal how race divided our country. Fighting a World War for freedom and democracy by relegating Negro servicemen to separate ranks and unequal service did offer another example of our American dilemma. Then again, despite Nym's continued race-baiting, Rabbie helped Mr. Hayden continue writing poetry so he could complete his M.A. even after Strait drummed Auden out of Michigan. Rabbie hired Hayden as a teaching assistant for the first-year writing class and helped the young poet find a job in the library so he could support his wife at home with their baby. Together, they also persuaded Wayne State University to count some of his graduate classes toward the final requirement for his undergraduate degree.

Mirja and Angelyn Stevens embraced Mrs. Hayden and the lovely Maia. Odd how individuals often do better one by one in bridging differences than when organized into groups, whether hidebound faculty into departments or racist Aryans into conquest.

Ruthie and Angel shared a bedroom and regularly begged to listen to my poems or those that Auden, Roethke, and Frost sent. Ruthie and Davey became best pals, with Ruthie beating him as badly as she did me swimming all distances in the pool, but he outraced her skating on the frozen ponds and hiking up the west face of Sleeping Bear Dunes. They both thrived in the Leelanau School, and our little albino goddess, Angel, was the Ogichidaakwe for telling Ojibwe legends. She also led the student watch to protect the Sleeping Mama Bear and her dunes. Davey led the school science club in using the Peebles' observatory telescope to split the stars and in monitoring the buzz still recorded on Pip's old radio scoop on Empire Bluff. On Sundays we worshipped in the old kirk in Omena, the Ojibwe now sharing the pews and standing room with the rest of us.

ഗ

Suddenly, a wasp flitted through the attic. When it flew near my head, I shook my fist at it, but the wasp only buzzed me more. So I swatted at it but raised only a cloud of dust, glowing in the tunnel of light piercing the window. I thought back to Mama's death, not that much older than me when she waved farewell, and felt a shiver. I sang my three goodbye songs to her, but the pressure I felt on my chest only increased until a tremor of death terror overwhelmed me. I feared the wasp might be my little Grim Reaper, come to deliver the message if not the execution. I swung a broom with all my might and cleaved that poor insect in two. I sang:

> A pesky wasp flies round my room
> With plans to build its nest—
> "Not here," I say—and swing my broom—

I do not fear the sting of Death
As round the room it flies—
For I have Dreams—and Life to test.

Maybe no more lovers for me, but still dreams for my Pip and Ruthie; the Ahgosas; our delight of life, Leelanau; yes, for Paul and Mirja; maybe even for Rabbie, if not also Robbie, Teddy, and Wystan.

Dear Lord, thank you for giving me this time, and I pray you won't have to take me for a while: I still have so much more to live for. Maybe that's what makes the thought of dying so frightening—the fear I'll lose all this, forevermore.

The next Sunday morning broke bright, clear, and warm. The south wind shepherded us to the Omena Kirk and back to the Homestead for early Sunday dinner. After the long winter, the snowpack was deep, but the freshening warmth cut through the crust all afternoon. No need for caps, gloves, or coats, we donned long slacks and snowshoes and climbed in our shirtsleeves to the top of the ridge. Davey took the lead, but Ruthie followed close behind. Angel flew up the steep hill faster than I could, so Spring Blossom kept me company on our climb to the top of the ridge. Was it already 15 years since David Ahgosa, Dr. MacKenzie, and I plotted the golf course, more years than that since Frost and I stood two by two with buck and doe here?

At the clubhouse Davey, Ruthie, and Angel donned skis and carved deep furrows in the corn snow. They flashed down the slopes and across the valleys, skated to the rope tow, rose to the top, and skied down again. Spring and I sat on the west deck. I closed my eyes and heard the dripping of the snowmelt from the roof and the babbling of the rivulets below as they began to gather for their race down the hill. I must have dozed off because I heard a cascade of water. As my body warmed in the afternoon sun, I also dreamed I felt the surge of the first crocus thrusting through the snow and exploding its petals in a rush of ripe color. Could the huff of the buck and doe be far behind?

"You all right, Belle?" Spring asked.

I opened my eyes and looked north across the bay, still packed with white ice, to the darker waters of the now-open Manitou passage and then shifted my gaze west to the sandier dunes of Sleeping Bear, rising as they always did, so pure and majestic, pointing the way for the spring sun to set. "I'm too young for a hot flash," I replied. "Maybe, it's my body wishing I'm not too old to find a new lover."

Spring smiled. "Thanks for not stealing your old one from me."

I looked at her, so dark, still so lithe and beautiful, her long hair braided in two plaits dangling over her broad shoulders to her narrow waist. "When David escapes from D.C., he can't keep his eyes and hands off you."

Spring nodded but continued, "I'm grateful you left him to me."

"That myth won't fly. He chose only you."

"When the war ends, you can take your pick of the other returning veterans."

"Spring, you fixing me up with a younger man?"

"You should see yourself in that swimsuit, red tresses flying, eyes blazing, high cheeks flush."

I had lost 15 pounds trying to keep up with Ruthie in the pool and working so hard. When I heard the children putting their skis back in the rack, I almost chuckled.

That evening I retreated to the attic and sang my love lament anew:

Cascade

Spring melts winter away
and icy water swirls
down the mountainside—
the raging river rumbles
louder than thunder
outside my open window

keeping me awake
tumbling my thoughts
like broken branches
over boulders white with froth,
some wedging themselves
among gray rocks of memory,
others racing by—
just beyond my grasp.

I looked out the window, but all I saw was my reflection in the glass. Not a traditional beauty, with my unruly red hair and plain face, but still a good smile and, for a pale child of Scotland, clear skin and good color in my cheeks. I cradled my arms under my breasts, hugged myself, closed my eyes, and cried:

You bring me new spring
each time—
I feel the purple crocus
break through the winter's crust,
the tulip rise and bloom—
I open myself
to welcome your tongue.

Who was I kidding?

A Bee's sting festers
in my Heart filled with longing—
Martyr of loves lost!

Ha: all just imagined tingles, all gone awry. I slammed my notebook into Mama's chest, locked it tight, but didn't throw the key away. Even an Old Maid can still dream.

ᔓ

The next Friday we had our first accident in Empire. The line snapped on a crane lifting our furnaces onto a freighter. The cords holding one furnace onto a pallet also broke. Five hundred pounds of steel slid off and pinned one of our women. I heard her scream, looked out the back window, and saw a tall shadow flash across the pier. Beyond human force, the Dark Giant forced a crowbar under the furnace and lifted it up. Three other women dragged their compatriot out. Yes, the shattering of her leg was a terrible price, but Sven Surtr saved her life and limb.

I treated him to a beer at Art's Tavern in Glen Arbor to say thank you, but he declined the role of hero: "Ve may need you to keep most of our Day clan verking this summer iv ve're going to keep Glen Haven and our dune rides alive for the tourist boom ven ve vinally vin the var." How I could I refuse?

Sunday afternoon Ruthie and Davey stole me away to go fly-fishing. The Crystal River rushed in full-throat from the snowmelt. As we cast, our lines glistened and made a bright web across the water. First Davey and then Ruthie brought in a coaster brook trout, but she refused to stuff hers next to his in the creel I carried. She said hers wasn't near full-grown and deserved the chance to swim free. After she released the brookie, a big bald eagle swooped down, grasped the unsuspecting trout in its talons, and flew off.

Davey gave Ruthie his I-told-you-so look, but she argued all the more fiercely for releasing younger fish so they could add to the future bounty. Maybe on this spring day, with the beauty of stream, air, light, sound, fish, and bird, we should just give thanks for enjoying the fishing their fathers knew a generation before. No, Ruthie said, we all need to learn to be stewards of stream, shore, fish, and fowl. Davey caught and released another big brookie. We watched as another eagle circled overhead and attacked, but this trout dived deeper, to swim in the Great Lake.

That night after dinner I sat on Mama's chest and composed another song:

Fishing Lesson

They carried their gear to the stream:
rods, reels, waders—and a woven creel
just in case the fish were biting.

Her father looked at the sun
and figured by the time it was three
just maybe there would be bugs.

It was rocky along the shoreline
and water bubbled by at a steady pace,
then flattened where it was deeper.

She waded into the stream with her father
and cast her line the way he taught her,
playing it with the current, reeling it slowly in.

She felt the sun warm on her back
and then she saw a shadow rise
just the way her father said.

She cast again toward the current
and soon felt a tug. She tugged back
kept her pole up, and reeled.

They admired her twelve-inch brookie,
its silver scales, golden spots, and rosy belly
illumined by the afternoon sun.

Her fish lay helpless secured in a net,
flopping every now and then.
Her father opened the woven creel,

but after she removed the hook,
she tossed her brookie into the stream
and watched it dart in a silver flash

beneath the surface, swimming free.

ꝏ

In May we gathered front-row-center in the Rackham Amphitheater. Mirja Fitzpatrick sat on my right with Angelyn Stevens, Stella Brunt, and Dorothy Donne. Roy Cowden, Rabbie, and I had overcome Nym's vicious rants against Louise Bogan so she could deliver the first Hopwood Lecture by a woman since 1934. Theodore Roethke, home for a visit from his first year teaching at Bennington, sat on my other side. Teddy whispered he'd not won a Hopwood only because he graduated too early.

Rabbie, sitting on the other side of Ted, said, "Didn't matter." He ignored Roethke's shush. "Penn State hired him because they thought he *did* win a Hopwood."

After Cowden awarded the last prize, he introduced Miss Bogan as "the most influential American poetry critic for her long-running reviews for the *New Yorker*." He added she was also quite a poet, as attested by raves from the likes of Robert Frost. "Another former Creative Fellow and Hopwood Judge, Wystan Auden, captured her current poetic spirit—'to go on rather than under, to live dangerously or not at all.'"

Teddy led us in rising to greet Miss Bogan with applause. A tall woman dressed in a tweed suit coat and a skirt flowing to her calves, her dark hair pulled back in a soft chignon, her eyes gray-green and changing as the sea. Two years older than I, she fit much more comfortably in her solid frame. She must have a secret lover, I thought. She surveyed the amphitheater, all seats filled, with more students, mostly women, standing three deep in the back, as if she owned us.

Louise Bogan began in a soft but clear voice. Unlike most prior Hopwood Lectures, she didn't read a typed essay but instead talked with us. For 20 minutes she surveyed how the best poetry reconnected art with ordinary speech, as Rabbie Burns did with the folk ballads of Scotland and Yeats did with the Irish peasant stories. America was blessed with many more of these folk traditions, whether hard-scrabble tunes from the hollows and the plains, Indian lore, spirituals rising from chains, jazz, or blues. In contrast, bad poetry was too tame, too middling in tone, no wildness, no passion.

"As young poets," she concluded, "learn your own walk on the waves."

She bowed her head, and we rose as one, women and men, and cheered her inspiration. Oh, how I wanted to return up north to my attic, open my songbook, and compose poems in my voice, as Emily Dickinson had done for so many years in her Homestead, but first I had to complete my mission here for the University.

At the party for Miss Bogan at Hill House, I pulled Roy Cowden aside in the east garden. "When's the English Department going to hire more women?"

He explained how Rabbie and he had overcome the objections of Strait and all his hidebound Nyms to no avail: "The Chairman made three offers: Stella Brunt and Mrs. Donne begged off for personal reasons, and you headed up north to run your family Empire after too few semesters." When I countered that Dorothy might now be a better long-term prospect because her husband had been named to head the University Press, Roy asked me to help persuade her. When I asked about Bogan, Cowden replied, "You know Strait and his crowd will try to blackball her, but I'll talk to the Chair."

Thank the Lord, they didn't know about Roethke's sex jousts with her, but I couldn't resist asking, "Any chance he'll agree to bring Teddy back?"

"Teaching the new course at Bennington offers the only hope for repairing Ted's name here after all he's done to fuel Nym's charges."

Unless Teddy found an appealing woman on the faculty or staff there, he'd more likely attract one too many young women students and ruin his last chance.

I excused myself and found Mrs. Donne in the side parlor. "Unless one of us takes a real shot at it, there won't ever be a woman professor in the English Department."

"Helping Rabbie with his first-year writing course was great, but with raising three little ones at home, I didn't have the time to review 180 papers and hold 60 student conferences a week."

I shifted gears and asked what she thought of Miss Bogan's talk.

"After I put the kids to bed, I try to compose my own walk on the waves. Something comes into my head that starts vibrations, and I can't get it out until I write it in a poem."

I always knew Dorothy was a poet at heart. "What if the Chairman offers you a tenure-track position in poetry and essay instead?" She lit up with delight at first but then wondered aloud how to care for her children.

I returned to look for our guest of honor, but Angelyn Stevens intercepted me in the front hall. She handed me a copy of an Auden poem, "*Mundus et Infans*," dedicated to "Albert and Angelyn Stevens" and their new son they'd named in the poet's honor.

"Are your baby's seasons 'Dry' and 'Wet' as Wystan says?" I asked.

Angelyn laughed with me and then confided how Auden had "healed" her of terrible allergies by force of his "charismatic vibrations" so that she regained her "zest for life." While I was thinking how much I missed such "zest" in my life, she added, "I'll let you know the date when the godfather can join us for the Christening."

Angelyn was a fixture in the Philosophy Department as an

assistant with her Master's degree, and I asked whether she'd ever thought about doing a dissertation on Auden and joining the faculty.

A pained expression crossed her face. "Not enough time with my new boy."

I made my way to the front parlor and found Roethke practicing his Foxtrot on Louise, but Mirja intercepted me. She asked if I'd join her to help fund a war chest to defray the costs of child care for faculty families. She added that the Dow heir who founded the Children's Play School would join the campaign. "Including our Frost pledge," Mirja said, "the four chairs for women in Literature, Science, and the Arts still go unfilled." Outside Nursing School she noted there were only three women professors on campus: one in Psych, another at the Medical School and the third at the B-School. "Pip's pal, Doc Losh in Astronomy, is the only other woman who has a shot at tenure."

When I suggested Michigan would need many more professors when the war ended to serve all the returning vets, Mirja warned the University might reduce the number of coeds instead.

Before I could reply, Teddy rushed by us, across the hall, and into the sitting room and engaged Rabbie in animated discussion. "What are those two scheming?" I asked.

Mirja explained how Rabbie was joining Roethke for the summer term at Bennington, and they planned to make their first-year writing and poetry classes even better. When I asked if she was going, she shook her head.

"Staying to play with Pip?"

"Paul thinks he's finally going to beat your brother on the golf course."

"You didn't tell your son yet?"

She pulled me upstairs to her sewing room. "I did tell Rabbie, though."

"Didn't kill him," I noted sarcastically.

Mirja replied, "No, it's liberated him."

I didn't want to hear her complain about any sauce for her gander, so I only shook my head.

"We agreed not to tell Paul as long as things don't heat up again with Ruthie."

"Mirja, think we can risk you and Paul joining Pip for a vacation up north, too?"

"You couldn't keep us away," she said and hugged me close.

We strode down the stairs, and Teddy greeted me with a glass of rum punch. One glass followed another as he regaled me with stories about his teaching during the spring term at Bennington. The gist: he'd thrown himself into his new "Verse Form" course. "Thank God no one saw me shooting up my breakfast in the woods before class."

"Found anyone to replace Kitty to stoke your fire yet?"

"I'm only on leave from Penn State," he replied but lowered his sad eyes and conceded that Bennington's Dean had taken him in.

"Stick to her, and Cowden says you've still got a shot back here."

"What makes you think I want to leave my Vermont idyll to battle Strait again?"

"To be closer to your Mom and Sis, and your Big Mama." When he kissed me on the lips, I pushed away and asked, "What do you think Frost would say if I suggested Rabbie as his biographer?" Teddy chortled. "You don't think Rabbie could do it?"

"Frost already signed up a younger man, but rumors suggest there was some tiff between Frost and Mrs. Morrison before the lothario shipped off into the Navy."

I had to smile at that. "Take care of Rabbie this summer, will you?"

"I thought you wanted me to stick with the Dean of the College." When I only shook my head at the thought of these two aging bulls let loose among the college girls, he pulled out two pieces of paper with his green hen-scratching. "If you can type these tonight, I'll stop by in the morning to pick them up."

"Ted, do you have better plans after dinner?"

He handed me the two pages. "I'm finally writing the poems about growing up in the family greenhouse."

He left and joined our guest of honor, his sage and former lover. Maybe I was hurt Teddy no longer wanted to dance this Bigger Mama off my feet again. Rabbie approached and asked if I was okay. I only raised Teddy's two poems and said, "You open to a new writing project, too?"

The Irish twinkle in his eye now matched his big smile: "Give me your best shot."

I poured us each a Jameson. "A biography of the literary life of a great poet."

"You have to publish your poems first," he replied.

I ignored his riposte. "Roethke, Auden, or Frost: Take your pick."

Ruth, Paul, and Pip burst through the door from the kitchen. Rabbie turned, picked up Ruthie, twirled her about, and set her down. "Lass," he said, "you're not a tad taller, but you've grown into a bloomin' woman." I had to admit she looked rather fetching. Unfortunately, Paul's gaze suggested he shared this view, but I heard Rabbie ask, "Got any short stories or essays for your old tutor?"

Ruthie smiled, glanced up to me, and said, "No, but I've got lots of new poems."

I gave Paul a hug and realized he'd grown taller than me but lean and lanky as Pip. Only his green eyes, dark complexion, and good hearing now belied their likeness. "I see you didn't fall to Dr. MacKenzie's lake, but did you beat your coach?"

"Pip had to birdie the last hole to beat me," Paul said. When Ruthie exclaimed she'd won a skin, too, the look they shared shot a hole in our plan to keep them apart.

ග

The last week in May, I sat in a hollow on the beach by Sleeping Bear Bay. Braced by the late spring breeze off the water and wrapped in an old Ojibwe blanket, I reread my treasures from Roethke and Frost. I pulled out a notepad and wrote Teddy:

Plan on a visit to Ann Arbor in September: Auden's coming for the Christening of his namesake, Wystan Auden Stevens. Sorry Louise won't be joining us as a Frost Fellow, because Strait dug up more dirt and blackballed her, too. If this War ever ends, I'm going to challenge that snot to a duel and kill him.

In the meantime I want you to know: you've really hit it with your greenhouse poems. The lost son can now explore and express untold wonders.

Hope you and Dean Garrett still play and Rabbie doesn't lead you astray: I do want you to join me back at Michigan before I grow gray. Why don't you sew up Rabbie as your biographer before Auden or Frost does? You know your greenhouse poems will earn a Pulitzer, and there's no one better to tell your story.

I opened Frost's *A Witness Tree* to page 13 and the lead poem of the opening section "One or Two." Under "The Silken Tent" he'd printed in his stubby hand,

TO BELLE, FOR YOUR PART IN THIS, WHETHER ELEGY TO A MOTHER LONG SINCE LOST, LOVE-SONG, THANKS TO A BELOVED WIFE, OR PERFECT SONNET TO BE READ AND HEARD FOR ITSELF, I ONLY HOPE THIS IS ANOTHER GOOD POEM THAT YOU WILL FIND HARD TO GET RID OF LONG AFTER I AM GONE, ROBBIE

I turned next to page 23. Under "The Most of It," he'd written,

TO PIP AND BELLE, FOR YOUR PARTS IN THIS: PIP, MAY YOU YET FIND THE DISTANT VOICES TO PROVE THAT WHAT WE SENSE HERE ON EARTH IS NOT ALL; BELLE, MAY YOU YET SHARE YOUR POEMS

SO THAT OTHERS IN THIS WORLD CAN HEAR YOUR VOICE IF THAT IS ALL. Frost

In 20 lines "The Most of It" told of a lone seeker trying to wake an answering voice but hearing only "mocking echoes of his own… Unless it was the embodiment that crashed in the cliff's talus on the other side," swam across the lake, stumbled through the rocks, and forced the underbrush. "Instead of proving human," this great buck, well, "that was all." Of course, Frost's poem resonated so it gave hope that was NOT all!

Thirty-some pages later, I found a curious note:

Dear Belle, I find I'm spending more time walking my Vermont fields and basking in the Florida warmth. After A Witness Tree, another Pulitzer thanks to Louis' inside suasion, and a bigger score in sales, my lover's quarrel with the world winds toward a truce. I even support FDR and worry less about filling Kay's cup.

All that's missing is a man—to mind my farms here and to walk and talk with me, day and night. I haven't found anyone since Van Dore decamped again. My eighth decade just around the corner, I decided to stick with Thompson as my biographer but with any publication delayed until I'm gone. If he makes it back from the Navy, don't give him or Kay more cause for catfights.

Give my best to Ruthie and Pip. RF

I doubted Frost's cantankerous moods would permit this equanimity to last. I also worried my darker spells would soon bury me again.

Sand pricked my face. When I put up my hands to protest, a rising storm pelted me with cold spears of rain. I gathered my belongings and raced to the shelter of my office. After drying off, I let down my guard long enough to compose:

Lost

Before the storm
Lake Michigan waves
smash the duney shore
a cold wind whistles
its woeful tune.

I huddle against driftwood,
wrapped in an old red blanket
tight as a tourniquet,
my face turned west
toward the roily sky.

Rain pelts my cheeks
mixing with tears
of raging sorrow—
My heart flows out
with every wave.

I folded my poem, took it to Mama's trousseau and wrote Frost:

Dear Robbie,
Thank you for A Witness Tree with your notes, but more years can't excuse your mellowing. Good Heavens, not only settling into your lot with Mrs. Morrison but also writing political poems as if you were campaigning for favor with FDR. Mr. MacLeish better watch out, or the President will ask you to read "The Gift Outright" at his Fourth Inauguration. What would The Moodie Forester say to that! The labors of love in the first 12 songs, though, should earn you every award here and, at too long last, abroad.

I didn't know whether Frost's discussion of young Thompson as his biographer offered an opening to suggest Rabbie as an alternative. So I adopted a different tone:

Rabbie's joining Teddy, teaching this summer at Bennington. You may want to drop by to see their composition and verse-form courses engaging students in writing. You may also want to pull Rabbie aside to explore whether you can persuade him to write your biography rather than Teddy's. Rest assured my lips, and correspondence concerning you, will be sealed shut to any Frosty biographer.

I enclose several poems I composed this spring.

As ever, your other Belle

That left Frost's odd reaching out to me about finding a man to help him in Vermont. He knew Wade Van Dore so much better than I did, but I couldn't imagine anyone else.

P.S. I hear Van Dore may be at loose ends. His marriage to Edrie over, he's seeing a former sweetheart in Detroit. Not sure whether a package deal is one triangle more than you can take or whether you want to compete for Wade alone. After my more exhausting days running Empire, this Old Maid also pines for a companion, albeit for wilder nights: any suggestions?

Summer 1943: Glen Arbor and Ann Arbor

We ate dinner in a semicircle around the east side of the campfire, our Peebles clan in the middle; the Ahgosas, including David home for a rare vacation, on our left; Mirja and Paul, joined by Trudy and Kurt visiting from New York, on our right. The corn, tomatoes, and lake perch and river trout roasted in husks by the hot coals never tasted sweeter. The sun, slowly setting, danced off the dark water in the Manitou passage, over the bright blue in the bay, and across the teal of the shallow inshore water. The evening breeze rustled through the pine, birch, beech, and maple, graced our ears with its familiar tune, and blessed our cheeks with the first chill that sneaks in early up north.

As soon as we finished savoring our late-summer feast, our chatter drowned out the hum of waves washing on the shore. I scooched close to Trudy and shouted in her ear, "You regret not trying the Aquacade and Hollywood with Johnny and Eleanor?"

Trudy shook her head with a big grin but asked, "Want to send Ruthie to Matt Mann's camp next summer so I can train her for the '48 Olympics?" When I shook my head with a bigger grin, Trudy yelled, "May be time to free her from your cocoon."

Kurt leaned in and hit me with another jab: "David says only an Act of Congress requiring reinstatement of veterans will unseat you as CEO when he comes back."

I only smiled at that. We'd need David's leadership, Pip's tinkering, and Kurt's financial skills to transform Empire into a competitive consumer company once the war ended. The sun began to sink into the distant horizon over Lake Michigan to the north of Sleeping Bear Point. The red orb bathed the sandy dune, the big bay below, and the wispy clouds above in scarlet, orange, and pink streaks. I looked around the faces of my family and friends and enjoyed their glow. Angel, now eight, flowed to the opposite side of the campfire and danced. Her white halo took on a crimson aura. When she removed her dark goggles, her pale eyes took us all in.

"Storytime," she sang, "adults, first; kids, last."

I joined Angel and pointed to the huge full moon rising in the east. I told how Pip always dreamed he'd search the heavens as a boy and built the observatory on the dune beside us and the radio scoop on Empire Bluff. Kurt recounted Trudy's crossing the English Channel, including acting out her refusing to be pulled out after battling the terrible tides. Not to let me be outdone, Pip rose and told how I swam through the frigid water after the seiche ripped the ice apart and swallowed up our mama, and David mimed how I struggled to match Trudy's epic crossing here on this bay, as the shifting summer storms blew me off course and I refused to quit. The children shouted for more, but I said, "No more about Marmie, thank you."

David silenced us all by telling the legend of Sleeping Bear. As the gloaming fell to dusk and the huge expanse of dunes behind him darkened, the Ojibwe sang, danced, and signed. When he finished, only the crackling of the embers in the campfire broke the hush. Spring Blossom rose and told how Davey and Paul had conquered the steep west front of Sleeping Bear Dunes and contrasted David and

Pip's rite of passage a generation earlier. Mirja showed us drawings, bright with charcoal and pastels on white paper. When she raised her sketches, we saw she'd captured the most striking image of each story.

Then the children began. Ruthie told how she swam with Trudy on several legs of the Great Lake–Erie Canal swim and rode in the ticker-tape parade down Broadway. When she finished by saying she'd been training all summer to join her Marmie and Trudy on another swim, tomorrow, to South Manitou and back, my heart fluttered, and the lump in my throat grew.

Paul and Davey acted the story of how David and Pip paired with Walter Hagen and Bobby Jones in the first match here. They closed by showing how they'd been practicing and looked forward to beating their elders tomorrow on the links. What was this, a conspiracy of youth to better their elders on the same haunts? When David and Pip rose and shook hands with their youthful counterparts to accept the challenge, I froze. Spring slid over and whispered she'd pilot the old Cadet to spot for Trudy, Ruthie, and me. Before I could protest, Mirja accepted on my behalf.

Angel capped the show. She danced, signed, pointed, and mimed the Legend of Leelanau and, before our eyes, became the lost daughter who fled the north shore of Lake Superior for this Delight of Life. The wind quieted, and the waves lapping on shore stopped to watch. Her limbs so agile and frame so light, she flew from the far side of Lake Superior, across the Upper Peninsula and Lake Michigan. When she glided across the campfire and landed, sitting cross-legged in front of us, we clapped.

Angel wasn't done. She spread her wings as if opening her stage for the next act, and the pulsing green of the Northern Lights unfolded. Her white hair flamed by the campfire behind, Angel stood as if in a tableaux, the flickering red and yellow flame and the pulsing green appearing to complete her show. No, she closed her arms over her head, and the night sky reappeared behind her: a meteor shower graced the inky black. Not a sound, not a peep, not the whistle of the wind, not the waves lapping on shore dared speak.

In the hush we gathered our waste and buried the last of the fire. Angel pulled me to the totem pole. I reached up and rubbed the stone for my Papa, polished white by so many hands rubbing it for luck over the years.

"Marmie, it's not your time yet."

After I tucked the two girls in bed, I stole away to Mama's chest in the attic to compose a new song, but my mind raced. I don't know why, but I tried to make Angel's dance fly across the Great Lake to a crescendo as loud as Emily Dickinson's "Wild Nights." The more I tried to sing so, the more I realized Angel's Fire came not from sound but light. I wrote in my journal:

Angel Fire

Around the campfire
Angel dances the tale of the Nibi
her golden hair a halo

stars spangle the night sky
and a huge harvest moon
rises over Pyramid Point

Angel sways in green glow
for overhead Northern Lights
pulse to and fro

a shower of meteors
adorns the indigo sky
with silver lace, mirrored

on the lake below.
We are held in Leelanau's spell
till the last ember glows

and a single shooting star
glides out to the horizon
fading into velvet night.

The next day Angel was there for me. While Spring Blossom piloted the vintage Cadet across the bay, Angel set off with Ruthie, Trudy, and me in the sporty, green Lincoln, top down, the rushing wind blowing a song through our hair. Mirja and Kurt, the referees for the golf challenge, waved to us from the deck of the clubhouse atop the ridge. Upon reaching Sleeping Bear Point, Angel helped us grease up. I worried this marathon crossing might prove too much for me but didn't want to share my doubt.

Spring brought the Cadet, luster deeper from all the years, close to shore. While Angel swam to the craft, Trudy directed Ruthie and me to stick together. I warmed up and began to feel the embrace of the water flowing under, over, and around me.

Five miles into our swim, the breeze stiffened and turned. The cold wind hit us head on. The big chop slapped me on the shoulders. I fell behind, lost touch with my mates, and began to panic. Angel, covered head-to-toe in a white robe with a hood, threw the rope ladder down and extended her hand. When I reached up, Trudy and Ruthie grabbed juice and bananas. I floated on my back in the lee of the boat, sheltered from the wind and chop, and they fed me. Trudy rubbed my arms and hands; Ruthie, my legs and feet. I began to warm again.

Ruthie and Trudy now swam in tandem in front of me, breaking through the wind and the rising waves, drafting me forward. An hour later, my stamina running out, I felt what must have been the sandy bottom of South Manitou but was too weak to stand. Ruthie and Trudy rose up under my shoulders, and we clambered ashore. After Spring threw an anchor over the side of the old Chris-Craft, our dark-goggled Angel appeared on the beach with more juice and bananas. I drank, ate, and warmed my body, the midday sun hot above and the sand warm below.

Sometime later, I woke, hearing Trudy say, "Time to go."

I tried to stand, but my legs wouldn't hold. I put one arm over Ruthie's shoulder and the other over Trudy's, and they dragged me into the water. When I thought to kick, my feet propelled me forward. When I thought to raise one arm and then the other, I stroked in time with every six slow beats of my feet. With the wind and waves at our back, we set out in a line, Ruthie or Trudy in front, and the other behind. The northwest wind pushed us on a course that, once again, would make Glen Arbor our landfall. More than two hours later, I swam easily, sure I would make it.

A pain shot through my left calf. I reached down but couldn't find any wound. As I clutched my leg, I didn't fathom why I couldn't breathe underwater. I began to open my mouth to scream for help, but a powerful body lifted me from below. I rode up on strong shoulders. When my face broke through the water, I gulped for air. Ruthie helped roll me onto my back. Trudy rubbed my calf, and Ruthie pushed my foot back toward my shin. Although the searing pain began to subside, the knot did not. I knew.

Spring brought the Cadet close. Angel pulled—and Trudy and Ruthie pushed—me up the ladder. Surprisingly, I wasn't ashamed I had to give up. Angel dried me off, bundled me, and pointed at our two swimmers. "We'll help them get to shore." One more rest for juice and bananas, and the ghostly remnants of the piers for the old dock at Glen Arbor began to rise in front of us. I peered forward, in search of the place where I'd lost and found Mama so many years before.

Suddenly, Ruthie's head popped up before my eyes. I threw off my blankets and dived into the water. It felt so cold, my whole body shivered. Or was it a tingle, so different from the first but more welcoming? We three, Ruthie on one side, Trudy on the other, swam slowly toward shore. I treaded water at the spot where the sturgeon pointed me before. We dived down and, although only the ripples of sand appeared below, the knowing squeeze of Ruthie's hand let me see again Mama saying farewell.

Oh, Mama, I still miss you so, but you'd be so proud of our boy Pip and our girl Ruthie!

Angel's goggled face appeared in front of us, her hair floating above her head in a golden spray. When she smiled and reached her hand out, Trudy made room, and we four rose to the surface together. We swam to shore four abreast and strode arm-in-arm onto the sandy beach to the cheers of the four golfers and their two referees.

ග

The next morning Major Huey stopped to see Pip and me. I sat behind my desk in Papa's study and directed the two Amherst grads to sit in the two easy chairs facing each other so my brother could read his mentee's lips. Major said he wanted to buy our interest in the inn, as well as the Homestead Golf and Outing Club—links, clubhouse, pool, forest and all—and to eliminate all the development restrictions we'd agreed to with Skipper Beals. He said he wanted to develop lots for homes hidden in the trees on the ridge, expand the clubhouse and inn, and build dozens of cabins close to shore.

Pip scowled, but I said, "You and Helen have done a terrific job managing the inn and the club, and we're grateful you helped Ruthie thrive."

Major nodded, smiled and relaxed in his chair. "Do you think we've been bad partners for you up to now?" I asked.

Major shook his head but more warily now.

"Major," Pip picked up, "we'll sign a long-term contract with you to manage our club, the resort, and the inn for a fair salary and half the profits." I added we'd also finance improvements to his school, camps, and the inn on good terms.

"Conditions?" Major asked.

I looked to Pip, and he nodded. "All the land-use restrictions we made with Skipper stand, including no new building on the ridge or between river and shore."

"Fair enough," Major replied, "for now." He told us his plans for expanding skiing and fishing. "Davey's a wonder on the slopes and in the streams. He makes the ski patrol motto 'Safety and Service' a big plus for our club."

Pip shared his long-term vision: develop the towns more densely; preserve the lakes, shores, dunes, ridges, forests, orchards, and meadows forever; and operate the Homestead Club, Inn, and Leelanau Schools and camps as premier destinations, year-round, for families to learn, to enjoy, and to treasure.

"Mr. Surtr will never agree to go along," Major said.

"I wish old D. H. were still kicking so we could work together to preserve our Sleeping Bear," I replied, but my brother said Sven and the rest of his Day clan did a good job helping at the plant and we should find a way to work with him. I had to concede the giant hadn't sabotaged our Empire.

Pip asked Major to have his campers watch like hawks to make sure Surtr didn't threaten our Sleeping Mama Bear.

After lunch I drove Ruthie, Davey, Paul, and Angel in the old green Zephyr, top down, to Empire, where David, Pip, and Kurt had been meeting with our plant manager. I stole David away for a walk. We got to talking so, we passed the Bar Lakes, up the steep hill, and through Major Huey's land with all the beech and maple, birch and new pine. We tiptoed atop the dunes to the cottonwood grove looking out to the Sleeping Bear pinnacle. The west wind continued to erode her west side, and hikers gouged deeper paths on the south and east sides. I told David about the talk with Major Huey.

"I hope you're not asking the fox to watch the chicken coop," he replied.

"Maybe Major should convert his wild campground here into a scenic drive, with hiking only on boardwalks over the dunes: Might kill off Sven's dune buggy rides."

Four hundred and fifty feet above the Great Lake, David sat down, cross-legged. "We're massing supplies and men to retake Europe, starting with Italy in a few weeks, France next spring."

I sat down on his lee side to avoid the freshening wind from the west.

David didn't flinch from the spray of sharp sand. "Is Paul going to volunteer?"

Stupid me, I hadn't even begun to worry about the boy who every day looked more and more the son of Pip he surely was. Paul was my kin, too, but what had I ever done for him, except to pry Ruthie away. Yet he was only 15 now—too young, I could hope, ever to fight in this war. "I don't know. What about Davey?"

"He's training for the mountain corps so he can take the fight to the Alps."

"When Davey comes back, do you want him to help you run our Empire?"

"That your way of saying you want me to come back as CEO?"

"No one else can lead us where we'll need to go after the war."

"Just needed to hear it from you, I guess." He dropped his head and added, "Davey wants to run the Ojibwe enterprises instead."

I had to laugh and teased, "Like mother, like son."

"Mind if I broach the idea with Pip of Ruth helping us at Empire?" When I said she was too young, he replied, "A year older than Davey."

"You think they might make a good pair?" I asked to cover my embarrassment at not encouraging Ruthie as a possible successor to run our Empire.

"I wouldn't object."

I wished he wouldn't have objected to me two decades before, but I only asked why he wasn't joining Casper Ance's petition to recognize the Leelanau bands.

"Once my federal service ends, I will join the fight for all our original peoples' rights." When I asked how much longer the war would last, he said, "We're all in Pip's debt on radar." He chuckled.

"When the navy nixed John Kraus's idea of wrapping every ship with copper, Pip got him cracking on better sonar, too."

"Both better than having Ojibwe scouts?" I asked.

"Still," David said, "two or three more years, unless we unleash the Bomb."

As the storm gathered offshore, we trudged back in silence. The sheets of rain rolled off Lake Michigan and pelted us by South Bar Lake. We ran and took shelter under the Empire dock, where several ships loaded up our finished goods. Within a few minutes, the clouds passed overhead, and we walked past our big plant to my car. Paul and Davey raced down the bluff, Ruthie following close behind, Pip and Kurt bringing up the rear. Ruthie pointed behind us. I turned and saw the double rainbow arching over the Great Lake.

"She could do worse than join us here," David said.

Paul reached us first. "Pip let us listen for God's voice." When Paul turned to greet Ruthie, the white spot in his hair behind his ear shined bright.

If David noticed, he didn't let on. Instead he said to Ruthie, "While your Marmie drives the others back, let me show you a few things here."

How could I be as biased about our girl as Papa had been about me? Probably more so: Ruthie gave no quarter to anyone, whereas I hid behind any shelter I could find. Why did I try to protect her so? That night I stole away to the attic and composed a song:

Blind

An aspen seedling
yearned to soar
over the forest
to distant fields
where larkspur grows

Stay close to home
warned Mother Seed
where the earth is loam
you can take root—
and grow.

But when March winds
began to blow
Little seedling—
twirling and swirling—
broke free to roam

Three days later I opened a letter from Mirja:

Pip got so busy reading Paul's lips in the rearview mirror, he nearly did us in. Failed to stop for the state highway or hear the horn of the Speedway Oil truck barreling east from Empire. Thank heavens the trucker slowed to make the turn: he slammed on his air brakes and missed our trunk by a hair's breadth. Pip apologized and offered to let me drive, but I was so shaken, I changed places with Paul instead and told them to keep all four eyes on the road until we got home.

If there's any good news in this, Pip said it's inspired him to tinker with smaller receivers. Rather than rely on those big tubes he built for Trudy, he's experimenting with some newfangled little "chips" he can hide inside an ear.

When we got home, Paul joined me in organizing, printing, and binding all my sketches. On our next visit up north, can we spend more time learning the legends of Leelanau? Those tales and the illustrations they inspire hold promise for our new publishing venture. Might also help preserve our Sleeping Bear.

Why hadn't I petitioned the Road Commission to put a stop sign on the county road at the Empire-to-Traverse state highway long before?

The rest of the summer I worked so hard in Empire during 12-hour days, I could barely make time in the evenings to meet with Spring and Major to learn how the Homestead and the Ahgosa enterprises made out. Thankfully, both were prospering without me, and Ruthie was thriving in the Leelanau camp as she had in school. I got so tired one Saturday, I had to retreat to my cottage for lunch. I sat on the deck and soaked in all the sights, sounds, smells, and tastes of my home and, at last, the gentle touch of the warm August sun. I couldn't help taking the afternoon off and composing a song:

Summer Symphony

Stretched out on an old green chaise,
I watch a summer breeze
Gently ruffle the placid lake

Bees hum along the daisies
While an a cappella choir of finches
Serenades me from the trees.

Warmed by sunshine
A lofty book rests beside me
A marker between its pages

I hear the ice cubes in my tea
Clink as they slowly melt
Filming the glass with cool spray

Inside, chores queue up,
And the whine of a ringing phone

Jars my reverie.

But I am busy outside
Watching lacy white clouds
Shimmer across the lazy lake.

ꕥ

That fall in our big kirk in Ann Arbor, Albert Stevens stood on one side of Auden, Angelyn holding their eight-month-old boy on the other. His brother and two sisters crowded close. Unlike the great poet's imagined infant, this godson didn't bawl.

Reverend Lemon welcomed the rest of us to the baptismal liturgy. Nodding to Auden, he noted its origins in the Anglican Church before the more independent Scots split off as Presbyterians. Speaking to the parents, he asked a series of questions ending with, "In the name of your child and on his behalf, do you renounce the devil and all his works, the vain pomp and false glory of the world, with all its covetous desires, and instead believe in God the Father Almighty; …in the Lord Jesus Christ, his only begotten son; …and in the Holy Spirit; … the communion of saints; the forgiveness of sins; the resurrection of the body; and life everlasting?"

Satisfied by the parents' affirmations, Reverend Lemon turned to Auden: "Do you promise to undertake the responsibility of assisting these parents as they nurture this child in the Christian faith and practice to the glory of God?"

Wystan said, "I do."

Oh, how I wished I'd had the opportunity to exchange those words at the sacrament of marriage with such a good man. Of course, Auden wished he could share vows with Chester Kallman instead, but that bad boy stayed home for this sacrament, at the place Wystan rented for him to finish school at Michigan.

The pastor dipped his hand in the font and graced the baby boy's forehead with the holy water. "Wystan Auden Stevens, I baptize you in the name of the Father, and of the Son, and of the Holy Spirit."

We all joined in saying, "Amen," and I gave thanks to the Lord for giving me the chance to join at Ruthie's baptism. I prayed He'd forgive me for failing in my vows to her and asked Him to remind me to do better by our girl going forward.

But, Oh Lord, what are my responsibilities to our boy Paul O'Bannon?

Baby Wystan broke my reverie. He let forth a howl of indignation, but his godfather reached out and handed him a small, silver drinking cup. The six-month-old baby clutched at the handle. Wystan brought the cup to his God-son's mouth, and the sanctuary quieted.

The reverend closed with the declaration from the 1549 edition of the *Book of Common Prayer*: "Let us receive this child in Christ's name. We pray that… he will manfully fight under the banner of Christ against sin, against the world, against the devil, and will continue to be Christ's faithful soldier and servant's to life's end, living the rest of his days according to this good beginning. Amen."

When we responded, "Amen," the Stevens family walked back to us and showed off their rosy-cheeked boy. In his little hand, he still grasped the handle of the silver cup engraved in old English letters with his full name, Wystan Auden Stevens. The baby looked up and beamed at his only other peer there, the beautiful Maia Hayden, whose smile now also blessed him.

I picked Auden up from the Stevenses' home on Marshall Court after their early Sunday dinner. As he stepped into the bright sun, he put on dark glasses. I drove him to Hill House for drinks with our hosts: Mirja and Rabbie; Dorothy Donne, now teaching a creative writing seminar; Ted Roethke, home for a visit from Bennington; Wystan's mentee, Robert Hayden, and former colleague Warren Ray; and Ruthie. Auden had asked that we not invite the Chair, Cowden, or any others from the English faculty, lest he look like he was campaigning for a job again. The poet still bridled at the locals here who questioned his preferences and thought the worst of him because of Strait's gossip.

I parked in back, and we entered through the side door into the kitchen. As Wystan removed his sunglasses, I saw the pain cross his forehead. "You okay?"

"Some rude beasty nesting on my optic nerve."

"Make time for a consult tomorrow at the eye clinic at University Hospital?"

"Only if you can find me a doctor who practices the Great Ostler's rule: Care for the individual patient more than for the particular disease from which he suffers."

I had to laugh. "Is that how you practiced on Angelyn to cure her allergies?"

"We-e-el-l-l," he said as if six-syllables, "my godson's proof."

Mirja rescued Wystan from my mothering, and we joined the others in the shade of the champion yellowwood tree at the back of the east garden. Drinks and conversation flowed easily for an hour. Although most of the talk centered on their experiences teaching different classes, Ray managed to pry out of Auden that his writing on another long dramatic poem—*The Sea and the Mirror*—was finally beginning to flow after a long dry spell.

"It's the best work I've done so far," the poet announced. "Picks up the mess where *The Tempest* left off and finishes it."

"Can you cure my writer's block so I can compose again, too?" Dorothy asked.

"Just read all Shakespeare's plays, as I did over the summer."

"Maybe reading all of your collected works would inspire us more," I said.

"Egad! *The Collected Poetry of W.H. Auden* sounds as if I'm finished composing or near dead."

Teddy tut-tutted, as if our guest were already planning such a collection.

As the sun passed over the canopy, a bright ray hit his eyes, and Wystan clapped his big sunglasses back on his nose. "My *deahs,* I've only just begun to write." He turned to Rabbie and added, "Another reason I won't cooperate with you or anyone else to write my life before I am dead and can no longer protest."

"I'm not worth writing about yet," Teddy interjected, "but I'd trust Rabbie."

Auden shook his head. "Knowledge of the raw ingredients of a writer's life doesn't explain the peculiar flavor of the dishes he cooks for his readers."

"Wouldn't you like a contemporary's biography of Shakespeare?" Ray pressed.

Auden scoffed, "Perhaps a gossip-writer, a satirist, or even one of those voyeurs who fabricates a new psyche and ascribes his subject's genius to the poor mortal's sins."

"I fear for Frost," Rabbie said. "The biographer he chose combines the worst of that sorry lot."

Teddy suggested that was Frost's scheme to sell more books.

"Only proves my point," Auden answered. "The taste in the reader's and critic's mouths should depend solely on the writing, not who the writer is or was." The furrows in his forehead from the pain in his eyes only added to his humor when he smiled and said, "Can you imagine the Fairy Scandal that sorry snob Strait would write about me?"

Roethke nodded but gave me a sour look, as if I were to blame for our nemesis. Whatever bloom Teddy had once seen on my rose must have long since wilted for him.

Throughout our conversation, Robert Hayden listened attentively. On another man I could see that his thick glasses might have made him a butt of jokes, but his friendly demeanor made him a sympathetic figure. Hayden turned to Auden, chuckled, and said in his deep voice, "Much as you appeared in agony your first semester teaching here, what with your brow drenched with sweat, eyes squinting, papers blowing on the floor, epithets flowing, you held us in your thrall: 'No note-taking. You don't want to miss what's important.' 'Learn these few'—FIFTEEN?!—'precepts of literature… and life.' You even played a Beethoven piece on your old phonograph to emphasize a point about the individual piano versus the orchestral group." Auden couldn't help smiling along, until Robert closed, "but you did make us join you on a deeper psychological, almost biographical, inquiry into Dante, Shakespeare, Goethe, Melville, libretti by—"

"No!" Wystan interjected, "no, a deeper inquiry into the *text*, not the *author*."

Hayden's eyes, already magnified fourfold by his thick lenses, only widened to welcome Auden's riposte as if a friendly amendment.

Wystan managed a smile, said, "Sorry, Robert," and asked, "How are you coming on that long poem you didn't finish in time for the Hopwoods?" When Hayden replied he'd nearly completed this final step to earning his Master's, Auden asked if he'd recite a few stanzas.

Robert's several different voices and narrative perspectives took us on a searing voyage into the slave trade across the Atlantic to America. Culminating several minutes later in the slave rebellion on the *Amistad*, "Middle Passage" left us in awed silence. Even Roethke appeared spellbound, speechless.

After a minute Wystan said, "Well," with his usual six syllables, "Robert's figured out how to write a poem that plumbs for the unknown rather than rants about the obvious." This intense young man could also compose poetry aslant with a punch.

Auden thanked his hosts; congratulated Dorothy on her new book of essays; encouraged her to read Shakespeare and urged her to compose her own poetry; and gave Robert Hayden an almost brotherly tap on the shoulder. We set out in my Lincoln, but Wystan asked to stop by Cambridge House first, "for a wee chat."

We closeted in my study, on opposite sides of my big desk. I poured us each a sniff of Laphroaig as he set his sunglasses on my desk. "You were right about Frost. He's the ultimate conjurer, perhaps better than Prospero. With his folksy diction and holding back, he does sneak up on you without telegraphing the punch."

"Did you tell him yet?"

He shrugged his shoulders. "The old bard's going to outlive us both." After a long pause, he pulled out a Lucky Strike cigarette and lit it with his Zippo. When I passed him an ashtray, he said, "Belle, I need to settle down with a more mature person, too."

"You didn't find a rich, forgiving surrogate mother at Swarthmore?"

"Well, my *deah*, she's much *too* old to be my wife," he replied without blinking.

"What about your Missus Mann?" I poured us each another Scotch.

He shook his head. His pale blue eyes, still watering from whatever ailed him, fixed on me with a beseeching look. "Will you and Michigan take me back?"

"Marshalling our allies to shut Strait up is a delicious prospect," was all I replied.

"Just as I cured Angelyn of her allergies so she could bear my godson, I can also minister to you so you can sing your songs in public and cross the pond again."

"You'd give new meaning to being a conjurer, then."

He smiled at that and added, "Just think, Roethke, Hayden, Dorothy, you, and I could have a great time composing here, couldn't we?"

"Until this war ends, I've still got to run our business and raise Ruthie up north."

He blinked, and tears dribbled from his eyes.

"I'm sorry, Wystan."

He knocked back his Scotch, stood, clamped on his dark glasses, and muttered, "Me, too. Me, too."

When I stopped the car in front of Kallman's house, Wystan said, "If I sell enough copies of my collected poems, I can afford a place in New York, another on Fire Island, and Chester will come back to me." His watery eyes brightened. "Pick me up tomorrow at noon for my consult?" When I nodded, he skipped up the front steps as if a teenager looking forward to rejoining his first and only true love.

Strange, I wasn't willing to exchange marriage vows with Auden and meet my vow to confront and crush Strait. If anything, the war had shown that women and others outside the mainstream, like Auden, Roethke, and young Hayden, must prevail over the chauvinists, critics, bigots and pedants who'd held sway in academia for too long.

Once this war ends, forgive me, Lord, I will find a way to get even with the Nyms at Michigan.

ఌ

When I returned to Cambridge House and burst into the living room, Ruthie and Paul greeted me from the couch. Thankfully, they still wore all their clothes. Paul rose, and I gave him a big hug as if he were my boy, too.

"Mirja" I said, "told me you're writing up-north stories to go along with her drawings, and I can't wait to see them."

Ruthie got up and punched his shoulder. "You didn't tell me."

"Haven't finished a whole story yet."

"You want to stay for supper, with Pip, too?" I asked him.

"Sorry, I'm singing vespers with my Da." Paul turned to give Ruthie a hug, thought better of it, and walked across the well-worn path in the little park to his house.

Ruthie joined me in the kitchen. She pared small potatoes, onions, and carrots, as I simmered the beef stew, always better if cooked the day before and given an overnight in the Frigidaire to flavor.

"Where do you want to go to college next fall?" When she didn't answer, I said, "Michigan, so you can spend more time with your Dad and Paul?"

Ruthie gave me one of her looks. "Paul's such a goody two-shoes, I wouldn't be surprised if he goes to Notre Dame to become a priest."

Well, that would keep him out of the war and assure there'd be no incest between these two, if half-sister and half-brother, but I replied, "I know Pip wants you to go here."

"He spends more than a hundred hours a week in his war lab."

"Want to join Trudy at Barnard?"

"I swim because it makes me feel good, not to train for the Olympics."

I had to nod at that.

"Marmie," she said, "is it okay if Mrs. Huey takes me to Madison to see the university and her sorority and meet her family? There's a big lake there to swim, too."

"Do you want me to talk to Pip?"

"Dad's taking me golfing tomorrow at dawn. We'll have the course to ourselves."

ꟹ

The next morning a letter from Frost arrived in the post:

Dear Belle,

Van Dore spent the summer working with me. I asked him to become my partner, but on his father's death, he returned home. I do hope Wade will return.

Maybe you've worn me down, but I now think it's a plus your poems sound better said aloud than read on paper. Don't tell your new pal, Auden, but my verse play Masque of Reason, about my good friend Job, will be finished soon. I'm also working on the other Bible ode about Joshua, for I know better than to tackle Shakespeare!

I'm stuck with my biographer, as only our contract shuts him up until after I die. By then Roethke may be a more noteworthy subject for Rabbie. Those two boys' excitement over their courses reminded me how much I enjoyed our arboreal time together. I do look forward to your inviting me up north again, but why not ask our big Teddy Bear to sport so wildly as a partner with you?

Warmly, RF

Rumors abound that Harvard's got the inside track on Madame Bianchi's cache of Dickinson poems and papers. Nary a word heard of the intentions of Mabel's daughter, but she's had well more than a decade to load up her guns.

> *Dear Robbie,* I wrote back:
> *Your flattery tempted me to publish a collection of my songs, but then I realized you're just mellowing in time. So I'll keep writing for myself and, every now and again, share a poem to see if you remember how to rage. I enclose "Angel Fire" as my invitation to our wilder play up north.*
>
> *Rabbie and Mirja hosted Teddy, Dorothy Donne, Warren Ray, and a young Negro poet for drinks with Auden. Wystan argued biographies of poets should be banned so poems sing for themselves, as yours surely will whatever Thompson may say. But no confidence between us ever escapes my lips: I trust none escapes yours, including that Teddy no longer calls me his Big Mama or anything else.*

I heard the once familiar knock. I looked at the grandfather clock: still a few minutes before I had to pick up Wystan for his appointment at University Hospital. I opened the door and invited Rabbie into my study. "Sorry Frost didn't sign you up."

"Ted and I came to an understanding." He paused. His dark eyes sparkled with his old Irish wit. "I've got a different proposition for you." I looked to the grandfather clock. "After you die," he asked, "may I publish all your poems and write your biography?"

"That only makes me want to outlive you."

"Then let's organize a summer writers' camp at the Homestead," Rabbie said, "while we're both still kicking."

"Oh! I'll get Frost to come and... botanize." My pulse quickened.

"Roethke, Stegner, Cowden, Robert Penn Warren, and Hayden, too," he said.

"Dorothy Donne, Bogan, Millay…" The heat rose on my face. The phone rang on my desk. "Good Lord, I forgot Auden." I picked up: "Wystan, I lost track of time talking with Rabbie about a summer writers' camp up north. You'll come, for a good fee?"

"Can't wait," Auden replied. "No, I mean we're late."

"I'll be right along. We're meeting with the best specialist, plus the medical student who audited your classes here with Angelyn Stevens and Robert Hayden."

"Nice young man." When I added David Protetch was moving to New York, Wystan said, "For a big enough fee to pay my consults, I will join your writers' gaggle."

I rose with Rabbie and asked after his mother. "The Queen will outlive us both," he said but hugged me for all I was worth. I walked out the back door, clicked my heels by the pool, and skipped out the glasshouse to my top-down green Zephyr. Head up, red hair flaming, heart racing once again, I gunned the old Lincoln to pick up Wystan.

Summer 1946: Ann Arbor and Glen Arbor

So many comings and goings since the war, I had to stop to catch my breath. I floated in the glasshouse pool at Cambridge House and let my mind wander. Ruthie, back from Wisconsin for the summer, showed me the fraternity pin of the captain-elect of the Badger's football team and star defenseman of the hockey club. She wore it only when Paul, graduated from St. Thomas and heading off to Notre Dame in the fall, appeared.

Paul told her he'd "enjoy meeting your new boyfriend on the ice next winter, at least if the Bucky Badger doesn't forget how to skate, running around the football field."

It took three years to organize, but Rabbie and I lined up a stellar cast for our first Up North Writers' Workshop at the end of summer, including three women writers. Yet we had lost ground on that front when the Ruthven Administration greeted the mass of returning vets by limiting the enrollment of women in the freshman class, for the first time ever, to the number of spaces reserved for coeds in the dorms. Yet many older women, who had worked during the war, demanded graduate education; Mirja helped organize scholarships for tuition and daycare for them. With Pip's encouragement she also bought a printing press, put it in the annex to the cottage she built below Empire Bluff, and called it Fitzpatrick Press. Mirja wanted a hideout with Pip when Rabbie ruled his new summer roost at the Homestead Inn.

David Ahgosa took over running our Empire, thank heavens. I was worn out after four years expanding the business to meet the war needs. He now faced the tougher challenge of retooling to meet the different consumer demands in peacetime and to reorganize the workforce to include the returning vets. Most of the women went back home, despite David's offer for work-sharing arrangements for all. With Pip's help tinkering and Kurt's help finding financing, David positioned our family business to expand and to diversify in the years ahead.

Davey returned from the war alive but not whole. He lost his left leg below the knee when he tripped a mine in the Italian Alps. No heroic act fighting the Axis, he walked in the wrong place on the way to the front. Lucky he wasn't killed, Davey resented being a cripple more. Hospitalized in Savoie, he spent his free time drinking the Alpine white wines from the local vineyards and those across the border in Switzerland. He spent six months at Walter Reed, fitting his stump with a newfangled artificial limb that looked almost a real leg, until he strapped it on and stumbled around. He substituted an old-fashioned wooden peg leg and stomped his protest until the Army let him go home. In Ahgosatown Davey drank too much, let his hair grow long, and took to wearing a bandana around his head. He looked more pirate than Ojibwe.

With Angel's inspiration Spring took over running the Grand Traverse orchards, fruit, jam, jelly, juice, and pie enterprises while Davey moped. David couldn't interest his son in our Empire, either. Davey avoided Paul and refused even to join in playing our Homestead links, and he rarely set foot near the schools, camp, shore, club, inn, and my cottage, where he'd spent so much time growing up. Angel told me Davey couldn't bear to hobble where he'd flown before.

Only Pip appeared to break through Davey's shell, if only for a while. Whether because a physical handicap marked each or they were both dreamers, Pip engaged Davey in the search for signs of life in the distant echoes captured by the old radio scoop on Empire Bluff. This ended the day they joined Mirja, Paul, and Angel at the new Press. Davey called Angel a traitor and stalked out when he saw her helping Mirja and Paul draw and write *The Legend of The Lost Daughter, Leelanau*.

Major Huey, aided by Helen, ran the Leelanau schools and camps and our Homestead Inn and Club. Smart, thorough, ambitious, and a born leader, he set his education and recreation empire to grow. I also had to concede, he designed and built trim wood cabins, dorms, and classrooms nestled in the trees on the far side of the Crystal River, away from the lake, beach, and dunes. He expanded the rustic inn along the base of the hill and added a low-slung wing to the clubhouse atop the ridge. The bustling harbor at the mouth of the Crystal River offered moorings for sailboats, canoes, kayaks, and motorboats in summer and iceboats in winter. The fishing in the river and big bay had never been better.

Next to Davey, I worried most about Pip. Not yet 40, he seemed lost. Oh, he still got up early to oversee his warren of buildings across the Huron River, but they were now mostly hollow shells. He offered to transform his war labs into a research institute with the University, but the Engineering School was more interested in turning out mechanics for the mass-manufacturing boom, while Astronomy and Physics were glad to get back to what they called basic research, untainted by defense needs. So he helped his War Lab colleagues find new jobs, at MIT, Stanford, Bell Labs, and other leading companies and universities, but he couldn't convince Michigan to hire his best inventors.

Pip also began to focus his research on what he called "chips." Once he completed the two sets of Little Ears, with sufficient amplification pouring through tiny "plugs" so he and Trudy Ederle could hear, he sent Bell Labs his prototypes and shared his musings. He said Ma Bell could race RCA, IBM, MIT, and Stanford to create new radios, connections, and amplifiers to fit into the receiving and sending ends of telephones, television, hearing aids, other communication devices, and business machines yet to be imagined. When I marveled at the small size of the wafers he built for his Little Ear, he said, "They'll double in power and halve in size every couple of years."

"We could sell America's Flame, invest the money to build new companies with Kurt's help from all your inventions, and cooperate with the University to find new—"

"No," he interjected, "Michigan's limiting its so-called 'applied research' to hush-hush military contracts hidden at Willow Run under cover of one of their professors."

Finally, I got it. Once again, the University decided to ride with a different jockey. Too much a tinkerer for the Astronomy Department, my brother seemed too much a dreamer for the Engineering School. Even if Pip had completed his Ph.D., neither would have hired a deaf man to teach their students.

"I'm sorry," was all I could think to say.

Pip shook his head again. "Michigan will force faculty who want to turn their research inventions into businesses to choose: be a professor or be an entrepreneur, never both." He paused. "Maybe it's harder for a state school. If the public ever cries out against the Willow Run Lab helping to fight less popular wars, Michigan will be forced to cut it off, too." He paused. "I'm quit with this University. John's going to Ohio State, and he's going to build our Big Ear there."

I should have consoled Pip but instead said, "Mirja's not giving up, and I won't either."

My brother's face twisted as if I'd lashed him. Recluse in my two safe Arbors, who was I to say such a thing to my boy, who'd overcome so many hurdles to contribute so much more? His pale blue eyes stared through me as if I weren't there. He turned toward the door.

"Pip," I shouted, and he stopped. "Don't ever give up on your dreams."

My brother gave only the barest hint of a grudging nod, his face looking longer as his cheeks hollowed out more every year. No doubt he headed to McKenzie's UM course for another round of golf alone. I feared my boy was falling into a dark abyss.

I probably should have pondered my fate, but I was too tired. Or, after so many months relieved of responsibility up north, Ruthie away during the school year, was I just lost in the darkness, having too much time on my hands? Almost every night now, just as I was about to fall asleep, I jerked awake in fright, thinking about what I'd feel in the last moment before I died. I was so tired during the day, all I wanted to do was sleep. On my last visit up north, Angel had climbed into my bed, held me tight against my fears, and said, "You need to help Pip and Davey, Ruthie and Paul."

As I floated in my glasshouse pool, I began to doodle with images and play with the sounds of all these transitions, comings, goings, moving on. I dreamed of seeing tadpoles change into frogs by the Crystal River, a young brookie flashing downstream to the Great Lake, an eaglet flapping its wings to fledge. Yet there was so much that was harder, especially for Pip, Davey, Ruthie, and, yes, me. The images began to form a song, "Wages of Peace," but I still could only see it. Sounds and words eluded me.

I heard Teddy's voice ask softly, no bravado, "Big Mama, you okay?"

I looked up and saw his big mug and sad eyes. I felt my side to make sure I wore my one-piece suit. Good Lord, was I worried *that* big a bear would see *my* paunch? He looked awful, almost ashen. Six months after his most recent breakdown and hospitalization out east, electroshock therapy to boot, he lived in his Saginaw home with his mother and younger sister. He survived off a Guggenheim. The whisper mill suggested Roethke had awed one too many of his students out of class at Bennington. Michigan shunned its crazy son again when Strait spread the rumors.

Teddy stuck out his notebook. I popped out of the pool, dried my hands on his shirt and took the book. His eyes wandered over the riot of colors of the plants. "You don't miss my gardening."

"I miss your voice." I opened the notebook and saw, neatly typed on 20 pages, "Lost Son." I scanned the poem through once, read each page more slowly again, and handed the sheaf back to Teddy. "Sing your song."

A smile lit his face. His voice rose and fell. His cadence picked up and slowed down. He paused to build anticipation. He spoke softly in a lower voice for emphasis.

I closed my eyes and listened to "The Flight," "The Pit," "The Gibber," "The Return," and "It was Beginning Winter." His voice danced me off my feet as he continued through his greenhouse as a boy, through his echoes rethinking those memories, through rhythms and sounds of Mother Goose, Yeats, Frost, Auden, Bogan, and more, to a voice all his own.

"The Lost Son found at last."

"Look out, Pulitzer, here I come," he exulted and held me tight, wet suit and all.

"Not so fast, Teddy Bear. Who's going to publish and promote your new book?" When he suggested Knopf again, I asked what they'd done for his first book.

"1000 copies, no advertising, no campaign." When I chuckled, he laughed too.

"And how're you going to play the politics of poetry this time?"

"Share bits with Louise, Wystan, and Robbie at the writers' conference up north?"

"Don't forget Rabbie, Roy Cowden, and Robert Penn Warren, too."

"Arrange a tour of readings?" I nodded again. "Find a home where I can write and teach, so I don't have to worry so about singing for my supper." I laughed with him as he put on Frost's most puckish air, pursed his lips, and whistled.

"Also find a good woman to hold you down when you get manic,"

I added, "to lift you up when you get depressed, and to care for you when all else fails."

"Big Mama, you willing to sign up at long last?"

"Tempted as I am, another aging woman mothering you won't do. One of the students you awed before must be old enough now to want to get to know you better."

"Haven't met her again," he grumbled, but with a big smile added, "yet."

"Stay for dinner to see Ruthie and Pip?"

"Got to get back to Mom and Sis."

I knew that feeling, the tug of home, a nest impossible to fledge. I sang Teddy my "Up North" song slowly as a lament, ending with a long, bittersweet dash. He asked me to sing it again, and I did, this time as my personal anthem, with an exclamation point at the end. He stood, lifted me up, and twirled me around.

"When I'm most in need of inspiration to compose, I'll remember your round both ways—so much better than Auden's villanelles as coy love songs."

"You've only just begun to write, Mr. Roethke." I kissed him as warmly as I dared on the cheek, but he only said goodbye, his head down. Lost Son? Lost love for me.

☙

Over the Fourth of July, Pip, Ruthie, and I returned to Belle Cottage for the summer. Without Paul, Mirja, Spring, Davey, and Angel underfoot, our family home seemed almost empty the first week, and Ruth complained every day about missing her Badger boyfriend. She begged to go back to Madison early, but I needed her here through the end of Labor Day, to help me host our first writers' workshop. She protested, but Pip backed me. Of course he wanted to share more time with her and took her golfing, fishing, sailing, waterskiing, and hiking. He also took her to Empire, although she played with Mirja's printing press and Pip's little radio scoop more than explored the plant.

Every Tuesday and Thursday afternoon, Pip disappeared, and Ruthie and I swam Sleeping Bear Bay. Pip said he was meeting with David Ahgosa in Empire, but my CEO confided my brother was busy tinkering again. The last Thursday in July, Pip showed up late for dinner, Angel and David in tow. He showed us three shiny metal devices, each with a different "foot" attached to a pole, the length of shin and calf, not much bigger around than a golf club shaft. The first foot, a dozen inches long, included a thin arched top and bottom, welded together with a thick spring in between. The second, five times as long, offered a much bigger version of the first. The third looked more like a ski. "Davey," Pip said, "will walk, run, and ski again, agile, sure, and quick."

After dinner, Pip and David displayed their new books for Davey on planting vineyards, harvesting grapes, and fermenting white wine. David showed us the different locations in the foothills of the Alps, in eastern France, in northern Italy, and in western Switzerland where diverse white wines, still and sparkling, had taken root. "Similar climate, soils, and potential here," he said.

Ruthie asked about vines to plant, and I pressed on barrels to ferment.

"The first vines should hit Empire dock in ten days," David said.

"Pip built a model of the first vat," exulted Angel.

"All steel," David added, "no oak. Grand Traverse wines will be crisp and fruity."

Angel grabbed Ruthie. "Let's sing songs again." Up the stairs they raced.

I looked to Pip and David. "Bless you both."

Pip nodded but said, "The harder part begins for Davey now with his new legs."

"Spring's got him tending the orchards more," David said, "and drinking less."

Ten days later the big freighter docked on schedule, no Davey yet in sight. The raw materials and parts for our stoves, furnaces, and camping equipment rolled off the boat for two hours. Still no sign of Davey, but Ruthie, Angel, Spring, and Pip stood on the dock and, as the time passed, peered more anxiously to the big dunes. As I demanded to know where Davey and David were, crates from the Alpine wine regions landed on the pier. The vines looked more like gnarled old roots, stalks and sticks. Angel looked up past me and pointed. I turned and searched far up the shore but saw nothing. Angel pointed higher, and my eyes rolled up the steep hill, past the forests and tall grasses in the distance. There, I made out two figures bobbing across the top of the dunes.

They disappeared among the trees and then reappeared, jogging down the sandy slope to North Bar Lake. After they crossed the narrow outlet onto Lake Michigan, they began to run, yes *run*, along the beach. One man had a hitch in his stride, but his longer hair flowing out behind seemed to propel him forward faster than the other man. As Davey approached, I saw he was wearing shorts, the metal peg leg, and the shortest of the three "feet" Pip had made. We all waved and cheered. Davey slowed to let his father, sweating more profusely and huffing much more from the final dash, catch up.

"What took you so long?" I asked.

I thought Davey would describe his rite of passage. Instead he smiled. "Marmie, I lost my footing for a long while." His red bandana, long black locks, dark face, arms, and one calf, now mottled with sand from his long journey, looked as if they belonged to him. He wore his shorts—and his new pole limb and foot—with pride.

Ruthie hugged Davey so hard, I thought she'd never let go, and Angel and Spring piled on, too. I heard the pop, and soon Pip and David handed each of us a glass with champagne, no more than a sniff and a taste. David raised his glass to his son, "To the new President of the Grand Traverse Enterprises, vineyard and winery included."

We clinked glasses and, following Davey's example, sniffed and sipped the bubbly nectar. Rather than ask for more, Davey stuffed the cork back in the bottle. He walked over to Pip and thanked him, then Ruthie and Angel, and finally his father. He stepped up to me, pointed across the vast expanse of Lake Michigan to the horizon. "We're going to work together to make sure our every action preserves this Nibi, for seven generations at the least." He looked south to Mirja's cottage behind the first two dunes. "Marmie, why don't you let Mirja and Ruthie draw illustrations for your songs?"

That night, I retreated to the attic and composed a new verse. Instead of the awful wages of peace following the war sticking in my craw, I sang my thanks for the new hope welling up for all of us. I composed a hymn:

Ode for Davey

Joyful are we for Your gift of love:
For Angel's gentle healing touch
That saved a life once lost, once dim—
For this blessing, to Thee we sing.

Like the trillium opens every spring
Our Angel's voice released his pain,
Unchained despair, unfurled his hope—
For this blessing, to Thee we sing.

Joyful are we in this dazzling sun
To watch our friend embrace the wind,
For Angel's dance has freed his soul—
For this blessing, to Thee we sing.

Joyful are we for the gifts You give:
This Lake and Land we hold so dear.
Protect this place, keep it secure—
For all our blessings, to Thee we sing.

❧

Six weeks later Frost said, "Your *Up North* songs still ring." I'd opened Ted Roethke's two-week verse-writing seminar that morning by sharing ten of my poems, much as Rabbie started his prose seminar by reading one of his short stories. We walked through the trees on the ridge overlooking MacKenzie's links and Sleeping Bear Bay. "A little early for a buck with a big rack to flush a doe, though," he said. His big head, hair now all white, his cheeks still ruddy and hands rough and strong, his body straight, his shoulders square, Frost looked a man chiseled rather than weathered by all his years. He turned and began his still-sturdy stride down through the trees.

I called after, "Don't you want to go back to the cottage to rest for your reading?"

"For shame, Belle, if you can't keep up botanizing with this old man."

At four o'clock the two groups, poetry and fiction, each 30 strong, assembled in the dining room of the inn. Frost and I arrived in the nick of time. Robert Penn Warren sat at the front table, nearest the windows overlooking the big bay. I slid into an open seat in back next to Rabbie and Roy Cowden, as Teddy rocked in the front row, center.

Warren, in his gracious Southern voice, introduced Frost. He noted his "mentor's *four* well-won Pulitzers" for writing the best American poetry, *three* decades helping young poets "find their own voices," *two* verse plays—"at a place and time in life when the most revered and accomplished writers rest on their laurels and reprint old works"— and "*one* call, long ago, recommending publication of my first poems."

Frost rose and looked out into the crowd. "How many of you are here to write poetry?" Thirty eager hands shot into the air. He looked down at the gentleman who'd introduced him. "After all the thanks I got from Mr. Warren for getting his first poems published..." Frost pursed his lips, whistled, and took us all in his confidence with his best stage whisper: "Can you believe it, he writes best-selling *political* fiction instead!" Frost paused again, and the audience, all except for Warren, Rabbie, Teddy, and me, let out its breath in one collective sigh of concern. Frost continued, "Yes, Robert Penn Warren will win his *first* Pulitzer for a *novel.* So don't any of you get any funny ideas about asking me to recommend *your first* poems for publication."

Warren laughed with glee, and the rest of the audience followed with relief. Many now expected the great poet to read from the much-anticipated second of his verse plays or his collection of new poems. Others, who'd heard him before, expected Frost to start by quoting from his essay, "The Figure a Poem Makes," and then recite a few of his exemplary lyrics. I knew better: on our walk botanizing, he compared his memories of my *Up North* poems with his musings on living in New England, north of Boston.

When the crowd quieted, he proceeded to sing his songs from memory, no book, no notes, not one piece of paper to distract us from his journey, starting with the first poem of *A Boy's Will* (1913), "Into My Own." He sang "Mowing" (also from *A Boy's Will*), "Birches" (from *A Mountain Interval* in 1916), and "Two Tramps in Mud Time" (from *A Further Range* in 1936). We listened as Frost's voice rose and fell, his cadence quickened and slowed, and his pauses lingered. Several times he repeated a part of a verse, whether a line or quatrain, and each time his voice offered a different tune.

The next poem, "After Apple-Picking" (from *North of Boston* in 1914), he sang more slowly. He paused and sang it again, even more slowly, softer, in a deeper voice. The literal figures of the "long two-pointed ladder sticking through a tree toward heaven," empty barrel, drinking trough, pane of ice, hoary grass, bending boughs, cellar bin, apple scent, "rumbling sound" of apples unloading, his aching instep arch pressed against a ladder rung, and the woodchuck all fused into our "drowsing off" in broad daylight with our narrator into his dream of a long sleep.

When Frost appeared to close with "Come In" (from *A Witness*

Tree in 1942), we clapped and began to rise, but he shushed us and bade us sit down. He proceeded to sing "Stopping by Woods on a Snowy Evening" (from *New Hampshire* in 1923). Only 16 short lines, the dreamlike quality of this lyric now came clear to all of us blessed as ear-readers, hearing the poet's voice. Dangerously tempting as the woods may be, "lovely, dark, and deep," the rider must move on, not for food and a stall, as his horse does—not even for the shelter and safety of the village, as the owner of the woods—but because *we* "have promises to keep, and miles to go," yes, miles to go, "before we can sleep."

Frost dropped his pale eyes and sat down. Robert Penn Warren pocketed his pen, rose, and led the rest of us in singing as one the last stanza of the poem. I couldn't remember Frost ever looking so alive and happy. At 72 Robbie was a virtuoso soloist, and our chorus lifted him to his feet. Even Ruthie joined for Frost's performance instead of helping Davey tend his vineyard, as she had every day since the vines arrived.

Major Huey's four waitresses brought in the refreshments: punch, soda, beer, and, yes, the last of Papa's best Macallan. Conversations broke out all over the dining room. Frost and Warren circulated. Teddy, Rabbie, Roy, and I introduced them to our guests, and we began the process of becoming one class—whether of prose or poetry, it didn't matter—each participant to write, write, write, and write over the next two weeks.

We proceeded in a closely linked line down the stairs, across the lawn to the bridge over the Crystal River, and up the beach and dune for a campfire cookout under the weathered birch box and totem pole. The feast of roasted fish and vegetables and fresh, hand-churned strawberry ice cream sated our appetites, but the fire, the talk, and the views over the blue bay to the rising sands of the Sleeping Bear Dunes and the green Manitou Islands inspired our imaginations.

I was delighted Ruthie joined us by the campfire. She sat with Angel on one side of Frost, with Dorothy Donne and her family on the other. Mirja and I bracketed Warren. I asked him whether he planned to write an essay about Frost's performance. When he nodded, I said, "Make it the lecture for our Hopwood awards next spring?"

I tapped Angel on the shoulder, and we crossed to the far side of the fire. As the reds and pinks in sky and bay fell to flatter grays and blacks, the firelight and shadows graced her as she took off her sun-goggles and turned her pale eyes to her audience across the fire. Her dance brought Leelanau, the delight of life, to our shore that evening. I accompanied Angel by singing "Angel Fire." Every eye focused on her dance; every ear listened to my song. Angel closed by leaping across the last glowing embers, landing without a sound and spreading her arms. No matter the Northern Lights didn't appear as she opened the curtain to the night sky and no shooting star accompanied the end of my song. Angel pointed east, her admirers all turned, and the glowing orange orb of late summer rose and looked three times larger than any moon ever had before.

I said my goodbyes to Mirja and the other guests and shepherded Frost, Warren, Ruthie, and Angel safely along the walk to Belle Cottage. Pip greeted us at the door, and Frost couldn't resist asking him to show how his new Little Ears worked. Pip removed his hearing aids, took one apart and explained how the thin wafers in the tiny plug worked as amplifiers. Before long Frost inveigled an invitation to see our plant at Empire so he could visit the old radio scoop atop the bluff. The bard regaled Warren with our observations from so long ago and his fights with the hidebound academics who refused to open their eyes to the deeper gazing into the heavens Pip and Frost proposed.

My brother chuckled. "I'm driving back to Amherst tomorrow to visit my freshman roommate. Remember, we hid Sabrina in the little barn behind the Astronomer's house?" When Frost nodded with a smile, Pip added, "Charlie Cole's President of the College, and we can make it a package deal if you want to join me."

I told Robbie that Pip's friend could do more than secure the Dickinson originals from Mabel Todd's daughter and convert Emily's Homestead into the Dickinson Library. He could also dedicate a new library at Amherst College for Frost's papers to assure an enduring legacy for the nation's most poetic fellow ever.

"My friends there did welcome me back for a lecture last spring," Frost replied, "but maybe I should stand with Auden and let my poems speak for themselves."

Given all the campaigning both Auden and he did for their poems, he couldn't keep his face straight long enough for me to retort. So I said instead, "At least Mirja can keep you company on the long drive."

He couldn't resist nodding now.

Angel and Ruthie excused themselves. After Pip returned from wishing his daughter and her best friend good night, I walked him to the front door. "If Mirja drives with us," he asked, "what should we do about Paul?"

Staying at Mirja's place in Empire all summer, Paul had been scarce at Belle Cottage. "I guess he can take Papa's old bedroom," I said. What could be the harm now that Ruthie and Davey spent so much time together?

Pip turned to leave, but then paused. "Think we should buy more of the shore, dunes, and forest here?"

I wasn't sure how to respond.

"In case you hadn't noticed," he added, "I bought the remaining land north of Empire to the Major's campgrounds south of the state park, plus the southwest shore of Little Glen." My boy hadn't been idle all summer. "You think we should try to buy out the Day heirs, too?"

"Maybe it's time we talk with Governor Osborn to get advice," I replied.

"About a national park or getting Michigan to join in our preserve?" he said.

"You found someone you trust at the University?" I asked.

"Kurt introduced me to another of you Michigan MBA's. Bill Pierpont's taken over as UM's CFO." I couldn't help shaking my head in disbelief. Pip continued, "I showed him a thing or two on the golf links, and he respected my honors."

"Good Lord, going to give him your land and labs north of the Huron, too?"

"No, but maybe we can negotiate a fair price for a sale." He paused. "He's joining us for a weekend of golf on the way back from our trip…to visit Chase at his Duck Island compound to explore the possibilities here." My boy Pip was going to be all right.

I returned to the kitchen and heard Robbie and Warren talking about how the former focused on verse plays and the latter on novels. Their mutual admiration flew back and forth until Warren sided with the few reviewers who applauded Frost's dramas.

"My damn biographer's review makes me the maddest. Called my *Job* unholy and, compared with Moby Dick no less, *slight*."

Warren reached over and touched Frost's shoulder. "Most critics today wouldn't get a new play by Shakespeare either."

"How do you explain Auden, then?" Frost barked. A grumble rolled from someplace deep in his throat. "Even Untermeyer's fallen in love with his verse plays!"

As much as I enjoyed reading Wystan's fantastical flights, I couldn't resist chirping, "Broadway and West End won't run any of his dramas either."

"The novel's a much likelier source for stage and screen today," Warren added.

"I figured that out the first time I met with a New York producer about the idea for my *Masques*," Frost replied, "but I'm such a stubborn fool, I refused to listen to myself."

Warren rose and smiled. "Robert, I've got to get upstairs."

"Oh, Red, stay awhile and make an old man feel good."

"I'm not going up to sleep, but to write up my notes on your talk…" He winked at me. "…for my Hopwood lecture next spring."

After Warren left, I asked Frost, "You need to rest up for your long ride home tomorrow?" He shook his head. I got the Macallan from the cupboard and splashed the Scotch in two tumblers. I told him about how Pip made a new leg and three different "feet" for Davey Ahgosa, David Ahgosa taking over our family business, and Mirja's new press in Empire.

Frost stopped sipping. "Do you find you compose more songs now that you don't have anything else to do?" When I shook my head, he continued, "I always found idle time makes for a lazy mind."

I looked at that dear man, still as vital as the day I met him a quarter-century before, and nodded.

"Cowden and Rabbie want you back in Ann Arbor to teach freshman writing this fall and a senior poetry seminar next spring."

"Why didn't they ask me, then?" I barked.

"Maybe they had to beat down our old Nym nemesis first."

I poured myself a shot of Scotch and threw it down. When I choked and Frost laughed, I felt like clobbering my old—what, friend?

He got up, raised my left arm, and paddled me on the back until I cried, "Uncle!" He walked over to the sink and returned with a glass of water. I took a few sips and then swallowed the cool, crisp northern drink. Refreshed, I said, "I'll consider joining the staff at Michigan again only if you come back for a class with my seminar and join me in thumbing our noses at Ned Strait."

The lids over his pale eyes blinked, but a sparkle did escape anyway. "Can you have Cowden make the request this time so Kay won't get mad?"

I chuckled and asked, "How's your next book of poems?"

"I like most of them, but Holt's not racing to publish." He recited "Directive" for me. His voice drew me away to a dream world "back in time." I wandered with his tune down the worn path, past the abandoned farms and town, roofs long gone. His dream became my home, too, when he put "up a sign CLOSED to all but" us. I joined him at the stream, "cold as a spring as yet so near its source," and drank its water from the goblet he stole from the children's broken playhouse.

"Back to your old west-running brook," I said, "but, oh, so much better!"

A flash of terror hit me, at the thought of the moment right at the end when I'd know I'd never again hear his voice nor sing my songs I hid in Mama's chest.

Robbie reached across and touched my arm. When he didn't draw his hand back, I told him about my frights. "Maybe," he said, "we all practice our dying, in different ways, at different times, but there's no way to avoid the thought. Write it if you can."

I walked up the stairs to the attic, withdrew my book from Mama's chest and sang:

Last Sleep

i

white trillium carpets the forest
the hum of honeybees
a newborn fawn on spindly legs
apple blossoms in the breeze

ii

buttercups in the meadow
sailboats on the lake
wheat fields turning golden
cherry pies to bake

iii

maple leaves turning scarlet
floating to the ground
harvest moon is rising
big and orange and round

iv

now the snow is blowing
its blanket soft and deep
outside the wind is howling:
I fear my final sleep—

v

I must return to Leelanau
prepare for eternal rest,
for like a goose and gander
it is where I make my nest—

❧

At 4:15 p.m. the following Sunday, after Ted Roethke's introduction, Wystan Auden began his reading from the draft of his verse play, *The Age of Anxiety.* In six parts, including prologue and epilogue, Wystan called it "A Baroque Eclogue." Behind him, a late summer storm dumped sheets of water into the bay while lightning flashed in the dark sky and thunder punctuated his words. In the front row sat his special guests, Ruthie and Paul with Davey and Angel, Angelyn Stevens, Louise Bogan, Roethke, and, right in the middle, the mate Auden brought with him from New York.

I'd worried that some of our campers might be offended by Wystan's odd relationship with Chester Kallman, and I'd reserved Papa's old garret in the inn. But his real guest surprised even me. Albeit also blonde and Jewish, Rhoda Jaffe—trim, long of limb, and graceful—displayed the figure and face of a Radio City Rockette. After lunch they'd stripped down to their bathing suits and strolled along our crescent beach. Wystan wore his big sunglasses but showed more interest in fondling Ms. Jaffe. When rain began to fall, they retreated to their love nest. Both showed up in the dining room at 4 p.m. sharp, hair still wet but neatly combed, fully dressed. Even Wystan's face appeared less wrinkled and craggy as he walked, hand in hand, with his new mate and deposited her in the front row beside Louise.

Cowden, sitting next to me in the back row, whispered, "A man of many surprises."

"Maybe the Chair will recruit him back as a full professor now."

"Not as long as Strait still slanders our friend." *Damn Nym*, I must have muttered because Ruthie, sitting with Davey, Paul, and Angel beside us, shushed me.

Not enough time to recite his entire drama, Wystan set the scene: one afternoon during the War, when all were lonely, Rosetta, an attractive British émigré working as a buyer for the Ladies section of a New York department store, happens upon a dashing younger medical officer from the Canadian Air Force and two older men in a Manhattan bar. They move to a booth with a "Wallomatic" jukebox, where their talk, occasional reports from the front, and too many drinks lead them from Rosetta's wish to return to her claimed pastoral England before the war into a fantastical journey through Old England's more fearful mazes in the countryside and blind alleys in towns. The frightening pilgrimage engages the four in various pairings, but they always come back together at key waypoints, even when Rosetta wants to continue alone with the dashing young man.

When the owner of the bar finally turns off the lights, Rosetta invites the other three to come back to her apartment. Disappointed that all accept, she entertains them with drinks, sandwiches, and the prospect of her awaiting bedroom. The three men try to recapture a bit of the higher spirits they shared in the bar, even if each knew "they were tired and wanted to go home alone to bed." The young cadet, Christian from head to foot, asks Rosetta to dance with him. The pair move as one, sit on the couch, coo to each other, kiss, and exchange the most ridiculous vows. Not to be outdone, the other two drunks rise to the euphoria, and each of the four offers manic hopes for a new day after the war. At long last, after all wear out, Rosetta escorts the two older men to the elevator. She returns to find the young cadet she so wanted has gone to her bed, but "passed out."

Wystan then recited Rosetta's 128-line closing soliloquy. She acknowledges that the dashing younger man's not for her. Nor is his WASP society that let the "bruised or boiled bodies" be "chucked like cracked crocks onto kitchen middens for so long" in the Holocaust. She admits she's not from the gentleman's family and pastoral bliss she claimed at the bar. No, Rosetta's from "the semi-detached brick villa in Laburnam Crescent" and a "poor fat father [with] appalling taste in ties."

Outside a storm roared as inside Auden smote the peace following World War II with his *Age of Anxiety*. No matter how troubling Wystan's dream tales, he composed and sang with passion that wouldn't let any of us "pass out."

No up-north campfire roast would cap this evening. Instead Major Huey's cooks prepared our feast in the kitchen while his servers poured drinks, iced tea, white wine, mixed drinks, and Scotch as we milled companionably around the dining room. Little groups formed, broke up, and reformed. Poets mingled easily with fiction writers, and different clusters gathered and dispersed around Bogan, Roethke, Donne, Cowden, and O'Bannon. Rhoda, looking every bit Rosetta, stood beside Wystan and beamed with the kudos we all gave Auden for this character.

"*Deah,*" Wystan said to me, "do you mind if Rhoda and I stay another night?"

"You're welcome as long as you wish."

"How's Ted holding up?" Auden asked. Wystan had just finished teaching the spring–summer session at Bennington, filling in for Roethke.

"Our boy's new book of poems will propel him far, and he's the best teacher I've ever worked with—you, Rabbie, Frost, and Cowden included." I paused. "But he's run through his Guggenheim money, and he doesn't have a position for the fall."

Wystan nodded.

"Will Bennington take him back?"

"Hard to put that Humpty-Dumpty he broke there together again." Wystan paused. "What about Michigan?"

"You know Nym." Auden nodded again, but this time at me. He knew I'd include a bonus to tide Teddy over for the fall. Ted had earned it. I could only hope one of Roethke's more influential and better-connected friends would help find him a sympathetic and permanent faculty home. "How's Mr. Kallman?"

"I wish he were more jealous." Wystan made me laugh. "Ruthie and Paul look terrific together again, though."

That brought me up short, what with all the time Ruthie spent with Davey all summer. I looked over and saw Louise and Teddy talking and laughing with Ruthie, Paul, Davey, and Angel, but I had to admit Ruthie rubbed up as close to Paul as Teddy did to Louise.

"Sorry you missed Frost," I said to change the subject.

"Ted said he's never been in better form."

"He's mad you get all the good reviews for your verse plays."

"I rather like his *Masques*," said Wystan. "Ted shared that 'Directive' poem Frost read. Makes me want to go back and write about my source, too." He paused. "Sorry young Hayden couldn't join us this year."

"I am too. The Chairman of the Department wouldn't match Fisk's puny offer, and Robert had to move his family to Nashville this summer. "

Rhoda entwined her arm in Wystan's and thanked me for being their host.

As I watched him leave for their garret, I knew Auden's poems about his homeland would prove more lasting than any of his plays, including the one with Ms. Jaffe as Rosetta. I only reminded, "Wystan, now that you're a citizen, your new verse play will surely win the Pulitzer next spring."

As the evening wound down, Ruthie again invited Angel to spend the night and kissed only Davey goodbye. When we got back to Belle Cottage, Ruthie took her little friend right up to her room. I sat down with Paul in the kitchen and heated cocoa atop the stove. His face, dark and handsome as Mirja's, and his eyes, inviting green in color, looked serene. Paul always displayed this aura, whether competing on the ice rink and golf course, singing in the boys' choir, or talking with his peers, teachers, or other adults.

I placed a cup before him, sat down with my own, and asked, "Looking forward to Notre Dame?"

He sipped his hot cocoa. "I'll miss Pip and you." When I asked about Ruthie, he said, "There's a line ahead of me."

I didn't much like that answer. "I bet you'll leave a dozen hearts pining in Ann Arbor and ignite the hopes of many an Irish lass at St. Mary's."

"I'm not much of a lady's man."

A boy of that *persuasion*, I wondered.

He smiled as if he read my mind and shook his head, not the least bit offended.

"Well, I hope you won't ever consider yourself a stranger here."

"Marmie, I consider you, and Pip and Ruthie, family."

What was this 18-year-old, a saint already? "Well, you are my boy, too."

After Paul retired to Papa's room, I called Spring to find out what she'd seen going on among our four charges while I was busy at the writers' conference. "It's like old times: Davey and Paul hiking, running, and working together; Ruthie fighting to keep up; the three older kids making sure not to leave Angel behind. I almost can't believe it."

I didn't. I knew Ruthie, and she no longer wore the Wisconsin crusher's fraternity pin.

✑

On the last Friday at 4 p.m., Rabbie and Teddy shared their views on writing, reading, listening, and teaching, but they also welcomed alternative views and suggestions. They'd created an environment in which the hard work of every individual writing alone was appreciated and encouraged by all. Rabbie and Teddy demanded much, but both threw so much of themselves into each session, every writer lifted his or her game up over the two weeks. Cowden and I handed out a personal note of appreciation to each camper. Louise Bogan closed the proceedings by reading the review for the *New Yorker* she'd drafted on her experience over the past two weeks.

I was stunned by the standing ovation the 60 participants gave us when Louise finished. The drinks flowed, dinner followed, and our celebration spilled onto the broad lawn in front of the inn. We took turns taking pictures of one another, standing by the tall trees as the setting sun and great bay reflected a rosy glow off the inn's tall windows.

I pulled Rabbie aside and handed him an envelope. "Give Teddy this bonus for all his work here, and sign him up for next summer, okay?"

He looked inside, saw my handwritten note with the bills, and asked whether I wanted to hand it to Ted myself, as Roethke felt hurt I'd paid so much more attention to others the entire workshop.

"No, this is your show, but tell him his Big Mama wanted to include a more personal thank you, too."

He looked at the note again.

"It's just an old poem I wrote about my papa when he died, but Teddy will understand." When he looked hurt, I added, "Rabbie, I haven't enjoyed working on writing so much since our first year together at Michigan." I gave him more of a hug than I should and remembered the tingles he gave me so long before.

"Come back to Ann Arbor to teach one of my first-year writing sections this fall," he said, "and lead a graduate poetry seminar in the spring." Rabbie added that Strait was advancing himself as a worthy successor to direct the Hopwood Program, but the aging Cowden wanted me to join as his successor-in-training so he could stay on a few more years. "Willing to join with Frost in my seminar and give Nym what for?"

"Why not Dorothy?" I asked.

Rabbie explained she was better qualified to become the first tenured woman and permanent holder of the Robert Frost Chair in Poetry.

I had to nod at that, but I squeaked in a fright at another thought, "Do I have to publish, too?"

He held me close for the longest time and whispered, "Not if you think inviting the Chair to our writers' workshop here will convince him you should succeed Cowden."

"Then let's see if we can bury Strait and all he represents, once and for all."

Rabbie lifted me off my feet.

I whispered, "We need to talk."

He raised me higher.

I began to tingle but managed to blurt, "No… about Ruthie and Paul."

He put me back on the ground. "Tomorrow morning? I told Paul we'd drive home after lunch, and he said he'd meet me at the pier in Empire."

"Perfect. I drive Ruthie tomorrow afternoon to meet the evening ferry to Wisconsin." I wondered whether Rabbie resented my spending so much time with Frost and Auden as much as Teddy. Good Lord, what was I dreaming?

I worried Paul and Ruth might party the night away but found them back at Belle Cottage, already packed for their separate trips, playing hearts with Davey and Angel. They invited me to join, and I delighted in their protests when I finally shot the moon to end the game. I hurried Paul and Davey off to bed in Pip's room and tucked my two girls in Ruthie's on the third floor. When they begged me to sing "Up North" and "Marmie's Lullaby," I did. When Ruthie and Angel kissed me goodnight, the touch of their lips reminded me how I sang these songs so many years before to two little girls.

I retired to the attic, opened my trousseau, and happened on Doctor MacKenzie's little book, *Spirit of St. Andrews.* I continued rummaging through the chest until I found every scrap of loose paper on which I'd ever composed a song. I organized the poems by subject, tied each packet with a neat bow, and returned them to their hiding place. I opened my several journal-books and also read those poems. I returned my songbooks and sat on top of Mama's chest. All my poems triggered so many imprints in my mind and, like the photos fading to sepia in so many family albums, jogged dreams of bygone days. Like footprints in the sand, though, the wind, rain, and surf would eventually bury these memories, too. If so, the Good Lord had already blessed me with my full share, thanks in no small part to all that David Ahgosa, Mama, Papa, Miss Schultz, D. H. Day, and Pip had taught me. I wrote a *tanka* to express our view:

leave only footprints
on these sacred Nibi shores
beside Nature's gift
crystal clear deep blue waters
to sing Her praise in your songs

I must have slept late. Only Angel greeted me at the kitchen table. She wore her dark goggles and didn't want to talk. I offered her Corn Flakes, but she declined. I poured myself a bowl. While I slurped, Angel fidgeted. When I asked about Ruthie, Davey, and Paul, she only shook her head.

After I finished, I said, "What's going on?"

Angel took off her goggles, and I saw her tears. "Ruthie packed a picnic and took Paul for a sail in the old boat. Davey packed their suitcases in his car and said he'd meet them in Empire. She put your Papa's firewater into the Thermos."

"How long ago did they leave?"

Looking at the clock, she mumbled, "Too long."

I walked with Angel into Papa's office, picked up the spyglass, and looked across the bay to Sleeping Bear Dunes. No whitecaps or white sails in sight. I told Angel I'd get Rabbie from the inn, and we'd take the Cadet to make sure they were safe. I asked her if she wanted to join us, but she shook her head and clamped on her goggles.

I pushed the throttle of the old Chris-Craft open. Rabbie and I raced from the mouth of the Crystal River across the bay. No sign of the sailboat as we passed Glen Haven, the Coast Guard Station, and the Point. We rounded the head of Sleeping Bear Dunes and, still no sailboat in sight, headed to Empire, 8 miles away. The west wind picked up, but I kept the throttle open full, even when the waves pounded our starboard. I pulled Rabbie close on the leather bench seat, and he held my hand, tight. Along the way we scanned lake and shore but found no sign of any wreck or landing. As we passed the dunes north of the mouth of North Bar Lake, I slowed the Cadet, but we didn't see anything. The mouth too shallow for my old inboard anyway, I opened the throttle to race our Cadet toward Empire pier, where a small sailboat might lie hidden. Rabbie put his arm around me, squeezed gently, and turned me to look back. There, at the far north end of the little lake, the top of a mast swayed. I felt such relief, I kissed him. I turned the Cadet and anchored 20 feet from shore. Rabbie and I dived into the warm water and climbed the dune. When we reached the top, we saw only the sailboat, sails furled, with a tarp rigged to shield the open cabin from the sun.

We approached quietly, the only sound the gentle pinging of the rigging. There, in the bottom of the boat, sleeping in each other's arms, legs entwined, lay Ruthie and Paul. Completely nude, tan all over, ripe, Ruthie never looked more voluptuous. Paul, darker but still fully clothed, pants zipped, Topsiders tied on his feet, and top collar of his long-sleeve shirt buttoned shut at the neck, never looked…

what, more like a priest? Paul's head fell away from us, and the white spot on his long dark hair appeared over his ear.

Ruthie opened her dark eyes, glazed from drinking. She looked up at us and smiled. She put her forefinger to her lips, gently separated from Paul, put on her short shorts and T-shirt, no apology, a wry smile on her face. Her breath reeked. As she walked ahead, Rabbie offered a gentle caress to my arm, and I squeezed his hand.

I joined Ruthie, and we swam the short distance to the Cadet. I pushed her up the ladder and clambered after. I pulled up anchor, threw a blanket over her, and made her sit next to me.

We passed Glen Haven before she said, "Marmie, much as I love him, he's too pure."

I pulled her close but didn't say a word, not when we moored in the Crystal River, not while she changed at Belle Cottage, not when she said goodbye to our Angel, not while we drove to Empire and she said goodbye to David and Davey Ahgosa. I didn't let go of her until we got to the dock in Ludington. Without looking back, she boarded the *S.S. City of Midland*.

Good Lord, why didn't I say, "No matter what, I'll be there for you?"

That evening in the attic, I thought of the two children, one girl, one boy, both growing too rapidly into adults. Both had always called me "Marmie." I composed a shorter *haiku*, and wrote it on a scrap of paper:

LOST
harvest moon, dark sky
a single swan sailing by—
uncharted waters

It probably said as much about me, my failing each of my charges and lonely with both gone, than about either of them. I was so angry with myself, I wanted to rip it up, but I couldn't. So I buried it in the *Spirit of St. Andrews* at the bottom of Mama's chest.

Next morning I made a copy of my five-line *tanka* and sent it to Frost with a note:

Dear Robbie,
I enclose another short poem I composed about my home. I hope it sings to you as David Ahgosa taught me. Thanks again for making our first Up North Writers' Workshop more than I ever hoped, even more fun than when Rabbie and I first served as your scribes. You inspired me to return to teach at Michigan: I promise not to stuff shot down my students' throats lest any lose their voice. As ever,
Belle

Later that evening I heard a scraping on the front porch and opened the door to find Major, Angel, and Davey. The Ahgosa boy apologized for his part in Ruthie's escapade with Paul.

Before I could reply, Angel said, "The Dark Ogre's making evil plans."

Major explained how his campers had seen Sven driving a half-ton Ford pickup right to the base of the Mama Bear.

"Did it have balloon tires?" I blurted.

"No, very heavy, with huge treads," answered Davey. "He left deep tracks."

I thanked Major and piled my two kindred Ojibwe spirits into the Lincoln. We cruised through Glen Haven and, lights off, parked across from the life-saving station and walked up the road. Under the cottonwoods sat one big truck with monstrous treads and three big benches. We buried the seats in sand, and I taped a note to the steering wheel:

Sven, I still appreciate your help and heroism working in Empire, but your operating this tank on Sleeping Bear violates our agreement. Don't ever run it across the dunes again, or I'll fill the gas tank with sand and thrash you in court.
Belle

Spring and Fall 1947: Madison, Ann Arbor, and Glen Arbor

Two hours into the voyage across Lake Michigan, the *S.S. City of Midland 41* hit high winds and heavy seas. The big ferry ship rolled, yawed, and groaned, and my stateroom bucked. The kielbasa I'd wolfed down in Ludington rebelled. I fought my way forward in the center passageway and pried open the bulkhead hatch. I crab-walked a few feet to a chaise fixed to the deck with cleats. The sky already pitch black, I couldn't see any sign of shore ahead, but the cold, wet blasts kept my mind off my stomach flipping.

I held on tight, closed my eyes, and tried to think how I could face what lay ahead. At least Pip, driving from Chicago, would arrive to help Ruthie pray for Paul several hours before I did. A rogue wave lifted the 400-foot-long ship up to the crest, and then the *Midland 41* slid down the mountain of water and crashed in the trough. Her 60-foot beam shuddered, but her double hull held. At long last the call whistle blasted *long-short-long*. The lights onshore flickered through the gloom.

We docked safely, and I called ahead to the University of Wisconsin Hospital. I reached Pip, but there'd been no change in

Paul's condition or Ruthie's anguish. I had too much time to think on the drive to Madison. I kept reviewing the crusher's check in my mind: Paul, racing down the ice to break the tie, split the defensemen, deked to his forehand, and, when the goalie followed, pulled the puck to his backhand. He tucked it into the net just as the captain of the Badgers' team cross-checked him from behind. The only thing that saved our boy's head from cracking like a robin's eggshell when it hit the crossbar was his stick. The blade caught the center post first. When the stick buckled, it slowed the speed of his headfirst crash, but the broken shaft pierced Paul's midsection.

Ruthie's call still seared. Not able to find Pip at Cambridge House, Hill House, or Mirja's cottage up north, she felt betrayed and alone. She also hated herself for falling for "that brute." I tried my best to comfort her, but she cried, "Marmie, I don't know what to do." I knew I had to go to her side. Maybe I could help Paul, too.

Mirja and Rabbie had arrived from Ann Arbor and joined Ruth by Paul's bedside, and Pip greeted me in the waiting room outside the intensive care unit. I finally told Pip why I thought Paul was his son.

"I've known for years," he replied, "maybe since I first watched him skate and swing a golf club." He paused. "For sure after I saw the white splotch when he bent to survey the echoes recorded from my horn scoop."

"Don't you think you should tell Ruthie?"

"She's so vulnerable." Pip paused again. "I don't know."

I didn't either. When Ruthie opened the door to the waiting room, she fell into my arms. I held her tight and noticed she'd put on weight. "Paul woke up." She paused. "He held my hand and said he was sorry." Ruthie pushed herself away and clenched her fists. "Why should he be sorry?"

When I didn't answer, she stepped back and looked at her father. Pip took his daughter's hand and walked out to the hall. I'll never forget the look Ruthie gave me just before the door closed. I'd failed her.

Mirja entered the waiting room and sat next to me. "He's going to make it."

"Pip's telling Ruthie," I said. "Does Paul know?"

"We never told him. This'll drive him straight to the seminary, though."

"What if Ruthie and Paul marry instead?"

"He believes Ruthie's beyond his grasp." She took me to see Paul.

Rabbie rose from the bedside chair and reached out as if to embrace me but only touched my arm as he left. A nurse entered and said, "Only a few minutes."

Paul looked far better than the report of his injuries. As he spoke, I leaned forward and dropped my head to hear him say, "You need to stay strong to help Ruthie."

I reached out my hand and asked if he was hurting. He only cupped my hand in his. Good Lord, was this kin of mine already a priest and seer? "You know I will," I said. I saw a single tear roll down his cheek. As I left, I added, "I'm here for you, too."

"Marmie, Ruthie needs your help more now." What did he know I didn't?

I took the elevator to the first floor and wandered past the main entry, looking for Ruthie, Pip, Mirja, and Rabbie. As I passed the front desk, I saw a stocky young man with a red jacket and big block "W" in white. He asked the receptionist whether he could visit Paul O'Bannon. He looked far worse than Paul. I knew it was the crusher. Ruthie stepped out of the cafeteria door, stormed up, and punched him in the chest; then she shook her head at me and walked toward the elevator.

I approached the young man, introduced myself and hurried him away to the main waiting room. Mick Shiller was a big man, as tall as Paul, but much thicker. He apologized for losing his temper and taking such a cheap shot at the person Ruthie said was a better man, "but I still want to marry her."

I wondered if that was part of his misguided pride but only asked if he'd ever hit Ruthie. Taken aback, he shook his head at first but then held up his right forefinger. That was once too often for me, and I rose to leave. He grabbed my hand. He pulled out a small box, showed me the engagement ring, and mumbled something about "doing the right thing." I didn't want anything more to do with this bruiser and left.

When I arrived at the waiting room upstairs, Ruthie argued with Mirja, Rabbie, and Pip about who should stay now that Paul was out of danger and sleeping soundly. Exhausted, I was ready to go to the hotel, but Ruth had other plans. "Marmie and I will be up talking for several hours anyway."

After the others left, I didn't know where to begin. Ruthie did. "I should be mad as hell at you for not telling me Paul's my half-brother." She paused, and I pondered whether I should share my nagging doubts. "Marmie, I'm in trouble." *That's* what else Paul could see: she was pregnant. Despite that, she looked as healthy and, although fuller, vital as ever. "I'm thinking about an abortion."

"How many months?"

"Four." She paused. "No, closer to five."

Major surgery and scarred for life. "Do you want your baby?" I asked, but she only answered it would be better if the baby had a father, too. "Who is the father?" Ruth dropped her head and began to cry. I knew it was Mick. I pulled her head to my shoulder.

After several minutes Ruthie said, "I'm so embarrassed."

I lifted her head up and said, "Not nearly as much as I was before." When she looked stunned, I added, "Never lucky enough to get pregnant, despite trying too many times to get a mate when I should have known better."

"Never with your brother!"

"Oh, Ruthie, I saw my Mama give birth to Pip and raised him as if my son." When she nodded, I said, "But I don't know for sure who fathered Paul, although I think it's more likely Pip than Rabbie." That much was true.

When she asked "What about me," I paused for a long time. "I guess I don't know that for sure either, but Pip's never expressed any doubt to me."

Ruth nodded with her first smile.

"Mick showed me the engagement ring he bought to give you after the game," I added. As Ruthie's smile disappeared, I asked, "Did he ever hit you?"

Ruthie said once and explained how Davey Ahgosa visited in the fall, beat Mick in a footrace, and danced her off her feet at Chi Phi. "The fraternity brothers razzed Mick for losing the race—and his sweetie—to 'a peg-legged Injun boy.' Mick took offense at the slur, decked one of the insulters, and began to pummel another. One of the bigoted boys shoved Davey, and Mick took after that one, too. When I tried to break up the melee, Mick just tried to push me away, but I hit my head against the bar."

That put a different light on my view of the crusher.

"Maybe I got pregnant that night, when Mick was so apologetic and attentive." She shook her head, but a smile again graced her. "It probably didn't hurt I dreamt the whole time about dancing under the full moon with Davey by Sleeping Bear."

"Ever consider marrying Davey?"

"Not with another man's child, and Mirja's tricks aren't for me."

Ruthie rested her head on my shoulder and yawned.

I must have dozed off. I heard the door to the waiting room open, and Ruthie entered. The clock on the wall already read 9 a.m. "Paul proposed to me," she said.

"Did you say yes?"

"No, I told him he's still too good for me."

I shook my head, pulled Ruthie close, and wouldn't let go.

"Then I told him about my baby." After a long pause, she sat up. "I decided to mother her." She stood and said she was going to the Delta Gamma house to get cleaned up for a class test and then long talk with the father. "Meet is at the Rathskeller at 2:30?" When I asked what that was, she answered, "The lower level of Wisconsin's Union. It's right on the lake, if you're ready for a swim with this ripe polar-bear-mama-to-be."

"I'll settle for beer, a brat, and being the first to congratulate you and Mick."

ശ

A month later Robert Frost stood at the podium of the Rackham Amphitheater. Earlier in the afternoon we'd traded barbs—and poems—in my seminar, when he challenged me to a competition of his "*North of Boston* lyrics" against my "*Up North* songs." I had to sing 12 of mine to only six of his. He'd barked triumphantly, "Takes two of this younger Belle's to equal one of this old bard's." At Rackham the packed house listened as he reminisced about our "welcoming Ann Arboreal clime, where I botanized in your Arb and gazed at the heavens from the Detroit Observatory."

Frost couldn't resist taking a few shots at the narrow-mindedness of academics and their unwillingness to embrace the dreamers and poets who could imagine a brighter world, a bigger universe, intelligent life in space, and the darker secrets each of us hides deeper inside. A ripple ran through the audience as more and more realized that Frost spoke of our university. He squinted toward the back of the hall. Ned Strait stumbled down the aisle, trying to find a seat.

"Why, here's Nym," Frost said. "You still spreading your gossip about us poets and dreamers?" In his best stage whisper, my Robbie added, "His ilk teaching led me to drop out of Dartmouth and Harvard, even if I've got several trunks full of honorary degrees to prove I'm no dummy." My Robbie stared down our nemesis until Strait turned and slunk up the aisle and out the door.

Frost proceeded to offer a heartfelt talk on the purposes of college, but he couldn't resist wondering why most teachers refused to accept that students "learn most when they find a pursuit for which they'll neglect their studies." He nodded to Pip and Ted Roethke, both now bobbing their heads while rolling side to side in their chairs. Frost's glance fell to Stella Brunt and the Three Graces sitting on my other side before he continued, "Many here may think I'm partial to boys after all my years at Dartmouth, Harvard, and Amherst, but you must remember, I also had the pleasure of hearing your coeds' better tunes." He paused. "Does the gratitude we owe our returning veterans justify limiting the number of women we admit to our great universities?"

Frost looked down at me and smiled. "Enough of my questions about *higher* education. Let me close by talking with you about folks who think poems are good only if they're of immediate practical use or offer commentary on the larger social issues of our day." He paused and recited "Mending Wall." He chuckled. "I can't tell you how many times your so-called professors of English argued this poem's about everything other than what it says." He recited "Stopping by Woods on a Snowy Evening." He turned, cocked his head at an angle, and said in his stage whisper out the side of his mouth, as if including each of us in his secret, "Can you guess how many times that good poem has been ruined by being pondered over too much by the critics and academics?"

Turning to face the audience, he concluded, "It's okay for poems to leave us with a dash of uncertainty in the midst of the narrower-minded academic search for order. It's okay in your writing, as in your life, to mix in a dash of tumult, at least as long as you never give in so to confusion as to admit you're licked." He paused. "As with the Michigan Union, don't be afraid to question bastions for one kind only; and remember to write, write, write. You just might get lucky enough to contribute to forming that more perfect union the *Constitution* committed us to nearly 8 score years ago." The packed house, men and women, faculty, students, staff, and friends of Michigan, rose to salute our 73-year-old curmudgeon. April 1 it was, but Frost was no one's fool.

Rabbie and Mirja hosted a small reception at Hill House afterward.

Teddy, home from Penn State for spring break, confided that the University of Washington had begun to court him to serve as a professor of English. Frost assured our Teddy Bear he'd call his friends at Dartmouth to see if they'd "get the ante up." I had to laugh when Robbie pulled Cowden and Rabbie aside and whispered, "Washington and Dartmouth are courting your Mr. Roethke: this is your last chance to land him." Then again, with the Chair heading back to the faculty in the fall, maybe we could convince the new Department head to give Roethke a shot before he landed in the west for keeps.

Robbie paid particular attention to Paul O'Bannon, home recuperating from concussion and the removal of his spleen. When Paul explained his plans to join the Old College Holy Cross Seminary at Notre Dame in the fall, they traded jibes about the Catholic faith and religion in general.

When Frost asked about Ruthie, Paul looked to me and explained how she'd rejected his proposal and married a Badger instead. Frost chuckled. "Much as I've admired watching Ruthie grow to a woman with all her Marmie's wit and wile, that's still no reason for you to take to a sack cloth and celibacy."

Soon Frost asked me to take him back to Cambridge House for the night. He said he needed to get up early in the morning for the long drive with my brother to a secret meeting with President Cole tomorrow night. "Did Pip tell you he's also persuaded Cole to award his Negro pal an honorary doctorate at commencement?"

I had to shake my head, but I wasn't surprised. My brother, as odd and often-moody a loner as any person I knew, was very willful in remembering his friends. So, too, Frost had a long memory: no matter how many times he'd quit before, Amherst was his home. Pip would help the College take our Robbie back so he could ramble with boys who would keep him young until his last go down. "Thanks for defending Pip, Teddy, and us girls this afternoon."

"My dear Miss Belle, I don't know what you're talking about." He pursed his lips. "Where's Ruthie going to have her baby?"

"She and her husband plan to stay at Belle Cottage all summer."

Frost raised his blue eyes, paler and sadder than I remembered. "Please keep Ruthie here, close to University Hospital." I kissed him on the cheek and tasted the bittersweet of a single tear at his loss of Marj.

ℭℌ

May 28, Robert Penn Warren graced another packed house in the Rackham Amphitheater for his Hopwood Lecture on "The Themes of Robert Frost." Fresh off winning the 1947 Pulitzer Prize for fiction with *All the King's Men*, Warren began, "The important thing about a poet is never what kind of label he wears but what kind of poetry he writes."

Starting with "Stopping by Woods on a Snowy Evening," through all the poems Frost read at our writers' conference last summer, Warren read each, repeated stanzas, and showed how the particular facts and the literal scenes dissolve into a dream. He finished with his favorite, "After Apple-Picking." The narrator's dream, albeit troubled as only a human's can be, is no nightmare: he "*cherished*" every aspect of his "apple-picking" and "the harvest." Thus a "poem defines an attitude, a basic view… It defines, if it is a good poem, a sort of strategic point for the spirit from which experience of all sorts may be freshly viewed." In Frost poems, "the reader realizes not only that the natural world transmutes into the dream world" but also that the poet "plays between the two worlds," and the reader "feels the reverberations." Warren concluded, "This *interpenetration* of the two worlds is itself the theme of these poems."

I wished Red had come right out and described their most important trait: different phrasings and tones that spoke aslant with a pang or a punch. As much as I appreciated Red's insight into eye-reading, I still preferred the varying sounds a good poem can make for us ear-readers. For me, Frost and Dickinson were the greatest American poets not because of the images and dream worlds they conjured but because of the sound and beat, pang and punch, in the different tunes they composed. I said as much to Ted Roethke and Dorothy Donne.

"You tell him, Big Mama," he said.

"There's a role for eye-reading, too," she replied. "Maybe cultivating seeing and hearing offers another resonance, as we sense the echoes of sounds reverberating with the reflections of images." Mrs. Donne was already a good writer, poet, and teacher. Cowden and Rabbie were right: No better woman to break the glass ceiling by becoming the first Robert Frost Professor of Poetry at Michigan.

At the Hill House party afterward, I shared our discussion with Red. "Maybe I should stick to fiction and writing plays then," he replied with a smile.

"Imagine what you'd accomplish if you composed poems again," I retorted.

He blushed as only a fellow redhead can but shook his head. "Not much singing going on in my life now, so I'm heading off to Italy to work on another novel." He held up his lecture. "Think Frost would like a copy?"

"Worried he'll snap at you for making more of his poems than the words say?" When he blushed again, I added, "I'll be glad to send it along with a cover note saying how much we arboreal sorts here enjoyed your praise of the figures his poems make."

Then Teddy asked me to dance, but I tried to beg off.

"Big Mama, I promise to sing for my supper up north again even if I move to Seattle to teach."

I mumbled something about how this would pay his way back to see his family.

"No, Belle," he answered, "I want to thank you for helping me all these years."

Thank goodness, Mirja started another Foxtrot on the piano. My big Teddy Bear swept me off my feet and reminded me how much I loved dancing with him, manias and all. So why didn't I tell him that? Nym had won again, so there was no future for Ted at the University so he could join me. Damn!

ᔕ

The first day of fall broke at Belle Cottage with a caterwaul from baby Marty. Louder than a cock crowing, only her mother's milk could quiet her. When damp, she demanded clean diapers but screamed at being washed, dried, and powdered, whether changed by her Mama or Marmie. Only the sight of Angel's halo of white hair and the magic touch of the Ojibwe Ogichidaakwe calmed Marty in the bassinet. Mick was useless: all thumbs, he couldn't even get the baby to suck a drop of mother's milk from his too stubby forefinger. So I'd take the crying baby with a bottle into the study. After Marty feasted, I'd sing her to sleep with my *tanka*, "Up North" anthem, and a lullaby.

Paul and Davey invited Mick to play golf and fish, but Mick preferred the role of lone outcast. He ran on the beach and sailed solo. I offered to play tennis, but my son-in-law said, "Hand-eye coordination isn't my game." I invited him to readings, lectures and dinners at our writers' workshop, but he only joined Ruthie and the baby for the two cookouts at the campfire in front of the totem pole. Around Belle Cottage, he cleared his plate, helped with the dishes, and never complained. He even refused Pip's invitations to scan the heavens with the school telescope or the horn scoop, David's offer to visit the Empire Plant, and Davey's request to enjoy the Grand Traverse orchards and vineyards.

With only five days left before we'd load Mick, Ruthie, and baby Marty into their car and see them off to their new apartment in Madison, I couldn't take it any longer. I asked to go along on his sail. He hugged the shore with short, awkward tacks into the west wind. I ducked my head to avoid the boom as it whipped overhead. After a painful hour, he wrenched the center board up and ran the sailboat ashore at Glen Haven.

With pride he walked me to the Day general store, purchased two tickets, and jumped into the backseat of the next Ford convertible with balloon tires. Major and his campers had made sure no more trucks or gravel roads marred Sleeping Bear Dunes. Pip, bless him, had apologized to Sven for me but confirmed the conditions on our loan.

The Dark Ogre pulled the Day boy out of the driver's seat and hopped in. Sven motioned, and I climbed in front. As we turned by the life-saving station, he gunned the motor and sped up the dune. As we approached the crest where we could see the eroding crown of the mound in the distance, Mick shouted, "Faster!" Despite my protests, Sven careened too close around the base of Mama Bear. The big tires threw out rooster-tails of sand and, in their wake, left a track all the way back to the General Store.

Sven hopped out and opened my door. "A taste of the thrill our Scenic Ride will offer once we pay you off."

"Better read the fine print, lest you forfeit the remains of King David's Kingdom to Pip and me." I slammed the door and walked off.

I bought an orange Nehi for Mick and grape for me in honor of D. H. Day. We sat on the beach next to our boat and looked over the decaying pilings of the old dock. "Belle, mind if I drive a dune buggy for Sven next summer?"

"Only if you're still staying in my home then," I snapped.

Mick swallowed some of his orange drink down the wrong pipe.

"Mick, may I show you what this place is really about?" Still red in the face and catching his breath, he couldn't say no.

I stood up, dragged the sailboat back into the bay, hopped in, and grabbed the tiller. Mick splashed hopped over the transom. I handed him a towel and tacked into the west wind until we rounded the point. I set the sails for the long reach down the steep west front of the dunes.

"Looks different from here," Mick said. We sped along at a steady 10 knots as I trimmed the sails to maximize our speed. As the breeze picked up, the boat heeled far over. I showed Mick how to sit on the windward side so we could race at our hull speed, 13 knots. With the wind, the spray, the vibration and movement of the living beast under us, he held onto me tight, all the way past the magnificent west face of the Sleeping Bear Dunes to the mouth of North Bar Lake. There I luffed the sails, coasted ashore, hopped out, pulled the boat out of the water, and danced to the crest of the shore dune. When Mick caught up, he said, "Okay, maybe that's as big a thrill as the dune ride."

I pointed up the steep hill to the north and set off at a brisk pace through the sand, the dune grass, and the maple, beech, and birch forest of Major Huey's campground. A half hour later, we reached the summit and headed down to the cottonwood grove. We sat down in the shade to cool. When he started to speak, I shushed him so we could listen to the wind rustle the leaves, feel the flying sand sting our face, and taste the sweet majesty of this haven. I pointed to the eroding pinnacle of the Sleeping Bear in the distance, still standing watch over the twin Manitous. I told Mick the legend of Sleeping Bear. "The wind might erode her in time, but we made a deal with Sven his dune rides won't destroy her before her time."

As we walked back, I stopped at the point where we could gaze over Little Glen and Alligator Hill to the ridges above our Homestead and east across Big Glen to the tall forest now stretching as far as we could see. The many layers of blue rippling in Lake Michigan and Glen Lake, the sandy ridges and hills in the dunes, and the blanket of emerald from the trees painted a glorious scene. I pointed south to Empire and the sea of green bordered on the west by the steep bluffs and Great Lake. I explained how D. H. Day, my father, and our families brought the logged forests back to life.

We trotted down to our boat, and I sailed the short distance left to Empire dock. There several big freighters unloaded raw materials and parts and loaded our finished appliances and furnaces. After mooring, we walked up to the plant.

I asked David to show Mick around, while I talked to the only three women who still worked on our teams. It was good to be with them again, and they bantered about how much tougher a boss I was than David. The few older men from my father's day job piled on, albeit with affection: "Aw, she was a softy compared to her Papa." I missed these people, but I loved working at the university, encouraging young men and women to write, write, write and composing my songs.

When David and Mick returned, I borrowed my CEO's car to drive back to Belle Cottage. I drove around the south shore of Glen Lake, headed north at the big lake's eastern shore, and turned up Miller Hill road to the lookout. I hopped out, and Mick and I sat on the hood of the car. If the sight of the emerald and sapphire gems and white pearls forming a necklace on the bluest body of freshwater in the world couldn't win my son-in-law, I didn't know what would. I told him about the legend of the lost daughter and how she made this delight of life her home we now call Leelanau.

When we got back into the car, Mick said, "I grew up on the wrong side of the tracks in Green Bay, never learned how to swim, let alone fish, sail, golf, or play tennis. I was lucky to grow big and thick-skinned enough to become one tough brute on the gridiron and the ice so I could escape to Madison."

He paused, and I told him the story of how my father, with much the same background and no college, married my mother and took over the family business.

"Too risky for me," he replied. He explained how he was going to law school, to work in a Chicago skyscraper and bust the unions. "I'm going to buy a house in Lake Forest, so Ruthie can stay home and raise our kids."

Better to learn he didn't have Papa's ambition, Kurt's smarts, or David's sense than let him run down our family business. "Why do you want to live there?"

"Big houses along the shore, and Ruthie can teach our children to swim, sail, golf, and play tennis." He patted my arm. "Don't worry, we'll visit you and Pip here two weeks every summer, and invite you to visit us any holiday you want."

I felt like clocking him as hard as he'd checked Paul but only said, "What if Ruthie wants to take this year off and train for the Olympics?"

He shook his head.

"You didn't know the coach of the women's swimming team called her?"

"Who'd mother baby Marty then?"

I felt like telling him he could handle changing diapers and feeding his baby with a bottle but only said, "Why do you think Pip and Ruth call me Marmie?"

"You'd keep Marty in Ann Arbor?"

I refused to answer.

"And Ruthie'd go to New York to train with Miss Ederle?"

I drove down the winding, dirt road back to Belle Cottage.

Eventually Mick said, "I couldn't live with that."

"Then you help more with the baby and accept my paying for regular help in Madison so Ruthie can graduate from Wisconsin and get a teaching certificate by the time you finish law school." He nodded. "And at least let me teach you how to sail for the time we've got left together here." Thus did Mick and I forge an uneasy truce.

ꟷ

Ten days later Pip brought Wilbur Pierpont, the university's Financial Officer, to dinner at Belle Cottage. A man of much lank and little girth, Bill's big smile made me forget his owlish glasses. I was inclined to like him, as he brought our mail from Cambridge House, including the new books from Auden and Frost with their cover letters. Pip had already shown Bill his new land along Empire Bluff and south of Little Glen. Tomorrow morning Pip, Bill, David, and Ruthie would play our MacKenzie links.

Young Pierpont shared our enthusiasms, for the forest, shore, and fresh water to be sure, but also for the enterprises in Empire, not just our family business but also Mirja's Fitzpatrick and (now) Son Press, Pip's horned scoop, and the possible uses for Pip's new tracts. Bill also wanted to learn about the "economics" of the Leelanau Schools and Camps, the Homestead Inn and Golf and Outing Club, our Up North Writers' Conference, and the other towns Pip envisioned thriving along the coast from Empire to Northport. Paul O'Bannon would have relished this talk about the place that had become his second home, but he'd returned to seminary in South Bend.

Ruthie piped up to suggest a new camp associated with University Hospital for kids recovering from surgery or sickness. Baby Marty cooperated, resting comfortably in Ruthie's lap or mine throughout dinner, and even let Mick cradle her without caterwauling. Ruthie excused herself to feed the baby, and Bill engaged Mick in a discussion of the University of Wisconsin's ongoing expansion following the war.

Pierpont also knew several contemporaries in the big accounting and law firms in Chicago and offered to introduce Mick if he wanted to serve as an intern next summer. "Be sure to take tax and finance courses, too," Bill advised. "There's a lot more opportunity in those big firms if you specialize in corporate law."

Mick listened hard, and I realized he'd cause less damage working in a law firm than driving Sven's dune buggies.

I excused myself after dinner and retreated to my bedroom to review my prizes from Frost and Auden. I first opened Auden's *Age of Anxiety* to the title page, saw his hand-written inscription, and took out his note.

My Belle,

I've a confession. Good as Rhoda may be for me, it's a sin: I'm cheating on myself and on her. Just one night reveling in a carnival at the Fire Island Hotel dressed up as Cardinal Pirelli, and I remembered my truth: unfaithful as Chester is to me, that's no excuse for me being unfaithful to myself.

Enough with my confessions, or you'll call me a Catholic. The first run of Age of Anxiety sold out. Stravinsky wants me to write a libretto. The pain in my optic nerve has subsided, thanks to your Dr. Protech

But I have neglected my duties to my godson horribly, so give him a sweet for me and my best to Angelyn. We can all meet at your writers' conference, at least if you'll have me as an honest man this time and send me more of your Up North songs.

As ever, Wystan

To meet his challenge I composed a dialogue in verse. Then I wrote back:

My Dear Wystan,

Now that you're finally eligible as a citizen, even Frost will concede your Age of Anxiety will win the Pulitzer, but don't let Stravinsky's wooing turn your head. You promised a poem about your limestone source: write it and many more. Remember how you revised the Marx duo's crazy chorus in F6? Your "Funeral Blues" made me cry. I want to hear you sing such new short lyrics at our writers' workshop. The Homestead garret will welcome you and yours again, but you may not appear in costume as Cardinal Pirelli, thank you.

I enclose an Up North poem I composed for Ruthie and her new baby. She shares much with the bawler "Infans" you composed for Angelyn and your godson. If my little river debate meets your challenge, I look forward to seeing you here, as will Angelyn and your namesake.

As ever, Belle

I opened *Steeple Bush*, the thinnest of Frost's books, to the first poem he marked, "Directive." I sang it and danced along with Robbie once again. From his secret goblet, I greedily drank the sacred water of his source until I felt "whole again beyond confusion." Several pages later, he'd inserted a letter:

Dear Belle,
Our boy did us proud at Amherst. President Cole dedicated the renewal of Fayerweather Hall as Charles Drew Science Center and thanked your brother for paying for it. Kay enjoyed the scene at Amherst, but there's not been much joy at Noble Farm since. Even Untermeyer found my Steeple Bush wanting, and Time's bad review sent me to bed for 10 days until the old Bread Loaf doctor issued his diagnosis: Nothing the matter with me except my head.

Poor Irma suffered much worse. She fell into a depressed state so bad she couldn't care for herself. Her estranged husband John had to take over the care of their boys, and I had to commit her to the State Hospital in Concord, New Hampshire. I couldn't have managed without Kay standing with me to help all along this sorry way. What kind of luck is it that only Lesley among my children escaped my family curse? Counting my father and sister that means 6 of 7 of our Frost lot died too young or went insane. Not sure yet where I may fall in this, but don't you think it's enough for three generations in any family tree? Oh, how I hope so, because Robin and the rest of the Frost grandchildren deserve better.

I do have good news. President Cole and I see eye-to-eye, so I can go back home for my last days. Roethke's tenure job also came through in Washington, but I still wish Michigan had the smarts to invite him home instead. Then, at long last, our big Teddy Bear could share the glasshouse Eden with you.
Now, you write and tell me Ruthie's well and her baby's fine. I hope the poem I enclose with this note will cover the new baby with health and protect her from misfortune.
As ever, Robbie

"Skeptic" offered another of Frost's pithy wonderings on the stars, light and science. I reread the concluding lines about the narrator feeling the universe, "very immense or not…tight against my sense like a caul in which I was born and still am wrapped." From the phrasing I knew 'caul' must be some kind of cover or veil. I took out my *Webster's* to find out what else he meant. The word described a baby born with the placenta over the head, still protected from any foreign threat for yet a while longer. Over time, being "born in the caul" became a sign of good luck and good health, and the legend grew that sailors born under this good omen wouldn't drown.

Frost had added a postscript: *Thanks for the copy of Red's talk. Glad to know my poems inspired him to invent his own dream world: reminds me of your even dreamier slants on The Silken Tent. With any luck we'll get Red back to composing his own dreams so I can write about the figure his poetry makes. About time you compose another of your songs and share it with your erstwhile preceptor, too.*

My Dear Robbie, I wrote back:
Ruthie and her girl are both fine, thank you, but never has a friend offered a better gift for a newborn than your Skeptic's song. If not a believer, you're a Burns Bard through and through, wishing our girl such good Scots luck. Ruthie and I will make sure the newborn learns to swim so she never drowns either.

Do not bother about any review of your new book: gain revenge by publishing your collected poems. Pip will send the Nobel but tone-deaf Swedes several pairs of his little ears so they can finally hear all your different tunes and slants of meaning.

You know Ted flies too high and far for this arboreal nester, but he is joining us again up north. I'll invite Wally and you bring Kay. She can then witness your losing another World Literary Tennis Championship.

I do hope Irma recovers, but please take as good care of yourself, Lesley and all of your grandchildren as you can. As with the blessing of Ruthie's little Marty, I now appreciate more fully the joy and hope for a brighter future such grand-children offer us. Come what may, remember that your lot is to keep writing: I look forward to your next stay against confusion. I will keep composing, too. As ever, your other Belle

P.S. I am teaching writing with Rabbie again this fall and a poetry seminar in the spring. I enclose a dialogue I wrote for Ruthie and her baby.

After lunch the next day, we brought in several chairs from the dining room and met around the kitchen table. I sat at the head, Ruthie, David, Spring, Davey, and Angel on one side, Pip, Bill Pierpont, and Major and Helen Huey on the other. First, Pip presented his plans to work with the University: on the south shore of Little Glen, a camp for handicapped and sick kids and their families; and on the coast, bluff, and forest south of Empire, a biological station and research institute. Bill said University Hospital would support the camp and the Regents would welcome the forest preserve, but Michigan needed a few years to consider a freshwater research institute on the Great Lakes. "In the meantime," he concluded, "you may want to reserve a piece of land on Empire Bluff for another golf course." Pip whistled with glee.

Major piped up, "This Magic Wish Camp going to compete with my Leelanau camps and Belle's writers' workshop at our Homestead?"

I had to give Major credit for making it sound like I had an equal stake in his question. Before I could reply, Ruthie told him Pip's new camp would lead to more kids enrolling in Major's camps and schools, more applications to our writers' conference, and more families wanting to stay and play at the Homestead.

Major nodded a tad too easily: what new idea did this ever-ingenious but maturing and increasingly independent young pup have up his sleeve?

Davey and Spring then described how they hoped to expand their holdings east and north of Ahgosatown, all the way to Miss Schultz's preserve. "We need to protect Sleeping Bear first," David interjected.

Major Huey only smiled without saying a word.

So I asked him, "What's your plan for your campground south of the state park to Pip's land in Empire?"

"From what Mr. Pierpont says, sounds like I should build a golf course."

Reminded me why we needed him on our side. To my surprise, David said, "It may be time to explore whether a national park will help us acquire the key parcels."

Davey scowled at that and barked, "And renounce our fishing, hunting, and gathering rights while the Feds continue to refuse to recognize our band?"

"I worked with the Secretary of Interior at the War Production Board," his father replied. "He's a good man. We should try working with him so it's not either-or."

"All of our private land, like Miss Schultz's Leelanau Conservancy," Pip added, "will continue to respect Indian rights in any event."

"Be careful what you wish for," Major scoffed, "lest the Park Service henchmen go after all your land and businesses as well as mine."

"Whoever heard of a national park," Davey added, "with towns, schools, camps, golf resorts, factories, publishing companies, research institutes, a port, and great Ojibwe orchards, vineyards, and enterprises!"

"You and Major want to join Pip and me to ask?" David said.

Angel and Ruthie looked at each other and said as one, "If they don't, we will."

Spring and Helen nodded at that, and Davey and Major could hardly object.

As our meeting broke up, I steered young Mr. Pierpont into the study. "I hear Chase Osborn's counseling you and Pip."

He nodded but said, "The governor's daughter gave me an earful at dinner after Robert Frost's talk at Rackham." He offered his apologies for not getting to know Pip and me before, because the University made "big mistakes letting his war lab, John Kraus, and their Big Ear get away and reducing the number of women admitted as freshman after the War." Good Lord, this CFO was no ordinary accountant. "Miss Belle, I have a young daughter, too. I don't think the League excuses the Union's limiting its front door to men or the many Hopwood Awards won by coeds excuses the University's depriving qualified women of serving as English professors."

"Mr. Pierpont, are you here to ask me for more money for the University?"

"Miss Belle, you make what I like to call the Michigan Difference. Will you finish endowing the English chair for a woman?"

"You need it to hire good candidate from another school?"

"A promotion from inside," he said with a knowing wink.

Oh, Dorothy Donne will be the first nail in Strait's coffin; Rabbie and Cowden have done very good work with the Chair.

"The candidate will need to publish a book of great poetry first."

"Mirja and her press in Empire will be glad to oblige."

When Bill Pierpont gave me his big smile and stuck out his hand, I shook it and asked, "Think we need to take our Empire public?"

"Kurt arranged private debt financing for your expansions thus far?" When I nodded, he asked, "Why not ask Kurt to compare the risks and rewards of selling Empire to your competitors with selling shares to the public and going head to head with them?"

"I couldn't ever sell out from under David Ahgosa." Bill didn't argue, but he didn't give in either. "Care to join Kurt on the board of our conservation trust here?"

"When Michigan accepts Pip's gift of land," he replied, "I hope to join as a representative of the University, but you shouldn't wait to add your girl."

"Ruthie?" He nodded, and I did, too. "Want to go with my boys to meet the Interior Secretary to see how a national park might enhance *your* biological station, research institute, and new Magic Wish Camp?" When he nodded with a chuckle, I shared my poem about preserving Leelanau I composed for Ruthie and her baby:

Conservation Conversation

"To catch a trout," said the angler,
"wade into these crystal waters
quiet, and flick your wrist.
Work the line back and forth
near that outcropping there
where you see a silver flash
till you feel a strike.
Set your line, then reel,
steady, and once your fish
is in hand, gently remove the hook
and let it go."

"You have it all wrong, Sissy,"
said the eagle high on his perch.
"From this aspen branch
you watch the waters
for movement. From up here,
I can spot a trout a mile away.
You take flight and soar,
then swoop down
when a nice brown rises
and hook its meaty flesh tight
with your trusty talons."

"Then you let it go?" said the girl.

"Hell, no!
I've a family to feed
not to mention
my own needs to nourish."

"But future generations
depend on the trout
making the swim upstream
to spawn," said the angler.

"Yes, the best eating season of all!"

"Have you no respect for nature?"

"I AM nature," said the eagle,
"and where I fly
it's hunt or be hunted."

"I'll remember that.
My gun has more grit
than your talons any day,"
said the more determined girl.
"You, Bub, could end up
on my table!"

"When I visit next spring," he said, "will you take me fly-fishing with Ruthie and Pip on the Crystal River?" When I nodded, he added, "Belle, can we catch sight of a feisty eagle, too?" Mr. Pierpont and I would do more business together.

Spring and Summer 1950: Glen Arbor

David, Spring, and Angel Ahgosa sat with me on the deck of the clubhouse atop the ridge. The noon sun turned the crusted snow from ice to corn. Davey slalomed through the trees on his steel shin and artificial foot-ski. Engaged to marry a second cousin as darkly handsome as Spring in the fall, he would expand opportunity for another generation at their burgeoning Grand Traverse enterprises.

Almost 15 now, Angel still looked a pixie. Her dark goggles and big floppy hat protected her pale eyes and skin from sunburn, while her frizzy golden hair peeked out from under the brim and framed her face. This fairy sprite's grasp of her heritage made her the band's acknowledged Ogichidaakwe and heir apparent as next Ogema to succeed David. Angel leavened her second sight with a curiosity to learn everything she could about the history, geology, geography, flora, and fauna up north. She also worked closely with Mirja and Paul O'Bannon on writing and illustrating the native legends for a broader audience. Published by Fitzpatrick and Son Press in Empire, these gorgeous books sold in increasing numbers throughout the Midwest and Ontario.

I worried about David. Our All-American Flame brand, and sales of our stove, dryer, camp products, and heating, air-conditioning, and refrigeration systems continued to expand, but he'd become distracted, even careless. At the Empire warehouse he twice ran into the corners of crates and needed stitches over his right eye. Twice, the right side of the pickup truck he drove clipped a parked car. I asked him to make an appointment at the eye clinic at University Hospital, but he put me off. Angel confided he sometimes got lost in a dreamland, and Spring conceded he tired much more easily.

A cloud passed over the sun. I looked out to the big bay, blocks of ice still piling inshore, but the passage open, the water dark blue from the cold. Within a few weeks, all the snow would melt, rivulets would race down to the Crystal River, pools would form under the trees, and the ephemerals would spring to life.

I turned back and said, "David, I'm driving back to Ann Arbor tomorrow for my seminar. Why don't you—"

Before I could finish, Angel cried, "Davey's down." His one wood ski slithered to the bottom of the hill, and Davey lay crumpled at the base of a big pine. I ran down the hill with Angel and Spring. The deep, wet snow slowed our progress.

David flew by on his long skis. Angel shouted, "Stop," but her father didn't listen. He barreled straight down the hill and barely missed several trees in his mad dash. As he approached his son, he jumped in the air and turned sideways as if to make a flying hockey stop. The lowest branch of a big birch on his right clipped his head. He and the limb fell like two stones and buried in the soft snow.

We didn't hear a sound, but Davey turned and dragged himself up the hill to his father. We tramped down as fast as we could, but Angel already keened as Davey cradled his father's head. The gash extended from David's right temple to his cheek. A bloody socket stared back at us.

"Still breathing," Davey said.

"I'll get the toboggan," I said and climbed back up the hill. Angel flew by me, and pulled a toboggan from the shed under the terrace. "You slide down," I said, "and I'll call Major for help. Meet us at the road by the river." The same place where we'd loaded Spring into a car and saved her life so she could give birth to this Angel.

Major drove the school van up just as Spring and Angel, pulling the toboggan, and I converged on foot. Davey held his unconscious father. Major folded the third-row seat flat. Major and Angel on one side, Spring and me on the other, we lifted one end of the toboggan and slid it as a stretcher in the way-back. Davey, his good leg propped at an odd angle, held his father and wrapped him in blankets. Spring and Angel climbed in the second-row seat, Major hopped behind the wheel, and I sat next to him to help navigate.

David began to wake as Major sped onto the jog of the Empire–Traverse City state highway, where my brother had crashed before and the police escort had greeted us when we drove Spring, pregnant with Angel. Although David never allowed more than a low moan, Spring urged Major to drive faster. Angel sang in a soft, calming voice, while Davey fought back his tears. When Major pulled into the Emergency at Munson Hospital 25 minutes later, the orderlies placed David on a gurney.

Major asked whether he should wait to drive me back. I felt so guilty for failing to get David to an eye doctor before this accident, I didn't know what to say. My mind also roiled with all the calls I needed to make to set up temporary arrangements. Good Lord, what if David never recovered? And if Davey lost his other leg, could he ever accept running the Ojibwe enterprises in a wheelchair?

"No, I'm needed here."

I waited with Spring and Angel in the hospital room with two beds. A nurse wheeled Davey in, his stump with a metal ski-foot on a footrest while his whole leg stretched out before him in a huge plaster cast. Only a clean break in his tibia and torn ligaments in the ankle, but Davey had a broken heart about his father. Angel pulled the curtain shut, and I couldn't hear what she said to her brother.

After several minutes Angel invited me in. Davey rested on the hospital bed, the plaster cast elevated in a sling.

He turned on me: "Why didn't you make him go see the eye doctor?"

"Oh, how I wish I had." I saw he also wished he'd pressed his father. Strange how life changes so quickly and, when it does, we blame ourselves for not doing what we could to try to rewrite such fickle fate. I sat down and laid my hand over his. "Davey, I'm so sorry." The tears flowed, and Spring and Angel joined us.

After we gathered ourselves, Spring joined me for tea in the cafeteria. I said I'd take over running our Empire and ask Pip to help until David recovered. She said she'd oversee Grand Traverse enterprises. I asked whether it might be better if her boy got back to work rather than blame himself for his father's accident.

"Oh, Belle, it's my fault, not Davey's or yours: David asked me not to say anything." She teared up. "Why do such bad things happen to such good people?"

All I could think to say was, "Angel will help us understand."

That brought a smile to Spring's face that spread to mine.

"I'll meet you back in Davey's room." Without my saying, she knew I had many calls to make.

I tried Pip at Cambridge House and at Mirja's cottage in Empire. No answer. I even called Hill House. No answer. I tried Kurt Knutsen at home. No answer. Finally, I reached him at his office and explained David's accident and my fears about a deeper disease at work.

"Terrible tragedy," Kurt said. He paused. "It also threatens our public offering." When I asked why, he told me how we'd have to disclose David's condition. "That'll make investors so skittish, we'll have to pull it."

"I haven't been able to track Pip down yet, but I think we need to wait to see if David recovers enough so we can get his insights, too."

All business, Kurt said, "Fair enough. We'll put the offering on hold." There was a long pause. "If David doesn't recover, I think selling's the best option."

So hard to lose the family business after all these years, I answered, "Kurt, one piece of good news. Pip invented a new gas refrigerator-freezer that will trump Amana."

"America's Flame won't do as our brand."

I couldn't laugh, not this day. "How about *America's Fridge*?" I managed.

"Hope Frigidaire won't sue us." He paused. "Belle, I'm so sorry about David."

I looked in my little address book and called Rabbie's office. He picked up on the first ring. "Think Professor Donne can take over my seminar for the rest of the semester and help you run the poetry section of our writers' camp?" I explained David's accident and injuries and my need to take over running the family business again.

"What about Cowden?" he said.

Hell Damn, my leaving would open the door for Ned Strait to press his campaign to become the next Hopwood Director. "Ask Roy if he'll stay on longer?" Rabbie paused for so long, I cut the silence by saying, "You okay?"

"Moved back to the family farm in Northfield Township."

That explained why no one had answered the phone at Hill House: Mirja had decided to live openly with Pip there, but they were away traveling. "Paul okay?"

"Graduates from the Holy Cross Moreau Seminary in June." There was another long pause before he said, "My Ma's dying, another week or two at most."

"No mother ever cared for her son more."

"You got that backwards."

I remembered the day we first met, when he took me to the cemetery at St. Patrick's to visit his brother's grave and his family home. "No, Rabbie, I saw how much the Queen loved you." When he greeted my statement with silence, I said "With Teddy confirmed, maybe I can get Frost and Stegner to join us for a rematch up north."

"That'll only begin to make up for you not running the poetry section." A long pause followed. "Good luck with David."

"Godspeed with your Mother."

"I'm alone at the farm if you…" There was a long pause before he said, "Belle, I'm sorry," and rang off.

I could still see the gorgeous violets by his front path rising to greet me the day we met, but why was he saying "sorry" to me now?

I called the plant manager, told him about David's accident, and asked for his help to run our business until David got back on his feet. Nearing 65, he'd worked for my father, Kurt, David, and me. "We'll manage, lass," he said, imitating a Scottish brogue through his heavy German accent. When I thanked him, he added, "Tell David he better get well quick before you get too uppity again." We'd get along fine.

A nurse walked up. "Miss Belle, a call for you in the office."

I followed and expected to talk with Pip. Instead I heard Ruthie's voice. "Angel called and told me about Davey and their father."

I heard something else in her undertone but said, "Yes, terrible accidents." I paused. "Have you heard from your father?"

She explained how she just got off the phone with him. He and Mirja were exploring a proposed national park on the Outer Banks, and their drive back wouldn't get them to Ann Arbor until tomorrow evening. I heard a muffled cry. "He told me he's moving into Hill House."

Maybe Ruthie viewed her father leaving the house in which she grew up as deserting her. "You know you and your family are welcome to stay with me."

"I'm leaving with the kids right now. Where should we meet?"

"Take the ferry, and I'll pick you up at the dock in Ludington this evening." I paused. "Ruthie, for you and the kids to join me now is a blessing."

"Thanks, Marmie, but you know we're running from Mick."

I could only guess what happened, but I respected her judgment.

I called Major and explained how I needed a ride to the car-ferry. He said he'd pick me up and asked whether we could talk on the way. "Why not?" I answered.

I took the elevator to Davey's room and learned that David was conscious and stable. Of course, his right eye was gone, but there was also a marked deficit in the peripheral vision in his left eye to objects on his right. Not a good sign, I knew.

"Can we fly him to University Hospital tomorrow morning?" I asked.

Spring nodded. When Davey looked uncertain, I explained we'd rent a plane big enough to carry all of the Ahgosas.

"I'll learn how to walk on crutches tomorrow," he replied, "and be ready to run our Grand Traverse enterprises first thing Monday morning." He was his father's son.

I left to see David in the recovery room. His bandages covered the top of his head and the right side of his face. His left eye, clear and dark as ever, focused on me. He extended his hand and bade me sit in the chair by his left side. He listened while I told him how Pip and I would help run our Empire business and Kurt would delay the public offering until he returned. I explained how I had to pick up Ruthie and her two kids at the ferry tonight, but Spring and Angel would fly with him to University Hospital in the morning and live in Cambridge House again. As soon as Davey was sure their band's enterprises were running smoothly, we'd drive down to Ann Arbor, too.

David Ahgosa nodded and turned his head away but extended his hand to me. He turned back and opened his left eye. "I'm sorry I caused you all this trouble." I squeezed his hand. "I hoped to see our Empire through the next phase, but when I saw Davey fall, I couldn't help flying to him." I stifled a sob. "Spring knew," he continued, "but I need your help with Davey and Angel to carry on after I'm gone." I raised my right hand to his mouth and hushed him, but he continued, "Time to sell Empire and use some of our gain to secure the future of our Leelanau, too."

I broke down, laid my head on his chest, and said we'd help him buy more land so his eagle could return for his band, too.

"Thank you for sharing," he said as he stroked my hank of still red hair. "Go to Ruthie now."

"Not goodbye for a while yet, thank you." Damned if he didn't nod with a grin despite his bandages, injuries, and worse. I began to feel one of my death frights coming, but I fought it off so I could wave to David at the door.

Major picked me up in my old green Lincoln Zephyr, but I was so tired I asked him to drive to Ludington. He didn't give me a chance to rest my eyes. After the briefest of preliminaries getting an update on David and Davey, he said, "Belle, I traded my campground south of the Dune Climb to the new lumberman for Alligator Hill."

Although I'd steeled myself for bad news, Major might just as well have poleaxed me, but I didn't dare flinch. Although we hadn't always seen eye-to-eye and he acted in what he saw as his best interest, he'd been a good partner and friend to us for too many years just to up and declare war now. So I only replied, "Not happy you didn't include me in your discussions."

No dummy, he didn't try to make excuses.

"Is he planning to log all that precious land between the dunes and Pip's Empire?" When Major shook his head and told me the new man might build a scenic toll road up through the forest to several outlooks, I said, "A damn sight better than the Dark Ogre's thrill rides. Tell your trading partner, I'll be glad to finance his new tourist attraction." When Major chuckled with me, I added, "Okay, what's your plan for Alligator Hill?"

"A four-season golf, ski, and hunting resort overlooking the bay, lake, and dunes."

"What the dickens do you propose for *our* partnership on the Inn and *your* management of *our* Golf and Outing club?"

"What I really want is to trade Alligator Hill to Pip and you for the rest of the Homestead."

I was so relieved, I laughed out loud.

"You don't think it's a fair deal?"

"Just amused by your manner of bargaining." When he smiled with me, I added, "Give me a chance to talk to Pip, but you know we'll never agree to let you subdivide any of our land for home lots." When he began to get into details of what development restrictions we'd want, I raised my hand. "Major, I'm too tired now, but you know Pip and I will come to good terms with you on how to support our shared goals for our little corner of paradise, including the Indian rights to gather, fish, and hunt there."

I must have rested my eyes then because I didn't wake until we reached the turn to the ferry in Ludington.

"One more thing?" Major said.

What could I do but nod?

"Sven's bought a whole fleet of Ford F150's and plans to build gravel roads across the dunes, all the way to Mama Bear and back." As I shook my head and thought, *Over my dead body*, Major pulled the car to a stop at the ferry lot. He opened my door and shook my hand. "Miss Belle, I will miss you as a partner when we complete our trade."

I leaned down and gave him a peck on the cheek. "Major Huey, you'll still have to put up with me as your best customer..." He smiled too quickly. "...and nosy neighbor."

*

I had to wait only 15 minutes before Ruthie drove Marty and the baby off the *S.S. Midland 41*. Ruthie looked drained, but Marty greeted me with a big smile, and the infant waved a rattle at me from his special carrying chair Pip had made. Refreshed by my nap and bargain with Major Huey, I offered to drive so Ruthie could rest in back with the two children. Within ten minutes of pulling onto the state highway, all three fell asleep and didn't wake until I pulled to a stop in front of our family home.

Pip raced down the front steps with gifts for his grandchildren. He gave Marty a stuffed sea turtle wearing a green T-shirt from Cape Hatteras and held two stone turtle's eggs up for his grandson. Little Paul reached his hands out, and Pip gave him the stones, too large to fit into the baby's mouth. Pip gave Ruthie and me a hug and shooed mother and baby up the steps. Past midnight, Ruthie retreated to Papa's study to feed Paul, and Marty yawned. Pip popped his head into the parlor and said to me, "I put the baby's crib and Marty's stuff in Mama's old room. That way Ruthie can get some rest in Papa's bedroom, and I'll be down the hall to help with the kids."

Made more sense than stuffing Ruthie and her family in her old bedroom on the third floor. "How'd you get here so fast?"

"Rented a plane."

With all my other worries that day, I'd forgotten that my boy flew all over the country to open our plants and to share his and others' tinkering.

He asked, "Will you read Marty a story so I can talk to Ruthie?"

I wasn't about to tell Ruthie's father I wanted to talk to our girl first. I took Marty by the hand, walked her up the stairs into Mama's old room, and helped her put on her pajamas. She fell asleep before we got halfway through the second of my river dialogues.

I didn't wake until I heard baby Paul's cry early the next morning. While Ruthie fed her hungry boy, I went to the kitchen, washed my face and hands, mixed the ingredients for flapjacks, and lit America's Flame under the griddle. Pip told me to sit down and poured five ladles, two for me, three for him.

"How's Ruthie?" I asked.

"She'll only talk to you about what Mick did, but there's no going back, ever."

"I wish Miss Schultz were here to advise us," I said.

"I already called Frank Devine in Ann Arbor." For such a dreamer, Pip could take charge. "If Mick thinks he's going to get admitted to practice law, he'll cooperate."

"You want to run Empire, too?"

"Sorry, how's David?"

I told him what I knew and what options Kurt put before us.

Pip asked me to step up again but said he'd help oversee operations at all our plants. "Unless David can get back to being CEO, I'm for selling, too." I shook my head, and he continued, "I asked Ruthie if she wants to learn the business so she can run it, but she says she's going to teach and raise her two kids." He paused. "She wants to compose poems and write legends, like you and Angel." He also explained how he'd called Bill Pierpont to intercede so Ruthie could also transfer to the Education School at Michigan. "I think she'll choose to settle in Cambridge House with you." He paused. "Marmie, I'm sorry I didn't tell you before that I was moving out so Mirja and I could live together."

"Fixing to get hitched?"

"If she can get an annulment, I'll convert."

For all his hiding out in his old garage attic in Ann Arbor and Mirja's new cottage up north, he was a far braver soul than I: he seized his main chances. I don't know why, but I blurted, "Maybe the son you share with Rabbie will conduct your catechism then." When he gave me a sour look, I said, "Sorry. What's Paul going to do?"

"I pray he doesn't disown us and serve as a missionary far away." He reached for my hand. "Mirja and I are going to make the cottage up here our main home."

As I reflected on how the University was such an important part of our lives, despite all the problems we both had, I must have frowned. "Marmie." He cleared his throat. "You've been the only reason Mirja and I stayed so long in Ann Arbor, but we've got to make our way up here now, okay?"

I swear there was a film of water over his blue eyes and, no doubt, over my dark ones, too. I hugged him close. I wanted to thank him for being my boy, brother, business partner, helpmate, best friend, and, more often than not, inspiration all these years. I said, "About time" and hid my head on his shoulder so he wouldn't see me crying. When I finally gathered myself, I added, "Just because you're finally moving out doesn't mean you're getting rid of your Marmie." I told him how much I looked forward to working with him to do right by Ruthie and the kids and our family business, helping the towns of Empire and Glen Arbor thrive and preserving as much of our delight of life up north as we could. I concluded by telling him about my discussion with Major Huey.

"We've got a bigger problem than Sven," Pip said. The longtime head of the Park Service opposed making Sleeping Bear a national park. "The new head of the Interior Department wants to overrule him and press Congress for funding, but…" He slumped.

"But we promised David," I said. After a long pause I had to ask what I didn't want to think about, our Ojibwe partner never returning: "If we have to sell our business, you going back to tinkering and searching the heavens full-time?"

He placed his long, thin, bony fingers to his face, grown gaunt through all the years, and shook his head. When he lowered his hand, though, he looked like a new man, as hopeful as the boy who left for Amherst College with such enthusiasm 23 years before. "I'm thinking about investing in new technologies now emerging from all the War research around the country."

"What would your Dr. Charles Drew think of that?"

"He'd join us in filling up every gas tank in Sven Surtr's new trucks."

I rose from my chair and embraced my boy. "Don't ever sell yourself short."

ᔕ

Three nights later I set off with Pip and Mirja in the old Lincoln, top down, while Ruthie stayed home with Marty and baby Paul. Once again I turned the lights off when I turned onto Michigan's shortest state highway, drove into Glen Haven, and parked behind the long-closed cannery. I said a prayer for King David as I tiptoed up the front steps to the general store he built so long ago and taped the huge poster Mirja made on the front door. A big Mama Bear, worn by wind and weather, sat atop a tall sand bluff. She flicked out her paws and flipped over dozens of little pickup trucks as they invaded her sacred domain, but dozens more kept coming. The caption read, "D. H. Day would never go to war against Sleeping Bear Dunes." Tears flowed from the Mama Bear's eyes and flooded the gravel road made by Surtr, all the way back to Glen Haven. Pip and Mirja taped their copies to the front doors of the inn and the blacksmith shop.

We hopped into my car, drove past the old life-saving station, turned up Surtr's gravel road, and pulled to a stop at the front of the long line of red F150 pickups stored beneath the cottonwoods. Each truck had an open cab in front, three rows of benches in the back, and four big tires with huge treads. They appeared to dwarf my green Zephyr in the dim light of the quarter moon. We pulled out the shovels and began piling sand up to the front wheel wells to block each truck. We started with the lead one and, four hours later, with my back, shoulders, and arms aching and my hands screaming with blisters, we finished the last one. Mirja walked back to the Lincoln and pulled the big teddy bear from the trunk. She returned and placed the Mama Bear in her watchful crouch in the middle of the gravel road 10 feet ahead, facing the lead F150. As Pip unfolded a paper with the pertinent deed restriction from our loan agreement printed in bold.

Pip leaned down to place the bold print in the Mama Bear's front paws, but a huge shadow fell over us. I turned and saw the Dark Ogre wielding one of our big shovels as a baseball bat to strike Pip. I screamed and rammed my shoulder into Sven's side.

Although I only bounced off, I delayed his swing long enough for Pip to turn. He stood and grabbed onto the shaft of the shovel, each of his hands inside Sven's grip. Although six inches shorter and 50 pounds lighter than the giant, my brother's arms were longer, his bony hands bigger, and his gnarled fingers stronger. The two men pressed, pulled, and twisted the shaft, but after more than a minute, Pip stood as the immovable object against Sven's irresistible force. Their faces contorted and their fingers, hands, and arms seemed to grow, but the shovel barely moved as the shaft vibrated for what seemed an eternity, until Sven began to push the shovel and Pip to the ground.

"Enough," said a voice I knew but couldn't believe. A light flashed and Davey Ahgosa hobbled forward on crutches, one leg in a big cast from hip to toe, the other leg bared at the knee, with Pip's metal pole and foot below, a red bandana on his head, and a Kodak in his hand. Sven let go, and Pip scrambled up and laid the shovel on the ground.

"I paid ovv your loan," Sven sputtered at me, "and I've got the state's permission to build this gravel road so my new Scenic Rides von't hurt the dunes."

Pip stepped back, leaned down, and placed the paper on the little Mama Bear's front paws. Davey flashed another picture of the bold print: "For 10 years after repayment, borrower shall secure lender's consent before purchasing or operating new equipment or building new roads to carry passengers across Sleeping Bear Dunes."

"The agreement says you can't unreasonably vithhold your consent," Sven said.

"You never asked us," I replied.

Davey snapped pictures of the teddy bear blocking the long line of trucks from driving up the dunes. Sven bared his fangs in rage, and Davey snapped that image, with the Dark Ogre glaring at the little teddy bear's warning in the background. Sven demanded we leave his property, but Mirja said we were all standing on state park land. Davey snapped that shot, with the line of F150s in the background, stopped in their tracks by the sand blocking their front wheels. Sven said he'd see us in court after he ripped the posters off his buildings in Glen Haven.

Davey patted his Kodak camera. "Already took snapshots of

all three, from my car in the middle of M-209, thank you." Sven stalked off, saying he'd sue us for any loss of business. Davey shouted, "Prepared to see all my pictures in the press stories first?"

ɞ

Frost's July 1 letter and package confirming his participation in our writer's camp contained fewer contraries than usual:

> *Although the Nobel Swedes and my former ally Untermeyer and his Pulitzer Committee refused to give me their prizes, the U.S. Senate acclaimed my poetry for "promoting understanding and love of our country" and sent "felicitations of the Nation" on my 75th birthday.*
>
> *I enclose a Limited Edition of my Complete Poems. Don't for a moment think the Christmas poem "Closed for Good" I put in the Afterword is my valedictory. I don't want your return to the helm of your Empire to go to your head either. I told Wallace Stevens the problem with his poetry is he can't escape the business exec he is and writes too much bric-a-brac. I therefore challenge you to compose a better Up North lyric I can use in my opening lecture there. Tell Wally Stegner I'm arriving Saturday evening, and I expect him to stay over Sunday so we can reclaim the World Literary Tennis Championship you stole.*
>
> *I look forward to seeing O'Bannon there, too. Ted says I made a mistake letting Rabbie be his biographer rather than mine. I hope all my friends and Holt will defend me against whatever Thompson may say, so the resulting controversy spurs sales of my poems long after I'm gone, as it has for Dickinson. Although Mr. Hampson did sell all of Madame Bianchi's originals to Harvard, President Cole continues to court Mrs. Todd's daughter for her Dickinson papers. Charley is also courting me for mine.*
>
> *Very sorry about David Ahgosa. Please make the time so*

> *we can visit him, his family, their orchards, and the old kirk in Omena.*

I reread the poem in his Afterword and felt, again, like I was walking hand-in-hand with this old friend down a long lane "cut… to last" by the "passers of the past." Yes, the old bard said he was glad they'd "left the road" to "his slowness" to enjoy the onset of winter snow, "till even I have ceased to come as a footprinter and only some slight beast so mousy or so foxy shall print there as my proxy." It reminded me I should reread Emily Dickinson's songs to see if the odd figures of her poems facing hope and death could help me come to grips with David dying.

Auden's letter and package confirming his regrets was no less challenging:

> *So sorry I'll be in Ischia when you need me to sub for you at your writers' camp up north. Probably just as well: Chester and I have been scribbling away on the libretto, and I wouldn't dare leave my bad boy to his own devices now. But give my best to Roethke up north. Why not ask young Hayden to join you two?*
>
> *Please thank Angelyn for me. Not sure her dissertation doesn't give too much meaning to my moral musings, but her colleagues showed good sense adding her to the philosophy faculty at long last. Give my godson a hug for me, too. Tell Frost I look forward to botanizing with him this fall. While he's rambling with his Amherst boys, I'll be a monk tutoring the Mt. Holyoke girls.*
>
> *Next spring Random House will publish my new shorter poems. I enclose the one you demanded, "In Praise of Limestone." Send me a new Up North lyric so I know your return to Mammon doesn't mean you lost your Muse.*

His poem rambled across two typed pages, 100 lines in 50 couplets. Daunted by its apparent density, I feared I'd get lost in the words. Instead he transported me on his journey through the delightful limestone land of rounded slopes and secret system of caves and conduits, nurtured by a mother who loved him regardless of his faults, to the more conspicuous fountains, jagged cliffs, and temperamental gods of his middle age in Italy. "When I try to imagine a faultless love or the life to come, what I hear is the murmur of underground streams, what I see is a limestone landscape."

I went up to the attic, pulled out my journal, thought of all my seasons overlooking the Great Lake. I sang until I made it right:

My salvation is

a rainbow of pure blues
all the way to the horizon:
gray-blue the early morning,
until the sun appears

to rim the shore with turquoise—
water so clear you can spot
schools of dancing minnows
and crayfish scuttling about—

Beyond, on summer days,
sunshine paves diamonds
from Empire to the Manitous
on the cornflower bay—

When clouds scatter by,
Lake Michigan becomes
the sky's periwinkle mirror
adrift with marshmallow puffs—

Should dark storm clouds
rumble in from the west,
turning the bay denim,
white caps will race for shore—

On clear autumn nights,
long after ribbons of salmon,
purple, magenta and pink
have faded away,

the rising harvest moon
casts a golden path
across the cobalt bay
to the inky shore—

December crusts the lake
with steel gray and pewter,
freezing waves along the coast
sculpted by a powerful wind—

Beneath this icy rime,
teal glints wink at me
giving joyful assurance
of my blue salvation!

Naturally, I called it "Blue Salvation II." I made two copies. The first to Frost: *I enclose my latest up north song and hope it won't embarrass if you choose to include it in your talk here. For our rematch with my Teddy and your Wally, do I need to lend you a racquet so you can blame my strings?* The second to Auden: *Your praise of limestone inspired me to drop my business pose for one night and dream a new song of Leelanau. If you like it, I hope you'll visit my Blue Salvation again here before you forget our Arbor days as you have your manners: Don't assume this Old Maid has lost her passion to sing!*

ꟷ

The day before the start of the writers' camp in late August, Paul O'Bannon knocked on the front door of Belle Cottage shortly after dinner. He'd been traveling for interviews all over the country since his graduation from the Moreau Seminary at Notre Dame and induction into the Congregation of Holy Cross. Wearing a becoming black cassock and clerical collar with a white tab, his dark hair trimmed, face and hands tan, and eyes pale green, he looked like the Latin priest he was.

"Do I call you *Father* now?"

"Not unless you want me to call you *Belle*."

"You're not free of your Marmie yet!"

He flashed his white teeth.

"Paul, may I offer you a sniff of Papa's Macallan?"

"Thanks, Marmie," he answered with his Irish smile. He followed me into the study, where I poured us each a small tumbler. I sat in the desk chair, and he sat in the leather chair on the other side, looking out the window, west across the sparkling bay to the crimson sun setting over the dunes. "Ruthie and the kids okay?"

"You can see for yourself if you want to join us for lunch tomorrow." When he nodded, I added, "Pip and Mirja are driving them from Ann Arbor."

His face grew so dark I turned in my chair to see if a sudden storm had blocked the sun. "You know Pip still loves you as his son, too." When Paul only stared at me, I said, "Let me get this straight, Father O'Bannon. You could bear the odd triangle, even accept knowing that Pip begat you with Mirja, but only so long as they didn't openly admit it and your mother and father kept up the front of being married?"

"Marriage is a sacrament; divorce, a sin."

"You're not welcome to tell Ruthie that at lunch tomorrow in my house."

"I wouldn't do that."

"I know. You offered to marry her when you knew she was pregnant with another man's child, and you couldn't help but suspect Pip was your father."

"I wasn't a priest then, remember?"

"No, you were closer to a saint." I paused. "When did you last see Mirja?"

"Grandmother O'Bannon's funeral at St. Patrick's."

"Your priestly vows compel you to disown your mother?"

He shook his head.

When I asked when he'd last seen Pip, he said, "My graduation, two weeks before that." Paul handed me a golf ball signed by Alister MacKenzie. "Pip told me to enjoy the game for the rest of my life, even if I never spoiled a good walk with him again."

"We've got an extra set of clubs if you want to join on the links here."

He took another sip of Macallan and looked out the window. When he finally said he'd join us all for lunch tomorrow, I escorted him to the front door. "Why don't you also join Rabbie when he introduces Frost a week from Monday?"

"I will if I've found a job somewhere up north by then." I couldn't help hugging the nephew by blood I wished I could have loved as a son all these years. Father O'Bannon skipped down the steps, his cassock flowing to his old beater of a Ford.

ග

Pip and I didn't escape our meetings and calls with Kurt and our lawyers until late the next Saturday night, when we wrapped up negotiations with the winning bidders. That meant Rabbie and Roy Cowden had to serve as hosts for the writers' camp during the first week, including at breakfast every morning and dinner every night.

Rabbie also emceed the talks on Monday, Wednesday, and Friday afternoon, starting with Stegner speaking on "The Problem of Fiction" and ending with Roethke reading several new greenhouse poems for his next book. Robert Hayden and Dorothy Donne helped Teddy lead the daily seminars for the poetry participants, and Wally helped Rabbie with the prose writers. Fortunately, Angel helped care for Marty and baby Paul. This gave Ruthie time to make all the participants feel at home as our personal guests. Ruthie also greeted Frost when he arrived Saturday in time for dinner, and Teddy, Rabbie, and Wally rambled and talked with their old friend in the evening until he retired at an early hour.

At 10 a.m. Sunday, I strolled onto the green Har-Tru court next to the Inn. Frost and Stegner already hit from the back court on the north side to Teddy, who volleyed at net on the south side. Having slept late, I skipped breakfast but remembered to bring an extra racquet for Frost. I held it up, but he raised his own.

"Won't need any excuses this morning, thank you, Miss Belle."

I spun my new Jack Kramer and said, "M or W?"

"What's wrong with 'Rough or smooth' this time?" Robbie barked.

"W," said Wally with a big grin.

I looked at the butt of the handle. "W it is." I turned the racquet around so Frost could see as he walked to the net. When he asked for the balls, I looked to Teddy to see if he wanted to aggravate the old bard by taking the other side again, but he only hobbled back to return serve in the deuce court.

"Could I hit a few balls to warm up?" I asked.

Frost pointed toward Teddy and shook his head. "You'll need all your energy to cover a lot more court this time."

Little did I realize how much. Teddy's knees were shot. I had to cover Frost's clever lobs over Roethke's head, sinister drop shots in front of him, and too much of the rest of the court. We won only one game the first set. Gasping for air on the changeover, I discussed strategy with my partner before he served to open the second set.

"Sorry, I'm so lame," he said in a whisper, his head down.

"You win your serve again, we don't waste energy on Wally's, and we try different tactics on my serve and Robbie's." Teddy didn't raise his eyes. "Look at me."

He raised his head, and I saw the sweat dripping and his big chest heaving.

"On my serve, play at the service line so you take away Robbie's lob and drop shot. On Robbie's serve, step a few feet back and step up again after your return."

His sad eyes brightened, and he won his serve easily. Although Wally breezed through both his serves, Teddy's midcourt position did frustrate Frost's touch game on the Old Bard's serve and mine. We won the second set six-two.

I suggested a celebration over lunch, but Frost again demurred. He whispered in the back court with Stegner, and they came out on fire in the third set. Wally won his serve easily as Frost positioned himself two feet in back of the service line and took away our lobs over his head. We lost Teddy's serve when Frost moved in front of the baseline and managed to chop back two returns deep, and Stegner poached Teddy's cross-court forehands. Frost served soft up the middle, but deep in the service box, and then toddled up to the service line. When Robbie managed to scoop our returns deep, Wally either poached our drives or knocked off our lobs for winners.

Down love-three, I won my serve by going to net on Frost's soft returns and hitting Stegner's hard returns back at Robbie's feet. Wally won his serve to put the bi-coastal team up four-one. Teddy proceeded to win his serve by acing Frost three straight times and getting lucky when Wally's flat drive on ad-in clipped the top of the net, bounced up, rolled along the tape and fell back. We broke Frost by returning the ball hard at his feet, and we won my serve again by hitting every ball at him.

At four-all Stegner was magnificent. His big serve overpowered us, except when he threw in a high-kicker and I lobbed back over

Frost's head. Wally just stepped behind his partner and sharply angled an overhead for a winner. Teddy served to tie the match at five-all. If we could win his serve, we'd certainly break Frost, and I'd serve for the title. The game proceeded with Teddy hitting his big serve for a winner every time against the tiring Frost but losing the next point as Wally hit sharply angled returns and blasts up the middle for winners. After the fourth deuce-ad, Teddy, his first serve losing its steam the longer the game went on, hit a slice on deuce point wide to Frost's forehand. Damned if Robbie didn't extend his arm beyond its reach and pop a perfect top-spin lob over my head for a winner.

Down four-five, ad-out, Teddy hit a big serve toward the far corner of the service box. As it bounced high and wide, I faked as if to poach, and Wally backhanded a soft lob down my alley. I stepped back and smashed the ball cross-court at Frost's feet. The ball rocketed off the Har-Tru clay, bounced up, hit his racquet, and, unaccountably, flew so quickly over Roethke at the service line he didn't reach up to smash it. I lumbered back cross-court, stretched as far as I could deep in the corner of Teddy's alley, and lofted the ball back. We all watched as the little white sphere floated over Frost and began to arc down behind him for a winner. Except an overhanging limb of a pine tree reached out and clipped my lob. Bough and ball fell together in his alley.

What an unfair way to lose a great match, but I had to give Frost credit for a terrific reflex volley. I turned to shake hands with my partner, but Teddy walked back to the baseline and took a ball from his pocket as if he thought the score deuce and expected to serve again. I shook my head, but Wally said, "Let's play two."

Frost walked to the net. Teddy protested, but I gave our bear of a boy a hug. When I returned to the net and reached out, Robbie took my hand. Whatever his usual phobia, he kept pumping it so I had to drag him off the court and sit him on a bench to make him let go. He couldn't stop talking about his two "great gets" and the divine intervention of the tree my Papa planted. Teddy sat on the other side and congratulated Frost.

Robbie looked up at Wally and said, “Good thing I got you to change tactics after that second set!” Frost lifted a full ladle of water as if to toast himself.

“Damn it,” Teddy said, “I thought you were at least going to concede the World Literary Tennis Championship, but no, now you’re going to compose so many more good poems, you’re going to steal so many Pulitzers there won’t be one left for me.”

Frost reached back as if to throw the ladle at Teddy. Inertia sent the water cascading over my chest and Robbie’s instead. Frost jumped up and sputtered. I was worried I’d have to shoo Teddy and Wally away again, but Robbie apologized, picked two towels off the net, handed one to me, and used the other to dry himself off.

“Sir,” I said to Frost, “your manners, like your tennis, improve in time.”

His pale blue eyes sparkled, but the bushy eyebrows seemed to weigh down his lids and shoulders, as he said with resignation, “Going forward, I’m leaving the Pulitzer field to Mr. Roethke and your younger generation. Untermeyer’s committee snubbed my *Complete Poems*, despite all three agreeing it was the best book by America’s greatest poet.” When Teddy said it was the best by far, Frost rose and shook Roethke’s big paw. Robbie winked and added, “Ted, trust me: Louis says your time will come, soon.”

Robbie and I repaired to Belle Cottage, and Teddy and Wally, to the inn. At 1 p.m. we convened in my kitchen to share lunch before Wally headed off for a seven-month teaching tour through Europe and Asia, sponsored by the Rockefeller Foundation. Stegner bemoaned the lack of sales and reviews for his new historical novel about Joe Hill, the much-storied labor organizer and songwriter who’d been eulogized as a union martyr wrongly convicted after being executed in Salt Lake City in 1915 for murder.

“The liberal critics,” Frost said, “don’t like to hear the uglier truth.”

"Like you," Wally replied, "I had to tell it as I saw it." He paused and added with a rueful smile, "Except you know how to milk the resulting controversy to multiply sales of your books, while mine die the death of being ignored."

"What's the difference, if you're true to yourself?"

"About a million bucks," Stegner said. "I'm beginning to wonder if I'm just pounding sand down a rat-hole, writing novels no one wants to read."

Teddy said, "I've only published two books. One sold less than a thousand."

"Enough," I said. Maybe Wally and Teddy felt a little guilty, knowing I published nothing, but they shut up. "You two just keep writing, and your rewards will come."

Frost said, "Amen." With a smile to Stegner he added, "Too bad you're leaving and won't hear what I have to say about our Miss Belle and her Blue Salvations."

"Enough," I said again, albeit with a smile now.

We got up, and Stegner embraced his mentor Frost and shared a big bear-hug with Roethke. I escorted Wally to his car, parked in front of the inn, and thanked him for joining us. I couldn't let him go without asking his advice. "Frost tells me your interest in conservation grows as much as your skill in telling a good story."

"Benny DeVoto," he replied with a shrug, "finally shamed me into speaking up for our Western wilderness against all the dam boosters."

"What do you think of a Sleeping Bear National Lakeshore here?"

"Frost had it right in 'The Gift Outright': we owe all to our land, even if we've pillaged her as we've crossed the continent. Better to preserve her as best we can going forward."

"Not sure Frost's hostility to big government doesn't extend to the National Park Service." Stegner chuckled. "I also worry we don't have a true wilderness here."

"Belle, the national park is the best idea we Americans ever had."

I met Teddy on the porch and asked whether he wanted to join Frost botanizing.

"Big Mama, you wore me out covering your side of the court." He kissed my cheek and tried to kick up his heels.

When he stumbled, I held him close and said, "I'm returning to teach at Michigan in the fall. If I manage to do Strait in, will you come back?"

"Already wrote 14 poems since my last bout, and there's no holding your Theodore Roethke back now." He turned away but then turned back. "Big Mama, your Teddy Bear will only come back for you."

He tried to dance me off my feet with his Foxtrot, but I had to hold him up. As I pushed him away, I said, "Ted, I will always love you."

He turned and bumped his big chest against mine, as if a boar rubbing against his sow. Good Lord, how could any woman bear such a mate?

I turned him away but smacked his butt. "I do miss you."

ꕥ

I pulled the old Lincoln in front of the house, lowered the top, and tooted the horn for Frost. He ambled down the steps but stood beside the car. "You're not taking me botanizing again through your Garden of Eden here?"

"Sorry, Champ, you already tuckered me out." As he opened the passenger door and hopped in, I noticed one of his sun spots looked distended. I reached in the backseat; grabbed the two big, floppy hats; and clapped one on my head and the other on his.

"I hate wearing a hat," he protested.

I reached over, touched the odd mark, and felt its jagged rise above his skin. I asked Frost if he'd stop in Ann Arbor so University Hospital could take a peek.

He didn't answer, but he didn't remove the floppy hat either. As we crossed the Narrows bridge between Big and Little Glen and saw

Sleeping Bear Dunes rising, he said, "Can it wait until Kay takes me to our farm?"

"You promise to go to the Hitchcock Clinic straight away then?"

Frost nodded. "You worried about me dying?" When I froze up, he added, "The surest sign of immortality I've found is the longer I live, the more time I have to burn."

I took the shortcut to the new scenic drive and paid the toll. We drove on the gravel road, up through the evergreens to the maple, birch, and beech sprouting a hint of their fall colors. At the first lookout, we peered through the trees across Little Glen Lake to Alligator Hill.

"When are we visiting David and his family, and the old kirk, too?"

I'd spent countless hours with David at his home in Ahgosatown since his return from University Hospital but stopped three weeks ago when I couldn't bear watching him fade away any longer. Not even rereading Emily Dickinson's poems took away the sting of his dying. "Tuesday morning Pip and Mirja plan to drive you for a visit."

I drove on until we reached the boardwalk that led across the dune to the cottonwood grove. Our feet clopped along the cross-ties, and the blowing sand pricked our ankles. The dunes flowed north three miles to Sleeping Bear Point, and the blue water of the passage spread another five miles to Manitou.

"You swam there?" I nodded three times, but they all seemed so long ago.

We continued to the cottonwood grove. I told Frost how different the flattened hump in the distance looked, compared to when David and I first gazed at her.

"Your Legend of Sleeping Bear," he said. He cupped his hands behind his ears. "No trucks roaring up to threaten her this summer."

I explained how, with Sven's new trucks stuck in neutral by our opposition, this new scenic toll road had filled the vacuum.

He listened hard and asked, "Have you brought David back to sit with you here?" I shook my head. "Don't wait, Belle."

When tears rolled down my cheeks, Robbie held me. "Can't you see? There are so many ladders pointing up, there must be something for them to lean against."

I remembered the opening line of his "After Apple-Picking" and sang, "My two-pointed ladder's sticking through a tree toward heaven still." I paused. "You make me want to believe, Robbie," but I hurried along the decking back to our car.

I drove up, up, and up and parked below a big dune. As we approached the top, I held Frost's hand. "Close your eyes." When we got to the summit, I said, "Open."

High above Lake Michigan, the view offered a 180-degree panorama of the Great Lake, blue, deep, mysterious, untamed. I felt his pull on my hand. "I've seen enough to include your Crystal Moment and Blue Salvation II in my talk."

"Which of your poems are you going to use?"

"Several from *A Witness Tree*, starting with 'I Could Give All to Time.'"

"Too bad Stegner couldn't stay," I interjected. "That's his favorite poem."

"Can't you help David cross to safety, too?"

"Can you include one of Roethke's poems?" When he looked at me puzzled, I said, "He's still recovering from his latest mental breakdown and hospitalization."

"Which do you suggest?" I handed him a copy of "Praise to the End," a long poem, covering four typed pages. Frost's lips moved, and his head bobbed as he read it as if singing aloud to himself. "Still a good ear for sound and rhythm in his verse, but I'll need to study this more to make sure I don't misread our boy."

"Your praise can help him win a Pulitzer."

"I'll ask him to read it here, but I'm going to end by saying my 'Silken Tent.'"

"You know that's my favorite poem!"

"Like your 'Crystal Moment,' it also begins in delight, inclines in impulse, runs a course of lucky events, and ends in a momentary stay against confusion..."

"...whether heard as elegy or love song," I interjected, grabbed his hand, and skipped back across the dune to my green Zephyr. As we drove down to a clearing in a stand of beech and maple looking south, I asked whether he'd had a chance to talk with Robert Hayden.

"Those glasses do make him an odd-looking fellow." He paused. "He read three of his poems to start one of the writing sessions. Don't know whether it was just the way he spoke, but the deep voice and vital beat of his 'Ballad of Remembrance' made Mardi Gras in New Orleans jump." He paused before grumping, "Nobody ever wrote such a good poem to thank me as he does for that middling Columbia U poet, though."

"Why don't you arrange to have Hayden join you at Bread Loaf, then?"

As we got out of the car, Frost couldn't resist a smile and nodded. "As one who's too often been pigeonholed as New England bard of rural scenes, I admire his stand in refusing to be viewed as a colored poet of the Negro experience."

I couldn't resist twitting him: "You both use your vernacular to rise above your different roots."

Now, he couldn't resist a smile. "As does that Chicago woman who stole the Pulitzer from my *Complete Poems*," he conceded with a rueful shake of his head.

We sat close together on the hood of my old Lincoln and looked down on the lighter blue of North and South Bar Lake and the bustling town of Empire. We scanned its big bluffs and green forest beyond, the ribbon of white sand curving in a gentle crescent around Platte Bay to Point Betsie 15 miles away. A big freighter turned and moored next to two others on the long Empire dock, jutting out 300 feet into the deeper blues of Lake Michigan.

"The last of those big ships will soon make its final stop there," I said. I wondered what Papa and Mama would make of the plant closing.

"What's going to happen to the town?"

I pointed to our big, long factory spreading back from the dock several blocks along Niagara Street to the state road and explained how we were donating the building and an endowment to the University for a Great Lakes Research Institute and a freshwater aquarium. I pointed to the new building in the quadrangle next to the Fitzpatrick publishing company and shared how we'd also helped Michigan establish a Biological Station to study the ecology of the forests D. H. Day, Papa, Pip, and I planted. I pointed west of Empire to the low-slung, cedar-shingle house and the much larger cedar building to the south. "The new clubhouse and inn for Empire Bluffs Golf Club, only a niblick shot from the back door of Mirja and Pip's cottage."

"You going to take Rabbie back to complete making a square out of that triangle?"

"I thought you told me to make room for our Teddy Bear instead."

"Judging from his decline, he can't keep up with you." Frost chuckled. As I smacked his shoulder, his blue eyes lit up. "Well, you did ask for my suggestions!"

"I wouldn't convert to Rabbie's Church 30 years ago to marry."

"Haven't you learned that personal faith and companionship matter more?"

"And the institution of marriage causes the least possible pain between the sexes?"

Frost couldn't help chuckling at the irony of this reminder and nodded. He pointed to the top of Empire Bluffs: "Pip building another observatory?"

"No, he arranged for a new Air Force radar station up yonder." I smiled and thought back to the times so long before when my brother and John Kraus played with their radio gizmos there and happened to find ships and planes hidden in bad weather.

"You mean Pip's given up listening for extraterrestrial voices?"

"Not a chance: With his favorite acolyte, he's built a really Big Ear, the size of three football fields, at Ohio State."

"*Our* boy *is* a wonder." Frost waved his hand, turned in a 360-degree arc and asked, "With all this, and the rest of your land, why would you ever consider a national park and all that federal folderol, anyway?"

"To protect our Sleeping Mama Bear, as Pip and I promised David Ahgosa."

ᔕ

The following afternoon I sat alone in Papa's study. Ruthie had driven over to Ahgosatown to say her farewells for the summer to Angel, Davey, and Spring and her final goodbye to David. I'd read to Marty and Little Paul until they'd both fallen asleep. I looked out the window to the Leelanau Schools, Glen Arbor, Glen Haven, and the dunes.

The meetings Pip and I held with Surtr to try to settle our dispute out of court hadn't borne fruit, even with Major Huey's sympathetic mediation. Pip and I offered to buy D. H. Day's heirs out of Glen Haven—and loan them additional money—to relocate and help build Glen Arbor into a bustling, four-season town to complement Major's burgeoning Leelanau Schools, Camps, and Homestead Resort. I held out the prospect we could also throw in the old Bell factory land and buildings so Sven could anchor his development right on the lakefront.

At our last session, though, Sven threw a wicked curveball back at us. He'd sold his modified F150's to dune buggy operators downstate after GM offered the new Oldsmobile Rocket 88 convertible and balloon tires: "Hell, Belle, vith no need vor gravel roads, no court vill ever tell me I can't run my *Dunesmobiles* vrom Glen Haven the same vay I did vith my old Vord cars vhen your loan vas in place." Maybe a national park did offer our last best hope to save Sleeping Mama Bear.

The knock on the front door broke my reverie. I opened it and saw Father O'Bannon in full priestly regalia. "Good Lord," I said in my best Scottish burr, "I'll not convert even if the Pope sent you."

"No, lassie," Paul answered in his family's best Irish brogue, "you'll get no confirmation into our flock until I hear your Penance and Confession of all sins and you complete the full Catholic catechism."

I invited him into the kitchen and set one cup of tea for him and another for me. "Where'd you get off to after Frost's fete Monday afternoon?"

"Took awhile to recover from the bard calling you and Roethke up and then conducting the dueling readings between you three," he said with a smile. "Yours made the best figure of a poem."

"Your Irish blarney will get you nowhere with this crotchety Scots Old Maid."

"I visited all the parishes in the northwest corner of the Grand Rapids Diocese."

"Find any that need a rookie?" I asked.

"Not one."

"Sorry," I replied, meaning it. "We'll miss you up north after all these years."

"Sorry," he said. "The bishop hired me to serve as the new itinerant priest for all of Leelanau County, as long as I also teach English to the students at St. Mary's."

"I'll be damned," I blurted.

"I'll pray you won't, if you let me stay smack dab in the middle of my circuit in exchange for my taking care of this place while you're in Ann Arbor."

"Oh, did you talk to Ruthie?"

"Pip told me she's going to teach at the new Tappan Junior High and raise the children at Cambridge House with you."

Now that Frank Devine had shamed Mick Shiller into skulking away to the Illinois Bar, I knew the children could use the influence of this good man but shook my head. "I plan to give Belle Cottage to

Ruthie." The minute I said that, I felt I'd wronged him again: he was at least as much my kith and kin.

He replied as if he read my mind: "Remember, I took a vow of poverty."

"I'll talk to Ruthie before we leave tomorrow and let you know."

ᔓᔕ

An hour later I heard a big knock on the front door. When I peeked through the peep hole, there stood my Teddy Bear in a red plaid shirt, khaki pants, and a brown tweed coat with leather on the right shoulder and big side pockets. I opened the door and said, "You looking for Rabbie to get your bonus or for me to go shoot a big buck?"

He emptied all his pockets to show me that only one check and not any shells fell out. He flashed his bonus and said, "I'm taking you to Art's to say thanks."

I hopped into the passenger side of my old car and tossed the keys to Teddy. He roared us into Glen Arbor, top down. At our friendly corner tavern, he ordered us pan-fried perch, a grilled cheeseburger deluxe, a mess of steak fries, and two Stroh's.

While we waited for our feast, he challenged me to a game of ping-pong. He took off his jacket and whipped the reigning king-of-the hill to get control of the table. His style of play wasn't much fun, as he loomed over his end of the table and blasted top-spin forehands and backhands past me on every one of my serves and returns. He made five errors, two long, two in the net, and one wide, but he also made 21 winners. I supposed his method saved his aching knees, as the points were short and he only had to roll right in his red-checkered shirt to hit his big forehand and left to hit his bigger backhand.

"Not sure that's any way to say thanks or introduce your girl to a new sport?"

I saw his eyes widen as they rose and peered above my head. I heard Sven Surtr behind me say, "Mr. Big Shot, iv you're Belle's wannabe beau from the southland, I'll show you whose king of this hill up north!"

Before I could retort, the Dark Ogre grabbed my paddle and cleared the crowd, all the way past a four-top to the booth by the wall, a good 15 feet from his end of the ping-pong table. Although Roethke was a big man, Surtr was taller by almost a head, and his wingspan seemed twice as wide. Sven gripped the little wooden paddle, stippled green rubber on each side, at an odd angle, almost as if he intended to use it as a shovel. He sliced under the ball, and it bounced once on his side, darted over the net, and skidded even lower on Roethke's side. Ted made as if to hit a big forehand blast but stopped when the ball looked as if it might bounce a second time. When the ball cleared the edge of the table, Teddy couldn't mount his big swing in time.

Soon it was five-zip, and Roethke rolled up the sleeves on his flannel shirt past his elbows. He served his top-spin version of his smash: The ball bounced on Teddy's side, dipped over the net and took a big bounce to Surtr, standing a dozen feet beyond the table. Sven shoveled it back over the net with a low slice that barely cleared the net, bounced, and then skidded beyond the end of the table, and Teddy blasted it back. The single point went back and forth 10 times, before Sven's slice didn't clear the net. So it went, through all of Teddy's five serves, and two more rounds of serves between the two.

By the time it was 15-all, Roethke was sweating buckets. He took off his shirt and handed it to me. He flexed his arms, and his big shoulders, chest, and, yes, belly, puffed out of his ridiculously small undershirt. Teddy continued to roll to the left and right, blasting his top-spin returns close over his end of the table, while Sven stood well back and coolly sliced shot after shot, tempting Teddy to hit harder and harder, with more and more top spin. On the last of Sven's next five devilish slice serves, Teddy leaned in even closer and scooped the ball back just over the net. Sven leapt forward, stretched his big arm, and managed to pop the ball back, but it bounced too high. Teddy's smash rattled the table on the other side of the net, shot up, and hit Sven on the nose.

Smarting now, Surtr determined to hit Roethke's top-spin serves and smashes back with an even more pronounced chop that made the ball skid with an even more wicked low bounce. On the second and fourth serves, Sven won the points after long exchanges, when his low shots finally skidded so low Teddy couldn't swipe them back before they bounced twice on his side. That made the score 20 for the Dark Ogre to 19 for my Teddy Bear. The last point seemed to go on endlessly, a big pong and a fast ball with each of Roethke's smashes, with a little ping and frustratingly slower retort from Surtr. Sven's final devilish slice barely cleared the net and skidded low after it bounced on Teddy's side. Roethke leaned forward and took a huge forehand swipe up, but his paddle caught the end of the table at same time it struck the ball. The thunderous thwack of the paddle was rivaled by the crack of the ball as it exploded in half between the back edge of the table and Teddy's paddle.

Surtr threw up his hands in victory and let out a Norse war cry. He doubled over with an even louder "Oof!" as the head of Roethke's paddle flew into his solar plexus. Surprisingly, I realized Teddy hadn't thrown his paddle in anger, as the handle still remained firmly in my big bear's grasp. Yet Sven was so mad from being struck in the gut, he leaped over the table and threw his shoulder into Teddy's out-size chest.

All hell broke loose when Teddy hit the floor. As Surtr straddled Roethke, my boy freed his right hand and blasted Sven in the nose with a straight jab. The rest of the crowd stepped back to let the two big men brawl, and Sven soon started pummeling Teddy. I jumped forward, placed Teddy's flannel shirt over Sven's face and pulled back as hard as I could on both of the empty sleeves. Before Sven could protest, the owner roared out of the kitchen wielding a big frying pan and whacked Surtr on the head. Art's wife, Mary, followed close behind yelling "Fire!" before her husband could knock any better sense into Roethke.

All the other customers fell over themselves clearing the tavern.

Ted, Art, and I managed to drag the woozy giant out as the flames exploded from the kitchen and pushed us out the front door. We collapsed in the middle of the road and watched as the blaze shot through the roof. Too soon, the windows blew out, and the exploding heat made us all pull back to the far side of the road.

Art stared at the blaze in silence as the roof collapsed. The volunteer brigade arrived, but all we could do was watch the fire die down until sure it wasn't going to spread to any other building.

When Art said, "Thank heavens, nobody was killed," I replied, "Whatever the insurance doesn't cover, we'll help you rebuild."

Sven, still glowering, said he'd buy the first round of beers, while Teddy, still red-faced, said he'd return to buy schnapps for all. After the fire brigade made sure no one else was hurt, Teddy and Sven even shook hands. Not sure we all parted as friends, but I managed to drag Roethke away before we contributed to any more "misunderstandings." We walked down to the end of Lake Street and sat together on a big silver tree trunk, weathered smooth by the Great Lake.

"I'm sorry," Teddy began, "but I had planned to ply you with good food and more drink and then beg you not to marry me again."

"Good Lord, Mr. Roethke, you mean Sven was right about you wanting to be my beau? I'm not sure I can take any more excitement on one evening out on the town, when we haven't gotten the first morsel of food yet."

He smiled, but his big shoulders slumped, and he turned his head away.

"I'm sorry," I added, "but what you said is a big mouthful." I grabbed his arm and made him look right at me. "Teddy, I'm not sure I could ever put up with you in the same house for long, but I would give it as good a go as I've got if you move in with me." His hands began to shake. "But you know I can't leave my family and my responsibilities here and in Ann Arbor to join you in Washington, and I haven't been able to kill off Nym or his slanders at Michigan yet."

Roethke rose. "I told you before not to marry me no matter how much I begged." He turned and began walking back along the beach.

When I called after and asked where he was going, he said to the inn to hitch a ride with Rabbie back to the train station in Ann Arbor for his trip to Seattle.

"Theodore Roethke, what's happened to your manners? You can't desert your date at the dance just because you begged her not to marry you, and she ignored your advice and answered she would say, 'I do,' but only if you move in with her."

My big Teddy Bear returned, his head still down, took my hand, and marched me back up Lake Street as fast as his sore knees and lumbering gait would allow. He threw the car keys at me and pouted, "You know, Frost is still way too old for you!"

On the short drive to the Homestead, he didn't say another word. When I dropped him off at the inn, he leaned down and kissed me on the lips, though. He stepped back. "Big Mama, you made me the best proposal I ever had, but I have to move on, to keep writing and teaching, even if it's all the way across the country." When I began to tear up, the gentle touch of his forefinger made me look up. His eyes looked sadder than ever, but he said, "Don't let Nym and the Old Guard beat you down at Michigan as they have me."

When I parked the car in back of my cottage, my spirits and head down, Rabbie surprised me by opening the car door. He said he'd talked to Cowden. Roy had agreed to stay on as Hopwood Director to mentor me, and Rabbie would join in pressing Chairman Ray to choose me over Strait.

"Oh, Rabbie," I began, but I didn't know how to thank him.

He said he was sorry Michigan had turned its back on Ted again, sorrier still that David Ahgosa was being taken too young.

I kissed him on the cheek. "Think we're still young enough to swim laps at Whitmore Lake together?" I asked.

Rabbie held me close and sang, "My Dearie Belle, till the day I die."

I smiled at his reminder of our first meeting, but then he got down on bended knee, pulled out a little, black velvet jewelry box, opened it, and showed me a gold band polished bright by decades of rubbing.

"My Ma left me her wedding ring. May I plight my troth to thee?"

Given the Queen's long opposition, I thought about saying, "How dare you!" but I couldn't muster the strength. Instead I reached down for him, and he stood beside me, his hand with the ring outstretched. I couldn't help smiling but shook my head and said, "Apart from the minor detail you need to get a divorce first, don't you think we should see how we do swimming and spooning again for starters?"

When I saw Rabbie's mouth broaden to an Irish grin, I couldn't resist planting a pucker on his lips that lingered longer than it should have. He nodded, pocketed his ring, and walked back toward the inn. Rabbie must have caught me in my weakest moment: what was I thinking?

I walked in the back door and saw Angel and Marty cleaning up dinner while Ruthie fed baby Paul in the kitchen. Ruthie asked how my date with Ted had gone, but I only told her about the ping-pong match, the head of Uncle Teddy's paddle flying into Sven's stomach on the last point, my pulling a shirt over the Dark Ogre so he wouldn't beat our Teddy Bear to a bloody pulp, Art belting Sven on the head with a frying pan, and the tavern burning down. Ruthie, Angel, and Marty laughed. Hard as I tried, I couldn't.

Harder to admit, but I now felt much worse about leaving for Ann Arbor in the morning without saying farewell to Angel's father than saying goodbye to Teddy or hello to Rabbie. I suggested to Ruthie we pack early, drive over to Omena in time to attend the Sunday service at the kirk, and leave from there. Ruthie said Angel had already agreed to spend the night and watch the baby in the morning so Ruthie could take Marty on their last swim in the bay instead. Maybe David put his shaman daughter up to making sure I wouldn't have to go through the agony of saying farewell.

After songs and stories, I asked Ruthie if Angel could help the kids to bed so we could talk alone. Ruthie joined me in Papa's study, and I asked her what she thought of letting Father O'Bannon stay to take care of the cottage after we returned to Ann Arbor. When Ruthie laughed and shook her head, I said, "I'll tell Father O'Bannon that Major Huey already assigned several of his students to live here, then."

"No way: my kids need a Father, and just because he's too good for me doesn't mean he won't be good for them." When I asked again about David, she replied, "Dad already talked with him about how best to split the sale proceeds, one share each for you three partners, one share for the workers, and one share for our Leelanau land trust."

"David Ahgosa could still understand?"

"David offered a friendly amendment and asked whether Davey could also represent the Ojibwe interests on our conservancy board." When I asked what her father had said to that, she replied, "Only if Angel also agrees to serve."

I managed a smile now.

Ruthie added, "After the closings in New York next Friday, Pip and Mirja plan to go to Washington to see if they can figure out how to get around the head of the Park Service. We'll know soon enough."

Suddenly, I wanted to go to bed for a long sleep. At the second-floor landing, I stopped to say goodnight, and Ruthie stood on her tiptoes and whispered, "Marmie, David Ahgosa already knows how much you care."

I confided how Roethke had begged me not to marry him again.

"Marmie, Uncle Teddy always loved you, too."

I nodded, but no way would I share that Rabbie also proposed this evening.

I climbed the stairs to my turret, kicked off my shoes, and fell onto my bed, too tired to take off my clothes. I must have fallen into a deep sleep because the dream woke me at 7:30 in the morning. I could see in the fog of my mind Angel, her frizzy white hair forming a halo, coming into my room, stroking my red hank of hair, and saying, "My father will meet you at the kirk at 9 a.m. He'll help you make this crossing to safety."

I washed up, drove the old green Lincoln to Leland and across the county road to Omena, took West Bay Shore north through the village, and stopped at the base of the hill in front of the white clapboard kirk with its tall steeple. The rising sun already warmed the crisp day, and I put the top down. Still a few minutes early, I walked up to the cemetery on the east side of the kirk, the maple and beech already showing a hint of color among the bigger green cedar. I stopped at the markers for David's parents and mine. His would be next, and, the good Lord willing, I'd follow before I had to bury Pip, Ruthie, Father Paul, Davey, Angel, or any from the next generation of children. I don't know how Frost managed to survive with his bad luck, but I began to tremble.

I returned to the front of our kirk and entered. David Ahgosa sat tall on the aisle seat in the left front pew. His hair, jet black, flowed in a ponytail between his shoulders. A colorful bandana formed a tight dome over his head. I walked up the center, around a small wheelchair with big inner-tubes for wheels, and slid by him. David, his left eye as clear and dark as ever, black patch on the other, nodded. We sat in silent prayer, our hips touching. My breathing slowed to match his.

David pointed to the wheelchair. I helped him in. I guided the chair safely down the grassy hill overlooking Omena Bay. The rising sun glistened off the water, navy blue, still as glass. I helped him into my car's passenger seat. As I began to fold the wheelchair, I saw a small cooler on the canvas tray beneath the seat. I picked it up, leaned over, and placed it next to David so he could use it as an armrest.

"What's in here?" I asked to break our silence.

He spoke in a gravelly, hoarse whisper that started deep in his chest and emerged very slowly from his lips: "Our last supper."

I folded the wheelchair into the backseat. "Where'd you get this little chassis?"

In that same soft, slow, deep rumble, he answered, "Our partner." Who else but Pip could tinker a wheelchair into a dune buggy?

I slid into the driver's seat, and David pointed north. We drove past the rows of buildings for the Ahgosa Grand Traverse enterprises that now spread on both sides of the state highway, down the slope to the houses and cove that had sheltered his great-grandfather's band so long ago, and up the hill to the new winery. He pointed west, and I turned up the gravel road that cut between his clan's expanding orchards and vineyards. When we hit the Manitou Trail, I turned and headed north on West Bay through Northport and then on the country roads to Miss Schultz's land and the lighthouse. I lifted the wheelchair out, set it on the ground, unfolded it, and helped David climb aboard. The big balloon wheels rolled easily over the gravel paths and down to the shore. He surveyed the scene as we had so many years before, when Miss Schultz's gift vested us with responsibility to conserve this delight of life. One of the big freighters carrying the last stoves from our Empire steamed across the Great Lake. The ship blew its horn, two longs, a short, and two longs. David raised his arm in salute.

We returned to the car, and I wound south and west along the old Indian trails through the rolling hillsides, with row on row of his fruit trees and vines. When we reached the road to Gills Pier along the shore that marked the western boundary of his holdings, a ribbon of sand appeared. David pointed, and I nodded: More land we needed for a national park or our Leelanau conservancy.

"A tribal reservation?" I asked as we passed over the friendly roar of a fast-running brook.

A tear formed, and he shook his head. I drove back to the Manitou Trail and headed south.

On the isthmus between Lake Leelanau and Good Harbor Bay, I stopped at the general store in Leland and bought two Nehis, one orange and one grape. David chose the grape and savored each drop. As we drove on, he kept pointing to the shore. When we rounded

Little Traverse Lake, he began to smile. I started to turn onto the road to Pyramid Point, but he shook his head. I turned on the road to the Leelanau Schools, drove past, stopped, and helped him into the wheelchair.

When I lifted the small cooler out of the front seat for a picnic on the beach, David shook his head, no. I wheeled him across the footbridge, over the dune, to the hollow with his birch box still flying high from a tree and the big pole he carved with Papa still rising toward heaven. He eyed these totems of his forebears, all the way from the Eagle watchers at the top to our generation at the bottom. In his hoarse voice, he said, "more stories to be written."

I looked up to the two eagles, one in the front of the birch bark box and the other atop the totem pole. How could the color still be so vibrant after all these years? He pulled my head to his lips and whispered, "I added new paint, at least a dozen times, always red, for you." He chuckled. "I had to rebuild the birch box with Davey as often, and Angel helped me repaint your visage atop the *odoodem* this summer."

David raised his hand and pointed to the round stone, still shiny from so many hands touching it since Papa died, but out of his reach. I helped him stand, he took my hand in his, and I guided him to the stone. Together we rubbed it. Through my tears I asked, "Want to ride the funicular up to the clubhouse to see the links you designed?"

He frowned. "Make sure you enforce the deed restrictions on young Huey."

I told him we would, but that Major had helped us acquire all of Alligator Hill and worked with us to try to persuade Sven to move from Glen Haven to Glen Arbor.

"Rid of the dune buggies yet?"

Not yet, but I told him about Pip and Mirja's mission in Washington, D.C. He pointed, and I wheeled his chair to the stream. He lowered his left hand and formed a cup in the rushing water.

Slowly, he lifted the Crystal River to his lips. He drank the clear, cold water greedily, put his hand down again, and yet again.

When we got back into the old Zephyr, he waved me west, past D. H. Day State Park. I asked if he wanted to go into Glen Haven, but he pointed the other way. He gazed up at the east front of the Sleeping Bear Dunes and the Dune Climb. He turned to the shimmering turquoise of Little Glen and the darker green now covering Alligator Hill. "Good trade," he said slowly, "you made with Major."

He waved me forward, and I asked if he wanted to tour Empire and see the colleagues he'd led so well for so many years. He mumbled something I couldn't hear, and I leaned closer. "Not enough time."

When we came to the new scenic drive, he motioned. I turned and paid the toll. When we passed Pierce Stocking's sign, he smiled. It read: "Take only pictures; leave only footprints." He clutched my hand and said, so haltingly I couldn't look at him, "Make that the motto for Sven and Major, too."

I drove slowly over the rough gravel road through each of the different forest types and ground covers as we proceeded up the great dune. We came to the lookout over Glen Lake, and he waved me on. When we came to the long winding boardwalk, he nodded. I parked the car, helped him into the wheelchair, and placed the little cooler in the canvas tray below his seat. I wheeled him along the deck to the end so he could see what was left of Mama Bear's hump. He waved me on, and the big balloon tires rolled easily over the sand, up and down the hills.

The wind blew hard off Lake Michigan, and the sand clipped my legs. He put his left arm down and invited the blowing sand to prick the back of his hand. The dune stretched miles to the north in front of us, Glen Lake and Alligator Hill to the east, the Great Lake still blue against the gray sky far past the horizon to the north and west.

I rolled him into the cool shelter of the cottonwood grove, where the blowing sand covered the legs of a lopsided, old bench. I sat down on the wooden seat and leaned back on the slatted back as he gazed steadily at the Sleeping Bear pinnacle. All vestiges of the ghost forest buried in time, only the east side of her humped back remained, her fur now only a gnarl of grasses and patches of sand, ready to be undercut by the expanding blowout on the west side. A tear rolled down the warrior's cheek.

A low, muffled "*Hoo hoo hoo hoododo hooooo hoo*" answered. A great horned owl peered down at us, his big, black pupils magnified by his yellow eyes, tawny-orange circles, and large ear-tufts. David's dark face broke into a big smile, and he hooted right back. Soon a chorus of bird and human calls reverberated in the shelter of the glade until the Ojibwe raised his hand, and the bird quieted.

"Let Angel guide you on the national park," he said in his slow, gravelly voice. "She will be the Chairman of our Grand Traverse Band." He paused. "Even if she marries one of the Peshawbestown Odawa."

"What if she were to marry an upstanding, redheaded Scots Presbyterian?"

"Too late for us," he answered, "but not for Angel." He held my hand as the tears leaked down my cheek. Eventually, David confided that he had passed title to the land and business of his Grand Traverse enterprises to his family. Haltingly, he added, "I don't know if the BIA will ever recognize our Ojibwe and Odawa bands here."

"What if the Park Service won't honor your fishing and hunting rights either?"

After a long pause he said, "Spring, Angel, Davey, and I talked." He took a deep breath and implored as best his slow speech could, "Belle, please protect our Sleeping Mama Bear, but don't let the Feds take any of our land or yours unless they respect our original rights and recognize our bands."

He grasped my hand. "Thank you for being my partner." His voice broke. "Hungry," he said.

I pulled the cooler from under his seat, and we shared an apple, a pear, a peach, and a handful each of grapes and cherries. He laughed when I spit out the seeds.

"Tired," he wheezed. I helped him out of the chair, laid him in the sand, and cupped his body in a warm spoon. "Sing," David croaked. I sang the sonnet I composed about the love we shared together in the snow here so long ago. From a long way away, deep inside his heaving chest, barely audible above the flutter of the cottonwood leaves, I heard his low rumble, "Oh, Belle, one more time."

Crystal Moment

We follow deer tracks into the silent wood,
The crunch of our boots the only sound.
Around us shaggy boughs of pine bend low,
An offshore breeze swirls wisps of snow.

Our campfire ring's a sculpted mound of white
Blazing bright with each shaft of morning light
Filtered through birches and ancient oaks—
Like memories that burn and fade in smoke

A crimson cardinal weaves among the trees,
A snowflake lands upon your ruddy cheek,
You kiss me once, your lips do not linger—
No fire for us this cold December.

Instead of repeating the final couplet about our love, I paused. I looked out to our Sleeping Mama Bear still eroding before us in the distance and offered a different vow:

Our pledge to Nibi—a promise we will keep—
Secure this sacred land before we sleep.

"Share that," David rasped, "with the kids and help them return the Eagles…" He gasped for air as he struggled to speak. I held my Ojibwe original until he quieted.

I placed a piece of paper in his hand. "A poem to remember me and you, always."

"Sing it," he said as he grasped the paper.

I sang as best I could through my tears, "When I see you…

the years peel away
like birch bark
and memory becomes
the moment—

I can feel
your hand in mine
your lips like velvet
the yearning—
like earth for spring

But then the wind blows…
the cry of geese
in this gray September sky
reminds me

our years tumbled
on divergent paths
with other hands to hold

But oh—
If only….

He squeezed my hand and more wheezed than whispered, "I will see you when…" The wind whistled through the cottonwoods, and David Ahgosa walked on.

Winter and Summer 1953: Ann Arbor and Glen Arbor

Dear Belle,
Good news, I got married and will soon ship out for a honeymoon to Auden's Forio villa on Ischia. Seeing as I crossed paths with my former Bennington student only a month ago, I didn't give her time to get to know me and beg off. Auden and Bogan stood up for us at the wedding. Wystan tried to spoil the nuptials by pretending he couldn't find the ring, but my one Gott in Himmel spurred him to hand it over.

Bad news, I won't be back from our grand tour (and a reading for the BBC) in time to join at your writers' workshop. But Beatrice and I will drop by this fall in my Flying Jukebox on the way to Seattle.

I enclose the title poem to my next book, The Waking. Honor me, Big Mama, by singing it to hear if my rolling refrains rival the tunes of your Up North's bittersweet lament and personal anthem. If you don't run up the flag to salute my villanelle, I'll show up in my gangster suit.
Theodore Roethke

P.S. I still carry my greenhouses with me wherever I go. On my visits to see Mom and Sis in Saginaw, will you still share our glasshouse pool?

Please, I thought, *give Beatrice the patience of a good nun, the caring of a devoted mother, and the sex drive of a college coed to nurture this aging but manic bull of a bear.*

I sang his poem in my study overlooking the little park. Six stanzas, the first five, three lines each, and the last, four lines, danced along with a good beat. Yes, growing up as boy and man, he kept learning from his greenhouse memories and his bouts with mania and depression: "This shaking keeps me steady. I should know. What falls away is always. And is near." The first and last lines of the first stanza repeated in the last two lines of the last stanza: "I wake to sleep, and take my waking slow. I learn by going where I have to go."

Ted, My best wishes to you and Beatrice. Rabbie and I will miss you at our writers' camp and do so look forward to seeing you both this fall, but do you really want your biographer to see your new bride dropped into our glasshouse pool from a flying jukebox? Save the Zoot suit, though: shortly after your first anniversary, The Waking will win the Pulitzer!

Our big news: Together with the Leelanau Conservancy honoring David Ahgosa and Miss Schultz, we'll make sure our Delight of Life will be here when you next return, while we keep fighting for a national park to save our Sleeping Mama Bear, her dunes, and two cubs. You and your Missus will be our guests up north, no singing for your supper necessary.

I enclosed a copy of my revised "Crystal Moment" but finished on a different note:

> *If you talk with Wystan before you head back, tell him he owes me a new poem, preferably one that includes a good beat and enough sound to please us ear-readers: Your Waking should rouse him if my song does not.*

I must have dozed again because the knock on the front door woke me. The long change of life was wearing me down, too many cramps, too little energy. I dragged myself up and opened the door to Bill Pierpont. "Hi, Belle, I need your advice."

I directed him to the study. The Engineering Dean had asked to honor Pip at the opening of the first lab on North Campus, but my brother refused. "I'd hoped the University's good work up north and purchasing his land here would heal the wounds Bill opened."

When I said Pip still couldn't forgive Michigan for letting the Buckeyes steal John Kraus and their Big Ear, he replied, "Harlan Hatcher was the provost at Ohio State then. To make amends for stealing Michigan's best, he can invite Pip to introduce John for a lecture on the Big Ear as a part of dedicating the first building on North Campus."

"Get our president to assign you as the University's representative to our Leelanau Conservancy Board, and I'll make sure Pip won't refuse."

He shook my hand: "Michigan does have to protect our investments up north."

A month later I sat in the front row center of the Rackham Amphitheater, this time with Bill Pierpont, Ruthie, Mirja, and Father Paul. Harlan Hatcher looked the University President, tall, hair graying, graceful in his demeanor, and gracious in his remarks. He thanked Pip for his many contributions to the University, for helping win the War, for donating the land for the University's Great Lakes Research Institute, Biological Station, and Camp Inspiration up north, and, yes, "for agreeing to sell his land for the North Campus, albeit for a fair market price." Hatcher concluded by apologizing for helping Ohio State steal John Kraus and Pip's Big Ear away from Michigan.

When Pip stepped forward, he stood even taller than the president. His blue-gray eyes, as deep as ever, looked over the engineering, astronomy, physics, business, and natural resource students and staff who filled the seats and stood in back. His latest set of hearing aids peeked out from his otherwise almost deaf ears. My boy had aged into a different man. A second streak of white now parted his hair in the middle, as our Mama's had. A neatly trimmed beard, no sign of gray yet, hid how gaunt his angular face had become. He towered over the microphone and gripped the sides of the podium with his long arms and huge, bony hands. If he donned a stovepipe hat, I'd have mistaken him for a ghost of Abraham Lincoln.

Pip spoke in a steady, slow, firm voice that belied the many years he could barely hear. My brother also one-upped Michigan again: he hosted his *two* favorite cosmologists for this celebration. He first introduced Abbé Georges Lemaitre, "a Catholic prelate by faith and a mathematician by profession." Pip described how they first met at Cambridge University in 1927, studying under Arthur Eddington, the secretary of the Royal Academy, who first confirmed Einstein's theories of celestial bodies warping space and time by observing solar eclipses. In the end the good professor rejected Lemaitre's theory of the origin of the universe because he couldn't believe "it all started with a bang." The Royal Academy nevertheless gave its first Eddington Award in Astrophysics "to our first speaker for his work 'on the expansion of the universe.' It used that phrase so Georges' Big Bang wouldn't wake Sir Arthur from his grave."

Lemaitre stepped to the podium in his clerical garb and thanked Pip for encouraging him to pursue his "odd but simple theory of the origin of the universe." His hands and arms flew from a small cup at his waist up and out to a wide reach to the heavens: a small but incredibly dense mass exploded, flinging spinning galaxies outward in space and forward in time. Georges ruefully acknowledged that

Einstein was also blinded by "the difficulty of accepting what Pip calls my Big Bang theory because it appeared, well, too akin to the teachings of most religions." The abbé closed with some advice: "As a Roman Catholic and a scientist, it's a mistake to argue that proof of my theory would show that God created heaven and earth. Rather, it's more than enough to leave the challenge of discovering what existed the day before there was no yesterday to you, the future generations of scientists and dreamers, poets, philosophers, and priests."

Pip's introduction of John Kraus was more pointed: "As you will soon learn, Michigan made a mistake when we failed to find a home for our greatest astronomer and engineer. Abbé Lemaitre rightly called one source of cosmic rays, 'the leftovers from the fire and smoke from the original explosion of the primeval atom.' John's going to tell you today about an even more important discovery our Big Ear has recorded."

Kraus began by thanking Pip for mentoring him for more than three decades, starting with their short-wave radio tinkering when John was a boy, all through his studies at Michigan and charting radio waves in Empire, their years working together at the "most important lab for winning the War and now at Ohio State with our Big Ear." With his arms and hands spreading wide and high, Kraus described their invention: a tilting flat reflector a hundred feet tall caught the incoming radio waves from space and sent them across to a 60-foot-tall fixed parabola that bounced the waves back to receivers in front of the reflector. More than three football fields wide, "our Big Ear's most important search is for extraterrestrial intelligence—SETI for short." He summarized the huge odds against earth being the only place in our universe, with trillions of stars and several times that number of planets, to support life. He then described the even greater challenges of distance and time for capturing any signal of intelligent life in the vast space-time cone of the cosmos, at least 14 billion years old, already 150 billion light-years wide and expanding: "Talk about finding a needle in a haystack!"

He paused, and we all moved to the edge of our seats. “Well, friends, I’m here to tell you we’ve happened on one ‘Big Wow’ already.” He described the unique nature of the one-time signal and its source, on the eastern slope of a ridge, not far from the center of our Milky Way galaxy. “To confirm such signals of intelligent life, we will need many more savvy anglers here casting in the vast cosmic pond out there.” He paused, “Or, maybe, there’ll be an angler out there who snags one of our signals and sends a radio-wave back we won’t receive here for thousands or millions of generations.”

Awestruck, we didn’t respond when John Kraus sat down. Only when Pip rose to the podium and clapped did we come to our senses and cheer.

Pip quieted the crowd. “I want to thank the president and the University for honoring me for the small part I played in opening the other side of the Huron River to a new campus. Most of the credit, though, goes to your vice-president and CFO, Wilbur Pierpont.” He made Bill stand for a round of applause. “Just as we have a Union, a League, a Bell Tower, a great library and concert hall, and this grand amphitheater to bring us together on this main campus, so too we’ll need a commons to bring us together across the river.” He paused. “We will raise the money to build it sooner if we call it Pierpont Commons to serve men and women alike.”

After President Hatcher joined the women in cheering, Pip continued, “I’d also like to introduce my family. First, my children, Ruth, a teacher at Tappan Junior High, mother of my two grandchildren and now Chair of the Leelanau Conservancy. Next, my son, Father Paul, the good priest for all the parishes in Leelanau County and the dean of St. Mary’s School there. This summer he’s going to officiate up north when Mirja Fitzpatrick and I share our vows in the holy sacrament of marriage.” The Pope must have granted an annulment to Mirja: Did the confusion over Paul’s father provide the basis in the canon law?

Pip looked down at me as if he saw my pondering. Instead he said, “Now hold the standing ovation for Belle until I finish speaking.”

I was stunned, but Pip quieted the rising roar. "You all know she's my sister, but my Marmie also raised me since my birth and is still my adviser, partner, and best friend. Despite her trying to avoid the public limelight and the University's gravity, she's a Lecturer in Poetry and the anonymous source of many improvements, chairs, and prizes here. She's also the force behind America's Flame, conserving Leelanau, our drive to get Congress to fund a national park to preserve the Sleeping Bear up north, and the inspiration for songs yet to be sung. Let me share one story about how she taught us all." He proceeded to tell how Robert Frost and I took on the Hussey professor at the Detroit Observatory. "My Marmie Belle taught me I could follow the beat of my drum and reach for the stars. I hope this university also learns from her it's okay to be a woman scholar and an athlete, to be deaf but not dumb, to stick up for what's right against prejudice even if it's not popular, to be a poet, a dreamer, a tinkerer, and, yes, a tough businessman and better teacher, because she lived—and taught me—all that and more."

Well, I admit I did rise in thanks with a wave when the audience stood and applauded, even if it was more to thank Pip for sharing his day with me. For I knew I'd failed my family, my friends, and myself more often than not.

When the pain stabbed my pelvis and innards again, I sat down even more quickly. I tried my best to make my grimace appear a smile, but Ruthie and Father Paul both sat down and held my hand until the cramp finally passed. I hoped only Bill Pierpont noticed, because I didn't want Pip worrying about me when he closed his show by inviting everyone to Mirja's Hill House for a celebration.

Ruthie and Father Paul drove me home. I felt weak but not in pain. I encouraged them to take Marty and Little Paul down to the party while I rested in the glasshouse on a chaise. I must have dozed off again, for it was already dusk when the knock on the back door woke me. I chuckled because it sounded like my Teddy Bear from so many years ago, but then I remembered he was honeymooning.

The door opened, and I saw Rabbie. "You okay?" he asked. He took off his shoes and socks, and we sat with our legs dangling in the pool. I'd forgotten how much I'd missed my element all spring, too tired to join him for our usual laps. I stood up on my own, walked into the house, and returned in my swimsuit. I slid into the water, tried one of my old crawl strokes, and realized floating on my back might work better.

"Belle, Father Paul and Ruthie called me, and I got here as fast as I could from the farmhouse."

I floated over and told Rabbie about the show at Rackham. He even laughed with me at several of Pip's zingers. When I got to the part where I collapsed at the end, he asked when I'd had my last checkup.

"Oh, this is just another change of life every woman who lives this long has to face."

"I arranged an appointment for you at University Hospital in the morning."

"Don't let anyone tell Pip," I blurted, already dreading the results. The lump grew in the pit of my core, but Rabbie now stood next to me in the water. He held me up until the water embraced me and then helped me out of the pool, wrapped me in towels, laid me gently down to a reclining position on a chaise, and sat down beside me.

"You need to let Cowden and Ray know." For two months I'd been putting off an answer to the Chairman's offer to become the second Director of the Hopwood Program. "Roy's already stayed two years extra so we could persuade Warren you're the right person rather than Ned Strait."

The thought of losing out to Nym after my final victory seemed assured made me want to scream. "Can we wait until I find out what ails me?"

Rabbie was a good friend for staying by my side after all that each of us had been through since he first captured me at Whitmore Lake 33 years ago.

"No, *rescued*," I thought I heard him say. Not sure I knew enough to know back then, but he surely had lately, when he made me his partner in our writers' workshop up north and his companion here in Ann Arbor.

When I told him about Pip's announcement of his plan to marry Mirja, he said with too lighthearted a voice that Father Paul could now marry us, too. He pulled out a little velvet jewelry box and held out that same damn wedding ring from the Queen. I didn't know whether to get angry, laugh, or cry.

Holding back a tear, I managed only to squeak, "Don't you think we should also wait until I find out what's the matter?"

He leaned over and cradled my head until I stopped crying and fell asleep.

ᔓᔕ

After the grim diagnosis and exploratory surgery, I holed up in my bedroom, feeling sorry for myself. Although I let Rabbie and Ruthie console me, I closed my door to the rest, even Little Paul and Marty. Ruthie must have gotten so tired shooing them away, she left one of my Dickinson songbooks on my nightstand. After nibbling at the cereal, tea, and toast on my breakfast tray, I opened the volume to the bookmark and my favorite poem. A bird's lovely call from my window sill interrupted my reading. Hell Damn, I wasn't going to live to hear Emily Dickinson's original lyrics. So I sang her song in a soft voice:

> "Hope" is the thing with feathers,
> That perches in the soul
> And sings the tune without words,
> And never stops at all.

I marked up all the stanzas with Emily's original exclamation points, dashes, and capital letters. I heard the call of the birds outside to sing again but loud, no matter the "Gale" or "storm," whether on "the chillest land" or "the strangest sea." Even in my "Extremity," I owed it to my family—and myself—to open up.

Ruthie knocked on the door and brought the mail to my bed, including letters from Frost and Auden. Thank heavens they didn't know, and I didn't have to tell them.

"Where you been keeping Marty and Little Paul?" I said. When she reminded I'd asked her to keep them from disturbing me, I replied, "Tell them to get their butts in here and read me stories, or I'm going to hop out of this deathbed and paddle them good."

Ruthie looked at me and held back her tears.

I sang "Hope." I pulled Ruthie onto the bed with me. "I know Pip won't be able to stand the sight of me dying, but if you think the kids can, I ought to get on with living a little until my last go down, okay?"

Ruthie folded into my arms and cried on my neck. I cried some too, and it made us both feel better. She hugged me and got up, and a few minutes later, Little Paul hopped up with one of his big picture books and pushed it at me. *The Legend of Sleeping Bear* never meant more to a grandmother or grandchild, even if we didn't fit the exact definition. I read Father Paul's story and shared Mirja's illustrations as if a new discovery. Maybe the legend grew with each telling, from David Ahgosa to Angel to the new books from the press in Empire. Maybe my fear I wouldn't be around to read much longer made me tell the story with an even more authentic voice. When I finished, Little Paul told me all about his day at the Towsley tot center, how Pitter had put finger paint on Adele's face and she had spilt her juice all over her dress.

"Other kids laughed," he said, "but I wiped her face clean and gave her my shirt."

I patted my little boy on the head, and Marty appeared on the bed. She looked at Paul, and they both nodded. I sang "Up North" as an anthem, Marty joined in "Marmie's Lullaby" she knew by heart, and Little Paul tapped my sleeve and mumbled words in time to my revised "Crystal Moment."

It had been four weeks since they'd cut my belly, my privates, and my head open and sewed me right back up. The cancer from my ovaries had spread all over. Ironic, the organ that failed me when I wanted to marry now failed me again when I wanted to live into old age. I promised this would be the first day of the rest of my life. I sang a new song about this season's "Renewal" to Marty and Little Paul:

robin red breast on the wing
bluer skies and gentle rain

violets on the forest floor
peepers in the pond now sing

newborn fawn behind a birch
a flash of silver in the brook

in the air a fragrant wind
Nibi's blessing—we call it spring

I also called forth an old tanka I'd composed:

birches' yellow leaves—
petals on the forest floor—
seven deer, asleep—
snowflakes flutter into drifts—
below, the trillium wait

They clapped for more, but I said we'd get another chance to sing up north soon.

∾

After they left, I picked up the letter from Auden:

Dear Belle,
Sorry, but Ted and Beatrice overstayed their honeymoon in Ischia so long, I won't be able to make your writers' camp. Poor things, if they put a pea in the pot for every romp there, and remove one for every tumble thereafter, they'll never get to the bottom. I do hope their embrace of the Forio passions provides dear Beatrice with some inkling of Ted's ups and downs.

I hope the enclosed poem sings for ear-readers. If nothing else, the song represents the admiration I hold for you and Pip because of your respect for your WOODS. Give my best wishes to Mirja and Pip, and I hope you'll agree it's not too late for you to say yes to Rabbie. The rumor mill swirls that Warner Ray will finally appoint you to succeed Roy Cowden as the Hopwood Director, but I'll hold off congratulating you until the announcement so as not to queer that deal either. Once anointed, I hope you bring young Hayden and Ted back to the alma mater you share.
Wystan

I opened the copy of his poem "WOODS" and saw below the title "(For Belle)." Nine stanzas, each six lines, the beat sure, and the sounds so clear. The first two lines hit me, hard: "Sylvan meant savage in those primal woods that Piero di Cosimo so loved to draw…" With a good beat his poem marched to the point, "The trees encountered on a country stroll reveal a lot about a country's soul.…A culture is no better than its woods."

Ruthie must have heard me because she knocked on the door. "You okay?"

I invited her to sit beside me, and we sang Auden's song. I handed her the copy and asked her as chair of our conservancy to share it with her father. "He'll get more out it if we sing it to him together," she answered. I hugged her tight and cried on her shoulder. Ruthie held me until I fell into a deep and restful asleep, the first that welcomed me in too many weeks.

I woke and read Frost's letter:

Belle, I offer a confession of thanks long overdue as to one of your several musings on "The Silken Tent." This past week I returned to the cemetery by the Old First Congregational Church in Bennington and said it over the site where I buried Elinor's ashes. Don't reckon she heard me, but it reminded me how much we shared and how much her steadfast support, surprising strength, sustained sacrifice and enduring grace blessed me for so many, many years. I guess you are right: a perfect sonnet can offer more meanings than the words and phrasings suggest. But don't let this one admission get you to hearing too much in the sounds, tunes and slants in any good poem may make, mine or yours.

The American Academy of Poets gave me a cash prize that at last tops the Hopwood check you won. My belated triumph emboldens me to offer a proposal: As Holt shows little interest in publishing a new edition of North of Boston *with drawings by Andrew Wyeth, will you ask Mirja to publish your* Up North *poems with her illustrations at the same time she publishes my* North of Boston *poems with Wyeth's? I will change my schedule to practice our readings during the second week of your writers' camp before we set off for a college tour. Past time we get you out of your sheltered Arbors and spread your songs around the world. Your Robbie*

Past time, all right: like Auden's suggestion I marry Rabbie, too late for me. I wrote my dear friend Frost:

Your sonnet is such a blessing! Better late than never for you to hear it as an elegy befitting Elinor. Mrs. Frost once told me how much a good partner is required to support the driven artist through all the years. I never had such a mate in marriage, but thanks to Elinor and you opening your home and your hearts when it mattered most, Pip, Ruthie and I are still together. Now also blessed with Ruthie's children and a few good friends in my two safe Arbors, I am thankful I have never had to live alone either. Yet I do wonder whether anyone will have loved me enough to say The Silken Tent at my memorial service.

Please send me a few examples of Mr. Wyeth's work, and I will get you Mirja's offer. Whether Holt then decides to publish the book, I leave to your better negotiating skills. No need for any rehearsal at our writers' workshop though: You know I can't stand the thought of publishing my songs. I enclose a story from the Michigan Daily describing how the University honored Pip: You'll enjoy the thanks he pays you for defending our boy against that huffy Hussey astronomer.

Ted Roethke's off on an extended honeymoon to Auden's villa, but he sent a note saying he's stopping in London on the way home to do a reading for the BBC. Hopefully, his voice will enable him to earn as big a buzz on his return across the pond as you did so many years before. Can you get the Pulitzer Committee to listen to our Teddy Bear's new Waking so he can win the Prize he deserves?

I will miss seeing you this summer, but I remain your only other Belle

Ruthie brought Pip into my room and, oh, did my boy look a fright: salt beginning to pepper his dark beard, cheeks hollow, hang-dog expression, so uncertain he barely raised his head to give me one flash of his blue-gray eyes. They were puffy and red. I bade him sit in the chair, and Ruthie hopped up next to me. I handed him Auden's letter. After he finished reading, our girl joined me in singing "Woods." By the end Pip snapped his fingers to the beat.

"We've done Papa, Mama, David, and Miss Schultz proud up north," he said and grasped my hand, "haven't we?"

"King David H. Day, too, but there's a lot more work to do." I turned to Ruthie. "Madame Chair, I charge you with convening a meeting of our conservancy board after your father and his lovebird marry in Empire."

"No, we're putting off the… until after you—"

"Better marry Mirja now," I snapped, "than wait until the day before you die, as Chase Osborn did with Stella. Besides," I chuckled, "Mirja's too old for you to adopt."

When he couldn't help nodding, I asked, "Ruthie, could you fix me a plate of fruit and cheese?" She hopped down. "Take your time. After I talk to your father, I'm going to wash up for a luncheon appointment in the glasshouse."

Pip and I talked and talked. I wanted to learn what he was going to do. Although he'd invested in stocks with good success, he'd spent too much time hitting a white ball over hill and dale, across water and sand, into a cup—including every damn day since I came home from the hospital. So I told him about my letter to Frost, sharing how we twitted Hussey. Then I asked, "What do you think the next big discoveries will be?"

"Not sure about all the science, or what the tinkerers will invent, but the greatest advances over the rest of my life…" He paused, blushed, and looked down.

"I won't begrudge you a long life even if I'm angry mine's ending too soon."

"Sorry, Marmie, I'm no good at this."

"Me either. Hold my hand so the silence won't kill either of us prematurely."

He gushed like the wide-eyed boy he was years ago, when he wanted to share every new insight. "The three E's," he began, "electronics, energy, and the environment." He pulled out the little ear hidden in his silver hair. His pale blue-gray eyes flashed as he explained how the tiny "transistor" inside was the primitive precursor to semi-conductors that would revolutionize computing, telecommunications, and wireless devices, all woven together like a globe-girdling radar network to form a worldwide communication web.

I didn't know enough to doubt him. "Can you invent two-way Dick Tracy radio wrist bands that will help me compose a song with a better tune, too?"

Rather than remind me I wouldn't last that long, he continued on to energy. He said natural gas would supplant coal and oil as the primary source of fuel because it was cheaper and burned cleaner, and there was more of it.

My boy was a dreamer if he thought all the Standard Oils and big coal boys would ever let America's new Flame rule the roost. So I asked his position on the much-heralded "peaceful use of atomic power."

"I'm going to fight to close the lid on that Pandora's Box before we incinerate the earth." Pip leaned in close. "Energy for the future should come from capturing the continuous power from the Sun and the magnetic field that already blesses Earth."

"That your plan for Empire?" He nodded. "Willing to take me in yet as your first outside investor?" He stared back at me as if I were crazy, thinking about such long-term plays. "If you get serious about this, nobody I'd trust more to invest my estate, for our conservancy, Ruthie, and our grandchildren."

I asked whether Mirja was selling Hill House and the newlyweds moving full-time to her cottage up north. When he nodded, I saw the gray beginning to overtake his thick hair all over his head. I had to laugh: soon he'd lose the white streak that had made him look so distinguished as a young man.

"What's so damn funny about you dying?" he said.

My often-distant and always stoic boy was near tears. "Nothing," I had to admit. One of my death frights began to rise. I squeezed his hand and took several deep breaths. "I want to be the Maid of Honor at your wedding before I die."

Pip looked at me with those gray-blue eyes without end.

"When we put it off until after..." He paused. "Mirja already asked Ruthie."

"I'll settle for Matron of Honor again, then."

He nodded at the memory of his wedding with Rachel.

"But only if you cut off that damn beard so you don't look too old for your bride."

He finally smiled and added Kurt was going to be his Best Man.

"Is it okay if I invite Rabbie to escort me?" I asked.

I already felt so much better, I didn't wait for an answer. I put my feet on the floor, but the room started spinning as I tried to stand. Pip caught me and sat me on the bed. Damn it, I'd already had enough lying around waiting for my doom to last the rest of my life. I focused on the bathroom door and held on tight to Pip as he helped me to the sink. I turned on the water and shooed my boy away.

ꟃ

One telephone call and a half hour later, face scrubbed, lips painted, and red hair brushed to a shine, I reclined in my chaise beside the iced tea and lunch. When Roy Cowden appeared at the door to the glasshouse, I waved him in. He stopped well short of the pool and made as if to look for any little boy in his way. He offered a courtly bow, extended his hand, and sat on the chaise on the other side of the table.

"You were smart to look both ways before crossing," I said. "Ruthie's Little Paul is a sinker, too."

He cut the pear into slices, added a couple of pats of sharp cheddar, and handed a plate to me. I tucked into the fruit, then the cheese, then a mouthful combining both. It all tasted so good, I licked my lips when I finished and put my plate down.

"I'm sorry you won't be able to replace me," he said. Not as sorry as I was. "I fear Ned Strait's now the only candidate left standing."

I wanted so much to say "Over my dead body" again, but that was no longer a threat. Instead I suggested, "What if Rabbie applied?"

"You think he'd give up directing his first-year writing program?"

"Leave that to me."

Cowden nodded and said he'd talk to the Department Chair.

"If you think it might help, tell Professor Ray I'm prepared to endow a chair for the Hopwood Director, a Hopwood writing fellowship in your honor, an Auden prize for long poetry, and a Roethke prize for shorter verse." If that wasn't enough to get Rabbie's appointment past the Chairman of the English Department, I knew what would.

"Belle, your 'Goodbye to Mama' is still the best submission never to win a Hopwood." Roy's big grin and affectionate tap to my hand made me smile. Before I could express my thanks for all his years helping me, Cowden told me he planned to write his long-simmering book on *The Creative Impulse*. He described how he would compare early drafts with final versions of Dickens, Hardy, Browning, Keats, Thoreau, and—if he could get access to the papers—"Dickinson, Frost, and you."

I had to admit I'd soon be dead, and I trusted Roy Cowden. "I'm honored you asked," I replied, "but I believe the composer's final lyrics should speak for themselves." I reminded him of how the editors butchered Emily Dickinson's poems, of the long feud between the Dickinson and Todd clans, and of the ongoing fight over her papers; and of how Frost was so worried about what his chosen biographer might say he got Thompson to agree to not publish a word until after the poet's death. "And Frost's already mounting a campaign with his friends to defend him posthumously against his biographer."

"If you let me be your literary executor and biographer," Cowden said, "I promise I won't change one dash, capital letter, or exclamation point."

I was tempted until a different idea flared in my head. "Roy, you've been a good mentor and better friend, but I'm making an arrangement with an Angel."

He shook his head with a smile. "I guess I can't compete with a higher spirit."

When Cowden left, I called Bill Pierpont and told him about the part of my conversation with Roy concerning the likely appointment of Ned Strait by default as the Hopwood Director and my suggesting Rabbie O'Bannon as an alternative. Bill listened hard and asked a number of questions but made clear this was an academic not a financial matter: "Your offer of endowing the Hopwood Program and its new director contingent on Rabbie being chosen won't carry the day."

I proceeded to summarize Nym's bad acts: his slandering Frost, Roethke, Auden, and even Robert Hayden; his undercutting creative writing; his obnoxious sexism, racism, and homophobia; and, yes, the professor's abuse of power, trying to dominate every woman student who caught his fancy, including me.

"Plan on sharing all that with the Department Chair?" Bill asked.

"Also with the Dean, the Provost, President Hatcher and, if need be, the Regents."

"If you must, share it with Warren Ray, but talk to me again before you go out blazing with the rest, okay?"

I didn't reply.

"Belle," he pressed.

"I promise." I'd come to rely on Mr. Peirpont's straight talk and better deeds.

That afternoon I scribbled a new poem in my latest songbook:

Final Choices

Who, who…who cares
about my broken limbs? wails an owl
from the branch of a felled oak tree—

Nearby, a mother deer
nurses her twin fawns in the hollow
formed by its curved trunk—

I could complain, curse the moon,
and shout at stars—or settle
my accounts for others' gain.

It would make me feel a lot better sharing what I'd stored up: Settling up with family and friends would also allow me to settle accounts with myself. That would leave only two accounts open. I hoped I could yet finish Nym off. After all the struggles with the Dark Ogre, though, I had to concede only my brother would be left to settle with Sven Surtr.

ೞ

The next afternoon Ruthie dropped me in front of Angell Hall. President Burton had commissioned Albert Kahn to make this classical structure *the* central building of the campus, and so it was, nearly 500 feet long, the broad entrance portico with eight huge, three-story Doric columns astride a wide esplanade of steps. I dragged myself through Angell to the English Department, now housed in the new Haven Hall behind. The secretary led me into the Chairman's office. Professor Ray, lean and authoritative as ever, greeted me.

"Belle, I'm very sorry you can't take Roy's place." He paused. "Choosing you over Professor Strait was very difficult."

"I know: an unpublished, non-tenured, intermittent Lecturer over a much-published, highly regarded Shakespeare scholar and long-tenured Professor." When he nodded, I said, "Rabbie should be a breeze, then."

"No, it's a post that doesn't require tenure, and I chose you on the merits. You have been an extraordinary presence for more than 30 years here, and you would have helped me take Avery Hopwood's bequest and this Department to a higher plane."

Given Ray's diplomatic touch and iron will, I wasn't sure how to proceed. I decided not to reiterate what I knew Cowden had already shared, about how Rabbie could elevate the Hopwood Program even more, while Ned Strait would drag it down. Instead I handed Ray my detailed dossier on Nym. I added, "As Director of the Hopwood Program, Rabbie can inspire Michigan's best students to write without requiring you to expend so much of your budget on 80 English I-II teachers."

"If I choose Professor O'Bannon, budget savings won't be the only reason."

"At the least, then, the appointment will inspire Rabbie to write great novels."

Ray nodded with a smile. "As I wished your being the Hopwood Director would inspire you to write epic poems of real drama, too." I blinked at that.

He opened the folder and read its contents thoroughly but without once changing expression. "I know Ned has made many enemies in his time here, perhaps none greater than you, although I'm not sure sharing your views matters now."

I almost screamed "Views!" but restrained myself.

"I also hope I have shown I am a good steward, should you decide to make any further bequests in our favor."

I nodded but said, "Dorothy Donne should not be the only woman whose merit will warrant tenure during your term as Chairman."

Ray placed his hands on the desk. "Professor Donne is an exceptional case. She was the best student of Milton I ever had and a superb academic analyst of literature, but we don't have many positions for creative writers." He must have seen I wanted to scream because he continued, "Even with your extraordinary support, it's proven nigh onto impossible for Mrs. Donne to find the time to be a housewife, homemaker, primary caregiver for three children, and teacher, writer, and scholar." When I only shook my head, he added, "I know I'm Old School, Belle, but..."

I interjected with what must have sounded a scream, demanding what he thought of Nym's blackballing Roethke and the English Department never bringing the Big Man back.

"I have high regard for Ted as a great poet and better teacher. Given his checkered record, however, I decided Mrs. Donne was a better bet for that slot." He paused. "Rest assured, I will find appropriate ways for Michigan to honor our lost son."

When I asked about Frost, Auden, and Hayden, Ray said, "Frost and Auden departed long before I became chair, but I doubt my predecessors could have kept either here for long, even if Nym had never whispered his shameful slanders. Their ambitions were larger than Michigan, and their lifestyles called each to a different place than Ann Arbor—the pull of New England for Frost, the anonymity of the big city for Wystan."

The Chairman paused. "Did you know that in the summer of 1938, I was on the panel of three judges that awarded Robert Hayden his first Hopwood in poetry?" When I shook my head, Warren Ray added, "I have very high regard for Robert as a person and as a poet. As good a scholar as Strait is, his comments about Hayden's appearance and heritage were shameful. I am watching Robert closely, and I still hope he starts publishing great poetry so I can invite him back to Michigan one day." His eyes locked on mine. "The competition for the very few creative writing slots the Department can afford is very stiff, though."

The Chairman was no one's fool, certainly not mine. I also hoped in the end not Ned Strait's, either. He handed my folder on Strait back with a bemused look of disdain, as if disappointed I had stooped to the level of Nym's slanders.

I told Professor Ray about the 30-year battle David Ahgosa and I waged to prevent Sven Surtr from destroying the Sleeping Bear by driving all over her.

Warren nodded and said, "What your Leelanau Conservancy can't protect, your continuing fight to fund a national park may yet enable your up north to forever thrive."

"Whether Congress ever appropriates any money or not, wind and storm beyond our control will continue to erode Mama Bear, but that doesn't excuse Ned Strait driving great poets from here before their time either."

Warren Ray smiled, rose, and shook my hand. "I will miss you, Belle."

"No matter who you choose to pick as Hopwood Director, I will endow the Cowden Fellowship, the Auden and Roethke prizes, and a Chair for Rabbie, as Robert Frost Professor in Creative Writing."

Too much a gentleman to embrace me, the Chairman smiled. "To the extent it's within my power, I won't tarnish your substantial legacy here either."

"Good Lord, Mr. Chairman, then loosen up the Department's purse strings, bring back Roethke and Hayden, and hire another woman to break into your Old Boys' Academic Club before it's too late for you, too." I gave him a firm tap on his shoulder, turned, and closed his door behind me.

I said my goodbye to his assistant in the outer office and opened the door to the central hallway.

Ned Strait ran into me. His briefcase clattered to the ground, and he grabbed the doorframe to avoid falling. He looked terrible, his face splotchy and jowly. His belly hung over his belt, and his undershirt bulged between the buttons of his silk shirt. The few strands of hair left on the sides of his bald head, he combed over the top. Only by sneering over his half-glasses down his nose while he craned to look up did he appear even to acknowledge me. Was this how our long death-struggle was to end, the anticlimax of an accidental run-in without a single word, let alone a duel?

I picked up his briefcase and handed it to him. "You got a ruler in there?"

He shook his head and said, "I appreciate your making way for me."

Did he mean that as a smart-aleck remark about our run-in at the door or a cutting comment about my dying so he could become Director of the Hopwood Program? "Sorry," I replied, "I could have used it to beat you to a bloody pulp."

ℭ

The summer flashed by in a blur up north. Although each moment seemed as fresh as if I were a child experiencing every sight, sound, smell, taste, or feeling for the first time, the days raced too quickly into weeks and months. Seeing Kurt and Trudy again was a joy, even if we knew my time was short. Fortunately, with Father Paul showing the way at the St. Neri chapel in Empire, the wedding became a time of celebration for the unlikely bride and the newly clean-shaven groom, the entire wedding party, and even this Old Maid and my escort, the new director of the Hopwood Program.

Angel, Spring, Davey, and Major stopped by to chat in the days and weeks that followed. Ruthie, Marty, Little Paul, and Father O'Bannon took me on outings, even in the last few weeks of summer, when they had to guide me around in David's old wheelchair with balloon tires, all the way from the Omena Kirk, through the Grand Traverse orchards and vineyards, to Miss Schultz's preserve and lighthouse, back along Good Harbor Bay to Pyramid Point, Port Oneida, Miller Hill Lookout, and the Crystal River, from its source in Big Glen and Fisher's Lake to its mouth in Sleeping Bear Bay.

At Rabbie's writers' camp, Ruthie, Marty, Little Paul, and Angel ate, danced, and sang me through a campfire cookout by David's birch box and totem pole. Once again, the Hayden and Donne families shared our delight of life, while Dorothy and Robert, Rabbie and Roy Cowden worked to inspire another group of writers Up North. Angel capped the evening by opening her arms at the end of her dance to a comet racing across the dark sky. She also won one of Michigan's five Indian Scholarships so she could leaven her Ojibwe second sight with the study of Native American history and art and our region's natural resources.

Major dropped by to see me in my office. As I sat behind Papa's old desk with his many carvings, Huey asked me whether Ruthie would chair the Board of Directors of the Leelanau School when he converted it into a nonprofit educational corporation.

"Only if she'll allow Pip and me to endow the school so it will thrive in perpetuity," I answered.

Inspired, Pip got Mirja and me to match him in building dorms at Father Paul's St. Mary's School and funding an endowment to provide free high school there for needy families throughout northern Michigan. Not to be outdone, Spring and Angel challenged Mirja and me to join in funding local history, poetry, and art competitions and a science fair to honor her father and his best friend, Pip.

As chair of our Leelanau Conservancy Fund, Ruthie's first mission was to persuade the owner of the scenic toll road to agree to a sale if Congress ever appropriated funding for a new national park. She advised Pierce Stocking, "We'll provide a match to double any offer so you can enjoy the rewards in this life from conserving Sleeping Bear, rather than fight Uncle Sam to the death and leave your heirs to wrangle with those penny-pinching Park Service henchmen." Unfortunately, the Congress was so stingy, it still refused to authorize any funds for acquisitions, and the lumberman saw no reason to sell to our conservancy before the true value of his land and improvements were fully recognized. Who could blame Pierce Stocking for fixing to hold on to his lands and scenic drive until the people's representatives anteed up? After all, we weren't going to sell any land until the United States also recognized the Ojibwe and Odawa bands here and the rights of the original people to hunt, fish, and gather there. I could only hope Congress and the National Park Service would get their heads out of their behinds soon after mine walked on.

I sneaked out of bed most evenings to the attic, where I organized my songs, correspondence, journals, and memoir and tucked them into Mama's old chest. I even flipped through the pages of MacKenzie's old book, *The Spirit of St. Andrews*, and remembered the good golf doctor sipping Scotch with Papa in his office and the Scots homeland they shared across the pond. Odd, but some of the scraps of paper I'd folded in the bottom of the chest so long ago now sang to me. I'd hid these with my last poem to David in my first songbook. I didn't want Angel or Ruthie learning of our forbidden love from reading "When I See You" in its proper time frame.

Mama and Papa, if you're listening, I hope you can still hear your girl singing about renewal up north.

Oh, I had my spats, the worst with Mirja and Rabbie. She said she wouldn't make an offer to publish a new illustrated edition of *North of Boston* for Frost unless I agreed to let her publish a collection of my poems as *Up North* with her drawings. Rabbie pressed me to share all my papers so he could write a biography about me. I told him our Teddy Bear was a big enough subject for any one biographer. Finally, I asked Ruthie to tell them both to stop trying to kill me before my time.

Mirja and I reconciled only after she said she'd match Pip and me in putting up money to purchase land for our conservancy until the powers that be in D.C. came to their senses. We sealed our deal in Papa's study with a little shot of his Scotch, my first sip in months. Burned going down, but tasted so good.

"You fixing to declare your more colorful heritage now?" I asked.

"Already have!" Her jade eyes sparkled at this liberation. "Pip joined me in co-sponsoring the first annual NAACP Freedom Fund dinner in Detroit, and Willis Ward introduced us to Thurgood Marshall. Once Mr. Marshall learned Pip went to Amherst, they couldn't stop talking about the two Lord Jeffs who'd mentored them, Charles Houston for Marshall and Charles Drew for Pip."

When I asked how I could help, she said, "Join Mr. Ward, Pip, and me in supporting the Legal Defense Fund to challenge the color line everywhere."

I thought back to all the barriers David Ahgosa fought to overcome in order to lift his Ojibwe band. "Introduce our Angel and Davey to him, and I will. The Ahgosa clan doesn't want to pass for white either."

Mirja nodded and poured another sniff of Scotch in our glasses. "Would you have approved if Paul and Ruth could have married?" she asked.

"I wish Paul would rip off his priestly collar and marry Ruthie right now." Mirja raised her glass. Whether Mirja had any idea her son had proposed to Ruth from his hospital bed in Madison, I didn't know. Rather than ask, I decided there never would be a better time to settle a different account: "What's your asking price on Hill House?" When she answered, I gulped the Scotch down. "I'll buy it."

"For Rabbie?" When I nodded, Mirja said, "I guess he's made it as much his home as mine over all the years, hasn't he?" When I nodded again, she continued, "I'll turn the deed over to him as part of our property settlement instead." She paused. "No sense giving the nosey-parkers in Ann Arbor any more grist for gossip."

Mirja stood up, walked around Papa's desk, and pulled me up close. She'd always been a better friend to me than I to her, and I told her so. We shared a good cry. She whispered, "Pip's so distraught at the thought of losing you."

I thought back to all the hurdles and slights my boy had overcome, how we'd worked together to raise Ruthie and her kids and to help Paul, how we'd built our family business and fought to renew our Great Lake shore, dunes, and forest. Yet he'd always been his own person, whether tinkering with radios and searching the stars, inventing the ways to win the lethal cat-and-mouse games in World War II, or thereafter working with the university that had turned its back on him to help build a new campus in Ann Arbor and a thriving new Empire up north. Yet he was still as odd a man as he had been as a child.

"I can't stand the thought of leaving my boy either." I held Mirja at arm's length. "You're his partner for life: please keep him young as you two grow old together."

After the special meeting of our Leelanau Conservancy Board, Kurt and I met alone one last time in Papa's study. He asked if I wanted him to help invest my estate for the benefit of Ruthie, Marty, Little Paul, and an anonymous trust to support Father Paul's parish work.

He outlined his recommendations, but I asked, "You bored with Lazard, yet?"

He began to shake his head but then nodded.

"Did you enjoy working with Pip, bidding up the price for our Empire and closing on the sale of our different lines to Whirlpool, Carrier, and Coleman?" He nodded again.

"How'd you find working with him on our other ventures before and since?"

"He's crazy good." I shared the gist of Pip's session at Rackham with Lemaitre and Kraus and summarized what Pip told me about investing in electronics, energy, and environmental inventions.

Kurt asked so many questions I couldn't answer, I put up a hand to make him stop. He paused but then began to muse, "If I were to stay in New York and Pip stays here, we tap all his tinkering friends at Michigan and hire two junior partners, one in Cambridge for MIT and one in Palo Alto for Stanford…"

Before he could get in another word, I said, "I'll put in a third of my estate, and you and Pip can each add an equal amount."

For a moment he looked so eager I thought he was going to jump across the desk and kiss me, but that wasn't any more likely today than 26 years ago. Instead, he walked around the desk, held my two hands, winked, and said, "We'll keep building your Empire." On a piece of paper he drew a three dimensional logo, a cube in perspective with an E on the top and E's on the two sides below. "E-Cubed will thrive!"

"Glad you learned something about marketing and building a brand after all." When he smiled, I added, "Put Bill Pierpont on your Board of Directors, and make sure a part of the return on our investments benefits our Leelanau Conservancy." I paused. "While you're at it, think you and Pip can also convince Mirja and Father O'Bannon to add Angel and Ruthie as partners in their Press?"

"They can now use Trudy's logo to keep America's Flame alive, too."

"No, the Sleeping Bear is their trademark. And they should adopt the name Empire Press." When he smiled with me, I stood and pulled this dear man close. He leaned his head against my shoulder. We'd shared so much more than most married couples. "Kurt, please make sure Trudy will be okay, too."

ꙮ

My last big regret was not helping Little Paul learn to swim. Marty, already a dolphin in water, swam far into the bay with her mother, but I didn't have the energy to do more than sit in the shallow water and make sure the little boy didn't go deeper than the bottom of his swim trunks. He didn't have his grandfather's fright of deep water, but I didn't give the boy any opportunity to learn to swim either. I tried to get Ruthie to teach him how, but she enjoyed her deep-water frolics with her daughter as much as I'd enjoyed my time swimming with her. Marty wasn't any help, as she always wanted to swim with her mother and said, "Don't worry, Marmie, I'll save my brother from drowning." I didn't have the heart to tell her a seven-year-old was not a likely life guard.

The last day up north, Pip and Mirja hosted Ruthie, Marty, Little Paul, Father O'Bannon, Angel, Davey, and me for a picnic supper in the cottonwood grove overlooking the eroding Mama Bear. I sat in David's wheelchair and surveyed the scene. Maybe it was my eyes fading and my temperature rising, but a hot haze dimmed my view and made me sweat. The sand dune melted the graying blue of water and sky into a drab dun color. The Ahgosa fresh fruit tasted flat. Even the wind died down, and I couldn't hear any flutter of leaves nor feel any blowing sand pricking my skin. Then it hit me. There wasn't any sound of engines roaring up as they approached Mama Bear or fading as they headed back to Glen Haven.

"What happened to all of Sven's Dunesmobiles?"

Pip nodded to Ruthie. "The Day heirs decided to sell after the Secretary of the Interior invited Sven to the White House for an autographed picture with Ike. When the Park Service went behind our backs and Congress once again refused any funds, our Conservancy upped the ante enough, he sold to us." Pip explained how he threw in the old Bell Stove Works and invested with the Dark Ogre to build a new hotel, restaurants, bars, and stores by the shore in Glen Arbor. "We're also going to conserve Glen Haven and the farm as a living museum to King David H. Day's reign, when there were no damn dune buggies."

I looked out to the Mama Bear, hoping she'd grow bigger with the news, but couldn't even find any sign of David Ahgosa smiling down on us. I wanted to say my thanks but couldn't. I'd miss this place too much. At least Pip and Ruthie had helped me keep our promise to David: Maybe the relentless wind and erosion expanding the blowout on the west side of the Sleeping Bear might eventually consume her, but no Dunesmobile would threaten Mama Bear's backside ever again. Odd how one of my supposed death feuds got resolved thanks to a new alliance, while the other ended in an unconditional surrender. Michigan had accepted Ned Strait's resignation, no emeritus asked or given. "Good riddance, Nym," I wanted to say, but Miss Schultz and Bill Pierpont had been right all along. He'd never been worthy of my concern.

I thought back to all the seasons I'd enjoyed up north, every summer except for my first year in Ann Arbor and almost as many winters, springs, and falls, too, with Mama, Papa, Pip, Miss Schultz, David and the rest of his Ahgosa clan, Ruthie, Father Paul, Marty and Little Paul, Skipper Beals, the Hueys, my three poet friends, and, yes, Rabbie. I wondered if the times we shared made the loss of never being able to enjoy another season here all the more painful.

I turned to Pip. "Make sure Sven serves the best fish: Past time you eat that mess of perch Mama planned for us her last day." I paused. "And don't you ever give up on getting Congress to fund a Sleeping Bear Dunes National Lakeshore here either."

I felt my boy's hand fly to mine and the prick of windblown sand on my wrist. I heard the flutter of the cottonwood leaves. I smelled the freshwater scent of the Great Lake as the breeze freshened on my face. The deep blue of the water came into focus, and the brighter blue of the sky spread across my dome of vision. The rolling shapes of the sandy dunes sharpened before me.

To Pip, Ruthie, and the rest of my family and friends, I said, "Praise the Lord and thank you all."

Soon the sun, as it fell to the horizon, turned into a crimson ball. A mirage formed as the blue water rose to meet the pink island clouds floating to the horizon in the reddening sky. Just before the red orb began to fall out of sight, a little green ball appeared on top and flashed its goodbye rays at me. Stunned, I turned, and Pip nodded, Ruthie smiled, and Angel, Marty, and Little Paul all clapped, crowded around, and hugged me close.

Little Paul pulled at a weathered board stuck in the sand but couldn't budge it. Soon, Marty dug beside him, and the back of the old bench began to emerge. It seemed only yesterday I'd sat there with David Ahgosa for our last supper but ages since I returned the next winter. I had so wanted to be with him again. On that clear, moonlit night, the moonbeams danced off the snowdrifts on the hills and the frozen ponds of snowmelt from a midwinter thaw in the valleys of the dunes. I found I was still adrift then and had composed a poem with that title.

I asked Davey, Ruthie, and Angel to roll me to the tilted bench. After they sat down with Little Paul and Marty and leaned back beside me, I sang my song:

seven brown leaves still
clinging to a bare branch —
Icy pond, a white matte

silent half moon hovers
in an empty gray sky—
geese, long gone.

the trail of my footsteps
stops where we once sat—
this lopsided wooden bench

adrift in the snow

As my last poem I'd sung to Angel's father at this very spot rang through my head, I wondered, Oh, David, will I see you beyond the veil? An eagle soared above, circled, and then headed west over the Great Lake. Was he showing me the way to walk on?

That evening, on the back porch of Belle Cottage, we sang my "Up North" anthem and revised "Crystal Moment" and reveled in Angel's mimes of her Leelanau legends. Eventually, we retired to our bedrooms. Although Angel would join us for our drive back to Ann Arbor in the morning, she stayed in my third-floor aerie this night.

I reached into the top drawer of my bedside table, pulled out the keys to the attic door, Mama's chest, and the locked box inside. "When you're next here," I began, "take the chest and hide it until Pip, Mirja, Rabbie, Frost, Auden, and Roethke all walk on."

I reached into the drawer and pulled out an envelope with my letter of instructions inside. I licked the flap, sealed the envelope, and handed it to her with the keys. I told her about Emily Dickinson leaving her poems and letters scattered around her Homestead and the awful editing and family feuds this spawned. "I don't claim my poems compare with Miss Dickinson's, but I won't risk embarrassing my friends and family with my songs, journals, and memoir." I paused. "Give my letter to Ruthie if she's still alive; if not, to Father Paul; and, if he's not alive, you read the letter and do what you think best."

"What if I don't last on this side of the spirit that long?"

"Give the letter and keys to your child you trust most, okay?"

"You see me with a husband?"

"Of your own choice," I answered.

She asked if I thought she could continue to serve as Ogema if she married one of my kind.

"Your father said you should lead your band no matter who you marry, although he hoped your husband would convert to our Kirk and join in your *mide* rituals." I added, "He said you'd thereby show your ways to us latecomers and grow your clan faster." Angel said she'd try to explain that when she joined in seeking recognition of the Grand Traverse Band of Ojibwe and Odawa.

I handed her the smooth, round skipping stone that joined her father and me for so long, through our rites of passage so many years ago, watching over Papa and our clans while embedded in the totem pole they built, and seeing David and me so well through his passing. Her fingers flew across the stone. I heard a gentle hum. She handed it back, and I felt the vibrations, as deep as those from the big bourdon in Burton's bell tower.

"Angel, will you place this on your father's marker when you think right?"

When she nodded and said she'd also work with Davey to return the Eagles of the birch box and totem pole to their eastern shore of Leelanau, another song began to well up, "Homecoming Dance." Unlike Frost's "Stopping by Woods," I hoped my poem wouldn't sound a death dance for any reader. It would embrace only the joys of returning home rather than worrying about promises left to keep in the time left. I rejoiced in singing the poem in my dreams throughout the night, hoping against hope I wouldn't have to suffer a cold winter purgatory in Ann Arbor before returning to join Mama, Papa, and David. Come morning, though, I couldn't remember the lyric or the tune. Yet I had to smile, for once again the process of composing had offered me salvation:

Mama, thank you for encouraging me to sing so in my own voice so long ago!

ᔕ

The last weeks in Ann Arbor at Cambridge House were hard, harder than anything I'd faced before, harder than my fears of venturing beyond my two safe Arbors, speaking in public, or publishing my too-personal poems, harder than losing Mama to the seiche or rescuing Pip from the cold grip of the bay so many years before, worse than the repeated dashing of my hopes for joining with a good man, worse even than losing Papa or David. I couldn't endure the crushing pain, the indignity of my bladder seeping and my bowels oozing, the death frights imagining the last moment before I would know no more.

Rabbie sat at my bedside and dozed for hours at night, awake in an instant to offer a cool cloth to my hot pains, a warm blanket and body to my chills, a soothing touch if my frights gripped me so I couldn't moan, let alone speak. All day Angel sang me her legends and my *Up North* songs. I asked her to read me other poems, Dickinson, Frost, Roethke, Auden, yes, even Rabbie Burns. When I was able, we'd talk about the verse, says the tunes in different tones and beats, and laugh or cry together. Afternoons, Rabbie would carry me to our glasshouse Eden, help me float in the pool and dry off, and lay me down in a chaise to take in the warm sun and fragrance from the exotic blooms. Ruthie spent lunches and dinners with me. She let me sing and read with Little Paul and Marty in the evenings until I tired and then let them share their stories, joys, falls, and tears of the day with me.

Nym refused to let me go in peace. One afternoon Rabbie left me in a chaise by the pool while he made calls in my study to enlist the national judges for next spring's Hopwood awards. I must have rested my eyes because I woke when I felt a shadow leaning over and saw Strait's lone mole hair twitching as he lowered his mouth.

"Good Lord, Nym," I blurted, "a little early if you want to molest a corpse."

"I wouldn't think of giving you the thrill, you Old Maid." He continued his descent and sat in the chaise next to me. He waved a manila folder. "I'm here to show you how I'm going to bury you after you're gone."

I read the three typed, single-spaced pages inside. I had to admit his dossier on me was much more inventive than the one I prepared on him. He included just enough facts and half-truths that his libels rang true. And, whatever else, I had to admit I wasn't ever a saint. Signed *Nym*, his screed made me look as evil, devious, and predatory as the worst Scots kelpie. Then it hit me. Strait had shared this before Chairman Ray had chosen me. I began to laugh, softly at first, but then louder, uncontrollably, right in Nym's face.

Rabbie must have heard me because he ran down the back steps, collared Strait, and looked so angry I thought he'd break my tormentor's fat neck. I managed to croak, "Take a look at his eulogy for me before you choke him."

Rabbie let go and began to read. His Irish dander rose as he read the charges, beginning with our premarital coupling and ending with my paying the University and flaunting my sex to secure lectures, appointments, and promotions for Rabbie, Robbie, Vincent, Wystan, Louise, Dorothy, and myself. By the time Rabbie finished, though, he guffawed and sent me into another fit of laughter.

"There's nothing funny about this," Nym screamed.

Whatever my failings, my deeds, good and bad, had already written the story of my life. Nym's words, as Warren Ray had already recognized, could no longer hurt me.

"Rabbie, please show Mr. Strait the door so you can take me in my bedroom."

Once there I lacked the strength to couple with my companion, but I shared what I could. I composed a love song to thank him for what we did share together:

Rendezvous

hand in hand
they stroll across
an Oriental bridge

peer beneath the quiet green
where golden koi meander
among snow white water lilies.

As she looks up
to watch an egret preen
he gently kisses her—

a whisper on her lips,
softer than dragonfly wings
of secret things…

although she knows
these stolen moments
float on slender strings—

That evening Rabbie had to go to his farmhouse, and I began to feel sorry for myself again, with no hope for enjoying any more seasons with him, my family, and friends, here or up north. I don't know if it was the chill in the fall air and the leaves dropping, but another song began to rumble around my head. I hummed the tune, mouthed the words as best I could and printed a final poem:

November Hike

Leaves crunch—
forgotten memories
beneath my feet—

I wind up gentle hills
and around the shells of fallen oaks—
watch a squirrel skitter

carrying its cache of acorns
into a hollow trunk—
back and forth it goes—

the birds sang
when we walked this path
one sunny day in April—

we carved our initials
into an elm tree trunk—
it died of disease years ago—

though you clung to me
like lichen to bark,
I journeyed on—alone—

now, autumn is in me—
its crimson, gold, and orange
its rusts and regrets—

the raucous cry of geese
pierces the air—
and I can't remember

if your eyes were blue

I tried to sing my poem to Ruthie the next morning, but my halting, gravelly tones didn't sound right. I handed the poem to her, and she read in a tone that sounded eerily like mine. When I told her, she buried her head on my shoulder. "Marmie, I already hear your echoes, and they'll haunt me for the rest of my life."

I held her close and whispered, "Oh, Ruthie, you just keep singing, and you'll find your voice." I asked her to share my song with Pip: I hoped it would help his blue eyes remember our time together as long as he could still see, for years to come.

ဗ

The last weekend was the worst. Pip, Mirja, and Father Paul drove down to say goodbye. I'd probably prove contrary enough I'd refuse to die, so they'd have to visit again. Ironic how the instinct to live takes over, even when you think you've had enough and just want to let go. In a haze of morphine, first the children and then Angel came to my bed, held my hand, and tried to talk with me, but I couldn't bring myself to mouth goodbye or mumble farewell. I hoped they felt the squeeze of my hand.

A while later, from some remaining corner of my eye, I saw Mirja approach, as exotic as ever, albeit darker in my dimming sight. "Take care of Pip," I heard my voice say.

And, then, her answer, "Thanks to your nurture… and weaning… your boy's grown stronger than you and me." I felt her hold my hand to her beating heart.

I heard myself say, "I'm sorry I couldn't be a better friend." She pressed a forefinger to my lips to shush me, buried her head in my neck, and cried me to sleep.

When I next woke, Ruthie held my hand. I heard her whisper, from a long way away, "Thank you for being my Marmie."

All I could do was cry, not just in thanks for all she'd meant to me, but because I would miss her, and Marty and Little Paul, so. I finally managed to say, "Take care…"

By some grace I recalled all my doubts about Mama's goodbye: I'd be damned if the last words I'd say to our girl were "…of Pip," the thought that had bedeviled me so many years before. I held

Ruthie's hand close and said, "I mean, thank you." I hummed the refrain from my personal anthem and said, "Take care of our up north, too."

When Ruthie squeezed my hand, I hope she heard me add, "I love you so, my child. Please, seize all the opportunities I couldn't… with…" I tried to say Paul as my bellows gave out.

I didn't want to let go of her, ever, but soon I felt Pip's big, bony hand clutching mine. He leaned awkwardly across me, his body tense, whether angry or forlorn at my leaving him, I couldn't tell. He couldn't bring himself to say goodbye, and neither could I. After a long while he whispered in his wee boy's voice from so many years before, "Mawmie, I'll leave the light on fo' you."

My heart skipped, remembering that night so long ago, after I swam him to shore. His cheek, once again soft, graced mine as he gently rolled me onto my side. He cupped me in a warm spoon as I had held him before.

Oh, Mama, you'd be so proud of our boy.

I must have fallen down to a deep sleep because sometime, much later it seemed, I heard Father Paul O'Bannon speak. I pried my eyes open and focused on his clerical collar. I must have made some sound because he lowered his head. A distant voice inside me said, "Last rites?"

He shook his head.

I moved my arm, and he brought his ear close. I tried to ask, "Why not?" I gripped his collar.

"I can't," he whispered, "unless you convert."

Hearing must be the hardest sense to kill because the sound was so loud my head rang. "I won't."

"I can't do it as a Catholic priest."

A last surge of energy welled up as I ripped at his collar with my claw. "Then do it as the better man you are!"

He removed his collar, crossed himself, and spoke in a calming tone. "Do you have anything you want to confess?" I didn't want to tell him. His touch graced me. "In the name of the Father, the Son, and the Holy Spirit, I absolve you of all sins."

"I'm sorry I kept Ruthie and you apart." I tried to catch my breath. "Marry her."

"I can't." He cried softly in my ear, "You know she's my sister."

I shook my head as best I could and tried to say, "No, I don't."

I felt his finger cross my forehead. "Through this anointing may the Lord in his love and mercy help you with the grace of His Holy Spirit." I felt his touch rub—what, oil?—on my hands. I heard him say, "May the Lord who frees you from sin save you and raise you up."

I wished I could say "Amen," but my withered fingers did squeeze his hand.

I felt his press back and his kiss on my cheek. "Marmie, I will remember your voice, always."

I tried to speak. He brought his ear close again, and I said, "Your father…"

My "Up North" poem rolled around and echoed in my mind, the bittersweet lament reminding me how much I'd miss my Leelanau forevermore.

I heard more than felt Rabbie beside me. I must have uttered my request because he picked me up and carried me down to our glass-house and into the pool. I felt the cool water as the light faded, and I began to feel the chill, the death fright I'd experienced, even practiced so many hundreds of times. I took a deep breath, another, and another. I felt Rabbie's heat, as strong as ever, and his big chest and arms held me up. The water began to embrace me, as it had so many times before, the warmth spreading from my toes, fingertips, and head, through my legs, arms, and neck, all the way to my core.

"Oh… my Dearie Belle…" I finally heard my Rabbie keen from a long way away.

The hum of the wind whistling through the trees and of the whitecaps lapping on shore beckoned me. I swam on alone, through Sleeping Bear Bay, past the Dunes, over the big sturgeon and the old fishing shanty, on my last crossing home again, home at last. I took one more breath, slowly, slowly, slowly in, and exhaled out, completely.

Ruthie's Seasons
Late Fall 1977: Glen Arbor

Dear Ruth, Marmie Belle's letter from 1953 began, *Please forgive Angel for serving as my trustee to hide Mama's chest till now. I decided it was best not to share the contents while any of my peers and mentors still lived, not just my three great poet friends, but also Pip, Rabbie, and Mirja.*

Father Paul O'Bannon and I sat on the chest that had disappeared on her death from the attic in Belle Cottage. We had already spent a long day memorializing Mirja and Pip. We buried Mirja's ashes beside half of Pip's in the cemetery by St. Philip Neri Catholic Church in Empire, and we buried the other half by Marmie, their parents, and their best friend, David Ahgosa, in the cedar grove by the old kirk in Omena. An early supper followed at the Homestead Inn with Marty and Little Paul's families, the Ahgosas, Kurt Knutsen, Bill Pierpont, Sven Surtr, and the Hueys.

Angel had stayed to talk with Father Paul and me, the last two occupants of Marmie's haven. We made an odd pair of housemates, what with our separate bedrooms and independent lives, but never a whiff of any illicit relationship because we were half-siblings as Pip's progeny. After Marmie died too young, Father Paul became the primary resident as well as the caretaker of her cottage up north. As headmaster of the St. Mary's School, he also helped most families in need throughout Leelanau County, regardless of faith. He moonlighted helping his mother develop Empire Press. Since the elder O'Bannon died in 1968, and I moved shortly thereafter from teaching at Tappan and raising Marty and Little Paul in Ann Arbor to Belle Cottage, he also assumed Rabbie's roles as a mentor for me, my children, and, now, grandchildren.

I am the aging schoolmarm, Marty and Little Paul grown and moved to new homes in Empire. I teach English at the old boarding school by the Crystal River and co-author Angel's stories for her illustrated *Legends of Leelanau* that sell more for our Empire Press than even the golf books prized around the world. I also chair the Leelanau Conservancy and spoil my grandchildren as much as Marty and Little Paul allow.

❧

"The time," Angel had announced, "is here for me to deliver on a sacred trust." She led us up the two flights of stairs, past Belle's bedroom on the third floor of the turret. She took out a key and unlocked the door to the attic on the other side of the hall. There, at the far end, appeared the old chest. Angel handed me Marmie's letter, and Father Paul and I now sat close atop the chest so we could both read it:

> *You must now decide whether and to what extent these materials should be kept in the family, lodged with research collections, or arranged for publication. If you find I wronged you in hiding them all these years, close the chest up, and throw it overboard in Sleeping Bear Bay.*
>
> *You may wish to consider one exception. The locked box at the bottom contains a very large envelope stuffed with the*

correspondence and poems Robert Frost and I shared. Although you will find the other letters and poems Ted Roethke, Wystan Auden, and I shared elsewhere in the chest, I believe Robbie is America's greatest poet, even greater than Emily Dickinson. Amherst was also Frost's home, the place that had to take him in whenever he went back. If you choose to deliver these Frost papers to the College, I ask you to cooperate with its president alone. Whatever you decide, I trust your judgment.

Father Paul shifted away as we read our Marmie's more personal words:

I've often wondered whether Mirja and I did the right thing in separating you and Paul O'Bannon when you fell in love as kids so long ago, the more so the nearer I get to walking on to my blue salvation.

As I write today, I rue I didn't seize one of my opportunities to make a nest with one partner, but I wasn't lucky enough to find any that could overwhelm whatever set me apart, until it was too late. Yet my regret over that loss is more than offset by my joy in sharing a larger and closer-knit family, including most importantly with you, your father, Father Paul, Marty, and Little Paul, and, in different ways, with David Ahgosa; his Angel daughter; son, Davey; and wife, Spring Blossom; Mirja; and, yes, my erstwhile Dearie, true in the end, Rabbie.

If you do choose to deliver the Frost papers to the president of the College, I hope you will also investigate the circumstances giving rise to your birth and your mother's death. More than anything in my life, I now regret not introducing you to your mother's family in Amherst. I can only hope you forgive me if you find I wronged you there, too. Love, Marmie

My mind raced with so many conflicting emotions, I didn't know what to think. Yet when Angel held up a second key to unlock the chest, I stood with Father Paul in anticipation. She inserted the key and lifted the lid. Five songbooks brimming with Marmie's lyrics rested on top. Dozens of packets of poems neatly bound together lay in the next layer. Correspondence with colleagues and friends organized by name in folders came next. Notebooks with a rough draft of a memoir and many journals, books of Dickinson poems, family pictures, old photos, a hand-drawn map and illustrations, silver, jewelry, and dolls followed. At the bottom I saw her Mama's wedding dress, with Alister MacKenzie's *Spirit of St. Andrews* hiding in the folds atop the locked metal box.

I looked up and saw Angel, still so small and white, staring at me with her pale eyes. She had been true to Belle and to me through all the years. I stood, hugged her close, and said, "Thank you."

Father Paul leafed through the good doctor's book. "Whatever else you decide," he said, "Empire Press will get one best-seller."

I fished the locked metal box from the chest and said, "Whatever else *we* decide, Marmie's correspondence and poems with Frost will go to Amherst College. They will answer the vicious personal attacks on the great poet and good man by his biographer."

Father Paul nodded. He reached over and put the locked box and MacKenzie's book back in the chest. A single sheet of paper fell on the floor, and I read "Marmie's Lullaby." From my first day to her last, she had cared for me as if I were her child.

The three of us proceeded to pore through the songbooks, folios, notebooks, papers, photos, drawings and correspondence, careful not to disturb their order, for several hours. When I found Belle's personal anthem "Up North," I read it aloud.

"Maybe," Father Paul said, "it's all worked out for the best. By Marmie hiding her poems, she gave you time to find your voice; and now you get to hear hers anew."

"A quarter-century trying," I snapped, "and my verse still sounds off-key, a tinny copy of hers." I saw from his stunned look he meant no offense. "Sorry," I said.

When Father Paul nodded with an encouraging pat to my hand, Angel pointed to a page from Marmie's oldest book of poems. She plucked an Indian Princess penny in mint condition from the binding and sang "Delight of Life," our Marmie's perfect sonnet about a rite of passage "as old as Eden's vine" by a campfire along the sandy shore:

> the flicker of fireflies sparking love's desire
> fading like tiny stars to memory, dear—
> as soon the imprint of our bodies here.

Belle's young voice rang of her never-forgotten love with David Ahgosa.

Angel held up the penny. "May I place this on Marmie's memorial to match the old stone from the totem pole I placed atop my father's marker when we buried her in the cemetery by Omena Kirk?"

I thought back to that day and remembered how Angel had placed the white stone, rubbed smooth by the Great Lake and concave by the touch of so many fingers, atop her father's headstone beside Marmie's grave. Davey had placed the old birch box and totem pole in the big cedar grove, so the Eagles could watch over Belle and David and both our clans forevermore. As I began to reflect on how we also strewed the rest of her ashes at the places we shared most with her, Father Paul's squeeze to my hand broke my reverie. More than 27 years after we'd buried David Ahgosa and 24 years after we said our farewells to Marmie, I answered Angel's question, "About time!"

She bade Father Paul and me join hands and hold the penny. "Also time to hear our Marmie and search for the truth about your pasts, too?" she asked. I didn't know what to say, but I felt his hand in mine. Angel retrieved the coin, handed me the keys, and walked away. The hall light danced off her white hair and formed a halo that seemed to glow long after she left. I knew the Ogichidaakwe of her Ojibwe band could see things we couldn't, but all I said to Father Paul was, "Whatever else, I have been blessed with the best father and Marmie ever."

"Rabbie and Mirja were good parents to me, too," he replied. "Marmie and Pip also treated me as if I were their child."

After a moment's reflection, I thought, so true for me with his parents. "Do you remember the day after Belle died, when Marty saved her little brother from drowning in the pool, and she said it was because Marmie asked her to watch over the 'sinker'?"

"And over the next several weeks, we joined to teach Little Paul how to swim."

"As Marmie's still talking to us, think we should listen?"

Father Paul didn't know whether to nod, shake his head, laugh, or cry.

Neither did I.

We kneeled down, looked over the chest and out the window of Belle's cottage to the moonbeams glistening off Sleeping Bear Bay, and held hands in prayer. We said our thanks to his mother and to the fathers and the Marmie we shared.

ᔓ

Three more surprises greeted us over the next week. First, as the executor of Pip's estate, I received from our family lawyer a copy of his recent letter of instructions:

> *Dear Ruthie,*
> *As the sands of time run out on my rickety ticker, I want to thank you and your children for helping me discover anew. For too many years, I envied John Kraus hearing the Big Wow sound of intelligent life in space with our Big Ear and Lemaitre learning before he died that Bell Labs with its different Ear recorded the noise of his cosmic egg exploding to create our still-expanding*

universe. What with my hearing and hope of discovering The Voice of God both failing, I began to lose faith, despite the prayers and encouragement of Father Paul and Mirja.

Yet the more I learn from you all, most recently our little Paul and his Ph.D. study at UM of the connections between biochemistry, the cosmos and life, the more I realize my quest has been misguided. For Creation can be seen as much in the evolution of stars, galaxies, the elements, and life on earth as in the origins of our Universe. Creation can also be heard and seen in the sounds and the insights of many human voices, not the least in the poems of Frost, Roethke, Auden, and Belle, who battled their different demons to a draw in seeing God's hand in nature's designs, large and small. My wish for you is to find your voice to add what you will to this great story we all share.

Oh, how I wished I already had, but I couldn't give up. His note continued:

As the executor and trustee for my estate, you will control ⅔ of E-Cubed with your shares from Marmie. Rather than selling, please consider adding: (a) bio-chemistry and related genetic discoveries to our three E's; and (b) our little Paul as partner to head our investments in life sciences.

If Kurt's alive but wishes to retire, and Marty and Paul wish to continue, you three can buy him out over time and still get the benefit of his sage advice. Please also consider changing the name of our fund. I suggest you go back to the name Marmie chose for our family business so long ago and on which all else we have done since has been built: Empire.

I wondered whether Paul would prefer to pursue his life science research at UM. Pip answered:

I am disappointed by the University's refusal to change its rules against professors becoming entrepreneurs while remaining on the faculty, its refusal to value patents as much as any other form of publishing, and its diminishing defense research. Despite our investments over the past 24 years in several dozen Michigan inventors to build new companies, the University treats each as a lay tinkerer rather than as an academic prize. If the new Empire is to thrive, I fear that Marty and Paul will therefore need to spend more time in Cambridge-Boston and Palo Alto-San Francisco with the private universities, research faculty, inventors, and new companies growing faster there. With Bill Pierpont's help, perhaps Paul and Marty can also work with our great public university better than I have, to seize the research and invention initiative it lost after the dark years of the Vietnam War. I do hope both will maintain their homes here so you can continue to enjoy your grandchildren growing up, as I have enjoyed mine.

His postscript offered one last insight:

Ruthie, with Angel, Davey, Sven, and Bill Pierpont, you have done a great job working with our former senator and guiding our Conservancy to honor the historic treasures of Glen Haven and Port Oneida, to protect the second-growth forests and trails around our thriving Empire, Glen Arbor, Glen Lake, the Leelanau School, and the Homestead, and to conserve the incomparable shores, wilderness, and vistas of the Empire Bluffs, Alligator Hill, Miller Hill Lookout, Pyramid Point, and the Crystal River around Sleeping Bear Dunes National Lakeshore, at too long last "officially" dedicated just this fall. And you've helped Davey protect Miss Schulz's legacy at the northeast reach of Leelanau Peninsula while he strives to run Ahgosa enterprises in tune with nature.

I also applaud Angel joining her Ojibwe band in Dodie Chamber's Odawa petition for recognition of their bands as a tribe, despite the refusal of the Feds since the 1836 treaty with the original Ahgosa Ogema to do so. Such recognition, however, may not include a guarantee that their original fishing, hunting, and gathering rights will be respected on any public land, whether national park or not: Remember to honor our promise to David Ahgosa. Yet, even if all federal agencies and the State of Michigan agree to respect these original rights, the Park Service's recent land-grab from old Pierce Stocking shows that the Conservancy will have more work to do. Hold out for a fair price before transferring any land to the national park so the Conservancy can preserve more of Leelanau's Delight of Life. I'm sorry Senator Hart retired: as he was the father of our national park (and our Marmie the mother), I trust you to continue as the steward, conserving our great heritage.

Most of all, I treasured Pip's closing:

Thank you for being my daughter and best friend, bringing Marty and Little Paul and their children into our lives, and making Father Paul and Mirja a part of our family. Love, Your Dad, Pip.

Second, the report came back from the State Police and the coroner's office in Traverse City on the accident that had claimed Pip and Mirja. The preliminary paragraphs merely summarized what Father Paul and I already knew: On Saturday, December 3, at 12:30 p.m., when most of our conservancy board had already gathered for lunch at the Homestead Inn before our annual meeting, I took the call from Kurt Knutsen saying he still waited at the airport for Pip and Mirja to pick him up. Father Paul called the State Police, and we set off in Marmie's vintage Lincoln, top up, big snow tires carrying us safely through the deep powder from the first Arctic blast. As we raced south on the county road past the old Coleman Farm, we saw the county sheriff car's lights flashing at the odd intersection with the state highway. The blowing wind had drifted snow over the stop sign Belle got placed there. A semi heading south had barreled straight through and crushed Pip and Mirja at their first 90-degree turn on M-72 from Empire to Traverse City.

The final paragraph told a different story: Pip had managed to stop where he had the right-of-way as a massive heart attack took him. Mirja, trying to breathe life back into him, died instantly when the speeding truck crashed through the driver-side door.

Father Paul looked ashen after he finished reading the report, but I wasn't shaken. Pip's heart had been faltering for years. To the end, my gangly father maintained the strength in his long arms and hands as he lashed the dimpled ball around MacKenzie's Homestead masterpiece and the Empire Bluffs links he had designed and built. Yet his heart had already broken down so, he had to ride a natural gas-powered cart because his legs couldn't carry him, not around the streets of Empire, let alone on the hills and dales of his beloved golf courses that he played with Father Paul and me, Marty and Little Paul.

Nor was I shocked Mirja died trying to save Pip's life. She knew much more about the odd genetic makeup that he battled to the end. She watched over him the last few years and fought for every beat and breath she could wring from her true love's heart and lungs, even after there were no more.

I tried to explain to comfort Father Paul, but not even a man of God can control his emotions at the loss of the mother and natural father he'd come to love so dearly.

Third, a letter arrived two days later in the mail. Although I didn't recognize the name "Mrs. Rebekah Brodsky" on the return address, my place of conception and birth and my first home did ring loud: Amherst, Massachusetts. Pip, Marmie, and Frost had told me stories of my first months alive there, but Pip had never taken me back to visit the town or his alma mater, and I had returned only once, with Father Paul, for Little Paul's graduation in June 1972.

When I opened the envelope, a copy of the *New York Times* report of the life and death of Paul I. Peebles and Mirja Fitzpatrick fell onto the desk. Given my mourning over their loss and pawing through the trove Marmie Belle bequeathed me, I hadn't paid much attention to the tributes, condolences, and newspaper articles that poured in for Pip and his beloved mate. I laid the clipping aside and picked up the letter. *Dear Ruth*, she began,

> *I read the article in the* New York Times *on your father's passing, two months after my husband died of lung cancer. On his deathbed Bernard revealed circumstances I wish I had shared immediately with Pip, but I felt too aggrieved to do so. So I now write you instead.*
>
> *My husband's mind was clear until the end, but his conscience was not. He showed me pictures of my sister Rachel, your mother, he'd kept secret. He confessed he still regretted her spurning his marriage proposals, the more so after she admitted she was pregnant with his child. Bernard and I had a good marriage, but we were never blessed with a child.*
>
> *I met you and your Aunt Belle with Pip twice at Rachel's grave in the spring of 1927. They were gracious, and we shared our grief at the loss of his wife, your mother, and my sister. I didn't then understand why Bernard ran off without saying goodbye after he put the tip of his finger in your tiny hand. I spoke with Pip only once thereafter, in Amherst when President Kennedy spoke at the groundbreaking for the Frost Library. He told me about you and your children and offered to introduce us, whether through bringing you for a visit to Amherst or my visiting you in Michigan. I so much wanted to accept, but Bernard wouldn't hear of it. Now I know why. He was jealous of Pip.*

I'm sorry you didn't get to know your real father: he was a good man, the longest-serving physics professor at Amherst, a good husband and better friend to me all through the years, despite his long-lost and longer-hidden love for my sister.

I know Pip also loved Rachel, and he rightly chose you as his child from your first day and, as made clear in the enclosed obituary, to his last.

I hope you will stay with me in Amherst. We can visit your parents' graves. I also hope to meet your children, but I understand if you decide you don't want to see me at all or let your children know.

Your Aunt Rebekah Goldberg Brodsky

My heart didn't pound, and I didn't get angry. Maybe I had always suspected something was awry, and Angel's question freed me to inquire. I thought back to the times as kids when Paul O'Bannon cut off my advances before we went too far, how I ran off to Wisconsin to get away from him, how he proposed to me in his hospital bed in Madison only after he knew I was pregnant with another man's child. Was that all because he, Mirja, and Marmie believed Pip fathered us both?

I quieted my mind and heard Marmie's voice in the UW-Madison hospital when I asked her whether Pip was really my father: "I guess I don't know for sure," she said, "but Pip's never expressed any doubt to me." Yet Marmie always had doubts, didn't she, right to the end when she said goodbye and tried to tell me but I didn't listen?

I also imagined Pip's eyes, pale gray-blue and unblinking, when he assured me so many years ago, "You were always my child." I now knew the more important truth. He paid me the highest tribute: He chose me as his child.

I spent the rest of the afternoon reading everything I could find in Marmie's journals, memoir, and correspondence about Pip's time with Rachel at Amherst, her illness, my birth, and the time Pip,

Marmie, and I spent together in Frost's house. This review made me more certain than ever: Dad, wherever you are, I thank you for being my father. Belle, I had to admit with a smile and shake of my head at her conspiring along the way, I also thank you for choosing me so you could be my Marmie, too.

I wrote my Aunt Rebekah:

> *I do want to see you again, and I hope you will become a part of my family. On Pip and Mirja's death, I received another surprise, this one from Marmie's trusted Angel: a big chest full of Belle's poems, more voluminous correspondence, unfinished memoir, and many journals. After I finish plowing through these writings, I will deliver to the President of Amherst College this spring a large package, still sealed, of the letters and poems Belle and Robert Frost shared. I hope to persuade Pip's son, my lifelong friend Father O'Bannon, to join me. I look forward to visiting the graves of your sister and husband, my mother and natural father. You can fly back to Michigan with us to meet the rest of the family, my children Marty and Paul and four grandchildren. Love, Ruthie*

When Paul O'Bannon returned from St. Mary's to Belle Cottage late that afternoon, I sat him down in the living room before a roaring fire. I handed him an Irish malt whiskey on the rocks and Rebekah's letter. When he finished, I read him my letter to Aunt Rebekah. He drained his glass and set it on the table before he screwed up the courage to look at me. "This complicates our situation, doesn't it?"

Oh, I'll say! After so many decades of safety in our deepening friendship as half-brother and half-sister, he was suddenly no longer forbidden fruit. I wanted to hold him, all of him, as badly as I did when only a teenager falling in first love with him. Yet he'd been married to the Catholic Church for decades and become the trusted priest to more than a thousand parishioners in his flock. When he began to cry, I wanted to comfort him, to take him to my bed and never let go, but I only had the courage to place my hand over his. When he flinched, I didn't let go.

Eventually, he wiped the tears away with his other hand and placed it over mine. "I've always loved you," he began, "but this…" He paused. "How much did Pip know?"

"He never ever brooked any doubt with me about my being his child."

"Mirja?" he asked.

"Nothing in Belle's journals or letters suggests your mother had any doubt Pip was my father," I replied. "Marmie had doubts from the very beginning, but she wanted to raise me so much she…" I paused. "At least twice, once when you were in the hospital in Madison and once on her deathbed, she tried to let me know, but I…"

"When Marmie tried to confess at the end," he interjected, "I didn't listen either."

He looked so troubled, I didn't know what I could say that would help—other than I didn't want to marry him, but I wasn't going to tell another lie to make his priestly vows any easier. So I told him the truth: "Paul, I want you, all of you, but unlike my father, I'm not willing to share a mate who's married to another, whether a person of flesh or the Catholic Church." I paused before adding, "I don't think you are either." When he nodded, I said, "I'm going to Empire for dinner and a family conference with Marty and Little Paul." His face clouded over. "I'm moving into a little cottage on the beach there until you decide whether you want to join me."

"No," he protested, "I'll move into the parish house at St. Mary's."

"I need you to stay here to help with Marmie's papers," I countered. "That way you can read her writings late into the night and leave me your notes, while I work on them here after my classes at the Leelanau School."

He took this in and nodded.

"Dinner's in the fridge," I said, "but I'd best be leaving." I walked to the hall closet, took out the bag I'd packed, and walked through the kitchen to the back door.

Before I could open it, he touched my right elbow. When I turned, he held both my arms firmly in his hands and said, "Ruth, this is hard for me."

Before he could stop me, I pecked him on the cheek and said, "For me, too."

ᔕ

After dinner in Empire with my family, I shared all the news with Marty and Little Paul, but they couldn't resist asking what Father Paul and I planned to do now. I didn't know for sure, but our odd courtship did begin. I taught at the Leelanau School during the day, but early every morning I stopped by Belle Cottage and read his notes. After school I reviewed Marmie's papers in her study until Father Paul arrived from St. Mary's. For the next hour, we faithfully discussed what we'd learned from our research about Belle, over one whiskey on the rocks each—Irish for him and Scotch for me. I joined Little Paul or Marty and their families for dinner. Thereafter, I worked on the chapters for Belle's unfinished memoir at my little cottage, often past midnight.

As the days, nights, weeks, and months wore on and I pieced together, wrote, revised, and edited the story of our Marmie Belle, I began to share my drafts with Father Paul. He offered his suggestions, with increasing respect and affection.

Along the way a strange thing happened. As the biography spoke more and more in her voice, I began to compose verse in my own. The different sound at Empire beach helped. The waves lapping onshore and wind rustling through the trees at Belle Cottage in the shelter of Sleeping Bear Bay usually offered a gentle hum; the wind and water building all the way across Lake Michigan crashed ashore. Most days a deeper rumble rose, but in a raging storm, the sound roared as if the howl of the Mama Bear high on the dunes keening for her two cubs, lost on this great inland sea.

As Angel Ahgosa drew the illustrations for Marmie Belle's collected poems, I began to capture the different sounds of the Great Lakes in my verse, and Paul O'Bannon became my muse. I never lost hope that one day he would answer my call.

Spring 1978: On the Road to Ann Arbor and in Amherst

The small, flat granite headstone read THEODORE ROETHKE 1908 – 1963. It rested in an open patch, as much dirt as grass, behind the larger marble monuments for his parents and sister in the Oakwood Cemetery in Saginaw. "Dust to dust," Father Paul said, the collar of his trench coat turned up to protect against the cold wind we'd brought with us from up north on our drive down south to Ann Arbor so early this May day.

"Your father escorted me to the burial here. We joined the reception at Uncle Teddy's childhood home down the street afterward," I said as I grabbed his hand, "but the big greenhouses behind, the ones that had lived so long in his mind, were gone." I paused. "That's when Rabbie told me he was going to write *The Greenhouse* biography to tell the full story of Roethke's life if it was the last thing he ever did."

"Maybe another Irish blessing my Da finished it before the cancer did him in."

"No," I said with a squeeze to his hand. "I visited him in University Hospital on his last day, tubes sticking out every which way. He'd just completed proofreading the galleys and glowed so, I knew he was ready to walk on after the months of hanging on against all odds."

I handed him the draft of my last meeting with his father:

"More fun than writing novels," Rabbie croaked from his hospital bed. "*The Greenhouse* has allowed me to explore the greater spark in a more tortured soul." He paused. "I hope you'll be even prouder of your Uncle Teddy when you see how he made his big highs and bigger lows a part of his genius."

He asked me to hand him the thick, leather-bound book on the bedside table, with three folded pieces of paper sticking out, next to a thinner paperback. He opened the edition of Shakespeare's complete works and handed me the first folded note, from Auden.

Ruthie Dear,
Rabbie tells me you've got some kind of a block about composing poetry. When I had that problem back in '43 while drafting a verse drama to clean up the mess left in The Tempest, I reread all of Shakespeare's plays. That helped me get back to conjuring The Sea and the Mirror. I also enclose the only two of the many poems Belle shared with me that I can still lay my hands on. After you finish reading Shakespeare, my play, and her two songs (as she liked to call them), take out your pen and start composing in verse again.

You don't have to write with the mania of the Big Man, and you don't have to worry about the echoes of Belle's voice haunting you. You can even try to imitate the Great Bard, Marmie, Ted, Frost, me, and so many other poets, too, as we all copy madly from each other. My best to Marty and little Paul, and give our dear Rabbie and his son hugs for me.
As ever, Wystan

I pulled out the other two folded notes and read aloud the two poems in Marmie's hand, "Museum of Bad Words" and "Hoo… Who?"

Rabbie tapped his fingers right along to the beat, but the first was so much cheekier, its after-mark hit me all the harder, while the second offered a much more plaintive call than the echoes of Belle's few other songs I could still hear.

Rabbie pulled out a little piece of paper and gave it to me. Folded and unfolded so many times there were more slits than creases, it barely held together. It was a love poem from Belle, titled "Rendezvous." After I read it three times to myself, I recited the poem she'd written for him. His eyes began to tear, and I draped myself across his chest.

"Now that Little Paul's graduated from high school and off to Amherst for college," he whispered in a halting, hoarse voice, "why don't you move back to Belle's cottage?" Could Rabbie read my mind?

Too bad Frost hadn't fired Thompson and asked Rabbie to serve as his "official" biographer. *The Greenhouse* revealed our Teddy Bear's craziness, his recurring episodes of mania and depression, his tough brassiness and self-aggrandizing lies, his temper tantrums, and his insults. But Rabbie's even more personal history did so in a way that wasn't vicious and made sense of the story of the poet and the man, of Uncle Teddy always striving to write great poems about little things. If Rabbie had the same chance to write the life of Frost, and explained how Robbie's lyrics sang on their own terms, it would have been both more honest and more telling than Thompson's hatchet job.

ཥ

When the good son and priest finished reading my draft, he handed the pages back and said, "If you introduce Robert Hayden at Rackham this afternoon with this story of your conversation with the former Hopwood Director, the audience will be all ears."

Indeed, it would invite everyone to listen harder to Robert Hayden's Hopwood Lecture on *The Enduring Friendship and Many Voices of Roethke and Auden*. "I'm also going to share Marmie's last letters with Uncle Teddy and Wystan."

He nodded and said, "Too bad Auden didn't live long enough to hear the different voices of the characters in the epic verse play you're composing. Act I's a stunner."

We walked back to Belle's vintage Lincoln, top up, still in mint condition. He hurried onto I-75 to Flint, where we kept going south on US-23. "My Da told me the story of the spring of '62, when Frost and Roethke descended on you two," he said, his eyes turning slightly to catch mine in his peripheral vision. "He said Frost came first, and you met in the living room at Inglis House before his reading at Hill Auditorium that evening. The old man just yelled because Pip wasn't there with a hearing aid for him, and Frost couldn't make out a word you said."

"I grant you Uncle Robbie did look, sound, and act the part of a tired, cantankerous old man of 88." I paused. "But as he sipped his ginger ale, he did say, 'Thank goodness it's not Vernor's!' and remarked that 'Belle's eye for nature was always better than mine: I'm colorblind, don't you know?'"

Father Paul chuckled, and I continued, "That's when I told Robbie how much Pip, Mirja, Marty, Little Paul, and I enjoyed witnessing his show at President Kennedy's Inauguration. That puckish old bard had tried to steal the show there: He acted as if so blinded by the sun he couldn't read the new—and too long—poem others thought he had prepared especially for the occasion. He appeared lost until he feigned trying to remember the words but said 'The Gift Outright' instead to give some heft to JFK's call for A New Frontier. When I finished complimenting Robbie, his pale blue eyes twinkled anew. He tapped my knee and said, 'As with President Kennedy, once or twice before I also had to remind Belle that *promises* aren't enough: she also had an obligation to *do* better by this great land of ours going forward.'"

When Father Paul nodded, I continued, "And Frost then asked, 'Wasn't it her odd friend Auden who advised a culture is no better than its woods?' I responded by assuring Robbie how Angel Ahgosa called on the spirit of her father and of our Marmie to guide the deeds of our Leelanau Conservancy and to complete the unfinished business of establishing a national park for Sleeping Bear Dunes and Lakeshore."

Father Paul took his right hand off the wheel and laid it gently on my left. "We've done our Marmie and her poet friends proud in both respects up north, haven't we?"

"Yes, but if you keep two hands on the wheel and both eyes on the road, I'll tell you the rest of that story." After he complied, I continued, "As Rabbie and I got up to leave, Uncle Robbie raised his hand to wave goodbye but rubbed one of the many dark splotches on his face and grumped at me. 'After all I did to greet you in this world, you tell that ingrate of a father of yours I'm mad he didn't join us.'

"'Oh, he would have,' I replied, 'except he made arrangements with Mrs. Morrison for you to stay at our Cambridge House when you come back in June.'

"Frost seemed puzzled until his blue eyes cleared and he said, 'For Commencement?' When I nodded, he huffed, 'About time.' Yet a smile soon spread across his face. 'Best earn my keep tonight then.'"

Father Paul stole a glance at me, put his right hand back on my left and said, "Da told me the old bard put on quite a show to a packed house at Hill that night." When I nodded, he continued, "But Frost couldn't resist getting too full of himself after the show ended. As the crowd streamed outside to wave goodbye, he raised his arms high and said 'Remember me!' As he disappeared into the back of his limousine, the admiring throng sang as if his chorus, 'We will! We will! We will!'"

"I put his right hand back on the wheel and said, "No, the young lion of a poet the Department Chair hired on the English faculty instead of our aging Uncle Teddy had to struggle to escort Frost safely through the large crowd pressing to get a last glimpse of the great Bard."

"Sorry," Father Paul interjected, "I guess my father once again didn't give me the full story."

"Not the bit about how Frost yelled, 'What do I want with that?' when Marty pressed through the throng and tried to hand him a note?"

Abashed, Paul just shook his head.

"I stepped forward and told Uncle Robbie it was a gift from Belle. After he read Marmie's anthem to our north coast, he waved Little Paul forward and hugged my two kids in thanks. He tucked the poem inside his coat pocket and said to me, 'Make sure your father brings his new-fangled little ears when I return so I can better hear Belle's poems...' Frost chuckled before bussing me on the cheek and whispering '... and Michigan's president reading my honorary doctorate degree.'"

Father Paul smiled and tapped my left hand gently with his right. "In your introduction at Rackham this afternoon," he asked, "are you going to share how my Da saved you from the manic Roethke delivering two huge bags of presents for Little Paul and Marty the day after Marmie's memorial in Ann Arbor?"

"No," I said with a laugh. "Uncle Teddy was so obsessed by his Big Mama's death he was just trying to make amends as best he could for not reciting at the service Belle's anthem and his latest poem. He kept crying that her 'Up North' villanelle inspired his 'Waking' poem of the same form that would win the Pulitzer. Yet Uncle Teddy's irrepressible spirit soon got us all splashing and playing in the pool, including *your* Da."

"Sorry," he said, "I guess he didn't share the full story of that adventure either."

"That's because losing Belle also crushed your father. When he took Teddy back to Hill House, they both got so much in their cups, I had to drive Roethke to the station to catch his train. When I got back from the depot to check on Rabbie, he had sobered some and said, 'With your Marmie gone, and Father Paul and your father up north so much, let me know how I can help you and your kids here.' When he stopped by Cambridge House several weeks later with gifts wrapped for you, Marty, Little Paul, and me, I told him, 'You're driving these up with us to Belle's cottage so we can all celebrate Christmas and make a New Year together with Father Paul.'"

I paused when I saw the film form over his eyes. "That's how Marmie's last love became *my Uncle Rabbie* and helped me raise Marty and little Paul at our houses in Ann Arbor and Belle Cottage up north."

He dropped his right hand from the wheel again and placed it more firmly on my left. "Ruthie, you sharing these more… personal… stories in writing Belle's memoir?"

Seeing his eyes stray to mine again, I nodded and grasped his hand firmly in both of mine. I never wanted to let go.

"How are you going to end the book?" he asked.

"Unless something better happens to strike me," I replied, "the memorial service for Belle in the big kirk in Ann Arbor."

He nodded.

After 15 minutes driving in companionable silence, I also shared how Bill Pierpont, Robert Hayden, and the new Chair planned to join us for dinner at the League later that evening.

He nodded and asked, "Taking up where Marmie left off there, too?"

"And after Rabbie, too," I added tartly. I explained how enrollments in the English Department had flagged substantially in recent years, what with no new women professors and too little writing and composing to attract more students.

He held my hand tight and said, "Ruth, thank you." He paused. "Rabbie and Marmie would be so proud you're going to invest to engage a new generation of students and faculty, men and women alike, in creative writing at Michigan."

"No more proud than Pip and Marmie both would be that Little Paul didn't give up on Michigan either," I reminded him.

He patted my hand and said in a softer tone, "I'm even happier that he and Marty arranged their lives so both their families can spend most of their time near us."

Eventually, he lifted his hand to the wheel again, slowed, and steered onto the exit ramp for North Territorial. After a quick jog to the right, he turned south. "Time for a brief stop at my Da's grave?"

I looked at my wristwatch—1:30 p.m.—and began to shake my head, but I didn't need to get to Rackham before 3:30. "Save me getting any more willies worrying about how best to introduce the nation's Poet Laureate returning from the Library of Congress to rejoin Michigan's English faculty."

He tapped my hand and said, "I'm only sorry my Ma and Auden didn't live to share this day with Hayden and you. Mirja would be so proud to see you introducing one of her color and one of Wystan's disciples as the Hopwood Lecturer and Distinguished Professor in Poetry."

I nodded with a smile and gave his hand a squeeze. "At least Mirja and Pip did live to help launch President Ford's re-election bid at Crisler Arena on the dais with their old friend Judge Ward."

"When those firecrackers exploded in the top bowl sounding like gunshots and everyone sat stunned, Willis Ward stood up as Jerry Ford had for him before," he said, "and the crowd joined in singing 'The Victors' for Michigan's only president."

"Quite a send-off and last hurrah," I replied. "President Ford will long be remembered as the stand-up guy who helped heal the country after Watergate and Vietnam, but he'd be the first to agree with Willis, Mirja, Pip, and Belle that we've got a long way to go to form a more perfect union."

Father Paul squeezed my hand before lifting his back to the steering wheel and pulling across the road to the black-painted iron fence in front of the cemetery opposite Old St. Patrick's Church. The rose bushes on either side of the entrance bloomed in pink. We walked up the shallow steps and opened the main gate. A few steps on the left rested the weathered granite headstones of the O'Bannon clan: Rabbie, his grandparents, his parents, and his little brother, lost to a farming accident when a boy.

The remaining O'Bannon namesake crossed himself, kneeled down, and folded his hands in prayer for his Da. Still standing, I placed my hand on his shoulder, bowed my head and gave thanks for how much Rabbie meant to Marmie, me, and my children. Oh, how I wished Paul would hold me right to the end, as Mirja had held Pip, Rabbie held Marmie, and Belle held David. After he stood and crossed himself again, he grasped my hand as if he didn't ever want to let go either.

❧

We flew to Bradley Field near Hartford early the next morning, rented a car and headed north on I-91. Turning east on Route 9, Father Paul wound around the outskirts of Amherst, headed toward the town center and jogged north onto Sunset. He made a quick left into a looping drive on the far side of the two-story, yellow clapboard home with black trim. He pulled to a stop between the white columns under the porte cochere.

Aunt Rebekah, her long white hair flowing over the side of her face, flew out of the double door and down the steps. Still ramrod-straight at 77, she towered over me as I got out of the car and hugged me. We'd exchanged such friendly letters every week with so much news and history, I already felt as if I'd known her all my life. I guess that was literally true but for the half-century hiatus after Pip and Marmie drove me as a baby from Frost's house back to Michigan.

When I shared that thought, Aunt Rebekah broke into a radiant smile: "His Sunset House is four doors down on the other side of the street. I'll arrange a tour for tomorrow morning before we drive to the airport for the flight back to Michigan."

She'd prepared a lunch of fresh egg, tuna and fruit salads in the dining room overlooking a lovely English garden, already in spring bloom. While Father Paul feasted, Aunt Rebekah and I talked and talked. When it got to be two o-clock, he finally had to pipe up: "We'd best freshen up for our 2:30 meeting with the College president."

My aunt and I continued to jabber while he deposited the bags in our separate bedrooms across the center hall on the second floor.

When he returned, Aunt Rebekah said she'd leave a stew warming in the oven for us when we returned. "You've got a lot to go over with Bill Ward," she added, "and I'm usually in bed within minutes after sundown." She pointed out the dining room window to the Berkshires rising in the west, where the view of the setting sun would shine its grace before her bedtime at the end of every clear day.

At 2:15 p.m. Paul and I walked up to the town center. We turned south on Pleasant and looked east two blocks on Main, to Emily Dickinson's yellow-painted brick Homestead and her brother's Italianate Evergreens. We continued south parallel to the long green of the town common. The fairest College rose on the hill ahead. We continued until we reached the large brick, Greek Revival home of the president across the street from the campus. John William Ward waved to us from the front door, and we climbed the two sets of concrete steps. He greeted us at the top, and I introduced Father Paul O'Bannon as Pip's son and my editor at our Empire Press.

"So good to see you both again," Ward said. When we looked surprised, he explained, "Hard to forget my first commencement as president here and meeting the mother and her brother, the good priest and uncle, of the Brodsky Science Prize winner."

Ward, perhaps the preeminent American Studies scholar, escorted us into his study: Little did he know what other surprises would follow! I pulled the big envelope from my book bag and placed it on the table. I handed him Belle's letter of instructions. After he reviewed it, I said, "Unless you have any objections, my son and I hope to lodge with the College the correspondence and draft poems Belle and Frost shared."

"Your son," Ward said, "was as outstanding a science student here as your father, albeit in biology and chemistry rather than astronomy and physics."

"Perhaps more so," I replied. "My daughter changed the name of Pip's E-Cubed Fund in order to get him to join as a partner to lead a new division." I gave him a clipping from an Ann Arbor News article with a photo of my son announcing a new program at the University of Michigan to help students make and deliver inventions and discoveries in life sciences to advance the health of people and the well-being of our planet.

Ward read aloud the lead quote from my son: "'Today,' Dr. Peebles said, 'we're going to build anew on the tradition of Michigan's great inventors before, the Francis and Salk vaccines, the Sarns Heart Pump, and so many others, including my grandfather's Little Ear hearing aids for the near deaf and bigger running blades for amputees.'" After he finished reading the rest of the article, Ward looked up and said, "Back to the original name of your family business, Empire?"

"Yes, and there'll be a time when UM rejoins MIT and Stanford in the defense and energy research that fuels innovation in the fields Pip explored. His grandkids may yet inspire another Big Wow and Big Bang, as Pip and his War Labs did before."

Ward couldn't help nodding with a chuckle, but then turned, pointed across the road, through the trees, and up the hill, to the brick and limestone building standing on the north side of the original College quadrangle. "I'm grateful you think adding Belle's Frost collection here is the right thing to do. Before you finally decide, I must share a letter my predecessor sent your father after President Kennedy's groundbreaking for the Frost Library." He handed over a yellowed carbon copy, and Paul and I read the letter:

Dear Pip, I regret that the great poet's daughter has directed us to send to her all his papers Mrs. Morrison delivered here for the Robert Frost Memorial Library. Although Lesley assures she will share items most relevant to her father's long tenure at Amherst, this is a blow to our plans. Although the College will continue to gather original material to build our substantial Frost collection, this is small consolation indeed. I hope our slain President's dedication will assure that the new Library will better serve your generous albeit anonymous gift and our students, faculty, alumni, and friends for generations to come. I apologize for my failure to bring the Frost papers home, where they belong. Cal

"Always some controversy or intrigue about Amherst's two greatest poets and their papers with the College," I said with a smile, "isn't there?"

"You know about the battle between Mabel Todd and the heirs to Emily Dickinson that also left Amherst with the minor portion of her archives?" When I nodded, Ward said, "I fear the College's failure to acquire Frost's papers was the last straw for your father. He never contributed to Amherst again."

"Not so," I reminded him, "Pip and I entrusted you with my son for four years." I couldn't resist adding, "If you've got any women professors in the hard sciences to attract my son's twin tomboy girls here, he might become a loyal alumni donor."

"Soon I hope, but after only three years being co-ed, we already have highly regarded women as professors in English, as well as Psychology, History, Art…"

"One in each?" I interjected. When he nodded, I said, "Michigan's larger English Department hasn't done any better, but we'll keep working to change that, too." I paused. "Think Amherst will name a woman president before Michigan?"

"By the turn of the century," Ward answered, "I hope both will."

"I can see why the trustees chose you president," I said, "but at least Michigan opened the front door of its student Union to all us women to honor Belle after her memorial service, a generation before this College decided to admit its first woman."

"Neither has a monopoly on denying equal opportunity to women in higher education," he replied, "but I hope we will both do better going forward."

I nodded, pointed to the large envelope on the table, and shared the stories of how Frost awarded the first Hopwood Prize in Poetry to Belle and how she thereafter endowed a Chair in Creative Writing for the Director of the Hopwood Program in his honor. "The first holder of that Frost Chair was Father Paul's other father, Rabbie O'Bannon, who returned to Belle as her mate in the end. My father's reaction to the loss of Frost's papers won't alter our decision to trust you and the College."

"Thank you," he said with relief.

"When we return in June," I asked, "may we review Emily Dickinson's papers and the other archives from Mabel Todd and her daughter here?"

Bill Ward brightened. "We now work with all the libraries that hold Dickinson and Frost papers. When you come back, I will also show you the Dickinson Homestead and the Evergreens on Main Street."

"I look forward to that," I replied. "We're staying at the Brodsky home on Sunset and Aunt Rebekah has already arranged for us to visit…"

"Oh!" Ward interjected. "I never realized Professor Brodsky was your uncle."

"Turns out he was my natural father." When President Ward gawped, I added, "My mother wanted Pip as her husband and the father to raise me."

Bill Ward looked at Father Paul and me: "So you're not siblings after all?"

I shared the gist of the secret Professor Brodsky confessed to his wife on his deathbed.

"Your aunt was a saint to him," Ward said. "He could also be very difficult and demanding in his legendary Physics I-II classes, so much so that generations of students will never forget him—most for the better, a few for the worse."

"Including my son, a late riser," I replied. "The crusty martinet locked Little Paul out of his lecture when the tower bells here chimed 8 a.m." I paused. "Thankfully, that sent my boy into the study of life sciences instead."

With a wink and a smile, Ward said, "Now I know why Bernard scowled so when your son stepped forward at graduation to claim the science prize at commencement."

After an appropriate pause, the president continued, "When you return this summer, I will introduce you to a more welcoming member of our faculty. In Professor Pritchard's first year as a teacher here in the mid-50's, he was still working on his Ph.D. dissertation for Harvard on Frost. President Cole assigned Bill to serve as a driver and escort for our Distinguished Poet for his annual visit that year. Pritchard finally got around to asking if Frost would review the draft and offer suggestions." Ward chuckled. "A few weeks later, Frost invited him for lunch at the Lord Jeff Inn. The old bard advised only, 'Keep it around and deepen it, deepen it.' Although Bill Pritchard took another four years to complete his dissertation, two decades later he's still writing the literary biography on Frost he hopes to finish soon."

When I told him that Frost gave the same advice to Belle on one of her poems in 1921 and she worked for more than decade "deepening it," Ward laughed with us. He looked around as if to make sure no one was eavesdropping and opened a drawer on his side of the table. "I've been writing in notebooks and on scraps of paper with ideas for a novel ever since I became president here. Now, I feel like an eyewitness to unraveling another great mystery: I can't wait to read everything Belle put in this envelope."

Father Paul put his hand up as if a stop sign. "We have one request: the exclusive copyright on Belle's poems in this collection, as we already have all her originals."

"Planning to edit them for your Empire Press?" Ward asked.

"No," I answered, "we're going to publish her songs exactly as she composed them." I pulled from my book bag the first collection of Emily Dickinson's poems, the one with the Indian pipe on the cover that Mabel Todd gave Marmie in 1923. I recited Mrs. Todd's inscription: "*To Belle: Publish while you can, for after you die only others can edit or destroy your poems as they please.*"

Father Paul also told him about our plans for Empire Press: to add Angel Ahgosa's illustrations to a book of our Marmie's poems and to publish the life story I was putting together from her memoir, journals, and old photos, "first-person-singular in our Marmie's voice. Ruth and Angel will launch a national tour this fall for both."

Ward poured each of us a finger of Scotch and raised his glass. "To Belle, Frost, and Dickinson: May your publications and campaign launch another great poet!"

I pushed the thick envelope to President Ward. He unsealed and opened the flap, read each letter and poem as Belle had ordered them, by date. He handed them one by one to me, and I passed each to Paul, who made sure they were returned in order.

We didn't finish until close to eight o'clock, snacks and more drinks included. "You two have an important job ahead of you with Belle, as does our curatorial staff." Ward said. "You'll also add to the lore of Emily Dickinson's long-running afterlife."

"And I've got to make some substantial revisions and additions, too," I replied.

He poured us each another sniff of Scotch and raised his in a toast: "I look forward to reading the rest of Belle's poems and the story of her life."

He opened his drawer again, pulled a yellowed clipping from *The Boston Globe*, and waved it. "Was the memorial service for Belle the last time you saw Frost?" I told Ward about going to President Kennedy's inauguration and how, two springs later, Frost stole another show reading at Hill Auditorium "to earn his keep for an honorary degree."

"Oh!" Ward said, "I bet the old bard basked in the glow of that commencement."

I pulled the research note from my book bag and told him the rest of the story: Michigan's Lost Son, Ted Roethke, joined Michigan's first Creative Fellow, some 8,000 graduates, and another 20,000 family and friends at Michigan's Big House. President Hatcher first awarded a degree to Robert Frost, A.M. (hon.), 1922:

> *Since an instinct for order and the power of vividly apprehending value are necessary to the commonwealth…, a man may become known as a public personage and a statesman by virtue solely of the exercise of poetic genius… [T]he University happily acknowledges the public offices of this sometime poet-in-residence and frequent and most welcome guest in the degree now conferred upon him, Doctor of Laws.*

Several others followed before President Hatcher got around to Theodore Roethke, A.B., 1929, A.M., 1936:

> *In a period when poets often free themselves from older and more general traditions only to borrow lavishly from particular compeers, Mr. Roethke has been at once of his own time and his own master… Celebrating the forthrightness that distinguishes him as a man, the University proudly tenders to this son of Michigan the degree of Doctor of Letters.*

"Not sure our Marmie Belle would have approved of the highfalutin prose," I added, "and the praise didn't capture a quarter of what Robbie and Teddy meant to us."

When Ward nodded with a warm smile, Paul told him how after the commencement, Rabbie O'Bannon hosted a reception for the two poets at Hill House. "Roethke seemed annoyed at having to share the stage with Frost's greater eminence and muttered, 'New England is a mere literary convention.' Ted then boasted, 'I'm at my peak and writing long poems. My next book's going to drive Frost, Auden, and all the rest *into the shadows*.'" Paul concluded with the arrangements Roethke made to share his papers and personal life with Rabbie O'Bannon "'so the true tales of Theodore Roethke can be told after I win the Nobel.'"

"Your late father's *Greenhouse*," Ward responded, "is the only biography that makes sense of the Big Man and his hard-won place in American poetry."

I picked up and explained how I hustled Frost back to Cambridge House for the night to avoid any more irritations between the two big egos. "Pip and I stayed up way past midnight sharing stories about Belle with him. Frost finally asked Pip about what he'd done with Belle's writings. 'If Marmie had shared them with me,' my father replied, 'Mirja would have published her songs for all to hear long ago.'

'Maybe just as well,' Frost replied as he shook his big head. 'Our correspondence would have given my biographer more ammunition to damn me.'

'No,' Pip retorted. 'Her letters would defend you against all your critics.'

'Oh,' Frost said but then pursed his lips. When his rheumy old eyes cleared, Uncle Robbie added, 'Let's form a scouting party and go out and find them!'"

President Ward laughed and said, "But none of you knew where to look then."

"Yes, but both Roethke and Frost displayed their true colors the next morning." I explained how Uncle Teddy stopped by to say goodbye to me and the glasshouse he'd built and shared with Belle. "He stripped to his drawers and floated in our swimming pool. 'I still miss our Big Mama,' Uncle Teddy said, 'but maybe she had it right all along, to sing only for us rather than campaign to sway the critics and win an audience.'

"There was a rap at the glass door. Rabbie O'Bannon entered with Frost. Roethke struggled to his feet: 'Did you ever think you'd have to call this big Teddy Bear, Doctor?'

'Frankly, the honor's long overdue,' Frost answered. With a chuckle he added, 'I'd embrace you to show how much, but I don't want you dunking me in your Big Mama's Garden of Eden again.' Roethke said he'd be right back. After he changed, I got out the Kodak and took several snapshots of Belle's Robbie and Teddy Bear standing close to each other, smiling and chatting, even one where the big man put his arm around his much older friend. I also took a picture of Rabbie with both, and then Rabbie snapped a shot of me with Marmie's poet friends."

I paused. "When I told them I still wanted to hold her songs again, Uncle Teddy and Uncle Robbie hugged me close as if I were the last living aspect of Belle. Her voice still haunted them, too." I paused again. "But we now know the truth: Our Marmie Belle was as fierce in protecting the privacy of her three great poet colleagues, her family, and her closest friends after her death as she was in protecting her poems during her life."

"Thank you for sharing that," Ward replied. "The story of Belle's life will also provide new material to keep Bill Pritchard working to finish his Frost book. It will also help lift America's most-read poet from the mire of the bad man his biographer wrote and broadcast after Frost's death."

"Robert Frost and his wife," I said, "opened their Amherst home to Pip, Belle, and me after my mother died while giving birth to me in the spring of 1927. The great poet was a good man to our family thereafter despite the many losses and contraries he faced."

Ward picked up the yellowed clipping, and handed it to me. "This newspaper account may help you end Belle's story by telling of her memorial service." He smiled with a shake of his head. "It appears Frost, the inveterate campaigner, couldn't help stealing another show even in paying his respects to her."

I read the article from the *Boston Globe* and shook my head. "The celebration of Belle's poetry and person at her memorial service in the big kirk in Ann Arbor on November 15, 1953, will end *The Belle of Two Arbors...*" I paused to hand the clipping back to him. "...but it's a much different story than your local paper reported."

"How so?" he asked.

From my book bag, I pulled the pages I'd typed describing that day and handed them to Ward. As he read the draft, he nodded, smiled several times but also dabbed a tear from his eyes. When he finished, he said, "The *Globe* did get it wrong. Roethke, Auden, and Frost were all magnificent, but the three joined together only to pay tribute to Belle by each sharing one of their poems and several of hers: she stole the show."

Ward reread the final paragraphs describing Frost's eulogy and teared up again. He looked away and gathered himself. He turned back. "The Silken Tent is my favorite poem, and Frost must have loved Belle dearly to say it as an elegy for her."

I nodded. "Frost also nailed it at the end of his eulogy for our Marmie Belle after saying her *four* elegies for her parents: 'Once published and heard, Belle's songs, as she liked to call her poems with their different tunes and sound sense, are going to be very hard to get rid of.'"

❦

The next morning Father Paul drove Rebekah and me northeast from Amherst to the old Jewish cemetery. As we opened the gate, the rising spring sun glistened off the stone markers. Rebekah led us a few steps in, to an old one with pebbles neatly piled on top. Due to the years of hand-rubbing, I could barely make out the name, Rachel Goldberg, my mother. I touched the pebbles and ran my hand over her name, but I couldn't imagine what pain she must have endured to will me into life as hers passed.

Rebekah pointed to two graves nearby, and said, "My parents." When I saw the name of her and Rachel's mother—"Ruth"—my stomach suddenly roiled with emotions, welled up into my chest, and stuck in my throat. My tears must have flowed because Paul put his arm around me, and Aunt Rebekah held my hand.

Eventually Paul let go, and my aunt led us to the back of the cemetery. We stopped in front of a new marker: Bernard Brodsky, my father. If my mother had chosen him rather than Pip, I couldn't help wondering how different my life would have been.

"Remember," Paul said, "Pip chose you."

I wondered if he could read my mind or if I had spoken, but I nodded when he grasped my hand. I pointed to the grave. "I'm sorry I never got to know… him." What else could I call him, Bernard, Professor Brodsky, Rebekah's late husband, or my father?

"I'm sorry, too," Aunt Rebekah said. "Although short in height and temper, he was a good teacher, a good man, and a good husband to me, despite his undying love for your mother."

That explained the pebbles still piled on top of my mother's headstone as if a cairn: Rebekah kept up her husband's tradition after he died.

She placed three stones on top of his marker and handed me a fourth. I placed it on top and paid my respects to the man who played a part in starting the first of the several odd triangles that had shaped my life.

We walked back to my mother's grave in the front. Paul kneeled before me, reached into the right side pocket of his coat, and pulled out a small black velvet box. "After you left my Da's hospital room his last day, he gave me his mother's wedding ring and asked me to give it to the couple whose marriage I most wanted to bless." A smile broke out on his face as he flipped the top up to reveal a gold ring, shining as only an antique band polished by the ages can. He held my hand and placed the little box in it. "May not be exactly what he meant," he said, looking up to me, "but I think he'd approve: Ruth Belle Peebles, with this ring may I plight thee my troth?"

I must have stood there dumbstruck because he kissed my hand before he added, "Da said that Belle spurned him twice when he asked her to marry him after the Queen died. Don't tell me you're going to continue that tradition."

I stifled a cry, not sure whether of joy or irony. Still clutching the little box with the ring, I pulled him up until he stood beside me. "That last day with Rabbie I told him how grateful I was for his caring for our Marmie Belle in her final years and for Marty, Little Paul, and me ever since. 'No,' he replied, 'I thank you for making me part of your family.' When I told him Belle loved him to her last breath, he said, 'Ruthie, please be good to my son, too: You know he loves you so.'" I paused. "I didn't have the courage then to bring myself to tell him that I'd never stopped loving you, even if I thought you were more my kin than his and married only to the Holy Trinity."

Paul grasped my hands. "If you're willing to convert to the Catholic faith, I'll petition the Holy See for laicization. If not, or if Pope Paul won't grant my petition, I'll divorce the Church, and we'll get married in the Omena Kirk, okay?"

Giving up the priesthood, his parishioners, and the teachers and students at St. Mary's would be hard enough for him, and I'd come to like the liturgy, singing, and fellowship of his parish churches more than our Presbyterian cant anyway. Besides, we could still join the Ahgosas in our old kirk in Omena whenever we wanted. We also had a precedent: Pip had become a Catholic to marry Mirja; why couldn't I?

As if only yesterday, I heard Marmie saying her last words to me: "I love you so, my child. Please, seize all the opportunities I couldn't…"

Even if waiting to take Paul into my bed until married would require all my willpower, I kissed him on the cheek and said, "I will, but we've waited this long, do you mind if I just keep the ring in my pocket until the day you're also free to say, 'I do'?"

❧

It's only right the Sleeping Bear logo and Empire Press will now carry Belle's voice around the world. "Up North" was our Marmie's anthem. May it sing as the title and lead poem of her collected songs for all to hear:

UP NORTH
By Belle

Illustrations by Angel Ahgosa

Paul Fitzpatrick Peebles-O'Bannon,
Ruth Belle O'Bannon-Peebles, Angel Ahgosa
and Paul I. Peebles II, Publishers

Empire Press, 1979
Empire, Michigan

UP NORTH

My yearning for Leelanau is like a disease—
the sun through my window bids me awake:
a chorus of robins sings from the trees

to return to Her bosom, where She offers ease
from the thorns and the thistly losses that ache—
my yearning for Leelanau is like a disease—

the shoreline's now free from its ice-sculpted frieze,
and frothy white waves roll, tumble, and shake.
Five or six finches peek out through the leaves—

I dream of the pond near our bubbling creek,
the nest of a wood duck and her handsome drake—
my yearning for Leelanau is like a disease—

a riot of flowers—the hum of the bees,
the honeyed fragrance of spring in their wake,
a redheaded woodpecker taps on a tree:

Soon Brown-Eyed Susans will sway in the breeze.
The squawk of the seagulls, the bluest of seas—
My yearning for Leelanau is like a disease—
A chorus of robins sings from the trees!

AUTHOR'S NOTE

When I began this adventure, I planned to write an historical novel where the fictional characters would fit on the canvas painted by the many real persons, events, and places of the time, 1913–1953. The more I researched this history, the more blank spaces and missed turns I found. The more I developed my fictional characters, the more I saw how they might influence what happened. After all, individuals help shape their families, friends, colleagues, communities, and events, just as accidents of birth and the shifting historical tides shape each of us and the future. This begs the question: where to draw the line between fact and fiction? Here's what I decided:

First, where my primary fictional characters do influence real persons, events, and places, I hope these changes read as authentic and credible. In particular, Marmie Belle, her brother Pip, and their best friend, David Ahgosa—and their nemeses Sven Surtr and Ned Strait—do change the course of events in this novel, for better or worse, several times, in many ways. Where they do not change history, it is because I did not believe they—or anyone else in their circumstances—could alter the outcome.

Second, I hope my portrayals of the historical persons, events, and places also read as credible and authentic. Three great 20th-century poets—Robert Frost, Ted Roethke, and Wystan Auden—are main characters in this novel. The specter of a great 19th-century poet—The Belle of Amherst, Emily Dickinson—also animates this book. I hope the interactions of my fictional characters with these real persons shed insight into each. Despite the four poets' different circumstances, large egos, manic urges, only sometimes-repressed doubts and dislikes, and other human flaws and surface warts of each, Belle shared their drive to compose poetry. For Belle, each is also an unforgettable character and kindred spirit that she respected, admired, and, yes in different ways, loved.

With the exception of the Higginson-Todd version of Miss Dickinson's poems and a few other poems that are in the public domain, quotation of all other poems is limited to a few words and phrases. The descriptions and snippets of the poems of the three great poets who share time with Belle in this novel are interpreted and deployed only as Belle read and reacted to them. I am, however, grateful to the executor of the Frost estate for the opportunity to review an advance copy of *The Letters of Robert Frost,* Volume 2, 1920-28. I am also grateful for the insights and suggestions of Donald Sheehy, the lead editor of this series of *Letters,* and for his earlier essay, "Refiguring Love: Robert Frost in Crisis, 1938-1942," *New England Quarterly* (June, 1990).

Readers may wonder what ailments and anxieties prevented Belle from publishing her poems during her lifetime, limited her times away from her two safe Arbors to a handful, and kept her single despite several loves. I don't know either, because Belle mostly wrote herself. Perhaps her heart was only big enough to care for her family and few close friends more than herself and to tend her two homes, one in the shadow of the Sleeping Bear up north and the other of the University of Michigan downstate. Perhaps her larger interior hopes and doubts and private fears held her back. But woe be to those who threatened her family, three poet friends, and two Arbors or tried to exploit any underdog, whether the Ojibwe and the sacred land in

Leelanau or the creative writers, tinkerers and dreamers, women and other minorities at the University. To such antagonists, Belle was an implacable foe, at least until they made peace with her.

In the end, Belle also learned from the long-running battles over the archives and legacies of America's two greatest poets, Dickinson and Frost: she made sure all her poems and papers, including her correspondence with her great poet friends, wouldn't be opened until long after her death in 1953 and even then entrusted them only to the niece she chose to raise as if her daughter. I hope you will wonder about Belle long after you put this book down, just as I continue to wonder about her after my last edit, many drafts, and more revisions, long after Belle started blessing me nearly a decade ago.

Of the hundreds of books, articles, and reviews about Frost, Roethke, Auden, and Dickinson I read, the following proved particularly helpful in illuminating their character and work, at least as portrayed here: Donald Sheehy, et al., *The Letters of Robert Frost, 1920-1928* (2016) ; W.H. Pritchard, *Frost: A Literary Life Reconsidered* (1984); Robert M. Warner, *Frost-bite & Frost-bark: Robert Frost at Michigan* (1999); Wade Van Dore, *The Life of the Hired Man: Robert Frost and Wade Van Dore* (1986); Alan Seager, *The Glass House: The Life of Theodore Roethke* (1968); John Fuller, *W.H. Auden: A Commentary* (1998); Charles Miller, *Auden: An American Friendship* (1989); and Brenda Wineapple, *White Heat: The Friendship of Emily Dickinson and Thomas Wentworth Higginson* (2008).

I am also grateful to the research assistance provided by Kate Hutchens and Special Collections at the Harlan Hatcher Graduate Library, Terry McDonald and Brian Williams at the Bentley Historical Library at the University of Michigan, and Andrea Beauchamp, Assistant Director of the Hopwood Program; the Special Collections at the Robert Frost Memorial Library and the Emily Dickinson Museum of Amherst College; the local history in the collections of the Ann Arbor District Library, the Jones Library in Amherst, the National Park Service, and George Weeks, *Sleeping Bear: Yesterday and Today* (2005); and The History of the Grand Traverse Band at www.gtbindians.org, Nodwesi Red Bear at the Eyaawing Center, and M. L. M. Fletcher, *The Eagle Returns* (2011). Alan Seager's life and book, *A Frieze of Girls* (1954), offered additional grist for Ann Arbor, Oxford, and the Rabbie O'Bannon character as they appear here, as did John Kraus, *Big Ear, From Backyard Telegraph to Edge of the Universe* (1995) for Pip's radio astronomy pal in Ann Arbor.

The late Wystan Auden Stevens, Ann Arbor's long-time historian (and Auden's godchild), also offered invaluable insights, as did Richard Huey, the son of Major and Helen Huey, who ran the Leelanau schools, camps, and Homestead. Julia Schaub, Leelanau County's first woman lawyer, offered a model for the character of Miss Schultz I created for this novel. I hope my invention of David, Spring, Davey, and Angel Ahgosa does not insult the Grand Traverse Band of Ottawa and Chippewa, who suffered so much more at the hands of us late-coming immigrants in so many ways for so many generations. I also hope my invention of Sven Surtr does nothing to diminish King David H. Day and the many contributions of his heirs to Sleeping Bear Dunes, Bay, and Lakeshore. Although Ned Strait is my invention, the 1926 student literary magazine did satirize a Nym on the English faculty, and a Nym secretly did his best to blackball Ted Roethke in 1935.

Too many persons to name individually read one or more of my several drafts of *The Belle of Two Arbors.* I thank each for their time, suggestions and encouragement to see this novel through. I hope none will be disappointed by where it ended up.

I also want to acknowledge the Bentley Historical Library and Special Collections of the Hatcher Library for the historic photographs and images of the persons, places and buildings on the Michigan campus and up north that appear here, as well as Special Collections of the Robert Frost Memorial Library at Amherst College for the historic photograph of Johnson Chapel and The Henry Ford Archive of American Innovation for the photograph of the Robert

Frost Home in Ann Arbor. I thank Brittany Mash for the illustrated map of Glen Arbor and her other drawings that bless this novel.

A final note: I hope readers and critics alike will read the poems of Martha Buhr Grimes composed for Belle on their own merit as well as in the context in which they appear here. Their different slants, sound sense and changes in tune, diverse forms and further ranging stand with the great poets Belle walks with in these pages. Marty will also publish her *Up North* collection in a separate volume. Although I am grateful to include her poetry here, she bears no responsibility for my prose.